HELP OUR HEROES

A MILITARY ANTHOLOGY

Help Our Heroes

Copyright © 2018
All rights reserved

Anthology Creator: Louise Rogers-Thomas

Cover Design provided by: JC Clarke

This content is for mature audiences only.

Please don't not read if explicit language, violence, sexual situations offend you.

All stories in this anthology are the work of fiction, any names, places, characters and other things that are mentioned in this book are the result of the authors imagination.

A Military Anthology

Content

My Sweet GI by T.L Wainwright	5
Wounded Hero by Ava Manello	73
Wreaked by T.A. Mckay	95
Dearest Betty by M.B. Feeney	197
Leaving Home by Alyvia Paige	213
Never Forget Him by Tracy Lorraine	239
The Flyboy's Girl by Michelle Rene	349
Battle Ground by Skye Turner	425
No Beginning by Sam Destiny	533
Man Down by Alice LA Roux	561
Riding Out the Storm by Lucy Felthouse	579
Hunter by S.M. Phillips	593
Chopper (Broken Deeds MC #4.5) by Esther E. Schmidt	603
The Do-Gooder and The Dropout by Bella Settarra	675
Outranked in Love by JF Holland	731

Help Our Heroes

A Military Anthology

My Sweet GI

T.L. Wainwright

When a handsome WWII, American pilot called Teddy stepped into the local corner shop in search of candy, sweet and unassuming Jenny's world went from boring to breath-taking. But with war threatening to put an end to their budding romance, there time together became precious, forcing them to live for the moment.

* * *

"All we have of freedom, all we use or know - this our fathers bought for us long and long ago."
Rudyard Kipling

"A hero is someone who has given his or her life to something bigger than oneself."
Joseph Campbell

Help Our Heroes

Chapter 1

"I'm off Mam," Jenny shouted as she stood in the hallway tying up the laces of her boring old black, flat shoes. The toes were scuffed and dull, so she pulled her cotton hanky from her pocket, spat on it, then quickly ran it across the well-worn leather.

"Jennifer Carter, make sure you come straight home after work," her mother called from the kitchen. "Don't be gallivanting around with that Nora." Jenny could hear her mother muttering under her breath. She couldn't make out what she was actually saying, but she had a good idea. Something in the line of 'Harlot' or 'Jezebel' and a few other biblical words for a woman with loose morals. Jenny's mam didn't swear. If you used blasphemous words, she believed the lord would strike you dumb, so that you would never speak again. If that was the case, Nora would have been silenced years ago.

Jenny's mum Gladys doesn't care for Nora, who happens to be Jenny's best friend. Don't get me wrong, she had other more casual friends, but with Nora, they'd been best friends since infant school.

Gladys just thinks she's a bad influence and in some ways, Jenny can see why. Nora has a right mouth on her. She's not the type of person that thinks before she speaks and some of the stuff she comes out with, well it would make a sailor blush. She wasn't in the slightest bit shy either, and if she wanted something, then she'd bloody well get it. Not a bad thing in general, but when it came to the opposite sex, then the other women of the village thought it scandalous. Many a time, Nora had walked straight up to a man and asked them out on a date. Women's equality? Maybe, but with Nora, more likely a case of impatience.

Jenny was in ore of Nora, herself a little quiet, most people describing her as a shy, well-mannered and polite girl. A credit to her upstanding parents, who were members of the church, and her mother on the village committee. She hated all that straight-laced rubbish. Jenny wished she could be more like Nora, standing on her own two feet, confident and not scared to take a risk or two. But whenever she was in the position to do that, the image of her mam would appear in her head, a face like a slapped bum, and a mouth like she was sucking on a sherbet pip.

Jenny grabbed her jacket from the peg and got out quickly, closing the door behind her without even answering. That way, it looked like she hadn't heard her mam's ramblings, which meant that in theory, she wouldn't be breaking the rules when she met Nora as usual. That's what she told herself anyway.

Jenny made her way towards her work place. It's only a ten-minute walk to get to the grocery shop, that she'd worked in since she was fifteen and still at school. It was just weekends back then, but when school was done, Mrs Armitage the owner, or Betty as she preferred Jenny to call her, asked her if she would work for her on a permanent basis. Mam was under the impression she would go into a more respected profession, and had tried to push her towards secretarial school or nursing, but Jenny for once, had put up a fight and in this instance, had won. She loved working with Mrs Armitage, and felt a sense of loyalty to the widowed shop owner. The shop was an important part of the community, as it was the only one in the village. Which meant that it stocked everything from salt to sweeping brushes. Mrs Armitage prided herself on being able to supply whatever the customer wanted. Rations permitting of course.

Pushing the heavy wooden door open, the ting of the bell that hung just above the frame, announced Jenny's arrival.

"Hello, Mrs Armitage," Jenny sang out in her usual cheery manor.

"Morning Jenny," Ms. Doris Ramsbottom replied, before Betty could get a word in.

Doris is the village gossip. It's no great surprise that even though it's quite mild out this morning, she's dressed in her usual thick brown wool coat, with a navy head scarf covering her grey wiry hair and tied securely under her chin. It made her face look extremely round and her cheeks are littered with purply red veins. Her lips are pursed into a thin line and her wool mitten covered fists, are curled up and resting on her hips.

"It's a disgrace. We don't need the likes of them no good Yankee soldiers in our village. Why don't they send them to one of the big army bases down south? Why here in our tiny little village? They're going to be nothing but trouble, you mark my words."

Jenny glanced over to Betty, who is dressed in a pale blue tea dress that is one of her own creations. Her auburn hair set in soft curls that frame her face and flows long at the back. She rolled her eyes and shrugs her shoulders, while Doris is busy testing the firmness of the crust on the freshly baked bread that's laid out on the counter.

"Does your mother know about this Jenny?" Doris asks, suddenly turning her attention to her.

"Sorry Ms. Ramsbottom, I'm not really sure what you're talking about."

"Didn't you hear all the commotion last night?" she huffs. "Must have been near on five hundred of the buggers, and the noise, it was enough to wake the dead."

"I didn't hear a thing," pipes up Betty.

"Me neither," Jenny adds.

"Mm! Well that does surprise me. Rumour has it, that they are taking over Harpers farm."

"Well that's not even in the village, that's Halswood not Elington." Betty adds.

"Yes, but I bet they'll be looking for the nearest pub and guess what?" She crosses her arms just under her large bosoms, which only made them look even bigger. "Our pub, is in walking distance."

"It's miles away Doris, I'd hardly call that walking distance."

"Maybe not," she retorts, "but they'll be whizzing around in them monstrous army vehicles, inebriated, running amuck and…"

"I'm sure that Constable Winchester will take care of any problems that arise," Betty says, cutting Doris off, her voice a little louder than usual. "Now, have you remembered your ration book Doris?"

Jenny slipped behind the counter and through to the short, narrow hallway that leads into the back room. Removing her jacket, she pops it on the peg, next to where the crisp white apron that Betty insisted she wears is hung. Pulling it over her head, she smoothed it down over her red dress, before securing it around her waist with a double bow.

The dress she had on today was lovely, another product of Betty's handiwork. Most of Jenny's clothes were Betty's cast-offs, and she counted her lucky stars that they were both of similar height, size and shape. In fact, they could quite easily be mistaken as sisters. Never would she have been able to afford to dress so nicely, if it hadn't been for Betty's kind generosity. Some items she had given her, she had to sneak into the house and felted them in her bedroom, as her mam would never approve of their more risqué style. Betty's impeccable sewing skills meant that she only had to take a quick glance at one of the latest styles in a glossy magazine, and she'd be recreating it in a flash. Jenny thought it was amazing, as she herself, couldn't sew a button on. Baking was definitely her skill.

Jenny couldn't help but revisit the conversation between Doris and Betty. American soldiers, just outside the village. She put her hand over her mouth to stifle the laughter that was bubbling in her throat. Nora was going to be over the moon and be getting herself into all sorts of trouble. By the time she goes back through to the shop, after putting the kettle on to boil, rinsing the teapot and putting two cup and saucers out ready. All she sees is the back of Doris, stomping out and slamming the door behind her.

"Oh! What's got her knickers in a twist?" Jenny can barely keep the smirk off her face.

"She's convinced that the Yankee's are the spawn of Satan himself and are going to drag us all to hell."

"No wonder she gets on with me mam," Jenny sniggers. "What do you think Betty?"

Jenny only called Mrs. Armitage by her first name when they were alone in the shop. To do so in front of others, seemed a little disrespectful, her being her employer and all. Truth be, Betty was like a second mam to her, and although she did care for her mother, Betty was much more... with the times.

"I think that most of them are young lads far from home, the least we can do is make them feel welcome. When it comes down to the nitty gritty, this war, well, we're all batting for the same side."

"Why do you think they're coming here though?"

"I'm not sure love, maybe they're already full to bursting in the south and they've got to put them somewhere."

Help Our Heroes

"Do you think they will come into the Village?"

"What's with all the questions?" Bettys voice wasn't harsh, because she could never be that way with Jenny. "Is that the kettle I hear whistling?" she added raising an eyebrow.

Jenny grinned, did a twirl, then trotted off back through the doorway to go make the tea.

Betty shakes her head at the girl that keeps her young. She loves Jenny like she's her own. Betty never had children, never got the chance. Her husband of only eighteen months, had gone missing in action, presumed dead. He was her one true love, childhood sweetheart, and it had been the hardest and scariest experience when he enlisted.

Betty still remembers to this day, the feeling of dread she felt when she'd waved him off at the station. It was as if she'd known that it would be the very last time she'd see him. The loss of him still laid heavy on her, every minute of every hour, every day of every week for the past six years. She hadn't been short of offers from eligible men. She'd even had some unwanted attention from some not so eligible men. At only thirty-one, she was an attractive woman and was quite a catch being a shop owner an all. But she could never bring herself to be with another man, at least not while her heart still ached so deeply for her William.

Jenny walked back up front slowly, so not to spill the tea that she was carrying. "I've been thinking?" she announces, not once taking her eyes off the cups. "What about making the back room into a café?" she placed the cups onto the shop counter, then rubbed the palms of her hands nervously down the front of her apron.

"A café?" Betty laughed. "What for? It will only encourage Doris into spending more time in her moidering me."

"Sorry, your right, probably a silly idea." Jenny's head dropped disheartened.

"Mmm. No, come on then, tell me what you're thinking." Betty sighed, giving Jenny's arm an encouraging squeeze.

"It's just that, the room is so big and it's a bit of a waste. If you moved the boxes into the cellar, cleaned it up a bit. Three or four tables with chairs, you could sell tea, cakes and… it's somewhere other than the pub, where the Yankee's could go."

"If what the papers say is true, the American's drink coffee, not tea. The only coffee I can get readily is that bloody awful 'Camp Coffee'. I can't see that going down well. Cakes? I know how to make bread, but never been any good at baking."

"I can bake. Mam taught me, she says that every mother should at least know how to make a birthday cake for their kid."

Betty's face dropped. Jenny didn't miss it.

"Bugger! Sorry Betty, I didn't mean…"

"It's fine. Maybe your right, maybe we should make something of that room. I could ask the Vicar if he could lend me a couple of tables and a few chairs. With the one we have already in there, and the spare I have in the cellar…"

Chapter 2

Jenny and Betty had the back room up and running before the first American Soldier came to the village. However, the cafe was not what they were looking for.

Every night, the pub was full to bursting with khaki keggs, brown leather jackets, peeked caps, and those folding flat hats that were tucked into pockets as they entered.

The village response was mixed. The landlord was as happy as a pig in mud, but the church goers where mortified, including Jenny's mother. Fortunately, Gladys was unaware of the reasoning behind the addition to the shop, and for the better. Not that it mattered anyway, no soldiers had stepped over the threshold.

Until one particular day that is.

The bell tinged, as the edge of the door hit the bell, and Jenny turned to greet the shopper. Her eyes almost popped out of her head, the heat and colour to her cheeks instant, as her eyes fell onto the tall, American pilot that stood right at the other side of the counter. When he pulled off his hat, you could see the short crop of corn coloured hair.

"Good afternoon ma'am. Do you have any candy?"

"Erm!" Jenny took a couple of steps back, bringing her back hard up against the shelved wall.

"Hey, I'm not going to hurt you." He held up his hand in submission. "I just want to buy some candy."

"Sorry." Jenny snapped out of her shock. "I... I... you mean spice, you want some sweets, chocolate, boiled sweets."

"Boiled sweets?" his laugh is deep and masculine. The way he talked with a strange twang to his voice, sent all sorts of sensations racing around her body and leaves her a little breathless.

Jenny pulled one of only three sweet jars from under the counter. Sweets were rationed, but Betty always seemed to have a little bit extra put to one side.

"Is this what you mean?" Jenny tips the jar and lets a couple of oval fruit sweets roll onto the metal scoop.

"Yes, hard candy," his smile curled up at little more at one side, and you'd be blind to miss the pearly white, perfectly straight teeth that illuminate his face. He took one and popped it into his mouth. "Damn, that is so good," he groaned in approval, his vivid blue eyes connected with Jenny's, as he sucked on the fruity sweetness. "You can only chew on so much gum before it makes you gag. I'll take a bag. How much do I owe you?"

"I can only let you have a few, they're rationed you see and the shop owner, well, she's not here at the moment."

"That's okay sweetheart, I'll take whatever you can give me." He gave Jenny another heart stopping smile. "Besides, it only means I'm going to have to come back and see you again," he finished with a wink.

Blushing, Jenny weighed out two ounces onto the scales, then shook a few more out making it up to four. Bugger that, she'd give up her own rations if she had to, to make up for it. Folding the top of the bag over a couple of times, she held it out over the counter. His hand came around hers, and held it a little longer than necessary, before retrieving the bag of goodies. In return, he placed the flat of his palm against hers, as he drops a few shiny pennies into her hand. The warmth of his touch tingled against her skin.

"Honey, I think you just saved my life." He bounced the bag in his hand a couple of times, before he turned towards the door.

"Do you like tea?" Jenny sputtered out. Stopping in his tracks, he turned back around to face her.

"I'm more of a coffee drinker, why do you ask?"

"We have a café, in the back. If ever you, or your friends fancy… you know, tea and cake, then the café… it's through there," she pointed to the back.

"Well I'll sure tell the guys back at camp. Although, I'm not sure that's a good thing." He gave Jenny a hot hard stare, before he moved to leave again.

"The cakes are really good, homemade," she shouted out, just as the door closed. She grabbed a handful of paper bags off the side and wafts them in front of her heated face as she spoke out loud to herself. "Bloody hell, Jenny, pull yourself

Help Our Heroes

together."

* * *

Over the next few day's every time the bell tings! Jenny's head would shoot up to see who had come into the shop. It would drop just as quick when it wasn't who she was hoping it would be. It wasn't long before Betty noticed.

"What in the world is up with you Jenny," Betty questioned her once the morning rush had subsided and they'd a quiet moment alone. "You've got a face as long as a week, and even poor Mrs. Jeffries couldn't get a peep out of you. Are you on your, you know… time?"

"No!" Jenny blushed at the mention of the unmentionable. "I'm fine. I'll just go put the kettle on." Jenny scurried off so she could avoid any more questions from Betty.

He smiled up at her, his handsome face with its straight nose, not too big, not too small and firm jawline that was clean shaven, not a stray hair to be seen. His blue eyes seem to see into the very heart of her, making her hand shake as she pores the tea into a china cup.

"Thank you, Jenny… Jenny…Jenny…"

"Are you going deaf or something?" Betty's voice makes her jump, bringing her out of her daydream, only to find that the tea had spilled over the edge of one of the cups in front of her. She quickly grabbed the tea towel to mop up the spillage from the work surface, tipped the tea that collected in the saucer into the cup, before wiping it down along with the outside of the cup with the dish cloth.

"Jenny, what are you doing in there?"

"Coming Betty," she picked up the two cups and made her way back up front. Her hand started to shake and the clinking of the rattling china cups against the saucers, could be clearly heard, when Jenny is greeted by the perfect smile and beautiful blue eyes that had appeared so vividly in her fantasy.

"Hi there." The American soldiers gaze was firmly fixed on Jenny, which only made her blush profusely and her hands shook a little more.

"Ahh!" Betty utters, as she rescued the two wobbly cups of tea from

Jenny's hand. "Now it all makes sense." She placed them on the counter, before addressing her customer. "Morning, what can I get you?"

"Morning ma'am," he replied. "I'm here to try some of your Yorkshire tea and cakes? I have it on good authority that they are home baked." He gave Jenny a wink. She did a half turn and started to awkwardly re-arrange the few tins of powdered milk on the shelf at the side of her. Not that they really needed it, but she needed a distraction.

"Well mister?"

"Theodore James Briscoe, ma'am, but my friends call me Teddy."

"No doubt after your former president?" Betty replied.

"Yes, my parents are republicans, as yet, I myself are still undecided. You're interested in American history Miss?"

"Mrs. Armitage. I've read a book or two about it, and as we seem to be on first name terms, you can call me Betty."

"Pleasure to meet you Betty," he turned toward the fumbling girl, that now began to look extremely silly. "Forgive me, I didn't catch your name the other day."

"Jenny," it came out in a whisper. She coughed and spoke again. "Yes, hello, I'm Jenny."

"Hi, Jenny. Pretty name for a pretty girl." Some might think his accent was a little harsh, but to her it was like silk. The small fluttering of butterflies that had started in her stomach, suddenly burst free and morphed into something quite different. All Jenny could do was stand there goggle eyed, at least until Betty, yet again, brought her back to reality.

"Well then Jenny, why don't you take Teddy through to the back and show him your buns." The smirk on Betty's face and the mischief in her voice had Jenny gawping at her, but only for a moment, at which she then scowled back at her.

Jenny couldn't bring herself to say anything, so she just walked through the narrow passageway that led to the makeshift café area, hoping that he followed. Immediately, she went to fill the kettle with water, before placing it on top of one of the rings on the stove. Turning, she found him standing, larger than life, barely a foot away from her. He was close, and Jenny found it a little uncomfortable, but also secretly wished he was even closer. Her eyes dropped to the floor for a few seconds, while she tried to regain her composure, and give a chance for the flush of her blush, that had tinted her face, to subside.

"Would you like it strong?" Jenny asked, suddenly finding her voice. He gave her a confused look. "The tea."

"Damn, I'm not sure. Never drank the stuff before. What would you recommend?"

"Not too strong, but enough so you can taste it. Mrs. Armitage likes hers stewed. It's bloody awful." The last bit she said in a whisper. That gorgeous smile lights up his face, as a soft chuckle escaped his lips. Jenny's eyes couldn't help but focus on his fleshy lips. Most people would think the perfectness of them was a waste on a man, but they fitted his face perfectly. Jenny shook her head to clear the idea away of how good it would feel to touch them with her own. "Bun?"

"Honey, I…"

"Or we have Victoria Sponge, Honey Cake or if you'd prefer, I have a few honey biscuits. Betty's favourites, so you're lucky there's some left."

"Oh, lord," he laughed.

"What's so funny?" Jenny asked, a little annoyed.

"Nothing, nothing at all. Why don't I try one of your… buns and a… biscuit," he replied, not quite sure what they were, but if it meant he could spend a little more time with Jenny, he would be more than happy to give them a try.

Just as she had finished plating up the baked goodies, the kettle let out a shrieking whistle. Putting them in front of Teddy, now seated at one of the tables, she then busied herself making him a cup of tea.

Teddy, positioned himself so he got a perfect view of Jenny's curvy figure as she moved fluidly around the room. The soft sway of her hips and the swish of the skirt of her dress, had his imagination on overdrive, wondering what delights were hiding beneath the red fabric. When Jenny bent over to get something from a low cupboard, the fabric became taught across her round ass. He cursed under his breath, knowing he should look away, but the hardening of his dick, told him otherwise.

"Did you say something?" Jenny asked, as she straighten and swirled around to face him. Her chin dropped, and her mouth made a perfect O, when she caught him watching her. Once again, the flush of embarrassment cloaked her face.

Teddy coughed, blinked a couple of times, and ran his hand over his face. The hand that is hidden under the pretty floral table cloth, adjusted his cock into a less uncomfortable position.

"Looks delicious," he turned his gaze quickly to the miss-shaped mound, of what looked to be a dense mixture with a few raisins in the top. It looked quite hard and crunchy. In comparison, the cookie that sat beside it was a perfect round. "Does this one have a name?" he pointed to the miss-shape.

"It's a rock bun. Don't you have them in America?" she replied, placing the china cup and saucer that's decorated with roses to the right of the plate.

"No honey." He took a bite and found that once you got past the hard exterior, that the inside was soft and incredibly light. It wasn't as sweet as he would like it, but the combination of the buttery taste and the tang of the raisins had him nodding his approval. "That's good," he mumbled, before taking another bite.

"Really?" A giant smile lights up Jenny's face, not quite believing the compliment that she'd just been given. "Try the biscuit, tell me what you think of them."

Teddy swallowed his second mouthful of cake, and for a second, considered taking a mouthful of tea to wash it down. However, it looked goddam awful, so he decided to go straight in and took a bite from the cookie. A few crumbs escaped onto the front of his shirt, but he didn't take much notice. The sweet, crumply goodness had his taste buds jumping in excitement.

Jenny watched intently, and almost clapped with excitement when she saw his eyes close and heard the soft moan of appreciation escape those perfect lips of his. She also felt the stirring of something deep within her stomach. Who wouldn't, when you had such a good-looking man, making noises that sounded like sex. Not that she would know, but she had once unwittingly come across Nora having sex with one of the lads she worked with. She'd gone to meet her from work as she did every night, and waited in the usual place. On hearing strange noises, she had walking around the back of the building where the bike sheds were, only to find Nora pinned against the wall. The sounds that came from them both were quite shocking, but it was obvious that Nora was enjoying every minute of it. That's how she found out what sex sounded like. It also made her realise why she was an only child, as she never heard sounds like that coming from her parent's room. Thank God.

"That is one goddamn tasty cookie," Teddy declared.

"Cookie?" Jenny put her hand over her mouth to try and stop the childlike giggle that threatened to escape.

"That's what we call these back home," he laughed. "I guess there are more than a few differences when you come to the American and British language."

"I guess," she let the laughter out. Without thinking she swept her hand over the front of his shirt, brushing the crumbs that had collected there. "Oh!" she gasped, suddenly realising what she had done. Lifting her gaze, she found Teddy watching her intently. His pupils were blown, the blue almost non-existent. When she went to remove her hand that was still placed against his firm chest, he stopped her by putting his own hand over hers.

"Jenny," he breathed out, "damn your pretty."

"Erm, you… haven't tried your tea yet," she babbled, sliding her hand from under his. Her eyes dropped to the tablecloth, she noticed a couple of small tea stains that would need a good scrub on the next wash. That's Jenny, that's what she does. Awkward situations, she distracted herself with some other immaterial rubbish.

The sound of spluttering and coughing caught her attention. Teddy's face was bright red.

"What the hell? Sorry Honey, but that's not good. It tastes like pencil lead."

It's enough to break the tension, and Jenny couldn't help but laugh out loud at the sight of his face distorted with displeasure.

"What's so funny?" Teddy questioned, but he joined in with the joviality.

"Your face, it's a picture."

"Well that's disgusting. I think I'll stick to coffee."

"We do have coffee, well it's that stuff made from chicory. Now that is disgusting."

"How about next time I bring my own coffee, you could make it for me and

I can try some more of your delicious cakes?"

"I can do that," Jenny smiled. "Could you tell all the other Yank... men about it too. It was my idea you see, the café, so if it gets a few more people in, then..."

"I'll see what I can do," he says standing, yet almost reluctant to go. "How much do I owe you?"

"I'll have to check. Mrs. Armitage has the price list. You can pay on the way out." Jenny almost kicks herself for sounding like she wanted him to go, when it's quite the opposite. Despite her awkwardness, she liked the attention that she's getting from Teddy.

Jenny moved first, walking towards the hallway that lead to the front, only to feel a hand slip into hers, stopping her and pulling her back around.

"Will you come for a walk with me?" Teddy asked.

"I can't, I'm working."

"What time do you finish? I'll come back and meet you."

"I'm sorry, I can't. I'm meeting someone."

"Damn. I should have known that a pretty thing like you would already have a guy."

"No," Jenny sniggered. "It's just my friend, Nora."

"So, can't you ditch her?" When Teddy saw the soft scowl on Jenny's face, he quickly changed his tactics. "Bring her along. I don't mind. I'd just like to get to know you a little better."

"Sorry, I can't." Jenny said defiantly.

"Okay," Teddy held up his hands in acceptance, but with great reluctance. "Maybe another time." Jenny's silence does nothing to spur on his goal of getting to spend more time with this beauty.

Once Teddy had paid at the till, spoke pleasantries with Betty, he said his goodbyes, disappointed that he was unable to catch Jenny's attention, as she busied herself behind the counter. Just as he stepped out of the door, he felt a soft tug of his jacket sleeve. Turning he found Jenny, timidly stood in front of him. She didn't say a word, just gave him a smile that's full of warmth and dare he say promise, as she shoved a fist sized paper bag into his hand, before turning away.

With the ting of the bell in the distance and the soft closing of the door, he looked to see what it was that she had given him.

"Candy," he said out loud to himself. Enough of a sign in his eyes for him not to give up on Jenny, not yet anyway.

Popping one of the sugary treats into his mouth, he started to hum the song that had just jumped into his head, that he'd heard many times on the radio. 'We'll meet again, don't know where, don't know when' but sure as hell, it won't be too long.

Chapter 3

Jenny got to the steps outside Taylor's a little later than normal, and found Nora sat on the third step down, with her legs out straight in front of her. You would have thought that the shapeless blue overalls she wore and the scarf around her head, would have impaired her attractiveness. But with Nora, it just seemed to make her look even more alluring. You could wrap her in brown paper and string and she'd still have Jenny feeling insignificant stood at the side of her.

Nora had started working for the small family run engineering company when she'd left school. It used to make an assortment of machinery parts, mainly for the textile companies, but was now supplying bullet shells. It was a blessing that they didn't get involved with the actual explosive part of the process, that was done at a factory in Leeds, where the shells were sent.

"Your late," Nora chirp's, while letting out a puff of smoke from between her bright red lips.

"Sorry," Jenny replied, taking the offered cigarette from her friends outstretched hand, bringing it to her own lips. She takes a long deep drag, letting the burn of the nicotine hit the back of her throat, before slowly releasing the smoke in short sharp bursts from her mouth. "We had our first customer in the café today. It took me a little longer to clear up."

"Who was it? Nosy Doris, come to give you advice on how to make a decent cuppa?"

"Actually," Jenny didn't really want to say, but she couldn't lie to her friend. "No. It was one of the GI's from the camp in Halswood."

"Really?" Nora jumped up from the step and took back the cigarette, her face lighting up at the mention of men. "What was he like?"

Jenny knew this would happen, that's the reason why she was reluctant to take Teddy up on his offer. If she'd taken Nora along, then one look at her, any chance she'd get with Teddy would be gone. Was that a bit selfish? Who's she trying to kid? It couldn't happen anyway. Her mam wouldn't have any of it.

"Jenny, come on, tell me." She held the butt of the cigarette between finger and thumb, then flicked it with her painted nail over the curb and onto the road.

"Didn't take much notice, I was too busy in the shop."

"Then why is your face all red?" Nora stood with her hands on her hips. "I think my girl has a crush on a sexy GI."

"Give over Nora." Jenny turned and started to walk away. Nora did a couple of skips to catch up with her.

"Guess what," Nora slipped her arm through Jenny's as they continued to walk. "Halswood Village Hall are having a dance to welcome the Yankee's."

"Oh! That's good of em!"

"And we're going."

Jenny stopped dead in her tracks and turned to face Nora.

"You've got to be bloody joking."

"Am I ekers like," Nora sniggered.

"So, how the buggery do you think I'm gonna get me mam to let me go?" Jenny cocked her head to one side. "She'll be screaming blue murder at me when I get in, because I haven't gone straight home from work, never mind letting me out at night." They start walking again, turning onto the main road that runs through the village and towards Jenny's house. "My mam thinks that if you're out after dark, you can only be up to one thing. Trouble."

"Tell her you're helping Betty with the stock take at the shop. I'm sure she'll back you up."

"What exactly am I backing you up for?" Betty questioned loudly, appearing out of nowhere behind them. They both jumped.

"Hello Mrs Armitage," Nora gave her an exaggerated smile. "Erm, it's just that…"

"Nothing, just Nora and one of her silly ideas," Jenny chipped in.

"Shut up you," Nora elbowed Jenny before giving Betty the gossip. "They're having a dance at Halswood Village Hall tomorrow and I was…"

"Come on Nora, I need to get home before me mam starts fretting." Jenny pulled at her friends' arm giving her no option but to move away. "See you tomorrow B… Mrs Armitage."

"Bloody hell Jenny," Nora spluttered, almost tripping over her own feet. "You're such an old lady. You need to start taking a few risks, break a few rules. If you don't, then you'll never get out of this village and have a real life."

They get to the junction, where they part ways in silence. Jenny going off to the right to her house, Nora to the left to go to hers.

"I'm sorry Nora, but you know what mam's like."

"Can't you sneak out?"

"You are joking, aren't you? Mam watches me like a hawk. I'm not even meant to meet you after work. Anyway, what will yah dad say?"

"What he don't know, won't hurt him," she winked. "Besides, he'll be in the pub." Nora flung her arms around her and gave her a quick hug. "I'll think of som'ert. If not, then I'll just have to give yah all the gossip. See yah tomorrow."

"See yah," Jenny replies, watching her go on her way, waving at her over her shoulder.

As soon as Jenny stepped into the house, her mother appeared. Her grey flecked hair was scrapped back into the tightest of buns, that sat at the nape of her neck, making her face look even harsher than normal. Her cheeks were flushed, her eyes stormy green and her mouth was so firmly pursed together, it was a wonder you couldn't hear her teeth cracking from the pressure.

"What time do you call this Jennifer?"

"Sorry mam, it took a bit longer to clear up today." Jenny felt a small pang of guilt in her stomach, but then pushed it away as she wasn't lying. Not really.

"So, you're telling me you haven't seen that Nora?" her tongue lashed out the words like a venomous snake.

"I bumped into her on the way home," Jenny snapped back. "Why do you have such a hatred for her mam? It's not like she's ever done anything to you."

"Because she's a trollop, she'd give herself up to any Tom, Dick or Harry. I don't want you being influenced by her wickedness. In fact, I forbid you seeing her."

"Mam," she screeched. "She's my best friend."

"Best friend indeed. She's got a right mouth on her, and her father, he's just a no-good drunk, letting her run wild he does. It's a disgrace. No wonder her mother left them."

"Stop!" Jenny yelled. "How dare you say that. Nora's dad does the best he can. Three kids, three kids she left him to look after. Didn't bat an eyelid, just took herself off with no thought about any of them." Enough was enough. She couldn't take anymore of her mother's holier than thou shit. Jenny took to the stairs at speed, her shoes making a clomping sound on every step.

"I forbid you, do you hear?" Her mother hollered from below, and Jenny took great pleasure in slamming her bedroom door behind her.

Jenny threw herself face down onto her bed at an awkward angle, her legs dangling over the side. The frustration that bubbled inside her, had her screaming into the wool blanket that laid over her cotton sheets. Normally she wouldn't dare talk back to her mother, she would just keep her gob shut and walk away, but she was sick of being treated like a child. She was nearly eighteen for god sake, an adult, and it was about time she got the chance to act like one. Come to think of it, maybe a good start would be to go to a dance.

Chapter 4

The next morning, Jenny was up uncharacteristically early. She'd even skipped breakfast, so she could avoid another tongue lashing from her mam. Quickly and silently, she got herself ready for work, slipped on her shoes and jacket before tiptoeing out of the front door, making sure she made as little sound as possible. It was earlier than she'd normally set off to the shop. There was a definitive chill in the air, causing her to pull her jacket tighter, wrapping her arms around herself, in an attempt to retain her body heat. In the cold light of day, her anger and determination that had burned so strong last night, was nothing more than a smoulder now. Her mind replayed the conversation she had with her dad, when he had come to her room after he'd had his tea.

"So, what's going on with you and your mam that's got you hiding up here?" He asked, his big frame nearly filling the doorway. Edward was six-foot-tall and built like a brick outhouse, but he was a gentle man, 'an anything for a quiet life' type of man.

"Nowt," Jenn replied in a hushed voice.

"Come on lass, you can tell your dad and there's no need to whisper, she's gone down to see't vicar."

"I'm fed-up of her treating me like a kid, dad. It's suffocating. And now, can you believe it? She's trying to stop me from seeing Nora. I'm not having it dad... I'm not."

"Love, you know what she's like. If a lass wears kegs, does a man's job and isn't in church a Sunday, then she isn't right."

"But dad..."

"I know lass, I know. Look, step carefully, try keep out of trouble for a bit, and I'll have a word with her." He rarely spoke up against his wife and never criticised how she ran the house, but when it came to Jenny, well, she was his

Help Our Heroes

everything. The time had come where he had to intervene, because he knew deep down that if things didn't change, she'd be gone. And that would simply break his heart. "Now, tea's mashin' and you must be famished, so why don't you get thissen downstairs and get sommat' to eat before yah mam gets back."

Jenny had sat on the floor beside her dad's armchair for a half hour, dipping toast in her hot tea, while listening to the crackling music on the wireless. She could have stayed there all night, she loved spending time with her dad, but she had kissed him on the cheek and taken herself back to her bedroom before her mam had returned home.

So, her plans to go against everything her mam preached, was just hot air that was now as cold as the morning mist.

Jenny went around the yard at the back of the shop, knowing that the front would still be locked up. Looking through the window, she could see the misshaped outline of Betty through the frosted glass, moving around in the back room. Jenny knocked lightly on the glass, not wanting to make her jump. The dark outline moved from view. As the backdoor opened, a waft of warmth and the smell of freshly baking bread hit her.

"Morning Jenny, did you wet bed or sommat?"

"Avoiding me mam," Jenny sighed, while breathing in the delicious aroma.

"Oh dear, like that, is it?"

"Yeah, better to keep out of her way. If she asks, you asked me to come in early this morning."

"Jenny!" Betty exhaled. "Bloody hell, it's Friday, she'll be in this afternoon and she's bound to question me. I don't like lying to her."

"I'm sorry, but I just couldn't face another row."

"Alright, but just this once."

"Ta."

"While I go sort out the shop, you better get on with making some biscuits. Do me a favour, keep an eye on them bread cakes, they should be done in about ten minutes." Betty instructed, before disappearing down the hall.

* * *

When Jenny eventually stepped into the shop, she found Nora head to head with Betty, talking in whispers.

"What you doing here?" Jenny asked. Afraid that she was missing something she added, "What you chelpin' about?"

"Nothing, I just called in for my ciggies," Nora replied innocently.

"Yeah and I'm a monkey's uncle. What's going on?"

"Nora was just telling me about the dance in Halswood," said Betty. "The one they've arranged for the GI's."

"That Jenny won't go to." Nora pursed her lips and flashed Jenny a look of distain.

"Bugger off Nora!" Jenny snapped, her hands firmly placed on her hips. "I can't go and that's that. Me mam would have nowt to do with it, so just forget it." She stormed off into the back room before Nora even got a chance to say another word.

It wasn't until she heard the door chime go, that she risked going back into the shop.

Nora may have gone, but someone else had arrived.

Teddy smiled as soon as he saw her. In return, she blushed, dropping her gaze and started straightening the newspapers on the counter top, that were perfectly laid out already.

"Hello Jenny." His deep voice made her tingle right to where she knew it shouldn't, but bugger if it didn't feel good. She took a deep breath before she dared to answer him.

"Hello," she replied. "Have you come for more tea?" Stupid, stupid, stupid. Jenny chanted in her head, wanted to kick herself. He hated the tea, so why the hell did she mention it.

"No, but I've brought my own coffee, if I could trouble you for some hot water, and of course some of your delicious cookies." Teddy moved his attention briefly to Betty. "That's if it's okay with you ma'am?"

"Of course. Why don't you both go through. Jenny has made a fresh batch this morning."

Teddy moved swiftly towards Jenny, at which she quickly turned, knowing full well she was already flush faced. His musky scent made her aware of just how close he was to her as they made their way through the hall and into the back room.

"I'll put the kettle on," she said, moving towards the sink, trying to put a little distance between them. His closeness was doing nothing to slow her pounding heart, or the pulse that was building between her legs. God, he made her senses reel and her body hum in ways that she'd heard about, but thought to be just silly girly gossip.

"Those cookies smell damn good." Teddy spoke so close to her ear, that it made her jump. So much so, that the grip she had on the kettle that she was about to place on the stove, was lost. Quick as a flash, Teddy put his hand over hers, re-engaging the hold that she had. His hand was warm and firm, yet the skin was softer than she'd expect for a man. "Steady there," he whispered, his soft breath blowing the loose wisps of hair forward and across her cheek. Teddy was tempted to sweep them away with his finger, but he checked himself. Just having his hand laid over hers, was making his cock jump. He wasn't sure he wanted to be displaying a full-on bulge in his pants to her, not yet anyway he thought mischievously.

Jenny slid her hand from under Teddy's a little reluctantly when he released his hold, the kettle now safely in its place. She liked the way it made her skin tingle.

Teddy put his hand into his pocket and pulled out a small round metal tin.

"Here," he said handing it to Jenny. She took it from his hand and read the label on the side…

COFFEE, INSTANT.
1 OZ NET WT.
HILLS BROS
Chicago, ILL.

"Oh, I erm," Jenny stuttered after opening the tin to find a brown powder. She breathed in the distinctive odour that smelt lovely, much better that the thick liquid stuff that they were used too. "I've not made this kind of coffee before." She looked at him with wide eyes.

"Hey, let me show you," he laughed lightly. "In fact, why don't I make you a cup of coffee."

Jenny watched as Teddy spooned coffee into two cups. When she went to grab two saucers, he shook his head giving a gentle no, and they stood waiting for the water to boil.

"Jenny, there's a dance tonight, in the next village. I was kinda hoping that you would allow me to take you?"

"Oh, erm…"

The steam of the kettle hit the whistle, taking both of their attention and also saved Jenny from having to respond to his invitation.

If truth be known, she would have loved to go with Teddy, but in reality, it just wasn't going to happen.

Teddy filled each cup with hot water, leaving half an inch clear at the top. The steam rolled and swirled upwards, bringing with it the strong aroma. Jenny leant forward, closed her eyes and inhaled.

"That smells so good," she hummed.

"Now I like mine black, but some people prefer it with creamer," Teddy explained. "But you need to let it cool a little first."

"Oh, well, why don't you sit down, and I'll get you some bisc… cookies."

Table set and coffee cooled, Jenny took her first sip. The bitterness hitting her taste buds, had her screwing up her face and shuddering.

"You don't like it?" Teddy laughed. "Here, try it with a little sugar." He popped a sugar cube into the cup and stirred it a few times before removing the spoon. "Try it now?"

"Ugh!" Jenny spluttered. "That's not much better."

"Maybe you should add a little milk?" he poured a little from the milk jug and stirred again.

"More." She held her cup to him after taking a sip.

"Damn, your mistreating good coffee here," but he added a little more anyway.

"Mmm, that's better."

"And cold no doubt."

For a change, Jenny was quite forward. She asked him about the base that had been set up on Coppers Farm and the other GI's that had come over with him.

Help Our Heroes

She reckoned, if she asked him questions, then it was only polite that he answered. Therefore, not giving him a chance to ask her that certain question again.

"So, where in America are you from?"

"I live in New York, but I have family scattered all over the south. What about you?"

"Me, I've lived here all my life. Yorkshire born and bred."

"So, you've never travelled?"

"Not unless you call a day trip to Scarborough, travelling."

"That's over on the east side, yes?"

"Yes, it's still in Yorkshire though, so hardly a mad adventure."

"That's a shame."

"Why'd you say that?"

"No reason, just that the world is a might big place that's all."

"Who knows, maybe when this war is over, I might go to London, see the Queen." Jenny giggled. The cups were empty, the biscuits eaten, so Jenny rises to her feet and starts to clear the table.

"Jenny," Teddy says softly, as he stands and moves towards her.

"I, erm, if you go through and see Mrs. Armstrong to settle your bill," she says a little curt. "Just let her know that it was just the two cookies that you owe for."

Teddy gives her a nod and a smile, clearly disappointed at her brush off, before walking from the room.

As she places the cups into the sink, she dropped her head in disgust at her rudeness towards Teddy. He had been really kind and didn't deserve been dismissed in such a rude manner. Dropping the tea towel back on the counter, she hurriedly made her way back into the shop. A bag of sweets was already waiting under the counter for when he came into the shop again. She didn't mind giving up her rations, the one thing her mam did allow her. Teddy was already on his way out of the door when she got to the counter. Grabbing the paper bag from its hiding place, she scooted across the shop floor at speed, yanking the door open.

"Teddy," she shouted causing him to turn back to face her. "You're candy." Walking back up to where she stood, he cupped her laden hand with his and squeeze it gently. Leaning into her, he placed his lips to her cheek and kissed it softly.

"Come to the dance with me Jenny?" his gaze was full of heat and when her eyes met his, her stomach flipped. Her head was saying yes, yes, yes. But her voice came out on a sigh.

"I can't" to which she spun on her heels, closing the door behind her.

The look on Betty's face and the way her mouth was shaped, told Jenny that she was about to ask questions, but she just turned her head and flounced into the back before she even had a chance.

* * *

"For god's sake," an already irritated Jenny mumbled under her breath, when she saw her mam stood at the other side of the counter. She was still mad at herself for her behaviour earlier, and for still not having the guts to do something wild and adventurous.

"What was that Jennifer?" Her mother snapped.

"Good to see you, mam. What can I get you?"

"Nothing from you, thank you very much," her mother huffed obviously still simmering from last night's clash. "Mrs Armitage has seen to me, but you can bring the sugar and flour home when you're finished here. No dawdling, straight home."

"Oh, I was wondering if Jenny could stay back tonight," Betty interrupted. Jenny opens her mouth to say something, but then snaps it shut just as quick. It's the first that she'd heard of any of this. "It's my cellar you see. Well, it's in a right mess and I was hoping Jenny could help me sort it out. It might take a few hours, but I'll pay her for her time of course."

"Well I don't know…"

"It would really help me out. Jenny is such a good worker. Being on my own, I don't know what I would do without her." Although a little underhand, Betty knew that Jenny's mother had a weak spot, and she was hoping it did the trick.

"Well, I suppose so, but if it gets late, make sure you're quiet coming in. Don't be waking me and yah dad up."

"No mam," Jenny replied, still not sure of what the hell was going on. She was positive Betty hadn't mentioning this before and the cellar looked perfectly fine when she had been down there yesterday.

"I better take my groceries with me then," Gladys pointed to the items still sitting on the counter. "Otherwise, your dad won't be happy if he hasn't got any sugar in his tea."

Once Gladys had left and the door was firmly closed, Jenny turned to Betty, but before she could get a word in edgeways, Betty spoke up.

"Put the closed sign on and come upstairs."

* * *

"I don't understand," Jenny muttered, as she stood in the middle of the bedroom. Betty held the beautiful dress up against Jenny, just under her chin. Jenny couldn't resist touching the soft silky fabric with her finger tips, letting them gently slide across the sheen of the surface. It was in the most unusual colour, it wasn't blue or green, but somewhere in between and nothing like she'd seen before.

"This is the perfect colour for you," Betty cooed. "I made this especially for when William came home."

"Then I can't take it." Jenny shakes her head, pushing the stunning dress away from her.

"It's not to keep Jenny, it's just to borrow," she swallows hard and her eyes become shiny and sad. "I could never give this away. It would be like I was giving up on him." She sits on the side of the bed. "I know I'm fooling myself, but I can't accept it Jenny," she looks up, a single tear rolls down her cheek. "I have to believe that one day I'll see him again, even if it's in heaven."

Jumping up, Betty wipes her eyes with the back of her hand, pushing away the sadness. "Now shoes. You're a four, I'm a five. Maybe if we pad the toes with newspaper, it might just work." Betty went into the bottom of her wardrobe and produce a pair of black heeled shoes with rounded toe and ankle straps. They looked like new, not a scuff or a rub, unlike the flat worn ones that she had on her feet.

"Betty, what's this all about?"

"You're going to the dance." Betty announced nonchalantly.

"No, no, no," Jenny gasped. "I can't go, my mam will…"

"Your mam thinks you'll be here helping me. Now, I know for a fact that I'm not going to tell her. Are you?"

"But I don't want to go."

"Don't try and kid me Jenny. I saw your face earlier and you've been sulking like a baby that's just lost its dummy."

"But, I can't go on my own. Nora doesn't…"

"Nora's meeting you here at half past six, so," Betty checked the pretty little watch on her wrist. It's the only item of jewellery she wears, other than her wedding ring of course. Both given to her by her beloved William. "We've just over an hour to fix your hair and get you ready."

"We?" Jenny giggled, partly with excitement but mostly with nerves.

"Well you don't think I'm going to let you out, looking like a cheap floosy do you?" She tutted. "I don't know why you didn't just accept the GI's offer."

"What?" Jenny gasped.

"Oh, I heard him asking you to the dance. I ain't deaf and I ain't blind either. I've been watching you mooning around over him."

"I was doing nothing of the sort," Jenny tries to defend herself.

"Pfft! Not that I can blame you, he's a handsome boy and quite the gentleman. Oh, and by the way, I saw the kiss too."

Jenny shuffled uncomfortably from one foot to the other, before blurting out, "it's a pity it wasn't on the lips." Betty looked at her with raised eyebrows and mouth agape, then they both fall back onto the bed in a fit of giggles.

Chapter 5

When Jenny walked into the village hall with Nora, she was shaking like a leaf. It was crowded, noisy and her heart was drumming faster than the beat of the up-tempo music. It was exciting and scary all at the same time.

Nora had been shocked and a little jealous when she first clapped eyes on Jenny in her stunning outfit. Betty had done wonders with her hair. Dark soft curls fell over her shoulders and down her back. The victory roll at the front gave it a little height, making it perfect. Her make-up consisted of a touch of powder, a little mascara, and a burst of red colour to her lips. It was just the right amount, so as not to cover her natural beauty. Neither did it hide the sprinkling of freckles and the soft pink glow of her cheeks.

Jenny felt like a movie star, and as nervous as one doing her first audition. That's how it felt. Her first dance, her first time out, with men, soldiers even. No, scrap that. GI's. The forbidden fruit in her mam's eyes.

A pang of guild hit her, but she quickly pushed it away, determined that now she was here, she was bloody well going to make the most of it.

It was mere minutes before they were approached by two young GI's, who introduced themselves as Bud and Harvey.

"So, are you going to ask me to dance or what?" Nora says, turning her attention to Bud, hand on hip, as precocious as ever.

Bud simply smiled, grabbed her hand and led her into the crowd of swaying couples in the centre of the room.

Jenny stood nervously, cursing Nora in her head for leaving her.

"Would you like to dance?" Harvey shouted over the loud music.

"No thank you," she replied.

"You don't like to dance?"

"I don't know how to?"

"Me neither," he laughed, scratching his head.

The silence that fell between them was awkward, but while he fidgeted, looking everywhere but at her, it gave her the chance to get a look at him.

His brown hair had a curl that made it look unruly. His eyes, when she did manage to catch a glance, where a soft green. His lips thin, teeth a little crooked. He was… nice, but he wasn't Teddy.

"Hello Jenny."

The voice behind her, had her spinning around. Forgetting that she was in heels, she lost her footing, but was quickly up righted, thanks to Teddy's strong arms.

What was it that her grandmother used to say… 'Speak of the devil and he will appear.' Although Teddy looked nothing like the devil. Not one single bit. His fringe flopped over his eyes, but not enough to hide the beauty of the blue,

"Hello," Jenny eventually managed to say.

"So, that's why you turned down my invitation. You already had a date."

"No, I… this is not my doing. Betty, I mean Mrs. Armitage, she… well let's just say, she convinced me to come."

"You came on your own?"

"With my friend Nora. She's over there. The one in the red dress, dancing with the GI."

"And what about your GI?" he flicked his gaze over her shoulder. Jenny turns to find Harvey already making a hasty retreat.

"Seems like you've scared him off."

"Good." The intensity in his eyes when he looked at her made her skin tingle. "Let me get you a drink." Teddy glanced around the room and decided that he wasn't willing to risk leaving her there, a sitting target for all the other horny soldiers. "Why don't you come with me?"

Gently he placed his hand in the centre of her back, and led her to the back of the room. Her body reacted instantly to the warmth of his touch through the fabric of her dress. When she felt a soft throbbing between her legs, it took her by surprise. If this was how her body reacted now, god only knew what sensations he could ignite if he touched her in other places.

Holding two glasses, Teddy gestured for Jenny to follow him. Walking out of the main room, the noise subsided once the door swung closed behind them.

Help Our Heroes

"That's better, I can hear your pretty voice now," he smiles, handing Jenny one of the glasses. Not sure how to react to his compliment, she took a big gulp of the brown liquid.

When Jenny started to cough and splutter, Teddy quickly removed the glass from her hand before it spilt on her dress.

"Oh, shoot. Don't you like beer?"

"I've," cough… "Not had if before," she confessed.

"Damn, I'm sorry. I should have asked first. Let me get you something else instead."

"No, this will be fine." She gave him a soft smile and took the glass back from him.

"It is an acquired taste," he laughed. "And the beer over here, is nothing like back home."

"Do you miss it?"

"The beer?"

"No, home silly," she batted his arm, then dropped it to her side, fiddling with the fabric of her dress, when she realised what she'd done. Teddy found it funny, but held back his laughter.

"Sometimes, yes." He looked deep into her eyes then added, "but right at this moment, I wouldn't want to be anywhere else."

Jenny dropped her gaze, her thick lashes almost rested on her cheek bones. Teddy placed a finger under her chin and gently lifted it, until she had no choice but to look him in the eye.

"You're very beautiful Jenny."

He'd watched her earlier, for a little while anyway, so he could look at her. When he had seen her stood with another man, the sharp pang of jealousy had surprised him. He just had to intervene.

Now, standing so close, he could really look at her, take in every inch of her. From her thick dark, almost black, shiny hair, big brown eyes full of innocence, and the soft pout of her red lips.

Damn, that mouth, what he would like to do with her mouth.

The neckline of her dress, that sat slightly off her shoulders, displayed her slender neck, collar bone and soft peaks of her breasts perfectly. Classy, not slutty.

God damn, how he ached to get his lips on her skin.

The way the fabric nipped in at the waist, skimmed her hips, flared out a little, until you got to those legs. Fuck, how he would like to get between those legs.

The slimness of her ankles, her delicate feet, that looked so small in the sexy black heeled shoes.

Holy fuck, how he wanted to sweep her off her feet, lay her down and screw her.

He couldn't hold back any longer. With his free hand, he firmly cupped her chin, bringing his lips down to hers.

At first, her response was a muffled gasp, but soon it turned into a completely different, more encouraging one, as she began to return his kiss.

"I've wanted to do that since I first saw you." His words were hushed but perfectly clear, mouth hovering just a fraction from hers.

"Have you really?"

"You're gorgeous Jenny, and the sweetest thing is, you don't even realise just how stunning you are." Taking the glass from her hand, he put them to one side.

Jenny, still a little dazed by the heat of his kiss and the whirlwind of sensations that are coursing through her body, stood rigid, but internally, she felt like jelly.

"Jenny." Teddy slid his arm around her waist, his hand went up to her face, brushing his thumb along her flushed cheek.

"Teddy?" when her eyes met his, she saw the fire in them, that took her breath away.

"I want to kiss you again."

"Then kiss me."

Teddy, not needing to be told twice, drew her into his arms, his lips crushed against hers, with a passion second to none. Jenny shivered as his hand moved down the centre of her back, following the line of her spine through the silky fabric of her dress. His hands circled her waist, holding her tightly.

If Jenny thought that the first kiss was special, then this was exceptional.

Help Our Heroes

"Jenny," he growled into her open mouth, as they both caught their breath. "I want to touch you, feel every inch of you." He murmured against her ear. His hands began to move again, one of them palm flat against her ribcage, just under her left breast. When he slid his thumb across the round, skimming the nipple that was already pushing the fabric, a surge of electricity shot through her body, straight to her most intimate part. It's enough to shock her back into reality, making her realise that things were getting a little too heated.

Jenny pushed against his chest, and immediately, feeling her pull away, he relaxed his hold.

"I can't do this," she cried. "I need to go." When she tried to turn away from him, he released her, but grabbed hold of her hand.

"Jenny, I'm sorry. I shouldn't have done that. Please, don't go. Look, if you really must go, then at least let me take you home."

"I don't know. I need to find Nora."

"Let me help you find your friend, then I'll take you both back to the village."

"Okay," she agreed.

They searched the main room and hallway, but it isn't until they stepped outside, that they found Nora clinging onto Bud like a winkle.

"Looks like your friends a little busy at the moment," Teddy pointed out.

"Nora," Jenny hissed quietly. "Nora," she hissed a little louder. "NORA! I'm going home."

Nora just waved her hand in the air, making it clear that she wasn't going anywhere.

"Hey, Bud," Teddy shouted over. "Can you make sure you get Nora home safely?"

Bud gave Teddy a 'thumbs up' without letting go or breaking the seal, he had on Nora's lips.

"So, will you please allow me to escort you home Jenny?" he asks turning to her. "Trust me, your safe with me."

Jenny fidgeted, unsure what to do.

"I promise, I won't touch you. I won't even hold your hand, if you don't want me to."

"I'm not sure what time the bus comes."

"Then we'll walk."

* * *

The first few minutes they walked in an awkward silence, but it's not long until Teddy breaks it.

"Have you known Nora long?"

"We've been friends since school."

"Really?" Even though the natural light was dimming, as night began to fall, Jenny still caught site of his raised eyebrows.

"Yes, why is that so hard to believe?"

"You're total opposites. Nora seems to be a bit of a wild one, whereas you, you're…"

"Dull?" Jenny filled in the hesitation. That's how she felt most of the time, compared to Nora.

"That's not what I was going to say. I was going to say reserved, unassuming and demure."

"Isn't that the same? Boring?"

"If that's how you want to perceive yourself, then fine. Although, I strongly disagree. But if it is, then I must happen to like boring. In fact, I like it very much."

Jenny bit her bottom lip, trying to disguise the smile that was forming on her lips. "She's not always been like that. When we were younger we were like two peas in a pod."

"What made her change?"

"Her mam going. Nora got up one morning for school and she wasn't there. Gone, just like that. At first, she just went really quiet. I knew straight away something was wrong, but however many times I asked her, she wouldn't tell me. Then one day, she just broke."

"Poor girl."

"Since then, what Nora wants, Nora gets. Been that way ever since." Jenny stopped and span around to look Teddy in the face, feeling the need to defend Nora. "But she's my best friend and she has a heart of gold. Her and Betty, I mean

Help Our Heroes

Mrs. Armitage are like family to me." As quickly as she'd stopped and faced him, she turned back around and began walking again.

Teddy fell back in step beside her. On doing so, the leather of his jacket sleeve brushed her bare arm causing her to shiver.

"You must be cold," he realised. This time it was his turn to stop, shrugging off his jacket.

"I'm fine," Jenny uttered, instantly realising what he was about to do. Yet, her body signalled otherwise with a sequence of judders. "You don't have to do that."

Standing behind her, he placed his jacket across her back, his hands lingered a little longer than necessary on her shoulders. "I know I don't have to Jenny, but I want to."

Jenny stilled for a second, instantly affected by his touch and the warmth of his body heat, still retained in the fabric of his jacket. As a distinctive smell that she immediately related to him hit her nostrils, she let out a soft, uncontrollable moan of delight. If she could only swop shoes with him too, as the soles of feet, not used to wearing heels, were beginning to burn.

The conversation for the rest of the walk was light, and Jenny started to feel at ease with Teddy again. He even told her stories from his childhood, and the mischief he got up to with his two brothers, much to his parent's disgust and his grandparent's amusement. That was of course, until they arrived outside the shop.

"Goodnight Teddy," she said, coming to a sudden standstill. "Thank you so much for walking me back." She added, before quickly turning away from him.

"Woah! Slow down." Catching her hand, he spun her back around to face him. "You live here at the shop?"

"No, I..."

"I didn't think so. I'll walk you to your home."

"Here's fine."

"Now, I wouldn't be much of a gentleman if I didn't see you to your door."

"That's not such a good idea."

"And why is that?"

"Well, erm..."

"Jenny. Is there a problem?"

"My mam." The words fell out of her mouth with a deep exhale. "She thinks I've been working late in the shop. She's really strict you see, and if she sees you then…"

"With all due respect Jenny, surely you wouldn't be wearing that pretty dress, all made up, with your hair all special if you were working?"

"Oh, hell's bells. I'm going to be in so much trouble." Jenny put her hands over her eyes and sighed. "I didn't think of that. What am I going to do?" Teddy took hold of her hands with his and slowly pulled them from her face.

"If I walk you to the corner of your street, watch you till you get to your door, do you think you can sneak in without being seen?"

"Maybe. I'm going to have to bloody well try, aren't I?"

"Sneaking around doesn't come natural to you, does it?" the corner of his mouth turned up in a half smile. "Come on sweetheart, let's get you home."

As planned, they stopped at the corner of the street opposite where she lived, but still in view of her door. If her mother did happen to look from a window, it was unlikely that she would be able to see them, as daylight had now gone, and they stood in the shadow of darkness.

Turning to face Teddy with the intention of thanking him again for walking her home, the words got stuck in her throat. Although it was dark, she couldn't miss his deep sensual breathing. When he stepped a little closer to her, she felt his hot breath against her skin.

"I know I said I wouldn't, but I need to kiss you again."

Jenny's breathing faltered, as a pulse of arousal cursed its way around her body, causing goose bumps to prickle across her skin and an awkward shifting of her hips as she tried to squeeze away the sensation that she had between her legs. Just words. Just his voice and a simple request from him, could have this effect on her.

"Can I kiss you goodnight?"

"Yes," she whispered, scarcely audible, but Teddy heard it as clear as if she'd shouted it out loud. Crushing his lips to hers, he brought her into his arms.

Jenny's hands gripped the fabric that covered his firm chest, needing something to hold onto, to steady her. When her hands moved up and around his neck, her fingers toying with the short-cropped hair at the back of his head, his jacket slid from her shoulders and fell to the floor. Neither of them noticed. Neither of them cared, as at that moment, they were utterly consumed with each other.

Jenny could feel a hardness against her stomach. She wasn't stupid. She knew exactly what it was, and although she knew that she should be shocked, it thrilled her that she had this effect on him. The temptation to put her hand there and explore was too strong to resist, but Teddy took a step back, breaking their connection. Jenny gave a deep whimpering sigh of disapproval.

"Meet me tomorrow?" Teddy growled out his request. "After work, even if it's just for a few moments."

"Okay, at the shop, six o'clock."

With one more quick but heated kiss, he pushed her gently in the direction of her house, before he lost all control. He wanted her so badly, but he knew that one more sweet taste of her lips, would make it too difficult for him resist.

When she got to the door, she slipped off her shoes and picked them up, before turning to see him one last time. There was no sign of him, but she knew he was there. She could feel his eyes on her and it filled her with excitement.

Slipping silently into the house, Jenny closed the door behind her, taking the stairs quickly, making sure she missed the second creaking step, and got safely into her bedroom without been caught. Undressing in haste, she bundled the dress and shoes together and stuffed them into the bottom of her wardrobe. Once in her cotton nightdress, she jumped into bed, and closed her eyes in search of sleep. Within seconds, her eyes flew back open and she smiled. Thoughts of the evening occupied her head and sleep was the last thing on her mind.

Chapter 6

Over the next week, every chance he had, Teddy would call into the shop for coffee, or meet her around the back after work. Although their time together was limited, both were growing closer and closer to each other. Each kiss grew more intense, but were only short stolen kisses, as they never had the privacy for it to be anything more.

It was Friday and Teddy hadn't been in the shop, which may have been a good thing, as Jenny had been on edge all day. Knowing her luck, both her mother and Teddy would have come into the shop at the same time, something she didn't relish in the slightest.

So, when it came to finishing time and she looked out of the back window into the yard, her heart sored as it always did, when she saw Teddy leaning up against the wall waiting for her. However, when she stepped outside to greet him, a feeling of dread swept over her. His body was stiff, his face soulful, his demeanour far from his usually happy self. When he did see her, he smiled, but immediately, Jenny knew it was forced. He walked towards her with purpose, taking her into his arms and holding her like he never wanted to let go.

"What's wrong?"

"There's a rumour going around that we might be moving out." He held her even tighter, so tightly, that she almost couldn't breathe. "I don't want to leave you Jenny."

"When will you be going?" she asked, her voice cracking with emotion.

"Nothing's certain, but usually when there's talk, it's a sure bet that somethings going to happen. It could be days, if we're lucky, weeks. I just don't know."

"Teddy." Jenny pushed up on her tiptoes and placed her mouth against his, a soft whimper of despair muted with a kiss. Teddy kissed her back with every desperate emotion that consumed him. His heart aching with the thought of leaving the girl he'd begum to have such deep feelings for.

"Take me somewhere where we can be alone," Jenny whispered. Teddy looked at her questioningly, not sure if he understood what it was that she wanted.

"Are you saying what I think you're saying Jenny, because, if I have you all to myself, I'm sure I will be able to hold back."

"I want to be intimate with you Teddy, not just the way we are now, but in every way, before it's too late, before the chance is lost."

"Jenny, are you sure about this? This means…"

Jenny placed a finger across his lips and blew out a soft "shh!" from her soft pink lips. "Now, today."

Teddy took hold of her hand and led her out of the yard. "I borrowed one of the jeeps, its parked a couple of streets down." Teddy, still holding her hand firmly, started in one direction, only to be pulled in the other.

"This way," Jenny tugged on his arm. "It will be quicker if we cut through the ginnel."

"The what?"

"The alleyway," she sniggered.

Sure enough, the short-cut got them to the military vehicle in no time. Jenny pulled a scarf from her pocket, wrapped it around her head and secured it by tying two of the corners under her chin. It was partly to protect her hair while in the open vehicle, but also if she kept her head down, hopefully if they are seen, no one would realise that it was her. It was one of the downfalls of living in a small village. Everyone knew everyone and quick to spread any juicy gossip.

Jenny wrapped her arms around Teddy's neck, when he scooped her up and placed her into the passenger side of the green vehicle. Walking around to the other side, he jumped into the driver seat, and as soon as the engine rumbled into life, he headed out of the village.

"Where are we going?" Jenny shouted over the noise of the engine once they had gained some distance.

"There's a little guest house about thirty minutes away, where we can rent a room." Despite the noise, the gasp that Jenny made instantly got Teddy's attention. He also didn't miss the way her finger nails dug deep into the seat beside her leg.

"Jenny, what's wrong?"

"Have you... ... ..."

"I can't hear you."

Jenny shook her head, then turned her face away from him.

Teddy swerved to the left, pulling into the side of the road and cut the engine. He placed his hand over hers, softly squeezing and caressing, until the tension in her grip relaxed.

"Do you want me to take you home?"

"No... no, it's just that." She slowly turned to face him, her eyes sad and questioning. "Have you taken any girls there before?"

"Fuck no." Jenny's mouth falls open, shocked by the swear word that flew so easily from his mouth. He brought her hand up to his lips and kissed the palm. With his free hand, he took her chin firmly, and looked in to her deep brown eyes. "Never, Jenny. Never. Guys talk about the place, but this will be the first time I've ever gone there," he hesitated for a moment, "that's if you still want to go." When Jenny didn't speak a word, he added, "I'll take you home."

"I don't want to go home," her voice now clear and full of determination. "Teddy, let's go."

* * *

Teddy parked the jeep at the side of a large detached house. A sign showed rooms for rent, and made a squeaking sound every time it was caught by the soft breeze. Leaping from his seat, Teddy walked to the other side of the Jeep and held out his hand to Jenny.

When her feet hit the ground, her legs wobbled a little, but however much her nervousness tried to take over, a deep and powerful need was winning the battle.

They walked with speed towards the painted black door that sat central at the front of the house. When Teddy tried the handle, it opened. His eyes connected with Jenny's. He could tell she was nervous, but the sure nod of her head and soft smile on her lips, reaffirmed that she wanted this too.

* * *

The room consisted of just a bed, a small single draw bedside table and a narrow wardrobe, which was about the only furniture you could fit bearing in mind how tiny the room was. A small sink was tucked into the corner, the communal toilet however, was just down the hall. Jenny was amazed that there was a sink in the corner of the room and an inside toilet.

Teddy however, couldn't help noticing the peeling wallpaper, the damp patch in the corner of the ceiling and the thread bare rug that would have once been vibrant in colour, but was now dark and dull.

"I'm sorry Jenny. I thought this place was better than this," Teddy voiced. "Maybe we should try and find somewhere else."

"It's fine," she slipped her hand into his and gave it a reassuring squeeze. "It might be a little tired, but it's clean." A shy smile played across her face as she added, "And we're alone."

Tugging on her hand he brought her into his arms. No longer able to hold back, he held her firmly around the waist as his lips found hers.

Jenny's response was just as needy, and she returned the pressure to his lips. When the tip of his tongue pushed into her mouth, sweeping against hers, she showed no resistance. In fact, she followed his lead and tried to match his every move.

A deep groan vibrated in his throat, as his hands moved higher, his thumbs skimming the underside of each breast. He hesitated, waiting to see if she would stop him, but when her body pushed back against his touch, looking for more, he cupped one breast, caressing it, squeezing it and teasing the little hard nub that was stood prominent through the fabric.

The way he touched her. The feelings she had when his fingers rubbed over the material that covered her nipple. His hands were on her breast, but the sensations. It felt like he touched her there, her intimate spot, right between her legs. She wanted more. Jenny broke the kiss, desperately needing to catch her breath. At first, Teddy thought she was pulling away from him, but when her hand moved over his firm shoulders, down his back and came to rest on his ass, he knew that this was far from over.

"Jenny, can I undress you?" His voice was thick with need.

"Mmh!" she murmured, as she sucked the corner of her bottom lip into her mouth.

A Military Anthology

Eager to see what was hiding beneath her clothing, he pushed her coat from her shoulders, not caring a damn when it just falls to the floor. The small fabric covered button at the top of the back of her dress, was not so easy. Jenny quickly took over, popping it free with her smaller nimble fingers, while kicking off her shoes at the same time. Once the button was free, she grasped a handful of her dress and pulled it up and over her head in one swift movement.

Standing in front of him, in just her pale pink underwear, was something she thought would terrify her, but the way his eyes roamed her body, made her skin tingle. The way it made her feel, left her only wanting to show him more.

Once unhooked at the back, she let the bra straps slip over her shoulders and slide down her arms. Slowly releasing her full round breasts as it fell to the floor. With her fingers hooked inside the waistband of her knickers, she pushed them down. Once past her hips, the loose-fitting pants freefall, laying in a pool around her ankles. Stepping forward out of them, left her naked and also one step nearer to Teddy.

Teddy was so aroused from watching her undress, that his cock pushed uncomfortably against the stiff course material of his pants, desperate to be released. He couldn't take his eyes from her. Her body is exceptional and much more than he had imagined it to be. The soft curves, the creamy skin, the gentle bounce of her full breasts from her rapid breathing. Her waist narrow, but her hips had just the right amount of flair, along with a gentle roundness to her stomach. A triangle of downy dark brown hair nestled between strong thighs, tapered down to her slim ankles.

"Damn, you're breathtakingly beautiful."

Desperate to feel her naked skin against his own, he shrugged off his leather jacket and threw it on top of the pile of clothes gathering on the floor. Tugging at the fawn coloured tie around his neck, he released it and slid it from under his lapel. Next came the shirt, his fingers struggled to unbutton it due to his haste. Jenny stepped forward and began unbuttoning it too.

Her forwardness took them both by surprise, no more so than Jenny herself.

Pulling at his shirt until it came out from the waistband of his trousers, she started to push it over his shoulders. While distracted by the sight of his firm chest, the lines defining the muscles along his abdomen, Teddy took control of removing his shirt, balling it up and hurled it to join the rest of the discarded clothing. Her hands shook a little when she unfastened his belt, but Teddy's wasn't sure if it was a sign of her own need, nervousness or that she was cold. Whatever the case, he was certain he couldn't wait to warm her with the heat of his own body.

Kicking off his pants, shoes and socks, left Teddy just in his flannel shorts. As Jenny didn't make a move to unbutton the waist, Teddy decided that for now, he would leave them on.

Stepping closer to Jenny, he tentatively put a hand behind her head, and brought his mouth to hers. As their bodies touched, Jenny shivered from both the warmth and feel of his skin against hers. This was new to her, the feel of a man's body against her, the intimacy and deep passion that was evident in his kiss and the way it had awakened her desires.

As Teddy moved forward, Jenny stepped back and in just a few steps her knees hit the side of the bed. He guided her until she was sitting on the edge, then dropped to his knees in front of her, not once taking his lips from hers. His hand cupped her chin, then circled her delicate neck, before laying the flat of his hands across her collar bone. Moving down to her breasts, he covered the full mounds with his hands, taking the weight of them in each palm. He squeezed, not too hard, not too soft, but enough to warrant a high-pitched squeal of surprise from Jenny. A pinch of one of her nipples got a stronger reaction, and has her pulling away for a few seconds before pushing her tit back into his hand. Two, three, maybe four more pulls of each nipple had her squirming in her seat. When Teddy replaced one of his hands with his mouth, her body arched into him wanting more. Much more.

Jenny gasped when she felt the warm wetness surround her already over sensitive nipple. Her head dropped back as her gasps of pleasure turned to a throaty moan when his teeth nipped at the fleshy skin of her breast, before taking the whole of her nipple into his mouth and sucking it hard.

"Oh!" fell from her lips when he eased her legs apart and moved his attentions further down her body. "Ooohh!" The sound seemed to drag out forever, when he pushed her legs further apart, his head dropped between them and his mouth covers her. Her thighs try to clamp together, but he held them firmly apart as he pushed further with his tongue. The tightness in her stomach, rush of warmth and wetness between her legs only intensified when he found her clit and began to tease it.

"No, no, ooohhhhhh!" she groaned, as her back arches and her legs began to shake. Uncontrollably, her hips moving forward to enforce more pressure, yet at the same time her hand tried to push his head away, as if her body was fighting between wanting more, and it being too much to bear.

"Let it happen Jenny, let your body feel." Teddy murmured, before he sucked hard on her swollen nub.

When she came, Teddy didn't stop, but lifted his eyes so he could watch her, she her face when his name spilling from her flushed face with a scream, as he lapped up the effects of her orgasm that spilled into his mouth.

* * *

Jenny was still in a haze, laid halfway across the narrow bed, when Teddy lifted her and moved her fully onto it. Laying down beside her, he cradled her with his arms, bringing her body flush against his. Holding her close, his hands stroked her dewy skin, while she slowly regained a steady breathing pattern.

Releasing his hold, he moved over her. With a hand at each side of her head, and a knee at each side of her hips, his shoulder muscles tight and flex as he held his body mere inches away from hers. The first touch was his lips against the silky skin that covered the pulse point at her neck. Along her chin his mouth roamed, until it pressed firmly against hers. She welcomed him eagerly, returning the kiss with a fierceness that only a woman wanting more would give. A deep, gravelly moan vibrated in Teddy's throat, as once again he felt the delight of her naked skin against his. Pushing his shorts over his hips, with a little shake and persuasion they dropped over his feet to the side of the bed. When his erect cock touched the soft down of her pubic hair, he couldn't help but tilt his hips, rocking his hardness against it.

It was now Jenny's turn to moan, instinct had her opening her legs and pulling her knees up, giving him more access.

"I want you inside me," she urged, her fingers clawed at his back, trying to find tenure, pulling him closer to her.

"Jenny," he gasps. "Is it your first time?" She nodded, a flush of embarrassment covered her face. "I want you so much Jenny, but I need to know that you're sure about this."

Jenny moved her hand between them, and touched his hard penis. At first, it was just a feather light touch, but when she curled her fingers around the already hard shaft, giving it a firm but cautious squeeze, Teddy threw his head back, hissing as he tried to supress his urges. This precious girl below him had his head spinning and was pushing him far too close to losing his control.

"Make love to me Teddy. Please I..." He cut her words with a searing kiss, of which she returned with equal potency. Bringing her hands up around to the back of his head, her fingers unable to get a firm hold of his short-cropped hair, dug into his scalp. Having given her a taste of what could be, the raging feelings, the sensual experience had lit a fire in her. A fire that demanded more.

As much as Teddy wanted to plough his hard, pulsing cock straight into her, he knew that she wasn't ready for that. He kissed her with a softness that had her wriggling beneath him. His tongue teased her mouth with precision, when he slid a finger inside her. A quick, sharp inhale, had Jenny taking in his breath as her body jolted and stiffened from the intrusion, but as he started to stroke her gently inside, she began to relax and settled back into his all-consuming kiss. Teddy slowly added another finger as he tried to prepare her for his cock. He wasn't huge, but he wasn't small either and when fully hard, his cock was thick and girthy. Jenny's body began to tremble under him as her arousal began to build. Unable to hold off any longer, Teddy removed his fingers. A soft whine of displeasure slipped from her, but was only short lived when he tilted his hips towards her, and his cock pushed up against her already glistening pussy. Sliding his shaft and head along her folds until his dick was covered in her juices, she was left gasping, muffled little whimpers of want. With his hand, he gave himself two quick strokes, making sure he was hard, and covered in her lubrication, before lining himself up, placing the tip at her entrance.

Teddy released her hands from her head, taking one in each of his own, lacing his fingers between hers, before pinning them to the pillow at each side of her head. He brushed his lips against hers. He gripped her hands firmly. His blue eyes sort out hers and as they connected, he held her gaze, with extraordinary intensity, as he thrusted in quick and deep.

Her strangled cry was partly muffled with the intensity of his kiss, and it took everything he had not to pump in and out of her deliciously warm, wet pussy with vigour. However, he stopped still, allowing her body to adjust to his intrusion.

Breaking the kiss, he watched as moisture collected along her thick dark lashes. When a tear began to fall from the corners of her eye, he released one of her hands, so he could catch it with his thumb, before it makes its way onto her flushed cheek. Putting his thumb to his mouth, he sucked in the salty tear, letting it linger on his tongue. His heart tightened, gripped with guilt for hurting her, but he could only hope that the short sharp penetration, had a less lingering pain and discomfort to a slow drawn out one.

"Honey, you look so fucking beautiful," he murmured, as he began to withdraw from her. When she bit the side of her lip, and her grip of his hand became stronger, he takes it slow. It pushed his restraint to the max, but determined to turn the unpleasant feeling into a pleasurable one, he took his time. When he was almost all the way out, he slowly pushed back in. Slipping his hand between them, with two fingers he began to roll and flick them across her clit.

Rocking in and out of her, teasing her clit with his skilled fingers, it wasn't long before the pain was forgotten and is replaced with sensations that are intense. Her body began to move in conjunction with his, wanting more, wanting everything.

First came the tell-tale sign of her legs shaking. Then the rapid volley of moans that spilt from her mouth.

"Come for me Jenny," Teddy growled, on the edge of his own orgasm. "Come."

Teddy's cock felt every internal squeeze, every spasm, every god damn contraction, when her orgasm hit. Her tightness as he stoked in and out of her just a few more times, is enough to have him plummeting toward his own release. Muscle's taut. Breathing rapid. Skin slick with sweat.

"Fuck, Jenny... fuck," he groaned out, as he shot his hot cum deep inside her.

Exhausted and spent, he collapsed to her side, eyes closed, panting like he'd just done a ten-mile marathon. Reaching out and retrieving his shorts, he used them to clean them both up, before taking Jenny into his arms, and placing a kiss to the top of her head. Her shoulders began to shake, and a soft stifled noise vibrated against his chest.

"Sweetheart," he cooed, "I'm sorry. I know I hurt you, but," he lifted her chin with his finger only to find a smile on her tear stained face. "Jenny?"

"It did hurt but… it was… bloody great," she stuttered between gentle sobs. "And you shouted fuck."

Teddy looked at her with amazement, his pinched together eyebrows slowly relaxed as he smiled. She placed a hand on the side of his face and stretches up to place a soft kiss on his lips. When she moves back, the smile is no longer there, only dark heavy eyes look back at her.

"What are you doing to me Jenny?" he growls out. Taking her hand, he places it over his hard cock. "This is what you do to me Jenny, you're so fucking sexy. My dick has been hard since the first time I saw you." He covered her mouth with his, sweeping his tongue along the seam of her lips, until she opened them, welcoming him in. His tongue forged forward, exploring her mouth with an urgency that left them both gasping for breath.

Jenny's hand still laid where he left it, but now it began to explore his firmness. Holding, stroking, fingers wrapped around the shaft, moving from hilt to tip. Her fingertips fluttered across the head, picking up a droplet of pre-cum and spread it across the smooth silky skin.

"Fuck," Teddy growled, before placing his hand over hers and stopping her from making another move. "You need to stop sweetheart, otherwise, I'm going to come again."

"Don't you want that?" Teddy removed her hand but kept hold of it, bringing it to his mouth and placing a kiss right in the middle of her palm.

"I'd rather be inside you, so you can feel it too." Wrapping his arms around her, he brought her close. Her head dropped to his shoulder, so he can breathe her in. "But I don't think that's a good idea, do you?" Jenny shook her head against his chest. "Are you really sore?"

"Just a bit," she mumbled, slipping her arms around his waist.

"What time do you need to be home?"

"About an hour ago," Jenny sighed. Her body shivered, and her apprehension was blatantly obvious.

"Maybe we should get dressed, get you back home before your parents start getting worried." Teddy moved to get up, but the hold around his waist only tightened. He increased his hold on her too, as they lay wrapped in each other's arms, only the sound of their breathing can be heard.

"Do you ever wish that you could freeze a moment in time so it would never end, even though the world outside is in turmoil?" He asked quietly.

"Mhm! Have you?"

"Not until now," she tilted her face up to him, her eyes glazed with emotion. "I wish we could stay here, like this. No orders, no interference, no restrictions. Just you and me, locked in each other's arms, kissing, making love, exploring our bodies and minds."

"If only," she choked out, clear emotion in her voice.

Teddy rolled them, until she was flat on her back, and he was above her, looking deep into her eyes.

"I wish I could shower you with promises Jenny, but I can't. The war makes all our lives complicated, unpredictable. I could be here for weeks, months, but then again, I could be gone tomorrow." Teddy's mouth was so close to hers when he whispered. "But I know one thing darling," their lips brushed against each other as he spoke. "Every moment possible, every chance I get, I want to spend it with you."

Chapter 7

Jenny slipped into the house quietly, closing the door slowly so that her return was as inconspicuous as possible. When she turned to make her way up to her room, she was stopped in her tracks by the sight of her mam standing at the bottom of the stairs. Dressed in her winceyette nightie, she stood ridged, arms crossed, and face full of thunder. Jenny, straightened her back, standing tall in readiness for the inevitable telling off.

"And where have you been till this time?" her mother shouted.

"Out," she replied sharply. Her mam grabbed her roughly by the arm when she tried to get past her.

"I told you to come straight home," her voice full of anger. "What has gotten into you Jennifer, you constantly disobey me. You've been with Nora, haven't you? Even though I forbade you to. She's trouble Jennifer and God only knows what you've been getting up to with her." The last couple of words she almost spat in her face. Her voice got louder, the pitch higher as her ranting carried on. "That's it Jennifer, and I mean it this time, no more hanging around with that girl."

Jenny shook her arm free, taking a step back and folded her arms across her body, mirroring her mother.

"Mother, I'm nearly eighteen, I have a job, I earn my own money, so I think I'm old enough to decide when and who I want to hang around with."

"I don't think so. In fact, from now on my girl, other than work and church, you are not allowed out of this house. Do you hear me?"

"I think the whole street can hear you." Dad gritted out as he walked down the stairs. "What's all the racket about?"

Her mam opened her mouth to speak, but Jenny jumped in first.

"Nothing new dad, just mam treating me like a kid. Don't do this, don't do that, come straight home, don't be hanging around with that Nora," she said in a voice that was not that dissimilar to her mother's when she went off on one. "It's not fair, I'm an adult, and it's about time she started treating me like one. She needs to back the hell off and let me have some freedom. I can't…"

"Don't speak to your mam like that, Jenny" her dad interrupted with a sigh. He was stood halfway down the stairs. Dark circles are visible under his tired eyes, a shadow of stubble on his chin that will undoubtedly be removed before his next work shift. He ran a hand through his unruly hair and yawned.

"Lord have mercy." Her mam makes the sign of the cross over her chest. "What if the women at church get wind of this. We'll be the laughing stock of the village. I can't be seen to have a daughter who carries on like this."

"Like what?" Jenny screamed back at her mother. "Like a young woman, who has a social life that might include a pint at the pub, a laugh with a few friends, a date with a man?" Jenny held her hands up. "Lord strike me down, for I kissed a soldier."

"You did what?" her mam shouted.

"Bloody hell mother…"

"Enough," her dad's voice boomed out. Jenny jumped, shocked at his outburst as he very rarely shouted. "Go to bed. We'll discuss this tomorrow."

Jenny gave her mam an evil stare, before stomping her way up the stairs. She stopped halfway when she came face to face with her dad. His expression was hard. Normally, she would kiss his cheek before she went to bed, but as he seemed to have sided with her mam, the feeling of betrayal rested heavy in her heart, as she pushed past him, and going straight to her room.

Once dressed in her night clothes, Jenny pulled out the pot from under her bed. Hitching up the bottom of her flannelette nightie, she crouched to wee. She hissed when it stung, but then smiled as she remembered the reason behind it and the all-consuming events of the day. Once finished, she placed the pot back under the bed, before climbing under the covers. Within minutes, she pulled herself up into a seated position and yanked her nightie back off. She wanted to be naked, be free from the restrictions of any clothing. Her hand reached between her legs, as she tentatively explored the area that still felt tender. The memory of how he held her so tightly, comforting and soothing her, showing her affection that she rarely experienced, pushed her to tears. This time it's tears not from pain or anger, but

Help Our Heroes

from a whirlwind of emotion and feelings for her American G.I.

Chapter 8

It was difficult, that was for sure. The time they had was limited, and not in the most romantic of settings, but when they were together, it was everything to them. A heated moment in the back room of the shop, while waiting for the kettle to boil. A stolen kiss when Betty was distracted. Not once did they get the chance to re-enact the incredible moments that they shared that day. All that did accomplished was to intensify their mutual desire for each other even more.

Rumours were still rife within the camp. It was now looking more like a when, rather than if, Teddy's platoon would be moving out. So, when they were granted a few hours leave, Teddy made his way straight to the shop to see Jenny.

He caught the door, holding it back for the elderly lady who was just leaving, then slipped into the shop.

Jenny stood halfway up some wooden steps, duster in hand, flicking the yellow fabric between the boxes stored on the top shelf. She was singing. He hadn't heard the song before, but it had a sweet, uplifting tone to it. However, her voice was a little out of pitch. Oblivious to his arrival and Betty was nowhere to be seen, he slipped quietly behind the counter. Leaning with his back against the counter, his eyes roam her body, from her dark glossy shoulder length hair, down her back to her narrow waist. His eyes lingered on her skirt covered ass, before trailing down to her slim ankles. Her legs were bare, but the line she'd drawn from the edge of her shoe, up the back till it disappeared under the hem of her skirt, gave the illusion that they were clad in silk. The temptation was too much. He placed his hand just above her knee and slid it under the fabric, quickly moving it up till it hit the plump round of her ass.

Jenny let out a scream, jumped and lost her footing. The steps wobbled erratically, and she started to fall backwards. Before she has time to realise what was happening, Teddy had caught her, scooping her up, with one arm behind her back and the other under her legs, holding her against him. His lips found hers and she melted into him. Mint flavoured kisses that were soft and sweet, and said 'I've missed you'.

"Can you get away?" Teddy whispered against her lips. Their breaths mingled with each other, between the peppered kiss that he placed on her natural soft pink lips.

"I don't know," Jenny panted. Her body already alight from his touch, already craving more.

"She'll meet you around the back in a couple of minutes." Betty interrupted, walking in from the back room.

They both looked at Betty, before turning their eyes to each other. Realising that they were still in a bit of a compromising position, Jenny smacked Teddy lightly on his chest and wriggled until he relaxed the hold on her legs. Her feet hit the ground enabling her to stand, but his hand stayed firmly around her waist.

"Well, go on then," Betty waved at Teddy. "Round the back like I said, so the gossip mongers don't see you together and put two and two together and make... Well I suppose in this case...," she tutted and shook her head, but you'd be blind to miss the gentle curl at the corner of her mouth, her attempt at supressing a smile failing miserably.

Teddy kissed the top of Jenny's head, before he made to leave. When the door closed behind him, Jenny brushed down the skirt of her dress and gave Betty a sheepish look.

"Don't look at me like that Jenny, I'm not stupid, nor heartless." She chided. "It's obvious you've fallen in love with the man."

"Love? I don't think..."

"Tell me. Does your heart beat faster every time you're near him?"

Jenny looked at her feet.

"When he looks at you, do you feel like he's touching you, every part of you, making your skin tingle, even though his hands are still in his pockets?"

Jenny gave her a delicate nod.

"When he kisses you do you feel hot, light headed, unable to breath. A million and one butterflies are dancing in your very core."

Jenny opened her mouth to speak, but the words seemed to get stuck on her tongue, like they were jumbled together and stuck with emotional glue. So, she nodded again, but this time it was clear and precise.

Betty walked towards Jenny and placed her hands on her upper arms, making slow, short soothing strokes.

"That's exactly how my William makes me feel," Betty's smile was tainted with sadness. "And I love him more than life itself. The times I've wanted to give it all up is ridiculous, but until I know for sure that he's gone, I can't give up on my love."

Jenny wrapped her arms around Betty who in turn, hugged her right back, as the silent tears stain both of their faces.

Betty released her hold first, pushing Jenny away from her before wiping the tears from her own face, with the back of her hand.

"Right come on. There's a handsome GI out there waiting for you, so why the hell are you still here?"

Jenny couldn't help but giggle at her incredible friend. If only she had this type of relationship with her mother.

Betty followed Jenny through to the back, watching her while she removed her apron, and replaced it with her coat.

With a hand on the door handle, Jenny stopped, turned to Betty and said, "Thank you Betty. You're right," she added, "I do love him, but the uncertainty of everything, the war, how much time we have, well, it scares me."

Betty covered her own mouth with her hand and swallowed down the choking cry that was threatening to escape.

"You know I love you like a sister and the last thing I would want for you is to be hurt, but if you do love him, my advice is to not dwell on the what if's, the maybe's. Grab every moment that you can, make magical memories that you can cherish forever."

Running back into Betty's arms, she hugged her with everything she had, before quickly turning and running out the door.

When Teddy saw Jenny's tear stained face, he brought her into his arms, holding her tight against his firm body. He tucked loose strands of her hair behind her ear, before brushing his lips against it.

"Why are you crying?" Her fingers sank into the leather of his jacket that covered his back, pulling him even closer to her.

"Just…" she pushed her face into his chest and breathed him in.

"Jenny?" using his index finger, her lifted her chin, so she had no option but to meet his gaze.

"Nothing, I'm just being a silly emotional girl," she smiled. "Come on?" clutching his hand with both of hers, she walked backwards out of the yard, bringing him with her.

"Where do you want to go?" he asked as he followed her.

"My house."

"Your house, are you sure about that? What about your folks?"

"Dad's at work and Mam's gone into town on church business. The house is empty." Jenny knew there was a chance that they might be seen by one of the neighbours, who would no doubt relish the chance of spilling the beans to her mother, but she had no intention on wasting the precious time it would take to get to the little B&B. She was fed-up with only having a quick fondle and a stolen kiss or two. She wanted to feel his body next to her, feel his hot, moist mouth on her naked skin. His fingers caressing her intimately, until he pushed her to that special euphoric place that left her breathless and sedated. The dreams that had plagued her sleep where just that, dreams. Now she wanted the reality.

The catch on the door to Jenny's room had not even clicked, before they were tugging each other's clothes off. Not once did they break their heated kiss, at least not until they fell back against the wall, the air in their lungs escaping in great big gasps.

"You are so fucking sexy," he growled as he took her nipple and sucked it deep into his mouth, instigating a high-pitched squeal from Jenny. He lets the hard bud pop from his mouth, then soothed it with a gentle sweeping of his tongue. "So, fucking sexy."

The soft moans that resonated from Jenny's lips, are in total contrast to the pressure of her finger nails as they sank into his scalp, while his mouth moved down her body. Hot wet licks, mouth sucking at her heated skin, are mixed with delicate feather light kisses, sending sparks of fire throughout her body. Too fast.

Too soon. Jenny wanted the moment to last forever. Pushing hard against his chest, Teddy backed off and stood at the side of the small single bed, wondering what the hell was going on. When she dropped to her knees in front of him, taking his cock into her mouth, his legs nearly buckled.

"Fuck," he panted out. His hand impulsively went to her head, his fingers grasping her hair, as she began to move her mouth up and down his hardness. When he felt himself getting dangerously close to exploding, he grabbed her hair, pulling her mouth free from him. "Stop... damn... stop Jenny," he panted.

"Oh my god. Sorry, doesn't that feel good?"

"Jenny, honey, it feels too good, that's the problem. As much as I'd love to come in your mouth, I'd much prefer to come in your pussy."

His dirty talk, shocked Jenny, but also caused a tightening in her stomach and pulsing between her legs.

"Sit on the edge of the bed and open your legs for me." Teddy's voice was deep, dominating and demanding. "I need to taste you."

With his hot mouth on her, his flattened tongue rubbing hard against her swollen clit, fingers pumping in and out of her already soaked pussy, her orgasm built fast. When her legs began to tremble, so close, so very close, he pulled away from her, only to replace it with his hard cock. She whimpered as he pushed into her, slow but precise, stretching her until he was full seated. The sting was still there, but nothing like the previous time. Covering her mouth with his, he kissed her deeply, the remnants of her juices still lingered on his tongue. Jenny tasted the subtle saltiness but didn't feel the disgust that she thought she would. In fact, it merely heightened her arousal even more.

"Damn, you're so tight darling, so fucking tight," he growled through clenched teeth, as he languidly moved his hips back and then forward again. "So good, so fucking good."

The more he thrusted in and out of her, the lesser the pain. The faster he moved his hips, the quicker the sensations raced around her body, bringing her more and more pleasure, speeding her closer and closer to what her body, mind and soul was craving. His touch. His passion. Him.

Bringing her leg up and over his shoulder, a quick twist of his hips and he was deeper than she thought possible, hitting a spot inside that ignited a whole new bundle of sensation. She moaned, his name spilled from her mouth, her back arched, vision blurred and body shuddering, as she fell into an abyss of pure bliss. Teddy followed her, the tight warm grip of her inner muscles, pushing him past the point of no return, that had him growling out her name.

They collapsed onto the bed, their bodies slick with sweat, holding onto each other tightly, afraid that if they didn't, they would certainly fall.

Once their breathing was stable, Teddy rolled onto his back bringing Jenny with him, until she was laid on top of him. Moving her body up, they came face to face. Her hands slipped around his neck, fingers cupping the back of his head as she placed her lips to his. The sweetness of her kiss had him tightening his arms around her, his hand stroking the round of her ass, before pulling it back and giving it a quick, sharp slap.

"Ouch!" Jenny cries out as she jumped back, but Teddy just pulled her back into him, bringing her mouth back to his, but with a much deeper type of kiss. With the heat of his tongue and a need to take her very breath. Rolling Jenny onto her back, his hand played with her breasts, teasing and nipping her nipples in turn, each time instigating a sharp gasp, of which he captured with his mouth. He made a trail with his fingers from her breast bone, past her navel, until it stopped at her pelvic bone. Running his fingers through the soft hair, he strokes a fingertip over her pussy lips a few times, before pushing into her folds that were still coated with his cum and her wetness. Again, he brought her to a point where she was just about to burst, before he switched, flipping them back over, moving her till she was straddling him. With his strong hands holding her hips, he rotated his own hips, so his hardness rubbed up against her pussy, wanting her so desperately to ride his cock. As if knowing exactly what he was wanting, she pushed up on her legs, lining herself up with the tip of his cock. It was barely inside her, before she dropped down, taking him all the way in. Coarse pubic hair grazed her swollen clit every time their bodies came together. Speeding up, her need for release grew, Jenny began to whimper with frustration, when her rhythm began to falter. Teddy dug his fingers into the flesh of her hips and with his strong arms and determination, he took control. Jenny grasped hold of his forearms, to steady herself, her body shaking so profoundly, her breathing erratic, strangled cries bursting from her lips. One, two, three... deeper, harder thrusts. Bodies crashing, skin slapping together with a force that's unmeasurable. Names cried out, moans, groans, bodies ridged, skin slick with sweat, as they came together.

* * *

"Are you sore," Teddy spoke into Jenny's mess of hair. She was laid at his side, her arm placed on his chest, dreamily tracing circles around his nipples. She didn't answer, just murmured. "Let me check for you," Teddy rolled to his side, his hand sweeping over her stomach about to move south, when they hear a sound from downstairs.

"Bugger, what was that?" Jenny jumped up, suddenly lucid.

"Who cares," Teddy smiled and tried to take up where he left off.

"Get up, get dressed," Jenny whisper shouted, slapping his hand away from between her legs. "Bloody hell, I don't even know what time it is. We need to go before my parents get back."

Teddy looked at her, taking in the mask of concern, all colour drained from her face. Sad that the beautiful, sexy post orgasm flush to her skin had gone.

"Please Teddy," she begged.

"Okay, but first..." he cupped her face with his hands, "one more kiss." Jenny blinked, for a second or two, not sure if she should indulge him, but then she leans forward and kissed him hard. "Damn!" he growled against her mouth when she pulled back.

Getting off the bed, Jenny gathered up Teddy's clothes and threw them into his lap, before collecting her own. Reluctantly, Teddy got up, using his shorts to wipe himself and then started to dress, but only because he hated to see the fear on Jenny's face.

Jenny sorted herself out, got clean knickers from her chest of drawers, then dresses quickly.

"I'll go first, check out what that noise was. God, I hope it's not me mam," Jenny griped.

"Surely, she's not that bad?"

"Are you joking," Jenny raised her eyebrows at him. "I'll never be let out again."

Help Our Heroes

"It's not like she can keep you prisoner in here."

"What? She'd have me locked up in't coalhole for weeks if she finds us. And Lord, if she knew what we'd been up to. She'd have me shipped off to the nearest convent, begging forgiveness and pledging my life to the church." Jenny put her forefinger across her lips and silently slipped through the door and out into the hallway.

Teddy had just finished fastening the last of his shirt buttons, and was looping his tie, when the door opened again.

"All clear," Jenny sighed. "It was just a note from one of the church do-gooders for my mother. We better go though, it's nearly four o'clock and I'd best get back to the shop to help Betty close up."

"Okay honey, let's go."

After sneaking out of the house, walking quickly to the end of the street, they slowed their pace, putting a discreet distance between them and headed towards the shop.

"You don't need to walk me back if you need to get back to barracks," Jenny said to him, while cautiously looking around to see who was about.

"That's not going to happen. Like I said before, every chance I get, I want to spend it with you," A soft smile played on his face. "But not being able to touch you, well that honey is kinda torture."

Jenny failed to hide the flush to her skin, the smile on her face, or control the butterflies from dancing in her stomach.

When they got to the back of the shop, a quick check around and Teddy pulled Jenny into the yard. Pushing her up against the wall, pressing his body firmly against hers, he kissed her. A soft, slow kiss. The type you see in the romance movies, that only last a few moments. This one lasted for what seemed like forever, but at the same time, finished far too soon.

"Damn, leaving you just seems to get harder," he whispered softly against her lips. "I just want to keep you Jenny, keep you close so I can see your smile, your beautiful eyes and watch your every move. You're like the air that I breath. You make me feel alive."

When he covered her mouth with his, hands laced in her hair, holding her, tilting her head, the power behind his kiss was explosive. Arousal crashed through her body, a million electric impulses shooting in every direction. Goose bumps covered her skin, her fingers tingling at the very tips. Her hands tightly grasped the lapel of his leather jacket, clinging on for dear life, the need to anchor herself to him overwhelming. "I feel it too," she murmured into his mouth, as a soft tear fell from the corner of her eye.

"I'll see you tomorrow sweetheart."

"Promise?"

"Baby, I promise." He sealed it with another kiss.

Walking away, their arms stretched out, hands still holding, until it's just no longer possible. Reluctantly they let go, palm against palm, fingertip against fingertip until nothing, when he disappeared out of the yard.

Chapter 9

Five days and nothing.

Every time the doorbell chimed, a rush of excitement hit Jenny, only to be crushed when it wasn't him. The look of pity on Bettys face did nothing to help her feelings of despair.

Every night, her mind replayed the events, dissecting every moment, looking for a reason why his promise wasn't kept.

Did she say something wrong? Was she too open with her feelings for him? Was she not good enough?

At first, she tried to explain it away with the fact that he might not have been able to come see her. Maybe any leave from the base had been suspended. But then, surely, he would have found a way to get a message to her. That was if he cared about her the way he'd said he did.

Then the doubts hit.

Was she just taken in by his flattery, so desperate for attention that she fell easily? Was it all a lie, just a way of get into her knickers? He knew that she was inexperienced. It was pretty obvious that she had been a virgin.

Had been. Not anymore.

Was she just another one of the many stupid girls, that got taken in by a good-looking GI?

What was it they kept saying?

"Overpaid, oversexed and over here. Maybe they should have added and over their stupidly naive women?" she said quietly to herself, while laid in bed. "What have I done?" Her hand covered her mouth, as she tried to dull the sound of her strangled sobs. Just like every other night, she rolled onto her stomach and pushed her face into her pillow to muffle the cries of her aching heart.

* * *

When Jenny walked into the kitchen the next morning, she was met by her mother.

"What's wrong with you, have you been crying?" her mother asked, her voice void of any true concern.

"No." Jenny let her hair fall over her face, trying to hide her red rimmed eyes. "I'm fine, just tired."

"Don't lie to me girl, I know exactly what this is all about," she hissed back at her. "Gallivanting about with that American man."

Jenny looked at her in horror.

"What? Didn't you think I'd find out?" she sniggered. "You should know better than that Jennifer. You can't keep secrets in this village my girl."

"That's not…"

"Not what, why you're crying? Don't lie to me. What's the matter, are you missing him already? Well, good riddance to the lot of them. Maybe now our village can get back to normal."

"He's gone?" Jenny's voice cracked as she started to well up again. Tears, so many tears.

"Of course, he's gone. Did you think he would stay around forever? Stupid girl." She stood with her hands on her hips looking back at Jenny with pure contempt.

"But he didn't even say goodbye."

"Oh, did I forget to mention that. I can't believe the cheek of him to be honest, coming here, knocking on my door."

"What do you mean he came here?" Jenny moved towards her mother, as her anger mounting.

"Apparently, they were shipping them out, down south somewhere, to another base. Mumbled something about no time to call at the shop and could I give you a message."

"What did he say?" Jenny grabbed one of her mother's wrists and squeezed it tight.

"Get your hands off me," her mother tried to yank her hand free, but Jenny just tightened her grip, pulling her nearer.

"Tell me what he said!" she screamed into her face, all her built up emotions ticking like a time bomb ready to explode.

Help Our Heroes

"Nothing, he said nothing. He just pushed a letter into my hands then left with the rest of them."

"What letter, where is the letter?"

"I. Burned. It," she spat.

"Jesus Christ mother, you're a fucking bitch!" Jenny screamed, her mother pulled back her free hand and slapped her hard across the face.

"How dare you speak to me like that?" her mother screeched back, grabbing a handful of Jenny's hair, ragging her head from side to side. "I will not listen to your profanities."

Many a time she had clashed with her mother, but never had she laid a hand on her.

Pushing hard against her mother, was enough to shock her into letting go, but not before she felt the sting at her scalp. As her mother fells against the cupboard, she steps back.

"I will never forgive you for this," she hissed, before turning her back on her.

Taking two steps at a time, she rushed up the stairs and burst into her room. In just a few moments she had collected most of the things she needed, while ignoring her mother's monotonous shouting and demands that she return at once and apologise.

"Over my dead body," she hurled back at her through the tears.

Stuffing the rest of the clothing that Betty had given her into an old laundry bag, she shoved it over her shoulder, grabbing the rest and made her way back down the stairs. Her mother stood hands on hips, waiting at the bottom. Jenny took great delight when her mother's expression went from cocky to surprised when she saw her laden bags.

"And where do you think you're going?"

"Out of here and out of your life," Jenny sniggered, barging past her. Slipping on her sensible shoes, she dropped one of the bags temporarily, so she could open the door. She didn't turn to look behind her, when she said clearly and precisely, "Goodbye mother," stepping across the threshold and slamming the door behind her.

* * *

"I'm coming," Betty shouted in response to the loud banging at the back door. "Hold your horses will you."

When she opened the door to find Jenny, crumpled in a heap on the floor, amongst bags of belongings, tears streaming down her face, a vice type grip took hold of her heart.

"Jenny, what's happened?" Bending to meet the shattered girl, she wrapped her arms around her and with all her strength, pulled her to her feet.

Once she was seated, she went back and dragged the bags through the door, before closing it behind her.

The deep heart wrenching sobs had Betty tearing up herself. It killed her to see her young friend shaken and so emotionally broken.

Standing behind the chair where she sat, Betty wrapped her arms around Jenny's shoulders and held her tight. With every deep, hacking sob that escaped her, Jenny's body jerked as the emotion spilled from deep within her. Slowly, and after quite some time, the tears subsided, and her heavy sobs became gentle cries.

"I've... left home," Jenny stuttered. "And I'm not going back. Please, can I stay here with you?" her pleading tearful eyes broke Betty's heart all over again.

"Of course," Betty gave her a gentle smile. "For as long as you want."

"Thank you," spilled out with another onset of tears.

"Wouldn't have it any other way," Betty patted and squeezed her hand. "Now, let me make you some sweet tea."

Epilogue

Eight weeks later

—

present time

Jenny

The billowing smoke obstructed the view from the train window, as it pulled into the Leeds station. With each hand, I grabbed the handle of the two suitcases that sat in front of me and joined the rest of the travellers making their way off the train.

The platform is a hive of activity, mostly people saying goodbye, not so many saying hello. Soldiers in their uniform, embracing their loved ones before they go on another journey to hell. My eyes fell on a young couple, a tiny boy child crying as his father holds him tight to him, while he kisses the tear stained face of the mother. I should look away, leaving them to their personal moment, but I can't help but stare, even though it hurt to watch. Impulsively, my hand goes to my stomach, even though there's no visible evidence to any onlookers, I know what's growing inside me. I'm well aware of the difficult journey I have in front of me, but it's one I need to take.

* * *

I was oblivious to my predicament, or was it ignorance? Who knew. When I had been sick four days in a row, Betty enlightened me. I don't know what I would have done without her. I cried, I screamed, I was adamant that I wanted rid of it. I wanted to seek out some back-street doctor that could put an end to it, without anyone knowing. Betty begged me to reconsider, pointing out that it wasn't a decision to be taken lightly. Betty opened up to me that day, told me things about her life, secrets that she kept hidden deep within her soul. It was then that I realised that I needed to decide for myself, for my future, and the future of my unborn child. One that would leave me with no regrets.

Would the baby remind me daily of my foolishness? Of the love that I had lost? Probably, but it was a pain that I was willing to live with. One that would be replaced with the joy and love for my child.

Betty wanted me to stay with her, so she could help me raise my child, but I couldn't stay in the village. Was it for my mother's sake? To spare her the shame of having a daughter, knocked up by her sweet G.I? I told myself no, but I'm not so sure. I certainly couldn't face the look of disappointment in the eyes of my father. So, I told myself it was for mine and my baby's sake. A new life and a new start.

* * *

I have a new job and somewhere to live, here in Leeds, all thanks to Betty. An old school friend of hers is in need of a live-in housekeeper and with two children, it's quite understandable. While the husband, a military man, is away on service, the mother, a doctor needs all the help that she can get. They're aware that I'm pregnant, although they're under the impression that my young husband is just one of the many victims of war. I'm sure it took all of Betty's powers of persuasion to get them to give me a chance. I'm hardly the perfect candidate.

Maybe they pity me. For once, I don't care. I know I'm one of the lucky ones to be given a helping hand, but I'm not too proud or stupid enough not to grab it with both hands.

* * *

My only regret is leaving my father. From him I feel love, even though he wasn't one to show it. My mother, well maybe the only love she will every have is for her beloved church. How my dad puts up with her, I'll never know. If only he was stronger and stood up to her from time to time, maybe things would have been different. Then again, he wouldn't then be my kind, gentle dad.

* * *

Was I just another victim of this god forsaken war? I wouldn't say that, I hadn't had to fight. I hadn't lost my life. In some ways, I had lost a love, but in reality, I was just given a different path through nobody's fault but my own.

Help Our Heroes

Nothing I have been or will go though could compare to that of the men and women who are up there on the front line. Fighting for our country. Fighting for our freedom and our way of life. If I can muster up just an ounce of their strength, then I know I will succeed.

So many lost and damaged lives.

Will this war ever end?

* * *

As I walk out of the station building, I notice a man in a black suit, holding up a piece of paper with my name displayed on it. Walking towards him, he gives me a subtle nod.

"Follow me madam."

I smile, he takes my bags and leads me to a car that will take me to my new life, my new start here in Leeds.

* * *

Although my life is under a cloud of uncertainty and it's not going to be easy being a single mother. I'll fight with everything I have, because I'll be buggered if I'm going to let it get the better of me.

The End.

A Military Anthology

Wounded Hero

Ava Manello

Ava first wrote about Declan in Declan (Wounded Heroes #1).

This short story gives you a little more insight into his feelings, and gives you an introduction to the full-length story.

As this anthology is in aid of Help for Heroes, she wanted to give you more of a feel for the PTSD that he suffers from, and how it affects him day to day.

Chapter 1

The therapist sat across from me, just waiting for me to speak. This must have been the third or fourth session now, and I'd yet to say anything. Still, she sat, waiting. There was no judgment, no condescension; to be honest there was nothing. I'm not sure why I kept going back. There was a part of me that wanted to get all this turmoil out, but there was a bigger part of me that wanted to keep it locked away, safe from exposure. It was like a poison invading my soul, and I wasn't sure how much longer I could keep fighting it.

The nightmares weren't restricted to my sleeping hours, not that I got much sleep. They'd started invading every part of my day. I knew that I had to do something; I almost killed a woman the other night before I came to my senses. Despite everything I've seen, everything I'd done in that hellish war zone, it's that night that scares me the most.

I was used to fighting a hidden enemy, but at least I knew they were there somewhere. I woke up every morning in that sand ridden hell hole knowing that each day could be my last. My life wasn't perfect, but at least it made sense.

And then, that day, it all changed. My life stopped making sense. I've not been able to shake the guilt that has plagued me since it happened. Every time I close my eyes I see the child's face, and I feel physically sick as the memory of what I did plays back in slow motion.

Gran threatened to kick my ass if I didn't pull myself out of my downward spiral, and knowing that I couldn't do it on my own was the reason I was sitting there in the therapist's office. If it wasn't for Gran I wouldn't be there, I'd have given up on life already, just like Max, the friend I let down.

The therapist reached for the water at her side, taking a sip before placing it back down on the table. I stared at the drink, watching a slow but steady drop of condensation meandering down the outside of the glass. Its path was full of twists and turns against unseen obstacles. Is that what was happening to me? I was fighting against things I couldn't see or understand. I didn't know which way to turn. If I was honest with myself, I wasn't sure there was a way out of this spiral of despair I was trapped in. When I contemplated what I'd done, I knew that I didn't deserve to find a way out. I didn't even deserve to be sitting there.

The clock above the fireplace quietly chimed the hour. I rose quickly, relieved that the day's session was over, whilst disappointed that once again, the words failed to come. The therapist was polite and professional as she booked my next appointment. Still she didn't judge me. I almost told her not to bother, but the memory of that night stopped me. I had to see this through before I killed someone. I took the appointment card and headed for the parking lot where I'd left my bike, clutching the heavy paper as though my life depended on it. It may well have done.

Chapter 2

The next session still hadn't produced any words. What would I say? What could I say? I'm a failure. I failed my guys in Afghanistan, I failed Max to the point he took his own life, and I failed Georgia, his widow when she turned to me in her grief. The result of that night haunts me almost as much as the face of the child.

It was raining again and the somber and moody sky on the other side of the window matched my spirit. I was thankful for the rain, the drops of water trailing down the pane gave me something to focus on, a distraction from the silent appraisal of the therapist sitting across from me.

I desperately sought out distractions, anything to avoid having to feel, to think. My fingers fidgeted uselessly in my lap, bereft of the iPhone game I'd been losing myself in. When I did sleep, what little sleep I had that wasn't haunted by nightmares, my mind conjured up the repetitive movements of the match three games I'd been avoiding life with. Like the memories from my nightmares it played out in vivid technicolor, the 'You've failed' message at the end of the level mocking not just my ability to focus on the game, but my failure to focus and participate in life in general.

I'm sure that the low, steady tick, tick, tick of the clock on the mantel piece was soothing to most of the therapists patients, instead I tried to lose myself counting the seconds, failing as always because I couldn't seem to concentrate on anything other than the iPhone game for longer than a few moments. The gentle thrum of the rain comforted me a little. There were days in Afghanistan when I longed to be home, sat on Gran's porch enjoying the rare thunderstorms that lit up the sky in my childhood. Back then we'd complain that the weather got in the way of camping out or other boisterous adventures, but in that barren wasteland of death and destruction I'd have given anything to have experienced it again.

Have you ever watched a raindrop slide down a pane of glass or a droplet of condensation travel down an ice-cold bottle of beer? If you haven't you're missing out, it can be quite mesmerizing, especially when you're head deep in avoidance. The raindrop disappeared as it reached the sill on the windowpane and I realized with disappointment that the rain had stopped. The clouds were thinning out and there was a tantalizing hint of blue sky peeking through. I wanted to shout for the rain to come back. I wanted the world outside to be as gloomy as the world I was currently residing in. I didn't want the flash of blue to be there. That cerulean ray of hope for the outside world reminded me that I was supposed to be able to function out there. I couldn't. For fuck's sake, I couldn't even get the words out in the therapist's office. I'd come in, respond to the cheery greeting from the therapist with mumbled acknowledgments, then sit there trying to lose myself in silent insolence for the hour, and mumbled some more as the next appointment was agreed. I'm not sure why she put up with it, but I guess it's what the army paid her for.

    The chime of the clock sounded the end of the session, another hour wasted, another reminder that I was a failure.

Chapter 3

The silence in the room was starting to taunt me; I'd lost count of the number of sessions I'd remained mute in. The need to let this poison out, to release the fear, the self-loathing, got greater every session. The guilt always outweighed the need. I didn't deserve to be free of the weight that I was carrying. It was my fault. Max was dead; Georgia could have been too. The child was dead. That was all on me.

The sudden noise from outside startled me. I rose quickly, hands searching the empty air for a gun that was no longer there to protect me. The therapist talking quietly to me, soothing me, her words easing me back into the sofa from my defensive position. There was no rain that session, or any condensation on the therapist's glass of water to distract myself with. My foot tapped with nervous energy against the oak flooring, and my fingers sought out a loose thread in the stitching on the arm of the leather sofa. I couldn't regain the fleeting sense of calmness I sometimes felt in that room. For an hour at a time, it was a temporary reprieve. Whilst the negative thoughts never left me; they somehow seemed less invasive in that room.

"Declan?" The therapist asked quietly. "Tell me why that noise unsettled you."

This was the way our sessions went. She'd ask a question occasionally, and every time I would fail to respond. Gran would have told me off for being ignorant, she'd say that even now I'm not too old for a clip round the ear. I can almost hear her voice saying the words. It's a sobering realization. She's one of the reasons I was there, that and the fact I almost killed Georgia. A moment of insanity, a desire to ease the grief of Max's widow, a sexual release that I shouldn't have let happen, and then… then the car backfired and I almost strangled her. What started out as a sensual massage became something more. Animal instinct had taken over for both of us. Grief, survivors' guilt, a need to not feel so alone. It had all contributed. Then that one noise had triggered a violent reaction. My fingers had tightened around her neck, pressing into her throat. She'd managed to break through the nightmare that had taken me back to that place, and I'd come to my senses to find my hands forcing the breath from her, almost to the point of suffocation. I'd run, leaving her naked and crying on the bed. A coward. A guilt-ridden, good for nothing coward.

Some days I could barely lift myself from the bed, the burden of guilt weighing so heavily on my soul it was almost tangible. Some days I gave in to it, drugging myself into unconsciousness with a bottle of Jack. It didn't help; no matter how much I drank the nightmares still haunted me. Is that what happened with Max? Is that why he turned to drugs? Is that why he chose to end it? Someone said he'd chosen the coward's way out, I don't think he did. I wasn't brave enough to do it. What he did takes more courage than I possessed, no matter how much I wanted the escape and oblivion of death.

I wanted to answer the therapist, I really did. I wanted to end this waking nightmare. The words wouldn't come. How could I say anything when I didn't understand it myself? How could I explain the visions that played on repeat in my head? How could I voice the self-loathing that accompanied my every waking moment? How could I share the failure that I was? I let my men down. And now Max was dead, that was all on me.

The therapist seemed to sense something, some subtle change in my demeanor perhaps and repeated her question.

This wasn't how it was supposed to be. She asked the questions, I ignored her and we'd sit the session out in silence. She wasn't allowed to get inside my head. She wasn't allowed to know my fears. She couldn't. I needed them. They were mine. They fuelled the guilt. If she discovered my fears she'd find a way to allay them. I couldn't have that. My fingers moved faster, I was no longer fussing at the loose thread on the sofa arm; I was pulling at it, trying to draw it free. I could feel my anxiety rising. I was scared. I was angry. I was defensive. I was also struggling to maintain my façade of silence.

She said my name softly once more. "Declan?"

Something inside me snapped, I jumped up from the sofa startling her.

"What do you want from me?" I yelled. "I fucked her, I fucked my friend's widow and then I almost killed her!" The words were torn from my throat and yelled in anger. Something inside of me broke. It was like a dam being opened and I fell to the floor, curling in on myself, trying to hold back the flood of grief and sobbed like a baby.

Chapter 4

I'm not sure which was harder, sitting in the therapist's office unable to get the words out, or staring at the empty page unable to write. I'd planned a road trip with Cam and the therapist had suggested writing a journal might help in lieu of our face-to-face sessions. She'd still be on the end of the phone if I needed her. I wasn't sure if that was a help or not. If I couldn't find the words to express myself when I was sat opposite her, how would a faceless phone connection help?

The blank page was mocking me. I knew she wasn't looking for war and peace, but there wasn't even a hint of a skirmish in front of me, just bright white empty pages. A part of me believed that I didn't deserve to feel better; I didn't deserve a 'normal' life. Max was dead. Georgia's life was ruined. The child was dead. What right did I have to enjoy life when I was the reason that they couldn't? Guilt consumed me.

After my breakdown in the therapist's office, I'd felt a little relief. It's like the pressure that builds in the air just before a summer storm, the hot oppressive, almost stifling feeling that's released as soon as the first downpour hits. But like the relief that follows the storm, it was short lived. For those few moments after breaking down I'd had someone listen without judging. I was tired of being told I'm not to blame. I am. This is on me. The therapist never told me that. To be fair she never told me anything, she just asked questions and left me to analyze my answers, on the rare occasions that I responded.

The empty sheet annoyed me, so in desperation, I'd picked up the pen and sketched the route we were planning on taking the bikes. We were heading to some place called Severed, near Mildura in Victoria. I'd never heard of it but Cam had some old family friend who lived there and it was an excuse to take the bikes on a scenic route along the coast. Being out on my bike was one of the few times I could forget. No, not forget, that's the wrong word. I can never forget. Out on the bike though I had to concentrate on the road, on what I was doing, and for that short period of time my guilt wasn't at the forefront of my mind.

Gran had given me her blessing; she just wanted her grandson back. I was hurting her, and that was just one more reason to feel bad. I was a failure in so many ways.

Chapter 5

The first day out on the bike had found muscles I'd forgotten about. The gentle ache was a reminder of how out of shape I'd allowed myself to become. The hum of the road beneath the bike wheels had probably been as therapeutic in one day as the multiple sessions I'd had with the therapist so far. I could tell that Cam was struggling with knowing how to act around me; he was there after all. He lost a friend in Max as well, but he didn't have the guilt that was my burden alone to carry. To be fair to him he wasn't telling me to pull myself together or buck my ideas up. He just treated me like he always had; I'm just not convinced that I deserved it.

The journal still had no words on the page, but there were several more sketches. I'm no artist, to most they would be an unintelligible squiggle, but I knew what they represented - the sun hitting the tree at a certain angle, the creek where we stopped for a break and the lizard that watched me carefully from its hiding place in the shade of a rock. It was a five-hour ride to Albany and we had chosen a backpacker hotel with basic accommodation. Compared to Afghanistan it was almost luxury.

Sitting on the deck, overlooking the ocean whilst enjoying a cold beer, I'd felt at peace for the first time since I returned from that hellish desert. Cam had buggered off with some young student who'd been eyeing him up since we arrived. I was left with her friend, who looked willing, but I wasn't. Part of me was scared of what happened with Georgia, whilst the other part of me just wasn't interested. I'd rather enjoy the tranquillity of the view and my surroundings.

Day two of our journey found me waking from the best night's sleep I'd had in as long as I could remember. I felt rested for the first time in ages. There was no hangover from a nightmare I could barely remember, but knew had terrified me. It was a refreshing change. We'd another five hours on the bikes that day, but were moving away from the coast. I persuaded Cam to stop off at Observatory Point where I sketched the bay and rocks before we headed inland. It's these moments that calmed me. The night was spent at an old country pub and was nightmare free again.

Caiguna was our stopping point for the next day. It's unlicensed and Cam was not impressed. It wasn't as peaceful as the previous two locations as it was a 24-hour food and fuel stop. I barely slept. I had to ask myself if I'd become reliant on alcohol to ease me into sleeping, or if it was just the noise and hustle and bustle of the location. I really hoped it was the latter. I'd woken shaking with terror, images of the vehicle burning at my back and the child standing innocently in the road ahead of me. There was an echo of Max's screams from where he was trapped in the transport. I could almost feel the heat from the flames and the smell of burned flesh tortured my senses. It had taken a cold shower and a good few hours on the bike for the flashbacks to dissipate fully.

An eight-hour slog finally saw us cross into Southern Australia, and whilst we had enjoyed the beauty of the coastal road, I was more than grateful that the hotel we'd booked into for the night had a swimming pool. Yet again Cam picked up one of the tourists and went back to her hotel leaving me to entertain her friend. Despite half a bottle of Jack Daniels earlier in the evening, I was surprised to find myself hard enough for her to start giving me a blowjob. She was pretty good at it, but my attention strayed. The sight of her on her knees and the cheapness of the motel room made the moment feel cheap and tacky. I pulled out of her mouth, and instead of feeling disappointment when she cursed at me and left, I just felt relief.

I opened the journal, hoping I could put what had just happened into words. Nothing came. I couldn't even think of anything I wanted to sketch. Looking back over the pages I'd already filled I could see that each sketch represented a moment or a scene that had inspired me. Nothing about that evening had been inspiring. Time was, and not too long ago, that I'd have been delighted to find myself in that position. What was wrong with me that I turned down a blowjob? That night my nightmares were of Georgia. Her naked skin felt real and soft under my fingers, right to the point where my hands closed around her throat, almost choking the life from her. There was no soundtrack to this nightmare; just the haunting look of absolute terror on her face when she looked at me after I finally released her. Sleep proved elusive for the remainder of that night.

We were close enough to Severed that we could have reached it by the end of the next day, but the prospect of a long drive didn't appeal to either of us. As enjoyable as the route had been it had started to wear us out. We stopped off in Port Pirie for the night. Having fallen asleep easily I was soon woken by yet another nightmare. They were still a frequent part of my nights. My journal showed a collection of scribbled dark clouds and unclear images to represent my nightmares. I couldn't write the content of them down, as I could only remember traces of them. A look, a touch, the only sounds were when I dreamed of Afghanistan and then it was the sound of Max's tortured screams. The fear of almost ending Georgia's life haunted me for the rest of the night every time, and when I dreamed of Afghanistan it was the knowledge that I'd ended a child's life that tormented me.

When we pulled into Severed the following day I was delighted to find it soothing, despite being so far from the coastal roads that I had craved. It had wide streets and old buildings that were kept cool by the shade of the trees. It was probably that there was nothing about the place that reminded me of Afghanistan. I think it was smaller than Harvey, perhaps that's another reason I felt safe there.

The first night sleeping in the old pub was dreamless, a bonus that my shattered body and soul desperately needed. I almost felt rested. It turned out that Severed wasn't as peaceful as it appeared. The local MC had lost a few members recently, and there were rumors of a drug gang trying to move into the area. The thought of drugs in this peaceful place raised my hackles. It was also a stark reminder of how we'd lost Max. I couldn't stand the thought of anyone else being lost to them.

Chapter 6

We'd been in Severed for a few days before I came up with a brilliant plan that I may well live to regret. The landlord of the pub we were staying in was an old friend of Cam's family and had been trying to sell the pub so he could go stay with his sister on the other side of the country. She had cancer and he felt he needed to be nearer to her. There was something about this town that made me feel sane. Whilst I still had guilt and self-doubt, the nightmares were a lot less frequent. I was putting that down to the peace and calm I felt there.

Cam didn't seem as enthused about my idea to buy the pub as I thought he would. He didn't think it was a good fit for me considering our history. That's exactly why I thought it was right for me. It was so different to the war zone. There were far fewer triggers for my flashbacks in Severed. The memories from Afghanistan were becoming more vivid. They felt so real. It was almost as though I was back there on that road. I could taste the dry grit of the sand, feel the heat of the fire, and hear the screams from behind me. I could see the child in the road ahead of me. He was barely a teenager. Friend, or foe? How was I supposed to tell in this hellish place? It had been drilled into us that no-one, man, woman or child was to be trusted. Simple human decency almost destroyed the whole team; I couldn't possibly shoot a child. Gut instinct saved us, and left me with guilt I wasn't sure I could ever overcome.

The hardest part of my plan was telling Gran, but being the strong character she is, she supported me all the way. Within days the deal was done and Luke, one of our team from Afghanistan, was on a flight to help me pick contractors, fixtures, and fittings.

Helping the contractors with the refit had left me exhausted at the end of each day, and my sleep had been better. Cam had gone home but frequently told me on the phone that I was using this refurbishment project to hide from my feelings. He was pushing me to go back to the therapist and actually talk this time. The journal had sat abandoned on my bedside table since I arrived. I understood where he was coming from. I wasn't dealing with my emotions and feelings; I was hiding them with strenuous effort and mental exhaustion. I didn't have time to think about them right then.

Being here in Severed was almost an opportunity for me to reinvent myself. When my new bar staff had asked me about my past I'd been almost curt in my dismissal of the subject. I decided there and then that the past was past. Unless I decided to talk to a therapist it was dead and buried just like Max and the child that I killed. It was time to invent a new me.

Opening night caught me out, not with how busy the bar was; I'd kind of expected that. It was the way a certain brunette brought back feelings I thought I'd never experience again. I actually felt sexually attracted to her. That's something that had been missing the entire ride here with Cam, no matter how many friends his conquests had left me to entertain. The girls had been attractive enough, and the old me would have had them in bed before you could shake a stick, but since the incident with Georgia, the mere thought of taking anyone to bed repulsed me. Until that night. Holly was part of the local MC, and that meant I'd have to tread carefully if I didn't want to upset the status quo around there.

I picked up the journal for the first time in weeks and sketched her, the memory of the way her hair fell on her shoulder and the smile in her eyes came clearly to me. The sketch was a pretty good representation of her, but I took my pen and scratched through it. I couldn't risk a relationship. What if it became a repeat of that night with Georgia? I needed to forget about her.

Severed lost a little of its shine the following day when the MC sent a couple of its guys to visit me. There was a touch of bravado from all of us, jostling for seniority, but we ended the meeting with a healthy respect for each other, despite my refusal to reveal my past. There was a drug problem in Severed, and they had wanted to make sure I wasn't it. I had made it very clear how I felt about drugs, without letting on why. The whole thing with Max was still too raw, the guilt too fresh.

The guys from the MC were unaware of the contacts I still had from my military days, and I decided to use them to find out what was going on in my new hometown. The news wasn't good. I may have left Afghanistan behind, but it

Help Our Heroes

turns out I hadn't escaped conflict, far from it in fact. I had a horrible feeling that the shit was about to hit the fan big time.

Chapter 7

Despite my caution about her, Holly had a way of drawing me in. Bit by bit she was capturing my heart and making me feel again. Good feelings, not the terror and horror that I'd become used to. Even though I needed to spend time concentrating on resolving the shit storm I'd walked into in Severed, I allowed myself to be talked into a moonlight picnic with her.

The evening was like something out of a cheesy romance, lying on a blanket under the stars at the side of a creek. She even looked the part in her tiny denim skirt and chequered shirt. We made small talk through the picnic, and it turned out she'd lost someone close to her as well. I could feel the guilt she was hiding. You can't bull shit a bull shitter, I could sense a kindred spirit, although I didn't think she was struggling as deeply as I was. Hers seemed a healthier and more natural level of grief. It was like fate had decided we should be together to heal each other.

I felt like a teenager again, back at the creek on my gran's farm, making out with one of the girls from school. I don't remember how it happened, but before long we'd practically undressed each other. She'd traced her nails down my bare chest towards the top of my jeans and it had felt like an electric current was running through my body. Before I could get my hand in her panties she'd undone my jeans and grabbed hold of my hard cock. Fuck, that felt so good. Managing to pull aside her panties I'd pushed my finger into her, using my thumb to tease her clit. God, she was so wet. She'd tried her best to give me a hand job but had become distracted by her impending orgasm. Watching her explode was amazing; it had made me feel warm inside. It had never been that satisfying for me before, normally I'd become too focussed on reaching my own release to take much notice. Removing her underwear I'd hesitated, waiting for her confirmation that she wanted more. No sooner had she whispered an acknowledgment than I was reaching for a condom.

    Thrusting into her felt so good, she fitted me perfectly. It was almost like we were made for each other. Her legs wrapped around me, pulling me deeper. Moving one of her legs down on the ground, the other still on my back, put us almost side by side facing each other and allowed me to thrust even deeper. Groaning in ecstasy, and unable to ignore her exquisite nipples, I'd drawn one into my mouth, biting down and relishing the sound of her crying out. I couldn't help the loud roar as my orgasm hit and my cock filled her warm pussy with its release. She had the smuggest grin I've ever seen on her face as she lay back sated afterwards.

Chapter 8

I wanted to see Holly again, I knew I shouldn't, but there was a connection there that made me feel whole again. The timing couldn't have been worse as the trouble had started escalating in Severed. The tattoo shop that the MC own got trashed along with several of their bikes. It was a response to them warning off a drug dealer. I was reluctant to get involved, but then the clubhouse of another MC got bombed and people died. This shit was way out of the MC's league. It was obvious that the dealers had some serious connections, and it had become time for me to call on mine before Severed turned into a war zone.

It was on a trip to Melbourne to see my old army buddy Chris that I realized I couldn't be with Holly anymore. Whilst staying at his apartment he'd woken me in the middle of a nightmare and I almost strangled him. He's a bloody tough guy and it was obvious that I'd scared the crap out of him. If he hadn't been so strong he might not have been able to fight me off.

If that had been Holly... the thought haunted me. I returned to Severed and tried to stay away from her. It was easy at first as I had the excuse I was helping her MC deal with the drug problem and needed to stay away from her to keep her safe. Holly's a strong character, that's probably why I was so attracted to her, and that meant she wouldn't take no for an answer.

Holly and I had a row on my return from Melbourne; she couldn't understand why I couldn't be around her. She'd caught me off guard when I was tired and apparently I'd fallen asleep on her. I'd woken up next to her, angry that she was still there after I'd told her to go home. She kept pushing me and I'd finally told her about having nightmares, although not the details or the reason behind them. I also told her that I thought I was a risk to her when I was in that state. She shocked the hell out of me when she told me I'd had a nightmare sleeping next to her, but that she'd held me and spoken to me and calmed me down. I'd touched her throat, tracing the unmarked skin and questioned why there wasn't any evidence of me trying to strangle her. Her response was that she'd hugged my nightmare away. I couldn't believe her. We'd had sex then, brutal, wild sex. I'd fucked her from behind, slapping her arse and we'd rutted like animals. It was harsh, hot sex and I'd hoped in a way it would scare her away. Instead, she'd loved it. We both had. We'd then had sex in the shower. I needed to end it with her, but she was like an addiction I couldn't give up.

The drug situation came to a head, and I called in support from Cam and the rest of my team. One night we joined forces with the MC and sorted the problem once and for all, the way only the military in us knew how. It was dawn the next morning before we walked away from the wreckage. Holly ambushed us as we returned, refusing to accept that there was nothing between us.

When she finally left, tears in her eyes and vowing to return, Cam collared me. He asked me why I was being such a bloody fool, and for the first time, I told him just how bad things were. How scared I was that I'd hurt Holly, that I couldn't keep her safe from the nightmares that haunted me, and that I was afraid of a repeat of the Georgia scenario. He didn't tell me I was stupid, he didn't tell me off. Instead, he begged me to see a therapist, to try again even though it had failed before. His argument was that now I had something to fight for – Holly – and that made all the difference.

I'd still not been able to write in my journal, but at least now I wasn't scratching out the images of Holly when I sketched them. Everything about her felt so right if it hadn't been for the nightmares and the guilt and shame I still carried deep in my soul, I wouldn't have thought twice about a relationship with her.

I'd also had a talk with Chris before he returned to Melbourne. He'd come to Severed along with the rest of my team to help us and brought a load of military hardware with him. He'd told me that I was the only one who could make the decision to be with Holly; but that he liked the Declan he saw when I was with her. He was right. I was the only one who could make the decision.

Sitting in the bar I'd looked around and realized that being in this place did make me happy. That was a feeling I didn't think I'd ever have again. It wasn't just the bar and Severed though, Holly was a huge part of that happiness. I made my decision.

    I picked up the phone and made the appointment with the therapist. I was a military man, it was in my core, and now it was time that I chose to fight for the most important thing in my life… my woman.

Help Our Heroes

Wrecked

T.A. Mckay

Ralph can only think of one thing. Returning home to the man he loves after being stationed away for five months.

Unfortunately it doesn't work out exactly the way he hopes. Abandoned at the airport and kicked to the kerb, Ralph is left with nowhere to go and no one to help him. Luck is on his side in the shape of Aiden. The kind driver takes pity on him and gives him a bed to sleep in until he can get everything sorted.

What neither of them expected was to find an attraction growing between them, the connection allowing secrets to come out and fantasies to be lived.

But when fear makes Ralph run from the one person who truly gets him, will he ever be able to win Aiden back, or is the whole thing completely Wrecked?

Help Our Heroes

Chapter 1

Aiden

I watch the soldiers walking through the arrivals area, most of them being met by family and loved ones. I swallow the giant lump in my throat as I see the happiness on everyone's faces, the love clearly seen between the arriving soldiers and the people waiting on them. I wonder what it feels like to be without someone you love for so long and to finally get to hold them, to know they are safely home with you. I don't think I could live like that, with the constant fear of getting that phone call, the one that would tell me that the man I loved wasn't coming home to me.

I re-adjust my hat as a little girl is lifted into the arms of some big guy and spun in a circle. A prettily dressed woman stands and watches them embrace, her cheeks wet with tears as her emotions take over. A few seconds later those same big arms are wrapped around the woman, the little family all back together again. I feel myself sigh as I watch the whole thing unfold and I'm distracted enough that I don't notice the person standing in front of me until he coughs to get my attention.

I'm instantly alert, holding up my sign like I should have been the whole time I've been standing here. When I finally focus and look at the guy in front of me, my mouth goes dry and I know I'm staring, but holy shit. I have to look up to see the guy's face, which isn't exactly a shock since I'm only five-foot-seven, but I think even if I were standing at six-foot I would need to look up at this one. His eyes are dark, surrounded by shadows and as he glares at me, I see they are full of shadows too. His hair is blonde and messy, and even with the short military cut, it's obvious he's been running his hands through it. I try not to let my eyes wander but I don't have any control over them as they slip down over his body. His shoulders are as broad as I am tall and where most gym bunnies waists taper in, this guy is thick and full the whole way down. Add that to his massive biceps and thighs that I'm not sure I could get my arms around, and I would say he is firmly on the daydream wank material list.

He points at the sign, and that's the first clue that I've been staring at him. "Who are you and why do you have my name on a piece of card?"

I look down at the offending sign, rereading it like I can't remember the name on it. "Are you Mr Finnegan?"

"Yes."

"Mr R Finnegan?"

He's starting to look at me as though I'm a little slow on the uptake, or maybe I don't understand basic English, but who the hell can blame him. I'm finding it hard to form any words as he stares at me with those unforgiving eyes.

"Sorry, my name's Aiden and I will be your driver today." At least I sound a little less like someone who has no idea what's going on, even if my response seems to confuse him.

"I don't understand, why do I need a driver?"

His question throws me because I'm not sure what to say. Uncle didn't tell me why I was picking this guy up, only that I needed to be waiting inside arrivals so he would see me. "Um, I don't know. I just get told where to be and who to pick up."

He continues to stare at me, and I'm beginning to feel a bit uncomfortable. I've helped my uncle out a bit by driving when he is down staff, but usually, I hold up my sign, carry a bag, and then take my passenger wherever they need to go. This guy is making things difficult. "I don't need a lift, my boyfriend will be here soon."

I want to pretend the knowledge that he's gay doesn't make him even more attractive, but I've always made a point of not lying to myself. He takes off towards the exit, his large bag over his shoulder like it weighs nothing, and it takes me maybe three steps to each one of his to keep up. Not only are his legs thick, apparently they are long as well. We make it to the exit before I start to sweat and I'm thankful when the brisk wind hits me.

The big guy looks around, searching the cars out the front looking for his boyfriend. I stand behind him and stay quiet, knowing I can't leave until I take him

Help Our Heroes

home but not wanting to be the one to tell him he's been stood up. It's the only reason that I would be here, and it's a pretty shitty welcome home. I don't know where he's been stationed or for how long, but going by the weary energy he's giving off I know it wasn't a fun time. So no, I'm not going to be the one to tell him that he is on his own because his boyfriend is a fucking arsehole who couldn't even be bothered to pick him up.

We stand for a while, but I know that he's already worked out that there's a reason I'm here. Finally, he turns towards me, his head dropped and looking more tired than he had when he arrived, and nods. "Fine, take me to the car."

I want to offer to carry his bag for him, but it looks fucking heavy, so I just turn and head to the valet area where I parked the car. At least it's close so he doesn't have far to go now. I unlock the car and the boot pops open, so I stand to the side so he can drop his bag inside. When it falls off his shoulder, it's like it takes the last of his energy with it and his shoulders drop. I quickly shut the boot and rush past him to open his door for him. His whole body relaxes as soon as he gets into the car, and he leans back and closes his eyes before he's even shut inside. His arm comes up and covers his eyes, making me feel sorry for him.

I slip into the driver's seat, trying to keep the noise to a minimum so he can rest. I already have the address to take him to his destination so I don't need to speak to him at all. I start the car and make my way through the slow traffic towards the exit. Three flights arrived at the same time as Mr Finnegan's and now the whole place is almost at a standstill. I hate that there's a delay in getting him home, but at least it gives him a little longer to rest before the inevitable fight that's going to happen when he gets there. If he doesn't call out his piece of shit boyfriend, he's a better guy than me. The only thing that would be an acceptable excuse for him not being here is death, mainly his own, but since he apparently booked the car, I know he probably isn't dead.

The car moves slowly, the nose to tail traffic in front of me not going anywhere quickly. I try to keep my eyes on the road, but they keep connecting with the rearview mirror so I can see Mr F – which is what I'm going to call him since I don't know his name – still lying back against the back seat. His arm is now lying across his stomach but his eyes are still closed, making me wonder if he's fallen asleep. I study his face, thinking that if he is sleeping, he still looks tense. Is that what happens when you're in the army? Do you always look stressed, like maybe you're worried that something will happen when you're asleep? And does that ever go away, even when you come home?

I jump when the car behind me honks, and I look out the windscreen quickly and see that the road in front of me is clear. I drive forward and stop at the security barrier, putting my ticket into the machine when I reach it. My eyes flicker to the mirror before I move again and I see Mr F's eyes open and he's staring at me. Hating that I've been caught I concentrate on getting past the barrier and out onto the main road. Now that I'm approaching the motorway I need to focus because rush hour is in full swing and that brings out the crazy fuckers who just want to get home. I indicate before exiting the slip road, slowing slightly behind a car in the left lane before being able to pull out and gunning the engine. I'm on autopilot but still acutely aware, so when Mr F speaks it takes me by surprise. He's been so quiet in the back seat that I wasn't expecting him to start a conversation.

"What's your name again?"

I keep my eyes on the road but raise my voice so I know he can hear me. "Aiden, sir."

"Please don't sir me, I'm not a sir. My name is Ralph."

I don't mean to snigger, but apparently, my brain to mouth filter has taken a momentary holiday. "Ralph? Like you know ..." I swear I hear him growl and I decide that maybe it's safer not to finish that particular sentence.

Chapter 2

Ralph

I know what's going to come out of his mouth before he even thinks it. Ever since that fucking movie came out, people have been comparing the two of us. It doesn't help that we are both pretty big guys, making the comparison even funnier. "Yes, like Wreck-It Ralph. I know, I'm huge like him."

Aiden smiles, and it takes a little of the sting out of the joke he was about to make. I don't usually get so pissed off when people mention the film, but I'm just so fucking tired today. I had spent the whole flight home from Canada thinking about being back home in William's arms. It's the only thing that made the nearly eight-hour flight bearable. Five months. Five long, tiring months without him and I was finally coming home. I could see other men from the deployment being met by loved ones and it made my heart start to race in anticipation. What I hadn't expected was to find my name written on a piece of card being held by someone I didn't know.

I just wanted to hug my man and go home to sleep for the next sixteen hours, I'm now sitting in a car with a complete stranger - albeit a cute stranger – but a stranger nonetheless. I want to get my mobile out and call William to see where he is but it ran out of power about four hours into the flight after I fell asleep listening to music. I would worry about the reason he isn't here, possibly an accident, but since he organised a driver for me, he must have known in advance that he wasn't coming. That doesn't explain why he didn't tell me though and as soon as I get home, he has a lot of explaining to do.

"Sorry, I take it you hear that joke a lot?"

"More than you can imagine. As soon as one person said it, it spread around the base quicker than a case of crabs. My team even started calling me WI."

"WI?" He asks the question, but I see the moment that he works out what it means. "Wreck it." His laughter should piss me off, but it has me smiling as I relax in the seat a bit more. "So I know nothing about the army, explain in easy words what you do."

"I'm a recovery mechanic."

"Is that what it sounds like?" He watches me in the mirror occasionally as he speaks, but he always has to turn back to watch the road.

"I go in to recover broken down vehicles and repair them. I'm a Lance Corporal, so I have a team that I lead and make sure they're safe."

"That sounds interesting. It's like an AA recovery man but with guns."

I laugh at his description, thinking that they really should use that description to recruit new people. "That's pretty close to what it's like, well apart from the cars are sometimes the size of combine harvesters, and there is always the risk of being shot."

"Shit, do you really get shot at? I thought you would go in after everything died down."

"We go wherever there's a vehicle that needs to be recovered. Sometimes that's under heavy fire from enemies." This time I'd been stationed in Canada for training and maintenance of the vehicles, so there had been none of that, but my last visit to Iraq had proved how intense things could get. When you have gunfire going off overhead, it's incredible how quickly you can get a crane in place to move an overturned foxhound.

"Wow, that sounds … crazy and brave."

I can feel the pride swell in my chest, and it's a strange feeling. I've gotten used to not speaking about my job with William. His eyes would glaze over whenever I mentioned the army, even if it's the thing we fought about the most.

"It must be difficult though, leaving your family behind when you get deployed. That's the right word isn't it?"

"It's really fucking hard." I stop talking, prepared to cut the story short before I end up looking like I'm complaining. He doesn't need to hear my sob story, but he continues talking like he actually wants to know about it.

"Where have you come back from, and how long were you there? I saw some of the men coming out and seeing their families. God, they all looked so happy to be back together."

My chest tightens a little when I think about not being met by anyone who loved me. "I was stationed in Canada for five months, helping train up another team with a new winch. It was a long haul but not as bad as some of the other deployments."

"What's been the longest?"

"Seven months but it felt like seven years."

"Why …"

He stops talking and indicates to move to the middle lane. He's concentrating really hard on his driving, and I'm pretty sure he's using it as an excuse not to carry on with what he was about to say. "Why what?"

Aiden stays quiet for a few moments and I think he's going ignore what I asked but he eventually takes a deep breath and lets it out slowly before speaking. "Why wasn't anyone there to meet you?"

Now isn't that the million pound question. "My parents live in Spain and it's difficult for them to be here. My brother and sister have their own families, so as long as they know I'm safe, they're happy to see me in a few weeks. Now my boyfriend William, I'm not sure why he didn't come to get me. Hopefully, in about twenty minutes, I will find out why he wasn't there." My mind fills with all the reasons that he was missing. Maybe something had come up suddenly at work, or perhaps he has a surprise planned. My hopes are on that one. We'd spoken a lot about possibly getting married before being deployed, saying that maybe when I got home, we would finally take the leap. We already live together, so it isn't a huge step but one that I want.

"I'm sure that he has a good reason." Aiden smiles at me, but I can't see any conviction behind the move. He doesn't look as though he thinks there could be a good enough reason, and part of me agrees with him.

Just under my predicted twenty minutes later we pull up outside my house. I scramble to get out of the car, not wanting to believe what I'm seeing. I run around the back end of the car and come to a grinding halt. I stare at the pile of stuff on the front lawn not understanding what's happening. I step forward slowly like I'm back out on patrol and there's a chance that I'm going to stand on a mine, but that won't happen here, the only fear is what I'm about to find in the stack of black bags in front of me. I rip open the top of the first one I come to and it's full of my clothes, confirming that I was right to have my fears. I open another one just in case I had made a mistake with the first, but this one too is full of my belongings.

What the fuck?

I don't think about what I'm doing as I go storming up to the front door and finding it locked, start banging on it. I never take keys when I go on deployment just in case I lose them. It's not like I will need them while I'm away, it's not like I can come home and surprise William. I'm starting to see my mistake by not taking them because now I'm locked out of my own house. I continue to hit my fists on the door, but I know William isn't inside. Who would do all this shit and then wait around for me to come home? Now the driver makes sense. He sent someone to get me because he's a fucking coward. I stop the attack on the door, all the exhaustion from too many hours travel taking everything from me.

I turn away from the door and sit on the top step, dropping my head and trying not to give in to all the emotions that are battling inside to be let out. Frustration, anger, and shock are all there, but the one that wins out is fear. I have no idea what I'm meant to do now because I have no idea what's going on. Does this mean that William has kicked me out? Okay, so that part is pretty obvious, I just can't work my head around the why. Before I left, we were planning marriage, and now all my shit is sitting outside our house in black bags. My biggest problem is I don't know what to do now, where to go. I don't have anyone close to here that could take me in, and because William didn't want to live on a base, I don't have accommodation on there. I run through anyone on base that might be able to take me in for a few nights, but since most of my friends have a family, I can't put them out like that. I also refuse to share a room with Tyson's toddler again. I did it one night after a party and it wasn't a fun experience.

I become aware of someone standing looking at me, and I lift my head to find Aiden standing there, his hands in his pocket while he pretends this isn't as awkward as fuck. I feel sorry for him. He didn't sign up for all this.

"Hey, so um … what do you want to do?" He chews the inside of his mouth and it makes me feel even worse for him. I wouldn't know how to handle this if I was him. He's watching my life implode spectacularly and it can't be fun to watch.

"You can just leave my bag with the rest of my shit. It's not like I have anywhere to go."

He looks sad as I speak but I choose to ignore it. If I give in to the tears that I can feel burning at the back of my eyes, then I'm going to be a sobbing mess and that's the last thing I need just now. Best to just let the exhaustion win over anything else.

"I'm not just leaving you here. Do you have someplace I can take you?"

I shake my head because even speaking seems like too much effort just now. I cover my face with my hands because I just want to vanish for a little while. Maybe if I concentrate really hard then I will wake up, because I'm praying that this is nothing but a bad dream.

Chapter 3

Aiden

    I don't know what to do. Ralph looks like he's fallen asleep sitting up and all his stuff is still strewn around the grass like it was thrown there in a hurry. The minute I pulled up in front of his house I knew that it wasn't going to end well but this is a shit show I didn't expect. Now as I watch every ounce of energy drain from his body, I can't believe that his boyfriend has put him through all this. What sort of guy just dumps and runs when their man has been away at war? Okay, it wasn't precisely war, but he was helping our country protect itself. Five months he went without his home comforts so he could help train up soldiers who would, in turn, protect our nation, and his fucking boyfriend couldn't even stick around until he got home.

    "Ralph?"

    He doesn't raise his head, adding to my belief that he might be asleep, so I decide without him about what needs to happen. He can't sit here the rest of the night, so no matter what, I'm going to drive him someplace where he can stay. I'm sure there's a friend that can take him in or even a local hotel where he can stay until he sorts something out.

    I head over to the black bags and pick two of them up, taking them to the car and putting them in the boot. I continue with my packing until the front grass is clear and the car is filled to capacity. I've loaded the back seat with his belongings so when we drive away, he's going to have to sit in the passenger seat next to me. Now just to get the big guy himself in the car and find out where I'm taking him.

    I kneel in front of him, getting my face level with his. "Ralph?" This time he opens his eyes, and he looks shocked that I'm still there. His eyes are a little unfocused and he looks worse than exhausted. "Come get in the car."

Help Our Heroes

He nods and stands but I'm pretty sure he's moving on autopilot now. I can only imagine what's going on in his head, the confusion he must be feeling about all this. I lead him over to the passenger side of the car and open the door, holding it open while he folds his massive body into the seat. When I close the door, he leans back and closes his eyes, so I just make my way around to the driver's seat.

"Where are you going?" I ask the question as soon as I'm in the driver's seat but he's gone quiet again. I stare at his chest as it moves up and down slowly, his face at peace for the first time since I met him. To confirm my suspicions that he's fallen asleep he lets out a small snort that's quite cute. As sweet as he looks now, it doesn't help me work out where to take him, and I hate the thought of waking him up. Fuck it. I put the car in drive and pull away from the kerb.

Thirty minutes later I pull into the driveway in front of my house. I put the car in park and turn off the engine. I turn to look at Ralph and for the hundredth time, I wonder what the hell I'm doing. This whole idea is insane, but here I am, taking a complete stranger home. Maybe I should rethink this, I mean there is perhaps a reason he got dumped by his boyfriend the way he did, he could be dangerous to be around, and it was safer for his ex just to kick him out.

Before I have a chance to change my mind and drive away, Ralph stirs in his seat and opens his eyes. He blinks several times while he tries to wake up fully. He looks like my nephew when you wake him up from a nap, those first few minutes where he's confused about everything. Eventually, Ralph looks out the windscreen and then back to me, but there's still confusion on his face.

"Where are we?"

"You fell asleep and I didn't know where to take you, so I brought you to my place. I thought you could maybe have some sleep and then sort out what you're gonna do."

His eyes go wide for a few seconds before they fill with anger. "You brought me to your place? Shit, you don't even know me. I could be a complete danger to you and you have led me someplace that I could do a lot of harm to you. Please tell me you don't do this all the time."

I try not to laugh but it bursts out of me without warning. "Holy crap, you sound just like my dad."

The look on his face tells me that I've said the wrong thing so I get out of the car quickly before he can yell at me again. I feel more relaxed about bringing him here now that he's told me off for doing it. I'm pretty sure if he were a real danger to me he wouldn't be warning me about it. Most attackers don't yell at you for letting them get close before they hurt you. I open the back door of the car and grab the bag that he brought off the plane with him. I try to throw it over the shoulder but the thing is so freaking heavy. The weight of it over my shoulder knocks my balance off centre and I take a step backwards trying to stop the inevitable. Unfortunately, it doesn't help and I end up landing on my arse on the grass next to the drive.

Laughter catches my attention and I look up to finally see a smile on Ralph's face. I would be pissed that he was laughing at me, but the sight of that smile on his face takes my breath away. He's been intense since I picked him up from the airport like he has the weight of the world on his shoulders, but now he looks a lot younger than I thought he was. Humour is dancing in Ralph's eyes, and it's a little sexy. Okay, it's a lot sexy, but I try not to think about that since his long-term boyfriend has just dumped him.

Ralph holds a hand out to me and I take it, letting him pull me off the grass until I'm standing. I don't attempt to lift his bag again, leaving it on the ground until Ralph picks it up. "I'll take this shall I?"

I can hear the laughter in his voice and I stick my tongue out at him before heading to the front door. I don't bother telling him to follow me, just expecting him to do it. I unlock the door and walk inside, throwing my car keys in the bowl next to the door. I kick my shoes off, sighing as soon as the tight leather slips from my feet. The door closes behind me and I see Ralph standing just inside the door. The smile is gone but he looks more relaxed now, even if he still looks tired. I'm taking it a half hour nap isn't enough to make up for the hours of travelling he's endured. "Come on, I'll show you to your room."

He doesn't say anything as he follows me up the stairs. I lead him along the hall where I point out the bathroom before opening the door to my spare room. My house isn't huge, but with my spare room, it's big enough that I won't have to move, possibly ever. I stand to the side and let Ralph step inside.

"Make yourself at home. There will be plenty of hot water so feel free to grab a shower, and there are towels in the cupboard in the bathroom. Help yourself to anything you need. I'm gonna go make some dinner, is there anything you won't eat?"

He shakes his head as he drops his bag to the floor. I stand a little awkwardly, not sure what to say, and he doesn't help my internal struggle when he slips off his uniform jacket. If I thought he looked muscly before, I now know for sure, and I'm showing my approval of his arms by practically drooling down my t-shirt.

"Okay ... um ...I'll go and ... shit ... food. Yeah, food. I'm going to make food." I turn abruptly and walk out of the room.

"Aiden." I stop instantly at the sound of his voice, looking back over my shoulder to where he's still standing. "Thank you for this. It's more than I can ever repay."

"It's completely fine. I'm happy to help." I give him a final smile before closing the door behind myself.

I make my way down the stairs and into the kitchen. I'm halfway through searching the fridge when my phone rings. I close the door and answer it. "Hello?"

"Hi, son. How did the job go today?" Uncle Eddie sounds cheery, and I can't help but smile.

"It went well, a bit of a domestic drama but it was all sorted."

"I hope there wasn't too much of a problem?" Uncle always worries about my safety when I'm out on a call, even though every one of his clients are aggressively vetted before we take their job. We aren't a taxi firm, and due to Uncle being in the business for over ten years, he can pick and choose who he works for.

"No trouble, well not for me. The client didn't have the best of days though."

"I'm sorry, son. Is that why you didn't return the car?"

Shit. It's not the first time I've finished a job late and not gone back to exchange cars, but I forgot to text Uncle to tell him. "I'm sorry, I completely forgot to let you know I would bring it back tomorrow. The thing is, well, it's full of the client's belongings."

"What?"

"When I picked the guy up at the airport and took him home, his boyfriend had dumped all his stuff on the front lawn. He had nowhere to go and had been travelling all day. He's in the military and was coming home from deployment, so I couldn't just leave him there. I'm going to take him wherever he wants to go tomorrow and then drop off the car."

"Tomorrow? So where is he now, I don't understand?"

Okay, so he doesn't sound so happy now. "Um, well …" I close my eyes and lean against the fridge, preparing to get chewed out by my overprotective uncle.

Chapter 4

Ralph

The water feels amazing on the back of my neck. Aiden's house looks older from the outside, but he's fitted a modern bathroom, and the shower is fantastic. After deployment any fitted bathroom is an improvement, so the fact that this is a top of the range power shower is just a bonus. I feel the jets of water massaging the tension out of all my muscles, and I just want to dry off and climb into bed.

I think of the strange situation I'm in, showering in a stranger's home when I should be at home making love to my boyfriend, or I suppose I should get used to calling him my ex-boyfriend. I still can't quite get my mind around what's happened today. I had no clue that William was unhappy, so for him not just to leave me, but kick me out of my home, well I'm at a loss. I need to try and get a hold of William, find out what's wrong and see if it's something we can move past. I can't stay here at Aiden's house, no matter how sweet the offer is. I don't want to impose on a complete stranger.

I reluctantly turn off the hot water and grab the towel I left on the edge of the sink. The softness feels fantastic against my skin as I rub it over me. It's the small things that I miss while away on deployment, things like fabric softener and soft mattresses. Thinking about soft mattresses leads me across the short hall and into the bedroom where all my belongings are. I lean down and grab my mobile from my bag, searching through my holdall for my charger. There's a socket next to the bed, so I plug in the charger and connect my phone. It doesn't light up straight away, but the charge symbol appears letting me know it's working.

Hoping the mobile won't take long to turn on so I can call William, I lie back on the soft bed and stare at the ceiling. I can't do anything until I speak to him because maybe this whole thing is a mistake. Okay, so I'm not sure how it could be a mistake, it's not like he forgot to buy my favourite type of coffee, but still, I need to speak to him. I yawn so widely that my jaw cracks. Holy shit I'm tired. I slept in the car but it feels like I barely closed my eyes, and even after my nap on the plane, it feels like I've been awake for about a week. I close my eyes, planning on resting until my phone buzzes back to life.

* * *

A hand on my leg pulls me from my slumber. I smile when I feel Williams's warmth on my skin after so long. God, I missed him so much. Five months is far too long to go without the man I love. I can feel myself harden just thinking about being inside him again. He is the hottest guy I've ever seen. His body rivals mine in size and his shoulder-length hair so soft and shiny. Falling for him went against my usual type, but he stole my breath the first time I met him. I never thought he would want to be with a jarhead like me and for the first month he wouldn't even look in my direction, but one night when we met in a nightclub he finally spoke to me and there was no going back from that. I know a lot of people think he's a dickhead, but to me, he's just William. Sarcastic, a little judgmental, but once you get past all that he is a good guy.

I groan in pleasure and roll towards the heat that's trying to leave my body. I feel a tickle against my waist but I ignore it on my quest to get closer to William.

"Holy shit. Ralph!"

My eyes fly open when the voice I hear isn't William. I'm so fucking confused as I look around the dark room, the single bedside lamp not helping me see clearly. When I meet Aiden's eyes, the shock in them very clear to see, and like the rushing tide, everything that's happened in the last twenty-four hours comes rushing back. Flying back, finding out I'm homeless, and the fact I'm staying at a stranger's house.

All that pales into insignificance when I see where Aiden is staring. I follow his gaze and find myself hard, which in itself probably isn't a problem, but the fact that I'm naked is. I remember the tickling against my waist and realise that it must have been the towel coming undone that I felt. I stare at my erection for far too long. I should be covering it and getting the fuck out of here, but I can't seem to get my mind to come together to make it happen. Too little sleep and my head just doesn't seem to be able to make my body do what it needs to.

Help Our Heroes

Aiden finally looks away, his cheeks bright red, and it spurs me into action. I sit up quickly, grabbing the towel and covering myself with it, even though it's about five minutes too late to hide my modesty.

"I... uh ... brought you something to eat. I know you're tired but I didn't know when you ate last."

The thought is really sweet. I've never had someone who thought of me like this, not even William. He's very much a look after yourself type of guy, but it works out well since we don't see each other all that often due to our work. "Thank you, but I'm not that hungry." I laugh when my stomach makes a complete liar out of me by rumbling louder than I thought possible. We both look at it and Aiden bursts out laughing along with me.

"Want to try again?"

"Thanks, Aiden. I'm ravenous so I think I should eat."

We both laugh as Aiden grabs a tray from the dresser and brings it over to the bed. He places it down and my stomach does a very unflattering growl when I smell the food. There isn't a tremendous amount but it's enough to battle my hunger before I go to sleep. There is a BLT, with what looks like hand cut bread, a bowl of coleslaw and a bowl of crisps. The bacon smells terrific and I can't wait to actually eat now, but I wait, noticing that there is only one meal here. "Are you not eating?"

"I had something downstairs. I'll leave you in peace and let you rest. If you need anything just help yourself, the kitchen is ... well obviously downstairs. I'm up early tomorrow so I'm heading to bed. Goodnight."

He doesn't even wait for a reply before leaving the room and closing the door behind him. It doesn't take a genius to know that he felt awkward after seeing me naked. After being in the army for so long, seeing another guy nude becomes second nature. When you are living in close quarters with hundreds of other men, there aren't always facilities to hide your modesty, and some guys just don't give a shit about walking around naked. Murray is the worst on the team, walking around like no one has invented clothes. I will apologise to Aiden in the morning because I just want to eat and then actually have more than a nap.

My first bite elicits a deep moan from me. Holy shit this sandwich is fantastic, and not just because I haven't had decent food in a long time. No, this would be the best BLT I've tasted even if I'd spent my life eating nothing but BLT's. The bacon is crispy and the tomato fresh, adding a bit of bite to the texture of the sandwich. The bread is the winner though, thick and crusty, making it hard to bite through but worth the hassle. I finish the whole thing in record time and I decide it was a good thing I didn't eat with Aiden because I would have looked even more like a greedy fucker than usual. I eat fast at best of times, a point that been picked up more than once by William, but today I devoured my supper like someone was planning on stealing it.

Ignoring the rest of the food I lift the tray and put it on the dresser before heading over to my bags. I know I have a pair of sleep shorts in there and after Aiden already getting an eyeful of what he shouldn't, I think it's probably best I wear them tonight. I pull them on while heading to bed. I'd planned on calling William tonight and sorting this whole thing out so I could go home, but I'm just too fucking tired. I don't know what's going to happen between us, but it's probably not going to be the misunderstanding that I'm hoping it is, so a good nights sleep is probably a good thing. Give me a chance to understand everything fully.

I slip under the duvet, enjoying the comfort of a proper bed. First night home after a deployment is usually tricky for me, the sudden comfort playing havoc with my body, but tonight I don't think I'll have that problem. Not only am I physically exhausted but I am mentally as well. I just want to hide for the rest of the night, finally get some sleep, so when the morning comes, I can fight whatever battle is on its way. I am under no illusion that it's going to be a battle, and I have a feeling it might be one of the hardest of my life.

Chapter 5

Aiden

I throw the last black bag into my small garage and close the door as quietly as possible. The morning is still dark, and I don't want to run the risk of waking half the street so early. I need to get the car back to Uncle before the office opens so he can have his regular drivers take it. I only jumped in to help out since Bobby had called in ill at short notice. Working from home as a graphic designer means that I can help Uncle even at such short notice. He doesn't ask often so I don't mind giving up a day for him, even if this time I got an extra houseguest out of my kind offer.

The thought of my houseguest brings heat to my cheeks, the image of waking him up so he could eat burned deeply in my memory. I don't think I will ever forget what Ralph looks like without clothes on, that hard body is something I've only ever seen in porn. I honestly didn't think men like that existed, but apparently, I've been looking in the wrong place all this time. I need to get myself a military man because holy hell, they are built. His cock was pretty impressive too, not that I want to admit to staring at it like I did. It was like as soon as my eyes hit it I couldn't look away. That led to a very unfortunate boner and I couldn't get out of the room fast enough. I told Ralph it was because I was going to bed, but I needed to use his image to get off. Am I proud? Not really, but the intense orgasm told me my conscience wasn't all that bothered.

Getting into the car, I turn the heating up full and reverse out of the drive. I think again that maybe I should have woken Ralph to tell him I was leaving but he looked so exhausted yesterday that I just left him, convinced I'll be back before he surfaces.

* * *

I was right in my prediction of getting back before Ralph woke up, in fact,

I've also repacked my car and he still hasn't come down the stairs. I recheck the clock and see that's it creeping closer to lunchtime and I decide to make us some food. I have no idea what the rest of the day will entail so I plan on eating while I know I can. People think that I don't eat since I'm quite slim, but they are very wrong. I can eat my big brother under the table and he got his larger build from my dad. He looks like he should be able to eat a whole cow but he gives up before I do.

Making something for Ralph is a gamble, but since he ate the BLT last night, I take the chance of making a grilled cheese sandwich for him. I had one for the first time when I visited New York a few years back and I fell in love. Now I have one at least twice a week and I'm pretty sure that Ralph will enjoy it, I mean who doesn't like cheese? I grab everything I need to make it and start preparing. I turn the radio on quietly, singing along with the song that's playing. I like quiet days, the ones where you can forget about the outside world and just be. There aren't enough days like this for me because even though I work from home, I seem to spend a lot of time with other people. Between helping my brother out at his café and then stepping in every now and again for my Uncle, my job tends to get done in the late night hours when I'm meant to be sleeping or possibly having a life. It has been so long since I went out to meet someone, but I never seem to have the energy these days.

I lean down to get a frying pan, my lack of social life threatening to put me on a downer for the rest of the day, and when I stand up my back brushes against something. The shock of it has me screaming and turning with the pan in my hand, ready to hit whatever is there. What I find is a fully dressed Ralph with his hands held out in front of him. I would think that he is indeed feeling threatened but the huge smile on his face is a dead giveaway that he finds me amusing.

"Morning." He tries to keep his face straight but I'm not buying it for a single second. Fucker.

"I could have hurt you there. You really shouldn't sneak up on me like that. It's dangerous." This gets a full belly laugh from him and I glare, showing him how pissed off I am at him. He might be bigger than me, but I could have done real damage to him. I just didn't want to.

Help Our Heroes

"Do you need a hand?"

I don't reply, just hand him the frying pan and butter. He starts humming next to me and it's such a difference from yesterday. "Sleep well?"

"I did actually. That bed is super comfortable."

"I would take that as a compliment but since you've been sleeping on … what have you been sleeping on?" It's only now that I realise I don't know that much about the army and the men in it. I know how sexy they look in their uniforms but that's about it.

"We sleep on bunks when on base, but it's a lot different out on the field. Thankfully the last five months have all been indoors."

"Have you been in battle?" I'm suddenly very interested in finding out about Ralph's life. He's the first soldier I've had a chance to speak to and I want to know everything.

"Yeah, I was posted in Afghanistan for seven months."

I feel my mouth drop open at that information. I watched stories about that war on the news, shocked at what was happening but feeling somewhat removed from it all. I knew that men were risking their lives being over there, but since I didn't personally know anyone that had gone over there, it all felt a little unreal. "You were there when they were fighting?"

He takes over the grating while I stand and stare at him. "I was there right in the middle of the conflict. I wasn't in the direct line of fire because we spent most of our time on base, but the times we went out, it was pretty intense. It was the first time most of my team had seen real war and it left its mark on them, and not just physically."

"Did you ever get hurt?"

"A few cuts and bruises, but I've been lucky so far." He reaches out and touches the wooden windowsill and I would smile at him touching wood but I'm still stuck with the thought of him being shot at.

"So no bullet holes?"

"None, but I've lost a few friends to them. We might not be on the front line fighting the bad guys, but if a vehicle gets overturned or breaks down, we have to go in to get it."

I just can't wrap my head around this guy in front of me being shot at.

Again, watching it on TV, you become kind of numb to it all. "Wow."

"I'm sure you've spoken to people in the forces before, you aren't that far from the base here."

I nod because he's right, but then he's also wrong. "I work at my brothers café occasionally, so I've spoken to soldiers before but I've not thought about what they go through. It's more just a hello and how is their day going. You are the first one I've actually thought about being out there like... well in danger."

"The best thing is to not think about it. If you had that in your head all the time, you would never go out and do your job. I just get on with it, and to be honest, driving in Manchester scares me more."

I burst out laughing, not expecting that answer. "Well, I don't blame you there." I finally go back to making the sandwiches, mixing the cheeses so they are all well blended. "I'm gonna make grilled cheese, that okay with you?"

"Yeah. And thanks again for all this. I'm not sure what I would have done last night if you hadn't given me a bed. I wasn't exactly in the best condition to be making good decisions. I feel well rested and ready to tackle the day."

I look him over and see that he's telling the truth. Even though I was watching him while we were speaking, I wasn't actually seeing him. Now that I am I notice that the dark circles have almost vanished, making his green eyes a lot more noticeable, and his hair isn't as messy. My eyes work their way down his body taking in the black jeans and white fitted t-shirt, and suddenly his camouflage uniform isn't the sexiest thing I've seen him in. There is something very appealing about him in regular clothes, or maybe it's just how relaxed he looks today. "So what is the plan? Or is that being too nosey?"

He huffs out a laugh. "I don't think it can be classed as nosey when you saw my life go to fuck yesterday. The real answer is I don't know. I need to talk to William and see what's happening. After that, I can work out what to do."

I can only imagine how that's going to go. "How long were you with him?"

"Two years. I thought William was it, the last man I would be with." He sounds sad and as much as I should change the subject to save his feelings, I can't stop the next question.

"Did you have any idea this might be coming?"

Help Our Heroes

He walks to the sink to wash his hands and I think I've maybe overstepped. I concentrate on putting the bread into the pan, covering it with cheese, and then adding another slice of bread. I add another knob of butter and jump when he starts speaking.

"I didn't see it coming. I thought everything was perfect. Okay, maybe not perfect but not quite at the coming home to all my belongings on the front grass stage. We fought sometimes, I mean he hated my job so that was always a problem between us, but we loved each other. I just need to know what he's thinking, but I'm sure that everything can be worked through." He sounds sad, and I suppose that shouldn't be a surprise. He just lost the guy he was with for two years.

Chapter 6

Ralph

The more I speak to Aiden the hollower I feel. I keep trying to convince myself that whatever is going on between William and me can be fixed and I can go home, but the fact that he hasn't reached out to me since I arrived back tells me that I'm probably wrong. I want to keep that little bit of positive thinking I have though because if I give in to the despair, I'm feeling it's a slippery slope into a hole that I won't be able to get myself out of.

"I'm sure you're right." Aiden doesn't sound convinced, but I let it go. He's a stranger and doesn't know either William or me. "Can you pass me two plates?"

He points to the cupboard behind me and I open it, grabbing two plates and placing them on the worktop. He slides the grilled cheese sandwiches from the pan and the smell hits me, making my stomach grumble just like the night before.

"Are you ever not hungry?" He laughs as he cuts through the centre of both sandwiches, the cheese oozing out of the middle.

"When I'm asleep. But to be fair, the food on base isn't exactly the best in the world and I'm a big guy, it takes a lot to keep me moving."

"Yeah, that big body must take a lot of filling." I don't know if he means his words to come out sounding like a come on, but as soon as he says them he knows. His cheeks go bright red and his eyes widen as he stares at me. "I meant your stomach. Like you must burn a lot of calories in a day with all those muscles. I didn't mean that you need filling by..."

"Stop talking, Aiden." I practically shout at him to get him not to finish that sentence. There is only one way to end that sentence and if he says what he's about to, there is a good chance that my mind will wander to where it shouldn't.

"Thank you." He genuinely looks relieved that he's finally stopped talking and I wonder if he always has a problem with word vomit.

"But yes, a lot of calories are needed every day. The food I eat doesn't look as good as this though." I grab my plate off the worktop and take a large bite of the grilled cheese. I moan and my eyes close as the taste explodes on my tongue. It isn't just cheese, the little slithers of onion add another dimension to it, and the little bits of bacon ... holy shit. "Oh my god. This is so fucking good."

Aiden smiles and it looks shy, like he's embarrassed about the compliment, and I try not to think about how attractive he is. "It's not that good, but I'm glad you like it. Working at Jer's café has let me learn a lot about cooking."

"Well anyone that can cook like this is a hero in my eyes. I can burn water so when I'm home I tend to eat out a lot. Having you cook for me is ... well, thank you."

Aiden takes a bite of his sandwich but his eyes never leave mine, and I can see a question building in them.

"Spill it."

He finishes the food in his mouth but he doesn't speak straight away, making me wonder if he's going to ignore me completely. He finally clears his throat and speaks. "Didn't William cook for you?"

I think back over the past few years, to the handful of times that he was around at meal times. "He was never really around when it was time to eat. His work took him away a lot. When he was there, it was more what was quick, anything that could be thrown in the oven."

Aiden gets a sad look on his face and for the first time, I think that maybe everything in my relationship with William wasn't as perfect as I thought it was.

I put the last bit of grilled cheese in my mouth and turn to the sink so I can wash the plate. I need to get out of here. I don't even know Aiden and he's here dissecting my life like he knows what he's talking about. I put the plate on the dish rack and turn back to Aiden. "Thank you for everything, but I should go and speak to William. I'm sure that this whole thing can be sorted out." I smile and start to leave the kitchen, determined to call William and then go home.

I take the steps upstairs two at a time, putting distance between Aiden and me. It's a dickhead move after everything he's done for me but I don't like to feel judged. I've spent too long with people looking down on me because of the life I live, and I won't take it from Aiden. I enter the room, refusing to think about my parents and their judgey ways. You would think that giving my life over to protect our country would make them proud but no, the only thing they can focus on is the fact I like men. They don't disapprove enough to cut me out of their lives but just enough to make sure I never forget that I'm never going to be accepted fully.

I shake my head as I pack up the few belongings I had removed from my pack, trying to clear the thoughts of my parents from my head. When I'm about to face my possibly ex-boyfriend the last thing I need is to have their words of distaste floating around my head. I grab my pack and put it on my shoulder, leaving the room and heading towards the front door. I open it and step outside, only then realising that I have no idea where I am. I was asleep when Aiden brought me here last night, and even if I wasn't, I have no way of getting home. The door closes behind me and I hear the jangling of keys.

"Come on, I'll take you home." Aiden walks past me and gets into a different car from last night. I'm not sure where this car came from, but I follow him down the steps, stow my bag in the boot, and get into the passenger seat.

"Thank you … again."

He gives me a sweet smile before driving me silently to my house.

* * *

I take a deep breath and knock politely on the front door of my old house. I can't believe the nerves that are attacking me as I stand and wait for William to open the door. I've faced gunfire as I towed vehicles out of ditches, always aware that there could be landmines within inches of me, and not once have I felt this nervous.

Hearing footsteps heading towards the door doesn't help how anxious I feel, but I smile, wanting to face William without anger. That thought dies the instant the door opens and I see a stranger standing there. It takes a minute for me to process what's happening and my mind is heading towards the fact that William has moved out and this is the new owner, when I hear Williams voice.

"Who is it, honey?"

The stranger looks a little confused as he stares at me. "I don't know."

The face I spent five months dying to see walks around the corner and when he sees me standing there he stops, his mouth dropping open like he can't believe I'm here.

"What are you doing here, Ralph?"

"Really? That's what you lead with after you kick me out of my own home?" The anger that I was trying to keep under control is starting to show itself and I swallow it down, trying not to let it explode out.

"William, who is this?" The new guy looks confused as his gaze flicks between William and me.

"No one. Could you just go inside for a little bit, Rickie?"

The first word he speaks has the rage finally spilling over, eclipsing any other feelings I might have for William. "No one? Fucking no one? I've been with you for two years, William. Two fucking years and we've lived together for over half of that. But now I'm no one?"

Rickie's eyes go wide, his head turning instantly towards William. "He lived here? For two years?"

"I will explain later, baby. Just go in and let me talk to Ralph."

I take a good look at William, the first proper one in five months, and it feels like I don't know him. He looks the same, his built muscly body looking hot in the tight t-shirt that he likes to wear, his blonde hair sitting sexily on the tops of his shoulders, and his confidence giving him an air of arrogance that always attracted me. Nothing is different, but he isn't the same. He isn't the man I thought he was and that makes me see him like everyone else does. They all told me he was a jerk, that I wasn't seeing the real him through my love fogged glasses. He was a dickhead, a self-absorbed idiot who was only out for what he could get from people, but I told them they were wrong. Now I will have to admit to everyone that they were right, that I wanted more from him and he moved on before I even knew we had ended.

"Wait, I'm not going anywhere. He said two years, but we've been dating for ten months."

William approaches Rickie and cups his cheeks. "Baby, I promise I will explain."

Rickie knocks his hands away and turns to me. I came here to get answers but they don't seem all that important now. The knowledge that he's been cheating on me should make me angry but I'm just numb. It's like half of my relationship with him has been a lie and that fact takes away the fight. I no longer want to fix this. I just want to cut all ties and move on with my life.

"You said you lived here, when did you leave?"

I don't know if I should give Rickie any answer since he's involved with the destruction of my life, but going by the look on his face he knew nothing about it. I have a feeling he was getting lied to just as much as I was. "I found my shit on the front grass yesterday."

"I don't understand, I've been here for two months and I haven't seen you before."

Two months someone else has been living in my house without me knowing. Eating from my fridge, watching my television, sleeping in my bed, and fucking my boyfriend. "I've been on deployment. I'm in the army."

If I thought Rickie couldn't look more horrified I would be wrong, when he hears I'm in the army the colour drains from his face. "Oh god, I'm so sorry."

I don't know how to answer him, his sympathy completely throwing me off kilter. I shouldn't feel bad for him but we're both kind of in the same boat. "Don't sweat it, at least now I know. Have fun with him." I don't even wait for a response before turning my back on my old life and towards a future I have no fucking idea about.

Chapter 7

Aiden

I don't know how Ralph is feeling, but my heart is racing as I watch the scene unfold in front of me. I'm trying not to pay attention to what's happening on the doorstep but it's like a car crash that I can't look away from. I knew something was wrong the minute that the front door opened, the confusion on Ralph's face telling me it wasn't William who he was looking at.

Each second after that brought more drama until the moment it all clicked into place for Ralph and the new guy, Rickie. It seems William's been having his cake and eating it too, and by looking at him, I can't work out why. I mean don't get me wrong, the guy is handsome in a very obvious way, but there is something about him that just screams arsehole to me. There's a cockiness to his posture like he thinks he's the shit and no one would be able to convince him otherwise. Even now as the two men are talking about the overlap in their relationship with William, he looks like he will be able to smooth everything over without any problems.

Ralph turns and walks towards me, but it's what's happening behind him that still has my attention. William reaches out to touch Rickie but Rickie pulls back, slapping William's hand away. I'm not an expert at body language but I have a feeling that William won't be getting laid tonight.

"Would you take me to … fuck I don't even know."

My attention is pulled back to Ralph who's now standing in front of me. He doesn't look as confident as he did when he walked away from William and I wonder if the shock is wearing off and reality is now hitting him. "I will take you anywhere you need to go."

Getting in the car, I wait until Ralph is in before speaking again. "So, do you know where I'm taking you?"

He gets his mobile out and starts messing about with something on it. "A hotel would be fine, just give me a second to check availability."

"Do they not have somewhere on base you can go?"

"Yeah, but I want a break for now while I'm not on duty. We always get some down time after being deployed, and it's nice to not be on base."

I get that. It would be like working all the time, even if you weren't wearing your uniform. Like living in Tesco while not on shift.

"Okay, this one has a room. I'll book it online and if can take me there I would appreciate it."

"Of course."

"Thanks, if you just start heading towards the town centre."

I pull away from the kerb and head in the direction he told me to. We spend a few minutes in silence as he goes about booking the room. I want to ask him what he's planning on doing with all the belongings that are in my car but I decide that we will deal with that when we get to the hotel.

"The fucking bastard!"

I jump in my seat as his angry words echo through the car. I look over at him, a little shocked when I see his cheeks red with anger and his hands gripping his phone. I haven't seen him angry before, not even when he saw all his belongings on the grass, but maybe he was just too tired to care then. Now he looks pissed off and ready to commit murder. I don't speak, scared of having all that anger pointed in my direction.

"I can't believe he did this. Turn the car around."

Now that I know I can't keep quiet I look at him as I continue to drive in the same direction as I was. "Who am I turning around for you to kill?"

He gives me a look that tells me who he's talking about but still, I continue onwards. "William. He's cleaned out our joint account. There is nothing in it. All my money is gone. Fucking low life fucker. I need to fucking hurt him, turn around so I can fucking kill him."

I want to comment on his use of the word fuck when he's angry but since I value my life, I don't point it out. "Do you have savings?"

"No, everything I had was in there. The only money I have now is in my deployment account, the one I use when I'm away if I need anything, and there is only a few hundred pounds in that. Nowhere near enough to live off."

Holy shit. Just when I think Ralph's life cant get any worse, another page turns and the horrors increase. I can't even imagine what he's feeling right now, the anger that he must have against William, and that's the reason I'm not turning around and taking him back there. No, we will find another solution to this whole thing without him beating the shit out of William. "Do you have anyone you can stay with?"

He drops his head against the headrest and sighs. "Fuck me." He presses a few times on his mobile and puts it to his ear.

I try not to listen as he speaks to someone on the other end of the call, focusing on the road as much as I can. The conversation carries on for a few minutes but I can tell it's not great news.

"I totally understand, Dean. No, don't be daft, family comes first. Will catch you soon." He hangs up and drops his phone onto his lap. I don't bother asking him how it went because it's really obvious. Instead, I just leave the motorway on the slip road and turn the car around, heading back towards my house.

"Take me back to my house."

"No."

"God damn it, Aiden. Turn the fucking car around and take me there, or stop so I can get out."

"No." I grip the steering wheel harder to stop my hands from shaking with nerves. I feel like I'm prodding a bear, and since I've only known the bear for just over twenty-four hours, I'm not sure how he will react. Deep down I don't feel that Ralph is any danger to me, but I've been known not to read people accurately. Not the first time I've had to call Jer to come and save me when a one-night stand has gone to shit.

"Arsehole."

I relax when Ralph huffs back in his seat, muttering under his breath about me as I drive us home. I flex my hands to release some of the tension there. At least this time my intuition is working and Ralph isn't going to be aggressive, or at least not towards me.

A Military Anthology

Ten minutes later I pull into my drive and turn off the engine, sitting quietly not sure what to do. I brought Ralph here to put distance between him and William, but that's as far as my plan got. Now I'm flying blind. "What happens now?"

Ralph turns towards me. "I had a plan but you wouldn't help me with it."

I roll my eyes at his grumpiness. "Like I am going to take you over there to beat the shit out of William. I'm sure that would go down well with your job if you end up in jail."

"Stop being so fucking reasonable. I just want to hurt him a little bit."

I burst out laughing. I don't mean to but he sounds so much like a stroppy teenager right now that I find it extremely funny.

"And now you're laughing at me?"

"I don't mean to. I'm sorry, honestly." Even as I try to sound contrite, I know it's not working because Ralph is struggling not to laugh himself. I'm happy that I have managed to remove some of the stress that's been plaguing Ralph for the last few hours, his smile settling the part of my chest that's been aching for him. His life might be shit just now but he'll be okay, I know he will.

"I need to call housing on the base and see if they have a room for me. I'm gonna end up rooming with someone, I can feel it."

"Aren't you a higher rank though, doesn't that get you better stuff?"

"I only get better if it's available. The last I heard the single rooms were filled when the new Warrant Officers transferred in." He takes out his phone again but before he has a chance to press anything I cover his hand with mine. The heat from his skin shocks me, making me pull back instantly. I look at my palm as the tingles continue to spread over my hand.

"Come inside to make the call."

He doesn't speak, just nods before getting out of the car. I take another few seconds just staring at my hands, wondering what the hell I'm feeling. I shake my head and get out of the car, walking past Ralph so I can unlock the front door. I kick my shoes off before heading to the kitchen and putting the coffee machine. Ralph doesn't follow me into the kitchen so I suspect that he's calling the housing people. I potter about cleaning up the mess from lunch, needing something to distract me until Ralph is finished. I check my watch, aware that I need to leave to go help Jer for a few hours, and not wanting to be late. An afternoon of cooking isn't exactly something to look forward to this afternoon, but I promised last week when he asked.

Chapter 8

Ralph

I hang up the call and bang my head against the wall next to me. I didn't bother to follow Aiden into the kitchen because he knew that I needed to make this call. I also needed a minute to work out what the hell had happened in the car when Aiden touched me. It was like there was lightening sparking all over my skin, spreading over my hand where we connected. I've never felt that before, and I'm not sure what to think about it. Nothing. I'm going to think nothing about it because the only thing that I should be worrying about is where I'm going to be sleeping tonight.

I head towards the kitchen to find Aiden cleaning up the pan he used earlier to make me lunch. He's singing along quietly to a song on the radio, and I smile at how happy he seems with life. I don't think I've met someone as sweet as Aiden before. He took me in, a complete stranger, all because I was having a shitty day. I mean who does that? Who opens up the safety of their own house because someone is in need?

Aiden must hear me as I approach because he turns and grabs a towel to dry his hands. He looks at me expectantly and it takes me a moment to realise what he's waiting on.

"Nothing. Housing won't have anything for a few days at least. It's okay though, if I get a cheap enough hotel then I can stay a few nights before I run out of money." It will have to be an exceptionally cheap hotel, probably a crappy rundown B&B, but I'm sure I can push my money to go for up to maybe five days. I just need to make sure that I go back to the base to eat my meals.

"Are you being serious right now?"

Confusion takes over as I watch his face go from friendly to slightly pissed off. "Um, yeah?"

"You think I'm going to kick you out to sleep in a shitty hotel until your money runs out? Do I look like that sort of person?"

"No I don't think you're that sort of person, but you've also done so much already. You gave me a bed last night when I was so tired I was pretty much out of it. You let me into your house when you didn't know who I was. I think you're a fantastic person who I don't want to put out any longer."

"Shut up." It's all he says before he leaves me standing alone in the kitchen. I hear his footsteps on the stairs as he storms away.

I don't follow him, not wanting to start a fight before I leave, so I help myself to a cup of coffee from the pot on the side. I lean against the unit and sip it until Aiden returns. I'm not sure what I expected when he did, but when he walks into the kitchen, I'm shocked. He's wearing a white chef's jacket that is tight around his waist and the sleeves are rolled up to sit just under his elbows. I know he said he helped his brother in his café, but I always assumed he meant maybe a server. I don't know why I thought that because we were talking about food at the time, so it makes sense that he's a chef.

"You're a chef." Damn, could I sound any dumber? I swear seeing him wearing that jacket has made me stupid. I don't typically have a thing for men in such a simple uniform, but he looks sexy with it fitting onto his body.

Aiden looks down at himself before looking up at me. "Eh, well a cook, not quite a chef yet but that's the dream. I thought I'd mentioned that?"

"You did, but I didn't think about you being one. Does that make sense? It's like telling someone I'm in the army, they know what I do, but once they see me in my fatigues, it suddenly clicks with them." I keep talking, trying to distract myself from the boner that's threatening to make itself known. I blame no sex for five months for my predicament. My tiredness is finally wearing off enough that my dick wants some action. That's definitely why I'm getting hard, it can't have anything to do with the guy standing in front of me looking hot as fuck.

"Well this is me. Trainee chef in my brothers café."

"You keep saying café, but I think it might be different than what I'm picturing. I see a little greasy spoon that serves cooked breakfasts and bacon rolls."

Aiden's laughter doesn't help my hardening cock and I want him to take me to a hotel so I can use my hand for some relief. "Don't tell Jer that. It's slightly nicer than what you think. I might say café but I suppose I should call it a Bistro, but I think that sounds pretentious."

"Yeah, a little fancier than I imagined. Once I get money sorted I should come and visit, see how well you really cook. It would be interesting to see if it's only sandwiches you're good at."

He gives me the finger and I can't help but laugh at his reaction. He walks to the small table in the corner and grabs his car keys, prompting me to rinse my mug and put it on the draining board. I haven't made plans about where he can drop me but I can search while we head into town.

"Help yourself to anything you need, there is food in the fridge and juice in the cupboard. It won't be cold but there is ice in the freezer. I don't know what time I will get home but it shouldn't be too late." He takes out his mobile and hands it to me. "Put your number in there and I will let you know when I'm heading home. If it's not too late, I will bring dinner."

I'm still trying to catch up but I grab his mobile and input my number. He smiles at me when I hand it back and a few seconds later my phone buzzes in my pocket.

"And now you have my number if you need anything. I will grab your bag from the boot before I head out. Remember, help yourself to anything." He turns and leaves the kitchen.

It takes me a second to work out that he's leaving. I take off after him and meet him as he returns with my bag in his hands. It's a little funny seeing him trying to carry my pack. The whole thing is about the size of him and I would bet all the money I have that it weighs more than him.

"Holy shit, how do you carry this thing?"

"It doesn't weigh that much." It weighs a lot less than it usually does when on deployment but I don't tell him that.

"Sure, you keep telling yourself that. Let's just say there would be no way that I could lift it without both hands and a good grip."

"So you are the liftee and not the lifter?" It comes out before I have the chance to check myself, my flirty, sarcastic remark coming out naturally. It's something I would say to my friends if we were bantering, but I don't know if Aiden will take it as a joke.

"That's something that is found out and not told."

I sigh a little with relief when he jokes back with me, letting me know that even though his cheeks have coloured slightly, he is taking my joke in the way it was intended.

He turns to leave and it reminds me why I came out here. "Aiden, what are you doing?"

"I'm going to work. I told you that."

I roll my eyes at him. "Yeah I got that part, but why are you leaving me here?"

"Because I can't take you to work."

I run my tongue along the front of my teeth. I know he's purposely being obtuse and I'm not impressed. "Again, I got that part."

"I don't have time for this titillating conversation, Ralph, I'm gonna be late for work. Will see you at some point." He turns and leaves me standing in his hall.

Arsehole.

* * *

I turn the water tap off with my foot, relaxing back into the hot water. I wasn't sure what to do when Aiden left but when the urge to go and confront William wouldn't let go of me, I decided that getting naked and having a bath might change my mind. I can't exactly go storming out of the house if I have no clothes on. The added bonus is my muscles are more relaxed than they have been in months. The downside to the whole thing is my mind has time to finally think over everything that's happened.

Two years I spent trying to make it work with William. Two years of listening to him complain about my job and tell me that I need to think about him more. At the time I put it down to him missing me and not liking it when I'm away, but now I'm not so sure. If it takes two men to keep him entertained, I think it was more about him being the centre of the universe. I wonder if that's why he cheated on me? Dean always told me that William was an attention seeker, that he wasn't happy until everyone in the room was looking at him, and it seems like he was right.

I went against my usual type when I went after William. He just wasn't the man I would usually be attracted to but there was something about him that stood out. I genuinely thought he was the kind of guy that I could spend the rest of my life with. I can't believe I made such a huge fucking mistake. When I finally decide to get myself back out there, I'm going to go after the kind of man that I usually do. Small, slim but fit, with dark hair and a smart mouth. Someone that can challenge me and not let me away with my usual shit, but someone who cares enough to be there for me. Someone who might make me a grilled cheese sandwich after letting me sleep late.

Groaning to myself I slip under the water, trying hard not to think about the hot little chef who is trying to sneak into my mind.

Chapter 9

Aiden

"One truffle mac and cheese and one smoked haddock and leek rarebit for table twelve." I put the dishes up to the pass, making sure that the plates are still clean before the servers grab them. "We have one lobster risotto, one duck salad and one butternut squash risotto for table four."

"Yes, chef."

I turn back to the cooker and start on the lobster risotto. "How long to the pass for table four?"

"Seven minutes, chef."

I turn back and add more stock to my risotto before shaking the pan. My mind is focused on the dish in front of me, the noise of the kitchen making me feel at home for the first time in days. The heat and stress of the kitchen soothes my soul, making me relax more than a good massage. I spent many years at University getting my degree in graphic design, and don't get me wrong I do enjoy my job helping people with their website and merchandise needs with a large advertising company, but when my brother bought this place, I realised I had a hidden love of cooking.

"Four minutes to the pass." I shout out loud enough for my team to hear me and I listen for the responses. It's been busy tonight, apparently, the local theatre has a play on so people are coming for a pre-show meal, but I trust my team to work the way they should. Okay, so not my team, it's Jer's team. It's not often that I feel jealous of Jer and his life, but when I see the place he's created here I can feel that little pang inside. He found his love of food early on in life, allowing him to train with several fantastic chefs around the country before returning here to open his own place.

"Plating the risotto." I walk to the pass and spoon the risotto into a round white plate, letting it ooze over the base before piling it up. A few shavings of Parmesan and it's ready to go. I smile as I look at the cleanness of the dish. This is what I want, to create food that people will enjoy.

"We need two cheese soufflés and a crab waffle for table six."

I turn to see Jer standing behind me with the next docket in his hand. He smiles as the kitchen goes to work preparing the ordered dishes. "How is everything?" He puts the docket in the queue so he can see what else is needing to go out.

"Going well. No complaints which is always a good thing, don't think they even noticed it wasn't a proper chef that cooked their meals." I try to keep the bitterness out of my voice because it's not Jer's fault that I chose the wrong path in life.

"Say the word, little brother, and I will have you in here training. You want to be a fully qualified chef and I will make it happen. We can run this place together."

It isn't the first time that Jer has told me that he will help me achieve everything I want, and I have enough money saved to take some time and do the training, but part of me feels like I'm stealing his dream from him. He was the one who always wanted to work with food and maybe he would hate it if I followed in his footsteps. "I know. How was the bank?"

His eyes lose their happiness a little but the smile stays on his lips as he tries to convince me that he's okay. "Went well, just have to wait now."

"Wait on what?"

"Nothing. Now get home and relax. You do far too much these days."

I let him change the subject, removing my apron and putting it in the dirty washing basket. "We will be talking about this, Jer, don't think we won't."

I hear his laughter as I leave the kitchen area. He knows that I won't risk the orders getting behind by pestering him about it now, but I will talk to him soon, and I won't give up until I know what's going on. When I get to the staff room I head straight to my locker and grab my bag out of it. Checking the time I see that it's just after eight, so text Ralph to ask him if he's eaten yet. I get a response before I manage to change my shoes, telling me that he hasn't thought about dinner yet, so I grab some supplies on the way past the fridge. Jer shouts something about it being theft but I just give him the finger. Since I don't get paid for helping him out I'm taking whatever the hell I want.

"Good night, little brother."

I smile as I leave through the back door and head towards my car.

* * *

I'm draining the pasta when Ralph appears in the doorway behind me. He was asleep on the couch when I arrived home which was a bit of a surprise since he'd texted me twenty minutes earlier. I left him to rest though. He's been through so much since he arrived home and he already looked ready to drop at that point. My imagination tells me that they don't get the rest they need when on duty, but I don't know. They might get twelve hours sleep a night for all I know and live in five-star accommodation.

Adding the pasta to the mushroom sauce, I mix it until it's all combined and heap bowls high with the finished meal. Just as I put the pan in the sink I hear Ralph walking fully into the kitchen behind me. I turn and see him stretching his arms above his head while he yawns. The move pulls his t-shirt up and away from the waistband of his jogging bottoms, leaving a bare patch of skin on show. My eyes drop to that area and I can't look away. His skin is slightly tanned, showing a tan line just under his waistband, and it looks smooth and soft. There's no hair that I see apart from the start of the perfect happy trail. It's dark and alluring, and I want to tug those joggers down to see how thick it is.

Ralph coughing makes my eyes dart back up to his face. I try to look at him like I wasn't just staring at his cock area, but from the heat building in my cheeks, I know that I'm failing. To try and distract him from what I was just doing, I turn and grab his plate of food.

"Hungry?" I take the plates to the small table that sits at the edge of my kitchen. Once I put it down I take a few minutes to gather cutlery and drinks for us both, and when I return to the table Ralph is already sitting there waiting on me.

"All you seem to do is feed me." He digs into the pasta like he doesn't have a problem with me making him food.

"I love to cook, and it's nice to have someone to cook for. It's never as satisfying when I have to praise myself."

Ralph smiles around the fork and chews the mouthful before speaking. "Well let me be the one that praises you. This is fantastic, in fact, everything you've made me has been better than anything I've eaten. You're a fantastic chef."

"Cook." It's become second nature to me to correct people when they call me a chef because I don't have the right to claim that title.

"You said that earlier and I don't understand the difference."

"Cooks tend to be self-trained, you know like people who own cafes and food carts. Chefs are trained and have the official qualifications." I eat while Ralph processes that information. I know a lot of people don't see the difference but I refuse to let people call me that when it took my brother years of training and late nights to earn the title.

"But you want to be a chef?"

My heart races a little when I think about following that particular dream. I've spent so long thinking about it now that it seems so hard to do. I've left it too late to start chasing it. "I would love nothing more, but it's not meant to be. I'm too old to be changing careers, and after spending all those years in university, it seems like a waste to go back to training for something else."

Ralph puts his fork down and gives me his full focus, which makes me feel a little under the spotlight. "It's not a waste if it's something that you care about. I always knew that I wanted to join the army, even as a young boy I would watch the soldiers and want to be them. You should do what holds that passion for you. What are you doing now?"

I put my own fork down, my appetite disappearing under Ralph's intense stare. "I'm a graphic designer with Red Door Custom Designs. I help with the website and merchandise design."

"And it makes you happy?"

I take a moment to think about his question. People have asked me that before, Jer, my uncle, and my mum, but I always just give them the standard answer. Yes, I'm happy, no I don't think I'm wasting my life, no I don't want to rock the boat by changing things. This time I think about my answer. "Yes, seeing that finished product makes me feel like I've achieved something."

"That's not what I asked."

Help Our Heroes

"Fuck you, Ralph." I get up from the table, grabbing both of the half-empty plates and storming off to the sink. Who the fuck does he think he is? He's known me for like two days, and even in that time we have barely spoken, so it's not like he knows me. I'm basically his landlord just now, not that he's paying me. God, he needs to mind his own business. I'm slamming the plates around in the sink when I feel him standing close behind me.

"I'm sorry. It's not any of my business what you do. You have been kind enough to open up your house when you know nothing about me. It just seems to me that food is a passion, I just wondered why you weren't following your passion." He sounds so sad that I turn around to face him, my anger melting away as he speaks.

"It's okay. It's just my parents did without most of their life so I could go to university, I don't want to throw that back in their faces. If I give it all up, then it's like I don't care what they went through." I shouldn't be putting all this on Ralph, only a minute ago I was telling myself that he was a stranger, but maybe that's why he's easy to talk to. He has nothing invested in the outcome of my decisions.

"I don't think they would be upset if you were following your dream. You don't want to be unemployed, just change the way you make your money. Does your brother know?"

"Yeah."

"And?"

Why is he pushing me for all these answers? And why does it feel so good to finally talk about all this? "He says he supports me and will train me so we can run the café together." Ralph stays quiet and I eventually look up, wondering why he hasn't said anything. His arms are crossed over his chest and he looks annoyed, like he can't understand what my problem is. Going by the look on his face he's about to tell me.

Chapter 10

Ralph

I have no idea what to say to Aiden. He's acting as though he wants to follow a life of crime and thinks his parents will be upset. He isn't telling the world that he's giving up his degree to become some hippy in a commune, he wants to retrain in a field that makes him happy. I see his face when he talks about cooking, and I've tasted his food, the guy has a talent that shouldn't be ignored.

As I stare at him, wanting to say so much, I wonder why it's bothering me so much that he isn't following his dream. He isn't a friend or a member of my family, so it doesn't change anything in my life if he doesn't become a chef. *So why does this bother me?* Maybe it's just that I can see the way his eyes light up when he talks about cooking, the obvious joy he feels for food. I don't want to see him miss out on being happy for some silly reason, even if the outcome doesn't affect me in any way.

"Why are you glaring at me?"

I wasn't aware that I was glaring, but apparently I can't hide my emotions from Aiden. "Sorry. It's just ... I don't get why you won't take your brother up on his offer."

Aiden rolls his eyes as he walks to the fridge and opens the door. He takes two bottles of beers from the shelf and hands me one after removing the top on the opener on the side of the fridge. I take it from him and enjoy a long drink, sighing as I have my first beer in months. It really is the simple pleasures that I miss.

"Why aren't you more upset about the William thing?"

I blink mutely at the sudden subject change. It came so out of left field that it's thrown me.

"If you're allowed to get personal then so am I. You were with him for two years and he was fucking someone else, that's got to hurt a little?"

"And as you said to me ... fuck you." I slam my beer down on the worktop and turn, planning on escaping before I lose my shit with him. I don't get a foot outside the door before my arm is grabbed and I'm pulled to a stop.

"I'm sorry."

I don't turn to look at Aiden, too angry to look at him. He may have been kind enough to give me a bed for the night but he doesn't get to invade my privacy like that. I sigh when I realise that I'm angry at him for doing the same thing I just did. His life is his business and I shouldn't be asking him such personal questions. "No, I'm sorry. How about we make a pact to leave these subjects alone?"

"Sounds like a plan. Want to finish that beer?"

I laugh as I walk back into the kitchen, grabbing my beer from the worktop as I follow Aiden to the table again.

* * *

I park my borrowed car outside Handy's house on base. Aiden was working all day from the little home office he has set up in his garage, so he said I could take his car to do a few errands. I took the chance to come into the housing office, thinking that maybe I could convince them to get me a room quicker if I was face to face with them. What became clear very quickly is that it doesn't matter if you call or go in person, if they don't want to give you a room they won't. So I'm still homeless, I just have a pissed off woman dealing with my request now.

"Are you coming in, shithead?"

I hear Handy shouting from his front door before he turns and walks back into his house, leaving the door wide open for me. I smile before getting out and locking up the car. I take the steps two at a time, eager to get inside to see Handy. He's standing in the hall when I close the door behind me, and I don't say anything before I pull him into a bone-crushing hug. He hugs me back, his arms wrapped tightly around me. Handy, or as his mother knows him Charles, is probably the best friend I've ever had. We met about ten years ago in a bar fight and we have been solid friends ever since.

"It's so fucking good to see you." I mean the words so badly. I miss a lot of things when I'm gone and Handy is right up there on the top of the list.

"Same, brother. Come on, let's get a drink." I should tell him no because I have to drive home, but one won't do any harm. As long as it's just one beer and I don't drive straight away, then I will accept his offer.

I head into the living room as Handy goes to the kitchen to get us a beer. I collapse on the couch, feeling relaxed for what feels like the first time in days. Finally, I feel like I'm home. I look up as a beer appears in front of me and I take it from Handy as he sits next to me. He holds out his bottle and I tap the neck of mine against his.

"To getting home safe."

I nod my head at the toast before taking a drink. "You do know I wasn't actually in any danger, well unless you count from frustration. I swear I'm not sure how some guys got their qualifications."

"Was it that bad?"

I groan, thinking of all the fuck ups that occurred while the men were training on the new equipment. "Let's just say that the hundred grand piece of equipment is worth substantially less now." And I had to write up every report to explain why people couldn't do as they were fucking told.

"Shit, so you're glad to be home?"

"Very." I take another long drink.

"So, how is William? Still walking?" He chuckles at his joke, not knowing that I'm now single and living in a strangers house.

"Not sure, but if he's had a good fuck, it was probably Rickie who did it. Actually, Rickie looked pissed when I went to their house, so maybe it was someone else."

Handy freezes with the bottle halfway to his mouth, the look of confusion and shock clear on his face. "What?"

I spend the next few minutes explaining everything that's happened the last few days, leaving Handy angry as fuck.

"I can't believe that little wank stain. I told you he was up to no good, I could see it in his cocky little face. Shit. How are you feeling?"

"Numb. I don't think it's fully hit me yet but I'm sure it will."

"How are you not angry enough to punch his cheating little face in?"

That's a great question. I haven't felt anything since I came home and discovered all my shit out of the house. Okay, that's a lie, I would have killed William if I had seen him after I checked my bank account, but Aiden helped me get over that. I should be angry though and I'm not sure why I'm not. "Honestly? I don't know. I should hate him with every single part of me, but there's nothing. Maybe once I find somewhere to live and I have less to worry about I will collapse. My only focus is finding a house."

"Wait, where the hell are you staying?"

"With Aiden."

Handy sits forward and puts his beer on the small coffee table before turning entirely and giving me his full attention. "And who is Aiden?"

Aiden's name hadn't come up when I was telling Handy about what had happened and his reaction makes me laugh. "Aiden is the driver who picked me up from the airport. I think he felt sorry for me and was worried about me having to sleep on the streets. He's been kind enough to give me a bed until I can get a room from housing… even though I think that's gonna take six thousand weeks." I humph when I stop talking and it's Handy's turn to laugh at me.

"I'll come back to the whole Aiden thing, but what did housing say?"

"Before I went in and complained today, they thought they might have a room this week, but after I pissed off the woman with the pen, it might be a few weeks. Apparently, they don't like it when you tell them how to do their jobs."

This causes Handy to burst out laughing. "Who did you speak to?"

"Margaret?"

The laughter increases and it doesn't make my confidence grow. "Holy shit, brother, you are never getting a bed. You just pissed off a woman that can hold a grudge longer than my mother."

Fantastic. Just what I wanted to hear. I need somewhere to stay and it looks like I'm getting further away from that.

"Look, if you can give me until Thursday to clean out the spare room, it's yours. I know it's not the biggest room in the world but the double bed is comfy, and there is no rush for you to move out."

"Are you sure?" I want to make sure he's thought this through. I need somewhere until I can find an apartment off base or get assigned accommodation on base, and god knows how long that might take.

"I wouldn't have offered if I didn't mean it. The room is full of junk so it's not like you will be taking space that I use, and it would be nice to have company for a change. Shame it has to be you but I will suffer through it."

He has a shit-eating grin on his face but I don't give him the satisfaction of reacting to his comment. Instead, I reply in the only logical way. "Thank you for the offer, but do you promise to keep your ... night time activities behind closed doors? I've already seen more of you than I've ever wanted to."

As always Handy's cheeks get red with the mention of how he got his nickname. Poor guy, he will never live that down.

Chapter 11

Aiden

I've been stuck in my office all day trying to catch up on the design for a tattooist who is opening his third shop. He needed a logo that he could use on all his forms and advertising. It's been interesting working with him, but he is so freaking picky that I've had to change it a few times. I finally managed to finish it to his exacting standards so now I can sleep, well until tomorrow when I need to spend the whole day on my next job. Helping everyone has put me a little behind, but I don't mind a few full days catching up, it's worth it to spend time in my brother's kitchen.

I stretch my back, groaning when it cracks in several places, but it relieves a lot of tension in the muscles. I rotate my neck as I walk through towards the kitchen, easing out the ache from the tightness. I've forgotten to eat today and my stomach is suddenly letting me know how much it hates me. A cramp goes through it as it grumbles loudly and I hear laughter, making me look up and meet Ralphs' eyes.

"See, it's not just my stomach that talks loudly." His smile makes my stomach react again, just in a very different way than the hunger did.

Shit. I need to get that under control because there is no acceptable reason to be finding my houseguest attractive, even if he is stupidly sexy. No, not finding him hot would be the better option.

"I made dinner." His smile grows as I step into the kitchen and the smell hits me, making my stomach growl again.

"You cooked? I thought you said you didn't cook?"

He walks to the oven and opens it, pulling a large cardboard box from inside. "Cook … ordered pizza and brought it home … same thing." He puts the large pizza box down and opens the top. The smell intensifies, and it makes me feel like I haven't eaten for days. I don't even wait for an invite before I grab a slice, the cheese dripping from it in large globs.

I moan when I take a bite, closing my eyes just to savour the taste. The spices all blend to give the tomato sauce a rich flavour, one of the best I've ever tasted on a pizza. I try to pick out all the different ingredients but my stomach wins out with its demands, and I take another bite just trying to fill it.

When I open my eyes I can see Ralph staring at me, his eyes slightly out of focus and staring at my mouth. I wipe at my lips to see if I have anything on them and the movement seems to pull Ralph out of his staring and he looks away quickly, crossing the kitchen to grab cans of coke from the fridge.

"So I managed to get somewhere to stay."

I swallow and grab the coke from his hand. "That's great. Did housing come through?"

He scoffs. "No, and I don't think that will be happening soon. The woman there doesn't like me." He rolls his eyes, and I suddenly want to know what he did to put his name further down the list. "But my friend Handy says I can move in with him. The room won't be ready for a few days so if you don't mind me staying here until then I would be eternally grateful."

So much information but my mind sticks on one thing. "Yeah fine... but Handy?"

Ralph laughs, his eyes lighting up in a very unappealing way. Yeah, and I'm a liar too. "Charles, but no one calls him that."

"Well now I need to know this story, Handy isn't exactly your usual nickname. Spill." I take another bite of my pizza and enjoy listening to Ralph talk.

"Oh god. I swear I want to forget the memory of it, but it's been stuck in there for too many years. It was one night after a party, maybe eight years ago, and we were all staying at John's house, that's my brother. We didn't want to go back to base while we were so drunk so we were just sleeping where we fell. John was away training in Belfast, he's a teacher, and I had his key, so of course, his house pretty much became where we ended up most weekends. There were about ten of us all lying around on the floor in sleeping bags, we never stayed in John's room because that was off limits, and the chatter had died off. I don't know if Charles thought we were all asleep but suddenly Eddie sits up and puts on the floor light. He curses up a storm, and we all sit up and see what he's pissed off at."

I'm mesmerised by the way Ralph is speaking. Since I met him, he's always had an air of sadness around him. It's understandable after the way his life is going, but tonight it feels different. Maybe it's having a place to finally go, or perhaps it's spending time with his friend. Whatever it is I'm glad that he's feeling happier.

"That's when we see Charles, the only one who isn't sitting up, and he has his dick in his hand jacking off. Apparently, Eddie was lying next to him, and the motion had alerted him to what Handy was up to. He didn't even notice that we were all staring at him and none of us knew what to do. When the groaning started, we all knew that shit had to stop. It was then that he got the name Handy and he's never lived it down from there. The funniest thing is he doesn't remember any of it."

I start laughing right along with Ralph, his humour infectious. I can hear how much he cares about his friends and it makes me feel better that he has people like that in his life. "So is Handy your best friend?"

"There is a group of us that have been friends for a long time, but yeah, Handy is my closest friend. He is the one that's the most like me so I can completely be myself around him."

"Are you out with everyone?" My eyes widen as the question slips out. I'm heading into the too personal region again, and I'm not sure how Ralph will react.

"I haven't been the whole time, but I joined after it was technically allowed, so I never had to hide it for the job. I kept it to myself for a long time because I was never sure how people would react. It might've not been an issue with the army, but it was still a problem with a lot of my colleagues. Now I'm out, and I don't care who has a problem with it."

I can't imagine having to hide who I am for my job, knowing that you can't be yourself in case they don't have your back when you need them. "Do you get any hassle for it?"

"A little, but it's mainly only the new macho men that join. You know the kind, the ones who think only real men should be in the armed forces. It only takes one night out, and they keep their mouths closed."

I screw up my forehead, not understanding why a night out would change the meatheads minds.

"Alcohol tends to make them run their mouths and then that mouth tends to bleed. Once you take them down, it's hard for them not to think of the gay guy as a real man." He winks, and I burst out laughing.

It's not that hard to picture Ralph using that large body to teach someone a lesson. He has muscles on top of muscles, his power evident even as he sits here eating pizza with me. I look down at my own scrawny body and feel a little bit envious of his build. I could work out every day for the rest of my life, and I wouldn't be able to build any muscle definition. I'm not made to be muscly, my slim tight body not changing no matter how much I try.

"Where did you go?"

I look up to see Ralph staring at me. I hate it when he gives me his full attention because it makes me want to tell him everything, and that feeling is strange. I don't have many friends because I'm not exactly a people person, and my brother is probably the only person I can speak to about everything. I love my parents, but they are those people who were born old, their old-fashioned views on everything not helpful when I need help. I can't complain though because when I came out, they didn't even bat an eyelid, just telling me that's great and that I needed to tidy my room.

"Aiden?"

I get up from the table and grab the now empty pizza box. "Sorry. I was just thinking about how … fuck it sounds so stupid."

Ralph's hand on my shoulder has me stilling. He turns me slowly until I'm facing him, but I don't look up, avoiding his gaze. "Okay so now I'm intrigued. What can be that bad that you are hiding?"

I take a step back, needing to put some distance between us. I think this is the closest I've been to Ralph and the heat from his body is driving me to distraction. That's before the smell of his soap or shower gel hits my nose, because when that happens, I feel myself swaying towards him. I shake my head trying to get some blood to flow back up to it and away from my now half hard cock. Shit, I can't be getting an erection in front of Ralph.

"I was just thinking that you would be able to protect yourself easily. I've never been able to add bulk to my body no matter how hard I work at it. I'm pretty sure my brother was born with muscles, but I take after my mum. Unfortunately, that means I have the body of a teenage boy."

Even if I couldn't see him do it, I would feel the heat from Ralph's scrutiny as his eyes graze over my body. My skin erupts in goosebumps and it feels like his hands are tickling over me even though he isn't anywhere close. I can feel my dick fill and expand, and no matter how much I will it to stop I can't. The urge to grab Ralph and kiss him almost overtakes me, and when he speaks, he doesn't help my problem.

Chapter 12

Ralph

I'm blatantly checking him out, and I know he knows it. His cheeks go redder the longer that I stare at him, but I can't pull my eyes away. He thinks he has the body of a teenage boy, but all I can see is a man. He doesn't have a large build, he's right about that, but his body is toned and sexy. Tight in all the right places and powerful in a less obvious way. I've always thought I looked like a typical jock. My body has always been bulky, and when I started working out, it didn't take long before the muscles began to show. It makes me stand out when I'm in a club and I've never lacked attention, but the downside is that people don't want to talk. I'm the alpha that men want to climb, but when it comes to the next morning, they are gone.

"I don't see a teenager." Shit. My voice comes out thick and husky with lust. I need to stop this. My brain is on board with my internal instructions, but I can't seem to get my body under control. My eyes still roam over his body like they wish they were my hands and my dick is aching behind my zipper, and my skin is tingling from imagining touching Aiden. I'm suddenly thrilled I'm wearing denim and not jogging bottoms.

"You must be the only one." Part of me is grateful that Aiden sounds as though he's having the same reaction as I am, but the other part wishes he would tell me to stop perving over him so I could get a grip of myself.

"I would bet all the money I have that I'm not the only one, it's just not possible." *Shut up, shut up, shut up.* I need to engage my filter and stop this pathetic flirting. The last thing I need is to jump into bed with Aiden. He deserves more than to be a rebound fuck.

"Thank you."

Help Our Heroes

Holy fuck. The breathy way he says those two words has my cock twitching. It's that reaction that has some common sense coming back to me, and I step away, smiling as I pretend the last five minutes didn't happen. "I'm sure that you have guys all over you when you go out." I turn to the table, pretending to clean it while I get my body under control. I need to get laid, preferably soon and hard.

"Go out, whats that?" Aiden laughs as he goes about cleaning up the already spotless worktop.

"You don't go out?"

"I'm not exactly a social butterfly. I've never really had a lot of friends, and truthfully, nightclubs aren't fun when you're on your own. All the friends that I used to go out with have settled down, and we've drifted apart. I'm the last man standing." He tries to make it sound like a joke, but there is a tinge of sadness to it.

"I would offer to take you out one night, but I don't want to scar you. Handy is a rather tame story." This makes him laugh, and I hope that it's eased a little of his pain.

"Are you the only gay in the town?"

I'm starting to enjoy Aiden's sense of humour. He might step over the line into private information sometimes but he's sassy and quick, and with just enough fire to make me want to fight with him. It's one thing I never had with William, that spark, the need to fight, maybe that's why we ended. I was always happy that we didn't have so much passion between us, worried that the spark would fizzle out if it burned too bright, but maybe it was too far the other way. I thought our sex was fantastic, but now that I think about it it probably wasn't that great. I couldn't even tell you what William's favourite position is, and since I was continually on top, I know he couldn't name mine.

"Dan is bi, but other than that, yes, I'm the only gay in town. Not the only one on base obviously, but the only one in our group."

"Dammit. So, is Dan hot?"

A surge of red-hot jealousy nearly floors me, and I have to hold on to the table to stop myself from dropping to the floor. *What the hell is that all about?* I'm not a jealous person, it's just not the type of guy I am, but I feel it now when Aiden talks about Dan. "Hot if you are into cocky fucks." Jeez, can I sound any more bitter?

"I'm into any fuck at the moment." His laughter doesn't take away the shock of his words, but I am determined not to react.

"Then Dan might be the guy for you."

"Wow, this conversation has taken a bizarre turn."

This finally gets a laugh from me because he's right, it started with my tale about Handy, and now I'm pairing Aiden up with Dan.

"I'm beat and gonna head to bed. I will be working most of the day tomorrow so feel free to borrow my car again if you need it. All your bags are in the front room of the garage if you want to start moving them out, if not no rush."

That's a really good idea. The more I can get to Handy's before I move in the better. It saves dragging Aiden out on the final day. I can easily take a taxi or Uber to Handy's house. "Thanks. I might try and get the bulk of it out your hair. I hate imposing on you since you know, I'm imposing on you."

"It isn't an imposition. I had a room, and you had a need. It's just a bonus that your good to look at, and you pick up your dirty towels."

I raise my eyebrow at his comment but he ignores me.

"So no rush to get out, take your time. I need to sleep though. Thank you for dinner."

He smiles and heads out of the room, leaving me standing there struggling to say something.

Arsehole.

* * *

I know I shouldn't be doing this, but it's the only way I'm going to survive the next few days here with Aiden. I drop my head to the cold tiles as I rub the shower gel into my hand before wrapping it around my cock. Even just that simple touch has me closing my eyes, a shiver going down my spine. I don't want to think of Aiden as I stroke along the smooth skin, but it's his face that appears without invitation.

He has that little smirk on his face that turns my crank and he's staring at me with heat in his eyes. I add pressure to my hand as I imagine pushing Aiden against the wall so I can feel his small body against me. He may think he looks like a young boy, but to me, he is all man. His muscles look like they would be tight and lean, that quiet sort of power that I love. I haven't seen him without his clothes on but that chef's jacket was fitted enough that I can use my imagination perfectly without any problems. He looks as though he could comfortably pin me down without any effort.

I groan as I imagine that it's his steady hand that's rubbing my cock, the pinch on my tip making my breath stutter in my chest. God, that feels so good. It's been far too long since I felt the touch of another guy, and even though this is my hand, using Aiden as wank material is getting the job done. As much as I know I shouldn't be looking at Aiden as anything other than a nice guy who helped me when I needed it, but the truth is I would give anything for one night with him. Shit, I would be happy with an hour with him. My arse cheeks clench at the thought of the hard fuck that I imagine he would give me. The power, the sweat, the pure fucking passion that would spark between us, that's what almost takes me over the edge into orgasm.

Pinching my tip, I try to breathe through the need to come, but the pain that I crave sends me over the edge. Oh god. My hand moves furiously as steam after stream of cum hits the shower wall. My knees threaten to buckle and I have to lock them so I don't end up in a heap on the floor. My muscles turn into rubber as I add more weight to the wall and slide/twist myself until I'm sitting on the floor of the shower, the water hitting the top of my head. I'm probably sitting in the remains of my release, but I just can't find a single ounce of energy to care. I will wash off once I recover from my mind blowing orgasm.

Sex with William the last few months before I left, shit if I think about it it was closer to maybe six months, had become boring. Twice a week we would have sex but it felt as though we were just going through the motions. I thought we were going through a typical lull in our sex drive, I mean don't most couples go through that? At times though it felt like I was just using his body to get off like it was a step up from my hand. Maybe that's why he needed someone else? Did I just not do it for him anymore? God, did I push him into the arms of another guy because I didn't please him?

My eyes start to burn as tears build in them. I've spent the last few days making sure I didn't feel anything, not willing to show anyone how much I'm hurting, but apparently all it took for it to catch up with me was a good orgasm. I laugh but it doesn't stop the tears from flowing down my cheeks. I don't bother to brush them away, just sitting there under the falling water allowing them to try and ease my pain.

How could I not see that William was becoming bored with me? I put everything down to just regular relationship drama but apparently, I was wrong. I think I may have been more committed to the relationship than he was because I never once looked at anyone other than him. He was my everything and now my life will never be the same. I've lost everything. My home, the man I love, and the life I wanted. It's not how I pictured my home-coming to be. I didn't exactly expect fanfares or anything, but being wrapped in William's arms had been high on my list of wants.

So as I sit on the floor of the shower, I allow myself a moment to mourn my losses, to finally feel the heart-wrenching pain that has been sitting under the surface, and I cry like I haven't done in years.

Chapter 13

Ralph

I grab the last black bag out of Aiden's car and take it inside Handy's house. I've been piling them up in his dining room, not wanting to get in the way of the cleaning of his spare bedroom. I swear it doesn't look like he's done anything since the last time I was here but he assures me that I'll be able to move in in the morning.

"Ralph?" I turn to see Dan walking in the front door. I smile before heading over to hug him. I try to ignore the pissed off feeling that's fighting to come out. It's not his fault that Aiden was joking about him being hot. What I didn't tell Aiden is that Dan is very hot. He has those boyish good looks that make him a hit with men and women, and I hate him a little for it. He's never without company, and because he's a genuinely nice guy, he treats every one of his partners with respect.

"When did you get back?" He pulls back but keeps his hands on my shoulders, looking genuinely pleased that I'm here, and making me feel even guiltier about feeling jealous.

"A few days ago. Sorry I haven't called, but it's been… interesting."

Before he gets a chance to say anything else Handy walks in and shares with the world why I'm here. "Dan, my man. Did shithead tell you he was moving in here? I say good riddance to Dick…that's what I'm calling him now by the way."

Dan looks at us like he's not sure what the hell is going on, and really who can blame him? Handy is not known for his discretion or secret keeping, so his verbal diarrhoea shouldn't surprise me. I put Dan out of his misery, filling him in with everything that's happened. By the time I've finished my tearful tale, we are all sitting at Handy's breakfast bar drinking coffee.

"I can't believe he did that. I've never understood people that cheat. If you aren't happy then just leave, it's what I would do.

"That because you're not a dick like Dick. I told you, Ralph, the guy is not worth your time. I'm glad that you aren't wasting any time being heartbroken by him."

I'm glad that I had my breakdown last night while on my own. I'd spent a long time on that shower floor, tears streaming down my face as I finally gave in to the pain, but once finished I felt better. Lighter. It means today I can put on a brave face again and pretend that I'm not affected by it at all.

"Handy, seriously?"

"What? I'm just telling him what we all thought. None of us liked Dick, but no one wanted to tell him."

I look between Dan and Handy. Handy looks pleased with himself, like he's trying to make me feel better by telling me how much he hated William, but Dan's cheeks are going red with embarrassment. At least he knows that the knowledge of everyone hating William isn't going to make me feel better. "Everyone hated him?"

"What did ..."

I hold my hand up and stop Handy from carrying on. I focus on Dan, knowing that he'll tell the truth but in a nice way. "I'm asking you, Dan."

He sighs like he doesn't want to answer but a few seconds later I get what I asked for. "It's not that we didn't like him, it's just that we thought he wasn't the guy for you. He was kinda shallow, and whenever we were out, he would spend the whole night checking out other guys. He never seemed to focus on you which is what you deserve. You should have someone who makes you the centre of their universe, and that just wasn't William."

Well, I suppose I asked for him to tell me, I just wish that it didn't hurt so fucking much.

* * *

I can't believe that I've let that fucker get away with so much. He threw me out of my own house and emptied my bank account, and what did I do? I ran away with my tail between my legs like some big fucking loser. Why didn't I say something? Why the fuck did I not knock him out?

I throw back another Vodka, hissing when the burn in my throat catches my breath. My nose is numb, and I'm surprised that I can still feel the heat as the spirit goes down, but I don't overthink it. I fill my glass, the liquid sloshing over the side as my aim goes wonky. I needed a drink when I got home after dropping my shit at Handy's and all I could find in Aiden's cupboards was vodka. It isn't a favourite of mine but I'm not in the caring mood right now, and if I finish the bottle I will just have to buy a new one tomorrow.

Listening to Dan and Handy talking about how much they hated William, that they saw him do some shit that made them have doubts about his faithfulness to me, got me angrier as the afternoon went on. Eventually, it all became too much and I managed to convince both of them that I had to return Aiden's car. I'm not sure they were one hundred percent convinced but by that point, I didn't care. I needed to get out of there before I either cried or threw a punch, and I wasn't sure what urge would win out.

By the time I arrived home, I was shaking with rage and wanted nothing more than to get fucked up enough that I stopped feeling. It backfired though, and all I can focus on now is the bitterness and anger I feel towards William. I would love nothing more than to go over to his, no my, house and show him how pissed off I am. Maybe that's what I should do. Go pay him a visit and finally have my say in this whole thing. I won't use my words to tell him, I'll use my fists.

I giggle like a teenage girl as I take out my mobile and open the Uber app. It will take about fifteen minutes for a car to get here which is just enough time to get comfortably shit-faced before I head out. I don't need liquid courage, but if I'm going to face William in an all-out brawl, I want to be numb enough that I don't feel his punches. I'm not naive enough to think that William won't fight back, the guy is built almost as big as I am, but I'm hoping that not being able to feel pain will help me to fight longer.

Uber booked, I pick up the bottle and decide to forgo the glass, getting my buzz straight from the bottle. I turn too quickly, and my arm catches the now empty glass. I curse up a storm as it hits the floor, shattering and covering the wood. I really should clean it up, but I just stare at it as I take another drink from the bottle. The burn has lessened now, making me feel like I'm drinking water. I don't mind that though because it's improving my experience of drinking the horrific spirit. I've nothing but bad memories of the last time I got drunk on Vodka and it's left me with a hatred that makes me want to vomit when I taste the stuff. The first few mouthfuls tonight made me want to heave, but I pushed through since it was Vodka or Rum, and Rum just wasn't an option.

Just when I decide that it's time to clean up the glass a horn sounds from outside the house. I stumble over to the window and see a car with an Uber sticker sitting at the kerb. Shit, this is going to lower my rating score. Uber drivers hate to wait. Snorting at that thought, I head out the front door, trying the handle to make sure I've locked it. It's only once I am outside that I notice I still have the bottle in my hand. I use my free hand to support me while I bend at the waist, putting the nearly empty bottle on the top step. I stand upright again and blink a few times to try and focus. My eyes have decided that seeing two of everything would be fun and if I don't get it under control, I won't be able to have my moment with William.

It takes far too long to get into the Uber, and after a warning from the driver not to vomit, we are finally on our way. I watch outside as we drive the twenty minutes to Williams house, and thanks to the driver for stopping briefly at a corner shop so I could pick up some water, my head is feeling slightly clearer. When we pull up at the pavement in the front of William's house, I sit for a moment, wondering if I'm about to do the right thing. All doubt vanishes when I see William coming out of the front door and kissing yet another guy.

I thank the driver and tell him to leave, not wanting him to hang around and be a witness. By the time he's gone and William notices me, his friend has driven away in his car, leaving the two of us staring at each other.

"Why are you here, Ralph?" He sounds pissed off and it makes my anger rise quickly.

"The last time I checked my name was still on the lease so technically I can come whenever I want."

"You don't live here anymore."

I barely stop myself from growling at him. He has a fucking cheek with the way he's talking to me, treating me as though I'm someone who's boring him.

"Only because you kicked me out to move your little fuck toy in. So tell me, how long was my shit sitting out front? It must have been tough to keep me hidden."

William crosses his arms across his chest and glares at me. "Not really, it's not like you were here all that often. Look, you need to get over this okay. It's kinda pathetic that you are over here trying to win me back."

This time it isn't a growl that escapes me, it's laughter. "You think I'm here to try and get your skanky arse back? Oh please, I'm here for the money you stole from my account."

"Our account."

Two little words and I'm storming across the grass, my fists clenched at my side as I try to resist the urge to punch him out. I think my night will end just perfectly if I see him bleeding.

Chapter 14

Aiden

I pull into the driveway behind my car and turn off my brother's car. I had no plans on leaving the house today, but when a client had a sudden need to see their logos in person, I scrambled to find a way to get there. When the call came in, Ralph had already taken my car like I'd offered, but thankfully my brother was available to come and pick me up. When he had to go back to work, he left his car with plans to pick it up tomorrow when he comes over for coffee.

I get out of the car and lock up, loosening my tie until it's hanging slack around my neck. I don't often wear a suit, but my employer requests it when we meet with clients. I like to flaunt the rules slightly, and instead of wearing the traditional three piece suit they would want me to, I wear all black. Black shirt, black tie, and then a fitted black three-piece suit. A lot of people would call it overkill for a work meeting, but I call it the only one I own.

Walking up the front steps, I slow my pace slightly when I see the near-empty Vodka bottle sitting just in front of the door. I turn my head and scan the street around me, but nothing else looks out of place. I lean down and grab the bottle, noting that it's the same make as the one that's currently sitting in my cupboard, or at least it was there when I left this afternoon. My stomach feels unsettled as I unlock my front door. Something just feels off, and as soon as I walk into the hall, I feel alone. Ever since Ralph arrived I could sense him in the house with me, but tonight it feels like I'm the only person in the house.

"Ralph?" I step into the living room as I call his name, but I already know I won't get a response. Silence greets me as I look around but nothing is out of place. The uneasy feeling doesn't vanish with the lack of evidence. Instead it increases, and I can feel my palms starting to sweat. I don't even know why I'm worried, Ralph is the size of a house so looking after himself isn't a problem, but something feels wrong. That feeling intensifies a hundredfold when I walk into the kitchen and see the broken glass on the floor. Yeah, this is not a good sign at all.

Stepping carefully over the glass I approach the cupboard where I keep my bottles of alcohol. I open the door, and as soon as I see the space I race for the stairs, taking them two at a time until I get to Ralph's bedroom. I know I'll find it empty, but I check anyway to confirm my suspicions and seeing it empty sets my anxiety levels to Defcon one. I rush through the rest of the rooms before racing down the stairs incase he had come home while I was searching. Pacing back and forth across the living room floor I try to think where he might be. Ralph's a grown man so I shouldn't worry about him, he's also practically a stranger so what he does is his business, not mine, but none of that makes a difference apparently because I'm still worried and have this urgent need to find him.

Where can he be? I stop my pacing suddenly when the answer to my question hits me. He wouldn't go there, would he? Of course he would, and if he's been drinking, then the whole thing is going to be a shit show of epic proportions. I rush out the front door and towards the car. I need to get to William's house as fast as I can.

* * *

I'm barely parked at the kerb when I have the car turned off and I'm reaching for the door handle. I can see the two men in the front garden and as soon as the door is open their voices hit my ears. Ralph is screaming at William, all his anger finally surfacing about everything William has done to him. I don't blame him for a second for being angry, but with the alcohol going through his system, I'm worried that he'll take it too far. Their voices get louder, and before I can reach Ralph, he rears back and punches William in the mouth. Thankfully William is a massive guy so he doesn't go down, but on the downside, he now looks like he will be only too happy to return the punch.

I increase my speed, slipping my teeny tiny body in between the two human mountains, only thinking about the consequences far too late. I keep my back to Ralph, feeling safer keeping my attention on William, and put my hands up in front of me in my lame attempt to keep the two men apart. "Stop."

Thankfully William stops moving, but his death glare doesn't leave Ralph.

It's a step in the right direction though, and all I need to do now is to get these guys in separate postcodes. "Get him the fuck out of here." Williams's words are rough and he reaches up to wipe the blood from his lip.

I have so much I want to say to this guy on Ralph's behalf, names I want to call him like cheat and whore, but I keep quiet so I don't start them fighting again. Unfortunately Ralph isn't having the same thoughts as I am.

"You'd love that, wouldn't you? If I just fuck off and vanish, maybe not come over and tell all your little fuckboys who I am. Actually, that's unfair, I'm pretty sure you're the only fuckboy around here. God, I can't fucking believe I loved you."

"Then who's the stupid one? If you cant see what's happening so blatantly under your fucking nose then that's not my problem. And you know what, Ralph, maybe try satisfying a lover for once in your life and they won't need to look elsewhere."

I feel the push against my back as Ralph tries to move forward but I dig my feet into the ground, acting on hope alone that Ralph won't use all his strength to shove me out of the way. I press back and feel Ralphs body give, increasing the distance between the two of us and William.

"Why don't you just walk away, William? Haven't you done enough to him yet?" I point to the house before turning my back on William completely. My complete focus is now the raging man that doing his best impression of a wild animal. "Ralph?" He doesn't pay attention to my voice, so I raise my hand and put it on his cheek, turning his head down slightly so he's finally looking at me.

"Hi." I smile, trying to relax the situation. His eyes flicker back to William who I haven't heard move, but it's only for a fraction of a second before I get his full attention again. "Get in the car and I'll take you home."

"Do as your little boy tells you, Ralph. Don't make him be up past his bedtime." I can hear the derision in his voice and a fraction of a second later it becomes clear that Ralph does too.

Ralph chest butts me until my back is almost against William, and if I thought he looked angry before I was wrong. Now it's like there is pure rage seeping out of his pores as he glowers at William. I need to stop this before I get stuck between these two and get myself hurt. Putting my hands on Ralph's chest, I push with all my might but I barely move Ralph at all.

"Don't fucking talk about Aiden like that. He is more man that you will ever be you cocksucker, but then again that's not saying much. My mother is more man than you are."

I try not to laugh because it doesn't feel appropriate at the moment but I can't stop the snort that comes from me. The noise catches Ralph's attention, and I use that to my advantage. "Get in the car."

Ralph doesn't move and I lean all my weight into him again. All I have to do is get him to start moving in the right direction and I think that will be enough. When he doesn't look like he's going to back off, I put as much effort as I can behind my words, using anger and power to add enough force to get him to comply.

"Get in the fucking car, Ralph." This finally gets his attention and I swear I see his anger deflate the instant I growl out the words. He stares for a few moments before turning and walking to the car and getting in. I take a deep breath to brace myself before I turn and face William. I'm not sure where my bravery comes from because he looks as though he could snap my little body in two without breaking a sweat, but I have to say something to him before I leave. Even if it earns me a punch in the face.

"How can you sleep at night knowing what you've done to Ralph? I have never met such a nice guy, and you took him for a fool. I don't often wish ill on others, but I hope you get a dose of VD that antibiotics can't treat." I don't give him a chance to answer before I turn my back on him and walk as calmly as possible as I make my way back to the car.

When I sit in the driver's seat I let out a stuttered breath, not quite believing I just said all that to William. I've never had the balls to talk to anyone like that, not even when I'm getting abuse thrown at me by strangers, but something in me needed to defend Ralph.

"Thank you."

I turn to see Ralph looking at his hands where they sit on his lap. I can smell the alcohol on his breath but nothing about his demeanour hints that he's drunk. I should feel sorry for him, and a little proud that he finally got his say with dickhead, but all I'm feeling just now is anger, and I can't explain why. Maybe it's because he put himself at risk by coming here tonight when he wasn't thinking one-hundred percent clearly, or perhaps it's that he didn't just jump in and beat the shit out of fuckface. I know neither makes sense but that's where I'm at. I start the engine but before I drive off I need to know something. "How did you get here?"

"I took an Uber."

Good, at least he didn't do something stupid like try and drive. Now to get home before I lose it with him.

Chapter 15

Ralph

The whole drive home is done in painful silence. There's so much I want to say to Aiden but I don't think now is the time. I want to say thanks for coming to get me, thank you for saving me from doing something stupider than the one punch I got in, and I also want to tell him how fucking hot he was when he got all growly with me. It's not a side of Aiden that I've seen up until now but holy fuck it made my dick hard. So no, now is not the time to tell him that. I'll just stay quiet until we get home and then I will have another jerk off session in the shower.

Pulling up beside Aiden's car in the drive is the first time I notice that we aren't in it. I hadn't felt drunk up until this point, but apparently, I'm not firing on all cylinders. "Who's car is this?"

"My brothers."

It's all he says before getting out of the car. I watch him as he walks up the steps and inside the front door. I take a few minutes to compose myself because I feel like a fight is brewing between us and I'm not sure why. I didn't ask Aiden to come and get me, even if I'm utterly grateful for it, so it's not like I put him out. I sigh and get out of the car, knowing that if he's going to kick me out, I want it to be before it's too late to call someone to come and get me. That's probably what Aiden's doing in there, packing all my shit in a bag and it will end up on the grass out front again. I should just sit here until he does all the work but instead, I get out of the car and follow him inside.

When I step inside the lights are on in the hall and Aiden is leaning against the wall with his hands in his pockets. The move pushes his suit jacket behind his hips and for the first time tonight I realise how sexy he looks. The waistcoat hugs his waist as though it's painted on, making his hips look broad and strong. The whole outfit is black, and where on some people it might drain the colour from their skin, on Aiden it makes his skin look like it's glowing. Holy shit. I don't know if I've ever seen anyone look as fucking perfect as he does now. He's not so much like a teenage boy at the moment and a lot more Nicholas Hault.

I shuffle my feet against the ground as I make my way over to where he's standing, leaning against the wall opposite him. The intense stare makes me wilt a little but it also makes my cock get hard. It's the power in his stance, okay, it's also the fire in his eyes that makes me want to drop to my knees to worship him.

"What the fuck were you thinking?"

"I was thinking that I finally wanted to have a word with William. I hadn't had a chance before tonight."

He runs his tongue along the front of his teeth and I want him to open his lips so I can see movement. When his lips do part, his tongue is hidden again and I nearly moan in protest until I hear him speak.

"Are you listening, Ralph?"

My eyes meet his and I lose all thought from my head. I'm stuck in his burning stare and I don't want to escape. I don't even know what happens next, who moves first, but as Aiden pushes me against the wall and attacks my mouth I know I don't care. He takes full control of the kiss, pushing his tongue between my lips and sweeps it into my mouth. I whimper when he grabs my throat in one hand, pressing me firmly against the wall and not letting me move. *Fuck me.*

William never understood what I wanted, what I needed, but Aiden just knows. The pressure of his hold tells me that he isn't just doing this because he's angry, no his grip is controlling without anger. He might not have the body that most people would expect from a powerful top, but he has the attitude and control, and it's doing delicious things to my body. He grinds his body into mine, his stomach brushing against my cock, the pressure and friction building my orgasm to dangerous levels. His erection is pressing to the top of my thigh, proving that he's as turned on as I am. His lips leave mine to brush over the skin of my jaw and down over my neck, and I get a whole body shudder as he scrapes his teeth along my tender flesh.

"Oh god, Aiden."

He moves his mouth to the outer shell of my ear, brushing his lips against it. "Do you like that, little boy?"

I whimper at his words. Little boy. I have spent my whole life wanting someone to call me that or something similar, but no one ever took the time to notice. A few minutes and Aiden can read me like a book, cranking my gears like no one ever has before.

"I think you do. I think you want to get on your knees and have me tell you how to please me. Maybe I should force my cock in between those supple little lips of yours until you choke on it."

I reach down and grab my cock, needing some pressure to try and stop myself from coming too soon. Every word Aiden says is like a stroke against my aching hard-on, bringing me closer and closer to release. I'm scared if he doesn't do something soon the night will be over before he's inside me. My arse clenches at the thought of being filled after so long. It's been far too many years since I was with a man who was willing to top. My size always leads to attracting bottoms who want to be overpowered, when what I'm looking for is the opposite. I want someone to hold me down while they fuck me, to tie me up so I'm at their mercy, leaving me vulnerable and entirely theirs.

"I didn't say you could touch yourself, so you better stop."

I pin my hands back to the wall behind me instantly, pressing the palms against it so I'm not tempted to move.

"Good boy. Now I need some answers from you."

I look down into Aiden's eyes as he puts a little distance between us, wanting some form of connection with him at all times.

"Do you want this?"

I nod.

"I want to hear you, boy. Do you want this, and do you want me to be in control?"

"Yes, very much yes, Sir."

He grips the back of my neck tightly, digging the tips of his fingers into my muscles, and pulls me closer. "If we do this I won't stop unless you beg. I will mark you and make you scream, but I won't stop until you orgasm harder than you ever have."

My knees buckle and the only thing that keeps me standing is Aiden's body, which in itself turns me on, knowing that he can use his power to pin me.

"If you agree to all this go to my room and strip, and once you are naked get on your knees on the floor. I will follow you up in a minute."

He steps back until he's leaning against the opposite wall again, acting as though he hasn't just lived out one of my greatest fantasies. Granted, he still looks like a fantasy come true standing there in his suit. He looks so fucking relaxed and calm when I'm struggling not to melt into the ground with lust.

I manage to pull my eyes away from him, remembering the words he said, and head to the stairs. I take them carefully since my legs aren't working correctly and I'm sure tripping wouldn't be the sexiest departure. God, I can't believe this is actually happening. This stranger who felt pity for me a few days ago when my ex kicked me out is now about to live out my wildest dreams for me, and I know I'm going to love every fucking minute of it. Imagining his fingers digging into my muscles, his palm stroking my skin, and his teeth marking my skin as he pounds into me from behind has my heart racing and my chest heaving.

Somehow I make it to Aiden's room and start to strip off my clothes. It seems surreal that I'm here when barely an hour ago I was letting my alcohol courage lead me into a possible fistfight with William, and now I am stripping off so I can be submissive to Aiden. How can things change so much in such a little amount of time? I'm not sure, but as I remove my boxer shorts and place them on top of my jeans on the top of the dresser, I know I don't care.

I take a deep breath to try and calm my breathing down, if I don't then there is a chance that I'll pass out from hyperventilating. I want this so I just need to get myself under control. I close my eyes and focus on my breathing but that all goes to pot when I hear Aiden moving about downstairs. I drop slowly to my knees, the rough carpet tingling against the skin on my legs, and it makes my whole body feel extra sensitive.

Footsteps on the stairs alert me to Aiden's approach but instead of making me even more anxious, it calms my erratic heartbeat. I feel calmer knowing that he's getting closer to me, that he will take care of me the way I need. He is what I need to let go, and I fully trust him with my body.

Chapter 16

Aiden

I watch Ralph as he walks painfully slowly up the stairs. My heart is about to beat out of my chest, but I refuse to give in to my nerves until he's out sight. I can't fall apart while he can still see me, I need to give the illusion of knowing what the hell I'm doing. He takes the final step and turns towards my room, the light clicking on and lighting up the hallway.

As soon as I know he's safely in my room I double over, my hands on my knees to try and stop me from collapsing. *Holy shit, that was intense.* When we arrived home, I only wanted to make sure he got to his bed before going to sleep. Okay, that's a lie, I was mad as hell and I wanted him to know it. That's why I waited in the hall for him, but what I hadn't expected was the look of lust in his eyes. When he leaned against that wall he looked fucking delectable and I needed a taste. That's why I kissed him, and that's what led to the discovery of what turned Ralph on. When he let me take over the kiss, melting completely into my body, I knew that he was letting go so I could lead the way.

What I didn't expect was for the feeling of liberation that came over me when I took the reigns. It was like I'd been waiting all my life for someone to let me take what I wanted, and I didn't expect it from such an alpha looking guy. He is the epitome of the growly soldier so to feel him be so compliant under my hands was a rush. That's where the words had come from. I'd been shocked when I called him boy, fully expecting him to punch me in the face for my efforts, but he melted and god it was exhilarating. As a small guy I've always had fantasies of being the Dominant partner, my choice of porn leading to the slightly darker side of the web, but I never imagined it would come true. Now I have a sexy as sin man kneeling in my bedroom and I just have to let my imagination run wild so I can please him. No pressure what so ever.

Pushing off the wall, I head towards the stairs. I have a mixture of lust and fear running through my body but the combination is making my cock harder than it's ever been. Just knowing that Ralph is up there kneeling, waiting patiently for me to arrive. I could make him wait all night and he would still be there when I stepped foot in my room. *Holy fuck.* Tingles spread through my body and I reach down to grab my erection. I need to calm down and make this perfect for Ralph. He's been through so much recently that I want him to let go and find his pleasure, which means I need to focus and give him everything he needs. The last thing he needs is to have a shitty night of sex.

Stepping over the threshold into my room is like a lesson in torture. Seeing Ralph kneeling there completely naked, his cock pointing to the ceiling, makes me want to push him to the carpet and take him, but I refrain. He wants to be dominated and I'm the man he chose for that. His eyes are downcast and I take a moment just to take him in. It's not the first time I've seen him naked but it is the first time I've spent time focusing on him. He's tight and toned, his skin looking smooth and soft. I want to reach out and touch him, and I smile when I realise I can do just that. I take a single finger and run it along his shoulders as I walk around him. He jumps a little when I first connect with him, goosebumps erupting all over his body, but soon he's swaying towards me as I move.

When I'm standing in front of him again I feel a surge of power that I've never felt before and I feel like I could ask for anything I want. This gives me a thrill and makes me want to test the boundaries. How much can he take before he stops me? I've never wanted to see if I could break someone before but standing in front of Ralph I suddenly want to test his limits.

"Look at me."

Ralph keeps his head dropped low but his eyes rise to mine.

"Unzip me." I'm still fully dressed in my suit and it makes me feel even more dominant, especially while he's completely naked.

Ralph's hands move slowly, shaking as they rise, until they grip my zipper and pull it down slowly. I clench my fists at my sides so I don't reach for him. It's taking a lot more energy than I thought it would not to touch him, to put us both out of our misery. When the zipper is fully open he stops, looking up at me for further instructions. Why is that so sexy?

Help Our Heroes

"Take it out." My voice sounds thick with lust but just thinking about him touching me is driving me crazy.

He does as he's told, gripping my cock tightly in his hand and slipping it free of my underwear. The heat of his skin against me has me groaning in sheer pleasure. It's been a long time since I've had sex but nothing in all my experiences has felt like this.

"Suck it. Slowly." I watch in fascination as his tongue flicks out and he runs it along the bottom of my cock. He takes his time working on me, teasing and nibbling before he takes me deep into his mouth. I finally give in to the need to touch him, my fingers gripping onto his short hair as much as I can. It feels so fucking good having his mouth around me, too good, and I thrust deeply twice before I pull him off. I can't do this, I need to take the edge off before I can concentrate on what he needs.

I drop down in front of him, cupping his jaw so he focuses on me. His lips are swollen and wet, and I lean forward to taste them again. His eyes are unfocused when I pull back and I swear I've never seen someone look so fucking gorgeous. Submission is a good look on Ralph and I want to see it again and again. I push that thought from my mind because I'm under no illusion that tonight is a one-time thing. "I want to give you everything you crave but I'm struggling. You're just so perfect, boy, you're driving me crazy. I want you to go and lean over the bed, arse up, and wait for me. I'm going to use your body so I can come, then I'm going to torture you until you beg for more."

His whimper makes my cock pulse and I resist the urge to kiss him. Instead, I move back and let him follow my instructions. I stand up and slip my suit jacket from my body as I watch Ralph take the position I requested. I'm about to remove my waistcoat when he looks at me, his eyes going wide for a second before he speaks.

"Please leave it all on."

It's not something I thought of doing but now that he's asked me I can't think of anything hotter than staying clothed. I nod and he turns back to face the mattress. I undo the button on my trousers and slip them and my boxers down over my hips slightly. I reach into the top drawer of my dresser and grab a condom and some lube. I spare a second to check the use by date on the condom. Yes, my sex life has been that sparse recently. When everything is safe I open it with my teeth and slip the rubber over my cock. I pop open the lube lid and drip a little onto my erection, just enough that I can stroke myself without any friction.

Walking behind Ralph, I place the lube on the outside of his leg so it will be easy for me to grab when I need it. I kneel on the bed, sitting back on my heels until I can get my mouth on the delicious man in front of me. I let my lips brush over his arse cheeks, watching in fascination as Ralph's muscles clench at the touch. I have the sudden need to mark him and I bite him, sucking the skin until I know that he will be seeing the hickey for a few days at least. His catching breath lets me know that he likes what I'm doing, and the taste of his skin in my mouth is all I need to know I love it. "How long has it been?"

"For what? Sex or other stuff?"

"How long since you bottomed, how slow should I go?" I torture him as he tries to speak, nipping and soothing his skin with my tongue.

"I …it's been … oh shit. Aiden … five years since I bottomed. God, do that again. But don't go slow ... please make me feel it."

I run my tongue over his hole and he nearly jumps off the bed. I hold him down by the hips, keeping him still as I use my tongue to relax the muscles that I want to slip past. His flavour is like heaven and I stiffen my tongue and push it into his hole, his groan making my balls tighten. God I love rimming a guy, just not that many men are into it, or at least not the ones I meet. Ralph is enjoying every second of it and I make a note to revisit this, but for now, I need to be inside him.

I grab the lube from the bed and pour a generous amount onto Ralph's hole and my cock. I use a finger to press inside his body as I kiss over his back, using my teeth to make imprints in his muscles.

"No more, I'm ready." His words come out on a pant and as much as I wish I could spend more time prepping him, but my body is screaming for release.

I kneel up and push my cock against his tight ring of muscle, breathing once before I push forward. That gentle pop as I slide into his body has my eyes crossing in pleasure and I ease in very slowly. Or at least that's the plan. What happens is Ralph thrusts back and I impale him in one long stroke. We cry out

Help Our Heroes

simultaneously and just when I think it can't get any better Ralph proves me wrong.

Chapter 17

Ralph

It's all too much. The taste of Aiden in my mouth, the way he's touching me, speaking to me, and the burn of the bite on my arse cheek as he pounds against it. It all adds together to make me lose my fucking mind, and I come with a roar as soon as he's buried inside me, the pain of his entry throwing me over the edge. My mind goes blank as every part of me is focused on the jet after jet of cum that's flooding from me. I feel like this is the first real orgasm I've ever had, the other ones dimming in comparison. I didn't think I could experience pleasure like this, especially with no attention to my cock.

Awareness comes back to me, and I can feel my back being pressed against Aiden's chest. The brush of the material from his suit makes me shudder, my skin still tingling from my orgasm. I don't know when he pulled me up onto my knees, or when he wrapped his arms around me, but it makes me feel secure, like he's protecting me while I let go.

"So fucking beautiful. I've never seen anything like that before."

Aiden's words are spoken softly in my ear, adding to the dreamy feeling that's making me want never to wake up. I want to spend the rest of my life right where I am, with Aiden's cock inside me and his arms wrapped around my chest. Safe and wanted.

When Aiden starts to slip from me, I panic and reach back to grab his hip. I stop his movement and release a little sigh of relief. "Don't."

He kisses my shoulder, and I lean my head back against him. "What do you want, boy?"

"I want you to come. Please."

His first movements are tentative and I know he's probably worried about hurting me. I need him to realise he isn't, so I use my hold on his hip to add pressure to his thrusts, and it doesn't take Aiden long to get the hint. He slides into my body with more power than before, his balls crashing against me with force, and it feels like heaven.

A little yelp comes from me when I'm suddenly pushed to the mattress. I'm lying flat out when Aiden lowers his body onto mine, the roughness of his clothes adding an extra layer to the feeling. Knowing that he's still fully clothed while I'm naked is such a turn on. It's a show of power, letting me know I'm the vulnerable one between us.

"You feel so fucking good. God, there is no way I can last this time, but next time I promise it will be better."

Better? If it gets better than it is now, there's a chance I won't recover, but I'm willing to take the risk. All thought rushes from my head as Aiden starts pounding into my body like he's trying to bury himself inside me. I can feel myself getting hard again, but the only thing I can focus on is Aiden. His rhythm starts to change, and I push my hands against the headboard to stop me from head-butting it as I move up the bed. This position also gives me a little more stability, and I press my arse up, opening myself to him so he can get deeper.

"Shit."

It's the only thing he says before he sinks his teeth into my shoulder and bites deep. I scream in ecstasy, the pain making my balls throb, and he thrusts one last time before his body shudders. Knowing that he's coming in me, albeit in a condom, makes my heart fucking soar. It feels like he's claiming me, and even though I know tonight is a one-time thing, I lavish in the feeling of ownership.

I feel something trickle down my shoulder but I don't have the energy to turn my head and look to see what it is, telling myself it's probably sweat from Aiden. I love the feeling of Aiden's body weighing down on me, pushing the air from my lungs, and I try to memorise how it makes me feel.

"Shit, I'm so sorry." His words bring me back to my senses, and back to the stinging in my shoulder. Holy shit, that hurts worse than the burn in my arse as Aiden slips from my body.

"Oh god, I'm so fucking sorry." Aiden rushes from the room as I watch him over my shoulder. He re-appears a few moments later with two cloths. He puts one on the bed next to me and then presses the other one to my shoulder. It's only then that I notice the red drips running over my skin.

"You made me bleed?" Laughter follows my words at the shocked look on Aiden's face.

"Yes! Again, I'm so fucking sorry."

I struggle to get myself upright and close to Aiden. I take the cloth from his hand and throw it to the floor. "Don't be sorry, I'm not."

Aiden's eyes heat and I want him to bite me again, this time in a more private place.

* * *

A car alarm outside wakes me from the deep sleep that I'm in. I stretch my body, moaning when all my muscles ache at the movement. What did I do last night that would leave me so sore? I snuggle into the pillow, enjoying the feeling of the sun against my back. The sun? But my bed isn't near the window.

My eyes open wide and look around the room. It takes a second to realise where I am and when I do, the memories from the night before come rushing back all at once. Aiden, his teeth, his skin hitting mine, and his dick pounding into me. My cheeks burn as I turn my head and I groan when I see Aiden still asleep next to me. He has scratches on his back and I remember them happening. He had me pinned to the floor in the bathroom as he fucked me again and I was gripping on to him, trying to keep him close. I felt the skin break under my nails but neither of us cared. It wasn't the first injury of the night and it turned out not to be the last.

Shit, shit, shit. I need to get out of here. As unbelievable as last night was, now in the light of day with no alcohol running through my system, I realise what a colossal mistake it was. I let Aiden see a side of me that I've kept secret up until now, never admitting out loud how much I'm turned on by the thought of being dominated. Okay, so after everything that happened last night I know it's not just the thought that turns me on, the experience makes me come harder than ever.

That doesn't matter now. What matters is getting out of here before Aiden wakes up. I don't know how to react to him, so it's simpler if I just leave. I know it's a shitty move but I'm confident he will understand. Last night was so fucking intense and I can't face having to talk about it this morning.

Help Our Heroes

I ease myself off the mattress, watching Aiden carefully for any signs of him waking up but thankfully he still looks sound asleep. I tiptoe around the room picking up all my clothes. I'm thankful that I spent time last night putting it all in a pile because it makes it easier to make my quick escape. I ease open the door and slip out of the room, closing it silently behind me. I keep quiet as I make my way across the hall into my room. As soon as I'm inside, I grab my mobile and text Handy, telling him to come get me. I don't wait for a reply, gathering the few things I hadn't previously packed and shove them into my bag. I look around to make sure that I haven't missed anything and when I'm confident that there isn't anything, I turn and leave.

I struggle not to go back and check on Aiden one last time, just to look at him while he's lying there looking so fucking beautiful, but I can't risk waking him up. Forcing myself to keep moving I head down the stairs and put my bag next to the front door. I take my mobile out and see that Handy is on his way. It will take him about thirty minutes to get here but I will be out before then. I put on my shoes and grab my jacket, throwing it over the top of my bag so I don't forget it. My keys and wallet are by the door and I pick them up, tucking them into the pocket of my jeans. If I leave anything today then it will stay left, I can't come back no matter what.

Taking one last look around, actually feeling a little sad about leaving, I say a silent goodbye to Aiden before I grab my bag and walk outside. I close the front door as silently as I can and start walking down the street in the direction that I'm sure Handy will come in. I can feel pain in my shoulder from the bite that Aiden gave me last night as well as a few other bruises and hickies that mar my skin, but the main ache comes from somewhere more surprising. My chest. It feels tight and the further I get from Aiden's house the worse it gets. The tightness moves up my throat and I'm suddenly struggling not to cry. I don't know what the hell is happening, I didn't even feel this way when I left William.

When I turn the corner at the end of the street, I stop and lean back against one of the trees that line the pavement. I've dropped my bag next to me because I seem to have lost all my strength and now I'm struggling to breathe deeply. *Holy shit.* I lean my head back and stare at the sky, watching the clouds as they move slowly across the early morning sky. The weather is clear so far but I can see the clouds getting darker which probably means it's going to rain later.

I don't know how long I'm focused on the clouds but a car pulls up beside me and I hear the electric window going down. I'm scared to look in case it's Aiden, but when I hear the driver shouting out at me my mouth curls up into a smile.

"How much for a blowjob?"

Just hearing Handy's voice brings me back down to earth. I lean down to grab my bag, realising how fucking stupid I'm being. Last night with Aiden was fucking amazing, something I will never forget for the rest of my life, but that's all it was. It was a night of fantastic sex and now I move on. It's time to enjoy my freedom and live my life like it's one big party.

Chapter 18

Aiden

"You here, butthead?"

I hear Jer's voice and walk out from the kitchen to greet him. I've picked up my phone at least a dozen times to cancel coffee with my brother, but I knew he wouldn't listen, so there was no point. I'm not in the mood for company today, not after waking up alone this morning. It was a shock when I opened my eyes to find the opposite side of my bed empty, but I didn't think he had actually left. In my head he had gone to get coffee or use the bathroom, but when I searched the house though there was no trace of Ralph. If it wasn't for the broken glass still on the kitchen floor and the ache in my body, I would think I had imagined the whole night. Finding the house empty was the turning point of my mood and I haven't been able to recover since.

"Who kicked your puppy?"

I give Jer the finger before walking back into the kitchen to refill my coffee cup. I probably won't be able to sleep for the next two days, but I need the caffeine to get through the day without killing someone. I don't bother asking Jer if he wants a coffee because that's like asking a policeman if he wants a doughnut. The answer is always yes. I grab his favourite large mug and fill it nearly to the brim. No room for milk but a ton of sugar, gross but it's the way he likes it.

"Seriously, Aiden. What the fuck is wrong with you?"

"Nothing. I just didn't sleep well last night." Isn't that an understatement? I leave out the bit about my lack of sleep being caused by the huge sexy soldier who I pinned to the bed and fucked like a man possessed. I'm sure he doesn't need to hear that shit. I take a large gulp of my coffee and my eyes water when it burns my mouth. I can see a smirk on Jer's face because he knows what's happening, but I keep my face straight so he doesn't get the satisfaction of seeing my pain.

"How did the work thing go yesterday?"

I think for a minute wondering what he is talking about before I remember about the meeting with my client. It had completely slipped my mind after everything that happened when I got home. "Yeah, it was fine. I have no idea why they needed to see me in person again, I've already met with him once."

"Him?"

"Yeah, Christian Gallagher. He runs a chain of fitness studios, and he wants to rebrand everything. Apparently, another gym has a similar name and he isn't happy about it." Christian is what I would call a control freak. No matter how much I tell him that I'm on top of the project, he can't let go, needing to meet me again and again so he can micromanage the whole thing.

"Ever think he might want to see you cause he likes you? Maybe he wants to see you all sexy in your suit." He wiggles his eyebrows and I wish there was something close at hand that I could throw at him.

"Don't do that, it's disturbing."

"I'm being serious though, little brother. Maybe he genuinely likes you and just doesn't have the balls to ask you out."

I roll my eyes, not wanting to have this conversation with Jer again. He is forever pushing me to go out and find someone, telling me that I will never meet the man of my dreams in my living room. Little does he know that I did just that. No, not the man of my dreams, just a man. A hot, sexy man who does strange things to my body and makes me want things I'd never wanted before, but just a man.

"I've told you before, I'm not a man that's in demand."

"Fuck that, Aiden. I know I'm your brother, and I think you look like the nerd you always were, but I've heard differently."

"What?" I have no idea what he's on about, and as much as I should try and get as far away from this conversation as possible, my warped curiosity wants more information.

"Do you remember Derek?"

I rack my brains to try and think of a face to go with the name but I'm at a complete loss.

"He supplies the flowers for the Bistro. Tall, curly hair down to his shoulder, thick-rimmed glasses. Ring any bells?"

The description brings to mind a face that I'm pretty sure belongs to said Derek. I've only met him maybe twice when he had been delivering flowers, but if I remember he was quite attractive. Not Ralph hot, but cute. Shit, I can't use Ralph as my measuring gauge for all future men, it's not fair to them or me. "Yeah, I think so."

"Well, he's been asking me to introduce him to you for months now. Apparently, he saw you one day when you were cooking alone in the kitchen and he has been smitten ever since."

"Smitten? Seriously, who uses that word?"

"Fuck you, Aiden. As I was saying, maybe I could give him your number and when he calls to ask you out you could say yes?"

I think about what he's saying. Maybe it's precisely what I need after what happened with Ralph. It was a mistake having sex with him, there were so many reasons I shouldn't have done it. He's a stranger, I was angry and he had been drinking. Those were huge red flags that told me I should have stayed away. Unfortunately, I let my dick do my thinking for me, and I suppose waking up alone was Karmas revenge for being so fucking stupid. "Okay."

Jer looks shocked at my answer, probably expecting a full on argument to get me to agree. "Seriously? Just ... okay?"

"Just okay."

He stares at me as though he's waiting on the punch line to some joke but I have nothing to give him. Going out on a date is probably what I need to get over last night and since I never go out, Derek seems a safe bet. Anyway, there's no guarantee that he will even call and this will get Jer off my back.

"Well, since you're being so agreeable, I want to talk to you about something else."

"No." I pick up my coffee and drink some of the thankfully cooler liquid. Jer kicks me under the table, a dickhead move if there ever was one, and I kick him back a little harder.

"Shut up and listen. I want to train you ..."

"I've told you ..."

Jer holds up his hand when I start talking. It's a fight we have all the time but apparently this time he's planning on being more forceful. "Listen to me. The Bistro is getting busier by the day, I have to turn people away, and it's made me come up with a plan. I need you on board for it to work."

Okay, so he's got my attention now. I lean back in my chair and let him talk.

"My appointment at the bank the other day, it was to inquire about a loan."

"A loan for what?" Jer has always prided himself on not having a loan outstanding on the business. All his money coming from savings and a small payout after an accident left him injured, so the loan angle is confusing.

"I want to expand the Bistro. There's a shit ton of room out the back and it sits empty most of the year. If I can extend the building back there and then add a covered patio area I could add another ten tables at least."

I can actually picture it in my head, it would make the whole place look fantastic and the patio would make them unique in the area. God, Jer really does have the brains for business. He can look at something and see where he wants to take it.

"The only problem is it will require another chef and I don't trust easily."

"No shit." I laugh at his statement because Jer has fired more chefs for no real reason than is considered normal. To say he's a control freak would put Christian, the gym owner, to shame.

"Shut up. Anyway, what I was thinking is I could train you while the extension was being built and then when we re-open you could join me. You would be doing me a favour because you are the only person I trust in my kitchen. The staff loves you and you respect them all."

I think about his proposal, not dismissing it instantly as usual. This could be my chance to follow my dream while helping Jer with his. I've always felt wrong about wanting to be a chef, like somehow I was taking away from Jer by doing the same thing, but he's here asking me to join him in such a fantastic project. "Are you sure?"

"Why do you not want to follow your passion, Aiden? I swear I've seen classically trained chefs that have been doing it for years with less talent than you.

You just have this ability when it comes to food and I want to see you do something with that."

"I don't want you to feel that I'm taking away your thing. God, I know how stupid it sounds, but you were always the chef in the family." Saying it out loud to Jer, especially when he's looking at me like I've lost my mind, is making me sounds ridiculous.

"Shut the fuck up. How would you becoming a chef take away from my skill? I said I want to train you, I didn't say you would be better."

And just like that, I laugh. Jer always has this way of making me feel better about everything. Ever since we were kids he had my back, making sure I followed my dreams and didn't let anyone fuck with me. He really is the best big brother ever.

"Okay."

He gets that shocked look on his face again. "Really?"

"On one condition."

Now he looks worried and I don't blame him. He's probably thinking I'm going to make him eat something gross or tattoo something on his dick –hey, we've had bets before – but it's nothing like that this time. "You don't get a loan."

"Aiden, I can't do this without it. I need the capital to expand."

"I know, and I want to give you the money. I want to help you in your dream while you help me in mine."

I worry again that Jer will think I'm stepping on his toes but instead he gets a broad smile on his face. "Yes. Oh god, this will be awesome." He holds out his hand and I take it, shaking firmly. "Partners."

Chapter 19

Ralph

I open the fridge, look inside and then close it again.

"I swear, dude. You do that one more time and I'm gonna tie you to a fucking chair. You have opened that thing about fifty times and not taken anything out."

I turn to look in Handy's direction, realising that I didn't even know he was home. I head to the living room and drop into the chair across from him. "Sorry."

"What the fuck is wrong with you?"

What is wrong? I wish I could tell him but I've just felt off since I moved in five days ago. It's not Handy, he has been nothing but his usual self, it's more that I don't feel like myself. My skin feels too tight, like I want to burst out of it at any second, like it doesn't belong to me any more and I need to escape. There is a constant itch that I cant get rid of now matter what I do. "Nothing. I think maybe I've had too much downtime since deployment. Getting back to work can't come quick enough."

Handy stares at me like he doesn't believe a single word I say, and really who can blame him. I have never had a problem taking time off before so we both know that's not the problem. "We need to go out."

I groan at the suggestion but I don't fight against it. I have never managed to talk Handy out of a drunken night in the whole time I've known him and I decided a long time ago to stop wasting my energy.

"You will love it. Go out, have a drink and find a cute little twink that you can fuck into the mattress. What isn't to love about that?"

Yeah, what isn't to love? Well unless you count the whole topping someone who is smaller than me, because obviously as a large guy that's what I'm

Help Our Heroes

looking to do. This is why I haven't told anyone what really gets my engine revving because I'm pretty sure no one will look at me the same again. That was the refreshing thing about Aiden ... he just knew. My stomach tumbles when I think about Aiden. I've been trying to not think about him but it's getting harder every day. I dream about him so he's the first thing in my head when I wake up in the morning and I cant seem to get him out for the rest of the day. He's always there, smiling at me, seducing me with those blazing eyes, and I swear I can feel his hand around my throat still when I concentrate. The bruises he left on my body have started to fade and with them is my determination to stay away.

Everyday I need to fight against the urge to go running back to Aiden. Explain to him that I was scared about the way I was feeling and that's why I ran, but then I chicken out and stay away. Why would he care about my feelings when I was just a way to get off, unless I wasn't just a hot body. Maybe he felt the same things that I did, that spark when our skin touched and the feeling when our bodies connected, the way we just felt right together.

"Tonight we head to Climate, I will round the guys up." With that said he gets up from the couch and leaves the living room with his phone against his ear.

Looks like we're going out tonight then.

* * *

"Hey there, sexy. Aren't you just a big lump of fantastic-ness?"

I don't even look at who's talking, just lifting my beer to my lips to have a drink before replying. "Not interested. Keep moving."

I hear a huff before the heat that was pressed against my arm vanishes. I knew coming out tonight was going to be a mistake and when I got out of the shower I should have given in to my urge to just get into bed. Instead I've been sitting here for far too long trying to fend off handsy men who want to get to know me better.

"Seriously what is your problem? He was just your type."

I take another drink hoping that Handy will take it as a hint that I don't want to talk about it. Unfortunately he doesn't and he continues on while I flag down the barman and order some tequila shots. I'm going to need to be a lot drunker than I am to survive tonight. I down two of them while I listen to Handy carry on.

"I just don't get you. Why aren't you making the most of the single life? You didn't even look at that guy, he was hot."

I turn to look at him as I slip a shot glass in front of him. He takes it and downs it. "How would you know if he was hot?"

"I'm straight not dead, dude. I can appreciate the physical form of a man without wanting to sleep with them."

I raise my eyebrows at him but don't comment, downing another drink. The burn feels good but the best feeling though is the numbness that's attacking my nose. The sweet oblivion of alcohol is going to catch up with me soon.

"Shut up, I can." He leans in towards me, lowering his voice so only I can hear him. "I'm worried about you. If a guy like that cant get your dick interested there is something wrong. You would usually jump at the chance to fuck a guy like that, why aren't you at home already pounding into him?"

I stare at Handy, like really look at him, and wonder how much I can tell him. Is it crossing the line if I let him see behind the mask that I've been hiding behind all my life? Will he look at me differently, think I'm less of a man, if he knew about my need to be dominated? I'm a soldier, I spend my life giving out orders and working with danger, but it all gets too much and I just want someone to take me out of my own head.

"Ralph, you can tell me."

"I don't want to fuck anyone."

Handy's forehead scrunches up and I know that he isn't getting what I'm trying to tell him. I take a deep breath and tell him everything.

"I don't want to top, it's not my thing. I want someone to pin me to a bed and fuck me until I scream. No one looks at me like that though, well no one except Aiden."

Now that gets his attention. "Wait. You fucked, sorry, got fucked by the guy who gave you a room?"

"Yeah."

Handy motions to the barman and orders another round of tequila's. This is why he's my best friend, he always seems to know what I need. "Okay, so now the sudden departure makes sense. I'm taking it that it happened the night before you left?"

I down a shot and hiss through the burn. "I ran as soon as I woke up and I haven't spoken to him since."

"Is this a problem? Is this why you've been in a shitty mood since you arrived?"

Wow, way to make me feel crappy. I didn't realise that I had been so bad, I actually thought I had managed to completely hide the fact I was hurting. "Sorry, I didn't realise I had been. But to answer your question, I miss him like hell and I don't know why. I barely knew him a week, he's a complete stranger, but fuck me I cant stop thinking about him. He just got me, saw who I really was. I know that sounds really stupid."

Handy slams his glass down on the bar and grabs the back of my neck, pulling me close enough that our noses are nearly touching. Anyone watching us would think we were having an intimate moment but that's never bothered Handy in the past. He is the most tactile guy I've ever met and he's never worried that someone would think he was gay.

"Listen to me closely. You feel what you feel. Maybe you feel a connection with him because he is the other part of your soul, who knows. But you're not stupid for finally feeling something. Dick treated you like shit so it's actually nice to hear you talking about someone who *gave you* something instead of always taking. Where I do think that maybe you are a little dumb is that you are running away. If this guy gets you, knows what your looking for without you needing to tell him, why aren't you with him now instead of sitting here with me?"

My eyes widen as he practically growls at me. I know Handy wants the best for me but I expected him to tell me not to fall for anyone, that I need to go out and enjoy being single for a while. This is a shock and I'm a little lost for words so I try and joke it away. "The other half of my soul?" I laugh but it sounds fake even to my own ears.

"Do you think about him all the time?"

I nod my head.

"Did he make your toes curl?"

I nod again.

"Did he think of you when he didn't need to?"

"He came to get me when I went to face William."

"Dick."

I laugh at Handy's almost Tourette's reaction to me using William's actual name. He shall only be known as Dick now. "He got between us so I didn't get into trouble."

"Then why are you here?" His question comes out on a quiet voice, like he genuinely wants to know the answer.

"Because I'm scared to want him. What if he turns out to be another Wil … Dick? I barely know him, what if I'm missing something?"

Handy leans back, dropping his hand from my neck but still giving me an intense look. "I'm not telling you to go and marry the guy. Maybe start with coffee then progress to a meal. Remember dating?"

I smack Handy upside the head and he rubs his skin while laughing. He really is getting too much enjoyment out of this. "What if he won't talk to me? I snuck out while he was still asleep, that's a cowards escape."

"Then you grovel. If it's anything like dating a woman you tell them how sorry you are and plead for their forgiveness."

He makes it sound so easy but maybe he's on to something.

Chapter 20

Aiden

'Can you cover for me at work tonight?'

The text throws me because Jer hasn't mentioned anything about needing a night off. Usually, he tries to give me at least a few days notice, especially since I'm working my one-month's notice at my job. The company wasn't exactly thrilled when I handed in my letter of resignation but there wasn't much they could do. They tried to offer me more money and benefits but after talking things over with Jer, there's nothing I want more than to be trained by him. Being taught by Jer is doing what I did before I invested into the business, just going in in the afternoon to learn new techniques. He's told me that's the best way to learn, by watching everything he does.

I type my reply to Jer, telling him I'm fine to cover for him but I want to know why. He answers with a simple see you later and I growl in frustration. I hate it when he only tells me half a story. I'm a natural worrier and my mind automatically goes to something being wrong.

Checking the time I see I need to get a move on if I want to get to the Bistro in time for prep. I know I can leave that to the prep chefs but I don't want them to feel like I'm better than them and don't have to help out. It might be different when I'm working full time but for now I enjoy learning all I can. I rush up the stairs two at a time and go into my room to grab my chef's jacket. I choose the black one tonight because if Jer comes in to join us he will wear white, and I want people to know that he's the senior chef. Yes, I still have a feeling of stealing his thunder, but it's getting better. One day I might feel comfortable with it all.

* * *

I look at the clock and see that it's just before nine. We have a large booking arriving soon, on top of our already full dining room, and it's going to hit us hard. Twelve people at one sitting is always hectic in the kitchen, and my biggest order at one time so far. I take a deep breath and Sebastian, the pastry chef, pats me on the back.

"You'll be fine, chef."

I nod in his direction but keep quiet. I know I can do this, I just need to focus and work through it methodically.

"Table for twelve has arrived chef. They are getting settled and I will take their order."

My stomach drops as Tony, the head server, announces the table. I let out a calming breath while wiping my hands on my trousers. Right, I have this.

An hour later the final dish has gone out for the main courses of the large table, and all but one other table is served. I feel sweaty and a little like I'm going to collapse, but I achieved the stressful goal without losing my cool with anyone. It was close at a few points, nearly snapping at the other chefs when they weren't calling out times accurately, but I kept it in and sorted out the fuck up. Now I feel like I can do this job without anyone here to bail me out. I've always been worried that I want this so badly but I'm not ready for it. Tonight proved I am.

"I need you at table sixteen, chef."

My head flies around to look at Tony. I don't leave the kitchen, especially to approach the tables. "Why?"

"There's a problem with a meal and they are demanding to see the chef."

My stomach drops and I swallow a few times to get rid of the feeling of wanting to vomit. This is part of the job, going out and dealing with problems if I'm needed, but that doesn't make me feel any better. I look around like someone might bail me out but all I get are sympathetic eyes. Fantastic. I wipe my hands on my apron and remove it, not wanting to take any of the kitchen mess out front with me. "Lead the way, Tony."

I crack my fingers as I leave the kitchen because I need to get rid of some of the nervous energy that's rushing through my body. Whatever the problem is I will apologise and offer to comp the dish, maybe get them a drink. It will be quick and straightforward, and then I can disappear into the kitchen again to hide out for the rest of the shift.

Help Our Heroes

When I walk around the bar, I stop dead. The table of four is filled with soldiers in uniform, and I have the sudden urge to run in the opposite direction. I try to focus on the men that are at the table, not the one who automatically filled my mind, but it's a losing battle. I can barely go an hour without thinking about Ralph on the best of days, but faced with men that are wearing what he was wearing the first day we met then I'm lost.

"Mr White, this is our chef Aiden."

I take a moment to take in Mr White before putting a huge smile on my face and approaching him. I hold my hand out to him and he takes it straight away. "Mr White, I'm the head chef here this evening. Is there a problem?"

He tilts his head while he looks at me, his eyes wandering over my entire body until I feel a little awkward. It's only then I notice he's still holding my hand and I want to rip it away but I do it as politely as I can. "I can see it now."

Confusion hits me at his words and I feel like I'm missing something significant. "Excuse me?"

"I didn't know what to expect but I can totally see it now. I know why he can't stop thinking about you."

Yeah, completely lost, and it doesn't help when I see Jer walking out of the office straight towards me. He has a shit-eating grin on his face, and it's equal parts worrying and surprising. "Jer?"

"If you didn't guess, baby brother, you're off the rest of the night." He pats me on the shoulder and walks past me towards the kitchen. "You can thank me later."

I watch him until he disappears and only then do I turn back to Mr White, who is now standing in front of me. "I have no idea what is happening here."

Mr White laughs and holds his hand out to me again. I take it without any real thought. "It's nice to meet you, Aiden. My name is Charles, but my friends call me Handy."

Realisation hits me square in the chest stealing my breath. Holy shit, this is Ralph's best friend. I don't know what to do so I just continue to stand there gaping at him like a fool. "That there is Dan and the idiot on the other side is Benny. There was someone else here, but he wanted to surprise you."

"Aiden?"

I recognise the voice instantly and I close my eyes. I haven't heard it in over a week but it still makes my heart jump in my chest. I shouldn't want to rush into Ralph's arms. I should want to turn and punch him square in his disappearing face. I don't though, all I want to do is run and hide.

Hands on my shoulders make me gasp and before I know it I'm turning and facing Ralph. He's standing there with a single red rose in his hand. He looks fucking stunning in his black suit, standing out against the other three men who are wearing their camouflage trousers and white t-shirts. Truthfully though, he would stand out in a room full of men in matching suits. There's just something about Ralph that speaks to me on a deeper level.

"Hi." His voice sounds unsure and I get a sense of satisfaction from it.

Lips at my ear make me jump but when Charles starts speaking, I can't help but smile. "This is where you say hi. Then he is going to grovel and tell you how sorry he is for being an arsehole and vanishing. Then he's going to say sorry again and ask you to go out for coffee, which you will say yes to. After that, you are on your own, unless you both fuck it up again and I need to step in."

I'm laughing by the time Charles has finished but my eyes haven't left Ralph. He looks so embarrassed because of his friend but it's his eyes that won't let me escape. They show me everything he's feeling. I can see the apology in them, but there is also heat, the heat I remember so well from the night we were together. I'm so lost that when I feel a shove on my shoulder, I wonder what's wrong. It only takes me a moment to catch up and I follow the instructions that Charles gave me. "Hi."

Ralph moves towards me and I'm pushed again, making me close the distance a little more. "I'm really sorry. I did a dickhead move running out on you, and it was all about me. I got scared. I've never let anyone see that side of me before and you ... you just saw me. I didn't know how to deal with it so I ran, and as Handy will tell you, I've not been fun to live with since."

"He's telling the truth."

Ralph glares over my shoulder and I bite my lips so I don't laugh. I think I could grow to like Charles, especially if he continues to help me with Ralph. "Anyway, I wanted to ask you if you would like to go out for coffee with me one day. No pressure," He hands me the rose that's he's been holding the whole time. "I really want to get to know you better because I like you, Aiden."

The blush on Ralph's cheeks is what seals his forgiveness with me. Seeing him look so vulnerable in front of his friends makes me think that he really means what he's saying. "Okay."

His face lights up with one simple word and it makes me feel like I've given him a million pounds. I want to rush to him and kiss him, to fill my mouth with his taste again but I keep standing in place. He's right that we should get to know each other, nothing good ever happens quickly. There is another thought in the back of my head, and this one isn't as innocent.

I look him over, taking in his entire body in that sexy suit. It's not too dissimilar to the one I was wearing the night we were together and it makes lots of memories rush back. Ralph must see the lust building in my eyes because he gasps quietly and my eyes rush back up to his. Burning heat flows between us and I smirk. Yeah, the other thing that happens over time is sexual tension. I can spend our time together making him need me, making him want to bend over the instant I say. My dick is rock hard now but I don't try to cover it. I'm facing Ralph so he's the only one that can see it, and I want him to see it, want him to know what he does to me.

"I will go for coffee on one condition."

"Anything."

I walk forward and grab him by the back of the neck, pulling him down the small distance until my mouth is at his ears. I use my teeth to nibble his earlobe, loving the gentle moan that comes from deep in his chest. "I will go for coffee with you, but you must promise to behave, boy."

Ralphs hands come out and grip the front of my chef's jacket like it's too much for him and he needs help to stay standing.

This is going to be so much fun.

Epilogue

Charles ... um ...Handy

I press my back against the back of the wall at the front of the house, making sure I blend in with the shadows so no one can see me. I don't want to draw attention to myself and to hiding my rather large body is difficult, but I'm managing it…just.

"What the actual fuck are you doing, Handy?"

I groan when Dan speaks loud enough to wake the dead, apparently not getting the whole we shouldn't be here thing. "Shut the fuck up and get over here. Try not to be seen."

It's probably too late for that piece of advice since he's currently walking up the front path in full view of everyone. When Dan gets close enough, I reach out and grab him by the arm, dragging him into the shadows to hide with me. He growls, but at least it comes out quietly this time. "What the hell are you doing here? And what was with the cryptic message about wearing black and meeting you here?"

"I'm visiting a friend."

I can't see him in the dark but I know he's giving me that look he's mastered over the years since I met him. "Your friend doesn't live here anymore."

It's a small detail, but I don't let it deter me. I move quietly to the side of the house, rushing down the side of it and around to the back. I hear Dan's footsteps behind me and I smile. He might not know what's going on, but he's following me into the fox den like I knew he would. Our group of friends is a great believer in do first and ask questions later, trusting that none of us will do anything that might get us court marshalled.

I head to the back door and try the handle, not surprised to find it locked. It won't stop me though, Ralph told me the secret of getting in just after they moved in here. There is a loose section of the door, and if you hit it just right, it will click the lock over and free it. I follow the instructions and the door creaks open in front of me. Dan grabs me by the arm and I turn around, looking in his general direction since I can't actually see his face.

"Handy, this is breaking and entering. You do know that leads to being arrested, which leads to jail, which leads to losing our job and being dishonourably discharged. None of that's a good thing."

I understand his worry but we aren't here to do any damage. "Trust me, Dan. No one will ever know we were here and even if they did they would never be able to prove it. I just think that it's time that Dick got his Karma for treating Ralph like shit. You remember what he did to your best friend?"

"That's fucking low." He curses a little more under his breath before pushing me in through the back door. When he closes it behind us, we both hold still for a few moments just listening. I checked the house out for thirty minutes before Dan arrived, so I know it's empty, but it pays to be vigilant.

"Right, I want to be out of here in fifteen minutes, no more. I don't want to risk being caught." I tug the bag onto my shoulder as I grab my flashlight out of my pocket. I know that if anyone sees the light beams through the window they will be instantly suspicious, but I thought it was a better option than being caught by Dick with the lights on.

"What's the actual plan?"

I move to the table and hand Dan the flashlight, leaving my hands empty to search through my bag. I grab the bottle I was looking for and give it to him. "I need you to go through every liquid product you can find and add this laxative to it. It won't work straight away so I need you to add it to everything you can." I can see Dan's smile in the light beam and he looks really fucking happy now he knows what I am planning. "What are you gonna do?"

"His underwear drawer is calling to me and my bag of chilies." His laughter follows me as I take another flashlight out and head towards the bedrooms. When I walk into the living room I see a brand new sixty-inch television and it just gets me more pissed. Ralph was left with no money and nowhere to live and fuckface is here watching things on a TV that is far too big for this shitty living room. I would steal the fucking thing but I'm not here for that, and it would be better if Dick didn't know anyone had been here. It will make him go about his business and revenge will be so much better.

Hurrying through the house so I don't see anything else that will want me to punch Dick in the face, I reach the bedroom and rush inside. I put my bag on the bed and reach inside to remove a pair of gloves and the chilies. I learned one night after making tacos while drinking too much beer that touching chillies then your cock hurts like a motherfucker, so I'm pretty sure that rubbing them into the crotch of all Dicks undies will make him think he's caught something. It might not work, especially if the fucker has been sticking his cock in randomers, I mean he might already piss fire but it's worth the chance.

I spend the time to make sure that I get a good coverage on every pair before I return them the way I found them. Again I remind myself that he can't know we've been here. With that task done and Dan working on the laxative angle, I move on to the third and final part of my revenge plan. I head back out to the living room and approach the large front window. This particular act is all dependent on what kind of curtain poles are fitted, and when I see it's the hollow type I fist bump the air. I would have hated to go home and not do this one.

Carefully removing the end fixture on the pole, I grab the plastic box from my bag and open it. There is no smell yet but I know in a few days there will be no escaping the stench. I giggle like a maniac as I fill the end of the pole with raw prawns.

"What are you doing?" Dan's voice shocks me but he has humour in it as he approaches. When he's next to me I show him what's in the tub and he bursts out laughing. "You are one evil fucker. Remind me never to get on the wrong side of you."

I fix the end onto the pole before dropping the now empty box into my bag. I feel like I've accomplished something tonight and I smile at myself. The smile only lasts a few seconds before headlights from the car parking in the driveway lights up the entire room. "Fuck, Dick's home."

Dan bolts from the living room like his arse is on fire and I laugh as I follow him. We make it out the back door, closing it quietly behind us before the front door opens. We lean our backs against the wall and try to stop the giggles that are threatening to reduce us to tears. Voices from inside has me covering my mouth but when he asks his visitor if he wants a drink I know I need to get out of here.

I push against Dan's shoulder and he moves instantly, leading the way down the side of the house and out over the neighbour's front lawn. We sprint down the road and by the time we reach my car we are both laughing hard. Collapsing into our seats, we watch the front of the house like we're scared that Dick's going to come out and find us. When a few minutes pass and we know we're safe I start the engine and pull away from the kerb. I wish I had a way to keep an eye on Dick for the next week, see him suffer as he itches his balls and shits himself inside out, all while his house smells like something's died in it. Yeah, I would pay to witness that.

"Does Ralph know you were planning this?"

I laugh at the question. "Shit no, and don't even hint that we were here. I don't need my arse kicked thank you very much."

With Dan's laughter in my ear and a smile on my face, I drive us back to meet with the happy couple.

The End

Dearest Betty

M.B. Feeney

When Lizzie Cooper's grandmother passes away, she is given the task of sorting through her belongings. When she finds a stack of letters address to her grandmother dated during the war, she finds out more about her Nana Betty than she expected, especially as the letters aren't from her grandfather, rather a man she only knows as Samuel.

Please note, this is only the first few chapters of the book, written for this anthology. The story will be expanded and released at a later date once the anthology is no longer on sale.

So, please. Don't tell me off when you get to the end...

Help Our Heroes

Prologue

The day my Grandmother died was the first day I felt truly alone— it was almost as bad, if not worse, as the day I found out I had lost my parents. I was a grown adult, but I cried like a baby when my grandmother took her final breath with me at her side, holding her hand.

When I said that to people in the few days following Nana Betty's death, they looked at me strangely before remembering that I'd lived with Nana Betty and Grandpa Albert for longer than I lived with my parents. I was with them the day my parents' car spun out of control on an icy road; was there when the police came to the door to inform them that 'there has been an accident', was there when Nana Betty collapsed in tears, Grandpa Albert trying to help her back to her feet but failing as he crumpled onto the floor next to her.

At five years old, it was hard to see, and I remember running to them unsure what was wrong. Now, at almost thirty-five, it sometimes feels like it was something I'd watched in a film.

Nana Betty and Grandpa Albert were my mum's parents and insisted I lived with them. Mum didn't have any brothers and sisters, and my dad's family lived in Australia— he'd come over to the UK for university in his twenties, and had never left after he met mum.

Being 'the kid with no parents' at school was tough. My peers couldn't understand why I loved living with relatives who were old, but it had never bothered me. I never missed out on anything just because the family members I lived with were so much older than me. They never realised that my Grandpa Albert had a wicked sense of humour, and that one of his biggest guilty pleasures were teenage dramas on channels such as Nickledeon and The Disney Channel.

Nana Betty was the most amazing cook, but no one ever wanted to stay over at our house when I was growing up. Every time the school had a bake sale for charity, I would take in boxes of beautifully iced cupcakes and they would sell out before anything else, yet my 'friends' never wanted to come to the house and thank her in person.

By the time I reached university age, I'd accepted that I'd never have the close-knit friendships I read about in the books of my early teenage years. Deciding that I didn't want to carry on with my education was easy. Finding a job, not so much. I ended up working in the local supermarket.

By the time Grandpa Albert passed away four years ago, I'd worked my way up from cashier to assistant manager. He'd always been proud of me for earning everything I got rather than expecting everything to be handed to me on a plate. At his funeral, as I held Nana Betty as she cried, I made him a promise that I would be store manager within the next five years.

Then Nana Betty got ill.

By the time she died, my amazing grandmother was able to put all her affairs in order. Considering her advance years, she organised her own funeral, her will, and anything else. All I would have to do was to notify friends and organisations such as the bank, the local council, and her insurance people. She did all the hard work for me.

Once her funeral was over, and she was reunited with Grandpa Albert once more, I hated being in their little two-bedroom house. It was so empty without their laughter, music, and the smell of Nana Betty's cooking. I wallowed for as long as I could, but then things needed sorting.

My grandparents had been council tenants their entire lives, and it had been requested that I was allowed to take over the tenancy. The council had agreed, so I gave up my little flat around the corner and moved back into my childhood home.

The first night was the worst. Lying in my old bedroom, with the house in complete silence around me. No Nana Betty shuffling around in her slippers to get a drink of water, no radio playing softly to drown out Grandpa Albert's snoring, and no whispered 'good night's' through the walls. I cried myself to sleep that night, my heart broken into a million little pieces.

* * *

In between being stuck at work— I still hadn't kept my promise of becoming a store manager, but I still had twelve months left, and working my way through the house room by room, I began to heal my grief at losing the only parents I knew.

It was cathartic, working my way through their belongings and organising them into trinkets I wanted to keep, items to donate to the local charity shop, and anything that needed chucking away. I was able to take my time, remember the good times and the love this house had given me, and slowly move on from losing them both.

I found the letters in the loft, hidden in a box tucked in the very corner. Not only were they addressed to *Miss Betty Perkins,* which was Nana Betty's maiden name, they were dated during the war and they *weren't* written by my grandad.

Chapter 1

It had been a month since I'd found the letters. I'd forgotten about them as I'd worked through sorting all Nana Betty and Grandpa Albert's belongings; deciding what to keep and what to get rid of was hard, but I did it. Then, I needed to decorate and 'put my own stamp on the place' the way Nana Betty had wanted me to do.

I was reminded of the box of letters one evening as I cooked myself a stir fry and the radio DJ mentioned a postcard he'd received from a friend. As soon as my food was cooked, I ran into my bedroom and grabbed the box.

I sat on the sofa, my food and the box on the small table in front of me, and did nothing. To open the box and read the letters would be intruding on Nana Betty's privacy... but, she wouldn't have kept them if... I wondered if Grandpa Albert knew about them.

Deciding to eat my dinner first, I stared at the box while I ate. There was nothing special about the old hat box. The pink was faded and the edges of the deep cylinder were scuffed. Something had been printed on the lid, but the lettering was indecipherable from age and being left in the loft for the forty plus years Nana Betty and Grandpa Albert had lived in the house.

When I'd finished my meal, I pushed my plate to one side, and then leaned forward and tugged the box towards me. Pausing for a moment, I finally pulled the lid off and reached inside to pull out the pile of letters.

There was easily fifty or sixty of them, carefully folded and placed back into the correct envelope. Slowly, almost with reverence, I opened the top one, knowing Nana Betty would have kept them in chronological order. The blue ink was still strong against the discoloured white paper, which surprised me when I saw the date. May, 1942... Nana Betty would have been seventeen, so I knew she hadn't even met Grandpa Albert yet.

Help Our Heroes

A sense of relief washed over me as I began to read.

* * *

19 May 1942

Dearest Betty,

    I hope you don't mind me writing you; what am I saying? You gave me your address, of course you don't mind. I can just imagine you hadn't expected a letter so soon. I'm running on three hours sleep in about the same amount of days, so I'll apologize now about my spelling, my going off on tangents, and anything else I get wrong in this letter. One I hope is the first of many, if you don't mind.

    Ever since I first met you at your friend Maggy's party, I can't get you out of my head. I know we spent a lot of time together the two weeks I was in London, but every time I close my eyes, all I can see is your dark hair that reminds me of chocolate, and your blue eyes that are like a stormy ocean back home in Darien, Georgia. Jimmy, the crazy red head who was with me that night, teases me relentlessly about how much I speak of you; which is often I have to admit. Jeez, now I'm starting to sound sappy – can I get away with blaming my previously mentioned lack of sleep?

    Sadly, I'm not back in London for at least another two months. All I want to do is to take you dancing again; to see you smiling and having fun. You have the most beautiful smile – I know I told you that before, but it's true. Your smile lights up a room, and makes others around you smile in return; it's a gift, believe me. Never lose your positive outlook on life. Even in these troubled times.

    When we left London, we were taken to RAF Bassingbourn in Cambridgeshire, not that I particularly know where that is – I guess it's lucky I'm not the navigator. I was just getting used to being in the capital, and now I'm in the middle of nowhere with the United States Air Force. My crew hasn't been out on any missions yet, but it won't be long. Most of the time we're helping the other crews maintain their crafts or being put to work in other areas. I just want to get back into the air.

    Did I tell you how amazing it is to fly? Honestly, it's the best feeling in the world, exhilaration flows through you from the moment you take off until the second you land. Looking out of the aircraft windows, down onto the clouds which looks fluffy enough to try and lay on is surreal. Every now and then, during a break in the clouds, you catch a glimpse of the world below you – houses and vehicles that look like they could only house ants. It's like being in another world. You tune out the noises of the engines and the people around you, and feel almost alone.

Can you tell I love my job? If I'm honest, I'm a little embarrassed with how sappy I just sounded. In many ways, it's hard to show emotions, even ones of joy or enthusiasm unless you have a gun in your hand or a beautiful woman in your arms.

Oh, I'm being called out. I'll try to write again soon. I hope you find some time to write me back and I hope we'll be able to see each other soon.

Samuel.

* * *

It wasn't the most personal of letters, but I still felt guilty for reading it; guilty to the memory of my Grandpa Albert. My grandparents had been in love, even into their old age, always hugging, touching, and teasing one another in the way that only couples could do; it was a relationship I'd often aspired to, and knowing that Nana Betty has someone before him made me feel a bit... unfaithful.

I had no idea who Samuel was, Nana Betty had never spoken of him to me, and I wasn't sure what to think. I'd always known that both of them had lived through the war, and that they had lives before they met one another after the war had ended, but this, this seemed intrusive.

With a sigh, I put the letter I had just read back into its envelope, and placed all of the letters back into the hat box. I'd decide what to do with them tomorrow; I needed a shower and to get to bed. I was on an early shift in the morning.

The following morning, I woke up feeling worse than when I went to bed. I'd tossed and turned all night, thinking about the letters. I didn't want to read them, but I also wanted to know more about Nana Betty and her life before marriage and kids. Was it wrong of me to read them, even though they were obviously private?

Help Our Heroes

Moving through the regular morning routine without thinking about it, I got myself ready for work. The only thing I could think about were the pile of letters sitting in the old box on my coffee table. In fact, I'd dreamed about a man in uniform and a young Nana Betty. In an attempt to put it out of my mind, I pulled my uniform on, grabbed my things, and went out to my car ready to start my day.

A busy day at work took my mind off what was waiting for me at home as I dealt with shitty customers with bad attitudes, staff calling in sick, and finally a power cut.

Twenty minutes before the end of my shift, the entire store was plunged into darkness and the sounds of the checkout lanes went silent. Within seconds, the crowd of customers were up in arms, moaning about being late to appointments, or claiming they should receive a discount on their shopping due to the delay. A number of people even came looking for me, as if it were my fault that the entire row of shops was without power.

Almost three hours after the end of my shift, the power was restored in our store and the others affected and I was finally able to leave. I trudged to my car on exhausted legs, and drove home, ready to stuff my face and collapse in a heap on the sofa. A bad night's sleep and a shitty day at work, I could barely function, but as soon as I walked into the front room of the house, all I could see was the box of letters, waiting for me.

Chapter 2

16 June 1942

Dearest Betty,

Thank you for writing back, it was great to hear from you. I guess not having to wait two weeks for mail is the one silver lining to being in the same country as the girl you want to hear from during wartime.

Your letter was the only bright light in some very dark days right now. Although my crew have been successful in our missions thus far, others haven't been so lucky. The sense of mourning for our fallen brothers is strong and thick in the air on the base at the moment, but each and every man here understands that it's a horrible part of the life we enlisted for; it could happen to any one of us at any time. It sounds morbid to consider this job in that way, but it a way to get through the time we're at the front line, so to speak.

Some days it's harder to keep going than others, but each and every day we all wake up, thank God for that, and get on with our work. Even the knowledge that each day could be our last doesn't deter us from our lives and our duty. Losing friends we consider family makes this whole situation so damn 'real' – that sound crazy doesn't it? War *is* real, but...

I don't even know what I'm trying to say, my thoughts have been all over the place the past few days. I'm sorry, I shouldn't be using these letters to you as a form of therapy. I'll stop now.

From your letter, it sounds like you've been so very busy and loving every moment. I do hope the factory is treating you and the other girls well. I've heard horror stories from the wives and girlfriends of the others in my battalion about how the women back home are being treated while 'the menfolk' are away. I don't want that to happen to you or your friends.

Help Our Heroes

I've been told that we may be being give a weekend off soon, which is unexpected, but I'm not sure whether it'll be in time for the party you invited me to. I do hope so, I'm in need of a good night out where I don't need to think about anything to do with aircraft or Adolf Hitler. Once I know for sure, I'll try to get on the telephone in the mess area and tell you. I know Jimmy's hoping we can get the time off, so you may want to warn Maggy hahaha.

I don't know if she told you, but she wrote to him a couple weeks ago, and ever since then, he hasn't shut up about her. Seriously, even the other guys are fed up with hearing Maggy's name – no offence to her of course.

Well, I better go and get to sleep. I wanted to get this letter written in time to catch the mail first thing in the morning. Hopefully I'll see you before you get a chance to write me back.

Yours,
Samuel.

* * *

Deep in thought, I put the letter down on the table. Samuel's words were a lot more heartfelt, open, and honest. It made me wonder what Nana Betty's response to his first letter contained. The tone of Samuel's words were a lot friendlier rather than the simple information dump that the first letter had been, which made it clear to me that Nana Betty had told him things that had made him open up a bit more.

I knew that Nana Betty had worked in a car factory during the war. Of course, car manufacturing had halted to make way for military vehicles and other equipment. Nana had told me that she sat on a production line stitching seats with about twenty other women. She'd been very proud of her wartime work, and had always been a proud supporter of the armed forces up until the day she died.

Grandpa Albert had been in the army during the war, but hadn't spoken about it much. Nana Betty said it was because he'd seen some horrible things during his time on the front line in France, had lost far too many friends in front of him.

I could never have imagined what it was like living during times like that, and didn't particularly want to. Rationing, air raid sirens, and not being sure if anyone you loved would survive the end of the day or week.

Sighing, I put the letter back into the envelope and resisted the temptation to read another. It was late, and my mind was going a mile a minute. I needed to get some sleep, but knew I would lie in the dark thinking about the war and the people who lived through it.

Waking up with a jolt, I fumbled with the lamp on my bedside table. Once the warm light filled the room, I took a look at the clock and saw it was almost three a.m.

Sitting up and rubbing my eyes, I tried to work out what had woken me up. I had been dreaming I'd been in London during the war, and an air raid siren had been blaring. Running from a nice warm bed to a local tube station to get underground and protected was the last thing I could remember before waking up.

Wide awake and knowing there'd be no chance of me falling back to sleep anytime soon, I climbed out of my bed, pulled on my dressing gown and slippers, and made my way down to the kitchen to make a drink. Once I was done, I went into the living room and sat on the sofa, sipping my drink and staring at the stack of letters still on the coffee table in front of me.

My fingers twitched as I gazed at the two I had already read, shifting my eyes slowly to the pile I was yet to read. Making the decision to read at least another, regardless of the time, I put my tea down and grabbed the next letter. Before I opened it, I shot off a text to my boss to tell him I was unwell, and wouldn't be able to make it into work for my shift. Feeling guilty at bailing for the first time my working life, I turned my phone off and opened the envelope.

* * *

18 July 1942

Dearest Betty,

I have a spare five minutes before we head out for a late-night flight... that's all I can say, sorry; so, I thought I'd quickly pen you another letter. It'll only be a short note, but I need to take my mind off what is coming.

I'm so glad me and Jimmy were able to get to London a couple weeks ago. It was the perfect tonic for feeling more and more wound up, and if I'm honest, the best bit was seeing you again. Holding you while we slow danced was the most amazing thing to have happened to me in a long while. You not only looked absolutely beautiful, you smelled gorgeous – is that a strange thing for me to say? I hope not, because it's one thing that has kept me going the past few days; well, that and the kiss we shared as I walked you home after the party.

Something I never said at the time, and should have, was that I was so honoured when you told me it was your first ever. Never have I felt so overwhelmed with emotion.

Jesus, I'm so sappy, but I make no apologies. You've humbled me and made me so happy all at the same time, and I don't think there's any way I could ever thank you.

Well, that's kind of all I wanted to say – I feel guilty I was unable to say it to our face, but it needed to be said.

Yours,

Samuel.

Chapter 3

Finally, I fell asleep at almost six a.m. I'd stared at the hastily scribbled note that had contained hints at Samuel falling in love with Nana Betty. For almost two hours, I wondered if she'd felt the same, wondered if his feelings were one-sided; I wished I had Nana Betty's letters to Samuel to get the whole story.

It had been a long time since I'd had a lie in beyond nine a.m., but that morning, I slept in until almost mid-day. Sitting up in bed, feeling completely disorientated, my head pounded from the extra sleep that was at odds with my usual routine. Glad I'd decided to take the day off from work, I made my way to the kitchen, so I could have a cup of strong coffee and some painkillers.

Without hanging around, I went into the living room to where the letters were still where I left them on the table. I picked the next one up and pulled it from the envelope.

* * *

31 July 1942

Dearest Betty,

Thank you for coming to visit me at the hospital last week. My leg is much better now; I should be cleared for duty very soon, so I can get back to my crew. I still feel so very embarrassed about the entire thing. I'm supposed to be here, defending mine and your country, but I can't even walk across base without slipping over and spraining my ankle.

Like I told you when you came to see me, the guys in my crew ribbed me relentlessly. Apparently, I'm the only one who would get injured during wartime, but not actually on the front line. Only I could injure myself enough to wind up in bed for almost two weeks. They enjoyed teasing me far too much, and all I could think about was you.

Help Our Heroes

You looked radiant that day, and I can't rid myself of the mental image of you in that dress you wore; not that I want to. The fella in the bed next to me told me, after you left, that you're a 'right looker' – I'm a bit smug that, not only do I know what that means, but you came to visit me.

Oh, I'm sure you already saw it, but I sent you a copy of the picture the nurse took of us in the gardens of the hospital. I bribed one of my crew with a pack of smokes to develop the roll of film from my camera, and he gave me two copies of that one without me asking him to. I hope you treasure your copy as much as I do mine.

Once I'm discharged from the hospital, I'll be straight back to the base and back into missions. I don't know when I'll get a chance to see you again, and I hope I'll have the time to write to you as regular as I have been.

Yours,
Samuel.

* * *

There was no photograph in the envelope, nor was it in the hat box the letters had been stored in. I hadn't expected it to be and decided to rummage through the piles and piles of photos and albums Nana Betty used to have scattered around the house. I'd gathered them all together and squeezed them into a bookcase in the small bedroom. It was a room I hadn't been in since she had died, and I was dreading setting foot inside it, but I *really* wanted to know if Nana Betty had kept the photo of Samuel, all this time.

Putting the letter down, I took a deep breath before standing and slowly making my way to the bottom of the stairs. It took me a couple of minutes to gear up the strength to put my foot on the bottom step, and to continue to the very top.

The smallest bedroom had always been used as an office when Grandpa Albert worked from home during his time as an insurance broker, but since he had passed, it was more of a dumping ground that Nana Betty hadn't bothered keeping on top of. When she had died, it had taken me days to sort through everything, but I managed it, then shut the door without going back inside since.

Opening the door, I paused once more. Everything belonging to both of my grandparents I couldn't bear to part with was stored in this room. There wasn't much, but enough to flood me with memories of both good and bad times in my life.

Sucking in a shaky breath, I stepped inside, and closed the door behind me. I went straight to the shelves next to the old desk, and began to pull out all of Nana Betty's beloved photo albums. My grandmother was meticulous with her organisation of her photographs. Every album was dated, and each photo had a caption listing the names of those in the shot, and the date it was taken. I finally found the album from 1942-3.

So many photos of Nana Betty and her best friend, Aunty Maggy – who obviously *wasn't* my aunt, but was as close as. She'd been mentioned in the letters from Samuel, but I hadn't made the connection until I flicked through the photos of the two women in their youth. I was disappointed when I reached the end and there was no photograph of the elusive Samuel, and I flicked the final page over in frustration. Stuck on the inside of the back cover was an envelope, unsealed.

Carefully, I pulled the contents out. There were a few ticket stubs from train journeys and dances. Then, what I was looking for. A small black and white photograph of Nana Betty smiling radiantly, sitting on a garden bench next to a good looking young man who was sat in a wheelchair, his legs covered with a blanket.

Due to the lack of colour to the picture, I couldn't tell what colour his eyes and hair were beyond dark, but he was very handsome. He looked nothing like Grandpa Albert who was very fair, and I found myself to be relieved.

Carefully, I put everything back in it's place, and took the photograph downstairs to where the letters were waiting for me. Now I had a picture reference of the man who wrote to my grandmother.

* * *

19 August 1942

Dearest Betty,

Just another quick note. Myself and my crew have just returned from another successful mission, and I wanted to speak to someone other than the guys. I know writing a letter isn't the same as speaking face to face, but it'll have to do

Help Our Heroes

for now.

    I received a package from my parents this week. Full of my favorite candy and other things. I've included some of the candy for you to share with Maggy and your other friends. I know, thanks to rationing, that you don't get much chocolate and other candy. It's not much, but I hope you enjoy it.

    Me and Jimmy may be back in London soon, but we're unsure at the moment. I wanted to let you know. I really miss you and can't wait to be back with you. Hopefully, I'll have the time to take you out for a proper date. I've been saving all my pay so we can get dinner, and maybe head to a theatre to watch a movie. Without Jimmy and Maggy, if that's okay with you. I love that red-haired idiot, but I would love some time with just you. I can promise your parents that nothing untoward would happen.

    I better sign off. It's crazy ass o'clock in the morning, and the adrenaline is wearing off. The crash is going to hit hard.

    Yours,

    Samuel.

To Be Continued…

* * *

    I honestly hope you have enjoyed *Dearest Betty* so far. I will strive to get it completed as quickly as possible, so I am able to release the full novel once the anthology is taken off sale.

Leaving Home

Alyvia Paige

She's my best friend's little sister.

I'd just enlisted in the United States Army.

The two reasons that I should stay away are the very same reasons why I can't.

The opinionated, headstrong, gorgeous woman captured my attention when she refused to back down from a challenge. I kissed her on the tarmac and murmured a quick goodbye.

All choices have consequences, it's how we handle them that morph the challenges we'll face.

The question is, will Teagan choose to back off of our newly formed relationship or will she rise to the challenge with me?

Chapter 1

Teagan

"Ben you promised!" I shout and stomp my foot like a five-year-old in the midst of a tantrum.

"Teag, I already told you Tucker is going so you'll have the next best thing to me. He'll also make sure to keep the douchebags at bay."

"It's just... Ben, it's our last year for Fright Night over Atlanta. Six Flags in the pitch black of night is a tradition!" My frustration turns to sadness as it hits me all over again. I'm graduating in a few months and my big brother decided it would be a great plan to enlist in the United States Army. At least he doesn't have to ship out to basic for a few months.

"Teagan, it's fine. We've got time," he soothes. "Now dry your eyes and get ready." He shoots me a wink and smiles as his phone starts ringing.

"Love you!" I call after him as I make my way to my room. Once I'm in my room, I move to the makeup desk I have set up. Mom and dad purchased it as a study desk, but I have clearly made better use of it. I have everything organized; each item in its place as if the process of makeup application only works if everything is in its exact order. I sit with my brushes to the right, primer, concealer, and foundation at the helm and to the left is my mascara, blush, and eye shadow. Taking a deep breath and wiping my face dry, I get to work applying my Bare Minerals products, giving myself a natural look for the night. My overall made up face is still very much me, I'm not a transforming application kind of girl. I like to feel as if there is nothing there and look quite familiar to the me without makeup.

My phone pings just as I cap the mascara.

Tucker: Hey. Wanna grab some dinner before the bus leaves?
Me: Tuck, you don't have to go. I don't want you strong-armed to be Ben's

stand in.

Tucker: I'll never be strong armed by Ben. I'm stronger. Now, dinner?

Me: I'll be ready in 20

Tucker: Just looked into your window, you're done with your makeup. I'll be there in 10.

The man staring at me from his bedroom window of his childhood home is none other than Tucker Elliot Hoyt. Ben's best friend, the golden boy both internally and externally and stands at least six feet. His athletic build and smoldering eyes, not that he uses them to his advantage, at least not with me. He doesn't see me that way. He's the sweetest guy I've ever known, even in comparison to Ben, and he's an amazing sibling. I'd crushed on Tucker since we were all kids. Nevertheless, I've given up on that fantasy when Tucker left for college two years ago. He has options I don't dare myself to compare to. But I have to say, he's always coming to the rescue. Even living two hours away at college.

"Teagan," my mother's voice echoes off the stairwell into my room. "Tuck is here."

Grabbing my jacket from the hall closet, I smile up at Tucker when I see his oversized hoodie over a plaid flannel and jeans. October in Alabama is beautiful but the temperature can drop at night, and then add in riding rides, it gets chilly.

Fine.

I'm being dramatic.

It's like 60 degrees, but that's cold.

"I'm ready." I smile brightly. "Bye parentals, don't wait up." I call out over my shoulder and push Tucker's tushy to move out the door.

"In a hurry, smalls?" Tucker's smile is teasing as he rounds his lifted truck. "So, I was thinking Figo. Is that alright?"

"Sure, though I'm not that hungry."

Tucker glances at me then returns his gaze to the road. "You'll eat. It's pasta; you've never not eaten pasta."

Help Our Heroes

"No *Dad*, not if I'm not hungry," I sass.

"I ain't your daddy, but you are skinnier than you were just a few months ago when I left for school. You need food."

I blush at his acknowledgment and turn my attention out the window. Warmth settles over me as Tucker's hand imprints on my thigh.

"Teag, you alright?" He chuckles; the jerk actually enjoys watching my discomfort.

"Uh, yeah. I'm uhm, I'm fine," I stammer and refuse to make eye contact.

"You need me to flip the air on? You're looking a bit flushed." His playful tone catches my attention and earns him a glare.

"Stop messing with me, dick." I laugh and push his hand off my leg.

"But it's so easy, and I'm pretty sure you like it."

"Ugh, just drive Romeo." I laugh at his scoff and then sigh as my body temperature begins to lower.

"Let's go, Juliette," Tucker singsongs as he holds the door open to the fast stop Italian and Panini press restaurant.

"Jerk."

We continue our playful banter back and forth in line as we order and while devouring our delectable carbs. Just another day. Tucker may be best friends with my brother, but we're close too. Sometimes, heart achingly close. I've trained my mind to not want Tucker Elliot Hoyt, but my heart sometimes forgets. A lot.

And God, he makes it so hard to remember it's a bad idea.

Chapter 2

Tucker

Teagan squirms under my gaze. She always has. I used to tease her for fun but now I have to remind myself to back off. To not lead her on. To be the best friend, not the boyfriend. Her life is about to change in more than one way. Ben was just texting me this morning about Nancy wanting to relocate to Minnesota. Who in the hell wants to move to Minnesota? It snows there. Balls freeze off there. No thanks. Not to mention it's a long fucking distance for a weekend trip.

"Now you look like *you're* thinking too much," Teagan's soft voice breaks through my thoughts.

"I was, but I'm good." Twisting a huge heap of fettucine noodles onto my fork, I ask, "How's school going?"

"School is school. Jameson asked me to prom, but I haven't given him an answer yet." Teagan's shrug is noncommittal as she continues to eat.

"Jameson? What a little shit." I mumble. He's not good enough for Teag. Hell, no one is.

Not even me.

"What was that?" she probes although I know good and well she heard me.

"He's trash. Say no."

"Tucker, he's fine. He's nice," she argues, "I'll be graduating in a few months anyway. Early grad, remember?"

"Mm hmm." I roll my eyes then continue eating until I've cleared my plate. I need to remember, I have no right to butt in.

* * *

"I still don't know why I couldn't just drive us, Teagan."

"Because it's fun to ride with the group. Just. Sit." Teagan pushes me into an old school bus bench seat and plops down next to me.

"If you say so." I shrug and make myself comfortable. I don't miss the current passing through our jeans as our legs rest snugly against each other. The only part of us not touching is our hands and heads. A peace I haven't felt in quite a while settles over me as I rest my head against the back of the seat.

About 20 minutes into the ride, I feel her eyes on me. She hasn't moved her body which tells me it's only her head turned toward me.

"What Teag?" I ask with a smirk.

"Nothing," she whispers in response then sighs softly.

I untuck my hands from the pocket of my hoodie, pull it off and toss it into a heap in my lap. Resituating myself, I settle and link pinky fingers with Teagan. When we were little kids, it was our secret code. Interlock and squeeze means all is well.

"Tuck," she whispers again, but I ignore the warning in her voice and rest our hands at the joining of our legs where no nosy ass could see that we had our fingers were interlocked. It's not that I mind the physical connection hidden by the hoody, but Teag needs a quiet, non-harassed life. These blood-sucking gossipers would make her life hell until the next story breaks. I close my eyes and relax again into the seat, enjoying the warmth from both the hoodie and the connection with Teagan.

***

"Alright, I know you're all grown, kind of, however, you need to shut your mouths and listen up." Roger, the church youth leader shouts over the rambunctious group of teens ranging in age from 15 – 18 as well as some young adults that were once in the youth department before heading off to college.

We've been members of the Brick Church of Cullman since birth. Every Sunday and Wednesday we were there, sitting in the front rows during service and on the couches during the teen sessions. We dressed in our best clothes and paid attention. Learning life lessons and building relationships in a safe place.

"Thank you. As I was saying," Roger pauses ensuring everyone's attention. "Stay in groups. Act and behave like the respectable kids you are. No dark blue, no hot pink and no purple. This is a boy – boy, girl – girl and boy – girl free-from-contact event. Remember we are watching and so is your Maker."

I cough into my sleeve as Roger drones on and receive an elbow to the gut from Teag.

"Now, go forth, have fun. We leave the park at twelve-thirty. Be at the entrance by that time."

All at once, the group of sixty-seven disperses in different directions.

"Does a group actually require more than two people? I'm good with being a massive group of two," I grumble as a handful of Teagan's twiggy gymnastic team members linger to see where she goes. She's the queen of this pack no matter if she wants to be or not. It's a Finley family quality, love it or hate it.

Chapter 3

Teagan

"Oh Tuck, it's fine." I snicker. He loathes when the girls blankly stand around as if they have no brain to take action without direction. I mean, I get it. It annoys me too.

"Mm hmm." Nudging me with his right side, he begins walking toward the Batman ride.

"Ugh, I don't like this ride, Teagan!" Bella George is already bellyaching. She lasted a whole ten minutes, folks.

"Then don't ride it," Tucker grumps.

"I don't think I was talking to you, Tucker Hoyt." She pouts and flips her hair over her shoulder then storms forward.

"Such a meanie head," I feign disdain and shove him. He barely stumbles before bending slightly and grasping me at the back of my thighs. Tossing me over his shoulder effortlessly, he laughs. "Put me down, you brute!" I shout through my own laughter.

"You should be nicer to your elders, Teagan Marie."

"Oh no! Pulling out the middle name. Shi…stuffs getting real now," I sass.

Tucker deposits me at the front of the fast pass line. Yes, we're those people that will pay more money to wait less time. Those that don't aren't normal. I mean, who willingly enjoys waiting in line? Oh wait… three-fourths of our group. That's who.

"Front of the ride, Teag. You know the drill," Tucker's deep voice tickles my ear as he nudges me forward. Gooseflesh breaks out covering me head to toe.

The random flirting and boundary pushing continued from one end of the park to the other. We rode the Goliath, my favorite ride three times and are in line for the fourth and final time. It scales over twenty stories in height then drops out going speeds of up to seventy miles per hour through 4,480 feet of track.

"Teagan, just ride the next cart back. Otherwise you'll be three ahead of us." Bella whines.

"It's fine. We'll wait for you at the exit," Tucker repeats for the second time, agitation lacing his words.

Seventy miles per hour. One minute and forty-five seconds. That's how long I treasured Tucker holding my hand. His long calloused thumb stroking mine gently. I wasn't scared; I've ridden this ride more times than I can count. Still, the comfort calmed me, gave me a sense of peace that I usually don't have.

The seat restraints unlock and we exit the loading and unloading dock quickly so the next group can go. I look back and just as Bella had whined, they'll be three rides behind us.

"Come on Teag, we'll wait on the exit ramp." Tucker places his hand on the small of my back again, causing a flurry of heat to course through my veins, settlings in my belly and at the apex of my thighs. Just down the first winding ramp, I stop and lean against the wood railing. Tucker stops just beside me, our bodies touching.

With a gentle sweep of his hand, Tucker brushes a few wisps of hair from my face tucking them behind my ear. "You're flushed again, Teag," he says standing in front of me now, his eyes roaming my face.

"Hmm, must be the adrenaline," I murmur. My tongue quickly darts out, wetting my lips, as I watch Tucker's eyes focus intently on them.

"Teag," his voice pleading, lusty, conflicted. "Tell me no."

I shake my head no to his request as his face moves toward mine I've been waiting for this moment for as long as I can remember. Even if my head knows I should be saying no, I can't, I can't tell my heart to follow. "Not saying no, Tucker," I whisper.

I inhale just before his lips caress mine gently, expertly. My body feels as if it's engulfed in flames. His hands find my cheeks and move into my hair. My lips part and our kiss deepens as I moan into his mouth, hardly aware of the people exiting the ride. Never in my wildest fantasies that I was kissing Tucker Elliot Hoyt, did it feel like this.

Help Our Heroes

Tucker is turning me to mush; I'm putty in his hands. Gliding my fingers up his stomach feeling the valleys of his abs, I reach his taut shoulders and squeeze his traps as hard as I'm having to squeeze my thighs to ease my pulsing and aching core.

"Teagan," Tucker murmurs against my lips. "Shit, I've wanted to do that for years."

"Years?" I whisper, panting as our eyes lock. Tucker moves in to kiss me again, this time a brief, firm peck.

"You're Ben's baby sister, one of my best friends. I've wanted you for well over a decade." Resting his forehead to mine, I get lost in his adoring gaze. That is, until the cackling of kids fly past us.

"Jesus, Teag, You drive me mad." Tucker exhales and leans in and pours his assault on my lips, tugging my hair from the messy ponytail, but then pulls away abruptly. "Shit!"

"Tuck," I gasp out. When he looks away, I almost burst into tears. A moment I've dreamt of so quickly vanishing. It's as if he's realized I'm his greatest mistake.

"Teagan, I shouldn't have done that… this. I just crossed so many lines. Shit."

Grabbing his face, I pull his attention to me. "Tucker Elliot Hoyt," I say definitively, "don't do that. Don't look at me like I'm a mistake." My eyes begin to cloud with tears as I wait for the final impact of his dismissal. What can I expect? I know he's got an ocean of opportunity in college. As he said, he shouldn't have done it.

Caressing my cheeks, he brushes away my tears. "No man, not even me, worth keeping or holding your attention should make you cry." Tucker's lips find mine quickly, biting my bottom lip before resting his forehead to mine. "This might be messy, me and you. But you'll never be a mistake." He assures me.

"I'm not scared of a little mess or hard work. I didn't make it to all-state by pussing out."

"That's the thing. It shouldn't be work. If it's meant to be, it will be. One promise, Teag. Promise we–"

"Where are they?" We hear Bella's voice before she sees us, thanks to the dark corner we're situated in. With heavy sighs and an unfinished conversation, we separate ourselves. And almost instantly, I miss his warmth.

"Hey guys!" I feign excitement when they approach us causing Tucker to burst into laughter as I fix my tousled hair.

Chapter 4

Tucker

Me: Hey
Teag: Hi
Me: Wyd?
Teag: Just got home from practice
Me: Nice and limber then
Teag: Tucker Elliot Hoyt
Me: I like when you use my full name Teag
Teag: You coming over for tacos and movies?
Me: Have I ever missed Saturday dinner and movie nights
Teag: Um yes, when you were dating big boobs Barbie
Me: Really? You refused to allow her in your house!
Teag: DUH!
Me: Aww Teag, you sayin you've been crushing on me just as long as I've been with you?
Teag: Maybe
Me: Mhmm
Teag: I've got to shower this stink off
Me: …
Teag: … what? Get real!
Me: …
Teag: … naked, wet, BYE!
Me: evil. See you in 30

After getting control of my painfully erected cock, I throw on some joggers and a sideless tank then grab my Vanderbilt fitted hat and make my way across the yard.

Knocking on the sliding glass door leading into the Finley's kitchen, I pull it open and greet Nancy and Bob.

"Hey Tucker!" Nancy beams and pulls me in for a hug. "Did you and Teagan enjoy Fright Fest?"

"Hey Mama, Hey Pops," I smile shaking Bob's hand. "It was a blast. I think we rode everything at least twice."

I sense Teagan before I see her, my head quickly turning toward the doorway. "We rode Goliath the most." she says before pivoting around quickly to take water bottle from the refrigerator, I smile as she continues, "although, it would have been more fun if Bella hadn't insisted on being clingy and obnoxious."

I smile as I take her in, tight as fuck spandex leggings, an open sided Vanderbilt tank with a neon green sports bra. Heaven.

"Aww now, Teagan, she's just sad you're graduating early without her." Nancy empathizes.

"No, she wanted to climb Tucker's leg and rub him like a cat in heat!" Teagan blurts out with jealously.

Not expecting the comment, I was mid-swallow with a mouthful of water. Effectively shocked, I spray water everywhere as I choke up the fluid stuck in my windpipe.

"Jesus, Teagan." I cough harder.

"It's the truth," she states firmly.

"Alright kids, here's the tub of popcorn, I'll clean up this mess. Ben and Marilyn are already in the movie room." Nancy chuckles as she shoos us away.

Halfway down the hall, I tug Teagan's ponytail, stopping her in her tracks. The hall is empty, Nancy and Bob can be heard in the distance, and Ben and my older sister Marilyn are already in the home theater.

"Tu–" Teagan begins before my lips crash down on hers.

"Remember what I said?" I whisper against her already swelled lips.

"Nope," she teases and drags her tongue over her jutted out lower lip.

"I missed you," I confess easily.

"I missed you too. I always do. Every time you leave, I miss you. But

Tucker, we can't..." I cut her off with another kiss only pulling away to catch our breath.

"You go back to school Monday and I know I don't compete with the college crowd. In so many ways, I don't compete." Teagan's voice is timid, unsure. We've not talked about what this is that we're beginning to explore.

"They've got nothin' on you, gorgeous." I smile as her cheeks pink. Kissing her forehead, I smack her ass and turn the doorknob to the in-home theater to see the always-awkward moment of my best friend sucking face with my sister. Guess that's a little contradictory now that I've acted on my desire to be with Teagan.

"Knock it off!" Teagan laughs as she throws a handful of popcorn at their heads.

I take my usual spot on the sofa, kick out the footrest, Teagan settles against the opposite end, and rests her head on the armrest, propping her feet onto my lap. Previously this was a move that I refused to take much stock in, but that's a bit difficult as the little minx is resting her bare foot against my hardening cock.

"Mari," I call out garnering my sister's attention. "Throw me that blanket, please?"

"Hold up!" Ben shouts, sitting up to look more closely at the opening of the movie. "Who the fuck picked this?" He asks, as the title *Fifty Shades Darker* covers the screen. Teagan and Marilyn erupt into a fit of laughter before my sister hops up and changes the movie to *Girls' Trip*.

"Why?" Ben moans as if he is in pain.

"Get over it ya big baby," Teagan sasses as I grab her feet and squeeze the arches.

Chapter 5

Teagan

Sunday, the day of church, family lunch, and game nights. I have to admit everything seems a bit bizarre. Ben swears in tomorrow and will leave soon after that. I'm still not okay with this, not even a little bit. Tucker seems to be anxious as well. I'm not sure what that's about, but as I stare at his profile, I see that he, too, has changed quite a bit this fall while being away. Ben says he's trying to one-up him.

"What's up Tuck?" I ask. If he fails to answer, I'm going to pull out his full name, since he apparently likes it when I say it.

"Just thinking," he murmurs and winks at me, which in turn causes my stupid cheeks to heat. Yeah, this between us has me acting all girly and weird. "Careful babe, you're blushing," he taunts.

"Shaddup," I laugh as we make our way toward the family fleet of vehicles.

"Tuck. Lunch, right man?" This comes from my brother as he hangs out the passenger side door from the back of my parents' Tahoe.

"Yeah, idiot, just like always." Tucker shoots back.

"Sis, let's go!" Ben claps his hand against the roof of the car.

Once we're home, I take off upstairs and change into some sweats and a t-shirt. Washing my face clear of makeup, I pull my thick locks into my signature messy bun. Mom's in the den when I get downstairs, watching the US trial ice-skating competition for the upcoming Olympics.

"Heya, mom!" I shout intentionally to startle her and laugh when she jumps.

"Darn it, Teagan Marie. Stop that." She smiles and takes me in. "Care to tell me anything?" she pries. You know that thing about moms always knowing stuff before you tell them? I swear, it's real. All. The. Time.

"No clue what you're talking about." I lie as Ben, Marilyn, and Tucker make their way into the room quietly arguing.

"What's up kids?" Dad asks from the opposite doorway.

"Oh just bitching about these damn basic training physical requirements," Ben grumps.

"Benjamin!" Mom scolds, "language."

"Sorry, mama."

"What's so hard about your physical requirements?" I ask.

"Two minutes of push-ups hitting thirty-five, minimum, then another two minutes of sit-ups and that count needs to meet, but should exceed forty-seven, and last, but certainly not least, a two-mile run in sixteen minutes and thirty-six seconds."

I think over what he's just listed off. It doesn't sound that hard. Pulling out my phone, I look up what he just said from memory, not because I think he's lying but because that doesn't seem that impossible. Then I see it. That's for basic training. They, meaning the United States Army, up the ante to graduate Advanced Individual Training.

"Teag," Tucker starts to warn me before Ben realizes what I'm thinking... a challenge.

"Oh, Lil' Miss Prissy seems to want a challenge. It's dancing in your beady little eyes," he laughs. "I bet by the time we – I – swear in tomorrow 'til whenever we bus out, and add the ten weeks of basic, you cannot surpass the female version of the physical aptitude test." Ben is so sure of his proposed wager, a cocky smile sweeps over his face. He'll never learn to stop underestimating me.

"No," I object and then up the ante. Listen I never said, I was a thinking-on-my-feet kind of gambler. "One-thousand bucks, when I surpass the male physical aptitude that is required before graduating Advanced Individual Training" My confidence knows no bounds, just as it doesn't when I'm competing in meets.

"Ha!" Ben barks out. "When you fail, you owe me... hmm Tuck, what should she owe me?"

I can't help the chuckle that breaks through my skeptical pursed lips. "Yeah, Tuck. What say you?"

My incredibly good looking, smoldering, holy shit what's going on with me? Tucker coughs, and with his brow arched and a smirk on his lips, he stares me down right back. A tingling sensation ripples over me, head to toe.

"Ben, you really shouldn't challenge her, I mean, she always wins." Marilyn adds.

"Nope, I win and you do my laundry for six months once I'm off barrack assignments."

He's so cute. All serious and cocky. Really, it's adorable. I'm going to smoke his ass. Not a single doubt in my mind.

* * *

Tucker: Hey
Me: Hi <3
Tucker: What's up
Me: I'm just staring at my ceiling
Tucker: Why?
Me: Trying to figure out what's going on with us, I guess.
Tucker: Huh, me too
Tucker: Open your window
Tucker: Teagan. Open it. Please
Me: I'm comfy
Tucker: I see you moving around
Me: Stupid hall light

I quickly close my door and flip the lock to ensure no one simply waltzes in, then make my way to my window and open it all the way, just as Tucker's head rises above the bottom frame. This isn't the first time my window has been used over the years. Being separated by a yard of maybe twelve feet wide, we kept a collapsible ladder tucked away for Ben, Marilyn, Tucker, and even me to escape out or come in either house.

"Hey." Before I can respond, Tucker's lips are on mine. Slow, passionate, intentional kisses that quickly deepen as our tongues fight for control. I sigh into

Help Our Heroes

Tucker's mouth as a dance of passion unfurls within me.

"Hi," I wisp breathlessly and smile. "Gotta say, that's a first."

"Hopefully not the last," Tucker responds ruefully.

"Whoa," I whisper and pull back to observe the sorrowful chocolate brown eyes watching me carefully.

"Sorry, long night," he tries to explain, pulling me into his arms, holding me tightly against his chest and rests his chin on the top of my head.

"Tucker?" I can feel the deep breath expel from his body, his muscles contracting against mine.

"Hmm?" he hums.

"I'm worried about Ben; that he'll be alone. That he doesn't get what he's signing up to do."

"I know you're worried Teag, but he gets it. He thought long and hard about it, weighing his pros and cons." Tucker's voice is like a balm soothing my heart, word by word through his certainty. "It'll be alright. I promise."

Tucker unwraps our arms from each other and tugs me toward the bed. Once we're both situated and tucked in together, his sighs and looks past me toward the wall. Bringing his eyes back to mine, he smiles and places a gentle kiss to my forehead.

"Teagan?" This is my Tucker, the part of himself that I choose to believe he only reserves for me. His voice void of playfulness, he's serious, compassionate, thoughtful. Oh, the personalities you can learn in a person over nearly two decades of friendship.

"Hmm?"

"I want this, us. Even when I'm not here."

"I do too, but how? You cant tell me you're okay with a long distance relationship, especially with me still here 'til the fall." I try to lay out all my reasoning and fears without showing my insecurity, that I'm not enough. Not for him.

"Really?" He laughs then kisses my nose before continuing. "Gorgeous, you graduate in a few months, you'll be eighteen by then, and college is college. If I wanted to date there, I would. But I haven't because what I want, is you. It's always been you, Teag, it's always going to be you.

"Yeah?" I ask tentatively, tucking my head in and against his chest.

"No matter where I am, where you are, it's home." Tucker fits his hand to my chest, resting it over my heart. "This is my home."

I move quickly, my lips slowly kissing up his neck, suckling my way up to his chin, and landing on his perfectly full lips. Hip to hip, chest to chest we lay on our sides, exploring each other without words. Tucker's free hand tangles in my still damp hair. Pull it roughly as he assaults my lips. His kisses feel needy, full of longing, and passionate, as if conveying the words he just said.

My bare hand presses against the corded muscles that line his frame. Wetness gathers at the apex of my thighs as my desire skyrockets out of this world. I've never done the deed, I'd always thought, felt, and been taught, that it should be saved for your one and only. Tucker knows this, and while I know he won't push me, a part of me prays he will.

Tucking his knee between my legs, I feel his hardness pressing against me. Our exploration continues, his hand finding my hip as I rock against his muscled thigh, and then slips into my baggy nightshirt.

"We should stop," he murmurs, his lips now assaulting my neck.

"No, don't stop. Please Tucker, don't stop." I pant. Removing my hand from his bare back, I stroke his hard cock from the outside of his joggers. Jesus Murphy, it's huge. I gasp, causing another warning to spring from Tucker.

"Teagan," he growls as he cups my naked breast.

"Tucker, make me come."

Chapter 6

Tucker

"Make me come," her whispered plea nearly causes me to misfire like a sixteen-year-old inexperienced teenage boy.

"Fuck," I growl into her neck. As much as I want to take her, maker her mine, I can't. I remind myself of all the reasons why as she continues to ride my thigh. She's unaware that I too joined to service with Ben. She's a virgin. She's not eighteen for a little over a month. But mostly, because I need her to know and understand the magnitude of this decision.

"Please, Tucker..." her seductive murmur blasts out my own logic almost entirely. *Almost.*

Pulling back slightly, I find her swollen lips turned up into a confident and playful smile. I can't resist. I'll never be able to resist when it comes to Teagan. Melding our lips together rekindles the embers that were my intentions to keep from igniting. I always knew we'd have this kind of passion if we ever explored it. My imagination did not let me down.

"I can't Teagan." I pull back, my breath heavy. "You're not of age yet, it's your first time, and I ..." I trail off as her eyes cloud with tears.

"Wow," she mutters, trying to look away but I pull her face back to mine with my thumb and forefinger.

"No, look at me Teag; I've loved you even before I liked you. Of that, I am certain. But your first time, *our* first time, will not be in your childhood bedroom where we'll likely wake at least one person, thus ruining the second most important moment of us."

"What us," she sasses. Anger. Embarrassment. Frustration. I see it all in her amber eyes. But mostly, it's hurt.

"You and me, us. You're worried about Ben finding out that we're even entertaining this idea, your parents. You ready to tell me your ready for this step?" With the moment now lost, I wipe her tears away and place a chaste kiss to her lips. "You're my heart Teagan. My home. If you don't want that, tell me now. I know you've got a lot more exploration in this life left, but I'm yours. I'll wait."

Teagan's mouth quirks up on the left, like it typically does when she's being sarcastic and playful. My heart finally begins to slow as I wait for her words. "You'll wait for me, yet here I am, drenched and ready, and you're making me wait?"

"Listen, smartass, you know what I meant."

"You're infuriating, Tucker Elliot Hoyt!" She growls out my name before kissing me into oblivion. My brain short circuits and before I know it we're both panting and pawing each other as if it's our last moment to live. Well, I guess it'll be mine if anyone busts through that doorway.

Repositioning us so Teagan is on her back and I'm pressed against her side, I move my hand from her tangled hair skimming her bare breast and across her trembling, taut stomach.

"Please," she whispers into my ear before capturing my gaze and lifting her hips. My hand slips into her barely there panties then brushes against her bare skin just before finding the pool of wet heat. Swirling her desire around and over her swollen sex, I quickly capture her moan with a searing kiss.

"Shhh," I order while pressing our foreheads together as I continue my ministrations against her squirming body. I smile as her gasps fill the room after I insert a finger relishing the tight wet center. Teagan's breathing is heavy as I pump in and out of her, watching her eyes burn into mine. I press my thumb to the enlarged bud causing her orgasm to detonate as she silently cries out in pleasure, grasping the pillow in one hand and my neck in the other.

I kiss her soft and slow as she comes down from her orgasm, pulling my hand away as she breaks the kiss and sucks in much needed air.

"Hey," she smiles.

"Hi," I chuckle watching her face soften.

"Um, yeah, so what you were saying earlier..." Her yawn cuts out the words she tries to say so I assume I know what she means in terms of me wanting her to be mine.

"Mm hmm?"

"I'm in. Yours. No other chick gets you. No part of you unless it's a platonic, and I mean *very* platonic, friendship."

"Shit," I laugh, "I give you one orgasm, and you come back swinging." I smile and kiss her temple.

"By the way," she whispers, "I'm pretty sure mom knows something is up. I just didn't want Ben to stress with his swearing in tomorrow."

"Let's not talk about your parents or Ben directly after a moment we just had, hmm?" Libido gone. Ice-cold water just doused any embers that were remaining. I need to tell her it's not just Ben swearing in tomorrow. But I can't. I'm a coward. I plant another kiss firmly to her lips and crawl from the bed.

Yawning she asks, "See you tomorrow?"

"You certainly will, now get some rest. You only have a few hours before practice and school."

Chapter 7

Teagan

My alarm jolts me awake. Once Tucker left, I sank back into my bed, soaked up his scent left behind, and quickly drifted to sleep. And I slept hard. Just as any other day, I reach for my iPhone, see the missed messages, and missed snapchats from my gymnast team.

Tucker: Sleep sweet, gorgeous. See you this afternoon.
Tucker: Good Morning, my plans for the day got sideswiped. I missed a few important emails and messages yesterday. I'll see you at Ben's swearing in.
Me: I hope everything is okay. See you in a few hours

I quickly open my group snapchat and laugh loudly when I see Bella eat mat after a tumbling pass goes bad at last night's optional late open gym. The girl tried to pull a Biles, two back flips followed by a half twist. Except she had a faulty take off and didn't make it out of the second flip. We can't all be Olympians.

* * *

"Hey mom, sorry I'm late. Did I miss anything?" I ask breathlessly.

"Oh sweetheart, you look beautiful this afternoon. Ben is in the second group."

"Don't I always look beautiful?" I implore then ask my actual question before she gets on to me about my sarcasm, like usual. "You're sure there isn't any bailing out, right?"

"No Teagan, he knew what he was doing when he signed that contract." My mother's answer is firm and her tone tells me there's no room for my childish inquisition today, but I usually always push the envelope. Challenges that are spoken, written, or assumed, I jump at them.

"Actually, I read that there are a few options."

"Teagan Marie Finley, hush. I will blister that bottom." She threatens. "Now, here comes Benjamin. Support him Teagan, be proud of him."

"I'm sorry, and I will," I whisper and lean back into my seat.

I feel Tucker's presence before I his greeting tickles my ears. It's mind boggling how aware my body is to his.

I smile and look him over. He fills out a suit way to well. Should I have dressed up more? I look from him to my mom who is wearing something similar to me, and shrug. Guess not.

"Hi," I smile as I look him over again. "Nice suit, handsome."

Tucker shrugs and links our pinkies as the officer begins addressing the fifteen enlistees.

"Recruits, remember both groups today are bussing out at thirteen thirty. That gives you about an hour or so to eat and get back to the main lot. Immediate family only to see the recruits off."

"Yes, Sir," they all respond in unison.

"Dismissed." And just like that we all file out of the room and head to lunch. Ben was initially supposed to bus out to basic training in January. After my birthday. After my graduation. But he got an email Saturday afternoon that revised his orders for departure to Fort Campbell.

Once back on the location of the recruiting office, we all make our way to the lot surrounded with families, some laughing, a lot crying. I hear a familiar laugh and my heart nearly pole vaults from my chest.

Why is Tucker here? And his family? Didn't the guy say immediate family only?

"Ten minutes," a man standing near the massive bus commands.

"That's our cue," Ben announces and starts his hugs, first to the Hoyt family skipping Tucker then to me. I fight back the tears when his arms loosen around me. "Hey, no tears. You've got quite the undertaking to go She-Hulk. I mean, I'm good with you doing my laundry too." Ben's words cause me to burst into laughter, sadness aside.

"In your dreams, Benny," I laugh as he pushes me back and moves on to mom and dad. I watch as Marilyn hugs Tucker tight but not until I hear my dad tell the boys to behave does it all click. My hand clutches my chest as my body is crashed against the one person who calms my world. Except he's the reason that I'm going into a tailspin.

"Tucker," I cry, "tell me you're kidding. Don't do this to me. To us. I just got you!"

"What's going on? What's she talking about?" I hear Ben growl just before mom tells him to hush.

"Teagan. You and me? We are stronger than a choice I made three months ago. I know I should have told you, but I didn't want to lose you before I could get you to see that we're meant to be. To try." Tucker's voice soothes me about as much as rubbing alcohol poured into a freshly opened wound.

"No," I sob, holding on as tight as I can, clinging to him in hopes that he changes his mind.

"Ten weeks, Teag. I'll see you in ten weeks." He promises.

"Why?"

"Because I needed to do this. Positive note," he chuckles, "Ben won't be left alone."

"You all lied to me, to my face." I conclude stepping out of Tucker's arms. I stand defensively as the man near the bus shouts a five-minute warning. It feels like we've been standing here for hours, yet seconds as I watch Tucker observe me. Hot streams of tears pour down my face as I look at my parents, Marilyn, The Hoyts, and my brother who looks as if he's about to murder Tucker. I guess that's one way to avoid enlistment.

"No," my mother rushes to try and fix this mess imploding in my chest.

"Round up. Let's go!"

"Teagan Marie Finley, I love you. I hope you know that and remember it often." Tucker's lips tentatively grace mine. "Ten weeks," he murmurs, "I'm betting on you. On us." His smile, while still beautiful, isn't as easy going as it usually is as he walks backward, keeping his eyes locked on mine

"Dude, what in the actual fuck!" I hear Ben roar as his closed fist collides with Tucker's face.

"Ben!" we all gasp in shock, all but Tucker. He shoots me a wink with his good eye, his right eye is already swelling, and shouts, "I love you Teag. Ten weeks and I'm coming home. I sure as hell hope you'll be there."

We all know he isn't literally coming home in ten weeks. Basic graduation then Advanced Individual Training commences. But it is in that exact moment that I truly understood Tucker's words from the night before when he said no matter where we were, no matter what we were doing, I was his home. I get it now, because he's mine.

The end!
… just kidding it's only the beginning!

A Military Anthology

Never Forget Him

Tracy Lorraine

Never Forget #1

I only knew him two weeks.

It was the best two weeks of my life.

He was the one.

He showed me what love was.

He taught me the pain of heartbreak.

He left something behind for me to keep forever.

Never Forget Him is the first instalment of Tracy Lorraine's steamy military duo, Never Forget.

Prologue

"Once upon a time there was a handsome soldier. He was strong and brave, and whisked the princess off her feet.

"The solider was a hero, fighting all the bad guys and giving people their lives back.

"He was more than that, though. He wasn't just the brave soldier, he was thoughtful and caring, funny, and a little bit of an idiot." I smile to myself as memories start playing out in my mind of his slightly wonky smile when he was winding me up, and the infectious sound of his laugh.

"One day, I'm going to be just like Daddy. I'm going be big and brave and rescue people," Denny says sleepily.

I stay where I am, sat on the edge of his bed, and watch as he loses the fight against sleep. Denny looks just like him. Most days I find it comforting, but there are times, like right now, after he's made me recite his nightly story, that it's painful. The memories of him threaten to rip me apart.

I gently sweep his hair from his forehead once I know he's fast asleep. "You already do that, baby boy. You rescue me every day," I whisper as I take one last look at his gorgeous, peaceful face.

Chapter 1

Five Years Ago...

"Erin, come on, at least look a little excited about this. It's your twentieth birthday, for fuck's sake," Frankie, my best friend, complains when I sit on her bed, looking less than enthusiastic about our night out.

"I'm good, Ki. I am looking forward to it," I lie. "It's just I'm—"

"Worried about your mum." Her words come out softer, showing she does understand. They still make me feel guilty, maybe I'm being a little too self-involved.

"I'm sorry. I'm going to forget all that and we're going to have an amazing night," I announce, summoning up as much excitement as I can muster.

Frankie is the ultimate party girl. She loves nothing more than spending all weekend either getting ready to go out, or being out and getting very drunk. That whole scene isn't really me; I much prefer to spend my Saturday night at home, in my den, working, but I don't have a chance in hell of getting away without going tonight, seeing as it's my birthday.

"Here, get this down your neck. It'll help chill you the fuck out," she says, thrusting a glass of vodka Red Bull at me.

"Haven't you got anything else?"

"Nope, suck it up. We're gonna get ourselves nice and drunk before heading out. Seeing as we're two weeks away from our next loan payments coming in, I'm fucking skint. We don't all have a cushy job like you," she says before necking her drink in one go. I, on the other hand, sip at the vile liquid before putting it down behind me. If I never taste vodka Red Bull again I'd be happy. "Although," she adds, with a wiggle of her eyebrows, "a little birdie told me there're some hot soldiers in town tonight. Maybe they'll buy us some drinks."

Help Our Heroes

I can't help but groan at her mention of soldiers. Frankie makes no secret of her desire to bed a hot army guy. She has some obsession with being the one to make a soldier's leave the best he's ever had, to let him use her to blow off steam before sending him packing to wherever it is he's based with some amazing memories and no intention of ever seeing him again.

"Oh, don't give me that, E. You know you'd want it if you had the chance."

I don't respond other than to lift my eyebrow at her. She knows exactly what I'd say, anyway. My dad was in the army and I watched what it did to Mum every time he left to go on tour. I vividly remember the day she answered the door and collapsed to the ground wailing before the men the other side had even spoken. From as early as I can remember, I've said I'd never touch a man in the army. Dad broke my mum—totally shattered her. I never want to experience anything like that. Ever.

"Anyway, what do you think?" Frankie asks as she holds a small piece of silver glitzy fabric in front of her.

"I think it looks about the right size to be a dishcloth, Ki."

"I don't know why I bother," she complains, throwing the dress on the bed.

Frankie and I are complete opposites. She's tall, I'm short. She's blonde, I'm some boring shade of brown—to say brunette would probably make it sound too good. She's outgoing and adventurous, and I'm shy and reserved. Our choice of clothing is also at different ends of the scale. Frankie follows fashion and must be seen wearing what the celebs are. I, on the other hand, love the 1950's look, so when I'm not in a pair of jeans and a t-shirt you can find me in something like the high-waist pencil skirt, white shirt, thick red belt with matching court shoes I'm about to change into. It's not exactly a look most of our fellow students rock on a night out, but it's what I love, so I go with it. I wouldn't be seen dead in the tiny scraps of fabric Frankie steps out of her flat in.

"Who told you that, anyway?"

"Lisa rang me this afternoon from a bar in town. Apparently, they came in all boisterous and sexy and offered to buy her and Tara a drink. Once they found out their plans for the night, they excused themselves to ring me. I can't fucking wait, E. Soldiers! Actual soldiers!"

"Yay," I say, feigning excitement.

Frankie throws her lip gloss at me. "If you're not excited for yourself then at least be excited for me," she says, before stripping off her robe and reaching for her dress.

"Ready?" she asks excitedly as she finishes off the drink I abandoned some time ago.

I take one last look at myself in the mirror and run my hand down the fabric of my skirt. My hair is pulled back into a sleek ponytail with my fringe swept to the side and pinned behind my ear. My eyes are lined perfectly and my lips are fire engine red thanks to Frankie's skills—I could never achieve this look on my own. I may be good with my hands but it doesn't seem to translate to putting make up on.

"I guess," I mutter as I grab my bag.

Frankie ignores my less than enthusiastic response and takes my hand to pull me through her flat to the awaiting taxi. She can barely sit still during the short ride to the city centre, and I hate to admit it, but her excitement is a little infectious. This may not be my kind of thing, but seeing my best friend this happy does make me feel better about everything.

"We're here," Frankie exclaims, throwing money onto the passenger seat and practically bouncing from the taxi.

I thank the driver and get out in a slightly more composed manner. I wasn't paying much attention to where we were going, but I groan when I see which club we've just pulled up outside.

"Smoke? Really?"

"Yes. This is where Lisa and Tara said the soldiers were heading."

I'm not a fan of nightclubs in general, but I have a particular hatred of Smoke and Frankie knows it, which is probably why she didn't tell me.

"We're meant to be out celebrating my birthday. Shouldn't I have the final say?" I ask, refusing to move from the curb.

"Yeah, I guess you're right," Frankie says, thinking about more than her sexy soldiers for a second. "Where do you want to go?"

I desperately want to say home, but I know that isn't going to go down well. I also don't know if it's actually the truth. The place I love being isn't the same now I'm watching Mum fight this losing battle with her business. I think where I want to be is anywhere but here. I don't want to be stood outside this club I hate, and for the first time ever, I don't want to be in Bristol. I need to get away from it all, from the stress and the pressure. Being in uni should be pressure enough, but that's not even half of it. Even my love of jewellery making has been tainted by it.

Frankie stands in front of me. I can see how torn she now is about tonight. She's a good friend, and I know that if I were to say I didn't want to go in there, she wouldn't. As much as she wants those soldiers, I know she'd choose me over them. I'm just not sure I can do it to her.

"It's fine, let's go."

"Really?" she asks, all hopeful.

"Really. But if one sleezeball tries touching me up on the dance floor again, I'm leaving right after kicking him in the bollocks."

"Fair enough. Just let me know which one it was and I'll kick him too."

I reach forward and grab her hand, and then together, we walk towards the end of the queue.

"It's fucking freezing," Frankie complains after a couple of minutes waiting in line.

I look over at her in the flimsy bit of fabric she calls a dress and raise my eyebrow.

"Oh sssh," she sulks.

"ID please," the bouncer demands when we eventually get to the front.

I can't lie, even I'm cold now it's taken us so damn long to get here. Frankie had a text from Tara ages ago to let us know they were inside, but there was no sign of any soldiers yet. That news didn't help Frankie's quickly depleting excitement.

"Thank fuck for that," she grumbles when we begin walking up the stairs. "I swear my tits were about three minutes from freezing the fuck off."

"Let's go and get a drink," I suggest, hoping some more alcohol will put the spring back in her step. For my own sake, I really hope these soldiers are real and actually turn up. I don't think I'm ever going to hear the end of her disappointment otherwise.

"Oh there they are," Frankie points to the other end of the bar when we get through the crowd.

We do the usual shouted greeting that always has to happen when in a club; we all nod and smile at each other like we have a clue what the other is talking about, but in reality, the music is so bloody loud I can barely hear my own thoughts, let alone someone talking to me.

When Lisa begins pulling something from her bag, I immediately want to run, but instead I'm forced to smile and look happy about the fact they've got me a happy birthday sash and flashing badge.

Brilliant. Now I really will attract unwanted attention. It's like they don't know me at all, or more so that they do and they're all finding this hilarious.

Tara hands me a drink and I stupidly take a sip assuming it's my usual Malibu and Coke. Huge mistake. "What the fuck is that?" I shout as I try to scrape the taste off my tongue with my teeth.

"Jagerbomb," Frankie announces proudly as she knocks hers back.

"That's disgusting, Kiki." And to think I was under the impression vodka Red Bull was the worst mix of drinks in the world!

"Here," Lisa says handing me another glass after I shove my previous excuse for a drink at Frankie. I sniff it this time, just in case, but I know I'm safe because I can smell coconut.

"Thank you," I say, before quickly taking a swig to hopefully remove the lingering aftertaste of the Jagerbomb.

The three of them stand and shout at each other for a few minutes. Every now and then, Tara and Lisa look around, I guess hoping to spot their soldiers. I can see Frankie's excitement waning as the minutes go by. I told her not to get her hopes up.

When the latest Pitbull song starts pounding through the speakers, Frankie perks up, grabs mine and Lisa's hands, and pulls us to the dance floor. We end up in the middle of the of the crowd, exactly where I don't want to be, just as the smoke fills the dance floor, blocking my vision of what people are doing around me.

I stand and dance a little but I'm still relatively sober compared to my friends so I don't quite get into the flow of it like them. When the smoke begins to lift, all three of them are bumping and grinding away without a care in the world. As I stand and watch, I realise I'm jealous. They are all able to put everything to one side and just enjoy themselves. I need that; I need to forget everything for just a few hours and chill out, but no matter what I do I can feel it all weighing down on my shoulders. Mum's business isn't really my problem, but I'm not the kind of person who can just let her deal with it. She's been my rock my entire life, and now I feel like it's time for me to return the favour.

I'm smiling at my friends' antics when I feel the need to look over to the bar. I don't know what it is but it's like something's calling me. When I look over, there's a guy staring right at me. Thinking I must be wrong, I look over my shoulder expecting to see someone looking back at him, but everyone's too engrossed in their dancing.

When I glance back, he's still looking my way. I'm just about to turn when one of his friends put his hand on his shoulder and distracts him.

I continue watching them for a few seconds before I hear Lisa. "Oh my god, they're here," she squeals, making Frankie immediately stop dancing and look around.

"Where?"

"Over there, by the bar. That group of lads."

"The hot ones?"

"Yes. Let's go."

I stand back and allow Frankie and Lisa to force their way through the crowd towards the bar. Tara and I follow behind, neither of us sharing their excitement. Tara has a serious long-term boyfriend and only comes out to spend time with us, unlike Frankie and Lisa, whose only reason for coming is to pull.

I watch from a few feet away as Lisa walks directly up to the guy who was just staring in my direction. I'm not going to say staring at me, because that can't possibly be the case, unless he's also amused by the girl wearing the bright pink sash and flashing badge. Frankie latches herself onto his friend and leans into his side shamelessly.

Tara and I continue to stand slightly out of the way and just watch as Frankie and Lisa make drunken fools out of themselves.

The four of them stand together talking, or shouting, for a few minutes before I see Frankie look up and point our way. It's the first time the guy has glanced up since they approached, and when he does, his eyes widen slightly as he looks at me before they drop and run down the length of my body. Tara moves when Frankie gestures for her but I'm frozen to the spot as the guy continues taking me all in. Usually, I hate being ogled by men but there's something about this one that doesn't want to make me kick him in the balls for looking at me the way he is.

Frankie scares the shit out of me when I feel her slide her arm through mine and tug me towards the group.

"What the hell is up with you? I know you're not interested in a soldier, but they won't bite," she says, coming to a stop when we're directly in front of him.

"I...I know," I stutter when I look up to find him still staring at me. Lisa's practically dry humping his leg but he doesn't seem to be noticing it.

"Bax," one of the guys shouts. "Hey, Bax," he repeats, until the guy looking at me rips his eyes away.

"What?" he snaps.

"Here," his mate says, handing him a small glass full of golden liquid.

He nods his chin at him before bringing his gaze back to me, continuing to hold my eyes as he slowly tips the glass up to his lips and drinks it down in one. My eyes break from his as he swallows, distracted by the movement of the muscles in his neck. I continue downward, taking in his grey striped shirt, stretched over his shoulders and chest, before dropping down to his black, almost skinny, jeans. I'm not interested for two reasons:

he's a soldier, and

I have enough drama in my life right now,

but even I can admit this guy's hot.

Telling myself those things is all good and well, but I don't think my body believes a single word of it. My pulse is racing and my palms are sweating from just looking at this guy. When my eyes connect with his again it's like everything around me fades away and it's just me and him.

***

"OH MY GOD!" Frankie squeals as the four of us walk into the toilets a while later. "Dean's so fucking hot. I mean, have you seen those arms? What I wouldn't give to see him in action, all army man," she says as she fans herself in front of the mirror.

I leave her to it and make use of the toilet. I smile to myself the whole time when she doesn't even stop for breath talking about him. Lisa is much less enthusiastic because, after getting the cold shoulder from Bax, she moved onto another of his friends, who also doesn't seem all that interested.

An hour or so later, I leave everyone dancing in favour of getting a glass of water. Frankie and Lisa managed to convince Bax, Dean and their friends to join us all on the dance floor. It's clear Dean is loving all the attention from Frankie, and Lisa has at last found herself a friend who is interested. Tara and I have kept ourselves to ourselves and danced with each other, but that doesn't mean I've lost Bax's interest. He still seems way too intrigued for my liking. I could feel his gaze while we were dancing and every time I looked up those dark eyes were on me.

"Thanks, E, I needed that," Frankie says, taking the glass of cold water from my hands and downing it in one. "Bax totally has the hots for you. You should go for it."

"I'm good, thanks."

"Oh, come one. You need someone to pop that cherry. I think it's got his name written all over it. Plus, not every woman can say she had her cherry popped by an incredibly sexy soldier; I bet he's well good with his hands."

"Enough," I snap. I really don't need her shouting the details of my love life—or lack thereof—out to all the strangers I'm stood at the bar with.

"A night with him will chill you right out." At that moment, Dean appears from nowhere and runs his hands down Frankie's sides. She spins in his arms and they both disappear into the crowd together. I shake my head and turn back to the bar to order another glass of water.

Chapter 2

I continue standing at the bar, watching everyone for quite a long time. I don't see the girls or any of Bax's friends—not that I'd recognise most of them—but this is fairly standard procedure. Eventually, I'll get myself in a taxi and head home, leaving them to party the night away.

I'm just getting myself ready to go when I feel something. I look over my shoulder and find Bax right behind me.

"Oh hey," I shout over the music. His eyes are intense as he stares into mine. Feeling awkward I smile at him and I'm just about to excuse myself when he speaks.

"Your friends just left," he says, leaning into my ear. His warm breath caresses my neck and makes me shiver, even though it's swelteringly hot in here.

"Oh, I'll just get a taxi." I turn to leave but stop when I feel his hand wrap around my wrist. I look back to see his eyes once again boring into mine. I'm not sure whether I should feel intimated by his intensity, but I don't, not one bit.

"No," he states before stepping up to my side, placing his arm around my waist and pushing me towards the exit. I feel his thumb gently stroking my skin and it ignites butterflies in my stomach, but not the type I'd expect to feel whilst being touched by some random guy in a club. I'm not scared, and I don't want to cause him physical harm; I actually kind of like it.

He directs us to the coat check in and hands over a ticket.

"You don't have one?" he asks when I don't make a move.

I shake my head and we wait in silence for the girl to return.

When she hands his jacket over, he drapes it over his arm, and with his hand in the small of my back, he gently moves me towards the exit. His touch burns and sends tingles racing around my body.

I don't feel the cold like I did waiting to get in. I try to push aside the thought that it's because he's touching me, but I'm not very successful.

"Here," he says, placing his leather jacket over my shoulders.

"No, it's fine, you have it," I try to argue, but now he's removed his hand, I'm freezing.

"You need it more than me, Skittles."

Skittles? I don't get the chance to ask, because his fingers thread through mine and he encourages me to start walking away from the club.

We walk in silence, past the closed shops and dodging other drunk partygoers who are trying to make their way home.

"Where are we going?" I ask eventually, not concerned in the slightest that I'm currently walking though the city in the middle of the night with a man I've just met.

"Nowhere. Everywhere," he answers cryptically, before falling silent again.

I can't really argue with him, because although what he's just said makes no sense, I kind of understand it and it feels pretty perfect. I continue to hold onto his hand and walk alongside him silently through the city.

I've never really spent much time out here at this time of night, but for a place that's usually chaotic, it's strangely calming with the orange glow from the street lights ahead and the twinkling stars above.

Nothing's said between us for the longest time, and it's weird, because it's the most content I think I've felt in a long time.

Bax eventually breaks the silence. "There's a takeout curry house. Do you fancy anything?"

I'm not really hungry, but the thought of eating something warm gets the better of me.

"Sure." He changes direction and pulls me across the road.

We both order a chicken curry and chips along with two cans of Coke before heading back out into the night.

"Come on," he says, and I follow along, our hands once again intertwined.

We come to a stop when we get to the harbour side. He walks down a couple of the steps that descend to the water before tugging on my hand to encourage me to sit with him.

"Here," he says, handing my food over once he's unwrapped it.

"Thank you. Are you sure you're not cold?"

"I'm fine, Skittles."

"Why are you calling me that?"

"Because it suits you."

"Why?" I ask, but he just shrugs his shoulder. After a couple of seconds of silence, I decide he's not going to elaborate. "You know my name's Erin, right?"

"Of course. Can I ask you something?"

"Sure." I'm a little surprised by his question because he's hardly said anything to me since I met him.

"Why did you come with me? I'm a stranger you just met in a club. You don't even know my name."

"It's Bax," I say, trying to prove I do know something about him. "And...I don't know. It just felt right."

"Hmmm," he hums before throwing a chip covered in curry sauce into his mouth. "You should be careful who you decide to spend time with in the middle of the night, Skittles. They could be dangerous."

"Are you?"

"Very."

For some reason, his warning doesn't scare me off in the slightest. He might be the quiet, brooding type, but I'm not sure he falls into the dangerous category.

Once we've finished eating, we continue looking out to the dark water before us. There's no noise out here, and we're the only sign of life. I have no idea what time it is, but to be honest, I really don't care.

"I used to come down here in the middle of the night when I was a kid. I'd sneak out of my house and spend hours looking out over the water," he says quietly. I'm not sure whether he wants me to respond or not, so I decide to stay silent and listen. "It was the only peace and quiet I could get unless I was under a car in the garage. I used to sit here for hours."

Bax falls silent. I guess his memories are taking him far away, so I allow him to do his thing as my thoughts drift once again to Mum and her gift shop.

"Erin?" he asks abruptly, and I turn to look at him.

"Yeah."

"I haven't wished you happy birthday," he says, staring deep into my eyes.

Before I know what's happening, I feel his cold palm against my cheek and he leans in towards me. My eyes instinctively close seconds before I feel his warm, soft lips against mine. He holds still for the longest time with our lips pressed together, but he doesn't push any further. When he eventually pulls back, I can't help feeling a little disappointed.

"I'm sorry. I should get you home," he says, quickly taking his hand away and leaving me cold without his touch.

"No," falls from my mouth, shocking the hell out of me.

His head snaps to the side to look at me. He doesn't need to ask; I can see the question all over his face.

"Can we stay here a little longer?"

"Yeah, if you want."

"So, are you on leave or something?" I ask after a few more seconds of comfortable silence have passed between us.

"Yeah, two weeks," he says, but he doesn't sound very excited about it.

"Would you rather be at work?"

"Quite honestly, yes."

"Why are you here then? Surely you could have gone somewhere other than Bristol?"

"It's my home, I guess. I didn't really think about it. Everyone goes home to their families when they're on leave. Plus, my mate lives down south, and wanted a night out here before travelling on, so here I am."

"Don't you have family?" I blurt out, and then instantly regret such an intrusive question.

"My mum's here."

"Well, she must be excited about seeing you."

"I doubt it. I think I might just grab my car and take off."

"And go where?"

"Everywhere. Nowhere," he says, just like he did earlier.

"Sounds amazing," I admit, revisiting my thoughts from a few hours ago.

Bax's movement as he turns to look at me catches my eye, so I do the same. As he stares at me, I can see a small smile tugging at his lips, and just like every time he's looked at me this evening, his eyes twinkle in excitement.

"What?" I ask sceptically.

"Come with me."

"I'm sorry, what?"

"Come with me," he repeats.

"Where?"

"Everywhere, nowhere, wherever we want to go."

"Are you crazy? I don't even know you."

"You knew me well enough to walk off alone with me in the middle of Bristol, so I can't be that scary. You're a student, right? So you're free the next two weeks. We could just disappear."

My heart's pounding in my chest the more he speaks. I shouldn't be getting so excited about the prospect of running away with this stranger, but suddenly, it's all I can think about.

"What if I have work?" I ask, trying to play it cool.

"Do you?"

"Nothing I couldn't do on the move," I answer honestly. Yes, I've got an assignment to write, and I've always got more jewellery to design or make, but there's no reason I have to be here to do that.

"So is that a yes?"

"This is insane," I admit with a laugh, but he doesn't say anything. He just continues staring at me intensely, waiting for an answer. I quickly run through every reason in my head why I shouldn't be doing this. Weirdly, any concerns about him being a mass murderer don't even feature on my list. "YES!" I blurt out.

"Yes?"

"YES," I scream into the night.

Suddenly I'm on my feet, my body pressed against his hard muscles as his lips find mine again. They feel the same as last time, only they don't stay still. I feel them part before his tongue gently sweeps across my lower lip. My mouth opens without any instruction from my brain, and in seconds, our tongues are tangling together. He steps forward and my bum hits the wall behind me, stopping my movement, but it doesn't stop Bax because he presses further into me. His hands run from my face, over my shoulders, and skim the sides of my breasts before they come to a stop on my waist.

By the time he pulls back, I can feel his hardness pressing into my stomach. The thought of causing that kind of reaction has butterflies exploding in my belly.

Our foreheads rest together while he catches his breath. His eyes don't stray from mine. "Your eyes are purple," he whispers.

"Violet."

"Stunning."

I can't help looking away as embarrassment washes through me. No one compliments me like that, and I don't know how to take it.

"Hey," he says, gently forcing my head back with his fingers on my cheek. "You're going to have to learn to accept compliments if we're spending the next two weeks together, because I have a feeling I'm going to be paying you a lot."

I feel heat rush up my neck to my cheeks.

"Fuck, you look so sexy when you blush."

I desperately want to pull my eyes away from his, but his stare is too intense.

"Are you sure about this?" he asks as he steps back away from me.

"I think so."

"No, Skittles, I need to know you're doing this because you want to. Do you want to get away from this place?"

"Yes."

"Are you sure you want to do this with me? You've no idea who I am or what I'm capable of."

"Yes," I answer, a little more forcefully than before. It might sound crazy, but I know he's not capable of hurting me—not physically, anyway. I may have only just met him, but I already feel as if I've known him my entire life.

"Okay then, let's go."

"Right now?" I ask in a panic.

"Well, no, not right now. I was thinking we should get some sleep first. You can get some stuff together in the morning, I can get my car, and then we can go."

"Everywhere and nowhere," I state.

"Exactly. Come on then, Skittles, let's go find us a bed for a few hours."

I take his out stretched hand and together, we head off into the night.

It's not long until we're stood in the reception of a 24/7 hotel getting that look off the middle-aged receptionist. She thinks we're just checking in for a late night hook up. The thought makes me panic and it only gets worse when Bax hands his credit card over to pay for the room.

I look away from the desk and allow him to take my hand to pull me in the direction of our room once he's finished.

"Bax, I—" I manage to say when he puts the card in the little machine to unlock the door.

"I got a twin room," he says, obviously seeing where my thoughts were going.

"O…okay," I stutter, following him in.

When I look up, true to his word, there are two single beds. I look around the room and try not to let my thoughts show on my face. I don't want to seem ungrateful.

"No wonder it was so fucking cheap," Bax says from behind me.

I let out a sigh of relief that he sees it too. The place looks like it last saw a decorator in the eighties. The walls and ceiling are definitely yellower than they're meant to be, and the few bits of furniture in here look like they're about to fall apart.

"I guess it'll be okay for a few hours," I say, slipping my shoes off and wiggling my toes as I sit on the corner of one of the beds. It creaks loudly, making us both laugh.

"I've stayed in some bad places, but this is up there," Bax says as he empties his pockets on the bedside table.

I watch as he undoes a couple of his shirt buttons before he reaches back and begins pulling it over his head. I'm fairly sure it all happens at normal speed, but I could swear time slows down as he reveals the most incredible body to me. His skin is a stunning golden colour, like he's recently been in the sun, and it flawlessly covers perfectly sculpted pecs and abs.

Help Our Heroes

I know I'm staring, but I can't help it. It's like my eyes are glued to him.

"Fuck, Skittles," Bax complains when he catches me ogling him.

"Shit, I'm so sorry," I say in a panic as I spin on the bed so I'm facing away from him. My face heats and I drop it into my hands in an attempt to hide my embarrassment. I shut my eyes, but it's like the image of him shirtless is burned onto the inside of my eyelids.

I noticeably flinch when his hands land on my shoulders. "It's okay, look as much as you want; just know that I can't be held responsible for my actions when you do."

I try to swallow but my mouth is suddenly drier than a fucking desert, so I end up nodding instead.

"Hey, stop hiding from me," he says, pulling my hands away from my face and turning my head so I have to look at him. He runs his fingertips over my cheeks and his eyes look over every inch of my face. His mouth opens like he wants to say something, but he must change his mind because instead, he drops his hand and steps away from me.

"Here," he says, holding out his shirt. He must sense my reluctance because he drops it into my lap before saying, "Well you don't want to sleep in that, do you?" as he gestures at my outfit.

"No, not really," I mutter as I gather up the fabric and head towards the bathroom. I look over my shoulder before entering to see Bax with his back to me, undoing his jeans. He's just about to drop them when he must feel my stare, because he glances over at me. My breath catches at the look on his face. His eyes are smouldering.

"Keep it up and you won't be getting any sleep," he warns.

His words spur me into action and I quickly step into the bathroom and lock myself in.

I rest back against the door and try to get my head together. How the hell did this night end with me in a shitty hotel room with a solider? I wonder briefly what happened to Frankie, Lisa and Tara. The only reason Frankie and Lisa ever disappear on a night out is because they've pulled, so I can only imagine they're both currently warming a soldier's bed. I'm happy for Frankie in a weird way; she's getting to live out her fantasy, I just hope she doesn't end up getting hurt.

She likes to make out she's all about easy sex and whatever, but I know her, and I know deep down she wants more than that, even if she won't admit it.

I eventually make use of the bathroom before stripping off my clothes and pulling Bax's shirt over my head. It's huge and almost comes down to my knees, but I'm grateful because it does a good job of covering me up. I do my best with the complimentary soap and water to remove what's left of tonight's make up, and comb my hair through with my fingers before plaiting it over my shoulder. I pull my thick-rimmed glasses from the bottom of my clutch and slide them on after disposing of my contact lenses.

I'm just reaching for the doorknob when I get a sudden bolt of nerves as I think about who's on the other side of the door. How do I trust him so much when I've only just met him? There's no way I should be this comfortable about spending a night in a hotel room with a man I hardly know. I shake the thought away because there's something telling me this is exactly what I should be doing, that for some reason I was meant to meet Bax tonight. I roll my shoulders and let out a breath before pulling the door open and stepping out.

He was obviously waiting for me, because he starts talking before I round the corner.

"So where did you want to…holy—" he stops mid-sentence when I appear. His chin drops and his eyes race around me like they don't know where to look first. I want to be all confident like Frankie would be in this exact situation, but unfortunately, that's not who I am, so instead of standing here proudly, I fold my arms over my chest and look down at the ground.

"Oh no you don't," he says. I expect to find him out of bed when I look up, so I'm surprised to I see him still sat there with the covers over his waist. "Never be embarrassed by looking that incredible."

Heat races up my neck and I feel my face flush red. I manage to break from his gaze and rush to get into bed. The way he's looking at me right now scares and excites me in equal measures.

I lie myself down on my side and pull the covers up to my neck before looking over at him. He's still sat exactly as he was, and staring where I was stood.

"Are you okay?" I ask after a few minutes when he still hasn't moved or said anything.

"I'm not sure," he answers honestly.

"I…uh…can go," I offer, thinking he doesn't want me here.

"Trust me, Skittles, that's the last thing I want right now."

"Okay then," I whisper because the emotion in his voice just then knocked me for six.

"Goodnight, Skittles."

"Goodnight, Bax."

Chapter 3

I wake to the weirdest sound. I lie there for a few seconds, firstly trying to remember where the hell I am, and then secondly to work out what it is that's woken me. As soon as I open my eyes, it's obvious. Bax is at the foot of our beds doing sit-ups, and the noise is his exhale every time he does a crunch. I grab my glasses silently and shift myself so I have a better view. I watch with delight as he continues. His muscles flex in the most delicious way. I lose count after fifty, but eventually he turns over and starts doing push-ups. I almost groan at the sight of his firm arse clad in only his white boxer briefs. Every woman should get to wake up to this every morning.

I stay still and watch every single push up, taking note of the straining muscles in his thick arms each time he drops to the floor. The longer I watch him, the more my sleepy body wakes up. My heart is pounding, and I'm dying to fling the covers off me, but that means telling him I'm awake and watching, so I lie here suffering. It's totally worth it.

After an insane number of push-ups, he jumps to his feet. He's got his back to me but the second he raises his eyes to the mirror in front of him, they stare directly into mine. I see them widen slightly in surprise before they darken. We're both frozen, staring at each other for a few minutes. I'm not sure if that means he's pissed off that I was watching him.

Eventually, he turns. I'm desperate to run my eyes over his body again but the intensity in his keeps mine held hostage. In seconds, he's inches from my face, hovering above me.

"You need to be careful what you wish for, Skittles," he warns, his voice deeper than it was last night.

"I...I didn't," I stutter.

"I told myself I wouldn't do anything until you were begging for it, but you're making it really fucking hard to keep that promise."

I swallow, but my suddenly dry mouth makes it a challenge. Does he mean…?

My thoughts are cut off when his lips brush mine. It's a kiss like the first one we shared last night. There's no movement, but it feels like there's a promise in it.

His lips are gone as quickly as they appeared, and when my eyes focus, he's walking away from me. I only get a quick glimpse of his arse before he disappears around the corner and into the bathroom.

I stay where I am, listening to the sound of running water and imagining how his body would look wet and glistening.

When he emerges I get a shot of exactly what that's like because he's still wet with only a towel wrapped around his waist.

"I thought you would've gone back to sleep," he says when he sees me still awake.

"It's fine, I don't sleep much," I admit. I've always been a bit of an insomniac but since things with Mum and the shop have been getting worse, so has my sleeping.

"We've only had two hours," he says, sitting on the edge of his bed.

Okay, I do usually manage a little more than that. "You shouldn't have woken me up with all that huffing and puffing then," I say with a smile.

"I can assure you, I was not huffing or puffing."

"Okay then, army man, whatever you say."

Bax narrows his eyes at my piss taking but he doesn't say anything about it. "I was going to find some coffee. Would you like one?"

"There's stuff over there," I say, pointing to the little kettle.

"Knock yourself out, but I want real coffee."

"Real coffee would be good, now you mention it."

I watch in amazement as Bax stands, turns his back to me, and drops the towel. I cough to cover my groan but from the movement I see in his shoulders, I don't think I do a very good job. Once his jeans are on, he turns back towards me.

"I'm gonna need my shirt."

"Uh…hang on," I say, diving under the covers.

I squirm around and manage to get his shirt off before I poke my head out, followed by my arm, and hand it over. My other hand keeps the covers pulled up to my neck, although it doesn't seem to matter because the way Bax is staring at the duvet, you'd think it was see through.

"Thank you," he mutters before pulling it over his head. "Motherfucker."

"What?"

"It smells like you."

"Sorry," I whisper, feeling embarrassed.

"Don't be. It just means I'm even less likely to be able to get the image of you wearing it out of my head."

"Oh."

"I'll make sure I'm gone for twenty minutes to give you time to get dressed and shit."

"Get dressed and shit?" I repeat with a smile.

"Yeah, well, I don't know what girly shit you might need to do," he admits.

"Okay, well…thank you."

Seconds later, he's gone and I'm left alone in this dingy hotel room, questioning my sanity once again. I try to put my thoughts to one side as I rush into the bathroom to shower and dress before he gets back.

* * *

"Skittles, are you decent?" Bax shouts through the crack in the door exactly twenty minutes later.

"Yes," I answer with a laugh.

"Fuck's sake," he grumbles, making me laugh even more. "Here, I made an educated guess," he says, handing me a Costa cup and McDonald's bag. The smell makes my stomach grumble.

"McDonald's coffee not good enough for you either?" I ask with amusement, looking at what's in my hands.

"No," he says after taking a sip.

"Aren't they at opposite ends of the high street?"

"And?"

I don't really have an argument so smiling to myself I pop the top off the cup to allow it to cool down. I'm not overly fussy when it comes to coffee but when I see what I think is a cappuccino, I can't help but smile. "Perfect," I say, and Bax's face lights up. My heart flutters slightly at the sight and I desperately want to tell it not to be so stupid.

I take a tedious sip and when it's even hotter than I was expecting, I put it down and grab the bag. "Yum," I say, opening up the muffin, "just what I needed."

We both polish off our breakfast in record time before falling back into a comfortable silence.

"So what's the plan?" I ask eventually, my curiosity getting the better of me.

"You're still up for it?" Bax asks, incredulously.

"Of course. I wouldn't have said yes if I didn't mean it."

I get another smile off him and it affects me no less than last time. What is it about this guy?

"Is it okay with you if we don't have a plan? My life is one strict routine; I'd quite like to go with the flow for once."

"Of course. So when are we going?"

"I thought once we're sorted here, we'd go, get our stuff, and head off."

"I thought you didn't have any plans?"

"Once we're in my car and driving out of Bristol, I have none," he says with a laugh. He looks away from me but not before I see a serious look fall over his face. "This is just a two week thing, no exchanging numbers or anything. Are you sure you're okay with that?"

My heart sinks a little at the thought of whatever this is having a time limit, but I'm aware that it's what I signed up for when I agreed to this last night. "Yeah, that's fine with me," I answer, although a little reluctantly.

It's still crazy early when our taxi pulls up outside Bax's mum's home. It's not quite what I was expecting after spending the night with him. In my head, I had the image of a standard three-bed semi with a cute little garden, but in reality, his mum lives in a flat in a seriously run down area of town.

"Thanks, mate," Bax says, paying the driver. I hop from the taxi and he follows behind me. "This way. My car's in the garage." He places his hand on the small of my back and pushes me towards a set of dilapidated looking garages. It's obvious which one his car is in because there's only one with a working door. The rest are all hanging off at odd angles or missing completely.

When he pulls the door up, my eyes almost bug out of my head. "You're a boy racer?" I ask in shock as I run my eyes over his immaculate white Peugeot.

"I can assure you I'm not. We won't be cruising with a banging bass or hanging out in any McDonald's car parks."

"Riiiight." I can't help laughing at the look on his face.

"I love cars, especially classic ones."

"I'm not sure a nineties Peugeot 106 is a classic, Bax."

"Maybe not, but she's a beauty. I've totally rebuilt her from the wheels up. You won't find a better 106 out there. Anyway, get in, get comfortable, and I'll be back in a few."

"You're leaving me here?"

"Yeah, I'll only be a minute or two. My stuff's packed already from getting back yesterday."

I agree, but only because I can tell by his stance that I don't have a chance in hell of going with him. He's decided that I'm staying here and that's what's going to happen. I realise I'm getting my first look at Bax the solider, and it's hot.

I've never been in a car quite like this before. I drop my clutch on my lap and look around. The red and black interior is a stark contrast to the perfect white paintwork on the outside. I've no idea when Bax last drove this, but it's sparkling clean. The black dashboard almost shines in the morning sun, and the red leather bucket seats look brand new. I continue looking around and come to the conclusion that Bax is a bit of a neat freak. There's nothing in the door pockets—not even an old packet of chewing gum—and the glove box is definitely different to any I've ever seen before as it only contains one very neatly folded cloth.

I'm distracted from his perfect car by some movement in front of his building. I look over, thinking I'm going to be able to ogle him as he walks this way. Only, when I look up, it isn't him on the doorstep. Instead, there's a woman. She's got to be in her fifties at least. Her hair is a mess and sticking up in all directions, and her make up is so heavy I can see it all smeared down her face from here, but the thing that makes her stand out the most is what she's wearing—or isn't wearing. The lace nightie covers nothing, and I mean nothing. The much younger man she's with hands her something before turning and walking away. I quickly look down, not wanting to be caught watching them.

I grab my phone as a distraction and send a text to Frankie to ask how her night was. I don't expect an answer for hours yet. If I get any contact from her before two o'clock this afternoon, I'll be amazed.

"Hey, you haven't run," Bax says as he drops down next to me after throwing a bag into the back seat.

"I'm not sure I'd want to around here." I regret my words instantly when I remember this is where he lives.

"Wise move. This place is a shit hole." His obvious dislike of it makes me feel a little better. "I didn't grow up here. We used to have a lovely house in a nice neighbourhood, but when Dad left, it all went to shit."

"I'm sorry."

"It's fine. I joined the army the second I could, and left Mum to ruin her own life." As the words leave his mouth, I can't help but wonder if the woman I just saw was her.

It turns out we can't go anywhere until Peggy the Peugeot—yes, the car has a name—has a thorough once over, so our first destination is to an ancient looking garage on the edge of town.

"Are you sure this place is still in business?" The old tin building looks like it's about to fall down. I'm not sure it's somewhere I'd want my pride and joy to be.

"Yeah, it's open."

I see he's right the second he pulls the car to a stop, because a door opens and an elderly man steps out with a huge smile on his face.

"Bax! I wasn't expecting to see you. What a lovely surprise on this sunny Sunday." The man's joy couldn't be any clearer.

Bax jumps from the car and I watch as the two hug it out. I've no idea who this guy is, but they're clearly close.

They're just pulling apart when I reach them. "Erin, this is Arthur, my grandad's best mate. Arthur, this is Erin, she's…"

"A friend," I finish to help him out, although calling us friends might be pushing it slightly.

"Well, it's nice to meet you, Erin. Bax here needs a good friend," he says, elbowing Bax in the arm and winking at both of us. I try to play it cool but I can feel heat rushing to my cheeks at his insinuation. "Let's go and get some coffees, young lady. If I know Bax, you're in for a long few hours."

It turns out he wasn't lying. I spend a couple of hours chatting to Arthur in his little make shift kitchen before venturing out to sit at a bench in the sun. The benefit of being out here is that I get to watch Bax bent over the bonnet of his car, and let me tell you, he has one fine arse.

I hear nothing back from Frankie so I can only presume she's had a good night. If she'd gone off with someone who wasn't Bax's friend, I might be concerned, but something tells me she's okay.

"I promise I'm nearly done," Bax shouts over as he wipes his hands on a rag.

"Take your time." His eyes light up and I can only assume that's because I'm not rushing him and his darling Peggy.

I look back down at the paper I asked Arthur for and smile. It's been quite a while since I've been able to just sketch for the fun of it. That's what this all the used to be: fun. I'd design and make jewellery because I loved it, but now I feel like I'm under pressure to deliver because it could be what keeps Mum's gift shop open. We both do well from my jewellery sales so I keep pushing for more. Unfortunately, that also means pushing my creativity out the window, and recently, I've found my designs getting more and more generic and boring. I used to thrive on being unique and different, and sadly those are the designs that sell and make money.

Once I run out of inspiration from my surroundings, I start work on something totally different. It's not the easiest thing in the world because he keeps moving, but I do my best.

"Fucking hell, Skittles, that's incredible," I hear over my shoulder, bringing me back to reality. I'd totally lost myself in what I was doing.

I drag my eyes away from the tiny section I was working on and look at my sketch as a whole. It's not too bad, I guess. I shrug my shoulders at Bax before looking up at him. What was a smooth shaven face when I first met him yesterday is now covered in a layer of stubble, and he has smears of oil on his cheeks and forehead. It's really pretty sexy.

"What?" he asks when I sit there staring at him.

"Nothing."

"No, go on, you're clearly thinking something."

"It's nothing. Are you finished?"

He leans forward a little more until our noses are almost touching. "Tell me what you're thinking," he whispers.

I look away from his eyes before muttering that he looks hot.

"What was that? I couldn't quite hear you," he says, grabbing my cheek gently so he can turn me back to look at him.

I try to move away from his stare but he holds me in place. "Fine," I huff. "You look hot, okay?" I force his hand off me and stand up, gathering the paper in front of me as I go.

"Now, was that so hard to admit, Skittles?" I can hear the humour in his voice and it makes me want to kick him.

"Shut up," I mutter. "Can we go now?"

"Yes, let me just say goodbye to Arthur."

When we arrive at my house, thankfully there's no sign of Mum. It's not that I don't want her to meet Bax; it's more that she'll try to talk me out of this. She'd probably be right, because disappearing off with a guy I've just met is a little nuts, and very out of character for me, but right now I don't care about any of that. I just want to get away. What we do find is the bottle of vodka and sleeping pills she's left behind on the dining table. The sight reminds me of everything I'm trying to push to the back of my mind, and a massive ball of guilt has me on the verge of turning Bax down on his offer to disappear.

One look at him stood in the doorway behind me and I know I'm doing the right thing. He glances at the items on the dining table, then gives me a sad smile. If my assumptions are right about that woman being his mum, I'm guessing he kinda knows how I feel right now.

I point Bax in the direction of the shower and strip out of last night's clothes in favour of something more suitable for a road trip before I start gathering my stuff together. I pull my suitcase down from the top of the wardrobe and bang the dust off. It's been quite a while since it's seen some holiday action.

I fill it with clothes before pulling open my pyjama drawer.

"Fuck," I mutter to myself when I see the only sets left are the silk lacy ones Frankie bought me for Christmas last year that I'd hidden at the bottom. I glance over my shoulder at my washing basket to see it overflowing. "Fuck."

I hear the water shut off and I know I'm running out of time. I really want to get out of here as soon as possible.

I grab the pyjamas and throw them in my suitcase. We'll get separate rooms, it'll be fine, I think as I pull my savings card from my desk. I'll pay for my own room. It'll be safer that way.

"Hey, you ready?" Bax asks when he pokes his head into my room as I'm zipping up my suitcase.

"I think so."

"Let's hit the road then."

* * *

"Where are we going?" I ask when we've been driving for twenty minutes. After spending all day at Arthur's garage getting Peggy ready for her road trip, the sun is already setting.

"I found this in my room." Bax reaches behind my seat before dropping a bottle full of two pence coins in my lap. "I thought we could have some fun with those," he says, pulling away when the lights change.

"Oh my god, are you serious?" I know I'm acting like an excited child but I don't care. My dad used to take me to the pier in Weston-Super-Mare when I was little. It's one of my best memories with him.

"I've been collecting them for years. Now seems like as good a time as any to spend them. I need food first, though." Arthur made us a sandwich earlier but it's definitely starting to wear off.

Bax parks the car on the side of the road in front of a row of B&B's. "Let's find somewhere to sleep for the night, then dinner."

I follow him into the first B&B to be told it's full, then the next, and the next. At this rate, we're going to be sleeping in his car. It's a nice car, but it's not good enough to be our bed for the night.

Thankfully, the forth B&B has a room left. I lose the argument about paying for it and Bax hands his card over after trampling any point I tried to make about why I should foot the bill this time.

"Up the stairs, right at the end of the corridor, then it's the door on the left," the lady behind the counter says, pointing us in the right direction. "I would take you but I'm here on my own and trying to make dinner for some guests."

* * *

Bax opens the door and gestures for me to enter. I take two steps into the room before I stop. Bax isn't paying attention and crashes into the back of me, his arms coming around my waist to hold me up.

"Shit, sorry. What's the…oh," he says when he sees what I'm looking at—a giant four-poster bed. "We can try somewhere else," he offers.

"We might not find anywhere else." We drove past loads of no vacancy signs and I don't fancy spending the night trawling the streets hoping to find something. This place is nice and clean, unlike where we spent last night, and although it's only one bed, it looks pretty comfortable.

"I'll sleep on the floor."

"You don't have to do that."

"Anything to make you happy." I swoon a little at his words.

After dumping our stuff, we head out to find a restaurant for dinner. There's a bar and grill not far down the street, and we grab the last empty table.

"So what do you do in the army?"

"Recovery mechanic."

"You fix vehicles?"

"Not really. We recover them when they've broken down or got into trouble."

"Oh, I thought with your car and everything you'd be working on them."

"I wanted excitement and my job definitely gives me that. The mechanics are usually at camp fixing vehicles whereas I'm out in the thick of it rescuing our men. I love it." I can see in his eyes how much he enjoys his job, even if the thought of him being somewhere dangerous makes my stomach flip.

"What about you?"

"I'm doing business and marketing at uni."

"I thought with what you were doing earlier you'd have said art or something."

"No,' I answer sadly, making his eyebrows raise in question. "My mum has a gift shop, it hasn't been doing so well since the recession so I went with business in the hope of helping bring it back to life."

"You don't sound like you enjoy it."

"It's okay. I just want to help. The shop's getting the better of her at the moment, it was her dream and she refuses to let go of it. If she carries on the way she is I'm convinced she'll put herself in an early grave."

"You can't do everything for her, Skittles. You've got your own life to lead and she shouldn't be holding you back from that," he says. It's not the first time I've heard similar words. Frankie's always going on at me.

"I'm not doing it because she tells me to," I snap.

"I know, but it seems to me that because you're nice and caring, she doesn't need to tell you. Hell, I doubt she even needs to ask—she already knows you're going to do it." I hate that he can see right through me. I didn't realise I was quite so transparent. He can tell there's something off, because he reaches across the table and grabs my hand. "It's not a bad thing, Skittles. You just need to make sure people don't take the piss, and I can't help but think your mum is, but probably without knowing it. Did you want do a business degree?"

"Of course."

"Honestly, if you had your pick of anything, you'd have stayed in Bristol and done business?"

I stare into his eyes for a bit as I roll the real answer to the question around in my head. "No."

"I didn't think so. You're too talented to be doing business."

"You've seen one drawing."

"All I needed to see."

We're silent as we eat. His observations about my life choices hit a little close to home and have shaken me a slightly. I always dreamed of moving away from Bristol and doing something where I could be creative every day.

Help Our Heroes

Unfortunately, I never even got the chance to look at possible courses because I got sidelined into business. Bax is right; Mum never told me to do anything, but things were hinted, and as he says, I'm too nice and I went along with it all because it felt like the right thing to do. It leaves me with the question I try to keep pushing to the back of my mind. What am I going to do when Mum's shop inevitably goes under? I'm left with a degree in a field I'm not interested in, and no qualifications in the field I want to go into.

"Erin?"

"Huh?" I look up to see Bax at smiling me and a bored looking waitress stood next to him with her hand on her hip.

"Would you like pudding?"

"Oh sorry, no I'm fine, thank you." I smile politely but she still huffs as she walks off. "Sorry," I say again.

"Are you okay?" Bax's eyebrows are drawn together in concern.

"Yeah. It's just what you said about my life."

"I didn't mean to upset you."

"I know you didn't, but you've nailed it. Everything you said is true, and it makes me wonder where it leaves me." It also freaks me out that he has my life pegged when he's only known me for a day, but I don't voice that.

"You'll be fine, Skittles. I think you're stronger than you give yourself credit for."

"You don't even know me."

"I don't think that's true. One look at you in the club last night and I knew everything I needed to know."

I open my mouth to respond but nothing comes out. How can he say that? I'm a stranger to him.

"Come on, let's go have some fun. There's plenty of time to deal with the serious stuff."

I can't argue with that, so after paying the bill, we head off towards the pier. It's so modern compared to the memories I have with Dad. I kind of like it though, because it makes me feel like I'm making new ones with Bax and not overwriting the old ones I'm so fond of.

"How long do you think this lot will last?" Bax asks with a laugh as we stand just inside the arcade.

"Two hours, tops."

"Let's see."

We don't get to find how long the two pennies would've lasted because we end up getting kicked out when they close for the night. We walk back down the pier hand in hand with wide smiles on our faces. I feel light for the first time in a long time.

"Walk on the beach?"

"Sounds perfect." And it is. The sun has set and there are a million stars twinkling above us. Amazingly the tide's in and the only sound is the waves crashing onto the sand.

We walk with our hands intertwined for a long time before Bax stops. He takes me closer to the water and we sit on the last bit of dry sand.

"Do you ever worry you're not going to come out of some of the situations you get put in?" I ask.

"Of course. I've been in the middle of some very hostile situations, but that's what I signed up for. It's also what gets my blood pumping. I feel alive in the middle of it all, and like I'm really making a difference."

"My dad was in the army," I admit. "He died in service when I was little."

"I'm sorry."

I give him a small smile and shrug my shoulders. What's done is done. "I've always told myself I'd never fall for a soldier. Mum fell apart after he died. It's an image I've never been able to rid from my head." When I look up, Bax has a shit-eating grin on his face.

"What?" I run through what I just said in my head and then panic. "Oh no, no, no," I say adamantly, shaking my head.

"We'll see about that. Now tell me, Skittles, when was the last time you did something wild?"

"Uh…" I think he already knows the answer is probably never.

I watch as he rises to his feet before pulling his hoodie over his head. "Come on, get up."

"Why?" I ask sceptically. I have only one idea as to what he could be planning on doing, and I'm fairly adamant I'm not up for it.

"We're going for a late night swim," he says.

"You can. I'll watch from here."

"Don't be so boring," he says as he toes off his shoes and drops his jeans.

He throws his discarded clothes up the beach a little before running full speed into the sea. He doesn't even flinch, and I know for a fact it must be fucking freezing. He splashes water everywhere and makes a right show of himself. Thankfully, it's dark and there's no one around to witness his antics.

"Come on," he encourages. "It's lovely."

"Nope."

"Strip and get your cute little arse in here, or I'll come and get you myself and you'll end up in here fully clothed."

We stare at each other for a full minute having a silent argument, him trying to convince me to join him and me standing firm with my refusal. It's not until he starts moving towards me that I cave, because as much as I really don't want to join him, surely being able to get out to dry clothes is preferable.

"Fuck's sake," I scream at him as I start unzipping my jacket.

"That's more like it! Strip for me, Skittles."

My face flushes red. It's only Bax who can see me but I think his eyes on my almost naked body are going to be worse than a stranger's.

The second my jeans hit the sand, I run into the sea, not wanting his eyes on me for too long.

"Holy fucking shit, Bax, it's fucking freezing," I squeal as the cold assaults my body.

"Keep moving, you'll soon warm up."

"I can't believe you convinced me to do this." I try to slap his shoulder but he's too quick and my wrist ends up trapped by his fingers. He gives my arm a quick tug and in a second I'm pressed up against his almost bare body. A shudder runs through me when I feel his heat against me.

"You need to let your hair down more. You're young, remember that."

"You're not," I say, pointing out the fact that he's clearly older than me for the first time.

"Hardly." His eyes flash as he lifts me up so my belly button is in line with his nose.

"Bax, no," I squeal in a panic. "Please no, Bax, please," I beg. I may be okay with water but I have a huge fear of my head going under.

"Okay, okay," he says softly as he lowers me slightly.

When I look down, he's gazing up at me but he looks lost in his own thoughts.

"It's Jay."

"What is?"

"Me. My name's Jay. Well, Jayden really. Bax is what the boys call me. My surname's Baxter," he says.

"Why are you telling me this now?"

He loosens his arms and I slowly start to slide down his chest. It's not until our eyes are level that he answers my question.

"You're not one of the boys."

"Who am I then?" I'm too lost in his eyes twinkling in the moonlight to put much thought into what I'm asking.

"Definitely not one of the boys." As he says it, his hands slide down my back and grab on to my arse. He pulls me tighter to him and I feel something press into my stomach.

I clear my throat, the sudden tension taking me by surprise. "No, I'm not."

"No, you're not," he repeats before running his nose against mine.

As I stare into his eyes, with our lips milometers apart, all I can think is how badly I want him to kiss me again. The memory of our kiss by the harbour yesterday isn't enough.

He stops moving and we stand stock still in the water with him holding me tightly, my feet a few inches from the seabed. He looks deep into my eyes and that saying about someone being able to see into your soul suddenly doesn't seem so stupid.

It feels like an eternity but eventually he leans forward and presses his lips against mine. I moan the second I feel their heat and he must sense my approval because he opens his mouth and runs the tip of his tongue along my bottom lip. I don't waste any time in responding.

Help Our Heroes

What started out as something soft and gentle soon turns into something much, much more. I lift my legs so they wrap around his waist, and my hands alternate between running over his short hair to gripping on to his shoulders. It's not until I feel the vibrations of his groan that I realise I'm moving my hips. Oh shit.

I pull back and immediately avert my gaze from him.

"What's wrong?" he asks, slightly breathlessly.

I try to let go of him but he holds me too tightly to be successful.

"Erin?"

I look up at the moon as I try to pull together what to say to him. "It's just…I haven't…uh…I don't…"

"Hey," he says as he nudges my cheek with his nose. He clearly doesn't want to let go of me in case I run. Reluctantly, I turn to him. The look on his face takes my breath away. His eyes are dark and hungry but he has this sexy smirk playing on his lips. "It's okay," he reassures. "I'm sorry, I shouldn't have pushed you. We can take this at your speed. This," he says, flexing his hips, making me gasp at the sensation, "isn't what this is about."

The look on his face is so sincere I have no reason to doubt him. "Thank you," I whisper. I lean forward slightly when I realise how badly I want to resume our kiss, but instead of doing the same, like I expect him to, Bax, or Jay, pulls back.

"Maybe we should get out."

"Oh."

"Trust me, Skittles, it's not because I want to, it's because I have to. We stay like this and I can't promise I won't do something I shouldn't." To prove his point, he flexes his hips again, pressing his hardness into me.

"Okay," I mutter as I unwrap myself from him and begin heading towards the shore.

It's not until I'm out of the water that I realise how cold I am. Jay had successfully distracted me but now my teeth are chattering, and try as I might, I can't get my skinny jeans up my damp, sandy legs. Jay doesn't seem to have the same issue; when I look up, he's almost fully dressed.

"Here," he says, handing me his hoodie.

I pull it on and just like his shirt last night, it almost comes down to my knees. "Thank you."

"Our B&B isn't far."

Once we've got our shoes on, we make our way back for two hot showers. Being the gentleman he is, Jay tells me to go first and I'm too cold and sandy to argue, so I grab what I need and head into the bathroom. I intend on being as fast as possible but once the powerful jets of water hit me, that goes out the window.

I spend longer than necessary putting moisturiser on my face and faffing with my hair, even though it will always dry exactly the same: straight as a die and falling just past my shoulders.

I give myself a once over in the mirror. My cheeks are still rosy red from the chill of the sea, and my eyes are still alight with the feelings Jay brought to life when he kissed me. I look down at the silky cami and short set I'm wearing. I feel completely exposed with my breasts only just covered and what feels like the bottom of my arse hanging out. If it's possible, I feel more naked than I did in just my underwear on the beach earlier, even though there's more fabric.

I take a breath and square my shoulders as I grab the doorknob. I am confident, I say to myself as I pull the door open. I'm a grown woman with a body I shouldn't be ashamed to show off.

The second I step into the doorway, he looks up. His eyes pin me to the spot and I stand there as looks over every inch of me. I might be barely covered in floral silk but the way he's staring at me right now, you'd think I was naked. My heart pounds as his eyes burn into skin, leaving tingles in their wake.

When his they come to a stop, staring at my tits, I manage to remember how to speak. "Your turn." I don't even recognise the sound of my own voice.

I move to sit myself on the edge of the bed, and eventually he gets up and disappears into the bathroom. He doesn't say anything—not that he needs to, because his eyes say it all, and I'd be lying if I said it didn't freak me out. It's not often I think this, but I wish I could be more like Frankie right now and be able to embrace what's happening between us, to put all my insecurities and fears to one side and enjoy everything Jay's offering, because I want it—of course I do. The feeling of his hands on me is incredible, but I'm scared to take it further.

Help Our Heroes

He doesn't spend as long in the bathroom as me, and when he emerges, he's just wearing a clean and dry pair of boxers. I've got myself into bed and pulled the covers up to my neck in a pathetic attempt to hide from him. It doesn't stop him running his eyes down my body. He knows exactly what it looks like, how it feels, even with the duvet covering me.

As he starts to walk around the bed, I roll over. I don't mean to shut him out but I've got so much going on in my head that I need the space. What I really don't need is him pulling me to him and kissing me like he did in the sea again. That will only mess my head up more. I shouldn't be feeling the way I am about him. I shouldn't like him this much already when I've only known him for a day. Plus, he's not just a guy, he's a solider—exactly what I said I never wanted. I'm not sure I'm strong enough to deal with an army relationship and all the stress that comes with it.

I have no idea how much time ticks by as I lie there thinking, but I know he's not asleep behind me. I can tell by his breathing. A huge part of me wants to turn around, to make the most of the situation we've found ourselves in, but another part is screaming at me that this is only going to end one way, and that's with me left behind with a broken heart. I may have only know Jayden Baxter for a day, but I already know he's going to change my life. I'm just not sure I'm ready for it.

Chapter 4

Once we've had breakfast the next morning, we decide to hang around instead of getting in the car and heading off to our next unknown destination. We spend the day wandering through town whilst Jay picks up a few things he didn't have in his case. We stop and have a coffee whilst watching some street entertainers, and then another one a few hours later watching an old couple fighting with their fish and chips and a swarm of seagulls.

We shy away from any kind of serious conversation about our jobs or our futures, and it amazes me how quickly I allow myself to forget about the stress of home and just enjoy this time doing pretty much nothing with him.

We spend the rest of the afternoon walking hand in hand along the beach, talking, watching families building sand castles, flying kites, and those who are brave enough to venture into the sea. I have first-hand experience of how cold that is, and no intention of testing it out again.

* * *

When the sun starts to drop, we decide we've probably walked far enough and start heading back. I've no idea how many miles we've covered, and I don't really care.

Once we get back into town, we opt for crossing over the road and walking past all the bars and cafés as we debate where we're going to have dinner. We eventually decide on a little Italian on one of the backstreets. It's quaint, the owner is someone you'd likely see on a comedy sketch show. He keeps us entertained for hours before we head back to our room and spend the night chilling out. Jay flicks through the channels whilst I sit with my sketchpad, coming up with some beach themed jewellery based on our day. His eyes flick over to my designs every few minutes and when he looks up at me I see him asking the same questions I do of myself regularly. Why am I doing a business degree? What am I going to do next if—or more so when—Mum's shop goes under? I don't answer his unspoken questions because I have no answers. I wish I did.

When we eventually get into bed, I can't help but have a smile on my face. I've had the most incredibly relaxing day and the fact that I've been able to switch off has everything to do with the man lying beside me.

"Jay," I whisper, a few minutes after turning the light off.

"Yeah?"

"Do you have to be so far away?"

Not a second later, I feel his body heat against my back, before his arm wraps around my stomach and he pulls me to him.

I have the best night's sleep I've had in years.

* * *

"Hey, sleepyhead," Jay says when the sound of the hotel room door shutting wakes me up.

It takes me a few seconds to register what's going on, but I soon figure out that he must have been for a run. His fitted t-shirt shows off his sculpted chest and a pair of slim shorts hug his thighs. It's quite a sight to wake up to.

"What time is it?"

"Almost ten. I asked June if we could have a late breakfast before hitting the road. She's keeping it warm for when we're ready."

"Almost ten?" I ask in shock. I don't think I've slept in this late before, ever. I sit bolt upright in bed and look to the clock at the other side of the room.

"Fucking hell," Jay breathes, making me look back over at him. Only, he's not looking at me—well, not my face, anyway.

I look down to see my nipple is just about to pop out from behind my cami. "Shit." I shift around and quickly cover myself up.

"You ruin all my fun," he says with a laugh, but then disappears into the bathroom for a shower. A wave of anxiety rushes through me as I think about how I'm acting. It's clear he wants more from me but I'm running scared. Will he eventually get fed up of playing this cat and mouse game? He said our time wasn't about that, and he's happy to take my lead, but is that really true?

I try to put my thoughts to one side as I get dressed and go down for breakfast. I know it won't make the situation any better, but at least I can ignore it for now.

* * *

"Where do you fancy going next?" Jay asks once we've polished off our fry up.

"I thought we weren't making plans?"

"No, but I'd like to have an idea of what direction I'm driving in. Would you like to carry on down south or…?"

"I'd prefer to go up, if that's okay with you. I'd love to see the scenery of the Lake District and Scotland. I've only seen it on the telly and it looks incredible."

"It's stunning."

"You've been?" I'm not sure why I'm surprised, because he's probably been to most places, but I'm a little disappointed it's not something we can discover together.

"I've had a few exercises up there. No holidays, though," he says, making me feel a little better.

"So you don't mind then?"

"Of course not. Anywhere you want to go, we'll go."

"Australia?"

"That might be pushing it. Maybe next time," he answers with a laugh. My heart does a little dance at the sight of his joy. I love seeing him smile and hearing his laugh. I feel pathetic even thinking it, but I think it's my new favourite thing. "Ready?"

"Ready."

We grab our stuff, say goodbye, and get ourselves into Peggy for the journey up north.

"I'm so excited," I mutter, more to myself than Jay when he pulls onto the motorway.

"You're too cute, Skittles."

"Are you going to tell me why you call me that?"

"I already did. It suits you."

"That's not a reason."

Help Our Heroes

***

It's late afternoon and we're just over halfway to our destination when my phone starts ringing. Our very loose plan is to get as far into the Lake District as we can, and find a B&B before the sun sets.

"Well, it's good to know you're not dead," I comment as a greeting to my best friend when I put the phone to my ear.

"I could say the same thing. I've just been to your house; your mum said you left a note saying you'd be gone for two weeks. Where the fuck are you?"

"Uh…I'm not entirely sure, other than on the motorway heading towards the Lake District."

"The fucking Lake District? It's all mountains, lakes, and sheep; why the fuck are you going there?"

When I said before that Frankie and I are complete opposites in every way, this is what I meant. She can't imagine a holiday that doesn't involve getting wasted in a club full of sweaty, drunk people. I want to see places and experience other cultures and their history rather than getting drunk off my arse and not remembering most of the holiday.

To save myself further scrutiny I change the subject. "Have you had a good weekend?"

"OH MY GOD! Erin, you have no idea how incredible Dean is." She squeals so loudly I have to pull the phone away from my ear. Jay looks over and raises his eyebrows in question. I shake my head at him and roll my eyes.

"So it was all you wanted it to be?"

"And some. Seriously, E, I thought he was going to kill me with all the orgasms. I can barely fucking walk."

"TMI, Kiki. TMI."

"I don't care. I'm telling you everything. I've been waiting my whole life for this and I want to relive it with you."

"Great."

"No need to sound so excited about it," she chastises. "So anyway, after we left the club…"

She talks for almost thirty minutes as she tells me the ins and out—literally—of her weekend with Dean.

"So, are you seeing him again?"

"Yes, he's on leave for another week, I think he said. To be fair, we haven't done much talking, but he's taking me out tonight. He's left to do some crap, thank fuck, I can finally take a shit now he's gone! Now stop changing the subject, and tell me why the fuck you're going to the Lake District."

"I'm going with Jay."

"Who the fuck is Jay?"

I let out a breath before explaining who he is.

"Wait…that seriously hot guy from the club? Dean's mate, Bax?"

I don't need to look up to know Jay's smiling beside me, I can feel his amusement. "Yes, that one," I confirm.

"WOOHOO! Way to go, Erin. I bet he fucks like a fucking stallion as well."

"Uh…"

"Oh my god, please tell me you had a go on that."

"I…uh…"

"ERIN!" she screams. "For the love of all womankind, you need to tap that. Fucking hell, what's wrong with you?"

"Nothing's wrong with me, thank you, Frankie." I want to say something like, what we have is more than just a quick roll in the sheets like you've had with Dean, but I'm suddenly very aware that Jay's listening to every word I say, as well as how those words would make this sound very serious and meaningful. I'm not ready to think about that kind of thing, let alone say it out loud.

"I'm sorry, but seriously, girl. You've got what, a week or so with him? Make the fucking most of it. You'll be a long time cold and lonely when he's gone back to wherever it is he came from. You may as well have some amazing memories to keep you company. Remember, you never regret something you've done, only the things you didn't do," she says, trying to sound wise all of a sudden.

"Thanks for the pep talk."

"What are best friends for if it isn't to tell you to fuck that hot as shit guy sat right next to you?"

I sit in silence for a few minutes, running the conversation around in my head. Is she right? Am I going to regret holding out like this? I soon distract myself when I think back to what I wanted to say about this being more than just sex, because it is. It scares the shit out of me to admit it to myself, but I feel like this is the start of something. Something serious. I don't want to just jump straight into bed with him. I don't want to rush whatever this is between us just because we've got a limited amount of time together. There's no reason we can't take this one step at a time.

I finally arrive at the depressing part of all of this as I think about him going back to wherever it is he's based, and not seeing him for god knows how long.

"So who exactly was that?"

"Frankie, the blonde girl in the silver dress Saturday night."

"I'm not sure I'd describe that as a dress, but yeah, I know the one."

"She's had this fantasy about having a fling with a soldier, showing him a good time and then sending him off to war. You know, like in the old black and white films. She just took great delight in telling me all about her weekend with Dean."

Jay's response is to start laughing. It's not the reaction I was expecting.

"What's so funny?"

"You just told me she has a solider fantasy and then backed it up by saying she spent the weekend with Dean."

"Right, and…"

"Dean's not in the army. He's a mechanic for Arthur," he says through his laughter.

My mouth drops open in shock.

"Fair play to him, though, he's clearly had a fantastic weekend pretending to be a solider."

"Wanker," I mutter.

"What? Don't you think it's kind of funny?"

"Yes and no. Frankie's ecstatic about her fantasy coming true and he's lied to her. What's he going to do next week when she's expecting him to put his uniform on and head back to work?"

"No clue. Knowing Dean, he probably hasn't thought that far ahead."

I'm not sure if I'm pissed off that Jay's mate has outright lied to Frankie, or if I'm amused by the whole thing like he is. Frankie is going to be gutted.

"So..." Jay asks. "Know anyone else with that fantasy?"

"Not that I know of. I don't think soldiers are all that hot, really."

"Ouch," he says, putting his hand over his heart, making me laugh. "That's a real shame because I know a solider who's got some moves."

"They also tend to be a little big headed."

"It's not my head you need to worry about the size of," he deadpans.

"Oh please. I'll believe that when I see it. What the fuck are you doing?" I squeal when he makes a show of taking his hands off the wheel in favour of his waistband.

"I'm joking," he says with a laugh as he takes control of the car again. "I've had no complaints though, just so you know."

"I'll keep that in mind."

* * *

"Do you have any idea where we are?" We went past the sign for the Lake District over an hour ago but soon found ourselves in the middle of nowhere with no phone or GPS signal. We haven't seen a house or any kind of life form other than sheep for miles.

"Not exactly."

"By that you mean no, right?"

"We'll come across something eventually."

"You really think we're going to find a B&B out here?"

"No. Maybe a town, though. There's got to be one at some point."

We continue driving through the gorgeous countryside as we watch the sun set over the mountains ahead. I get the feeling we're going to be spending the night in Jay's car. I was all for not planning this trip, but I'm now feeling a little stupid for not at least aiming for a B&B, or a town where we might find one.

"Look, there are lights over there," Jay says as we drop down a hill. It's been dark out for hours now, we're both starving, and I'm desperate for the toilet. I don't have the luxury of being able to relieve myself on the side of the road like Jay did a few miles back.

"Oh please, god, let it be somewhere to stop."

Jay laughs but continues driving towards the lights. For a building that looks to be fairly close, it takes a hell of a long time to get to with the winding roads. By the time we pull up to the somewhat derelict old farmhouse, I start to have second thoughts about stopping here.

"It's got a B&B sign," Jay points out sceptically.

"Hmmm." Said sign was missing most of its letters and hanging at an angle. If it's an indication for how unloved this B&B is, I'm not sure it's where we should be staying. It already looks like it could be the setting for a murder mystery programme.

"How badly do you need the toilet exactly?"

"Badly, but I'm still questioning this decision." Maybe peeing in a bush wouldn't be so bad.

"Come on. I'm sure it's owned by some lovely old couple who just struggle with maintenance."

I try to go with his way of thinking but I can't seem to get the idea out of my head that we could quite easily be killed here and no one would ever find us. I think I watch too many unsolved murder documentaries.

My desperate situation means that when he pulls the car to a stop and goes to get out, I rush to do the same.

We're just about to give up after standing at the front door for a few minutes with no response when there's some noise from inside. The door gets opened slowly to reveal the most hillbilly man I've ever seen in real life. His hair is long and greasy, his teeth are either black or missing entirely, and he's wearing the stereotypical checked shirt and threadbare jeans. He's not that old, so Jay's assumption of this place belonging to an old couple wasn't right. I'm fairly sure my idea about being murdered here could be closer to reality, because this guy has a look in his eye I really don't like.

"Hi, sorry, we're a little lost and need a bed for the night."

"And a toilet," I add.

"Oh…uh…yeah, sure." I swear I see an evil little smile appear on his lips. "Come in, toilet's down there on the right."

I give Jay a concerned look but he nods for me to go ahead. I really want to refuse but it's getting pretty painful now, so with an unsure smile at him, I head off.

It's a sight to behold. The toilet and basin are avocado green, the tiles are an aqua blue colour and covered in a layer of mould, and I can hardly see the taps for the limescale. Thankfully, I've got some anti-bacterial gel in my bag so I forego the hand washing facilities in favour of that.

When I find Jay, he's stood at a rickety old reception desk with a room key in his hand. My stomach turns over at the sight. I really don't want to stay here; it gives me the willies.

"It'll be okay," Jay says, obviously reading the look on my face.

We grab the bags from the car before venturing to our room; after seeing that toilet, I dread what it might be like.

I stand behind Jay as he puts the key in the lock and pushes the door. Nothing happens so he gives it a quick shove with his shoulder and after a loud creak, it opens. He doesn't give anything away as he walks in ahead of me, but even still, I hold my breath.

When Jay stands aside, I get my first look. I could already see the bare floor but the walls are almost the same. There are just a few bits of wallpaper here and there. When I look into the room, there is a double bed in the middle with a naked mattress, and a single chest of drawers in the corner. That's it.

"Uh…" I go to announce my refusal to stay here when there's movement behind me.

"I'm sorry it's not much. Here's some clean bedding though, and a new duvet and pillows," Hillbilly says, handing everything over along with a couple of soggy looking sandwiches.

"It's fine. We just need a bed."

"Well, the bathroom is down the hall. You're my only guests and Mother and I use the one upstairs, so it's all yours."

Jay thanks him again, because words elude me.

"This is very domesticated," Jay comments when we're halfway through making the bed together.

"None of this is what I was expecting to be doing this week."

Help Our Heroes

"Me neither," he says sadly.

"What were you planning on doing before we ran off together?"

"No idea. Probably would have spent it either in bed or at the pub with Dean. I know you saw my mum the day we left, so you understand why I wasn't happy about being there."

"Why come back? Why not book a holiday or something?"

"Same reason you didn't go off to uni like you wanted, I guess. Some kind of fucked up loyalty to my mother. She was an incredible mum. When I think back to my childhood, there isn't anything I would change. I had what I thought was the perfect family. My parents were still together, and as far as I knew, they were happy."

"What happened?"

"Dad suddenly announced he'd met someone else. He packed his bags that same day and we haven't seen or heard from him since. Mum fell apart. She started with alcohol, then came the drugs, and now…well, you saw the state of her. Every time I come back I expect to find her dead."

"I'm so sorry."

Jay shrugs it off and continues making the bed, clearly putting his memories behind him again.

"What's wrong? You look like you want to say something."

"It's not that, it's just…I really want a shower."

"Sooo…go have one."

"That guy really freaks me out."

"Well, don't invite him to join you then," he says with a laugh, clearly not understanding my issue.

"That wasn't what I meant, you idiot. I just don't want to go alone," I admit.

"You want me to shower with you?" I see a smile twitch at his lips and his eyes darken a few shades.

"Not with me, just be in the room."

"You want me to sit in the room whilst you're naked in the shower?"

"Yeah." Hearing him say it aloud makes me realise how pathetic I'm being about this, but I don't care.

"What if it's got a glass door?"

"You'll have to keep your eyes shut."

"You're shitting me."

"If I wanted you to see me naked, I'd have invited you to join me in the first place."

"What if I want to see you naked?"

"Jay," I huff. "Will you please just come with me?"

"Of course."

"Thank you."

I gather my stuff and we go to check out the bathroom. Much to Jay's disappointment, there isn't a glass shower door, just a mostly mouldy orange curtain which really sets off the blue bathroom suite.

I have to give him credit because he turns around when I ask him to, and I'm pretty confident he doesn't peek, either.

He spends the whole time I'm showering complaining about how torturous the whole experience is for him. It amuses me greatly.

When we're walking back towards our bedroom, I'm reminded of why I wanted Jay with me, because loitering outside our room is the hillbilly.

"Is everything okay?" Jay asks when we get closer.

"Oh…uh…yeah. I was just checking on you guys." The way he says it and the look in his eyes creep me out. He then notices me stood behind Jay, and his eyes drop to my bare legs. I made Jay give me his hoodie so I didn't have to walk out in just my cami and shorts in case this exact thing happened. I hear a weird growl-like noise come from the back of Jay's throat before the guy backs off down the hallway.

"You locked the door, right?"

"Yeah, but he owns the place, so I'm sure he could get in if he wanted to." Jay's answer doesn't put my overactive imagination to rest at all. "You're right, he's creepy," he admits for the first time.

Jay lets us into our room and hands me the key so I can lock it myself. I think he's beginning to understand how uncomfortable I am.

I turn back around after pulling the key out to find Jay stood right in front of me. He's looking at me with hunger in his eyes and a small smirk playing on his lips.

"What?"

"You've no idea, do you?"

"Uh..."

Instead of explaining, he reaches back and pulls his t-shirt over his head, throwing it onto the bed behind him.

"What are you doing?"

"Distracting you."

My mouth opens in shock.

"You tell me when to stop, and I will."

I nod at him to show I understand, but I can't form words because my heart's hammering so damn hard my brain's gone fuzzy, and I have a whooshing sound in my ears.

It's like time stands still as I wait for him to do something, but the second he touches me, someone presses fast forward.

He steps towards me and his lips go to my neck. They dance over my skin as he peppers kisses from my ear to my collarbone. I lean my head to the side to give him the access he needs.

My heart continues to hammer, and tingles fire around my body, but they all meet between my legs. I've never felt anything like it but I already know I don't want it to stop.

Jay moves his head back at the same time I feel him start to lower the zip on his hoodie. He stares into my eyes for a few seconds before he drops it and stares at my chest like it's not still covered by my cami.

"You've no idea how hot you are, do you?" I bite down on my bottom lip. I have no idea how to respond to a question like that. "Fuck." He lifts his thumb to my mouth and pulls my lip from my teeth. "Mine," he mutters before he crashes our lips together.

He kisses me with an intensity I've never experienced before. His tongue licks and caresses while his teeth nip and tease. His hands slip inside his hoodie and rest against my waist. I can feel his fingers twitching to move and explore, and in a moment of madness, I grab his wrists and encourage them to do just that.

Slowly, he slides his hands up my ribs before he grabs on to my breasts. A moan I wasn't expecting falls from my mouth as he squeezes. "Oh my god," I breathe against his lips. I feel him smile, obviously pleased by my response.

He kneads my breasts for a few more seconds whilst he continues to kiss me. Then, his hands lift off before I feel him pinch my nipples. I suck in a sharp breath as what I can only describe as a bolt of lightning strikes between my legs.

"You look so hot, coming apart. If my hands make you like this, I can only imagine what else I could achieve," he mumbles into my neck.

"Please," falls from my mouth. I think it shocks him as well because he suddenly pulls back from me a looks into my eyes.

I stare back at him, silently pleading for more.

"You sure?"

I can only nod my reply. What he's done to my body has turned my brain to mush.

"Okay then," Jay says before lifting me so I'm pinned against the door by his hips. He grabs my thighs and wraps them around his waist, making his hardness press into the exact spot that's pulsing with need. The pressure against my sensitive flesh makes my head fall back. "Has anyone ever made you come before?"

I keep my eyes shut and shake my head.

"Good. I'd want to kill any fucker who'd already had the chance to touch you. You're mine, and I'm going to make sure you know it. You'll be feeling the after effects for days," he promises.

His continued hip movement ensures I'm unable to respond with more than a moan.

His lips continue exploring the skin of my neck before he ventures down over my collarbone and alone the edge of my cami.

"Are you particularly attached to this?" he asks as he tugs at the strap.

At this exact moment, I'd tell him I'm not attached to my legs if it meant he'd continue what he's doing.

"I'll take that as a no," he says when I don't respond.

Seconds later, I hear a rip before cold air surrounds my boobs. My head lifts from the door and my eyes spring open. When he comes into focus, he's staring right at my bare chest. After a couple of seconds, his eyes lift to mine. They're dark and hungry, and I'm sure there's a warning in them. My mouth waters for him as I take in his pained face.

"You're so fucking beautiful and your tits are fucking perfect."

He leans forward and I feel the incredible heat of his mouth as he sucks on one of my nipples. The feeling of his tongue running slowly around my sensitive peak has me trying to close my legs, but the only thing I achieve is to press him harder into me.

"You taste like heaven," he says, licking across my skin to my other nipple.

I'm panting and moaning as he continues to torture me. My whole body's tingling and the tension inside me is beginning to get unbearable. I have no idea what it is I need him to do, but it doesn't stop me begging for it.

"You want more?" he grates out, his voice deep and gravelly.

"Yes, yes," I repeat.

All of a sudden, I'm moving. I'm pulled away from the door before being lowered to the bed seconds later.

"Tell me you want me to make you come," Jay demands.

Embarrassment flows through me and I have the sudden need to cover myself up. Jay must sense it because he straddles my hips and pins my wrists together above my head in one of his hands. The other slowly teases the skin of my breasts. I can't help myself and I shamelessly arch my back as I try to get more of his touch.

"That's what I want—you begging for it. Begging for me to tip you over the edge," he says as he stares down into my eyes. "Now, tell me what you want, Erin."

I can't find the words he wants me to say. This is all new to me and I can't help fearing I'm going to say it wrong or sound stupid.

"Tell me to make you come, or I'll stop. I need to know it's what you want." To drive his point home, he pinches one of my nipples and I feel heat flood my core as it continues to pound uncomfortably.

"Make me come," I whisper, so quietly I barely hear it myself.

"Louder," he demands.

"Make me come."

"What was that?"

"Make me come."

"Scream it." I don't know what it is, but the way he's looking at me leaves no room for argument, so I immediately find myself following orders.

"MAKE ME COME," I scream, and in seconds, he's off me. I feel his hand skim the skin of my lower stomach before it disappears into my knickers.

Embarrassment heats my cheeks momentarily as I think about what he's doing, but the second I feel him touch me, all thoughts leave my head.

"Fuck," I breathe as I once again try to close my legs.

"Nope." Jay pins one of them down against the bed with his as he stares down at me.

"You're going to come on my fingers."

I nod; I have no doubt what he's saying is true.

His fingers circle my clit and just as the tension in me builds up to breaking point, he moves and starts to tease my entrance.

"Please tell me I'm the first to be here."

I nod.

"Tell me."

"You're the—" I let out a sudden intake of breath as I feel him press inside, halting my words. "Shit." I don't know whether I like it or hate in those first few seconds. It doesn't take me long to make up my mind.

"Erin?" His eyes come back to mine from watching where his hand had disappeared.

"You're the first," I confirm. My voice quivers as I say it.

"Fucking hell."

"What?" I ask in a panic, thinking I've done something wrong.

"You're fucking perfect."

Jay leans forward and sucks one of my nipples into his mouth again as his fingers start to slide in and out of me faster. I feel his thumb graze my clit and all my muscles tense.

"You feel that?"

"Uh huh," I confirm.

"Fuck, you'll feel amazing on my cock," he mutters. Everything gets tighter as I think about what he just said, how it might feel, how he'd look on top of me. "That's it. Let go."

"Oh my god," I squeal as something inside me explodes.

When I come back to myself, Jay is sat next to me, running his eyes over my skin. What the fuck did I just do? I've no idea who that was a few minutes ago, but I'm sure it wasn't me. I grab onto the sides of his hoodie that I'm still wearing and wrap it over my boobs.

His eyes find mine and I see panic in them as we stare at each other. Part of me wants to tell him that shouldn't have happened, but a bigger part knows I'd be lying.

In the end, I go with offering a favour in return, even though I have no idea what to do.

"Do you want me to…?" I ask, gesturing to the obvious bulge in his chinos.

"What? No," he says, sounding horrified by the suggestion. "Shit, no I didn't mean it like that," he quickly adds when he sees the look on my face. "If you touch me, Erin, then there won't be any stopping until I've owned you."

My mouth snaps shut and a gentle throb starts up again down below.

"Fuck." He gets up from the bed and paces back and forth a couple of times. "I need a shower. Are you going to be okay?"

With everything that's just happened, I've completely forgotten where we are and why I was so freaked out earlier. I guess he came through with his promise of distracting me.

"Yeah, just lock the door behind you."

"Okay."

I watch in silence as he rummages through his bag for what he needs. He's just about step towards the door when he turns to me.

"Here, wear this." He throws me the shirt I slept in on our first night. "I won't be long."

The second I hear the door lock, I strip out of my ruined cami and shorts and pull his shirt over my head. His smell engulfs me and I immediately wish I'd told him not to leave me. I sit myself on the edge of the bed and look around at the almost bare room. This whole thing with Jay is utterly crazy, but I can't imagine being with anyone else right now. From the second I met him, everything just felt right. I knew I needed to get away, but I wasn't aware there was something—or someone—missing from my life. I'm starting to realise Jay is filling a gaping hole. If you'd have asked me about a boyfriend a few days ago, I'd have said I didn't have time, and although that's still true, after only a couple of days I'm realising that I would make whatever time Jay needed because he's somehow managed to creep his way in, and it scares me to admit that I don't see him finding his way out very fast.

"Hey, are you okay?" Jay asks when he steps back into the room a while later to find me in bed with my laptop.

"Yeah, I wasn't murdered by the creep whilst you were gone."

"So I see," he replies with a laugh. "That wasn't what I meant, though."

My cheeks heat a little. "I'm good."

"What're you doing?"

"Trying to work on a uni assessment. I'll stop now you're back," I offer.

He refuses because he doesn't want me falling behind, so we sit side by side, me trying to work and him playing on his phone until the early hours of the morning.

Chapter 5

"Let's get out of here," Jay says the second I open my eyes to find him looking down at me the next morning.

"Yes." I jump out of bed and start gathering up my stuff. He doesn't need to ask me twice to leave this shithole.

I make quick use of the bathroom before Jay grabs our cases and we sneak out. The place is in darkness, and thankfully it's silent.

We jump in the car and both start laughing uncontrollably. I'm not sure why he's so amused, but I'm just grateful we got out of that place alive.

"Where are we going?" I ask when it seems he knows what directions to take.

"I discovered I could get some 3G when I was sat on the toilet whilst you were asleep last night. I managed to get a map up."

"You left me alone in that room in the middle of the night?"

"It was either that or piss out the window."

"I think I'd have preferred that."

"I've found a route that will take us past some of the places you mentioned, and I've booked a room for the night."

"You're doing a lot of planning for someone who didn't want any."

"I thought you deserved to know you're going to be sleeping somewhere decent tonight."

"I appreciate that more than you know. You deserve that, too; you're on holiday, after all."

"That place was a million times better than some of the hell holes I've slept in in the past. Having you beside me made it feel almost like a posh hotel, much better than the sweaty men I usually wake up with."

"Is there something you need to tell me?" I ask with a laugh.

"Definitely not. I'd lay my life down for those guys but they aren't coming nowhere near my junk."

Jay quickly changes the subject after glancing over at me. My fears about his job and the memories of losing my dad must be written all over my face.

He efficiently navigates us to a fancy hotel in Windermere and treats me to a wonderful breakfast, consisting of an all you can eat continental buffet before a mouth-watering plate of American pancakes, while he polishes off a giant fry up.

He drives us around the lake once we've finished and I spend the whole time staring out the window at the incredible views. I knew it was going to be stunning up here from what I've seen on the TV, but it really is amazing.

"What are we doing?" I ask when Jay pulls off the road into a small parking area.

"I thought we could experience the lake close up."

I hop out the car and follow him down the track to a small beach like spot at the edge of the water.

The sun's shining, and in this secluded little corner, we're sheltered from the cold wind.

"If I ever win the lottery, I want a view like this from my house."

"I could live with that," he agrees as he rests back on his elbows next to me.

We're both silent as we soak it all up; the sound of the water, and the bird song from the trees above us. I allow myself to get lost in the peace this place has to offer.

Jay scares me when he suddenly jumps up. "What's wrong?"

"Nothing," he says as he pulls his hoodie and t-shirt off at the same time.

"What are you—" My question gets cut short when he slips his trainers off before dropping his jeans.

"Burning off breakfast. Join me?"

"No, you're okay." He may have got me in the sea before, but it's not happening again. Once was cold enough.

"Your loss," he says before he turns his back on me and drops his boxers.

My mouth falls open as I stare at his naked behind—he has the most perfect arse. I watch as he walks towards the water before his bottom half disappears into what I can imagine feels like an ice bath. It doesn't seem to bother him; he ducks under before swimming off into the lake.

I watch him but the image of his naked arse seems to be burned onto the inside of my eyelids.

Thankfully—or sadly, actually, I'm not really sure—he covers himself when he eventually emerges from the water. To be fair, it must've been so cold that I can't imagine there's much to show off right now.

He quickly dresses before asking if I'm ready to take off.

We spend the afternoon driving around and taking everything in. We stop in a cute little village bakery when we start to get hungry and indulge in gorgeous cream cakes, before getting back in the car to head towards our accommodation for the night.

"You booked a room in Gretna Green?"

"Yeah, I've always been intrigued by the place so thought it was the perfect opportunity to check it out."

To say I'm relieved would be putting it mildly when he pulls into the car park of a fancy looking hotel. "I thought we were keeping to cheap B&Bs?" I ask on our way towards the expensive room Jay had already booked.

"I told you earlier, you deserve it after last night."

"Last night wasn't good, but that doesn't mean you need to spend loads. I'd be more than happy with a bog standard B&B."

"I know you would, but I wanted to treat you."

I can't help but swoon a little at his words. I know I made a bit of a fuss about that place last night, but it wasn't because I expected to be staying in swanky places, just clean ones with a couple more pieces of furniture, and without the epic creep we had to share the building with.

"Thank you," I say sincerely when we come to a stop outside our door. I reach up on my tiptoes and give him a quick kiss.

"I know how you could thank me properly." My eyes widen and my mouth drops. "I'm joking," he quickly adds on. "No need to look so worried."

Was I worried? I wonder as I follow him into the room. No, I'm pretty sure the tingles I felt when he said it were more to do with excitement.

"Oh my god, look at that bath." Sat in the middle of the bathroom is a huge free standing tub just calling out to be used.

"Knock yourself out. We don't have dinner reservations until nine."

I don't need any more convincing than that. I get the water the right temperature before searching for the complimentary bubble bath. When I find it I let out a sigh of relief that it's not the standard lavender scent I hate. Instead, it's a fresh mandarin and grapefruit flavour that makes my mouth water.

I check to ensure I'm covered in bubbles before telling Jay he can come in when he knocks. He opens the door and peeks through before walking in with a glass of bubbles.

"Champagne and a bath full of bubbles. What could be better?"

"Well, technically it's prosecco, but close enough. And you forgot to mention the hot man."

"Must have been an oversight. Thank you," I say, reaching an arm out to take the glass. "What's wrong?" He's got an odd look on his face.

"I'm disappointed."

"Why?"

"I was at least hoping to see some boob."

"Oh, get out," I say, flicking bubbles at him.

"What? It's not like I haven't already seen them." That may be true but it doesn't stop me blushing at the thought of exposing myself to him.

"Get out."

"Or licked them," he mutters as he steps back. His eyes darken as they drop from mine down to where my boobs are hiding behind the bubbles. I raise an eyebrow at him. "Okay, okay, I'm going," he says with a pout but before he turns, he scoops up the bubbles covering me and puts them on my head. I manage to hold my smile until he shuts the door.

* * *

"Fuck me, you look good," Jay announces when I emerge from the bathroom a long time later. Luckily, I packed a dress just in case. It's a classic black prom dress, paired with a thin red belt and red peep toe court shoes. My only jewellery is a heavy silver bracelet consisting of a series of solid squares; it's one of my favourites but can only be worn with something simple because of its size. My make-up is done—nothing exciting, just a bit of mascara, blusher and gloss.

Help Our Heroes

The only thing left to do is my hair.

"Thank you." I run my eyes over him as he does the same to me. He's wearing a dark pair of jeans and a plain white shirt. He looks incredibly sexy, resting back against the headboard where he's been watching TV.

I sit myself down at the dressing table and pull the hotel hair dryer from the drawer. I feel his eyes on me the entire time; they burn into my skin and ensure the tingles he started when he came into the bathroom earlier continue to simmer just under the surface.

"Keep it down," he instructs when I go to pull my hair back. I mostly get on fine with my hair; it's easy and low maintenance because it's always straight, but when I get dressed up I always feel like it's lacking because I can't do anything fancy with it.

"Why?"

"Because you look sexy." His eyes hold mine in the mirror and the heat in them ensures I do as he says. "Come on, it's time to go."

The short journey in the lift is torturous with his scent filling my nose while the heat of his hand burns into my lower back. I feel his fingers twitching where I can only assume he's as desperate to move it as I am. The memory of how it felt when he had his hands on me last night is right at the forefront of my mind.

I let out a breath when the doors open and I swear I hear him do the same. He leads me towards the restaurant and pushes the waiter out of the way so he can be the one to pull my chair out. I try not to let his gentlemanly actions affect me but it's no hope, I swoon hard. When I look up into his eyes to thank him, I feel myself fall for him even more than I already have. That's the moment I know I'm never going to be able to get him out from under my skin.

He orders us more wine. I'm already buzzing from the two glasses I had in our room but I don't argue; it's not every day I get this kind of treatment so I'm going to enjoy it while I can.

By the time we've eaten and Jay suggests we sit in the bar, I can already feel the room spinning a little, so when he places a cocktail down on the coffee table in front of me, I know I'm making a huge mistake by drinking it, but I'm flying too high to care.

Some amount of time later, I feel Jay wrap his arm around my waist and attempt to get me to the lift. My legs are like jelly and I swear I'm going to hit the floor any second. I wrap my arms around him to stop me from falling.

"I could get used to this," he whispers in my ear as we wait for the lift.

"Hmmm, I think you'd better, soldier boy, because I'm not letting you go."

"And I definitely like the sound of that." His words are at odds with his previous warning about this being a two week only thing but I'm too drunk to read too much into it.

By the time the doors open, I'm stood in front of Jay, looking up in to his gorgeous grey eyes. I feel him push me back by my hips and my legs must do as they're told because a few seconds later, I feel the handrail in the lift press into my back.

Jay doesn't move until the doors shut. Then, he presses himself against me and takes my lips in a hot and dirty kiss. My hands grasp at his shirt as my leg lifts around his waist as I try to get closer to him.

I feel the vibration of his moan all the way to my clit. Fucking hell, this man is like a drug; I don't think I've ever craved something so much in my entire life.

I feel myself being lifted from the floor, and the next thing I know, I'm in his arms as we head down the corridor towards our room.

He sits me on the bed before I feel my shoes being slipped off. Soft kisses run up the inside of my leg before I feel him almost at my knickers. I suck in a breath as I prepare for what's about to happen but he pulls back, and seconds later I feel him undoing my belt and unzipping my dress. Then, my bra's gone, and I feel the burning heat of his palms against my breasts. My head falls back as I focus on the sensation of him squeezing and pinching.

I fall back onto the bed when he encourages me to do so. My alcohol filled brain doesn't let me worry about being totally bare for him when I feel my underwear slide down my thighs and over my feet. The mattress dips as he crawls on top of me, and when I look down I see he's gloriously naked, only I don't get a chance to see everything because he folds himself over me and kisses me senseless. I feel him at my entrance and my muscles clench as they prepare for what it might feel like having him push his way inside me. I watch as he sits back, and he's just about to thrust forward when my eyes spring open.

* * *

I stare ahead. The room's light and the side of bed next to me is empty. What the fuck?

Then I hear something. When I look towards the noise, I find Jay once again doing sit ups. My heart continues to pound at the same speed as my clit as the images that were just so vivid in my mind continue to play out as I watch him. His muscles stretch and pull with each movement and his damp skin glistens in the morning sunlight.

I'm almost back on level ground by the time he stops and stands. "Sorry, did I wake you?" he asks when he sees I'm watching.

The second his eyes land on me, I feel my face fill with heat. Fuck.

"What?" he asks, a small smirk playing on his lips.

"Nothing."

"Skittles, you're flushed as red as a fucking tomato and your eyes are wide as fuck. That's not nothing."

"I…uh…just woke up all of a sudden and I didn't know where I was," I lie.

His cheeky smile finally breaks free. "Right." I watch as he climbs on to the bed. He's only in his boxers so I get a nice close up of his chest and stomach. "How about you tell me the real reason?" he says as he runs his fingers over my cheek and down my neck to my collarbone.

"I was dreaming," I whisper.

"Do tell." He's got a wicked glint in his eye.

"I can't really remember it now."

"Liar."

I shift onto my side and realise I'm dressed in his shirt, and I'm wearing knickers. "Did you put me to bed last night?" I ask, because other than the dream I have no recollection of leaving the bar, and I'm thinking it was just that: a dream.

"You don't remember?"

My cheeks flush once again as I shake my head.

"That's a real shame, Skittles, a real shame."

"What happened?"

"I couldn't possibly tell."

"Wanker," I mutter.

He has a little laugh to himself but he doesn't say any more.

It was just a dream, I'm sure of it. He told me he wouldn't do anything until I begged for it so I'm pretty sure he wouldn't take advantage when I'm drunk. Right?

This question rolls around my head the whole time I'm getting ready and throughout breakfast. I'm fairly sure it was all a dream. I'm desperate to ask him more, but at the same time I'm scared he'll make me admit what I think may or may not have happened—or worse, the details of my dream.

When we get to the bit of Gretna Green where they do all the weddings, there's a bride and groom having their photos taken. We stop on a little grass bank and watch the happy couple posing and laughing. They look unbelievably happy about the new chapter of their lives they've just embarked on.

Nothing's said between us for the longest time as we sit and watch the world go by, so when Jay suddenly speaks up, it startles me a little.

"Wanna get married?"

"What?" I ask, thinking I just heard him wrong.

"Let's get married."

"It's weird, because I thought you just asked me to marry you…twice," I say with a laugh.

"I guess I did. What do you say?"

"I say you're crazy. We can't just get married."

"Why not? We're here and this is where all kinds of crazy shit goes down, marriage-wise."

"You can't just turn up here nowadays, say 'I do', and be on your way. You still need to register and stuff beforehand."

"Well, that wasn't a no," he comments with a laugh.

"I'm not going to respond to your craziness with an answer, Jay. It's totally insane."

"But the wedding night," he pouts.

"Seriously, you're nuts."

His focus is still on the couple and photographer in front of us but he has this wistful look on his face that I haven't seen since we started this road trip. The sudden moment of seriousness reminds me of everything I'm running away from and the plans I need to make about my future. It's unrealistic to think I'll finish uni next year and work with mum in her shop, because it's going to be gone unless she makes some drastic changes. I need a plan for me, not her. If I'm going to focus on my jewellery then I need to find more stockists, look at going to trade shows, get my name out there, a million and one things really.

"Ready to make a move?" Jay eventually asks, distracting me from thoughts of my future.

"Yes."

We grab a couple of takeout coffees from a café before getting back in Peggy and heading farther up north.

* * *

"There's a classic car show this weekend, look," Jay says excitedly as we drive towards Inverness. "Can we go?" I can't help but laugh because he sounds like an excited little child.

"Sure."

"We can stay here somewhere tonight, and then go tomorrow."

His excitement is infectious, and I find myself looking forward to a day staring at old cars—not because I want to, but because more than anything I want him to be happy, and right now he's buzzing.

We spend all afternoon driving around the country roads, taking in the scenery before heading into town to find somewhere to stay for the night.

"What about there?" I say, pointing to a vacancies sign on the side of the road.

We continue up the long driveway to reveal a quaint bungalow. It definitely doesn't have the grandeur of the hotel last night, but equally, it looks loads better than the dilapidated farmhouse from the night before. We may have found a happy medium, even if it does look more like someone's home than a B&B.

We stand hand in hand waiting for someone to answer the door, and eventually an elderly lady pulls it open. She shouts something behind her but fuck knows what she says because her Scottish accent is so strong she may as well be speaking another language. I glance over at Jay, whose eyebrows are raised slightly, showing he has no clue either.

"Good evening, come in," she says to us. Thankfully, it's slower, and easier to understand.

She ushers us into their living room where her husband is sat watching TV.

"Good evening. I'm William, and this is my wife Mary. Are you looking for a room?"

"Yes, we saw your vacancy sign. I'm Jay and this is Erin."

I stand awkwardly as Mary looks us both up and down. She gives her husband a nod before he asks what kind of room we want.

"Double would be great," Jay answers without missing a beat.

"I presume you're married," Mary says, looking down at my left hand.

"Uh…no." Thankfully Jay doesn't elaborate and tell this obviously traditional couple that we've only known each other a few days.

"You're welcome to stay but only married couples will share a room under my roof," Mary says when William fails to do his job by the look of the stare he receives.

Jay looks over at me. The expression on his face makes me smile, because I can tell he's begging for me to apologise and be on our way so we can find a double bed. Unfortunately for him, I do the opposite. I'm not sure if it's for my own amusement or torture, but I tell Mary it won't be an issue and that we'll have a single room each. As the words leave my mouth, Jay's chin drops and his eyes narrow at me. I just smile at him.

"The rooms are next door to each other but there will be no sneaking into each other's in the middle of the night."

"Of course not," I say politely, earning me another death stare from Jay.

We stand by our doors as we watch Mary retreat down the hallway after offering us dinner.

"What the hell, Erin?"

"What?" I ask innocently. "I didn't want to carry on looking for us not to find anything, or worse, another shithole. This will be fine and it's only for one night. I'm sure you can cope."

"You're gonna pay for this."

Help Our Heroes

"Maybe you should have told me what happened last night."

"Oh, so this is revenge, is it?"

"Maybe," I say as I unlock the door and walk into my room. I put a little extra swing to my hips, leaving him muttering about getting me back for this.

When the door shuts behind me and I'm alone in my room, I can't help but feel like I've made a mistake. I suddenly feel lonely and I don't like knowing he's the other side of the wall. I sit down on my bed and let out a sigh.

I have a quick shower before changing and knocking on Jay's door.

When he opens it, he's only in his boxer briefs, giving me a great show of what I'm missing alone in my room next door.

"I know what you're doing, and it's not working."

"Really?" he asks as he bends over to put his jeans on.

I want to look away and not be affected by the show he's putting on but it's not working. Damn him.

By the time we get to the dining room, Mary and William are sat waiting for us with a steaming cottage pie in the middle of the table.

"Sorry, he wasn't ready," I announce when we walk in.

We spend the next few hours chatting away. We learn all about Mary and William's five children, as well as their nineteen grandchildren. Yes, they may be a little old fashioned, but they stay true to what they believe in and they're such a lovely couple, I can't help but warm to them.

* * *

"I guess this is goodnight, then," Jay says when we stop by our doors.

"I guess it is. Sleep well." I go to push open my door but my wrist gets grabbed and in seconds, I find myself up against Jay's chest.

"I don't think so," he mutters before slamming his mouth down on mine.

I worry for all of about two seconds that we're going to be caught, but as soon as I feel his tongue against mine, all thoughts vanish as I lose myself in his kiss.

When he pulls back, we're both panting with need and the images I still vividly remember from my dream last night are at the forefront of my mind. I desperately want to follow him into his room and let him get his hands on me, but I know we can't, so instead, I bid him goodnight and bolt to the safety of my room before I do something Mary and William wouldn't approve of.

I change into Jay's shirt, because I can't imagine wearing anything else to bed now, and toss and turn as I imagine what we could be doing. I should be using the time to do some work but all I can picture is him looking down on me.

I eventually fall asleep at some ungodly hour, but it's fitful and full of lustful dreams I shouldn't be having in this religious couple's home.

* * *

After being treated to a home cooked English breakfast, and somehow agreeing that we'll spend tonight with them, we head off to find the car show. Jay's like a kid on Christmas morning as we queue to park in a muddy field. I don't share his enthusiasm as it's cold and drizzly out. The last thing I want to be doing is walking around in the rain looking at cars. I think my lack of sleep—and lack of Jay—has made me a little moody.

I follow him around for just over an hour before he suggests I get a coffee and sit in the café to warm up while he continues to ohh and ahh. I'd love to share his excitement but they're all just cars to me.

I pull my sketchbook out and sit there coming up with ideas as I look out at the cars in front of the marquee.

I get lost in my car inspired designs and jump a mile when Jay places his hand down on my shoulder hours later. "Sorry," he says, sitting down next to me and grabbing one of the fresh coffees I notice he's placed on the table. "Let's have a look."

I hand over my sketches and he flicks through the pages. "These are incredible. There are loads of female car fanatics who'd love something like this."

"You think so?" I ask sceptically.

"I know so. I know it's none of my business but I think you need to let your mum deal with her business, and you need to focus on this. You've got a talent you could really make something of."

I let out a breath, because the reminder of what I've left behind sits heavy on my shoulders. I've had a couple of texts from Mum telling me she's had more final demands come through. I've been too scared to call her back and find out how things are really going. It's much easier living in denial as I flit around the country with Jay, but with every day that passes, I get more and more aware that I'm closer to going back and dealing with it all once again. Unfortunately, these two weeks will only last so long before I fall back to reality with a bang.

* * *

"What are you two all dressed up for?" I ask when we arrived back at the B&B later that evening to find Mary and William all ready for a night out.

"Susan's nephew runs a dance class at the village hall on a Friday night. Highlight of our week," Mary says happily. "Oh, you two should come. We've been working on a rhumba; I think you would enjoy it," she adds with a wink.

"Oh, I don't know," I say, thinking Jay's going to tell them where to go, because I can't imagine him wanting to go ballroom dancing.

I almost get whiplash where I turn to look at him so fast when he says, "Sure, sounds like fun."

"Fantastic. We need to leave in ten minutes, so go and get changed quickly."

"What the hell?" I ask Jay once we're out of earshot.

"What? I thought it might be fun, seeing as we'll be sleeping apart again tonight. I'll get to have my hands all over you."

A shiver runs through me at the thought. Okay, so credit where credit's due, he does have a point.

"Doesn't seem such a bad idea now does it?"

"I guess not," I say on a sigh, trying to appear less excited about it than I really am. It's been years since I danced properly, but the prospect of doing it with Jay definitely piques my interest.

I quickly change into my black dress and red shoes. Mary and William are looking dapper, ready for their night on the tiles, so it was my only option. When I meet back up with Jay in the hallway, I find him in the same outfit as that night as well.

He comes to a stop in front of me and runs his eyes from the top of my head all the way to my toes. He gives me tingles without even touching me.

"You look hot as fuck in this dress," he whispers in my ear when he steps up to me. "Do you know what's sexier, though?"

I shake my head, knowing he's about to tell me anyway.

"Taking it off you."

My mouth goes dry, and I have the sudden urge to drag him into my room and demand he does just that when I hear a voice asking if we're ready because we're going to be late.

"Fuck," Jay mutters before I watch him rearrange himself in his jeans. He must feel my stare because he looks up at me. "What? I can't help it. Have you seen yourself?"

I shake my head at him because I don't want him to know how happy it makes me to know I affect him so much.

The village hall is exactly like I was expecting. Every surface is covered in pine panelling, and the chairs and tables around the edges of the room look like they should have been replaced about thirty years ago. At the far end of the room, there's a guy who stands out amongst the elderly couples, not only because of his age but because he's wearing skin-tight black trousers and a shirt undone almost to his belly button. I guess he's the instructor.

"Are we ready to go? Do you all remember the moves?"

"Wait!" Mary shouts. "We've brought some friends."

The guy's eyes light up when he sees us. I can only presume it's because we're close to his age.

"The more the merrier. We'll soon get them caught up."

He starts the music and the sounds of Aerosmith's 'Don't Want To Miss A Thing' fills the hall, and all of a sudden each couple pairs off and starts a well-choreographed rhumba routine. I had plenty of dance lessons as a kid so I know what a rhumba looks like, but I was not expecting these elderly church going couples to move quite like this. This instructor must be having a whale of a time getting couples of this age moving their hips quite like that.

"Holy shit," Jay mutters next to me.

"It's quite a thing, huh? You're never too old for a little bit of that," the instructor says, wiggling his eyebrows and nudging Jay's arm. "How about we get you some tonight?"

"Uh…" Jay stutters as the instructor grabs both our hands and pulls us on to the makeshift dance floor.

Help Our Heroes

"I'm David, by the way," he says. He teaches us the first few moves as the couples continue with their dance. I'm amazed when I find that Jay's a natural dancer and we move together flawlessly.

"How much Viagra do you think is in this room tonight?" Jay whispers in my ear when David walks off to see how the others are doing.

"Oh god, don't," I say with a laugh as I look to the side to see the couple closest to us grinding away against each other.

"It's a good job they're all past it. Otherwise, there could be more than ten kids conceived tonight."

"Oh, please stop." The image that brings into my head is too much. "Anyway, where'd you learn to dance?" I ask, because this clearly isn't his first time.

"Promise you won't laugh."

"Of course."

"A year or so ago, my sergeant was getting married. He'd been having lessons with his now wife but when we got deployed a few months before the wedding, he needed a partner."

"Oh my god," I mutter quietly, trying not to smile. "You took her place while he practiced?" I really want to laugh at the image of two strapping army men ballroom dancing around whatever war torn country they were in, but what he did was too cute.

"That was so nice of you."

"You never say no to a favour when the next day that man could be the one to save your life," he says, but I can see he instantly regrets bringing his reality into this.

"Well, you're very good."

"What about you?"

"I had dance lessons until I was about fourteen."

"That's it, perfect hip action," David says as he stares at Jay's arse a little too intently. Jay narrows his eyes at him and I try to hold in my smile.

The dance class goes on for two hours. I never would've thought some of those old couples would've lasted that long, but they all look more awake than I feel.

"Right, one last time, all the way through from the top," David announces after everyone's had a quick drink.

Jay pulls me flush against him and places one hand on my waist and the other in my hand. He lowers his head so our noses are touching and he looks deep into my eyes as we wait for the music to start. We're not saying any words, but I feel like we're having a conversation, communicating just through our eyes how much we've come to mean to one another after only a few short days.

I don't hear the music start, I'm too lost to him, but when he starts moving I quickly catch up.

"Don't step away from me," Jay warns when the song comes to an end and the other couples separate.

"Why? We've finished."

"Unless you want David and everyone else in the room to know as well as we do how much I want you right now, you'll stay here." To nail his point home, he flexes his hips and pushes his erection into my stomach.

"We can't stay like this all night."

Once all the couples have walked past us, Jay pushes me in front of him and we head over to join them, me acting as his human shield.

"I can't believe we've got to sleep in separate rooms tonight," he whispers in my ear. "You've no idea how badly I want you right now. The thought of making you come again is fucking painful." His words don't help the throb that's going on between my thighs, nor his hard on that's now pressing into my back.

Jay fidgets the whole journey to the B&B in the back seat of Mary and William's car. I feel for him because he must be uncomfortable, but I'm equally amused by the situation.

"Would you two like a nightcap before turning in?" William asks once we're all inside.

"That's very kind of you, but I'm exhausted," I respond, thinking Jay won't be up for it, but to my surprise, as I say no, he says yes.

I watch as William pours Jay a generous glass of whiskey, but I decline when he offers it to me. Instead, I say goodnight to them all and head to my room. Jay watches me leave and I know he's desperate to follow me, but it's best we're

Help Our Heroes

separated right now.

Chapter 6

I stand under the spray of the shower for the longest time as I think about Jay and our time together. I still can't quite figure out why it all feels so natural. It's like I've known him my entire life. Everything's so easy and relaxed when we're together, and I can't help thinking I'm starting to enjoy it a little too much.

I think again about how fast the last few days have gone, and try not to focus on how quickly the rest of our time together is going to pass, because that leads me to the question of what next? What comes after our little road trip? Does he go back to army life, wherever that may be, and do I go back to trying to save an inevitably doomed business just because it's Mum's and I can't bear to see her lose her dream?

I'm in a bit of a sombre mood when I get out and start getting ready for bed. I pull the other cami and short set I brought with me from the bottom of my case, but at the last minute, I shove it back in favour of Jay's shirt. The desire to be encased in his smell all night again is too much to deny. I give my hair a blast with the dryer before jumping into bed. I'm exhausted after everything, and surprisingly, I find myself dozing off to sleep much quicker than most nights.

When I wake up, it's pitch black in my room. I expect there to be a noise as I feel like something woke me, but as I lie there, everything's silent. I'm just falling back to sleep when I hear something, and I instantly know exactly what—or should I say who—it is. I've no idea how I know, but my body seems to be aware whenever he's close. Seconds later, I feel the bed dip and his lips brush mine. It's gentle at first. I guess he has no idea if I'm awake, but as soon as I respond to him, he turns it into something else entirely. It's like he's trying to consume me, and as my hunger for him reignites, my actions match his need.

I free my arms from the duvet and run my nails down his back as he continues to kiss me. He doesn't part our lips even as he pulls the duvet away from my body so he can begin running his hands over my skin.

Eventually, he breaks our kiss, but his lips stay connected to me. He kisses and sucks a trail down my neck and across both of my collarbones. His hands come up to the top of his shirt and as his kisses descend, I feel him undo each button. Once my breasts are free, he runs his tongue over each one before flicking my nipples and sucking them into his mouth. He starts off gentle but it's not long before he's sucking harder and harder, making my back arch off the bed with the need for more. I hear myself moan and whimper as he continues to torture my body with just his mouth. Tension builds in my lower belly just like before, only he hasn't touched me down there, but fuck if I don't need him to.

It seems like forever but eventually I feel him start to move down my ribs before kissing around my belly button. My muscles clench as I think about where he might be going. I'm panting and squirming with need, and the image I'm conjuring up in my head of him between my legs only makes it worse.

I hold my breath when I feel his fingers wrap around the fabric at my hips before they slowly descend, and just like in the dream that's still haunting me, he starts kissing up the inside of my legs. Tingles shoot around my body every time he makes contact, and they only get stronger the higher up he gets. I should be embarrassed; he's inches away from my most intimate part and I don't know if it's the effect he has on me, or the fact I know he can't see anything, but I don't care. If anything, I want him closer. I want to know what it feels like to have his mouth on me.

I don't have to wonder for long, because seconds later, I feel the heat of his mouth against me before the sensation of his tongue licking me makes me melt into the bed.

Oh fuck, that's good.

I grab onto the sheet below me as he continues. I whimper, moan and writhe beneath him so much he has to put his arm across my hips to keep me still.

My hands let go of the sheet in favour of grabbing his head; unfortunately, his shaved hair is too short for me to thread my fingers through, although I've no idea if I'd want to pull him closer or push him away.

He changes his angle slightly and sucks hard on my clit as I feel his finger begin circling my entrance.

Oh shit, oh shit. A small voice in my head tells me to I need to be quiet, to at least try to be respectful of where we are, and as my orgasm crashes into me, I have to fight to not let go and scream out in pleasure.

Jay continues sucking until my body stops pulsing and I somewhat come back to myself.

Holy shit, that was incredible.

I expect him to do something else, or at the very least climb back up to kiss me, so I'm shocked when I just about see him wipe his mouth with the back of his hand before he gets up and walks out, almost as silently as he came in.

What the fuck?

I lay totally still and bare for a long time after he's disappeared. I know for a fact that wasn't a dream, but why did he just leave like that? There could've been more, I could have…

I eventually move when my previously hot and sweaty body starts to chill. I get myself back in the shower before powering up my laptop and getting some work done. I know my body and I know I'm not going to be sleeping now, so I may as well do something useful.

I lose track of time and end up late for breakfast; I'm surprised Jay didn't knock to make sure I was up. I'm even more surprised when, after getting no response when I knocked for him, I find only Mary and William sat in the dining room.

"Good morning. Did you sleep well?"

Flashbacks play out in my mind and I have to clench my thighs together. "Yes, thank you," I reply politely, even though it's far from the truth. "Have you seen Jay?"

"No, not yet, dear. Is there a problem?"

I shake my head and sit down as Mary pours me a coffee.

I manage a little bit of the breakfast but I've got this feeling in my gut that something's very wrong, so eating is the last thing on my mind. After a while, I excuse myself and head back to my room. I knock on Jay's door. I know it's stupid because we'd have seen him come in, but I feel the need to try.

After packing all my stuff, I sit myself down on the edge of my bed and try not to worry. I'm sure he's just gone for a drive and lost track of time or something.

We had planned to move on today, but as the time starts to get closer to lunch, I decide that I'll probably be sleeping in here again tonight and it stops me packing my last few bits. I look down at my phone and remember his warning from when we first met, this is only a two week thing, no promise of a future or swapping phone numbers. My heart drops knowing that our time together is slowing coming to an end.

I'm just powering up my laptop in the hope of finding a way to get home when I hear a car engine outside. I lean across the bed and pull the net curtain back to reveal what I hoped I would see. Jay's Peugeot has pulled up in the space we've taken over the past few days. He's in the driver's seat but the scene isn't what I was expecting because he's leant forward with his forehead resting on the steering wheel. I may not know that much about him, but the last few days have given me the impression that what I'm seeing isn't normal, that he doesn't get down very often.

After a few more seconds, I allow the curtain to fall back into place so Jay can have his moment in peace, whatever it is.

Footsteps echo down the empty hallway and the second I hear his door open, I do the same. He must hear me but he doesn't react. I just about manage to get my foot in his door before it slams in my face.

"Jay?"

He walks over to the window but doesn't turn around or acknowledge me in any way.

"Jay, what—" I don't get to finish my question because he turns and looks over his shoulder. His eyes are dark and tired and there's a deep line between his eyebrows. He looks stressed. "What's wrong?" I finally ask when I'm able to find my words.

Jay continues staring at me as if he wants to say something important, but no words leave his mouth.

"It's—" he pauses and takes a breath, but in the end he just shakes his head and says, "nothing."

"You can tell me. Maybe I can help."

"No," he snaps harshly, but one look at my shocked face has him apologising for his abruptness almost instantly. "It's not something you can help with, Skittles."

"Okay. I could listen at least, be a sympathetic ear," I offer.

"It's fine. Honestly," he adds when he sees I'm not falling for his blatant lie. "Anyway, what are we doing today?"

I sit on Jay's bed whilst he gets himself ready. It didn't escape my notice that he was wearing the same clothes as last night. When we emerge a while later, we bump into Mary in the hallway, who insists on making Jay something to eat as he missed breakfast. I can see that he wants to get away but the lure of her home cooked food is too much.

"You can drive," Jay says, handing me the keys to his baby as we walk towards where she's parked.

"Uh..."

"You can drive, right?"

"No."

"No," he repeats, like it's the craziest thing he's ever heard. "How?"

"It's not that I don't want to, I've just never got around to it. Public transport's pretty good in Bristol and there's no parking at uni." The way Jay's face screws up as I say the words public transport makes me laugh.

"How about some driving lessons?"

"Here? Are you serious?"

"Why not? Once we get out of town, the roads will be practically empty. It's perfect."

"But they're all windy," I say in a panic. I don't want to be responsible for wrecking his beloved Peggy.

"You'll be fine, trust me."

I stare at him for a few seconds as I wait for him to tell me he's joking, but his eyes don't waver, so eventually I grab the keys he's still holding out and unlock the car.

My nerves treble once I'm sat in the driver's seat. My palms are sweating and my feet are shaking.

Help Our Heroes

"I'm not sure this is a good idea," I admit, looking over at a tired Jay who's getting comfortable in the passenger seat.

"You'll be fine."

He talks me through the basics, most of which I already know. I may not have had any lessons but I'm not a total idiot.

"Okay, gently ease off the clutch as you press down on the accelerator."

I do as I'm told and in seconds, the car begins to move. My heart bangs in my chest as we slowly start to back out of the space.

Once we get on to the country roads, I relax a little, but only slightly because although there's less chance of me hitting another car, there's a pretty high chance we could end up rolling down a cliff if I were to come off the road.

"See, I told you you'd be fine. You're a natural," Jay says with a beaming smile.

His praise makes my confidence grow and I press the accelerator a little harder. He may be egging me on but it hasn't meant I've missed his whole body tense up a time of two at his lack of control.

I'm buzzing by the time I pull into an almost empty car park in Inverness town centre.

"Did you enjoy that?" Jay asks with a smile on his face. I'm relieved to see he's lost the sad, stressed look from an hour or so ago.

"Yeah, I really did. Thank you."

"You're welcome."

After getting a coffee, we wander off through town, looking in shop windows.

"Have you been here before?" I ask, when I get the feeling Jay knows where he's going.

"No." He's got a twinkle in his eye that makes me question his answer but I leave it there.

Once we're happy we've soaked up enough of the town centre, we hop back in the car—Jay driving once again—and we head out to the couple of spots Mary and William suggested we visit.

We arrive at Brodie Castle just as the sun's beginning to descend for the day, and it's beautiful. After walking around the grounds, I drag Jay inside. He looks bored as hell, but I love all the old furniture and patterns. As we walk, I sneak a few pictures for inspiration for some vintage style jewellery.

We have the most amazing day together. His mood when he returned this morning has vanished and he's been back to the Jay I've known the last few days.

"Aren't we heading back for dinner?"

"Nope. I told Mary I was taking you out tonight."

I look down at my ratty jeans and scuffed boots. "I'm not dressed for dinner. I look a mess."

Jay turns to look at me briefly, his eyes run over my face. "You look perfect," he whispers before turning his focus back to the road.

The compliment warms my body and ignites something inside me only Jay's been able to. I squirm in my seat as memories of my midnight visitor assault me.

"I'm sorry about last night," Jay says so quietly I almost think I mishear him. "I shouldn't have pounced on you like that."

"It was fine."

His eyes come back to me. "It was fine?"

I can't help but laugh at the look on his face. "Yep."

Turning away from him to look at the countryside beside me, I smile to myself. It was a lot more than fine.

"What's this place? It looks fancy." I say as we stand in the entrance to what I thought at first was a church is actually a restaurant.

"The Mustard Seed," Jay says, reading the sign in front of us. "It's meant to be incredible."

"I love this building, it's stunning. I'd love to live in a converted church or something one day. I love all the history."

Jay smiles at me, although he looks to be miles away; it's a reminder of this morning and whatever it was to cause such a serious reaction from him. I'm just about to question him when we're shown to our seats.

The food's incredible but it's slightly overshadowed by Jay's mood. I can tell he's trying to push through whatever it is that's bothering him. I wish he'd talk to me, even if it's so I can be a listening ear, but I can tell it's not going to happen.

Help Our Heroes

If I've learnt anything about Jayden Baxter over the past week, it's that he's stubborn and always gets what he wants.

* * *

The kiss he gives me before we part into our separate rooms causes even my toes to tingle. I desperately want to drag him inside with me and try to take is mind off his worries, but I do what I should and wish him goodnight before shutting my door behind me.

I don't get a midnight visitor. I don't hear anything from him at all, so when I wake up the next morning, the first thing I do is pull back the net curtain to make sure he's still here. I let out a huge breath when I see Peggy sat where he parked her last night. It's not lost on me how gutted I would've been if he'd gone in the middle of the night. I both love and hate the way he seems to have crawled inside me, but at the same time, our impending separation is never far from my mind. I can wish this trip's going to last forever as much as I want, but I know that's impossible. Real life is just a few days away now, waiting to throw god only knows what at me.

I reluctantly pull my phone out from under my pillow and open up the messages from Mum I ignored last night. I reply with similar words of encouragement I usually say when she tells me how quiet the shop is, but the words are all fake, my enthusiasm that things are going to turn around holding no weight. The only way to save her beloved shop is to make some major changes I don't think she's ever going to agree to.

I drop my phone onto my chest and think about what we should be doing—looking for different premises, streamlining our products, online shopping and marketing.

When I pick my phone back up, I notice I have another message. I click on the icon and Frankie's name appears. I open it and then regret it instantly. It's a photo of her and Dean, obviously naked in bed, and the caption says 'me and my sexy solider'. As I stare at Dean's face, I swear I see a little glint in his eye. Cheeky little shit. Frankie's going to skin him alive when she finds out.

I fire back a message telling her how happy I am that she's enjoying herself before getting up and showered. We'd agreed we'd move on today and I'm excited about our next destination—Edinburgh. It looks like the most stunning city and I can't wait to discover it with Jay.

After a quick breakfast we say our goodbyes to Mary and William and head off, hoping to get into the city before lunchtime. As it's Sunday, the roads are fairly quiet and the drive's straightforward.

As the scenery starts to change from countryside to city, butterflies start up in my belly. This is somewhere I've wanted to visit for a long time and I'm more than ready for the adventure to start.

We park at one of the hotels I found on the drive here and secure a room for the night, although we can't check in until later.

"What do you want to do?" Jay asks as we walk out of reception. The hotel's in a central location to almost everything, which is why I chose it, and I know exactly what I want to do.

"Just walk. I want to see everything, I want to feel the city, soak up the vibe."

Jay's eyes sparkle at my response. I know he's trying to contain a laugh at my over-excitement about being here. "You're so cute, Skittles," he comments before kissing the end of my nose. The smile he gives me as he pulls away lights up his face. Thankfully, when I met him for breakfast this morning, he was more like his old self again; there was no sign of yesterday's stress.

"How long can we stay here?" I ask. I hate to bring up anything that involves our ever-ticking clock, but I need to know how much I can squeeze in.

I watch his gorgeous face as he has the same realisation. We're into our second week and our time is running out. Fast.

"Two days," he answers after a few seconds. "I'd love to give you longer but we really need to start heading south."

"It's fine. I understand." I look back out over the stunning city below so he can't see what I really think about us heading back. My eyes fill with tears threatening to break free. I'm not ready for this to be the end for us yet; I feel like we're meant to have so much more time together. The word forever floats around in my head but I bat it away because thoughts like that aren't going to help me. This was always going to be a two-week thing, I knew that from the beginning, but it's a shame my heart didn't get the message, because it seems to be getting more and more attached to Jay as our time together continues, and I know that it's going to shatter into a million pieces when he leaves.

I push my depressing thoughts away and try to focus on the here and now. We're stood in the incredible Edinburgh Castle, looking down over the city below as the sun sets and the lights of the city begin to bring it to life.

I let out a sigh and soak it all in. I want to remember how this moment feels because I know what I have ahead of me isn't going to be easy. Jay must sense my mood because he stands a little closer and wraps his arm around my shoulder. He doesn't say anything but I know he's thinking the same.

Chapter 7

"Skittles, wake up. We need to get going," Jay whispers.

I stretch out my aching legs and groan at the prospect of getting out of this incredibly comfortable bed. "Another hour?"

"You've already had that."

I groan again.

"Come on, you can sleep in the car."

I begrudgingly swing my legs out and pull my aching body to a sitting position. I have a quick, hot shower to try to freshen myself up but I'm still sleep fogged, which is seriously unlike me. There's something about having Jay sleeping next to me that seems to solve my sleeping issues. I'm not looking forward to my long sleepless nights returning when he's gone.

The last forty-eight hours were by far the best of my life. Exploring a city as amazing as Edinburgh with Jay was a thing dreams are made of. I've wanted to see the city for years and I'm so glad I never made the effort before, because this has been perfect; even with my now exhausted body after walking god know how many miles. Jay doesn't seem to be affected one bit, but then I guess he's trained for a little more than just walking around a hilly city; his toned body certainly points that way. He looks as limber as ever while I hobble my way out to the car to start our long journey back down south. He hasn't told me where we're going next, and I'm more than happy for it to be a surprise.

I think I make it about an hour into the journey before I'm asleep again. I've never been able to sleep when travelling before and I put my new ability down to Jay's presence.

I wake up and fall back to sleep more times than I can count; songs on the radio blur into the next one and the view hardly changes as we fly down the motorway. The only constant is Jay sat next to me, silently driving. He feels my stare every time I glance over and immediately looks back at me. It makes me sad because although he smiles, I can see the dark clouds he's been trying to keep hidden resurfacing. He's had a couple of phone calls over the last two days that's he's excused himself to answer, and when I've asked about them, he's tried to play it off like it's nothing, but I can tell it's not. I asked if it's his mum but he said as far as he knows she fine, but the only way to tell for sure is to turn up because she doesn't answer the phone unless it's her dealer. I'm not sure if he was exaggerating, but I'm hoping so.

"Are you sure you're okay?" I ask for the millionth time.

"Yes, stop worrying. We're nearly there."

I sit myself up and look out the window to see a Welcome to Cambridge sign approaching.

"Cambridge?"

"Yep. You loved Edinburgh and this place has some great history too, so thought you'd like it."

"Jay, what the hell?" I ask when he starts heading up a posh driveway I would assume is to some fancy manor house, only the hotel sign at the entrance was a bit of a giveaway.

His answer is to shrug at me. I've tried my hardest to pay my way but other than the odd meal and a couple of coffees, I haven't succeeded. It bothered me in the cheap B&Bs we stayed in, but this place looks like it's going to cost a bloody fortune.

I let out a sigh as Jay pulls the car to a stop in front of the grand building. As I take in its vastness, I feel the weight of our impending separation pressing down on my shoulders.

"Hey," he says, reaching up to grab my cheek. His hand encourages me to look at him, and when I do, I see his face drop at the sight of the tears in my eyes. "I want to treat you, okay? I want you to have something to—"

"Remember you by," I whisper, cutting him off.

He instantly gets this guilty look on his face so I know I hit the nail on the head.

"I'm sorry, Erin."

I'm not entirely sure what he's apologising for. It could be a number of things but I feel the need to do the same. "Me too."

"Come on then, I've already reserved a room."

"Jay, it's too expensive. Let's just go and find a B&B."

"No," he snaps, a little more harshly than intended if the look on his face is anything to go by. "I've got this all planned."

"Okay."

* * *

"I have a room booked under Baxter," Jay says to the lady behind reception.

They continue chatting about the booking but I zone them out in favour of looking at the interior of this incredible hotel. The building's ancient and inside's just as gorgeous as the exterior. The decorations around reception are all deep ruby and gold. Butterflies flutter in my stomach as I take in the appearance of a couple of guests. I don't fit in here in my worn jeans, scuffed boots and slightly bobbly jumper. I pull my sleeves down over my hands as I start to feel more and more out of place.

"Come on then, our room's waiting," Jay says, stepping up to me and distracting me from my extravagant surroundings. He grabs my hand and pulls me towards the lifts. I don't realise he doesn't have hold of our cases until a very well dressed employee wheels them in behind us on a trolley. It all seems a little much for Jay's duffle and my tiny suitcase but I go with it.

Jay keeps a tight hold on my hand the entire ride to the top—yes, the top—of the hotel.

"Jay?" I question, when the bellboy backs out of the lift.

"Shhh…come on, you're going to love it."

He's not wrong, because from the second I step foot over the threshold, I'm in love. The room—or should I say suite—is incredible; totally over the top for the two of us, but still incredible.

Jay thanks the bellboy and I watch as he smoothly slips him some money before he quickly leaves us to it.

"Jay, this must be so expensive."

"Stop going on about the money. It's fine. I'm usually stuck on base and spend nothing. I want to enjoy ourselves, make tonight special."

The question about this being our last night together is on the tip of my tongue, but I don't want to know the answer so I snap my mouth shut and nod at him.

"Just so you know, I'm not one of those girls you need to spend money on to make something special."

"I know you're not, Skittles. I didn't do this because I thought it was what you wanted. I've done it because it's what you deserve."

My heart flutters and I know in that moment the last little bit I was holding on to has gone. I stare into his grey eyes and in one sense I can see my entire future, because I know he's going to stay with me forever, but at the same time I feel like I'm looking at the end.

"Don't get upset." His hands drop mine in favour of holding on to my cheeks. "I want to show you how much our time together has meant to me, how much you mean to me."

Thankfully, he doesn't give me a chance to answer because I probably would have burst into tears. Instead, he lowers his lips to mine. We stay motionless for a long time with our lips connected. As nice as the connection is, I need more of him. Our hours are counting down and I'm desperate to spend them as close to him as possible.

He must have the same thoughts because within seconds I feel his lips move against mine before his tongue sweeps in. He kisses me deeply, passionately, until my entire body is alight. My nipples peak and every time his chest presses against them, little bolts of lightning shoot off around my body. Jay's hands slide down my neck before descending until he grabs on to my arse. He pulls my body tightly against his, allowing me to feel his hardness pressing into my stomach.

When he pulls back, we're both breathless. "Jay, I—" I start, but a phone ringing stops me.

I stand and watch as he walks over to answer it. I can't help but smile when I see him try to rearrange himself in his jeans—kissing me caused that! This man is gorgeous, strong, kind, brave, and he wants boring ol' me. Even after all the time we've spent together, I still can't quite get my head around it. He has the most exciting life, shipping off all around the world, saving people's lives, yet he's spent the last ten days or so being the kindest and sweetest guy.

"Yes, she's on her way," he says, pulling me from my thoughts.

"Where am I going?" I ask when he's put the phone down.

"I've booked a couple of surprises for you."

"Isn't this enough?"

"Nowhere near." He's in front of me again and before I realise he's moved, he's pulling me back to him for a short but amazing kiss. "I told you I wanted to show you how much our time has meant to me, how much you mean to me."

After grabbing his duffle bag, he takes my hand and together we head back into the lift—only this time, we descend to the basement.

It's obvious what he's done when the lift doors open because we're greeted by a giant spa and wellbeing centre sign.

We just step out when he tugs my arm and pulls me up against him. "You go and relax, I'll be in the gym next door. I'll meet you back up in the room when you're done." He presses a second room key into my empty hand before giving me a slightly impropriate kiss and pushing me towards the spa entrance.

"Erin?" the lady behind the desk asks.

"Yes."

"Okay, if you head through that door you'll find a robe to change into and some lockers to put your clothes in. When you're ready, come back out and have a seat on one of the loungers. Kristy will come and get you."

I glance over to where she pointed and see a series of loungers in a garden room looking out over the grounds. "Okay, th...thank you," I stutter. This has taken me by surprise and I feel totally out of place, having never stepped foot in a spa before. I need Frankie here; this kind of thing is a weekly occurrence for her. As I walk through to find the robe, I realise how much I miss my best friend. We've hardly spoken since I left with Jay, and the only thing I know about what's going on with her is that she's shagging Dean, Jay's non-solider mate. Before getting undressed, I grab my phone from the back pocket of my jeans and write her a message.

Erin: You would not believe where I am! Jay's booked us a suite in this insane hotel in Cambridge and I'm currently stood in the spa. I've no idea what I'm doing. I think this is our last night.

I'm surprised when I immediately see three little dots on my screen.

Frankie: Make the most of it; you deserve it. Is tonight going to be the night?

Butterflies erupt in my belly as I think about what's in store for us tonight. That kiss earlier sure pointed towards more. The memory of him coming into my room in Inverness still haunts me, and I'd kind of hate to not have the chance to experience that again, only I'd like to be able to see him this time.

Erin: Only time will tell.

Frankie: If he's half as good my soldier, you're in for a good night.

I still don't have the heart to tell her over the phone that Dean's a liar, but I'm going to have to as soon as I get back.

Erin: See you soon. Love you x

Frankie: You're not going to get away that easily without telling me the details once you're back. Love you too x

I stare down at my phone and let out a sigh. Sharing what Jay and I have done together seems weird somehow. It's been about us, and part of me wants to keep it that way. I feel like we've experience something no one else is going to understand. I know most people are going to think I'm crazy for going with him in the first place, let alone falling for him when I don't really know much about him, but I have, and I think it's time I stopped denying how much. I try not to think about it because then it leads to me thinking about him leaving. I really want to ask about where he's based, what he's going to be doing and when his next leave is, but it makes everything too real.

I'm stood there with my phone in my hand staring at the blank screen for so long that eventually there's a knock on the door.

"Are you okay in there?"

"Shit," I whisper. "Yes sorry, I had a call. I'll be two minutes."

I quickly strip out of my clothes and stuff them and my phone into the locker before slipping into the thickest, softest robe I think I've ever worn.

When I step out, two women are chatting at the reception desk. The door shutting behind me alerts them to my presence and they both turn to look at me. I feel my face heat. "I'm so sorry."

"Don't worry. Come this way." I follow Kristy down a short corridor, spending the whole time wondering how she gets her blonde hair quite so perfect, before heading into a softly lit room full of candles and the same relaxing music filtered throughout the spa.

"Have you had a massage before?"

I shake my head, too busy looking around the room at everything to answer.

"Okay, well in a minute I'll leave you to get comfortable. You can remove your robe and lie face down on the bed, and cover yourself with the towel here."

"Okay," I whisper.

"We'll do your facial afterward."

Kristy does as she said and disappears out of the room and I stand there feeling totally overwhelmed. She may have only given me a couple of instructions but I have no idea what I should be doing.

I follow my instincts and get onto the bed.

"Are you ready?" I hear asked in a soft voice.

"Yes."

I'm face down and it kills me not to be able to see what Kristy's doing. I'm too damn nosey for this.

It's only a minute or two before she softly starts telling me what she's going to do, and then I feel her warm hands on my feet; I all but jump from the bed.

"Sorry, are you ticklish?"

"Yes," I say, trying to squirm out of her hands.

Thankfully, she changes her technique before swiftly moving on to my legs. It takes a while but eventually the soft music and her repetitive actions relax me.

"Erin?"

"Huh?" I ask, lifting my head from the hole.

"We're done."

I blink a couple of times as I try to figure out where I am. Kristy looks at me with an amused but knowing smile. Clearly, I'm not her only client to fall asleep on her table.

"I'll give you a couple of minutes to relax and then we can start your facial. You'll need to be on your back for that one so you can again cover yourself with a towel. I've put a clean one over there. I've left you a glass of water but would you like anything else?"

"That's perfect, thank you."

I just about manage to stay awake to enjoy the facial and I soon realise why Frankie does this kind of thing regularly. By the time Kristy has finished, I feel amazing. I swear my face has never been so clean.

"Thank you so much; that was incredible."

"You're welcome."

"Is that it?" I ask, seeing as she hasn't talked about anything else.

"No, you have appointments with Charlie and Ronnie, but you need to go and get showered first as I'm sure you won't want to once Charlie's done your hair."

"My hair?"

"Yes. If you go back to where you got the robe, you'll find showers. All the products you need will be in there. Then, just wait out on the loungers."

I follow her instructions and in a couple of minutes I find myself stood under a waterfall shower, silently thanking Jay for organising this for me. As much as I want my hair done, I'm also desperate to see him. Is it crazy that I miss him? I'm also kind of desperate to see him working out in the gym. I've loved waking up in the mornings to find him doing his sit ups next to the bed.

My thoughts run away with me and I once again find myself rushing to get back out before someone has to knock for me.

I've barely sat my arse on the lounger before I hear my name being called. When I look over my shoulder, there's a young slim guy with the silkiest locks I think I've ever seen stood smiling at me.

"Are you ready, darlin'?"

"Sure am."

Charlie leads me to a hair salon at the end of the corridor, sits me down and hands me a glass of bubbles. I could get used to this!

"So, darlin', what are we doing?"

"It could do with a trim."

"Okay, what else? How do you want it for your big night?"

"My big night?" My mind runs away with me and all I see is Jay and I in a huge bed. Embarrassment flushes my neck and face.

"Yes, I'm presuming you have dinner reservations with a sexy young man, and if your blush tells me anything it's that the plans don't end there," he whispers, making me flush more. "Just as I thought."

I change the subject and explain to Charlie how my hair doesn't do anything so it's not worth his effort, but he tells me that's rubbish because he can work magic. I give him permission to do whatever he wants and sit back with my bubbles.

"Tell me about this sexy man, then," Charlie says, once I'm back from the basin.

I hesitate for a second but when I meet his soft, kind eyes in the mirror, I find our story falling from my mouth. I tell him everything about meeting Jay in the nightclub to our road trip that has found us here.

"OMG, that's so romantic," he coos as he cuts a few millimetres off my ends. "A two week road trip with a sexy solider. Sounds like my kind of week," he adds with a wink.

I find it way too easy to talk to Charlie, because without realising it, my fears seem to fall from my lips. "What's going to happen next, though? We never talked about what would happen when our time was over."

"You've fallen in love with him, haven't you?"

I avert my gaze because Charlie's stare is too intense. It's as if he's reading my thoughts.

"Yes," I whisper. "What am I meant to do now?"

"You need to talk to him, darlin'. See if he feels the same way."

"What if he doesn't? I mean, he says all the right things, but what if this really was just two weeks of fun for him whilst he's on leave? What if this is it?"

"From what you've said, I don't think that's the case."

"I don't even know where he's based," I huff, thinking of all the times I've tried to bring the subject of his work up only to have him side step it.

"What do you think?" Charlie asks when he holds up a mirror behind me.

"It's gorgeous. I don't know how you did it."

"Pure genius."

I stare at my reflection with perfect curls framing my face. Charlie's not only cut and curled my hair to perfection, but he also added some highlights that give it a real sun kissed look. It's stunning, it really is. "You are. Thank you."

"You're welcome, darlin'. I hope it knocks his socks off."

Charlie has just walked off when a slightly older woman approaches. "Erin, I'm Ronnie, I'm going to do your nails and make up for you."

"Okay." I get up and follow her to her station at the other side of the room.

"Nails are to be red," she states. "Let's see your hands then, love."

I do as I'm told and lift my hands so she can inspect my nails. They're not in bad condition per se; I don't chew them or anything but I don't exactly look after them. "Why have they got to be red?" I ask.

"That's what I've been told."

"By whom?"

She shrugs, but it's kind of obvious, really.

Ronnie's easy to chat as well—not as easy as Charlie mind you, and thankfully she steers clear of any talk of relationships. By the time she's finished with me, my fingers and toes are fire engine red and my face is flawless. I thought Frankie had a way with make-up, but this woman seriously has skills. As I stare at myself in the mirror, looking better than I ever have in my life, I have the sudden desire to take a selfie, which is very unlike me.

"Do I need to pay for all of this?" I ask before leaving the spa.

"Nope, it's all sorted." I'm torn between being really grateful for what Jay's done and annoyed that he's spent even more money on me.

As I make my way to the lift, I see the frosted windows hiding the view of the gym goers behind. Something tells me he's right there on the other side of the glass, and I wish I could see him. I'd love to watch him putting everything he has into his exercise, watching his muscles bulge and the sweat pour from him. I shake my head to clear the thoughts. Who is this woman I'm turning into? I've never before even considered what a guy would look like working out.

I hit the button in the lift for the top floor with frustration, although I'm not sure if it's fuelled by my straying thoughts or still lingering after our kiss earlier.

I let myself into our room and just as I expected, I'm alone. I take the opportunity to explore the suite, as the only thing I explored before was Jay. I walk through the living area to find a bedroom with the biggest bed I've ever seen in my life. Seriously I think about ten people would be able to sleep in it. It seems totally over the top for two; we're gonna have to shout at each other, we'll be so far apart. Through a door on the other side of the bedroom there is one impressive bathroom with a two-man Jacuzzi bath in the centre. I may have just had the most relaxing couple of hours of my life but still, my body aches to be laid out in that with the jets massaging my muscles.

Regretfully, I turn and walk back into the bedroom. Something catches my eye that I didn't see before. Hanging in front of the mirrored wardrobe door is a black dress. I walk over and run my fingertips down over the satin fabric. It's plain, simple, and way too slinky for my liking. It's more like something Frankie would pick, not me.

I lift it from the wardrobe and turn it around, and not only do I find that it's almost backless, but there's a label hanging from it.

"Wear me."

I put it back and take a step away. I look at the dress before looking down at myself. It's going to look awful clinging to all my lumpy bits. I glance in the mirror at my perfectly done hair and make-up, and the sight gives me some courage.

After quickly stripping out of my clothes and changing into a fresh pair of knickers, I pull the dress on. Thankfully, it doesn't cling like I was expecting it to; it skims over my skin perfectly.

I spin to look at my back and notice the most horrendous VPL. "Shit."

I rummage through my small case but only find what I was expecting: more cotton knickers. Fuck.

I lift the skirt and regretfully pull my knickers down my legs before smoothing the fabric back into place. It looks much better but I'm hyperaware of my bare skin.

Help Our Heroes

I slide on my red court shoes, telling myself there's no way Jay will know I'm not wearing any underwear. I spritz myself with some perfume before sitting on the edge of the bed. I'm just about to grab my phone to take a photo of myself to send Frankie when I hear the door open.

My heart begins to pound as I wait for him to round the corner into the bedroom. I listen to his footsteps for a few seconds before he begins to get closer.

My breath catches the moment he appears in the doorway.

"Wow," I breathe, taking him in from head to toe.

He's dressed in a perfectly pressed white shirt with a slim black tie and black trousers. It's a million miles away from how he's looked in his jeans and hoodies.

"I could be saying the same thing. You look stunning," he says, his eyes running over every inch of my body. "I knew that dress was made for you."

"When did you get it?"

"That morning I went off in Inverness."

"Oh."

"I saw in it a window and it had your name written all over it."

"It's gorgeous."

"You are."

He steps up to me and cups my cheek in his hand. "How was I so lucky to find you?" Tears pool in my eyes. "Hey, none of that. We've got reservations." He leans in to kiss me but when he glances at my red lips, he changes his mind at the last minute and goes for my neck instead. He kisses and nips down my neck and across my chest until he's skimming the swell of my breasts with his soft lips.

"I wish you understood how sexy you look to me." As he says this, he runs his hands down my back and squeezes my arse. I feel his head lift from my cleavage and when I look up, his dark, hungry eyes are gazing at me. "Skittles?" he questions as he continues caressing my arse.

"Shit." My face flushes, knowing I've been caught without underwear.

"Oh, no. Never apologise for being this incredibly sexy. If I wasn't so fucking hungry I'd have made you come already; I can still taste you from the last time. I was so fucking desperate to have you that night but caving to it has only made it worse."

He drops to his knees and presses his nose between my legs. I want to be embarrassed but one look in his eyes when he glances up and I feel anything but. He presses his nose in a little harder and sparks shoot from my clit. My knees threaten to buckle but thankfully, Jay stands and pulls me to him.

"Dinner?" he asks, as if that didn't just happen.

"Uh...sure."

* * *

Dinner was amazing—from what I can remember of it. Having those grey eyes looking at me over the table had me pretty distracted. Every time I looked at Jay, I was back upstairs with his hands and lips on me. It doesn't help that every chance he gets, he places his hand high up on my thigh or runs his foot up my leg. I'm sat here just about ready to combust.

I thought we were done and was eager to get back upstairs to have him alone when he accepts the waiter's offer of coffee.

"Didn't you want coffee?" he asks, although I can see a glint in his eye.

"Sure."

"Or is there something you want more?"

I squirm in my seat and a slow, sexy smirk appears on his face.

"Tell me what it is you do want, Erin."

I break my eye contact, too embarrassed to vocalise what I'm thinking.

"Now's not the time to be shy, Skittles. If you want what I think you want, you're going to have to tell me. I told you I'd only do anything once you were begging. Well, now's the time to start, baby."

My chin drops open and I look back into his eyes. Am I about to beg for more of Jayden Baxter? Yeah, I'm pretty sure I am. A little voice sparks up in my head; it's now or never. I swallow down the never part because I don't want thoughts of our fast approaching end ruining tonight, and I focus on the now.

"I want you."

He raises his eyebrows as if he wants me to continue.

"I want you to do what you did before."

Another eyebrow arch.

"With your tongue," I whisper as I fight to keep eye contact.

"And..." he encourages.

I drop my eyes down to his crotch before slowly climbing back up to meet his amused yet hungry eyes. "I want all of you."

He stares at me, looking totally unaffected, but his darkening eyes tell me he's very much interested.

"Thank you," Jay says, confusing me, but seconds later two coffees are placed on our table.

I sit back and glance around the room as I try to relax. I jump when Jay's hand lands on my thigh. "Come on, drink up," he says as his little finger starts to stray until it's gently rubbing against my mound. "I'm not opposed to getting you off right here," he warns before sipping on his coffee.

I have two sips of mine before I push my chair out behind me, grab my bag, and begin to walk off. I feel him behind me in seconds, his heat warming my bare back and his hands landing on my waist.

"I didn't think you were ever going to move," he whispers in my ear.

Jay crowds me into the corner of the lift once the doors open and he's just about to lean in to kiss me when I feel someone else step into the small space. Jay looks into my eyes before reluctantly stepping back from me. That one look holds a promise, a promise that makes my insides quiver.

As soon as the doors open, he grabs my hand and pulls me to our room and through to the bedroom.

"Jay, slow down," I complain, when my heels stop me moving as fast as him. "What the fuck?" I squeal, when my feet leave the floor.

"Can't wait for you," Jay mutters once he has me over his shoulder.

One of his hands squeezes my arse while the other one shoots up under the fabric of my dress and slowly starts to slide up my leg. Heat pools between my thighs with every inch closer he gets.

I just about manage to contain my moan when he stops and throws me onto the bed. "Hey," I complain, but when I look up to see him pulling at his tie, I shut my mouth in favour of watching him strip.

His tie hits the floor before he starts working on his shirt buttons. I follow his hands as he makes his way down. The white fabric soon joins the tie and I expect him to start on his trousers but, to my surprise, he drops to his knees instead.

He grabs one of my ankles and gently slides my shoe off before it drops to the floor with a thud, followed by the other.

"You have no idea what kind of images have been running around my head with you looking like this tonight. The things I want to do to you…"

I groan at his words. He could suggest almost anything right now and I think I'd say yes.

When his lips touch my ankle, I fall back onto the bed in favour of focusing on the sensation. Before I know it, he has my dress around my waist and my legs spread. I'm totally exposed to him.

"Beautiful," he mutters between kisses up my inner thigh. As he gets closer, my muscles start to clench in anticipation. "I've dreamt about doing this every minute since I first tasted you."

"Jay," I moan just as his tongue connects with my sensitive skin. "Shit, ahhhh."

It's as good as I remember but when I open my eyes and see Jay between my legs, it becomes so much more. I scratch my nails over his short hair as I moan and rock against his mouth.

"Come on my mouth," I hear him say against me, and the vibration of his words gets me right on the edge of my release. He presses his thumb to my clit before sliding his tongue inside me, and it's the final straw. Light bursts behind my eyes and my entire body twitches and shakes as my release hits. Jay says something again and the vibrations make my orgasm stronger.

I'm panting when he pulls away from me and stands. I feel his stare but I can't open my eyes, not yet.

"Fuck, you're beautiful." I'm not sure I believe him in this instance, as I'm sweating with my dress hitched up around my waist. "Erin, look at me."

When I do as I'm told, Jay is gloriously naked before me. I take my time running my eyes over every solid but perfect inch of him. I've never seen a man naked in the flesh before, so when I get to his waist, I'm not sure where to look. That is, until he takes himself in his hand. Then, I'm fascinated.

"Get up," he demands, and I do immediately.

Help Our Heroes

I step up to him so my breasts brush his chest and he wastes no time in taking my mouth. I can taste myself on his lips. For a second, it makes me want to pull away, but as soon as I feel his tongue against mine I forget all about it. His hands lift to my shoulders and he pulls the straps down over my arms, allowing my dress to pool at my feet. The second it hits the floor, he pulls his lips away from mine and stands back.

"Fuck," he mutters as he runs his eyes over me. "So fucking perfect." My skin ignites as his eyes burn a trail into me. "You ready for this?"

I nod, because the way he's looking at me renders me speechless.

"You sure you want it to be me? You don't want to wait for someone special, someone who can give you everything you deserve?"

I'm desperate to tell him he is special, that he's given me everything and more during our time together, but the words get stuck on my tongue. So instead of speaking, I step back into him and show him. I run my hands up from his waist, across his chest and over his shoulders so I can pull him to me. I kiss him as I walk us back to the bed. When I feel the mattress against my legs, I fall back and pull him with me.

Jay allows me to scoot up the bed before crawling over me, ensuring he kisses every bit of skin he can on the way up.

"I don't think this will last very long," he admits as he runs the tip of his tongue around the shell of my ear. "I've been waiting for too long."

"Don't care."

Jay's fingers run down my stomach until he finds my swollen clit. He teases me until I'm squirming under him again before pumping his fingers inside me to ensure I'm ready.

"Okay?" he asks when he's in position between my open legs with his cock in his hand.

I nod. I know what he's really saying, this is going to hurt, but I'm okay with that. This is right; there's no one else I'd rather be here with right now, no one else I've ever really considered. I didn't know it before, but I was waiting for him.

A second later, I feel myself stretch as he presses inside me slowly. It doesn't hurt like I was expecting. It actually feels nice, and I'm seriously relieved.

"Okay?"

I nod and he presses farther, and just as I think everyone exaggerates about the pain, it hits me.

"Ugh," I grunt.

"I'm sorry." Jay leans forward to kiss me before he quickly thrusts forward again. I moan against his lips and dig my nails into his back. He continues to kiss me as the pain subsides.

"I know you're hurting right now but you have no idea how fucking incredible you feel," he whispers in my ear.

"I'm okay," I say as I flex my hips slightly.

"Yeah?"

"Yeah."

"Thank fuck." His hips are moving before he finishes speaking.

Just like he warned, it doesn't last very long. It's only a few thrusts before he groans; his entire body goes still, and then I feel him releasing inside me. The look on his face as he comes is an image I'll never forget as long as I live.

When he's finished, he falls on top of me, panting; he's heavy, but I love the weight of him on me. I wrap my arms around his back and make the most of this time.

After a minute or two, he pulls his head from my neck and sweeps away the hair that had fallen across my face. "Are you okay?" he asks, so softly it makes tears sting my eyes.

"Yes. Was that...?"

"Incredible, Erin. Fucking incredible."

I smile wide.

"Next time, I'm going to make you scream," he promises. "But first," he says, as he gets up and walks to the bathroom. The sound of running water gets me moving and in seconds, I'm stood in the doorway, watching him leaning over the bath, adjusting the water temperature.

"Hey," he says when he turns around and sees me watching.

"Hey."

He looks at me like he wants to say something else, but he must change his mind because after a few seconds, he walks over, lifts me into his arms, and kisses me before gently placing me in the soothing warm water.

"Where are you going?" I ask in a panic when he starts to leave the room. I thought this was going to be a two-person bath.

"I'll be back," he says before disappearing and leaving me alone. Reality hits me hard in that moment. After the high of tonight, knowing this is all about to come to an end is a hard blow to take.

"What's wrong?"

I look over to see Jay stood a few feet from the bath with a concerned look on his face and a bottle of bubbles and two glasses in hand.

"This is our last night together, isn't it?"

"Erin," he says, setting the bottle and glasses down and getting in with me. He pulls me to him and starts kissing me.

For a few hours, I forget all about what's to come, and focus everything I have on him.

Chapter 8

"Morning, Skittles," Jay says with a wide smile from the floor where he's doing his daily sit ups when I wake.

"Morning." I try to sound all chipper. Although he never confirmed it last night, I know I've just woken up to our last day together and I'd rather cry than smile right now.

He gets himself up, then crawls over to me.

"Morning breath," I complain.

"Don't care." He bats my hand out of the way and presses his lips against mine. "I've ordered breakfast to the room. We need to be out by eleven."

"Okay," I mutter sadly as there's a knock at the door.

When Jay reappears, it's with a trolley full of food. My stomach grumbles right on cue, and we both tuck in. We may have had a three-course meal last night but we did plenty of exercise to burn it off after. My face heats as I recollect everything we did together. Once Jay was happy I'd recovered from our first time, he made sure to show me how it should be, and true to his word, he'd had me screaming—more than once.

"It was pretty incredible, right?" Jay says when he looks over and notices my blush.

"Yeah. Jay—"

"I can't put it off any longer, can I?"

I shake my head. "It's our last day, isn't it?"

"I'm sorry, Skittles. I've got to head back."

"Where's back?"

"Germany," he admits.

"WHAT!"

"I'm based in Germany."

My heart sinks. I've no idea if carrying this on is even a possibility but I was under the impression he at least lived in this country. "Oh."

"That's not it."

I look up at him as a ball of dread starts to grow in my stomach. The look on his face isn't showing he's about to share some good news.

"I'm about to go on a six month tour of Afghanistan."

I drop the pastry in my hand and I vaguely hear the thud as it falls from the bed.

"We fly out on Monday from base. I'm so sorry," he says when he watches my first tear drop. "I didn't want our time to be tainted by it. I was so looking forward to going, getting back into the thick of it and then…and then I met you." My first sob erupts. "Erin," he whispers as he grabs my hands. "I wasn't expecting this to turn into anything. I thought we'd have a little fun and that would be it. I wasn't expecting to…"

"To…"

He looks up to the ceiling and lets out a long breath. "To…fall in love with you."

I collapse onto his chest and cry. I cry like I haven't in years, since that day we found out my dad had been killed. The thought of that brings on another round of sobs. Jay holds me the whole time and whispers sweet things in my ear, rubbing my back.

"I…I love you, too," I manage to admit eventually. And for the first time since I met him, I see Jay get a little choked up. It does nothing for my fragile state to see tears in his eyes.

"I'm so sorry. I should have told you."

"No. I don't think you should have. If I knew before we left, I probably wouldn't have come with you, and then I wouldn't have ever experienced any of this. I wouldn't have experienced you."

"Fuck. I wasn't expecting this," he repeats. "I don't know what to say. I don't know what to do next," he admits, looking totally lost.

"I'll wait for you."

"I can't ask you to do that."

"I'm not asking you to. I'm telling you it's what I'll do. This has been everything to me. You are everything to me. I'll wait."

I watch as Jay chews everything over. I can see all his thoughts and concerns rolling around behind his eyes, and I sit quietly and allow him the time he needs.

"Come on, let's get moving. We still have time to figure this all out."

"When are you leaving for Germany?"

"Tonight. Johnny's picking me up in town later this afternoon."

"Okay," I whisper, trying my best to keep my emotions locked down. It won't do him any good, knowing how affected I am by all this. I don't want him to leave, knowing I'm so upset. I'm going to have plenty of time once he's gone to fall apart.

It's just before eleven when we walk out of our fancy suite hand in hand. The journey down to reception and then out to his car is a total blur. I want to cling on to every second but they seem to speed by too fast, and before I know it I'm sat in the passenger seat waiting for Jay to start the car for the trip home.

The car roars to life before I hear a loud clunk.

"Fuck."

"What?"

"The clutch has just gone."

"What do you mean it's gone?"

"It mean it's fucked," he snaps.

"Well, can't we just get it fixed?" I'm not stupid enough to realise it will probably take longer to find a new clutch for his car than we have, but the words are already out of my mouth.

He turns to me and is just about to snap at me again when his face softens. "Sorry, this isn't your fault. Fuck, I need to get back. Shit."

"It'll be okay. Can we get a train or something?" I grab my phone to start looking at other options.

* * *

"Where are you meeting him?" I ask as the train pulls to a stop.

What was meant to be a three hour drive has turned into an almost six hour journey. Jay is seriously agitated. I don't think these kind of last minute issues sit right with his strictly planned army life. He's had to put his friend off and I know he's here in the city waiting on him. I can see Jay's trying to keep himself in check for my benefit, and I appreciate it, but I wish he'd chill out a little.

He grabs both of our bags and I try to keep up with him as he finds us a taxi and barks at the driver to head towards Cabot Circus.

"I'm so sorry. This has totally ruined our time together."

"It's fine, Jay. There's not a lot we could've done about it. We're almost there."

Jay pays the driver, and hand in hand we walk past the shops down Broadmead until he pulls me to a stop by the seating area in the centre of the walkway.

"I need you know how much this all meant to me, Erin," he says sincerely as he places his hand over my heart.

"I know. Me too," I say, trying desperately to keep my tears at bay.

"But I need you to promise me something."

"Anything."

"If someone better comes along, I want you to go for it. Don't put your life on hold for me."

"Don't be crazy, I won't—"

"Promise me," he repeats, a little harsher.

"Okay, I promise," I say, but I have no intention of following through on it because I know for a fact there won't be anyone else.

"But if in six months' time you still want me, then I'll be here, right here in this very spot, waiting for you."

I lose my battle and my tears fall. Jay reaches up and catches them with his thumbs.

"I have something for you." He drops his duffle bag on the floor and pulls something from the pocket. My breath catches when I see a little black box in his hand and my eyes widen in shock. "It's not that kind," he says with a sad laugh. "But it's a promise. A promise that I'll be here waiting for you no matter what you decide."

Jay grabs my shaking hand and slides the stunning vintage ring onto my finger. I choke back a sob as I study it. "It's my birthstone," I say, looking at the opal sat in the centre.

"BAX!" I hear shouted, but Jay doesn't turn around or even acknowledge it.

"Here," he says, popping a piece of paper inside the ring box and handing it over. "I love you, Erin, and I'll be back for you. I promise."

"I love you, too," I stutter out as a guy I vaguely recognise steps up to us.

"I've got to go." He pulls me into a tight hug and we hold each other for a long time before he lets go and gives me the most incredible kiss. "I promise," he repeats again before stepping back.

It happens all of a sudden and I know it's how we both need it to, but he grabs his bag, turns, and marches away. Johnny's hot on his tail and the only thing I hear him say is, "Whoa, mate, it looks like you had fun."

I stand on that exact spot for the longest time after they've left. I feel lost. I don't want to go home, I don't want to go anywhere, not without him.

I feel like half of me just left.

I don't notice the people walking around me or the sun starting to set and night descending. All I can focus on is the empty feeling in my chest that only seems to be getting worse the farther away I know he's getting.

I lift my hand with the box in and open it before pulling the piece of paper out.

13/10/2012

I promise x

With that piece of paper gripped in my hand, I make my way home, towards an unsteady few months and one very long wait.

Chapter 9

6 months later…

I understand why Jay said he wouldn't be in contact, that he wanted me to live my life, and if we were meant to be then we would be. But fuck, these last six months have been the hardest of my life.

The shop is right on the cusp of going under, Mum's health's deteriorating by the day, but she still point blank refuses to give it up. I get that she's chasing her dream, but there has to come a point where it's just not worth it, and I'm pretty sure we're there.

I swipe a coat of gloss across my lips and as I put the cap back on, my ring catches my eye. I haven't taken it off since the second he slid it on my finger six months ago.

I try to keep my butterflies under control, but as the days have been counting down, they've been multiplying faster and faster. I'm excited as hell but I'm also nervous. What if it's not like I remember? What if it was only meant to be those two weeks? All these questions fly around my mind as I step out the front door and look at Peggy sat on the drive.

Two weeks after I got back, the last thing I was expecting was to find Dean stood at my doorstep with Peggy's keys swinging from his fingers.

"He told me to drop it off here." Dean said, handing them over. "There's this, too."

When I opened the envelope, there was a receipt inside for an intensive driving course, and a note telling me to look after his baby until he got back.

I jump inside and start her up. She purrs just like she did when Jay drove her. I've made sure I've kept on top of all her maintenance and she's perfectly clean, ready for his return. I have to admit, I'm going to be sad to see her go. Since setting up my website and getting my jewellery into more stores across the city,

I've managed to get enough orders to have a little stash of money put away ready to buy myself a car of my own. Mum hated that I was no longer selling exclusively through her shop but I can't go down with her. I need to think of my future, now more than ever.

I'm a nervous wreck as I sit on one of the benches waiting for him. Town is packed, as there's some kind of event going on. There were signs on every post on the drive here, but none of them held my attention. There are street entertainers on every corner, and people chatting, laughing, and joking as they go about their day. They have no idea the importance of who I'm waiting for as I sit here.

I wait.

And I wait.

I look around through the hordes of people waiting for his face to appear, but it doesn't.

I check my phone. I have no idea why, because as he promised the night we met, we never swapped numbers.

Maybe he's delayed, so I wait a little longer.

I sit there until the sun's long set and the street's practically empty, still holding on to a small shred of hope that he's going to appear, while trying desperately hard not to think he changed his mind—or worse. Not one second of the past six months have I been able to forget that he left me to enter a war zone. No, I can't think like that. He's strong, nothing will have happened to him.

He's coming.

I know he is.

Something deep inside me tells me he's fine; I have to trust my instinct.

Eventually, I need to move. I'm stiff from sitting on the same bench practically all day, and I'm starving after having eaten through the snacks I brought with me hours ago. I stand up and stretch my back out before rubbing my hand over my ever-growing belly. He's been kicking the whole time I've been sat here waiting for his daddy, but I can only wait for so long. In my last ditch attempt in case he's really late, I pull a piece of paper from my note book and scribble out a message for him before tucking it into the bench. I have one last look around the dark street before I walk away.

Help Our Heroes

I've got to be strong, I tell myself. This isn't just about me anymore. But the second I shut the car door—his car door—I break down and cry like I've never cried in my life.

Epilogue

Present...

I take one last look in the mirror before opening the bathroom door to join Alex in the living room.

"Did he go down okay?" Alex asks.

Denny hasn't been great at going to bed for the last few weeks and it usually takes me having to lie with him until he drifts off—that's after his nightly story, of course.

"Yeah, he was okay."

"E, what's wrong?" he asks when he looks up at me.

"Nothing, babe. I'm just tired."

Alex has always been able to tell when something's wrong; he's too perceptive. I knew I shouldn't have gone and dug that scrapbook out, but something about talking about Jay with Denny tonight had me wanting to remember. I've never told Alex the whole story about Denny's dad, just that I had a fling with a soldier, and I don't intend on telling him the details now. What's the point? Denny's going to be five soon, and it's not like he's ever coming back.

Most days, I'm okay, and I feel like I dealt with everything that happened after Jay didn't come back, but others threaten to break me.

I look up to the last photo I have of Mum and me on the mantelpiece. She has her hand on my pregnant belly and is smiling up at me. She died a couple of weeks later. The stress of it sent me into early labour. Denny was in hospital for weeks before he was strong enough to leave. Everything went to shit pretty quickly but Denny saved me. Every day, he saves me, and now we have Alex, and life is good.

"Come and sit down, baby. You need to relax a little, you're working too hard."

I fall down next to Alex and give him a kiss when he leans in.

Life's good. I've got a good boyfriend, a great business and an amazing son. My only problem?

I'll never forget him.

Erin story continues in Never Forget Us, available now.

Never Forget Us: Never Forget #2

I thought I'd found my forever.

I believed he'd come back to me and we'd have our happily ever after.

He didn't.

Instead, he left me with a lifeline and a reason to keep going.

I'll never forget us, what we had, even if it was only for a short time.

Never Forget Us is the conclusion of Tracy Lorraine's steamy military duo, Never Forget.

Find out more at www.tracylorraine.com/never-forget

The Flyboy's Girl

Michelle Rene

Family treasures and cherished memories both can be found in the corner of the attic tucked away in a box long forgotten.

That's where my daughters found an antique tin full of old photographs and keepsakes. With their curiosity piqued, they are desperate to find out the stories behind them.

The only person I recognize in the photographs is the one person who lived through it.

Let's just hope she's ready to tell us her story.

Help Our Heroes

Chapter 1

Natalie

Present Day

Sitting in the pick-up lane at school, a crisp fall breeze blows through the window as I watch an elderly man across the street rake the leaves in his yard. The ringing of the dismissal bell catches my attention as students begin pouring out the doors. Moments later, Alana comes into view, long blonde hair pulled back in a ponytail, purple backpack slung over her shoulder and a bright smile on her face that took me three years in braces to obtain, while hers is completely natural.

Laughing and talking with her friends, Alana slowly makes her way to the car, flute case in hand. At twelve years old, Alana is every bit the social butterfly her sister is, even with the almost five-year age difference.

Finally saying goodbye to her friends, Alana opens the car door and climbs inside, dropping her backpack on the floor between her feet while reaching for the seatbelt.

I wait for the greenlight from the parking lot monitor and greet her, "Hi honey."

"Hi Mom," she replies while buckling her seatbelt.

"How was your day?"

"Oh, my gosh Mom, you are never going to believe what happened today," she gushes while turning to face me as she talks in her seat with a bounce. "So Justin, you remember Justin Harris that I've known for like ever? Well Justin asked Marissa, who asked Amber, who asked me, if I would like to go to the Harvest Moon dance with him!" she squeals in delight, eyes shining, barely taking a breath between sentences.

"Oh Alana, how exciting!" I tell her as I turn the car toward home.

Glancing over at her and then back to the road I ask, her excitement so contagious I find myself almost bouncing in my seat as I turn to her, my smile mirroring hers. "So I guess this means we need to go shopping for a dress this weekend?"

"Actually, I thought I'd see if Zoey would design something for me. Do you think she will, you know if I beg?"

At nearly seventeen, our oldest daughter Zoey is determined to become the next big name in fashion design. Of course, taking into consideration the dress she created for me for the charity gala Mark and I attended in the spring, she is incredibly talented, if I do say so myself.

"I'm sure she will. You know how much she loves designing. Just remember, Dad and I have to approve of it first."

"Okay," she readily agrees before her excitement takes over again. "Let's see… today's Thursday, so Zoe will be home early. Oh! Maybe we can get started tonight."

"Alana, I hate to rain on your parade, but don't you think you should wait until Justin actually asks you to the dance himself before you start on a dress?"

"Mom," she drawls out with a roll of her eyes. "He's going to ask, this was just his way of finding out if someone else had already asked me. Which they hadn't, by the way."

"Okay, if you're sure, just let me know what I can help with."

"Thanks Mom," she says as she continues to talk about her day as I drive us home. Of course, everything else in her day faired in comparison to being asked to the dance, even if it was via three people.

Pulling into the driveway, I put the car in park as Alana gathers her backpack before we make our way to the front door. Stepping inside, I drop my keys in the basket by the door as Alana starts up the stairs. "I'm going to go get started on my homework so Zoey and I can start planning tonight."

"Don't you want a snack first?"

"Maybe later," she calls back just before she reaches the second floor, her foot hitting that all too familiar squeaky step.

My siblings and I spent our entire teenage years trying to avoid that step. My parents considered a built-in alarm, alerting them when one of us was either trying to sneak in past our curfew or out when we were supposed to be sleeping.

When Mom and Dad decided to retire and move to Florida, they offered Mark and I the chance to buy my childhood home. At the time, we were contemplating a move to a bigger place, so we jumped at the chance to raise our kids in a house that already held so many memories for both of us.

Once Mom and Dad were settled into their new place in Florida, Mark and I began renovations. We added an in-law suite, upgraded the electrical and the appliances, refurbished the floors, and gave everything a fresh coat of paint, both inside and out. But even with all the upgrades, we both insisted that squeaky step be left alone.

* * *

Standing in the kitchen peeling potatoes, I hear the front door, followed by, "Hi Mom, I'm home."

"In the kitchen," I call back just before she enters and we begin our afternoon routine.

Since the day Zoey started kindergarten, we've spent every day after school the same way. Of course, in the beginning it was I pouring her a glass of milk and giving her a cookie or two. I can still see her sitting at the kitchen table, blonde hair pulled up in pigtails, crayons scattered in front of her telling me about her day as she colored while I prepared dinner. Now at nearly seventeen, which is almost impossible for me to believe, Zoey has traded the glass of milk for a bottle of water. And even though fruit is now the front runner of in the world of after school snacks, Zoey still treats herself to a cookie or two.

"Hi sweetheart, how was your day?"

Making a beeline to the refrigerator, she takes out a bottle of water and takes a seat at the island. "Ugh," she says on a sigh as she pushes her shoulder length dark blonde hair behind her ears and rolls her brown eyes. "Long. Mr. Rickman decided now would be the perfect time to assign a term paper on early American civilization."

"Well that sounds like loads of fun," I reply sarcastically.

"Right! Because it's not like this isn't the most social time of year. I mean, the holidays are right around the corner, and homecoming is in a few weeks." She lets out a sigh and slumps forward, elbows on the counter. "At least he gave us until the Monday before Thanksgiving to complete it."

"That's good. Hopefully you can get the bulk of it finished early and still have time for everything else."

"I hope so," she says as she takes a cookie from the jar.

The rapid sound of feet coming down the stairs reminds me and I warn, "Brace yourself."

"Zoey, my favorite sister in the whole wide world," Alana says while wrapping her arms around Zoey from behind.

"Let's not forget only, so that automatically makes me the favorite," Zoey counters.

"Yeah, there is that," Alana replies causing Zoey to laugh.

Knowing Alana has nothing left to argue, Zoey takes pity on her and says, "What can I do for you my favorite little sister?"

I smile as I listen to Alana tell Zoey how, by way of three other people, Justin asked her to the dance, then finally asking Zoey to help her come up with an amazing dress for the dance.

"This wouldn't be Justin Harris would it?"

"Um, yeah," Alana replies shyly.

"The same Justin Harris that you've had a crush on since the first grade?"

Biting my lip, I glance up to see Alana blushing before turning my attention back to preparing dinner.

With a sigh and a roll of her eyes, she says, "You know it is. Will you help me Zoe? Please?"

A slow smile spreads across Zoey's face, "Of course I'll help you! Now we have to come up with something completely fabulous so Justin won't be able to take his eyes off you."

"Zoey," I warn, "keep in mind she is only twelve, so nothing too provocative. And I've already told Alana, Dad and I have to approve of it."

Looking at her sister, Alana gives Zoey a nod in agreement to the terms. "We can live with that," Zoey says as she hops off the stool. "Come on, let's go up to my room and brainstorm until dinner."

As they scramble out of the room, I hear them say, "Hi Dad," moments

Help Our Heroes

before Mark enters the kitchen.

""Hey, gorgeous," he greets, just as he has every day of our marriage, as he walks over to my side and kisses me.

"Mmm, hey you. How was your day?"

"Much better now," he replies giving me another quick kiss. "Do I even want to know where the girls were headed in such a rush?"

Slipping into my best twelve-year-old girl impression I say, "Well, Justin asked Marissa, who asked Amber if Alana would go to the Harvest Moon dance with him."

A slight scowl mars his handsome face as he asks, "Do we know this Justin?"

"We do. Justin Harris, they live a few streets over from us. He and Alana have known each other since kindergarten."

"Why didn't he ask her to the dance himself?"

"I've been assured that he will. Apparently he was just trying to make sure she didn't already have a date."

Mark groans and rubs his forehead. "Did you have to use the D word? I'm not ready to think about Alana dating, I'm still in denial about Zoey."

Laughing, I dry my hands and make my way over to my husband. Wrapping my arms around his waist, I lay my head on his chest. "You knew this day was going to arrive sooner or later."

Sighing, he rests his chin on the top of my head. "Yeah, yeah. I was just hoping for much later than twelve." Stifling a giggle, I try for a comforting tone as I attempt to ease his mind. "It's only a school dance. I'm pretty sure they are just going to meet there, stand awkwardly along the wall, maybe even dance once or twice. I'm willing to bet he doesn't even kiss her."

"That's true. If he's as nervous as I was at our first dance, I'll get to save my gun cleaning routine for a few more years.

Mark and I met our sophomore year in high school. He was the new boy that had all the cheerleaders vying for his attention. I was the shy studious one admiring him from afar. With all the girls swooning over him, I knew there was no way I'd ever have a chance. I always enjoyed going to the dances to hang out with my small group of friends, all of us wallflowers. Until the night I watched Mark cross the gym and head straight for our group. Stopping in front of me, he introduced himself, like I didn't already know who he was, believe me I did, and asked me to dance. After a moment of stunned silence, I accepted, and let him lead me out to the dance floor. We've been together ever since.

Laughing, I step up on my toes and kiss him. "I still remember the look on your face when my dad pulled that on you."

A slow sexy grin makes its way across his face as he takes my head in his hands, his thumbs gently caressing my cheeks. "He was testing me. I was more afraid of him telling me you couldn't go out with me, than I actually was of your Dad. Little did he know it was going to take a hell of a lot more than a gun to keep me away from you."

With our twentieth wedding anniversary just days away, this man who stole my heart at sixteen, is still surprising me. Just as they did when we were dating, his sweet words cause my heart to soar. "My parents knew that day it was over for me. Mom said she could tell by the way we looked at each other, we were meant to be together."

"Hard to believe it's been almost twenty years," he says sweetly. "You're still as beautiful today as you were the day we met."

"And you're still the same sweet talker that stole my heart," I say with a smile.

"Only speaking the truth babe." Nodding towards the kitchen he asks, "What can I help you do?"

"Set the table and then call the girls down for dinner, everything should be ready by then."

* * *

Setting the last bowl on the table as the girls enter the dining room, I notice the sketchbook in Zoey's hand. Taking our seats, we join hands as Mark says grace blessing the meal before we begin filling our plates.

"How was school today girls?"

"Good," they answer in unison as they begin eating.

Knowing that teenagers are anything but forthcoming, and that tonight's dinner conversation needs a little prompting, Mark initiates a round a of high-low.

Help Our Heroes

A little game we've played over the years to get the girls to participate in dinner conversation. "Who wants to start us off on high-low?"

"I got asked to the school dance today," Alana says a little nervously.

"That's great," Mark says trying to calm her nerves. "Who are you going with?"

"Justin Harris."

"I'm going to design Alana's dress," Zoey says trying to take some of the attention off her little sister. "Mom's already told us that you two have to approve of it before I begin making it."

"Zoey drew up a few choices for you to look at," Alana says, excitement coming back into her voice.

As the tension begins to wane, the conversation continues to flow. Mark and I add in our highs and lows as well, and when the girls tell us what they considered their lows of the day, we talk about how to turn them around and learn from them.

* * *

After dinner, the girls begin to clear the table. Before they make their last trip to the kitchen, I remind them. "Don't forget girls, your dad and I are going out to dinner tomorrow night for our anniversary."

Chapter 2

Fastening my earrings in place, I take one last look in the mirror just as I hear the front door close and Mark call to the girls that the pizza is here. Smoothing my hands over my strapless black dress, I smile in surprise of the fact that after nearly twenty years of marriage, my husband still gives me butterflies.

As has been our tradition, Mark and I alternate years planning our anniversary celebration. This year, Mark was in charge and the only information he gave me was to be ready at seven for our reservations. And to dress up.

Picking up the small black clutch from the dresser, I toss in my driver's license, lipstick and phone, and then start down stairs to meet Mark.

Halfway down the stairs, Mark comes into view. Dressed in my favorite black pinstripe suite with a crisp white shirt, his blue eyes roam over my body as a low whistle sounds from his tempting lips. Stepping up on the last step so we're eye to eye, Mark wraps an arm around my waist. "Natalie, you look incredible," he murmurs as his eyes dance over me once again.

"And you look incredibly handsome," I reply running my hands over his lapels, before leaning forward to kiss him.

Taking my hand, he helps me down the remaining stairs, "You ready to go?"

"Whenever you are," I confirm while getting my wrap from the hall closet.

"Girls, we're leaving!" Mark calls as he helps me with my wrap.

"Wow Mom, you look beautiful," Alana says as she steps into the foyer.

"You really do, Mom," Zoey confirms.

"Thank you, girls."

Feigning hurt Mark places his hand on his chest. "What, nothing for Dad? I see how it is."

"You look very handsome too Dad," Zoey says as she stretches up to kiss his cheek.

"Thank you sweetheart," Mark replies.

"Okay girls, you know the drill, doors locked, no visitors, call us if you need us. We won't be too late."

"Got it," they say in unison.

Checking the locks on the front door one last time, Mark leads us through the kitchen to the door leading to the garage. Opening the door Mark pushes the button to raise the garage door before walking me to the passenger side door and helping me inside. Rounding the front of the car Mark climbs in behind the wheel and starts the engine. "Are you going to give me any hints as to what you have planned for tonight?"

"I'll give you two," he says giving me a quick smile as he glances over at me. "There will be dinner." He grips my hand in his and kisses the back of it. "There will be music." Another kiss. "Other than that, you will just have to wait and see."

Mark planned the perfect evening. Starting with dinner at Mon Véritable Amour, a French restaurant with a wait list that spans months. As part of the surprise, Mark had preordered our menu. Once the maître d showed us to our table, our waiter arrives with a bottle of champagne. Pouring us each a glass of the crisp bubbly, while detailing each course of our meal, he wishes us a happy anniversary, before he places the bottle in an ice bucket next to the table and turns toward the kitchen to check on our meal.

Raising his glass Mark began, "Happy anniversary Natalie. I can't imagine the last twenty years without you in my life." Touching his glass to mine, we both sip our champagne, before

The meal consisted of a wonderfully light cheese soufflé, beef bourguignon so rich and full of flavor with roasted vegetables, and a classic crème brulee for dessert.

After dinner, we spent the evening at the performing arts center, enjoying a rare performance of the only symphony composed by César Franck.

At the end of the evening, as we wait for the valet to retrieve our car, Mark asks, "Did you enjoy the evening?"

Looking up at him, the glow of the streetlights making his blue eyes sparkle, I smile and reply, "Yes, I did. Thank you for an amazing night. There's no one else I would have rather spent the last nineteen years with."

"Me either," he says as he strokes my cheek. "I love you Natalie, now and always," he whispers just before he kisses me.

The sound of a car door interrupts our moment as the valet arrives with the car. Assisting me inside and closing the door, Mark tips the valet and climbs inside turning the car toward home.

*　*　*

Arriving home, Mark clicks the garage door opener and pulls the car inside before turning off the ignition. We walk hand in hand to the door, inserting the key and turning the lock, Mark ushers me inside before locking the door for the night. The house is quiet as we walk from the kitchen to the foyer, but the lights are still on, alerting us that the girls are still awake. "Girls, we're home!" I call as I return my wrap to the hall closet.

Confusion appears on Mark's face as he checks the game room and then the living room. "They're not there," he says looking slightly worried.

"They're probably in one of their bedrooms with earbuds in and didn't hear us come in," I say as we head upstairs in search of the girls. "Zoey? Alana? We're home!" I call as we reach the second floor.

Nothing.

Checking both of their bedrooms, we find them empty as well.

As panic starts to build, Mark's voice booms through the second floor as he calls out one more time, "Zoey, Alana, where are you?"

"Up here!" Alana replies finally hearing us call for them.

Breathing a sigh of relief, Mark and I look at each still confused but greatly relieved. "In the attic," Zoey clarifies.

Making our way up the stairs and into the attic, we find our daughters sitting on the floor, various items strewn around them. "There you are, you girls almost scared us to death when we couldn't find you," I chide as we step further into the attic.

"Sorry," Zoey grimaces, "we didn't hear you come in from up here."

Looking around, Mark asks, "What are you two doing up here anyway?"

Help Our Heroes

"Alana and I were discussing her dress when I remembered seeing a box of patterns up here when we got the fall decorations down. So, we came up here to see if we could use any of them for her dress."

"That's a great idea," I reply. "Your Grandma would love that you are using them. But what's with all this over stuff?"

"While we were looking for the patterns, we found this old box of photos," Alana says as she holds up the box.

"I don't remember ever seeing this one, do you Mark?"

"No, must be one of your parents' that they left behind."

"I don't know who this is," Zoey says looking at one of the old photos, "but she was beautiful. She kind of looks like you Mom," she says handing me the picture.

Taking the picture from her, I look closely at it with Mark looking on over my shoulder. "There is a family resemblance," he says as I flip the picture over.

Seeing the date on the back, October 1941, it dawns on me who it is, "It's Grandma Ruby."

"Really? She's beautiful. No wonder the girls thought you looked alike." Mark says as he kisses my cheek, making me smile. "October 1941, that would have been a few months before the United States declared war on Japan and joined in World War II."

"Oh yeah," Zoey says. "We studied that last year in my American History class. The attack on Pearl Harbor is what launched the United States involvement in World War II."

"That's right, Zoe," Mark says. "Nat, did you have relatives involved in the war?"

"My Great-Grandfather was in the Navy and I think both of Grandma Ruby's brothers fought in it."

"Who's this with her in the picture Mom?" Handing me the picture, Alana asks, "Is that Grandpa Calvin?"

Looking at the picture, I say with both certainty and confusion in my voice, "No, that's definitely not Grandpa Calvin."

"Then who could it be?"

"I don't know, but I know how we can find out."

Excited at the thought of solving this mystery, they ask in unison, "How?"
"We'll go to the source."

Chapter 3

Pulling into the gated retirement community of Sunny Meadows, I maneuver the car down the winding road toward the assisted living facility. What started out as a typical retirement community, Sunny Meadows has grown into a premiere community with multiple levels of care for its residents.

In addition to the housing development, there's a full-service care facility and an assisted living complex that gives residents freedom, while also providing peace of mind to loved ones by having staff members check on them on a regular basis.

That's where Grandma Ruby resides. She and Grandpa were among the first residents in the Sunny Meadows community. When Grandpa passed away, Grandma moved into one of the deluxe suites in the assisted living facility. At ninety-four, Grandma Ruby is as socially active as I am, and sharp as a tack.

Pulling into a parking space, I put the car in park. As the girls and I walk toward the entrance, I turn to them. "Grandma Ruby is going to be so excited to see you two. I think this is the first time since summer break that you've been able to visit with me."

Walking into the lobby, Eve, one of the receptionist greets us. "Hi Natalie. We weren't expecting you today."

"Hi Eve. No, this one was a spur of the moment visit." Gesturing toward the tin Zoey is carrying, I explain the reason for our visit. "The girls found a box of photos in the attic, and we were hoping Grandma Ruby could tell us about them."

"Oh, what I wouldn't give to be a fly on the wall to hear her stories," Eve says. "She's the most entertaining resident we have."

Laughing I reply, "I'm sure she is. You wouldn't happen to know if Grandma Ruby is in her room, would you?"

"On a beautiful day like today? No, she's in the courtyard, giving the gardener tips on how to care for the roses." She smirks.

"Oh no, poor thing," I say with a laugh. "Maybe there's still time to rescue him, come on girls. See you later Eve."

"Enjoy your visit," she calls as we start toward the courtyard.

I can't help but laugh as the girls and I step outside into the courtyard to find Grandma Ruby explaining that the dead blooms need to be pinched off and not cut.

"Wait here girls," I instruct as I walk over to let Grandma know we're here. "Grandma Ruby, are you giving this nice young man a hard time?"

Turning to see who dares to challenge her, her face lights up with a smile. "Natalie Jean, you know better than that. I'm just trying to impart some of my old lady wisdom before he kills these beautiful roses," she teases.

The gardener laughs, "I appreciate the tips, most of the time."

Laughing at his honesty, I turn back to Grandma Ruby, "How about we let Rick get back to work. I brought you a couple of visitors today."

Looking around me, she smiles again, as the girl's wave. "Well if those two aren't the prettiest sights I've seen lately. You girls get over here and give me a hug," she demands opening her arms to them. Immediately obeying, Zoey and Alana make their way over and give her a hug. "You girls get prettier every time I see you," Grandma Ruby says as she holds one of their hand in hers.

"Thank you," they say in unison, blushing slightly at her compliment.

Looking at each one of us, Grandma asks, "So to what do I owe the pleasure of this visit?"

Holding up one of the bags, Alana says, "We brought lunch."

"And we were hoping you could tell us about this," Zoey says as she holds up the old tin box that they found in the attic.

A look of nostalgia washes over Grandma Ruby's face as she reaches out to run her hand over the top of the box. "Where did you find that?"

"It was up in the attic. Zoey and I found it when we were looking for some of Grandma's old dress patterns," Alana says.

"Dress patterns, huh? Well that sounds like a story I want to hear too, so how about we go up to my room, eat lunch, and swap stories?"

Smiling, the girls nod and turn toward the lobby. Threading my arm through Grandma's I walk with her to the elevator. "I should probably warn you that, like me, they are hopeless romantics, but don't sugar coat it for them."

She laughs and pats my hand. "Now have you ever known me to sugar coat anything?"

"No, that's one thing you never did, and I always appreciated your honesty."

Reaching the lobby, we enter the elevator and ride up to the fifth floor, making a couple of stops first. Opening the door to her suite, we step inside and the girls begin unpacking lunch, setting it up on the table surrounded by four chairs.

The deluxe suite is more like a small two room apartment. The door opens into a living room dining room combination, and a small fully equipped kitchen. Down a short hallway is a full bath and a large bedroom with a walk-in closet. The walls are full of family photos and memories of Grandma and Grandpa's travels.

Sitting down at the table, Grandma says, "Now tell me why you were looking for dress patterns."

"I was invited to a school dance by this boy I've known forever!" Alana exclaims. She begins telling Grandma how she's going to her first dance with a date and how Justin finally asked her himself yesterday during lunch. Smiling proudly at her older sister she finishes with, "Zoey is going to make my dress for me."

"Oh, I remember going to school dances. They were so much fun." She takes a few bites of her lunch before asking, "So this boy, does he have a name?"

"Yes, it's Justin," Alana says smiling, as her cheeks turn slightly pink.

"What about you Zoey? Any boys I should know about?"

Zoey smiles. "A couple, but no one special yet."

"Smart girl," she laughs, reaching over to pat her arm. "Play the field. You're both young, you have plenty of time. Enjoy it while you can."

Small talk continues as we eat lunch. Alana talking about how she was selected to perform a flute solo during the annual Christmas concert they're preparing for.

Zoey tells Grandma of her love of fashion. Her eyes lighting up as she talks about how she enjoys sewing, and watching one of her designs come to life. Of course, this leads our discussion back to the attic. Both girls tell Grandma how they were looking for Mom's old dress patterns for Zoey to use when she makes Alana's dress for the dance.

"Then we found a box of old photo albums and started looking through them. They must be Grandma and Grandpa's, because there were a lot of them when they were young and when Mom was little," Alana explains.

"That's how we found that box," Zoey says. "It was in the bottom of the box with the photo albums."

"These two almost scared us to death. Mark and I had gone out to dinner for our anniversary, when we came home we couldn't find them anywhere. We searched the entire house hollering for them the whole time. Finally, when we got upstairs and Mark called out for them, they answered from the attic. I recognized you in the pictures, but there were some people I didn't know, and we were curious," I admit. "Would you mind telling us about them?"

A wistful smile appears on Grandma Ruby's face, "I'd love to," she says. "Let's finish our lunch and get this cleaned up, then we'll get comfortable and I'll tell you all about it."

Chapter 4

    Sitting on the sofa, Alana on one side of Grandma Ruby and Zoey on the other, I sit beside Zoey as anxious as they are to hear the stories that accompany the photos inside the box. Carefully removing the lid and placing it under the antique tin, Grandma begins to sort through the pictures in search of where to begin.

    When she finds it, she holds up a photo of a family for all of us to see. "I'm not sure how much you know for our family history, so it's best to start at the beginning." She points to the couple in the middle she says, "These are my parents Doreen and Edgar Thorpe, and these are my brothers Eddie and Billy, my sister Tess and me. I was the youngest, and the only one of my siblings that would be moving with my parents to California. My father was a Captain in the Navy and had just received orders to report to Point Mugu to become the commanding officer. Along with the new post, came a promotion. Rear Admiral Edgar Thorpe. It was a huge accomplishment. We were all so proud of him," her voice takes on a wistful note.

    Confused Alana asks, "Why weren't your brothers and sister going with you?"

    "My sister had just gotten married and she and her husband were moving to Colorado. My brothers were both in the Army. Eddie was stationed at Fort Bliss, in Texas and Billy was stationed at Fort Sill, in Oklahoma."

    Studying the picture for a few minutes, Zoey asks, "Grandma Ruby, how old were you in this picture?"

    "I was about your age," she says smiling at the photo. "It was taken just before my fifteenth birthday."

    Taking in the snowy landscape in the background of the photo I ask, "Where were you living before the transfer to Point Mugu?"

    "We were living in Illinois. Being in the Navy, we moved around quite a bit. Each one of us were born in a different place. I was born in Maine, and we lived there until I was three, then we moved to Maryland and lived there until I was eight, and then to Illinois, and were there until we moved to California."

"Did you mind moving around? I would miss my friends if I moved now," Zoey says.

"When you are a military family, you get used to it. I did miss my friends at first. Given the choice between living on the lake in Illinois where it snowed and was below freezing almost five months out of the year, and living in California. I'd make the move every time."

Sorting through the box Grandma Ruby takes out another photo. "Dad was only allowed to take leave when it was approved, so we didn't go on many vacations. On our way to California we stopped at the Grand Canyon." Looking at the photo she says, "It was one of the most beautiful places I'd ever seen."

"What was it like living on a military base?"

She shrugs her small shoulders. "To me, there wasn't anything unusual about it. It was all I had ever known. The friends that we had were all like us, growing up on military bases. You learn how to make friends quickly and how to have friends without getting too close. It's always in the back of your mind that you could be transferred to another post at any moment."

Grandma pulls out several photos of her brother Eddie, the first one of him standing proudly in his uniform. "This was taken when Eddie made Sargent. We were all so proud of him."

"Why didn't he join the Navy?"

"He wanted to make a name for himself. He was afraid that if he joined the Navy, he would be given special treatment because of Dad. At least that's what he told everyone. Eddie wasn't a big fan of boats or open water. I think he didn't like the idea of being stationed on a ship in the middle of the ocean."

Smiling warmly as she looked at the next picture, Grandma says, "This picture was taken on one of the rare occasions that both Eddie and Billy had leave at the same time." Pointing to the first couple she said, "This is Eddie and his wife Sue, and this is Billy and his wife Joan. Eddie and Sue told us on that visit that they were expecting a baby. They had a boy, and then three more after that one. Billy and Joan had their first child the next year. The first granddaughter, followed by another grandson."

"What about your sister, did they have children?"

Grandma nodded, "They did. Tess and David had two daughters and a son."

As Grandma Ruby continues to relay our family history, the girls and I listen intently, hanging on her every word, until my cell phone rings interrupting her latest story.

Rising from the sofa, I dig my phone out of my purse. Seeing Mark's name on the screen I answer it. "Hey, everything okay?"

"Yeah, everything is fine. I was just wondering if you all wanted to pick up something for dinner on your way home, or if you wanted me to start something here?"

Looking around for a clock and not finding one I ask, "Dinner? What time is it?"

Mark chuckles in my ear. "Babe, it's six-thirty."

"What! No, it can't be that late," I say as I walk to the window and peer through the blinds finding the sun has already set. "I can't believe we've been here that long. I'll pick up a pizza on the way home."

"Sounds good, no rush though. Say hi to Grandma Ruby for me."

I smile into the phone as I reply, "I will. See you in a little while." Ending the call, I turn back to the sofa, "Girls, we need to be going."

"Awww," Alana says. "Do we have to?"

"But Mom," Zoey says, "we didn't find out about the picture?"

Grandma Ruby looks first at me and then to Zoey, "What picture?"

Reaching into the box, Zoey pulls out the photo of Grandma Ruby embracing a pilot and hands it to her.

"Oh," she says as she runs her fingers over the photo, a look of nostalgia settling on her face.

Lying my hand on Grandma Ruby's arm, I bring her out of her memory. "Grandma, are you okay?"

Looking up at me, she smiles. "Yes dear, I'm fine. I just haven't thought about Paul in such a long time."

"Maybe you could tell us about him sometime," I say as I squeeze her hand.

"Oh, you all don't want to hear about that."

"Yes we do," the girls say in unison.

"Please Grandma Ruby," Zoey begs. "We'd love to hear about how you two met."

Looking to me for approval, I nod and she agrees, "Okay, I'll tell you, but another day."

I pick up my purse and drape it over my shoulder then gesture for the girls to stand. "Come on girls let's walk Grandma Ruby down to the dining room on our way out."

Chapter 5

The next morning, by the time Mark and I come down stairs, the girls are dressed and eating breakfast.

"Wow, you two are up and about early for a Sunday," Mark says as he kisses the tops of their heads on his way to the coffee pot.

"We want to get there earlier today so we had more time," Alana says before taking a bite of her waffle.

Pulling two mugs out of the cabinet I ask, "Get where?"

"Sunny Meadows. Grandma Ruby said she'd tell us about the picture."

"Oh, honey I don't think she meant today," I try to reason.

"But she said she would tell us another day, and today is another day," Alana whines.

Glancing over at Mark, who offers no assistance but only grins knowing I've created a couple of monsters and they won't relent until they've heard the whole story, I sigh and shake my head. "You're right, she did. I'll give her a call and see if she's up to us coming back over today."

"Thanks Mom," Alana says as she continues eating her breakfast, while Zoey silently grins, leaving me with the feeling that I've just been played by my darling daughters.

* * *

True to my word, after breakfast I called and asked Grandma Ruby if it was okay if we could visit again today. She was more than happy to hear that her great granddaughters actually wanted to spend more time with her and listen to her stories.

As we settle back into the same spots we were in yesterday, Alana looks into the box and pulls out the photo on top of the stack. "Who's this Grandma Ruby?"

Looking at the photo of a young couple she says, "That's Millie, she was the first person I met when we moved to California, and my best friend, and that's her husband Don." Grandma Ruby smiles, "Millie met Don the same time I met Paul."

Looking at my daughters, I can practically feel the excitement vibrating off them, waiting for Grandma to continue with her story. Slipping off the sofa, I take my phone and capture the moment, knowing this will be a favorite memory for them in the future when they look back with their own children.

Resuming my place beside Alana, I muse, "I bet you two got into all kinds of trouble."

Grandma laughs, "Millie was something else. Like me, Millie had grown up in a military family. We both had older siblings and had learned a few tricks from them over the years. Of course, that also meant we had to be extra careful, because our parents had already dealt with most situations."

Looking over Alana's shoulder at the picture Grandma holds in her hand I ask, "How did you meet Paul?"

"We met at a dance. As I told you yesterday, my Father had been promoted to Admiral, so not only was he well known on base, so was I." Grandma Ruby laughs, "Of course I was also off limits to any of the enlisted men, because I was the Admiral's daughter, and no one wanted to face the wrath of Admiral Thorpe for attempting to court his daughter. Not to mention that I had just turned seventeen when we arrived in California."

Confused Alana asks, "What's court mean?"

Smiling I run my hand over her hair, "That's what they used to call dating."

"Oh," she says before turning her attention back to Grandma Ruby.

"At the end of my first week in California, Millie decided that I needed to see more than just the base and dragged me to a dance in town. Of course, the most exciting thing about going to the dance was that there would be boys there, boys that I could actually talk to and dance with, without my father scaring them off."

Grandma Ruby smiles, and then continues, "During the time my father was in the Navy, when a new commanding officer arrived on base there were ceremonies and dinners nonstop for a month. Millie and I spent almost every Friday and Saturday night at the dance in town. Our mothers used to tease that we were joined at the hip, because wherever you saw one of us you saw the other."

Taking Zoey and Alana's hand in each of hers, Grandma Ruby says, "I hope one day you both have a friend like I did in Millie."

Alana lays her head against Grandma's shoulder and reaches down and squeezes her hand, essentially melting my heart, and asks, "Do you still hear from Millie?"

"A few times a year. She moved to South Carolina with her son and his family after Don passed away."

Having heard enough backstory, Zoey says, "Grandma Ruby, tell us about Paul. By the way it looks in those pictures, you two were pretty close. Was he your first love?"

Smiling she pats Zoey's leg, "So much like your mother, she was never very patient either," she half whispers to Zoey making me laugh. "And you're right, Paul was my first love."

Grandma picks up one of the photos of her and Paul and gently runs her finger across the picture of the two of them. Eyes shining with remembrance, she says, "This old mind might not remember what I had for breakfast most days, but I remember the night we met like it was yesterday."

"We had been in California for a little over a year, and Millie and I attended the weekend dances in town whenever we could." Laughing she says, "Having a dance partner was one thing neither Millie nor I had to worry about. We met and danced with a lot of nice, respectful boys, but no one special until that night." Knowing Zoey is the future fashionista, Grandma leans her way and says, "You know, I still remember what I was wearing. A pink plaid dress with buttons down the front and a matching belt, with black patent leather shoes. I always like that dress, but it became my favorite after that night."

Grandma Ruby smiles at the memory then again squeezes the girl's hands, "It was just a few weeks before my eighteenth birthday."

Chapter 6

Ruby

July 1941

Stopping to look in one of the car side mirrors, Millie asks once again, "Are you sure my hair looks okay?"

Last week, Millie spotted an absolute dreamboat, on our way out the door, and it's all she has talked about this week. She even went so far as to assure me that she would have spoken to him, but we would have broken curfew, and neither of us were willing to do that. Our parents were sticklers for rules, and we knew there was a price to pay for breaking them.

"Yes, for the fifth time, your hair looks perfect," I say in mock exasperation. Although Millie has probably asked more like ten times so my exasperation was warranted. "Come on," I say, taking her hand and dragging her toward the door, "or that guy you've been fawning over all week is going to find someone else to dance with."

Gasping Millie's hand flies to her chest, "Bite your tongue Ruby Thorpe!"

Laughing at her response, I tug on her hand and continue to the entrance. The minute we step through the door, Millie's eyes begin scanning the room. Grabbing my hand, she whisper squeals, "He's here!"

Following her line of vision across the room to where the object of Millie's affection stood speaking to someone. I watched as their eyes met and the smile on his face widened. Millie was right he was dreamy. Tall, with dark hair and a chiseled jaw, it was easy to see why Millie had been swooning over him all week.

Then it happened, the man he had been speaking with turned looking first at Millie and then locking his gaze on me. Unable to tear my gaze from his, I hear

Millie mutter, "Well, well it looks like my dream guy brought a friend with him tonight."

Swallowing to moisten my suddenly dry mouth, I finally manage to respond, "Looks like it."

Not until Millie tightens her grip on my hand, do I look away and focus back on her. "They're coming this way!"

Before I can comprehend what's happening, they're standing in front of us.

"Hello ladies, I'm Don and this is my buddy Paul," he says as he introduces both of them.

"Hi," Millie says while effectively batting her eyelashes at Don. "I'm Millie and this is Ruby."

"It's a pleasure to meet you both," Don says not taking his eyes off Millie. "So Millie, can I get you a drink?"

"That sounds like a wonderful idea," Millie says as she threads her arm through Don's and they walk toward the table holding a punch bowl.

Turning a dazzling smile my way, Paul says, "Well it looks like I've been left alone with the most beautiful girl here."

Blushing, I shyly look down then back up through my lashes. "Thank you."

As the music begins to slow, Paul turns to me. "Ruby, would you like to dance?"

I smile at his invitation. "I'd love to."

Paul takes my hand in his and leads me to the dance floor, twirling me once before pulling me into his arms, causing me to giggle.

"Well that might be the best sound I've ever heard," he says causing me to blush yet again.

"You may need to get out of the city more," I tease.

Throwing his head back, Paul laughs, a rich deep sound I'm sure I could get used to hearing. "Beautiful and quick-witted, I could be in trouble."

Smiling back into his sparkling blue eyes I reply, "As long as you mind your manners, you should be fine."

"I'll keep that in mind."

Paul's voice was filled with laughter, joy even, but there was also the hint of an accent I couldn't quite place. "What brings you to California Paul?"

"What makes you think I'm not from California?"

Raising a brow at him in question I ask, "Are you?"

Laughing he shakes his head, "No. What about you, are you a California girl?"

Shaking my head, I admit, "No, I've only been here a little over a year."

"Still, it sounds like you are the perfect person to show me around this week while I'm here."

I can't stop the wave of disappointment that crashes over me. "So you're just visiting?"

"No, I'll be around, but I may not have as much free time after this week."

"So more work and less dancing is that it?"

"Something like that. Although I would always make time for dancing with you."

"You sir, are very charming."

As the music begins to pick up, Paul pulls me close and says, "Come on, let's get something to drink and you can tell me more about yourself."

Placing his hand on the small of my back, Paul guides us over to the drink table. "What would you like to drink?"

"Just punch please."

Taking two cups of punch from the attendant, Paul leads us over to an empty table in the corner. Placing the cups on the table, he pulls out a chair for me before taking his own seat.

"You never told me where you're from," I say before taking a sip of my punch.

"Neither did you," he challenges with a smile that makes his blue eyes sparkle.

"That's true, I didn't. My father is in the military so I've lived in a few places. All stateside. Before moving to California, we were in Illinois."

"That must have been quite a change for you moving from the cold of the mid-west to sunshine."

"It was, but a very nice change. I'll take the warm sunny days anytime." I take another sip of my punch before prodding him to tell me about himself. "Now you know where I'm from, tell me about you."

He chuckles a bit before looking up from his cup. "I was born and raised in Nebraska. Grew up on my parents' farm, where we raised cows and corn."

"So what are you doing in California?"

"Getting ready to start a new adventure."

"That sounds exciting."

"I hope so. Of course, I have to admit," Paul says as he reaches across the table and takes my hand in his, causing me to look up into his mesmerizing blue eyes. "It has been so far," he replies causing me to blush.

Caught up in the moment, my voice barely above a whisper, I ask, "How's that?"

Paul leans in close as if he's about to relay a secret, so I do the same. "Because today I met the prettiest girl I've ever laid eyes on, and I'm hoping that I get to spend more time with her."

Searching his blue eyes, I see nothing but sincerity in his words. "I have a feeling she would like to spend time with you too."

"I'm glad to hear that, because I think it's time for another dance." Standing from his seat and extending his hand to me, Paul leads us back out to the dance floor, where I spend to the next three songs held within his arms.

When the last song ends, we make our way back to our table, only to be stopped by Millie and Don.

"Hi you two," Millie says as they step up beside us. "Having a good time?"

"We are," I readily reply while leaning into Paul's side. "What about you?"

"It's been a perfect night," Millie dreamily replies while gazing up at Don, who matches her starry gaze with his own.

"We should be going soon Millie, we don't want to be late."

With a sigh and a slump of her shoulders, Millie agrees. "You're right, we should or we won't be able to come back tomorrow."

Paul's arm tightens around my waist, causing me to look up as he asks, "So we'll get to see you tomorrow night too?"

"Yes, as far as I know," I answer and watch the smile on Paul's handsome face grow.

"Hey," Don says gaining our attention. "Why don't you girls meet up with us early, and we'll grab a bite before the dance?"

Millie's head snaps in my direction, "Oh can we Ruby?"

"I don't see why not, we can get our chores completed in plenty of time."

Don chuckles, "Chores? How old are you girls anyway?"

"Ruby turns eighteen in two weeks, and my birthday was last month." Popping her hand on her hip Millie gives Don a stern look. "Is that a problem for you?"

Don laughs and raises his hands in surrender, "No, not at all. Just making sure we aren't breaking any laws."

Now that we are on the subject, and my curiosity has been piqued, I ask, "How old are you guys?"

"Twenty," Paul says and then looks to me and says, "I hope that's not a problem."

I smile and shake my head, "No, it's not a problem at all."

Chapter 7

The next evening, Millie and I met the guys for dinner then went dancing. Walking through the door to the dance hall, with Paul by my side, it struck me that this was the first time Millie and I were attending the dance with dates. All the other times we had attended by ourselves and had our choice of dance partners. Last night all that changed. Paul spun me around the dance floor and all thoughts of any other dance partner fled. We fit together perfectly as we danced. It was as if we were specifically created for one another. The disappointment I thought I'd feel knowing I would only be dancing with one person all night never came. Instead, all I felt was pride that I was the one walking into the dancehall on Paul's arm.

We had no sooner stepped inside; when the music slowed and began playing the same song that we first danced to the night before.

Leaning down to whisper in my ear Paul says, "They're playing our song." Looking up at him, I smile as he asks, "Dance with me?" Caught up in the moment I can only nod, as Paul's smile grows wider. Taking my hand, he leads me out to the dance floor. As we begin to move to the music, Paul pulls me closer. "I'm not sure if I told you earlier, but you look beautiful tonight."

"Thank you and thank you for dinner."

"It was my pleasure. I really enjoy spending time with you Ruby," Paul says as we continue to dance.

"I've had a great time too," I reply shyly.

Paul and I, as well as Millie and Don stayed to ourselves, each enjoying the time we got to spend in their arms on the dance floor.

When it came time for the evening to end, Paul and Don walked us to our bus stop so we could return to the base.

As Paul and I walked arm in arm he said, "I had a great time tonight Ruby, I'd really like to see you again."

"I'd like that too," I admitted

"I won't know when I'll be free again until later this week. How can I get in touch with you?"

"Millie and I volunteer at the library in town on Tuesday afternoon, when you find out your schedule you can leave a message for me there. If I don't hear from you, we'll plan on meeting back here next weekend."

"I like that plan," Paul says as he caresses my cheek. "But I'll find a way to see you before next weekend."

Butterflies take flight in my stomach from both Paul's gentle touch and the intense look in his eyes.

As the bus pulls up to the stop, Paul leans in close to my ear and whispers, "Thank you for giving me all your dances," before brushing my cheek with a kiss.

Looking up at him I smile, "It was my pleasure, I had a wonderful time." Before I step up into the bus, I look back and him and say, "Goodnight Paul."

"Goodnight Ruby," he replies.

Taking a seat by the window, behind Millie, Paul waves as the bus pulls away and I wave in return.

The minute the bus is on the road, Millie bounds into the seat next to me. "Tonight was amazing! Ruby we have to see them again! Don is just so nice and funny and, and just dreamy," she says as she lets out a dramatic sigh.

"Paul said he wants to see me again. I told him we volunteered at the library on Tuesday, so he could leave a message there letting us know when."

"Oh Ruby, you're a genius! We certainly can't have them showing up at the base looking for us. My father would have a fit and I can't even imagine how the Admiral would react."

"That's definitely something I don't want to think about."

* * *

The next morning, I readied myself for church and went to the kitchen to have breakfast with my parents. I rarely saw Millie on Sundays, unless of course it was at church. We spent most of the week together, but always seemed to act, as if it had been a month since we last spoke. Growing up in a military family, there are seldom opportunities for everyone to gather at once. Unless of course you were a Thorpe. In the Thorpe household, Sundays were reserved for family time. If by chance Dad couldn't make it because of his assigned duties, we were still expected to carry on without him. It was also one of the few times Dad stepped out wearing something other than his Navy uniform.

"Good morning," I greeted kissing both of my parents on the cheek before taking a seat at the table.

"Good morning sweetheart," my mother said as I poured myself a glass of orange juice.

As I placed pancakes on my plate my father said, "Don't forget we have the installation of new servicemen tomorrow morning at zero-nine-hundred with a lunch reception following."

"Yes sir, I remember."

"I'm sure I don't have to remind you what is expected," he said casting a glance my way before taking a bite of his pancakes.

"No sir, I'll be sure to welcome each one and not hide in a corner talking to Millie."

Smiling at me he said, "Thank you, that's all I ask. But not too friendly young lady," he continued with a teasing wink, "you are almost eighteen and you know my rule about dating men under my command."

"Yes sir, I remember."

My voice must have held more excitement than I realized, because I see my parents exchange a look.

I hadn't told them about Paul yet in case it was just a chance encounter, which I really hoped it wasn't. There were a lot of things that made Paul appealing. His charm, his smile, those blue eyes that seemed to look right into my soul and of course the fact that he wasn't in my father's command, may have been the most appealing of all.

Chapter 8

One thing you learn quickly about the military is that they stand on ceremony. Protocols must be followed and standards achieved at every one.

The installation of service members is always a special ceremony, but this particular one happened to fall on the 4th of July.

The celebration would begin on base and carry on into the evening as the fireworks displays lit the night sky. Millie and I had plans to watch from the beach, and with any luck, we would run into Don and Paul. As I checked my hair one last time, I heard my mother call.

"Ruby dear, time to go."

Making my way to the entrance, I find my mother slipping on a pair of white gloves. Ever the Admiral's wife, my mother was dressed impeccably in a navy blue dress and matching hat.

Smiling as I turned the corner she said, "Ruby dear, you look beautiful."

"Thank you, so do you. Dad is going to be too distracted to give his speech," I tease as we walked to the door.

My mother laughs as she places her purse on her arm. "His distraction is going to be his beautiful daughter and trying to keep the servicemen away from you."

"Thank you, but I'm pretty sure that rule number one when meeting with those new to the base is, 'no approaching my daughter'."

Nearing the waiting Jeep, Mom laughs again, "I'm certain it is. Good morning Ensign Jones," she greets as he opens the door for us.

"Good morning ma'am, Miss Thorpe," he says nodding at me as well.

"Good morning," I reply before climbing into the backseat followed by my mother.

We ride in silence to one of the aircraft hangers on base that has been transformed for the ceremony. When we arrive, Ensign Jones assist both mother and I from the vehicle, and we make our way inside. Greeted by another of my father's staff members, we are shown to our front row seats located directly in front of the podium. When the call to attention sounds, I sit a little straighter in my chair as I hear the sound of marching feet enter form behind us. Each of the new service men take their position on the stage remaining still and at attention until being otherwise ordered. Once the Color Guard has taken its place, my father and those in command under him enter and take their places beside him as he steps to the podium.

"Good morning, welcome and thank you for joining us today. As you can see behind me, we have a very special class of service men we will be installing today. And it is my honor to welcome and recognize each one of them personally." Turning to his second in command, my father says, "Now it is my pleasure to introduce Captain Steven Bishop who will read the names of those we are honoring today. Gentlemen as your name is called, please step forward to receive your honor."

Stepping forward, Captain Bishop salutes my father before exchanging a handshake and moving behind the podium.

"Good morning," Captain Bishop greets the audience. "We will begin with the installation of the Seaman Apprentice."

As Captain Bishop begins to read the names, each recruit steps forward for my father to add his newest honor to the board on his chest, steps back and salutes my father. Each one looks as fetching as the next in their white dress uniform.

When the name of the last Seaman Apprentice is read, I begin to focus more intently on those being honored before me.

"Donald Edwin White," Captain Bishop says as the final Seaman Apprentice follows protocol by stepping forward to receive his honor, steps back and salutes.

However, it's the reading of the first Airman receiving Apprentice status that causes me to pale. "Paul David Babcock."

As my father steps to the next Airman, crystal blue eyes find mine, and wink. A mix of emotions flood through me, least of all joy in seeing him again so soon. As my father moves down the line of Airmen, my focus remains on only one as I take in how handsome he truly is.

Light brown hair, crystal blue eyes that seem to look into my soul as we danced just a few days ago. Broad shoulders, tan skin, no doubt gained from working long hours on his parents' farm, all coupled with a smile that would melt any woman's resolve, including this Admiral's daughter.

It's not until my father moves back to the podium that I steer my focus away from Paul.

"Ladies and Gentlemen," he begins, "please join me, the entire staff and those currently serving in the United States Navy here at Point Mugu in welcoming our newest class of both Seaman and Airman Apprentices."

As the audience and officers begin to applaud, the newly promoted apprentices step forward, beaming with pride in their accomplishment. When the applauding begins to die down, my father turns back to the podium to address the audience.

"Ladies and gentlemen, thank you for joining us today for this very special installation. The administration has arranged a lunch reception and ask that you all join us as we get to know our new servicemen."

Turning to salute the newest residents of Point Mugu, my father dismisses them to begin the celebration.

"That was a beautiful ceremony," my mother says as she places her handbag over her arm.

"Yes it was," I agree as my eyes flit in Paul's direction only to find his watching me as he talks with one of the other airmen.

"Ruby," my mother says gaining my attention, "it looks like your father needs me. Are you okay on your own?"

Giving her a reassuring smile I reply, "Yes ma'am. I saw Millie sneak in late so I'll enlist her to mingle with me."

"Okay sweetheart, I'll see you later," she says as she makes her way to my father's side.

Knowing my father will keep one eye on me from across the room, I make my way out of the row and down the aisle to find Millie.

"Ruby," she nearly shouts, as I get closer.

Help Our Heroes

"Millie, I didn't think you were coming today."

"I wasn't planning on it, but changed my mind at the last minute," she says eyeing the appointees in their dress uniforms. "And I have to say, I'm certainly glad I did."

Grabbing her hand to gain her focus I whisper, "Millie, they're here."

"Who's here? What are you talking about Ruby?"

Sighing I clarify what I'm talking about. "Don and Paul. They're here."

"What? No, they can't be," she says in disbelief. "Surely they would have told us they were in the Navy."

"You were probably too far back to recognize them, but trust me, it's them." Pulling her in closer, I whisper, "Paul winked at me from the stage."

Grinning from ear to ear, Millie grabs my hand, "Well come on, let's go talk to them," she says as she begins to walk in their direction only to have me stop her.

"Hold on, we can't just march over there and start speaking to them. That would look too suspicious. We'll stop and speak to a few others on our way to them, okay?"

"Okay, that sounds good. Now let's go."

With our plan in place, we make our way over to a group of three apprentices, waiting until one stops speaking before stepping up to introduce ourselves.

"Hello," I say gaining their attention, "I'm Ruby Thorpe and this is Millie Bishop. We wanted to welcome you to Point Mugu and congratulate you on your promotions."

Seaman Apprentice Novak is the first to step forward and offer his hand. "It's a pleasure to meet you Miss Thorpe, Miss Bishop. And thank you for the kind welcome."

"It's our pleasure," Millie says, "and thank you all for your service. The lunch will be set up shortly, so please help yourselves."

"Miss Thorpe, Miss Bishop, Airman Apprentice Sanders," he says before introducing the third member of the group. "This is Seaman Apprentice Turner."

Smiling, the two of us shake their hands, "It's a pleasure to meet you both."

"Thorpe and Bishop," Seaman Turner questions, "as in Admiral Thorpe and Captain Bishop?"

"Yes, that's correct," Millie says, "the Admiral and Captain are our fathers."

I watch as recognition moves across their faces and I know this is the last time we will speak freely with these three.

Straightening his shoulders, Seaman Novak says with a nod to each of us, "It was a pleasure to meet you Miss Thorpe, Miss Bishop. Thank you again for the kind welcome. Now if you'll excuse us, it looks like lunch is ready."

Smiling politely, while trying not to laugh, I reply, "Of course, enjoy your lunch."

As they walk away, I catch Paul watching me wearing somewhat of a frown.

"Uh-oh," Millie says, "someone doesn't look happy."

"Well, they'll be even less so when they find out our last names. Come on, might as well get this over with," I say as Millie and I walk towards Don and Paul.

"Hello gentlemen," Millie says saucily, taking the lead this time. "I'm Millie Bishop and this is my very best friend, Ruby Thorpe."

Biting my lip to contain my laughter, I watch as both Don and Paul pale slightly.

Don swallows hard before asking, "Bishop as in Captain?"

Turning his focus on me Paul asks, "Thorpe as in Admiral?"

"Yes, they are our fathers," I reply my gaze solely locked on Paul's.

"Jesus Millie," Don whisper yells. "Why didn't you tell me?"

"If I had, you wouldn't have so much as looked at me, let alone dance with me and you know it."

Letting out a defeated sigh Don admits, "You're right."

"I know," Millie says, "and I didn't want to chance that. Besides I don't remember you telling me you were in the Navy."

"That's true, I didn't," Don says.

"I guess this means I won't be able to see you again," Paul says softly as his fingers tighten their grip on his hat.

"What? No. Look Paul, yes, my father has a rule about me dating men under his command. However, he can't control who you see on your time off.

"I see what you're saying Ruby, but I don't want either one of us getting in trouble with your father."

"We won't. We'll just need to be careful when we're on base."

Considering my words, Paul looks down before slowly looking back up at me. "If we get caught, we'll all have hell to pay."

A slow smile pulls at my lips, "Then we'll just have to make sure we don't get caught."

Chapter 9

Before we left the reception, Millie and I found out that Don and Paul didn't have to report in until zero-eight hundred Tuesday morning. Excited to hear that, we made plans to meet on the beach and watch the fireworks together.

Walking down the beach, Millie stops and asks, "What about here Ruby?"

"That's perfect. We should have a good view of the fireworks from here."

Unfolding the blanket, Millie took one end while I took the other to spread it out on the sand, and then we repeated the process with Millie's blanket.

"I'm hoping to be making fireworks, instead of watching them," Millie says.

Laughing I shake my head, "Millie Bishop, you're awful."

"Oh, come on Ruby, don't tell me you haven't thought about what it would be like to be kissed by Paul."

"Oh, I've definitely thought about it," I say as visions of Paul begin to flood my mind.

"Thought about what," a deep voice asks from behind me as strong hands rest on my hips.

Turning to face him, I smile and shake my head embarrassed he heard my confession. "It was nothing."

Cocking his head to the side, he studies me. "Oh, it was definitely something or you wouldn't be blushing," he teases.

Playfully slapping his arm, I retort, "I'm not blushing. I've just been in the sun."

"No," Paul laughs while wagging a finger at me. "You are definitely blushing."

Turning away and pretending to pout, Paul grabs me around the waist and hauls me back to him causing me to squeal and giggle. "Oh no you don't. Now I know it was something and you have to tell me," he says as he turns me to face him, still holding me securely in his arms.

Closing my eyes, I take a deep breath and confess to him what I said. "I admitted to Millie that I have thought about what it would be like to have you kiss me."

Lifting my chin so I am looking in his eyes, Paul says, "Ruby, you're all I've thought about since the night we met. You and what it would be like to kiss you."

"What's stopping you?"

"I'm afraid if I start, I won't want to stop."

My breath catches at his admission. We've only known each other for a few days, but there's an undeniable connection between us. At first, I thought it was a passing infatuation, but the more time I spend with him, the harder I feel myself falling for him.

"Ruby," Paul says while caressing my cheek with his thumb. "Why didn't you tell me who you were?"

Shrugging my shoulder, I ask, "Would you be here now if I had?"

"I don't think I would have had a choice."

Smiling I tease, "There's that charm again."

His grin widens. "Would you like to go for a walk before the fireworks start?"

"I'd love too."

Taking my hand, we walk down to the shore. "What made you want to become an airman?"

"I love the idea of flying and the thought of becoming a pilot excited me even more."

"Are planning a career in the Navy?"

"Nah, I'd like to stay long enough to become a pilot, get some flying experience. Who knows, maybe I'll find a nice girl, settle down, move back to Nebraska and start my own crop dusting service so I can still fly." Paul squeezes my hand causing me to look up to see him smiling down at me. "What about you?"

"I'm still undecided. I'm not sure if I want to continue going to school, or join the work force."

"Do you want to stay in California?"

"I suppose, if I have a reason to."

"Would I be reason enough?"

"You'd be the best reason of all," I answer honestly.

My answer both surprises and delights him, as is evident by the smile on his face. "Then maybe you should leave it up to fate," Paul suggests. "If you find the perfect job before it's time to apply to school, you'll know it's meant to be."

"I like that idea," I say as I mull over his suggestion in my mind. "Fate seems to be treating me well lately, maybe it will continue."

"I certainly hope so," Paul says.

As the sun begins to set, we turn around and head back to the spot we had picked out earlier to watch the fireworks.

When we return, we find Don and Millie snuggled up together on her blanket.

"Hi you two," I say as I kick my shoes off and take a seat on the blanket. "Having a good time?"

"We are," Millie says casting a glance at Don. "How was your walk?"

"It was nice," I say as Paul sit beside me.

Watching the sun drop below the horizon, Paul puts his arm around my shoulders and draws me closer to his side. Leaning my head on his shoulder, he turns and kisses the top of my head making me smile.

Along with the setting sun, the temperature had also dropped and now the ocean breeze caused me to shiver.

"Are you cold?"

"A little, but I'll be fine," I insist.

Shivering again, Paul moves away from me taking the warmth with him. "Come here," he says as he scoots behind me. Looking over my shoulder at him, he pulls me to sit between his legs, and wraps his arms around my shoulders effectively cocooning me from the cool ocean breeze.

"Better?" he asks close to my ear causing me to shiver for an entirely different reason.

Help Our Heroes

"Much, thank you."

When the first firework explodes in the sky, so do the oohs and ahhs from the crowd around us. Each magical display is more beautiful than the last. Leaning in and resting his cheek against mine, Paul points down the beach. "Look."

Turning my head to see the display from a neighboring town brings me face to face with Paul. Between the fireworks reflecting in his blue eyes and the air sizzling between us, I can't look away.

Leaning in, Paul kisses me softly before drawing back as if to ask permission to kiss me again. Giving him an almost imperceptible nod, this time I meet him halfway, eager to feel his lips on mine again. Shifting our position without breaking the kiss, Paul pulls me into his lap, my arms wrapping around his neck on their own accord.

Pulling apart to catch our breath, Paul's hand cups my face as his thumb gently caresses my cheek. "I knew once I kissed you I wouldn't want to stop," he says, a smile tugging at the corners of his mouth.

"Then maybe you shouldn't," I suggest as my fingers weave into the soft hair at the nape of his neck.

Dropping his focus to my mouth, Paul smiles. "You, Ruby Thorpe, are trouble." He lowers his mouth to mine again.

While the fireworks continue to light the night sky, Paul and I are unaware of anything happening around us.

When the rumble of the fireworks cease, Paul pulls away again. "As much as I want to keep kissing you, we should stop or these beautiful swollen lips of yours are going to get both of us in trouble," he says while running his thumb across my bottom lip.

"You're right," I agree as I lay my head on his shoulder. "I don't want to have to answer any questions tonight."

After a few moments of comfortable silence, Paul asks, "How did you two get here?"

"We walked. It's not far from the base."

"Don and I will walk you back. You're not walking back alone in the dark."

"One day and you're already being bossy."

Chuckling Paul kisses my head, "Just keeping you safe so I can keep kissing you."

"Well, since you put it that way," I tease, the smile evident in my voice.

"My, don't you two look cozy," Millie says as she and Don walk up to where we're sitting.

"Mmm, we are," I practically purr as I snuggle deeper into Paul's chest.

"We should be going soon Ruby," Millie says.

"I know, we don't want to be late."

"Don," Paul says, "the girls walked here. I told Ruby we would walk them back to the base."

"You sure that's a good idea?"

"Maybe not, but we can't let them walk back by themselves in the dark. If anyone asks, we'll just tell them we were making sure they got back safely."

"Okay, sounds good to me," Don agrees.

"You could always let us walk through the gate on our own and then follow us a few minutes later," I suggest.

"That's up to you. I think the Admiral would take more issue if we left you to get home on your own, than if we delivered you there safely."

Paul helped me fold the blanket, and carried it back to the base for me. We talked the entire way back, me telling him about my brothers and sister, and him telling me about his family and growing up on a farm.

As we near the base, Paul slows his steps. "We report in tomorrow morning and are off duty at fifteen-hundred Friday until zero-seven-hundred Sunday. I'd really like to see you again."

"I'd like that too. Millie and I could meet you and maybe see a movie?"

"I like that idea, and then we can make plans for Saturday."

When we reach the base, Don and Paul walk through the gates with us. Since our house and Millie's are practically across the street from each other, we stop between them to say goodnight. Handing me the folded blanket, Paul lets his touch linger on my arm.

"Thank you for walking us home, I had a great time tonight."

"Me too. Goodnight Ruby."

Help Our Heroes

"Goodnight Paul," I say before turning to walk to the door.

Chapter 10

The anticipation of getting to see Paul again, coupled with working with my mother on a summer party for the children of the bases military families, made the week go by surprisingly quick.

While we worked, my mother asked, "Do you have plans with Millie this weekend?"

"Yes ma'am. We're going to a movie tomorrow afternoon, and I hear there is a carnival in town this weekend so we're thinking of going there on Saturday."

"Oh, that sounds like fun. Would you have time to help me with a few things Saturday morning?"

"Of course," I told her with a reassuring a smile. We worked in silence a few minutes before I asked something that had been on my mind, and even more so after to talking to Paul during our walk along the beach. "Mom, I was thinking of applying for a job."

"That's wonderful sweetheart. What did you have in mind?"

I'm not sure, maybe something secretarial or at one of the stores in town. Perhaps I'll go next week and see what's available."

"That's a good idea."

* * *

When Friday finally arrived, Millie and I completed what we needed to at home as quickly as possible and then left for town. While we wait for Don and Paul to join us, I tell Millie about my desire to get a job, so we begin looking into who's hiring. As we pass by the bank, I saw a help wanted sign in the window.

"Millie look!" Pointing to the sign that caught my attention across the street. "I'm going to go inquire about it."

Stepping inside the bank's lobby, I make my way over to desk occupied by a well-dressed woman. Reading the nameplate on her desk, Mrs. Masterson,

Help Our Heroes

Executive Secretary, I address her personally. "Excuse me, Mrs. Masterson? I'm Ruby Thorpe and I'm inquiring about the help wanted sign posted in the window."

Looking up from her typewriter, she silently assesses me before explaining, "It's a clerical position. Filing, typing and secretary for our newly appointed assistant manager. Do you have any experience?"

Nervously interlocking my fingers, so I don't fidget, I admit, "No ma'am, however I did take a typing class in high school as well as shorthand. I assist my father with correspondence when needed and I volunteer at the library, so I'm used to filing."

"Very well Miss Thorpe, come back Monday morning, nine o'clock sharp, you can meet with Mr. Palmer."

Trying to contain my excitement, I smile and offer my thanks. "Thank you so much, I'll see you on Monday."

Practically floating out the door, I find Millie on the sidewalk. "Millie, you won't believe it!"

"Did you get the job?"

I shake my head. "Not yet, but I'm supposed to come back on Monday to speak with Mr. Palmer."

"Ruby, that's wonderful! I'm so excited for you. Now I just need to find something."

Threading my arm through hers I say, "Well let's get going, maybe we'll find something for you on our way to the theater."

By the time we reach the movie theater where we planned to meet Don and Paul, Millie had already secured a position at a new boutique in town.

Approaching the theater, I hear Don say, "Look there Paul, here come our beautiful girls now."

"Yep, and they do look beautiful," Paul says, his gaze never wavering from me.

Walking straight into his arms, I smile up at him, "Still working that charm I see."

Smiling Paul tucks a strand of hair behind my ear and shakes his head. "No, just telling the truth," he says before he leans down to kiss me.

When the kiss ends, I pull back and my excitement returns. "You'll never guess what happened today," I begin, excited to share my news. "Millie and I were walking through town and I saw a help wanted sign in the window of the bank. I went inside to inquire about it and they asked me to come back on Monday to speak to the assistant manager."

"That's great Ruby! See I told you fate would work it out for us. What would you be doing?"

"I'd be the secretary for the assistant manager," I reply proudly.

Paul looks down a little sheepishly, "Does that mean I won't see you as much?"

Stepping closer to him, I entwine my fingers with his. "Not necessarily. It should make it easier for us to sneak around, because you boys can meet us in town."

Pulling me closer Paul smiles down at me, "I like the way you think Ruby Thorpe."

"You two ready to see the movie," Millie asks from her place beside Don.

"Whenever you are," I reply moving to Paul's side.

Stepping inside Paul purchased our tickets from the attendant and we made our way into the theater. Taking my hand, Paul leads us back to two seats in a dark corner of the room. Once we are seated, Paul whispers in my ear, "I thought I'd have a better chance of kissing you if we sat in the back."

"I think your chances are pretty good no matter where we sit," I whisper back.

My reply was the only confirmation Paul needed that I wanted to be kissed just as much as he wanted to kiss me.

His kiss is soft and slow as his lips linger on mine. When he pulls away he whispers, "I've missed you this week."

"I've missed you too. I saw you once on base, and all I wanted to do was run to you. But I had to remember where I was and that I didn't want you to get in trouble."

"Oh Ruby, I think I'm already in trouble."

When the lights dim and the movie begins to play, Paul puts his arm around my shoulders and pulls me closer. Reaching up and placing a kiss on his jaw is enough to ignite the spark between us. Turning to place a kiss on my temple, Paul leaves a trail of kisses down my jaw making his way to my lips.

Paul wasn't the first person I'd kissed. That honor belonged to Brian Franklin my sophomore year of high school. But those were kisses from an awkward teenage boy. Paul is no teenage boy, he's all man and his kisses could easily set me on fire. What started out as slow and almost reverent quickly became more. We can't seem to get enough of each other. When Paul tries to slip his tongue into my mouth, I gasp and jolt away from him, only to have him calm me instantly.

"Oh Ruby, shhh, come here." Urging me back to his side, Paul lifts my chin as he asks, "You've never been kissed like that before, have you?" Embarrassed, I shake my head as his thumb caresses my cheek. "Let me show you then."

Searching his eyes, I nod giving him permission, because I really didn't want him to stop kissing me.

Leaning in, Paul captures my lips again and this time when his tongue runs along my lips, I open for him, allowing him inside. It feels strange and wonderful at the same time. Each time his tongue brushes against mine, I become bolder until I had taste every inch of his mouth. When he pulls back so we could catch our breath a whimper escapes me making him smile.

"I'm guessing you like being kissed like that," he whispers a smile playing at the corners of his mouth.

"Very much," I whisper back, my focus dropping to his mouth ready to have is lips on mine again.

"Good, so did I." The words are barely out of his mouth before he's kissing me again.

When the movie ends and the lights come back on, I begin to tidy my hair. "I must look a mess."

"No, you look beautiful."

"You don't have to charm me for kisses you know, I'll give them to you freely."

Paul chuckles. "I'm a lucky man, all your dances and all your kisses."

Smiling I lean in close so I can kiss him again. "Yes, they are only for you."

Before I can attempt to deepen the kiss, Paul moves away. "We need to get out of here." Offering me his hand Paul says, "Let's go find Don and Mille and go get something to eat."

Taking his hand, we walk out of the theater and find Don and Millie waiting for us on the sidewalk.

As we walk toward the restaurant Paul asks, "Will I get to see you tomorrow?"

"You will if you want to," I tease.

Smiling he says, "Just tell me when and where."

Grinning up at him I ask, "How do you feel about carnivals?"

Chapter 11

Monday morning, I dress in my favorite navy blue dress, slip into a pair of white heels and walk into the kitchen.

"Good morning sweetheart," my mother greets me.

"Well, what do you think?" I ask while doing a pirouette. "Do I look professional enough to be an assistant manager's secretary?"

"You look beautiful, and I'm sure they will hire you on the spot."

"Fingers crossed," I say as I take a seat at the table where a plate with a stack of pancakes waits for me. "I'm not sure when I'll be home," I say as pour myself a glass of orange juice and then drizzle maple syrup over the stack of pancakes. "Millie begins work today too, so I'll wait for her so we can ride home together."

"That's fine, your father and I have our weekly dinner with the Bishops tonight."

Finishing my breakfast, I take my plate to the sink and wash it before turning back to my mother. "Okay, I'm off to meet Millie. Thank you for breakfast." I lean over and kiss her cheek.

"You're welcome sweetheart. Good luck."

Thanks Mom!" I call before walking out the door. Closing the door behind me, I see Millie walking down her drive. Wearing a pink dress with white buttons, her blonde hair bounces from the excitement in her walk.

"Millie, you look beautiful," I say as she reaches me.

"Thank you, so do you. I'm a little nervous," she admits.

"Me too." I nod as we walk to the bus stop.

We have a short wait until the bus arrives, taking our seats, Millie opens her purse. "I brought this with me for luck," she says taking out the small lion Don won for her at the carnival.

"That is adorable."

"He tried so hard to win me a bigger one," she says laughing, "but it just wasn't his lucky day."

"It's perfect. Now you can carry it with you."

"Thank you for suggesting the carnival. I hadn't had that much fun since I was a kid."

"Me either, I think Paul really enjoyed it too."

"I know Don did. It was nice to see them loosen up and just have fun."

"It really was."

As the bus pulls to a stop halfway between the bank and the boutique, Millie and I make our way down the aisle to the exit.

Stepping out onto the sidewalk, Millie turns to me and takes a calming breath. We're both a bit nervous, given this is our first day. Giving me a hug Millie says, "Good luck today."

"Thanks, good luck to you too," I return her hug. "I'll meet you at Luigi's afterward and we can have dinner before going home."

"Okay, see you then." She turns toward the boutique and I spin in the other direction toward the bank.

I make my way down the sidewalk, trying to relax. Reaching the front of the building, I take a deep breath, grip the door handle and pull it open to step inside. Glancing at the clock on the wall, I see that I am five minutes early. That should help me make a good first impression.

Walking up to Mrs. Masterson's desk, I wait for her to acknowledge me. Sensing my presence, she asks? "Yes, may I help you?"

"Good morning Mrs. Masterson," I say trying to exude confidence, I only somewhat feel. "I'm Ruby Thorpe. I have a nine o'clock appointment with Mr. Palmer."

"Good morning Miss Thorpe, you're right on time," she says as she steps from behind her desk. Indicating toward the seating area she says, "If you'll have a seat, I'll let Mr. Palmer know you're here."

"Thank you." I watch as she walks to what I assumed to be Mr. Palmer's office.

When she returns, she smiles politely. "He will be with you shortly."

Nodding my appreciation, I return her smile and wait. A few minutes later,

Help Our Heroes

Mr. Palmer emerges from his office and walks to the waiting area to meet me. "Miss Thorpe?"

"Yes." I stand to meet him.

He's younger than I expected, perhaps in his early thirties. Sandy blond hair cut short, and a black suit that fit him perfectly, his kind brown eyes smiled as he offered me his hand in greeting. "Dwayne Palmer, it's a pleasure to meet you."

"Likewise, Mr. Palmer," I give his hand a firm shake like my dad has taught me. "Thank you for seeing me."

Releasing my hand, he indicated towards his office, "If you will follow me, we'll get started."

Following him inside his office, Mr. Palmer offers me a seat as he closes the door before making his way around his desk and taking a seat.

"Mrs. Masterson tells me you were inquiring about the secretary position."

"Yes sir, that's correct."

"What experience do you have?"

"Honestly, this would be my first time being employed. I recently graduated from high school, but I did take both typing and shorthand."

He's silent for a moment, no doubt considering what I've said. Sitting forward he leans his arms on his desk, "I was hoping for someone with a little more experience, Miss Thorpe."

Stealing myself against the disappointment of rejection, I listen as he continues.

"However, since I am also new to this position, I'm willing to give you a try."

I breathe out a sigh of relief. "Thank you, Mr. Palmer," I reply trying to contain my excitement.

"No need to thank me. Mrs. Masterson spoke very highly of you and is willing to take you under her wing."

"She did?" I ask, unable to hide the surprise in my voice.

Chuckling at my surprise he says, "Yes, it seems you made quite an impression on her. And, believe me, that is no easy feat. Now, let's go over what is expected of you, shall we?"

"Yes, of course."

"Mr. Meyers our manager opens the bank in the morning and I close, so you'll be expected to stay until closing. Your hours will be from nine to five daily, and the bank is closed on weekends and recognized holidays, with an hour for lunch. You'll be responsible for taking care of my appointments and correspondence as well as filing and other duties with which I may need your assistance. Any questions?"

"When would you like me to start?"

He laughs lowly at my eagerness. "How about today?"

"Today would be fine."

"Great," he says as he rises from his seat. "Let's get you out to Mrs. Masterson and she can show you around and get you settled in."

Rising from my seat, once again I express my appreciation, "Mr. Palmer, thank you for giving me this opportunity. I won't disappoint you."

"It's my pleasure Miss Thorpe," he says as he opens the door and ushers me back to Mrs. Masterson.

"Mrs. Masterson, say hello to my new secretary, Miss Ruby Thorpe."

Looking first to Mr. Palmer and then to me, Mrs. Masterson smiles, "Welcome Miss Thorpe."

"Thank you."

"Mrs. Masterson, if you could show Miss Thorpe around and get her settled in, I would appreciate it."

"Of course, Mr. Palmer," she replies while rounding her desk.

"Miss Thorpe if you'll follow me I'll give you the tour and introduce you to everyone."

*　*　*

When the workday ends, I head down the street to meet Millie. Just as I begin to step inside, I hear her call my name. Turning to see Millie walking up the sidewalk, I step away from the door to wait for her.

As soon as she reaches me, Millie threads her arm through mine. "You got the job, didn't you?"

"I did, and I can't wait to tell you all about it. But first, let's go inside and you can tell me all about your day."

Chapter 12

Paul and I continued to see each other over the next couple of months. Having a job in town helped keep me occupied and my mind on something other than Paul, although he was never far from my thoughts.

It had become our routine, on their days off, Don and Paul would meet Millie and me at either the theater or one of our favorite restaurants.

As Mr. Palmer and I are leaving for the evening, from behind me, I hear, "Hello my beautiful girl." When I turn around, I see Paul standing, looking handsome as ever, with a bouquet of flowers.

"Paul!" I exclaim as I fly into his arms. "What are you doing here?"

Laughing at my reaction Paul lifts me off the ground and spins me around. "I wanted to surprise you."

"Well you certainly did that," I say as he sets me back on the ground. Remembering my manners, I turn to introduce Mr. Palmer. "Paul, this is Mr. Palmer, my boss and assistant manager of the bank."

Offering his hand, Paul says, "It's a pleasure to meet you. Thank you for giving Ruby the chance. I know she is enjoying working with you."

"It's nice to meet you Paul," Mr. Palmer returns, "and believe me when I say Ruby is doing a wonderful job. Well, I should be going so I'm not late for dinner. You two enjoy your evening."

"You too Mr. Palmer," I say as I move closer into Paul's side.

We turn to walk down the street. "He seems nice."

"He is," I agree, "and so is his wife," I add so there is no misunderstanding. Hugging him closer I say, "I can't believe you surprised me! I thought we were meeting at the restaurant."

"Well, I wanted a little alone time with my girl. Don and I thought we'd shake things up a bit. He's surprising Millie too."

"I'm really glad you did." I look up at him, which Paul takes as his cue to kiss me.

We make our way down the street to a different restaurant than we normally frequent. Once we are seated and have been given our menus, I can't help but comment. "Wow when you said you wanted to shake things up, you really went all out."

Paul laughs and kisses my hand, "I have to keep you on your toes."

When the waitress returns, we place our order and Paul reaches across the table and takes my hand in his. As his thumb skates back and forth across mine, he says, "I got some exciting news today and I wanted to share it with you first."

"Really? Is everything okay?"

"Yes, everything is fine. My commanding officer told me today that I'll be included in the next group being sent for flight training."

"Paul that's wonderful! You'll finally get to fulfill your dream of becoming a pilot. Where are they sending you for training?"

"The training takes place in Hawaii, at the Kaneohe Naval Air Station. I'm really excited about that part, but it's the leaving you behind part that I'm not looking forward to."

"Oh Paul," I say as I squeeze his hand. "I'm not looking forward to that part either, but this is the reason you joined the Navy. And you are going to be the best Flyboy the U.S. Navy has ever seen," I say proudly.

"You know," Paul says with a mischievous gleam in his eye. "If I'm a Flyboy that means that you will be a Flyboy's girl."

"I like the sound of that," I say beaming up at him.

Paul smiles and his eyes sparkle as he asks, "Does that mean that I get to pin up a picture of you in the cockpit?"

My cheeks turn pink, because I know exactly the kind of pictures pilots pin up in the cockpit to keep them company. "You never know, I may surprise you," I whisper just as the waitress returns with our meal.

* * *

Over dinner, I tell Paul about how much I'm enjoying working at the bank, and he talks about the flight training he'll be taking part in. His excitement is evident the more he talks about it, and I couldn't be more proud of him. Becoming a pilot so quickly is truly an accomplishment.

Help Our Heroes

"You know," Paul says, "I saw a place that does day trips down the coast. We could spend the day on a boat, cruising down the coast, and take in the sites."

"Would I be able to hold your hand and steal a few kisses?" I ask shyly, thinking about how cautious we usually are when we are together.

"You don't have to steal kisses remember, they're given freely," he smiles, giving my own words back to me.

"Well in that case, that sounds amazing."

* * *

The next morning, Millie and I ride the bus into town to meet Don and Paul. Millie and Don had plans to picnic in the park, while Paul and I were on a boat cruising down the coast.

"Ruby, I have to say I'm a little jealous that you get to cruise down the coast."

"I know. I'm excited. It was all Paul's idea, which makes it even more special."

"You know, now that you mention it," Millie says, "it was Don's idea to have a picnic. If I didn't know any better, I'd think those two were up to something."

Somewhat surprised that Millie hasn't heard, I tell her Paul's news.

"Paul had some exciting news he's going to be in the next group sent for flight training."

"Oh Ruby that's so exciting!"

"It really is, I'm so happy for him."

"But?"

"Nothing, I really am happy for him."

"And I believe you," Millie says. "But come on Ruby, I've known you for a long time and I can tell that there is more that you are not saying."

Sighing I resign myself to the fact that Millie can read me like a book. "It's just that I'm going to miss him so much while he's gone."

"Oh Ruby, of course you will. You and Paul have spent the last four months together. Not to mention that you make an adorable couple."

Laughing I have to agree with her, "We do, don't we?"

"Yes, you do and you'll be even better together when he gets back from training."

As we get closer to our stop, I muster up the courage to ask Millie to help me with a surprise for Paul. "Millie, would you mind helping me with something before Paul leaves?"

"Of course, not. What is it you need me to do?"

Just as I finish explaining to her about the picture, the bus comes to a stop and we make our way to the exit and step off the bus onto the sidewalk.

The bus pulls away, revealing Don and Paul leaning against a car across the street. My smile widens as Paul spreads his arms and asks, "Well, what do you think?"

Millie and I look both ways, cross the street and walk right into their waiting arms. "I love it! Where did you get it?"

"Don and I thought we should be able to take our girls out properly, so we bought it from one of the guys being transferred."

"Are we still going on the boat?"

"Sure, if you want to or we could all drive down the coast."

I can tell he's trying to hide his excitement and really wants to drive instead of going on the boat. "Let's drive, then we can stop whenever we want."

Smiling Paul kisses my quickly, "Are you sure you don't mind?"

Shaking my head, I confirm, "As long as I get to spend time with you I don't care what we do."

Smiling, Paul leans down and kisses me again before turning to Don. "Don what do you think about all of us driving down the coast?"

Looking to Mille for confirmation, she smiles and nods. "Sure sounds good. It'll give us a chance to get a feel for this beast," Don says as he pats the roof of the car.

"Great," Paul says, "I'll drive down and you can drive back."

"Sounds good, let's go," Don says as he opens the door for Millie and they slide into the back seat.

Adjusting the seat back in place, Paul sweeps his arm toward the car. "After you," he says to me and I giddily slide inside, stopping in the middle of the seat so I can sit next to Paul while he drives.

Help Our Heroes

The drive down the California coast is breathtakingly beautiful. Clear blue skies stretch out over the Pacific Ocean with just touch of a chill in the October breeze. When we reach Malibu, we stop for lunch and a walk on the beach. As Paul and I walk hand in hand along the shore, I realize I haven't asked him when he is leaving. Though I really didn't want to think about Paul leaving, I did want to know how much more time we had together.

"Paul, when do you leave for flight training?"

"November first."

Feeling the tears well up in my eyes, I whisper, "That's too soon."

Pulling me against his chest and resting his chin on top of my head, he holds me as he murmurs. "I know, but I have to go."

"I know, but I'll miss you so much while you are gone."

Pulling away, Paul cups my face in his large warm hands, his thumb brushing away the tears that had fallen. "Oh my beautiful Ruby don't cry. I'll only be gone a little while and then I'm coming home to you."

Willing my tears to stop falling, as I look into his eyes I whisper, "Promise?"

A smile pulls at his lips as he answers, "Yes, I promise," just before he kisses me.

Chapter 13

October 31, 1941

With only a few weeks remaining until Paul left for flight training, we spent as much time together as possible. We had several more dates after our drive down the coast with Millie and Don. Paul even chartered a boat that took us out to one of the islands off the coast for a picnic so we could be alone.

The day before Paul was to ship out seemed to drag by, making the anticipation of our goodbye even more daunting. Preoccupied with thoughts of Paul, Mr. Palmer tried once again to gain my attention.

"Miss Thorpe?"

Jumping at the sound of his voice, I apologize, "Mr. Palmer, I'm sorry. What can I do for you?"

"Can I see you in my office please?"

"Yes sir," I reply rising form my seat and making my way into his office.

"Miss Thorpe," Mr. Palmer begins before stopping and giving me a sympathetic smile before he continues. "Ruby, it seems you've had a few things on your mind lately and I just wanted to make sure you were okay."

Embarrassed that my personal life has affected work, I begin to apologize. "Mr. Palmer, I am so sorry. I promise I'll be more focused…"

Holding up his hand to stop me, he says, "Miss Thorpe, I didn't call you in here to reprimand you, I am merely concerned about you."

Breathing a sigh of relief, I smile and reassure Mr. Palmer. "Thank you Mr. Palmer for your concern. Again, I apologize for letting personal matters interfere with my work."

Sitting up and leaning forward he says, "Ruby you are one of the hardest working people I've ever met. Your work is stellar and far from affected by whatever is going on. I just wanted to offer an ear if you needed to talk."

"Thank you, Mr. Palmer, I appreciate that. I may take you up on that while Paul is gone."

Shock evident on his face, Mr. Palmer asks, "Wait, Paul is leaving?"

"Yes sir. He's in the Navy and leaves in the morning for flight training."

"Tomorrow? Then what are you doing here?"

"Paul had some things to take care of today, and working helps keep my mind off him leaving. He's picking me up after work tonight." Hesitantly I continue, "I'm not supposed to date men under my father's command, so I stay quiet about our relationship. Our best friends are the only ones that know."

Confused, Mr. Palmer asks, "Your father's command?"

"Yes, my father is Admiral Thorpe, who happens to be in charge of the naval base. Something else I tend to stay quiet about," I say with a shy smile.

"I'll say. I had no idea. So your parents don't know you are dating Paul?"

I shake my head, "No, not unless someone else has told them. And I assume they haven't or they would have confronted me."

"That's impressive. Your secret is safe with me."

"I appreciate that, and thank you for allowing me to speak freely, I feel much better now."

"Good," he says smiling kindly at me. "Remember, my door is always open for you, and if there is anything we can do for you while he's gone, let me know."

Rising from my seat, I make my way back to my desk to finish out the day.

* * *

At precisely five o'clock, Mr. Palmer locks the doors of the bank as the tellers begin balancing their cash drawers. "Miss Thorpe," he says from his position by the door. "It looks like your ride is here and you don't want to keep him waiting."

Smiling, my heart does a little leap in my chest at the thought of seeing Paul. Quickly gathering my things, I walk to the door where Paul and Mr. Palmer are conversing. Opening the door wider so I can step through, Mr. Palmer shakes Paul's hand. "Good luck to you Paul."

"Thank you sir," Paul replies as he wraps his arm around me drawing me into his side.

"You two enjoy your evening," he says before locking the door behind us.

Walking me to the car, Paul opens the door for me, stopping me before I get inside. Smiling down at me he says, "Hi. You look beautiful."

"Thank you," is all I manage before he kisses me.

Pulling away Paul says, "We better get going."

Sliding into the front seat, Paul closes the door before moving to the driver's side and climbing in behind the wheel.

"Where are we going?"

"You'll see," he says giving me a quick smile before pulling out into the street.

A few minutes later, we pull into the parking lot of the diner, where we had dinner the night after we met.

Laughing I say, "I haven't been here since…"

Paul's smile is infectious as he finishes my thought, "Since our first date?"

"Yes," I reply confirming that he indeed can read my thoughts.

"Me either, come on let's grab a bite to eat so we can get to the rest of what I have planned."

Finding a table in the back of the diner, our waitress is there within minutes to take our order. Ordering a burger with fries and a vanilla shake for both of us, Paul sends the waitress on her way.

"You remembered what we had that first night."

"I remember everything when it comes to you Ruby. Where we've been, what we've done, what you were wearing the first night I saw you."

Smiling I shyly look down at my fidgeting fingers. "When you turned around and smiled at me from across the room, I thought I'd faint dead away."

Returning my smile, he says, "Well I'm certainly glad you didn't," Paul says as he leans in to kiss me.

"So am I," I reply as I our lips part. "Oh I almost forgot." I scramble to retrieve my handbag. "I have something for you." Taking an envelope out, I hand it to Paul trying in vain to control the blush I feel creeping up my neck.

"What's this?" he asks as he begins to open it. A slow smile begins to spread across his face as he sees what's inside. "Wow, Ruby… These are…

Help Our Heroes

Wow."

"Do you like them?"

"Like them? Ruby, these are incredible. When did you take these?"

Shrugging I shyly confess as he continues to look at the photos, "You had mentioned having a picture to pin up in the cockpit, so I asked Millie if she would take them for me, so I could surprise you."

"Rita Hayworth's got nothing on my girl," he says as his smile widens and he shakes his head. "I can't believe you did these for me."

"Well, I couldn't have you going off to Hawaii and falling for an island girl. I had to remind you what you have to come home to," I tease.

"Ruby," Paul says taking my hand and looking straight into my eyes. "There is nothing or no one that would ever make me forget you."

* * *

After dinner Paul says, "I have one more surprise for you," as he ushers me back to the car.

Making the short drive down the street, Paul pulls into the parking lot of the dance hall. "I thought we would spend our last night together where we first met."

Throwing my arms around his neck, while trying to keep my tears at bay, I whisper, "It's perfect."

Stepping inside the dance hall, Paul leads me out to the crowded dancefloor, and begins to spin me around the floor to the lively Tommy Dorsey tune the band is playing. The song ends just as Paul pulls me back in and dips me back over his arm. Lifting me back up and against his chest, now breathless from the up-tempo song, the band slows things down playing the very song we first danced to, all those months ago.

Pulling me back into his arms Paul whispers, "They're playing our song."

There are no words spoken as we sway to the familiar tune, eyes locked on one another. None are needed. There on the crowed dancefloor, as the song ends, Paul leans in and captures my mouth with his. Everything and everyone around us fades into the background, leaving nothing but the two of us caught up in this moment of time, neither of us will ever forget.

When the kiss ends, Paul whispers, "That was the best night of my life."

"Mine too," I whisper back.

"Come on. Let's get something to drink."

Accepting two glasses of punch from the attendant, Paul leads us over to an empty table. After a short break, Paul excuses himself to go and speak to the bandleader. The band begins to play Big Crosby's I'll Be Seeing You, as Paul makes his way back to me. When he reaches the table, Paul holds out his hand and asks, "May I have this dance?"

Smiling I place my hand in his, "I'd love to."

Curious I ask, "Did you ask them to play this song?"

Paul shakes his head, "No, but it's fitting, because no matter where I am I'll be thinking of you."

"Oh Paul, that's the sweetest thing I've ever heard."

As the song ends, the band begins to play Yours by Jimmy Dorsey.

"This is the song I requested," Paul says gaining my attention. "Ruby, these last few months spent with you have been better than I could have imagined. I love you Ruby Thorpe. I'm done hiding our relationship, and when I get back, I want to tell your parents that I'm in love with you. Because now and forever, Ruby, I'll be yours."

"Oh Paul, I love you too," I exclaim, "and I'll be yours for as long as you'll have me."

Taking my face in his hands, Paul kisses me thoroughly, before pulling away and whispering, "Let's get out of here."

Chapter 14

November 1941

Paul's flight to the training center in Hawaii took off at nine o'clock Saturday morning. Even though we had said our goodbyes the night before, it crushed me that I wasn't there to see him off. Paul had promised to write as often as he could, and I promised to do the same.

Each day I rushed home to check the mail, anxious to hear from Paul and to hear how his training was going.

The first letter arrived the following Saturday.

My Beautiful Ruby,

After a long flight, we arrived in Hawaii safe and sound. The view of the Pacific Ocean from the plane was incredible and I can't wait for you to see it. Once I'm officially a pilot I want to share it with you. I guess we can add that to the long list of things I want to share with you.

Our training begins bright and early Sunday morning. I guess the Navy doesn't abide by Sunday being a day of rest. I know that made you laugh and I wish I were there to hear it.

I miss you already and will be counting the days until I see you again.
All my love,
Paul

I read the letter twice more before tucking it away in my dresser drawer. Pulling out the letter I started the day Paul left, I add to telling him that I too, would be counting the days until he returned.

The next morning, I can hardly wait to tell Millie that I had received a letter from Paul. Being the amazing friend that she is, she allows me to go on about it the entire ride to work. When the bus comes to a stop, Millie and I part to head off to work, but made plans before to meet afterwards for dinner.

Arriving at work and settling in behind my desk, cheerfully greeting Mr. Palmer when he arrived.

"Good morning Mr. Palmer."

"Good morning Miss Thorpe. I'm guessing by that smile on your face you've heard from Paul."

"I have and I have a letter ready for the postman when he comes in today," I reply holding up the addressed envelope.

Mr. Palmer laughs, "I had no doubt you would," he teased as he went into his office.

Working at the bank had become my salvation. I had made a few more friends, none that would ever replace Millie of course. We had known each other far too long for that to happen. And though Paul was never far from my thoughts, work helped occupy my time and kept me from dwelling on the fact that he wasn't here.

* * *

Over the next couple of weeks, the letters continued and on the third week, I received two letters because he couldn't wait to tell me about his first time piloting with an instructor. His excitement poured off the page as he described the feeling of being above the clouds. To think that he wanted to share that with me warmed my heart.

As the weeks went by, my excitement built at the realization, that Paul would be coming home soon. I missed him terribly, and even though Millie and Don included me on some of their outings, I knew that they needed time alone as well. There would be plenty of time for us to go out together once Paul returned.

When the next letter arrived, I feel giddy all over again. Taking the letter to my room, I settle on my bed, open the envelope and remove the letter, ready to hear the latest on Paul's flight training.

Help Our Heroes

My Beautiful Ruby,

I can't believe I'm halfway through my training. Last week the instructor took us up to get us used to being at the controls. This week, we went back up only I was in control giving the instructor readings and determining when and where to land. My first landing was a little rough, but by the end of the week, I was landing like a veteran pilot. Even the instructor commented on how much I improved over the week.

The last two weeks of our training, we'll be teamed up with a rear pilot and graded on how well we work together. And before you ask, you'll be right there with me, pinned to the panel reminding me why I'm doing this.

I did get a chance to explore the island a bit, and it is a beautiful place to see. One I hope I get to share with you. Everywhere I looked, I saw something that reminded me of you. I couldn't help but think about our last night together, the song we danced to and how I held you in my arms.

I probably shouldn't mention this, but we've been working extra hours in hopes of being home in time for Christmas. If not, then you can bet I'll be there to kiss you at midnight while we ring in the New Year.

I love you Ruby and miss you more than I ever imagined. In only four short weeks, I'll be coming home to you. I can't wait to hold you in my arms once again.

All my love now and always,
Paul

    Unable to contain my excitement at the thought of Paul being home in time for Christmas, I take off across the street to tell Millie. Running up the sidewalk, I knock on the door and wait for someone to answer. When the door opens, Mrs. Bishop greets me.

    "Hello Ruby," she says with a smile.

"Hi Mrs. Bishop, may I speak to Millie for a minute?"

"Of course," she says opening the door wider. "Come on in, she's in the kitchen helping me with dinner."

"Thank you," I say as I step inside and follow Mrs. Bishop to the kitchen.

"Mille dear," she says, "Ruby is here to see you."

Looking up from the potato she is peeling, Millie smiles, but I can see the confusion in her eyes as to why I'm there, until she sees the letter in my hand.

"Hi Ruby, everything okay?"

"Yes, everything's fine. I just needed to talk to you for a minute."

"Sure," Millie says. "I'll be right back Mom."

"You girls take your time. Ruby would you like to stay for dinner?"

"Oh, thank you Mrs. Bishop, but I think Mom already has something started."

Following Millie to her room, she closes the door behind me and asks, "Is that a letter from Paul?"

"Yes," I practically sing in delight. "Millie, he said he might be home in time for Christmas!"

"What? Ruby that's wonderful!"

"I know! He said they've been working extra hours a day so they can finish early before the holiday. There's still a chance he won't be here for Christmas, but he'll definitely be here for New Year's Eve.

"Oh Ruby, I'm so happy for you. I know you've missed him terribly."

"I have, but once he's back we won't have to keep things secret. We're going to tell my parents and start planning our future. And I'll officially be a Flyboy's girl."

Chapter 15

December 7, 1941

When Sunday arrived, I was still floating on cloud nine at the thought that Paul may be home for Christmas.

Dressing for church, I made my way to the kitchen to have breakfast with my parents.

"Good morning, sweetheart," my mother says as I enter the room.

"Good morning," I cheerfully reply before kissing my dad's cheek on the way to my seat at the table.

Placing a few pancakes on my plate, my dad asks, "Ruby, how's your job going?"

"Really well. Mr. Palmer is so nice, and since he's new to his position, we are learning together."

"Good, I'm glad to hear that."

Just as Dad starts to ask me another question, the telephone rings, and Dad excuses himself to answer it.

Concerned of the timing of the call, Mom and I listen to Dad's side of the conversation.

"Thorpe," Dad says as he answers the call and listens intently to the caller has to say.

"They what?" We watch as Dad sighs, his shoulders slumping at what he's been told, and runs his hand across his forehead. "Casualties? Yeah. Call the Captains and have them meet me at HQ in fifteen minutes, and send the car." Hanging up the receiver, and looking completely defeated, Dad turns back to us.

"Edgar, what's wrong?"

Standing with his hands on the back of his chair he says, "The Japanese just attacked Pearl Harbor."

"Oh dear Lord," my mother says as my chest begins to tighten and tears fill my eyes.

"Number of casualties are unknown at this time, but expected to be many."

"What can we do?" my mother asks.

"Pray," he says as he turns to go to their room to change into his uniform.

"Mom," I murmur, voice filled with emotion.

"Oh sweetheart," she says taking my hand. "Let's not worry too much just yet. You heard your father, the best thing we can do right now is pray."

When Dad returns dressed in uniform, he kisses the top of my head and then my mother. "I'll update you when I can. I don't know how late I'll be."

"Do what you need to, we'll be fine. I expect the other children will call soon, I'll tell them what I can."

Watching my parents together, I can see the worry in my father's eyes, but his shoulders relax the tiniest bit just knowing that Mom is here to support him. Tears begin to fill my eyes again as I begin to pray harder that I'll have the chance to support Paul in the same way.

* * *

We didn't see Dad again until the next day when he came home to shower and change before heading back to his office. According to the Joint Board, the President would be making a declaration of war against Japan today in his address to the nation. Casualty numbers were still coming in, it would likely be a few days before the final numbers, and names of those injured or killed were released.

Arriving at work on Monday, Mr. Palmer met me at my desk.

"Miss Thorpe," he asks, voice filled with concern. "Have you heard anything from Paul?"

Giving him a weak smile I reply, "No, not yet."

"If you need to leave, I completely understand."

"Thank you, but if it's okay with you I would rather be here. It helps if I keep busy instead of sitting around waiting on word to come in from Hawaii."

"Of course. Let me know if you need anything."

"Thank you, I will."

* * *

Help Our Heroes

Wednesday evening after dinner with my parents, as I began clearing the table, Dad said, "We received a list of damages today. Four battleships were sunk and we lost more than one-hundred-fifty aircraft." Dad clears his throat of the emotion, so he can finish what he needs to say. "Four of the men we sent for training last month were killed during the attack."

"Oh Edgar I'm so sorry," my mother says as she squeezes my father's hand. "Do you know who they were?"

"Jenkins, Carver, Simmons, and Babcock."

The plates I had been carrying to the sink slipped from my hands, shattering on the kitchen floor at my father's words. Both of my parents turned their focus to me as I felt the blood drain from my face and tears fill my eyes. "P-Paul Babcock?"

"Yes, why?"

"No," I say as I begin shaking my head while sinking to the floor among the broken plates. "No, not Paul," I repeated as I began to cry hysterically. Lifting me from the floor, my father places me in a chair as my mother wraps me in her arms and tries to comfort me, unaware that I just lost the man I love.

"Oh sweetheart," she whispers. "I'm so sorry." She continues whispering soothing words as she holds me, allowing me to cry. When I finally run out of tears, she asks, "Do you want to tell us about him?"

Drying my tears on the handkerchief Dad hands me, I tell them how I met Paul, and had been secretly seeing him. How after he returned from his training, we were going to tell them. As tears once again begin to run down my cheeks, through my sobs I say, "But now you won't get the chance to know how wonderful he was or find out how I could have fallen in love with him after such a short time. Now someone will have to break the news to his parents that he won't be coming home."

The worry that has been present in Dad's eyes is now gone and sadness takes its place. Sadness for the loss of men under his command. Sadness for the loss of the man I love. Sadness that there will be many more lost before it's over.

"Daddy, do you know if Don White was told about Paul? They were best friends."

Reaching over he squeezes my hand, "I'll make sure he knows."

"Thank you. If you don't mind, I think I'm going to go to my room now."

Giving me a tight hug, Mom says, "Of course sweetheart."

Walking into my room and closing the door, I lie on my bed and before I cry myself to sleep, I ask God to look after Paul until I see him again.

* * *

Two days after receiving the news about Paul, while eating dinner, there was a knock on the door. Rising from his seat, Dad leaves the table to answer it.

Opening the door, I hear Dad say, "Seaman Apprentice White. What can I do for you?"

"Good evening Admiral. I was wondering if I might have a moment with your daughter, sir."

"Of course. Please come in and have a seat, I'll let Ruby know you're here."

"Thank you sir," I hear Don reply.

When Dad walks back into the kitchen, he clears his throat. "Ruby, Seaman Apprentice White is here to see you."

Grief and sorrow grip my heart as I rise from my seat to go speak to Paul's best friend.

Don rises as I step into the living room. "Ruby," he says and that along with the sadness I see in his eyes is all it takes to send me into tears once again.

Wrapping me in his arms, Don holds me as I cry, and whispers, "I am so sorry Ruby. He loved you so much."

"I loved him too," I say around my sobs.

"I know," he says as he directs me to sit on the sofa. "Ruby, I know Paul was trying to get home to spend Christmas with you. But in case he didn't get back, he wanted me to give this to you to open Christmas Day."

Don holds out a small wrapped box and an envelope, and with shaky hands and tears silently streaming down my face, I accept it. Giving me a sad smile Don says, "I think he would be okay with you opening it now, if you want."

Running my hand over the box, I express my appreciation, "Thank you Don. I'm so glad Paul had you as a friend."

"I'm honored to have called him my friend," Don says as he stands, preparing to leave. "Ruby, if there's anything I can do for you, just let me know."

"Thank you, I will," I reply as I walk him to the door. "Don," I call out, gaining his attention just before he opens the door. "There is one thing you can do for me."

"Sure Ruby, name it."

"Go tell your girl how you feel."

Giving me a weak smile, Don nods before saying, "I'm heading there now. Wish me luck."

"You don't need luck, you've got love on your side."

Saying goodnight to Don, I close the door and resume my seat on the sofa. Opening the envelope, I read the words Paul had written.

My Beautiful Ruby,

If you're reading this, then I didn't make it home for Christmas, and I'm still away at training instead of giving you this in person. I hope this gift keeps you company until I see you again. I found it on my first outing on the island and knew you had to have it.

Merry Christmas Ruby, I love you and will see you soon.

Forever your Flyboy,
Paul

Folding the letter, I place it back in the envelope. Carefully unwrapping the box, I slowly lift the top as tears cloud my eyes once again. Nestled on black velvet is a necklace with a pendant of entwined hearts. My breath catches at the beautiful gift and thoughtfulness behind it. Securing the necklace around my neck, and laying my hand over the hearts I whisper, "I'll always love you too, Flyboy."

Chapter 16

Natalie

Present Day

When Grandma Ruby finishes her story, Zoey, Alana and I are all sobbing surrounded by a sea of used tissues.

"Grandma," I say my voice thick with emotion. "That is the most beautiful, heart-wrenching story I've ever heard."

"It was heart-wrenching to live through," she says as she wipes the tears away from her own eyes.

Through her sniffles, Alana asks, "So you never saw Paul again?"

"No sweet girl, I didn't," Grandma says to Alana

Focusing on the box that held Grandma Ruby's memories, Zoey asks, "How did you get your letters back?"

"When Paul's things were returned to the base, Don made sure the letters I had written Paul and the photos I had given him were given back to me before everything else was sent to his parents."

"It must have been devastating to lose your true love like that."

"Oh child," Grandma says to Zoey, "I didn't lose my true love. I lost my first love. There's a difference."

"What's the difference?"

"Your first love teaches you what it means to love and how to love. How to think of someone else first and be considerate of their feelings. But your true love, they're the one that sweeps you off your feet when you least expect it. The one that constantly tells you that you've been on their mind. The one you think about when you buy a new dress, because you can't wait to see the look on his face when he sees you in it for the first time. The one you imagine building a life with, and sharing a home with, and having children with, that's who your true love is."

"But didn't you have all those things with Paul?"

"I did to some extent. Being with Paul was exciting. Mostly because I wasn't supposed to date someone on base. Even though I loved Paul, I eventually understood our love just wasn't meant to be, and that he would want me to be happy, even if it was with someone else."

"How long did it take you to get over Paul?"

"I don't know that you ever really get over you first love. Your first love will always be a part of you, just like Paul will always be a part of me. But once you find the one you are meant to spend the rest of your life with, the relationships of your past become life lessons."

Alana, who has been listening intently to every question Zoey has asked, finally gets to ask a question of her own. "So if Paul wasn't your true love, who was?"

Grandma Ruby smiles and her eyes light with love. "That honor belonged to my Calvin."

Excited to hear another story, Alana asks, "Will you tell us how you met Grandpa Calvin?"

Hugging Alana to her side she laughs, "I would love to, but that's a story for another day."

"Awww," the girls say in unison.

"Besides, I think I'm out of tissues," Grandma Ruby teases making us all laugh as we gather up the mountain of used tissues.

Looking at my watch, I'm surprised to see how late it is. "Come on girls, let's get things cleaned up, we need to be going soon."

"Aww, do we have to?" Alana whines.

"Yeah, I'm afraid so. But I bet Grandma Ruby would let us come back and visit again."

"Of course, you are welcome any time. I have plenty of stories to tell. I might even have a few to tell about your mother."

"Now there's something I'd like to hear," Zoey teases.

"We'll save those for much later," I tease back as Grandma laughs.

Walking us to the door, both of the girls hug Grandma and thank her for sharing her story with them.

Hugging her myself, I kiss her cheek. "Thank you. I'm sorry you had to go through that loss."

"Don't be sorry. It's the trial we go through in life that builds character. Paul was just the first of many trials in my life. Even after I married Calvin there were trials, the difference was having someone to go through them with me."

"You are an amazing woman Grandma, and I'm so glad my girls get to know you."

She smiles and pats my hand, "Me too sweet girl. Now you go home to that handsome man of yours and give him a kiss for me."

I laugh lightly. Grandma has always had a soft spot for Mark. "I will."

"And next time," she continues, "bring him with you. It's been far too long since I've seen him.

"I'll make sure I bring him along," I promise.

After another round of goodbyes, the girls and I make our way to the car to head home.

* * *

The drive home is quiet, reflective even. Once again, I'm thankful for the women who came before me. For the trials and heartaches, they endured and their willingness to share their stories so that future generations might learn from them.

Our journey to Grandma Ruby began because my daughters found a forgotten box of old letters and photos hidden away in the attic. One day my grandchildren will find the same box, tucked away in the corner of the attic covered with dust, and my girls will be able to tell them how the Admiral's daughter became the Flyboy's girl.

Help Our Heroes

Battle Ground

Skye Turner

The Fitzgerald Triplets

Rea Badeaux has always been best friends with the Fitzgerald triplets. Growing up alongside them, she's been there for all three. But, she's always yearned for more than friendship from the gorgeous, daredevil of the group, Luka.

Luka has always counted on Rea to nurse his various wounds, both physical and mental. Until he joins the Marines and sets his sights on becoming the best of the best… Special Forces.

While on a top secret reconnaissance mission overseas, tragedy strikes and his position is compromised.

Upon returning home, he must come to terms with the changes to his body and life.

Rea is once again there for him, though she's now involved with someone.

Luka quickly realizes that the one thing he's been fighting so hard for has been right there all along.

Only, he's battered and broken, a mere shell of the man she knew. He pushes Rea away only to pull her back in.

Is Rea willing to take a chance on the one man she's loved her entire life?

Help Our Heroes

Love is a battle and sometimes we have to lose to actually win.

# Prologue

Rea

Thirteen years ago

"Luka! Are you crazy? Don't you dare jump from there! You're going to break your neck!" I scream at Luka as he climbs even higher up the tree on the bank of the Mississippi River.

Leila, Luka's fourteen-year-old sister, another of the Fitzgerald triplets, and my best friend, rolls her eye and mutters, "Why are you even wasting your breath, Rea? You know damn well that he's an idiot and he's not going to listen to you."

My hands cover my eyes as I peek through my fingers and snap at her, "Don't cuss, Leila. Ladies don't cuss!" I groan as Luka grins down at me with his trademark smile. The one that normally makes my stomach flutter and my breath catch, but right now, I'm too scared he's about to die in front of me to care. He gives me a thumbs up from way up in the old tree and I whisper, "Oh, please don't kill yourself..."

Leila slaps her hands on her hips as she laughs at me. "Well, it's a damn good thing I'm no lady." Then turning, she yells at her brother, "You better not break anything else, dumb ass! Daddy will beat your tail. He specifically said that he was *not* going to the hospital on his day off!" She mutters again, "Damn, fool!"

* * *

A chuckle from beside us has me peeking over. Laeten, their brother and the last of the three, is lounging on the ground with his pencils and pad, sketching his brother's antics in the tree. "Leila, you know Luka does what he wants. He thinks he's Superman."

I'm only half listening to them as I breathlessly watch Luka scale another branch. He walks out on the far too thin wood and calls down to us, "Y'all ready to see something awesome?!" And as usual, without waiting for a reply... he jumps.

I squeal and my hands clutch at my throat as I watch him fall. His arms and legs are dancing with the wind as he heads toward the water.

That's way too high! Why would he do that!?

He's Luka, Rea. That's why. He doesn't think anything through and just does what he wants. The more dangerous, the better.

Stupid fool!

He whoops until he hits the water. My eyes are glued to the brown ripples, from the silt being all stirred up, on the surface of the river.

He doesn't pop back up.

Oh, God. Where is he? Did he hurt himself? Did the current grab him?

Oh, no. Where IS he?

Leila leans forward as her eyes worriedly race over the surface of the water; the ripples still. She chews her lips and gasps. "Oh, crap! Where are you, Luka?"

The three of us all watch the water for any sign of him.

Laeten suddenly jumps up and pulls his shirt off as he races toward the river. His pencils and sketch pad scatter in the river sand. I start to pray. Just as he reaches the edge of the bank, a loud cheer breaks the silence and Luka's brown head pops out of the murky water. Water rivulets are running down his face as he throws his head back laughs. He casually swims back toward us.

I exhale loudly and with effort, remain standing on legs that feel like that lime Jell-O Luka loves. Laeten harshly shoves him just as he walks out. His breathing is still uneven with worry and the quickness with which he sprinted to the water. "You, *asshole*! I thought you were dead!" His fingers are cupping Luka's shoulders and he shoves him again. "I should beat your ass right now!"

Leila screams at him as she charges him. Laeten sees her coming and steps to the side. No one wants to be at the mercy of Leila's temper. Luka catches her before she can make contact with him. He wraps her in a hug, pinning her arms to her side, before she can punch him in the face. Her temper flares brighter as she yells and fights against him, trying to break free. "You stupid, asshole! I'm going to whip you! Why do you do stupid stuff like that? You're so stupid!"

He laughs as he holds her, preventing her from wailing on him, but his expression is sheepish as he glances at her with love and apology, before he looks at Laeten and then me. "Aw, I'm sorry y'all were worried about me. I'm fine."

Leila calms down some and stops flailing with the effort to connect with his sun-browned skin. He pulls her close to hug her again before he releases her, keeping his eyes on her to make certain she's not going to wallop him. Looking over at me, he flexes his impressive young arms and winks. My heart pitter patters in my chest.

Ah, there you are...

"The water was deeper than I thought, but I'm sorry I worried you." He again looks at all three of us and shrugs. "I think I was a little too high."

Laeten growls at him. "Ya think, jerk wad?!"

My eyes travel over him to make certain he didn't break anything. I see dark red blood dripping down his leg and my eyes widen. "Luka, you're bleeding! You cut yourself. Come here! You need to clean that. That river water is disgusting!" My voice heightens at the sight of his injury.

He looks down with surprise and then grimaces as he sees the long slice on his calf. He takes a step toward me and winces. "Ok, that freaking hurts. Rea, do you have your first aid kit?"

I nod and sigh. "You know I do. Come on, let me clean it out and bandage you up before it gets infected."

He shuffles over and plops onto the sand as I get my handy first aid kit from my bike. Kneeling before him, I swallow as I rip it open and apply an alcohol pad to his most recent wound. Normally, I'd remind him the alcohol will burn like fire, but I'm still mad at him for scaring me. His breath hisses from between his teeth as the antiseptic sizzles on the open wound and his breath lifts my hair. My heart rate once again picks up.

Don't even think about that, Rea. Never going to happen.

Just patch him up and stop with the stupid dreaming.

After carefully cleaning his cut and applying ointment and a bandage, I lean back and breathlessly say, "There you are, Luka. All fixed up... until next time."

He bumps my shoulder with his and pulls my dirty blonde ponytail as he grins at me. "Thanks, Rea. You're such a good nurse. What would I do without you?" He stands and turns toward his own bike before calling back at us. "Come on, y'all. I'm hungry and I need to go show off my bandage. I bet the babes across the street will love it!"

Sighing as I stand, I mutter, "I'm sure they will…"

Leila is watching from her bike. Her lips twist in a sad sort of smile and she shakes her head at me. "Rea…"

Ignoring her, I grab my bike and we all head back toward home.

I know… I don't need the reminder.

* * *

Luka

Ten years ago

We can hear the crowds as they leave the field and we listen to coach talk about how well we played tonight, our last game of the season. My last game ever…

Laeten, my brother, leans over and says, "So, where are we going tonight?"

Turning my head, I look into the green eyes exactly like mine. It's obvious that we're brothers. People probably assume we're twins. That is, until they see Leila with us. We look exactly alike other than the fact that my hair is slightly darker. Leila's hair is the same color as Laeten's, a lighter brown, though hers is longer and well, she's a girl. Not only are we triplets, we're best friends. Add in Rea, our next door neighbor, and Leila's best friend, and the four of us are inseparable.

I shrug. "Don't know. Don't care. But, I'm starving."

He chuckles. "Ok. Once coach is done, we can hit the showers then grab the girls and see what Leila and Rea want to do."

Grab the girls… Ugh.

Hayley… my girlfriend.

I need to end things with Haley tonight. While Laeten is off to LSU and the art program, I'm heading to the Marines in a few months and I don't want anything to distract me. I'm *going* to be Special Forces. I'm determined.

I've already spoken to my recruiter. This is what I've always wanted. Haley was a good girlfriend, but it was never going to be a forever thing. Sure, I like her, but I don't love her. However, lately she's been hinting at a long term commitment.

I always knew that anything I started in high school would have to end before I left. I don't want anything back home distracting me once I leave. Tonight is as good a night as any to end things. And the longer I wait, the more attached Haley will be and that just spells a shit storm of drama. Drama I don't want to deal with right before I head out.

I nod at Laeten. "Sure. Rea bringing anyone tonight?"

Laeten's brows raise in surprise and he shakes his head as he says, "I don't think so. Why?"

I grimace. "I'm ending things with Haley.

"With her and Leila there, hopefully things won't get too crazy. You know Rea is always the one who keeps things under control." My hands reach for the back of my neck and squeeze. "Haley will be itching for a scene so... I need Rea to play negotiator and well, stop that from happening."

Laeten whistles. "Oh, shit. You want to break up with Haley... in public?! Damn, tonight is going to be interesting. But, you know you're a big boy, Luka... Rea isn't always going to be there to keep your messes under control. And... that's not her job."

Well, of course it is. That's what she does. It's what she's always done.

We all have our parts in this circle and her part is to make certain the rest of us don't fuck up too badly, and when we do, she keeps things from getting completely out of hand.

Coach ends his speech at that moment and we all clap though I honestly have no idea what most of what he said was. Leaning over, I jostle Laeten's shoulder and laugh. "Of course it is. She loves us. We're her best friends. We'd do it for her, too."

Laeten stands, shakes his head and mutters, "Yeah, like we'd ever have to..." He pierces me with his eyes. The green seems to sparkle as he stares at me. His expression gets serious and he growls, "Luka, you're a real idiot." Turning, he

Help Our Heroes

heads to the showers.

What in the hell is he jabbering about?
Why the hell am I an idiot?!

Chapter 1

Rea

Present day

"Mr. Demonte, you're such a flirt." I chuckle as I tighten the cuff around my patient's thin upper arm. "Your blood pressure is looking so much better! Are you taking your meds as you should be?"

He nods and waggles his bushy grey eyebrows. "Yes, pretty lady. Thanks for the three month supply at my last appointment.

"Rea, when are you going to leave this hell hole and run off with me?"

Laughing, I play along with him. I love my patients. My work at the Baton Rouge VA Clinic puts me in constant contact with some real characters. Mr. Demonte is a favorite of mine, though not all of my patients are quite so jovial. Many of my patients are older or disabled veterans who feel like they've given so much to their country only to be forgotten and shoved aside after returning home.

Not that I blame them. We are so overloaded here, but I love it. I truly do. I love my patients and do my very best to show them that I *do* care and I'm eternally thankful for their service and sacrifice. After all, they're the reason that I'm able to do this.

Smiling down at Mr. Demonte, I chuckle and wink. "You don't really want me to do that. You're free as a bird the way you are and we'd break the other ladies hearts here if I snatched you up for myself." He laughs along with me. "Besides, that would make it very hard for me to do my job if my co-workers hated me."

He throws his head back and laughs as the door cracks open. "Are you trying to steal my best nurse away again, Mr. Demonte?" Clive, the head doctor here at the VA… and my boyfriend, walks in.

I shake my head as his dark eyes meet mine and he winks at me. He's so attractive and such a good man. His dark brown hair, angular face, athletic build, and witty personality have caused many a heart palpitation here at the office. Add in his genuine caring about people and he's the bee's knees.

Hell, he gets a reaction everywhere he goes. I'm still shocked he's so interested in me. And we've been together for about six months now.

Mr. Demonte laughs again, "Your best nurse, my ass, Doc. You're worried I'm going to sweep your girl away." Clive chuckles and his eyes meet mine quickly though he ignores Mr. Demonte's glib statement. I shake my head in embarrassment as I feel my cheeks pinken. I don't know how Mr. Demonte knows that. We try very hard to keep our relationship private. Clive asked me out repeatedly for months before I finally decided to take a chance and accept.

"You know back in the day, I was quite the ladies' man. Hell, I'd have given you a run for your money, son. I'm not much to see now, but back in my prime, I could have taken you on for our girl, Rea, here."

Clive grins at him and chuckles. I sigh as I hand him the chart.

Damn. That smile… Ahhh…

He reaches out, but before looking down at it, he replies, "I don't doubt that for a second, Mr. Demonte." His fingers brush against mine as he takes it from me. He looks down at the notes I've written on the new report. He hums as he reads through it and then looks up and smiles at Mr. Demonte. "You've gained a couple of pounds and your blood pressure is looking much better. You've been taking your meds as you should?"

Mr. Demonte nods and rubs the stub of his arm. "I've been eating good. My neighbors have been bringing me meals a few times a week when they cook too much.

"Thank you for giving me all those samples of that medicine last visit and that coupon you found really helped. Took the pills down from over two hundred a month to only six dollars. I can afford to take them now. My disability isn't much and well… it's pretty much what I rely on. Sometimes if I have to choose between food and my meds and my neighbors aren't overcooking… well, I gotta eat."

My heart pangs at his words. That's a scenario we run into a lot here. We prescribe the meds these vets need, only most of them can't afford them without special assistance. Clive goes out of his way a lot to make certain that his patients have access to the medicines and supplies they need. He takes the time. Just one more reason he's so *perfect*.

I listen as he talks to Mr. Demote and answers his questions. All the while, I'm jotting pertinent information onto the chart Clive handed me.

I'll enter it into the ancient computer later. Most of what we do is still old school. We write everything down by hand and then manually enter everything when we have time, often late into the night, after the clinic closes. The work never ends. Maybe one day, we'll be upgraded to the twentieth century technology and not have to do everything twice.

Clive shakes Mr. Demonte's hand as he stands and says, "Alright, Mr. Demonte, you keep taking your meds. Keep going to your therapy. Keep eating that good food those neighbors are sharing with you.

"Call me if anything else pops up or you run into any issues." His eyes meet Mr. Demonte's. "I mean it. You call if you need to." Mr. Demonte nods at him. "Otherwise, I'll see you again in three months."

He answers a few questions and tells Mr. Demonte not to let the Saints games get him too excited on Sundays, then, he leans in to tell me to grab a few more samples of the blood pressure medicine he's prescribed from the supply cabinet.

Just in case anything comes up and that six dollars is too much to spend on them.

I nod in recognition and understanding and he once again smiles at Mr. Demonte. He salutes before leaving to head into the next room.

I can't stop myself from watching him exit the room. Mr. Demonte nods and smirks at me as I turn back to him. He saw that. Feeling myself blush again, I chuckle in embarrassment. "Ok, Mr. Demonte. This was a great appointment. Dr. Evans is going to send you home with another two to three months' or so worth of samples, should you need them, and he wants to see you back here in three months. Let's go ahead and schedule that now so you don't have to wait out front, okay?"

Help Our Heroes

He nods and we make his appointment amongst a little more general chatter. Not that I mind. I know that sometimes, we're the only people who pay any attention to him and human contact and conversation is a must for everyone.

After writing his appointment time on the card and handing it to him, I tell him to go ahead and get dressed while I head out to the supply closest to bag up more samples of his medicine. I'll see what we have in the closet. The Rep is due any day now, but since we get the leftovers, sometimes, we run pretty thin.

As I enter the hall and close the exam room door behind me, Clive walks out of his office. We dance around each other a bit and with a laugh, I slip under his arm and into the supply closet. He stops and leans into the room to quietly say over my shoulder, "Are we still on for dinner tonight, Rea?"

Turning my head, I meet his eyes. My breath once again catches at his pure magnificence. I swallow quickly and nod. "We are. Unless you have something better to do."

He smirks and quickly looks over his shoulder, down the hall, before swooping in and stealing a quick kiss. It's fast; a quick mere pressing of his lips to mine. But as his warm breath bounces off my lips, it causes my insides to squirm. I sigh and his eyes crinkle as he smiles down at me. "What's better than spending time with you?" One of the other nurses calls his name from the hall and he winks at me. "Duty calls. Think of where you want to go. You're picking the place tonight." Smiling again, he backs out of the small closet and calls out that he's coming.

Another sigh escapes me as I'm left alone in the closet with the subtle scent of his woodsy cologne and the pressure of picking the place we're eating tonight. I lean against the shelves at my back and try to get back on task.

Damn. How the hell is he interested in me? He's fantastic.
And why, oh why, am I not completely in love with him?!
What is wrong with me?!

He's seriously perfect for me. A doctor. Someone who shares my passion for our patients. He's interested in me and shows me all the time that I matter to him. He goes out of his way to make me feel special... yet, something holds me back.

Stop it, Rea. Don't go there. It's utterly pointless and Clive IS your boyfriend. Hell, he's the perfect boyfriend. I'm so lucky to have him.

I guess I need to figure out what I want to eat. I never pick the place.

A chuckle invades my musings as I reach for the blood pressure medicines I'm supposed to be getting for Mr. Demonte. My head turns sharply and I smile at Leila with chagrin, as if she can read my thoughts. She's leaning against the door jamb and grinning at me. "Ah, God, I hate you sometimes. I saw Doctor Dreamboat mosey on out of here a second ago. How scandalous." She covers her mouth with her hand in mock shock.

Doctor Dreamboat. She's always called him that.

A very fitting name.

Laughing, I roll my eyes. "Oh, yes. So scandalous. Because you know he just ravished me against the shelving, with the door open, and patients waiting on us."

She uncovers her mouth and wiggles her fingers together in front of her. "Oh, that would be something, wouldn't it!?"

Shaking my head at her, I laugh again. "You're ridiculous. You look like an evil mastermind." I bump her with my hip and she moves. "What are you doing back here anyway? Want to help me with my patients?" She shakes her head and follows me as I walk back to the room to give Mr. Demonte his medicine so he can head on home.

"No. I'm fine handling the books. You know I can't handle all of the grisly details..." She shudders. "I came to find you actually. Doctor Dreamboat just distracted me from my mission... Ahhhh.

"Anyway, back on track. Laeten is here, well in town, and he wants to take us to lunch. Can you get away for an hour?"

Laeten is in town. He didn't tell me that. Lunch would be awesome. We can catch up. I rarely see him since he moved to New Orleans to work on his art and that gallery is displaying his stuff.

Nodding, reply, "That sounds great. I've missed him. I can probably scoot out a little before noon. That good?" I knock on the door to make certain Mr. Demonte is dressed before I walk in.

Leila nods as he calls out to come on in. Hovering over my shoulder, she pops her head into the room. "Hey, Mr. Demonte. Stop by my office on your way out, ok. I just so happen to have some cranberry and lemon scones from Java and Sweeties. Lexi just made them this morning. I know how much you love them and I'm thinking you just might be able to talk me into sharing them with you.

"You know, since you're my favorite patient and all."

His eyes light up and he shuffles to his feet. Laughing, I hand him his bag and paperwork and wave him off. "Go on. Steal him away from me then."

He laughs. "Ah, two beauties fighting over me. Reminds me of old times." We're all chuckling as he slowly shuffles past me.

I look at Leila, "Save me one of those scones! Please."

Leila grins at me. "Now you, I don't want to share with. I mean, you have Mr. Demonte's affection… and my dream man. I'm just the sloppy seconds." I laugh at her banter as I blush and catch Mr. Demonte's wink. I'm shaking my head as she mutters, "Ok, but only half of one and only because we're best friends. About quarter to noon, ok?! I'll drive."

Offering him her arm, she leads him down the hall as I nod at her with a smile. After watching them for a second, I grab the chart on the next door before knocking and heading in when the patient calls out.

Chapter 2

Luka

Present day

"Two teams of six men. Going in dark at o-four-hundred. Today's recon shows them to be in the back barrack on the left. Eye in the sky is currently picking up six heat sources. Two in the front of the compound. Two in the artillery room, right here. One at the door and what we're told is the target is in the left back barrack…"

I'm listening intently to the recon specialist as he preps us for the mission. He's pointing at the areas on the massive projection screen as he goes over the specs.

This is supposed to be an extraction and capture, but there have been some questions about the information we're receiving. More heat sources keep appearing in the structure and no one is moving in or out through the doors. We have eyes everywhere so there's something we're missing.

Scooting forward in my cold metal seat, I stare at the screen, looking for what it is that we're missing.

The drone is hovering over the structure, so we have a birds-eye view.

Where the hell are you coming in at?

My eyes focus on a section of the ground near some outlying buildings that appears to be disturbed. "The far right of the frame, near the mercantile… Look at the ground. Does that earth look different than it did in the scan from yesterday? Can we pull that up?"

Everyone leans forward as the video from yesterday is played on a split screen. I point again. "Yes, look. Right there. That ground was undisturbed yesterday. Possible tunnel?"

Chatter escalates as everyone compares the videos. Finally, it's determined that the ground is most assuredly different. As if some of it has caved in... from a tunnel being dug underneath it.

Specs for the mission are reassigned with slight changes and we go over it until we all know our positions and actions like clockwork.

Another hour of preparation ensues and then we're dismissed to prepare for the mission.

* * *

My blood is pumping. My head is clear. And my focus is strong. This is what I *do*. This is what I'm *here* for. I *made* it. I'm a *Raider*. This is the *mission* and the mission is the *life*.

My team is in the hull of the plane and we're all lost in our own heads as we fly high above the clouds enroute to the rendezvous point. Everyone is going through the various motions of mentally preparing for the impending mission.

Culkin, my buddy and the guy who's saved my ass more times than I can count, is being his usual asinine self and cracking jokes as he checks his scope and chamber. We all know that for as much shit as he talks, he's the best of the best. He's the best damn shot around and he's always got my back. And I have his. Together, we're a well-oiled machine.

Finally, it's *go time*. We head to the rally point and break into our smaller teams. Everyone assumes their positions as we listen to our orders through our earpieces. Our team has cover across from the compound. The other team is on the opposite side of the compound, closer to the mercantile, in the shadows of the buildings, with orders to take out those who may be utilizing the tunnel either to aid or escape before using them to assist us in acquiring the target.

We're in the deserts of Afghanistan, but the nights are cool. It doesn't stop the perspiration from forming from the adrenaline. The smell of goat shit and sweet hay permeates the air, mingling with our sweat.

Radio silence ensues from both teams as mission command gives the green light. We're to rely on hand signals and eye contact to communicate. Brief, clandestine light signals are to only be used in dire circumstances.

Culkin and I are tasked with taking the right side of the compound to clear the route to the target. Nodding in understanding, we ready our weapons, tap our ears to secure the earpieces we wear to hear commands from mission command and communicate with each other, and pull our face shields down. We need to be ready for anything.

Mission command signals it's time. Muttering under my breath, "The strength of the wolf is in the pack," so quietly no one but me can hear it, I nod at Culkin. Together we flank the building, hugging the walls. We wait at our entrance point for the signal. Through my earpiece, I hear sounds of the rest of the team as they bust through the front doors and also enter through the kitchen on the right. That's our cue.

Culkin and I look at each other briefly and nod in readiness. We charge the door. I try the handle. It's locked. With extreme force, I kick in the heavy wooden door as Culkin readies his weapon for whatever may be on the other side. It flies open and drags against the dirt floors of the room. Culkin flanks me and checks the room as I cover him. It's empty.

Moving swiftly, but carefully, we stop in the doorway to the corridor and check it. It's also empty. The guards must have raced to the front to engage in the fire fight. My eyes quickly but thoroughly scan the walls and floor, toward the target's last known location.

The lack of resistance has the hairs on the back of my neck standing on end and my head is buzzing, screaming that something is off.

Culkin's head turns toward mine. I can't see his eyes through the shield of his mask, but I'm certain his eyes would be as apprehensive as mine must be. Waving with two fingers, he signals me to check the door to our left. It should lead to a new corridor that we can access the barracks from. The sounds of gunfire out front are echoing around in my head, amplified by the earpiece.

Counting down, *three... two... one...* I hold my weapon at the ready and fling the door open with my other hand... Culkin passes me and assesses the situation, ready to disarm or take out anyone in the way should bullets start flying. Only, the corridor is empty...

Culkin looks at me sharply. I signal with two fingers to head to the room down where our target should be. Together, we race down the empty corridor. The

Help Our Heroes

sounds of our own breathing and our stealthy steps seem to echo. Culkin arrives with me hot on his heels. He signals that he's going in. The door is ajar. I know what he's going to do. I'd do the same thing. Raising his booted foot, he kicks it and pauses for a brief second to scan the room. As I flank his back to also scan the room, his frustrated voice fills my ear. "Son of a bitch... Where the fuck is he? Where is everyone? He got the drop on us! Where'd he go?!" I can hear the astonishment in his voice. He snaps. "There is no way he got past us! And the other team is in the tunnels so he couldn't have gone that way, either." He frantically looks around the room at the floor and walls, trying to see if there is something, anything we missed. "There's no tunnel here, so, where the fuck is the bastard?!"

A faint sound behind us has me whirling. We're trapped in the room. If we're ambushed from the corridor, we're fucked. There's nowhere for us to go. We've backed ourselves into a corner. We know better than this. We were trained better than this...

My finger is on the trigger of my firearm, as I see the silhouette of a man in the corridor. But, I'm too late. He tosses something into the room and I see him take off, back down the corridor and away from whatever he just tossed into the room with us.

I know what it is before I see it.

Oh, shit! Fuck, this is not good!

A grenade rolls across the packed dirt floor in front of me. Diving to the side, seeking some cover, any cover, I scream out, "Culkin! Grenade! Take cover!" But, it's too late.

It's hastily made and very sensitive. There's no time for anything. Not even to pray.

The blast flings me backward. I don't even know where Culkin is as the sound reverberates in my brain. He could be next to me or behind me. Pain explodes throughout my body. I feel like I'm on fire. My leg... something is wrong with my leg... The wall catches my backwards trajection.

I try desperately to stay conscious as unimaginable pain envelopes me.

Culkin, where's Culkin?

I fucked up... I missed something...

Dear, God, I'm being ripped apart.
No one can endure this amount of pain...
Oh, God...
Blackness consumes me.

Chapter 3

Rea

I'm laughing at Leila and Laeten as they bicker as only beloved siblings can.

"No, that was *your* fault! How was I supposed to know that your crazy ex was afraid of butterflies? I mean, they're dainty, pretty, and colorful little things that flutter around and look beautiful. All I did was suggest we go to the Audubon Insectarium. That bitch almost passed out from hyperventilating at the thought. I mean, bitch almost went down... who does that?" Leila is pointing at him with her fork while her voice rises with ire. "*That* was an Oscar worthy performance."

Laeten chuckles as he wipes his mouth with his napkin and holds his hands up in surrender. "Yeah, ok. That was my fault. I'll own up to *that* one. I should have told you she was scared of winged insects. But you laughing at her until you almost fell over and then being unable to catch your breath and holding onto me as she sputtered...

"You calling her a 'fucking moron' and asking if she was 'serious or if a camera was rolling because that was too weird even for some blonde ass bitch', was mean, Leila." He chortles and tries to look stern. "Momma raised you better than that."

Leila rolls her eyes and snorts. "Whatever. I would think that you would be aware by now that I have no control over my mouth. I think it and it just comes out. My filter was broken at birth by you and that idiot brother of ours, Luka..."

My heart rate speeds up at the mention of his name.

Luka.

Leila continues with her tirade and I struggle to pay attention and not let my mind drift off to thoughts of Luka. "Besides...a winged insect is like a wasp, a fly, a cockroach... even a freaking dinosaur sized ant... *not* a damn butterfly." She

Dear, God, I'm being ripped apart.
No one can endure this amount of pain...
Oh, God...
Blackness consumes me.

Chapter 3

Rea

I'm laughing at Leila and Laeten as they bicker as only beloved siblings can.

"No, that was *your* fault! How was I supposed to know that your crazy ex was afraid of butterflies? I mean, they're dainty, pretty, and colorful little things that flutter around and look beautiful. All I did was suggest we go to the Audubon Insectarium. That bitch almost passed out from hyperventilating at the thought. I mean, bitch almost went down... who does that?" Leila is pointing at him with her fork while her voice rises with ire. "*That* was an Oscar worthy performance."

Laeten chuckles as he wipes his mouth with his napkin and holds his hands up in surrender. "Yeah, ok. That was my fault. I'll own up to *that* one. I should have told you she was scared of winged insects. But you laughing at her until you almost fell over and then being unable to catch your breath and holding onto me as she sputtered...

"You calling her a 'fucking moron' and asking if she was 'serious or if a camera was rolling because that was too weird even for some blonde ass bitch', was mean, Leila." He chortles and tries to look stern. "Momma raised you better than that."

Leila rolls her eyes and snorts. "Whatever. I would think that you would be aware by now that I have no control over my mouth. I think it and it just comes out. My filter was broken at birth by you and that idiot brother of ours, Luka..."

My heart rate speeds up at the mention of his name.

Luka.

Leila continues with her tirade and I struggle to pay attention and not let my mind drift off to thoughts of Luka. "Besides...a winged insect is like a wasp, a fly, a cockroach... even a freaking dinosaur sized ant... *not* a damn butterfly." She huffs. "You should be thanking me, brother. I did you a favor. She stomped off like a fool in those ridiculous ten pound wedges... Her tripping on the cable car tracks and shrieking as she wobbled, and tried not to fall, with her fake tanned legs going every which way, was hilarious. She looked like a gangly octopus." She snickers and pins him with her green eyes. "Even you laughed. Don't even try to act like that wasn't gut bustlingly hilarious!"

I try unsuccessfully to cover my mouth to hold in my giggles. It *was* funny. I never understood why Laeten was dating that woman anyway. They were the worst match in the history of the world. She was some dumb blonde bimbo with fake hair *and* boobs, not to mention Leila is right about the tan. I mean, she *was* orange.

He's so smart and artsy. Any woman would be lucky to date him. Though he never dates anyone he should...

Laeten sees me giggling and smirks as he nods in acceptance. "Ok, yeah, it was funny. But, it was still *mean*. You're horrible to the women I date, Leila. You never like any of them. You always manage to find something or another wrong with them."

Leila crosses her arms over her chest and huffs at her brother. "Well, that's because something *is* wrong with them and you're too good for them. I'm not the one shagging them. I don't give a hoot how great of a lay they are. You date dumb ass Barbie bitches with cantaloupes on their chests. You have nothing in common with them other than the fact that they all look exactly the same and have the IQ of a gnat. If they can wake up your nether regions, you're game.

"You've always dated down. Never once have you dated anyone of quality. If they don't look like they could be the centerfold in Playboy, you aren't interested. Dumb ass hoes, the lot of them.

"Am I right, Rea?"

Both of them look at me. Leila wanting me to back her up and Laeten waiting for my response to his sister's bluntness. I cough and try to appease them both. This is a seriously old argument and neither of them will give an inch. "Um, well... It doesn't really matter. Laeten is an adult and he can date whoever he wants..."

She's so right though. He's so smart and artistic. Yet, he dates the dumbest, shallowest women on the planet. And they DO all look the same. I doubt I could tell them apart if I had to.

Leila raises her brow at me and snorts again. "Oh, please. Tell the truth, Rea. He dates the completely *wrong* women! He goes for the casting couch, arm candy when he needs to be dating a woman with a damn brain. Hell, even half a brain is better than the idiots you find, Laeten. Everyone you *ever* date looks like they'd want to live with Hugh Heffner. You know what I'm saying?!"

She points at him again. "Where *do* you find them? Do you have a dating profile or something that says, 'Only dumb chicks with big tits need apply'?" If he were closer and not across the table, I'd be scared she's stab him with her fork the way she's gesturing to emphasize her point. "Why do you think it never lasts, brother dear?"

"I'll answer that one for you. Because no matter how happy your dick is, eventually you're bored with the airheads." She laughs. "Most people need at least some sort of mental stimulation to get their juices flowing. I mean, a cherry red mouth around your dick or airhead moans can only work for so long..."

Laeten groans. "Ok, stop it." His eyes widen and he shakes his head. "The fact that my sister just said something about my dick makes me want to vomit."

Leila sits up straight and nods as she laughs. "You should just let me find you a woman. I'd have you dating Rea."

Both Laeten and I look at each other in shock and alarm. I shake my head. "Um, no way…"

Laeten grunts, "That'd be equivalent to me dating *you*, Leila. Rea is just like a sister. I love her, but that's gross. Almost as gross as you talking about my manhood!" He grimace as he looks at me, "Sorry, Rea."

I mutter, "No worries. I agree with you on that!"

Me date Laeten… Oh my, God. No way. He's right. That's like borderline incest.

Too bad I never felt that way about Luka… While Laeten inspires feelings of sibling love and affection, Luka has always caused a much different reaction. Much, much different.

I haven't heard anything from him in a long time. It's been over a year since we last communicated. I know that he's busy and his job is top secret, but I still like to know he's ok. For a while after he left, he'd check in pretty regularly. We even exchanged a few letters. Just normal stuff. What he was doing and seeing; women he was meeting in his travels. What was happening with me?!

But then, he was accepted to the Marine Corps Forces Special Operations Command and was focused on making the Raiders. He was so excited and I was excited for him. But also worried.

Months and months went by and then I heard he made the Raiders from Leila. He didn't even tell me himself.

I reached out, but a year went by with no response, so I stopped expecting to hear from him at all.

I now get my info from Leila though I always try to make it seem as if I'm not fishing.

Should I ask his siblings if they've heard anything lately?

No, Rea, you shouldn't. Besides… if he wanted me to know anything about him, he'd tell me himself.

Luka isn't my concern.

He never really was…

Leila laughs again and I struggle to pay attention and catch up to the conversation.

Shit! I'm not even remotely paying attention to them.

What did I miss?

"Rea is taken anyway. She and Doctor Dreamboat are doing great. Right, Rea?"

What? Taken? Why are they talking about me?

Oh, yes. Clive.

Yes, of course we are.

Clive is perfect. Totally perfect.

I nod. "We are. Things are going really well for us. He's great."

Leila sighs, "You're a lucky bitch. If you weren't my best friend, I'd hate you, you know. I saw him first and he's just *so* perfect… Ah."

Laeten just looks at me. His green eyes crinkle at the corners as he concentrates, but he says nothing. He always does that when he's trying to read me.

I smile at them both and shake off any lingering thoughts of Luka. There's no point. "Speaking of Clive, I need to pick a place for dinner. He says I have to pick the place tonight.

"Any suggestions?"

We chat about it a bit more and then my cell phone alarm goes off. Glancing down at it, I see that it's time to go. I turn it off. "Well, I need to wrap this up. The clinic is jam packed this afternoon and we need to head back."

Laeten stands and pulls my chair out. Pulling me to him, he hugs me tightly before letting me go. Leila asks where her hug is and he jokes with her before giving her one and grabbing the check as she reaches for it, saying he's got it. We both thank him and head back to work to jump back into the day with Laeten's promise that he'll be around more.

since we last communicated. I know that he's busy and his job is top secret, but I still like to know he's ok. For a while after he left, he'd check in pretty regularly. We even exchanged a few letters. Just normal stuff. What he was doing and seeing; women he was meeting in his travels. What was happening with me?!

But then, he was accepted to the Marine Corps Forces Special Operations Command and was focused on making the Raiders. He was so excited and I was excited for him. But also worried.

Months and months went by and then I heard he made the Raiders from Leila. He didn't even tell me himself.

I reached out, but a year went by with no response, so I stopped expecting to hear from him at all.

I now get my info from Leila though I always try to make it seem as if I'm not fishing.

Should I ask his siblings if they've heard anything lately?

No, Rea, you shouldn't. Besides... if he wanted me to know anything about him, he'd tell me himself.

Luka isn't my concern.

He never really was...

Leila laughs again and I struggle to pay attention and catch up to the conversation.

Shit! I'm not even remotely paying attention to them.

What did I miss?

"Rea is taken anyway. She and Doctor Dreamboat are doing great. Right, Rea?"

What? Taken? Why are they talking about me?

Oh, yes. Clive.

Yes, of course we are.

Clive is perfect. Totally perfect.

I nod. "We are. Things are going really well for us. He's great."

Leila sighs, "You're a lucky bitch. If you weren't my best friend, I'd hate you, you know. I saw him first and he's just *so* perfect... Ah."

Laeten just looks at me. His green eyes crinkle at the corners as he concentrates, but he says nothing. He always does that when he's trying to read me.

I smile at them both and shake off any lingering thoughts of Luka. There's no point. "Speaking of Clive, I need to pick a place for dinner. He says I have to pick the place tonight.

"Any suggestions?"

We chat about it a bit more and then my cell phone alarm goes off. Glancing down at it, I see that it's time to go. I turn it off. "Well, I need to wrap this up. The clinic is jam packed this afternoon and we need to head back."

Laeten stands and pulls my chair out. Pulling me to him, he hugs me tightly before letting me go. Leila asks where her hug is and he jokes with her before giving her one and grabbing the check as she reaches for it, saying he's got it. We both thank him and head back to work to jump back into the day with Laeten's promise that he'll be around more.

Chapter 4

Luka

The noise... and the pain.
Oh, God. It's so loud.
My head is ringing and my entire body is convulsing with unimaginable pain.
How is it humanly possible for a mortal to experience such pain and not die?!
So many voices.
What are they saying? Who is talking? Where I am? What happened?
I can't breathe. Why can't I breathe?
I hear bits and pieces of frantic conversation though I can't concentrate on anything. Liquid warmth flows through my arm and drowns out the fire covering my entire body. I start to get woozy. My head rolls and I see Bones, our medic, at my side. Before I can ask him why he looks so worried, the blackness welcomes me again.

* * *

My eyes struggle to open and it takes me what seems like several minutes to focus. When I can see, everything is hazy. A bright white light is directly above me. It's surrounded by a stark white ceiling.
What the hell? Where am I?
What the hell happened?
I hear the clanging of metal on metal and the beeping of lots of machines. It smells like bleach. Soft voices merge with the other sounds and smells and I slowly realize I'm hearing the sounds of a hospital.
A hospital?

Help Our Heroes

My head turns ever so slightly and pain blankets me at the movement. Closing my eye and trying to steady my breathing, I realize that my breath is labored and my throat feels funny. Opening my eyes, I squint through the bright light.

Are they trying to signal space from in here? Jesus. Why is it so bright?!

Through the pencil slits of my eyes, I see a tall IV pole with tubing attached to a bag. My eyes slowly follow the tube down and I see that it's connected to an arm... my arm.

My arm? I'm the patient?

Why am I in the hospital?

Angling my head, I close my eyes as nausea threatens to choke me. Squeezing my eyes tightly shut, I slowly open them and with great effort, I look down at myself. I see white stark sheets, consistent with every hospital I've ever seen, in real life and on television, on the bed.

Why is my memory so hazy? I can't recall why I'm in the hospital...

I feel like there's something important I need to remember, but my brain is so fuzzy. I can see the sheets on the bed and the tubing attached to my arm, but I'm looking through everything as if I'm in a bubble. I can see it. I know it's there; but, I don't know why. Nothing is clear.

I'm trying so hard to concentrate and pop the bubble. If it would just pop, I could see clearly and I'd know just what the hell is going on.

Someone has to be here... I hear people though their voices are faint.

Where's a damn nurse? A doctor? Anyone really?

I can't lift my head. All I can do is roll it and search the room with my straining eyes. I feel as if I've been on a bender. I'm about to puke. Concentrating really hard, I try to force myself to regain the strength to move... to sit up... hell, to lift my damn head.

A slight sound to my right gets my attention. Moving my eyes delicately, I see a pretty young nurse standing at my bedside, checking the fluid bag attached to my IV. She must sense my slight movement because she quickly looks at me and jumps with a start. Her eyes meet mine and she gasps, "Oh, you're awake." Her voice is fluid... and foreign.

I nod. Or, I think I do. I try to swallow and open my mouth. No sound comes out. Trying again, I manage to rasp. "W……ater."

She nods and says, "Of course. I will get that for you. I am sure you're parched. I will be back in just a brief moment."

She leaves. I lean back against the hard pillow and try to keep my eyes open. I hear her return a short time later. Turning my head again, I see her approach the bed with a cup with a straw in it and a pitcher. The cup rattles as she sets it down and I hear the sound of crushed ice. Tipping the ugly green pitcher, she pours a small amount of water into the cup before slowly lifting it to my mouth while she murmurs softly, "Small sips. Do not take too much. Just enough to wet your throat. Too much at once will do more harm than good."

Taking her advice, I swallow a small amount of the cold water. She's right. It hurts and I cough, which hurts even more. Gasping, I fall back against the pillow and try once again to speak. "Wh—what happened… to… me?"

Her eyes widen and she says calmly. "You were injured… Let me find the doctor…"

Before I can say anything else, she quickly sets the cup on a bedside table. I can barely make it out it's so blurry and she leaves the room.

Obviously I'm injured. I'm in the damn hospital and I'm hooked up to machines and lying in a bed.

How was I injured?

Closing my eyes, I try to recall what happened.

I struggle to remember something… anything.

Dammit. Why is this so hard?

I remember readying my equipment for the mission. I remember the smell of goats, hay, and sweat. I remember adrenaline as we breached the building. I remember looking at Culkin as we entered a hallway that was empty… and then another hallway. It was empty, too. Then, we went into a room…

My memory freezes.

There's something else… something important.

Concentrating with all my might, I will my thoughts to formulize.

Dammit! Why is this so hard?!

My eyes fly open and I gasp as everything comes back to me. My brain struggles to keep up as information is overloaded. I can't breathe.

Oh, God.

The target… the sound… the grenade… yelling at Culkin to take cover… and then…

The pain.

Oh God, the pain.

The fire… I was on fire.

Was I on fire?

Oh, God.

And what about Culkin?!

I need to reach my body. I need to check myself for my injuries.

I was injured, yes. I remember pain. So much pain.

How badly was in injured?

If I could just reach my body. My hands won't move. It's as if they're glued to the bed.

Am I restrained?

I try to look down at my hand, but my head won't cooperate.

Dammit, my head is connected to my neck and all my neck needs to do is move so my head angles down.

Why can't I move?

I can't really feel anything.

Am I paralyzed?

Oh God. I can't be paralyzed.

I'm having a panic attack. I can't breathe.

The nurse comes back in, followed by a doctor in a white coat. He smiles at me but his smile fades as he sees me on the bed.

"You must calm down. Breathe. One breath in. One out. Do it with me. You must calm down." He stares at me, willing me to listen to him. Finally, I am able to control my breathing and I look at him. He smiles slightly.

Don't smile at me. Tell me what happened to me, dammit!

I snap harshly, though my words are broken and my breathing is still very labored. "Wh… what… hap… happen…ed… to… me?"

The doctor only looks at me. His eyes search mine and then he sighs. "You were injured. During a mission... an explosive detonated and you were in its path... You have serious injuries."

Serious injuries?

Dear God, I AM paralyzed.

My eyes flash and my words are surprisingly clear as I rasp, "How serious?"

The nurse looks nervous as she looks over me, lying on the bed. She looks from my chin down the bed and then back at the doctor without meeting my eyes.

Women always meet my eyes.

He says calmly while ignoring my question, "You must rest for now."

"No!" My voice is loud, louder than I expected. I startle myself. With great effort, I shake my head, or I think I do. "Tell me... How...ser—seri... ous?"

He sighs again and closes his fingers over the clipboard he's holding. It seems like forever before he speaks. Finally he says, "Serious. You were directly in the blast zone. Your body absorbed much of the impact. You have some serious burns on your left leg, both thighs, and your right arm. Some internal injuries... Your ribs punctured your lung... And..."

He stops.

My lung was punctured?

And I have burns across my body?

That's not enough!? And what?

I snap as harshly as I can in my present state. "A..n...d — what?"

He looks at me. I can see in his eyes that I don't want to hear whatever he's about to say.

It's bad. It's really bad.

He sighs and says, "And... we were unable to save your right leg..."

Huh?

Unable to save my leg? What?

I don't have a leg?

They removed my leg?

I'm all fucked up...

My leg is gone? No, that's not right. It can't be.

Help Our Heroes

I can feel my leg. If I concentrate really hard, I know I can feel my leg. It's there. He didn't take anything.

This is a nightmare. I'm having a nightmare.

Squeezing my eyes shut, I concentrate with all my might to feel, ignoring the pain. Ignoring the fact that I'm about to lose consciousness. My chest hurts. Probably from my punctured lung. My stomach feels as if someone is pulling at my sides and trying to rip me apart. My hips…

Dear, lord. This is excruciating.

My thighs… I can feel them. They hurt. They hurt so badly. I can't feel anything else.

Dammit, concentrate Luka.

I can't… I can't feel anything beneath my thighs. I scream out in pain and rage.

This is bullshit!

My bed slowly raises. Opening my eyes wide, I look down. I don't want to, but I have to. My breathing stalls in my chest and I feel like my heart is being squeezed by a vice. I try to take stock of what it is I'm seeing.

My eyes widen and then close before opening again.

That cannot be right.

My thighs are wrapped in gauze. Both of them, as is my left leg. From my left hip to my shin is one massive gauze. It's so white. Everything is white. My toes are visible. They aren't white. They're bruised and they are ugly. But on the right side… on my right side, beneath my gauze wrapped thigh… there's nothing there… It's a stub. My leg is gone… the bed is empty.

My leg is gone. The thigh is wrapped in thick gauze and then it just stops…

My leg is gone. They took my leg… My career is over. Everything I've worked for… it's over.

This cannot be happening.

This isn't happening. No way this is real.

Only as I once again stare at the empty spot in the bed, where my leg is supposed to be, the harsh reality sucker punches me…

My leg is gone.

My military career is gone.

It's over...

My life is over...

Unable to hold my head up any longer, I fall back against the bed and welcome the pain that brings back the darkness.

Chapter 5

Rea

Two weeks later

I'm once again sitting in my office at the clinic, staring blankly at a screen, trying desperately to concentrate on what I know I need to be doing. These charts need to be entered into the ancient computer. The clinic closed about an hour ago and most of the staff left soon after. I stayed behind, as I often do, to organize and enter the data from the patient charts.

The chart I'm "working" on, that I've been working on, for the past hour… is open on my desk, but I have yet to enter the first note into the system.

The patient is a thirty-nine year old man in excellent physical condition, other than the fact that he's refusing to show up to his physical therapy. He's also refusing to attend his group counselling sessions.

He was injured in a training accident on base and his leg was removed at the hip because the damage was too great to repair. He's angry at the world and in the past week, he's missed three appointments with us, his physical therapy session, and the group therapy session he's mandated to attend.

Every time I try to enter his chart, my mind drifts…

It was a crazy busy day, as usual. Leila and I were having a quick lunch in the break room and she was joking about Laeten's new girlfriend. We were supposed to head down to New Orleans that weekend to stay with Laeten and enjoy the city and the slight break.

Laeten had group texted us both that morning that he'd been seeing another artist he'd recently met at the gallery when he was dropping off some pieces and he wanted us to meet her over the weekend.

He and Leila had been blowing up the conversation all day with their various sibling jabs at each other. I'd been snickering all day when I'd check the text and read through their ridiculousness.

Leila's phone went off with the notification of a new text. Mine didn't buzz, so I knew it wasn't the group text.

She reached for it and her face went white as she read what was displayed there.

I immediately thought something happened to Laeten or one of her parents. So, I jumped up and rounded the table to hug her and offer her whatever comfort and support I could.

Before I got to her though, her phone rang.

I looked down at the display because I had to know what was happening.

The call was from Laeten.

Her stricken eyes met mine and I frantically asked, "What's happening, Leila? What's wrong?"

She held the phone out and I immediately understood that she wanted me to answer it. I punched the button to connect the call and leaned in. "Laeten, what the hell is wrong? Are you hurt? Are your parents ok? What's wrong?"

My voice was shrill with worry. And Leila wasn't saying anything. She was just sitting there staring at the phone like it was poison, which had me even more panicked.

Her eyes rose to meet mine and the absolute fear and desperation I saw there had my blood freezing in my veins. I immediately knew that whatever Laeten was about to say was going to gut me. In her eyes was worry, stark fear, pain, and... compassion.

She shook her head and grabbed my hand. I held hers tightly.

Laeten's voice was broken as he spoke. "I'm fine, Rea. So are my parents... it's... it's Luka."

Leila gasped his name, "Luka..." and my knees went weak.

I felt like the ground had been pulled out from underneath me and I was free-falling into an abyss. I couldn't breathe.

I gasped out as my knees buckled and I sat in the chair with Leila, practically on top of her. Through shaky breaths, I managed to say, "What do you mean, 'It's Luka'?" Leila's fingers clutched at mine. Her hands were like ice and her nails were cutting into the back of my hand.

Laeten inhaled before speaking so rapidly, I had trouble following him. His voice was so raspy. as if he was choking back tears. He said, "He was on a mission. Something went wrong. There was an explosion..."

All I could think was, "An explosion. He's dead?! No way. Luka is larger than life. There's no way he's dead.

Is he telling me that Luka is dead?"

I interrupted him harshly. "He's not dead!"

His breathing hitched and I heard him swallow. His words were rapid as he then said, "What? No, no. He's not... dead. A mission. A grenade... It detonated. He was virtually on top of it. He's hurt. He's hurt bad." He inhales and his voice is broken as he says, "He's hurt really bad, Rea.

"He... he was thrown by the blast and he has some internal stuff wrong. I don't know all the technical stuff. But, he's burned. And... and he lost his leg.

"He's not dead. Thank God, he's not dead. But, he's... he's really messed up.

"It's bad."

Leila was sobbing beside me and rocking as I hugged her tightly. I didn't even realize I was also crying until water splashed onto my chest.

I looked down with surprise but I couldn't deal with my own emotions then. If I had stopped to think it through, I'd have lost it.

I was fighting my own urges to curl into a ball and cry. There was no time for that.

Leila and Laeten needed me.

So, pushing it back, I asked them both, "What do I need to do? What do you need? Are you going to him? Where do I need to bring Leila?"

Laeten told me to bring her to their parent's house and that he would meet us there.

I left the clinic early and drove my best friend to the house that I lived at as much as I did my own growing up. Her family was my family and I needed to be there for them.

All of them.

Luka... Luka was hurt.

He was hurt bad. He wasn't dead, but was he going to die?

I learned what they knew, which wasn't a lot. The Marines weren't that willing to part with details on his injuries.

Luka was hurt. He had burns on a lot of his body. His lung had been punctured by one of his ribs, but they were able to repair it. And his right leg was severely injured. It had to be amputated. Without a leg, he could no longer serve. His military career was over. But he was alive.

As soon as he was able, he'd be transferred back to the states and then when they deemed it safe, he'd be home.

Home...

Luka is coming home. But, thank God, it isn't't in a pine box with a flag draped over the top.

He is coming home and I'll be here for him.

I'll be here for all of them.

I'm so lost in my jumbled thoughts that I don't even hear Clive come in to my office. I don't realize he's there until he perches on the edge of my desk and touches my shoulder. "Rea..."

I jump a mile and shriek as my heart pounds. "*EEK!* Oh my, God..."

His eyes widen and his hand jerks back. He quickly says, "I'm so sorry I startled you. I was calling you.

"Didn't you hear me?" His eyes searching my face. He's worried.

Inhaling swiftly, I shake my head. "I didn't. I'm sorry." I gesture to the charts all over my desk. "I was hoping to get these entered by tonight, but I'm afraid I'm not even close."

No, I'm not even close. Because I'm not even thinking about these charts...

He smiles at me and reaches out to tuck a piece of hair, that's somehow escaped my ponytail, behind my ear. His eyes crinkle. "Yeah, they can wait until tomorrow.

"What do you say we get out of here? Call it a night?"

I sigh and smile at him as he asks, "Hungry? How about I whip something up for us? We can go to your place or I probably have enough to make do at mine."

Ah, he's such a good man.

I nod.

"That sounds great. Your place is perfect."

Leaning down, he kisses me softly. I lean into the kiss and within seconds, my body is humming and I'm no longer drowning in worry and thoughts of Luka.

Clive's hand cradles the back of my neck before his lips leave mine. "Great. You can just ride with me if you're planning on staying the night."

* * *

Luka

I've accepted my fate. My life is over as I knew it. Everything I've worked for and toward is gone... My dreams, my aspirations, my life goals... gone.

Everyone keeps telling me how lucky I am. And I know that I am. I should be dead... There is no reason I should be here right now, but I am.

I should be happy about that and maybe one day I will be... but right now... I'm not there yet.

Not even close.

Chapter 6

Rea

Four weeks later

Closing the door to the exam room behind me, I sigh and reach for the next chart. I'm exhausted and I've been fighting a headache all day. Glancing at my FitBit, I see that it's only a little after two.

Ugh. Three more hours until I can go lay my head on my desk.
Well, suck it up, Rea.

Nodding at the voice in my head, I mutter, "Yeah, suck it up, Rea. This is your job and you love it. So, I'm having a craptastic day. No need to take it out on my patients."

A laugh beside me startles me and I drop the chart I'm holding. Swiveling, I glare at Leila as some papers scatter at my feet. She smiles and I can see she needs to share something. I grunt, "Well, while you spill whatever it is you need to say, help me pick up this mess." I look at her and then at the white, yellow, and pink pieces of paper on the floor in a six foot radius. "After all, you made me drop the chart."

She grins and squats down to start collecting the papers that managed to escape the fold-clips in the chart. "Well, if you hadn't been talking to yourself in the middle of the hallway, maybe you would have seen me coming straight for you and this mess wouldn't be here."

Rolling my eyes, I kneel to help her collect the last of the papers and sigh as I arrange them in the proper order before slipping them back on the eye-tooth clips in the chart and giving them an extra squeeze to make certain they're down. I mutter as I work. "Ok, so while I have a minute, talk."

Help Our Heroes

She doesn't say anything. In frustration and slight annoyance, I look up at her and raise my brows. "Well?! What is it, Leila? I have patients. I can't just stay out here. We're insane in here today." My voice is testy, but it doesn't faze her in the least.

Her eyes are almost dancing from whatever she's holding in. Finally, she smiles and claps with excitement. "Luka will be here on Friday! He's coming home! He's well enough to travel and... he's coming home, Rea!"

What?

Luka is coming home?

Oh my God.

Luka is coming HOME!

If he can travel, then that means he's getting better. And he's coming... home...

Oh, shit.

Luka is coming home.

Breathe, Rea. Don't you dare pass out in the middle of the hallway!

You knew he was coming home. Where else would he go? Home is where he needs to be.

Yes, but home... like he's coming here... and he can't go back to the Marines, so he's coming... HOME.

Oh, shit. I'm going to need a minute.

Reaching out before I fall over, I grab onto Leila's arm to steady myself. Her eyes flit over my face, taking everything in. I can actually *see* her trying to read my mind. She frowns at me. "Rea, what... I'm confused. Aren't you happy he's coming home?"

She's confused... Hop into my head, Leila!

But, I nod. "What? No, of course I am. That's awesome. It's great. If he is doing well enough to travel, that's really awesome. I mean, I knew he was coming back, it just seems... sooner than I expected." I'm rambling. I can hear myself and I know that I must sound insincere and flaky. But, I'm honestly just floored.

Why am I reacting like this?

I did know he was coming back and I'm so glad. But, I'm also terrified. I've felt so much for him for so long and now he's going to be here... all the time... and he's going to need help.

Hell, he'll probably be a patient here.

And I'm a nurse. The head nurse. So, he'll be my patient.

He's going to need a lot of help. It's a huge transition.

Of course, I'm happy.

I am... happy.

Of course, I'm happy. He's alive and coming home.

Luka is coming home...

Leila's eyes widen as she looks at me. Determination overcomes her face and looking over my shoulder, she calls to Denise, one of the other nurses, to come take the chart from me and handle the patient. Denise crosses to us with a smile and reaches for the chart. Without conscious thought, I hand it to her. I smile at her. "Hey, thanks. I'm just going to take a quick break, ok? You ok with taking this one?"

She nods reassuringly and says, "Of course I am." She knocks and opens the door when the patient calls out. As she slips into the room, she shoots another smile at us before it closes behind her.

Leila immediately takes my elbow and mutters, "Come on. Let's go to my office for a bit."

I can't help but follow along as she pulls me quite forcefully. Even if I wanted to refuse, she's not giving me a choice. Leila's office is at one end of the "T" shaped corridor while my office and the chart room, where we keep all current patient charts, is at the other. Clive's office is at the end of the hall, centered on the wall, between our two offices. Leila calls out, "I need her for a minute. Denise is filling in. Room Four." She doesn't even allow him to respond as she herds me past his office. I guess she already knew he was in there.

Hell, I barely had time to glance at him and see him look up with surprise from the chart he was reading while leaning on his desk front, as we passed the door.

Then, we're in her office.

She pulls me into the small room and then closes the door. She stares at me. "What's wrong? I could see everything you were feeling on your face, Rea."

Help Our Heroes

Leaning back on her heels she watches me as she crosses her arms. "I've known you my entire life... Why does Luka coming home scare you?" I just stare at her as I worry my lip and debate my answer.

Why does it scare me?

Because my entire life, my entire life, I've loved him from afar. He was always right there, but so untouchable.

At least as far as what my heart wanted from him.

He left. He went to the Marines and I knew that was for the best. That was the only way, my foolish heart was ever going to give up.

But he did and I moved on. I finally found someone... I have someone. Clive is so... perfect. I know he's perfect and I know that he's the guy I "should" want to commit to. He wants it... I should want it.

I do want it...

I was on the way to reaching it... and now, here comes Luka.

Here comes the man that has always turned my life upside down. And now, he's going to be in my world.

I'm going to have to help him.

I want to help him. My job is to help him and those like him...

But, it's Luka...

Luka isn't just anyone... he's the boy I loved who turned into the man I loved. He's the main character in the book of unrequited love. He's the guy who loves me back... but as a trusted friend...

I don't say any of that. Instead, I say, "I'm happy he's coming home, Leila. I'm just worried about him. He's going to need a lot of help... a lot of support... his life is going to be so different and that's not going to be easy... for him, or anyone around him."

Her lips purse and she nods though she doesn't look at all convinced. Finally she sighs. "Ok, fine. If that's your story, ok. I'm not pushing you." My chest thumps with my rapid heartbeat. She can see right through me. She sighs again and leans against the wall. "That's all true. But when you want to talk to me..." she pauses and her eyes lock on mine, "About whatever... you know I'm here. I'm always here, Rea."

A sigh of relief escapes me and I swallow. "I know that, but I don't need to talk about anything, Leila." Standing tall, I ask, "So, when is he going to be here? For dinner on Friday? We need to plan something... dinner. I'll cook so your parents don't have to worry about it. My momma will, of course, help."

Everything I said was true... but it was also a lie.

I have so much to talk about, but this isn't something I want to talk about with Leila. She's my best friend. My very best friend, but she's also the last person I would ever hit with my plethora of feelings about everything concerning Luka Fitzgerald... her brother.

* * *

Luka

Friday

The wheels make that eerie grinding noise as we the hit the tarmac at BTR, the airport in Baton Rouge, home, and the plane bounces twice. Then, I'm flung backward in my seat as my white knuckles grip the armrest of the seats on both side of me and the wing flaps raise to slow the plane. The noise is making me crazy. My head is pounding and my heart is about to burst from my chest.

We slow to a crawl and the pilot's voice comes over the intercom, "And welcome to Baton Rouge, passengers. We are awaiting confirmation to proceed to our gate and appreciate your patience. It's a beautiful seventy-two degrees with partly cloudy skies in the Red Stick..." He continues to jabber as we taxi to the gate, but I'm no longer listening to him. Instead, my gaze drifts to the window at my right and I stare at the hustle and bustle of the small airport in my hometown. People are ferrying baggage and workers around on the white carts. One of the tarmac controllers is dancing as he points the orange lights all tarmac controllers use to direct the planes. He's signally my plane to head to the gate directly in front of us. He seems to be in pretty good spirits for someone whose entire job is to stand out in the elements and direct planes all day.

The cabin air is oppressive since they cut the power to the air conditioning when they started the landing. I feel like I can't breathe. Leaning my head back

Help Our Heroes

against the headrest, I inhale deeply and hold it in for ten counts before releasing it slowly and starting all over again. It's one of my steps from therapy to calm my head and heart when I feel as if I'm going to suffocate. Sometimes it works, sometimes it doesn't. Right now, I'm kind of in the middle. I still feel like I can't breathe, but I am rational enough to know that I actually can breathe and as long as I concentrate on my breaths, I'll come out on the right side soon enough.

I'm in Row Four, which is actually the first row of the plane, but it's the only place on a plane I can get in and out of now…

The flight attendant approaches me and smiles. "Captain Fitzgerald, the Captain would like you to know we're going to deboard the other passengers first so that we can assist you. Do you need anything before we start disembarking?"

I shake my head. "No, that's fine. Thanks."

Of course they need to get everyone off this thing before I can get off. It takes me over ten minutes to get into that damn chair. And then someone has to push me to where I need to go.

They would have a mutiny on their hands if I held up the other passengers. Fine with me. I'll just close my eyes and ignore them all.

That way, I can't see their curious stares. I fucking hate that!

Nope. I am fine with waiting. I just wish I wasn't in the front of the plane so everyone could get off without coming near me.

She smiles at me again and grabs the phone mounted on the wall to assist the passengers with the information for the one connecting flight and where baggage claim is for the others, while the plane stops.

If anyone needs damn directions to Baggage Claim in Ryan Field, then they should be denied the right to breathe. You take the one escalator down and turn the corner, bam! Baggage Claim.

Reaching for the cell phone that was waiting for me when I touched down stateside almost seven weeks ago, I punch in the number and send a text.

"Luka

Just landed. Everyone has to get off before they can 'assist' me. Probably be about half an hour. Meet me at Baggage Claim. If the bags have made it, mine is the military one. I'm sure it's the only one.

Can you grab it?"

Before I can set the phone in my lap, I see the moving dots meaning he's already typing a response.

It pops up.

"**Laeten**

Sure thing. I would come to the gate to get you, but I can't get past security without a ticket. I'll meet you right outside of it though. We're already here. We'll take the elevator down.

The girls can head down now to grab your bag. See you in a few minutes."

What the hell? I told him to pick me up by himself.

What girls?

Son of a bitch...

My phone buzzes again.

"**Laeten**

Glad you're home, bro. I missed you!"

Yeah, I missed you, too. But, I can't say I'm happy to be home...

Closing my eyes, I ignore the loud chatter, smells, and constant jarring of my seat as the rest of the plane starts to get off.

Chapter 7

Rea

Laeten smiles at Leila and me as he nods at his phone. "He just landed." He's been bouncing with anticipation for an hour. "Can you two head to baggage claim and get his bag if it comes through?" He chuckles. "Though, that's pretty doubtful."

Leila frowns. "No! I'm not leaving. I want to stay here with you to get him. We can just head down when we have him. I doubt anyone is going to steal his bag."

I quickly speak up. "Why don't you both stay? I can go to Baggage Claim. I don't mind."

Yes, I can go to Baggage Claim and try to prepare myself for seeing him again... after all this time.

I NEED that time and Leila staying with Laeten is the perfect way for me to have my internal freak out AND then regain control without anyone being the wiser.

Laeten looks at me curiously. "Leila is right. You should both stay here. We can all go down together when we have Luka. It's *not* like the bags will even be down there before we get there anyway."

No. I can't be here when they see their brother for the first time in forever and like... well, different from what they remember. That's private for them and I NEED the time for myself.

I've been with these two all morning. I took the day off to prepare food for the Fitzgerald family for tonight. My momma is at my house right now... still cooking. I wish I was there with her, but Leila guilt tripped me into coming with them.

They are his siblings. I am not. I'm just someone he used to know.

Yeah, someone he used to know.

A friend. A friend who doesn't need to encroach on their reunion.

I'm a fourth wheel.

Smiling at them both, I shake my head and reply firmly, "No, you two stay here. I'm going down. I'll see him in a bit. You need to see him first. You're his family."

Leila frowns. Hard. Her head cocks to the side and she crosses her arms as she stares at me. "Um, so are you, Rea. But fine. Go. I'm going to embarrass him anyway with my tears, hugs, and kisses to his stubborn face."

Laeten mimics Leila's head tilt. They are *so* related. He speaks slowly and I can see in his eyes that he knows what I'm doing. He nods. "Ok. Go ahead. We'll probably be at least half an hour. If not more." He shrugs. "If you get bored... or antsy, just come back up."

Nodding, I quickly turn on my heel and scurry away.

* * *

Oh, God... Oh... God...

Luka is back. He's here. He's actually in a plane, on the ground, in the same place I am. Like on the other side of this building.

What is wrong with you? You're losing your damn mind, Rea. And why?

Ok, so Luka is back.

Luka... your childhood friend is back. That's all it is.

Yeah... uh huh. Sure... My friend is back.

Nothing to be all crazy about.

Besides, Clive is coming with me to dinner tonight.

Clive... Clive, my amazing boyfriend.

Luka is just my childhood friend.

Yeah, keep telling yourself that...

I'm driving myself crazy as I stand at the edge of the room, near the round seats for people waiting for their bags to come through once they are taken off the plane, seats I should probably be sitting on. I've been down here about fifteen minutes and so far, nothing. Most of the plane is down here, shuffling around, going to the restrooms, and looking at the televisions and advertisements for loads of local restaurants and things to do while here.

Some people are getting a coffee at the PJ's Coffee right here as they wait.

The coffee is calling to me, but for as jittery as I am, I'm scared that if I drink anything with caffeine, I'll have a heart attack. Not that caffeine even affects me on a normal day. A normal day... when I'm not a candidate for the mental hospital.

My eyes drift over everyone assembled in Baggage Claim. Baton Rouge is a relatively small airport, so only one plane at a time is usually on the ground. Many people here have family or friends who came to pick them up. Why park and pay to leave your car here when someone can just drive you and be back home in half an hour?! Of course the travelers and tourists either rent cars or use the hotel shuttles. While the airport is kind of *away* from what is considered central Baton Rouge and Downtown, everything is still really close together and the farthest hotel is like twenty minutes away, using the interstate, on a good traffic day.

I'm just people watching and trying not to overthink anything while I wait for Luka's bag or the Fitzgerald triplets to make their way down the elevator and meet me.

I'll see Luka for the first time in about four years any minute now.

Whooooo... Sah....

It's all good, Rea. It'll be fine. Totally fine.

People are staring at the conveyors as if watching them will automatically make them come on and deliver their bags.

Playing on my phone, to occupy my hands and stop from fidgeting, I keep glancing around just waiting for that first glimpse.

An older man standing beside me, wearing an old fashioned jacket with elbow patches, and a felt like brown fedora catches my eyes. He smiles at me and I smile back. He takes it as an invitation to walk over. As he reaches me, he nods at the still conveyer belt. "I don't recall seeing you on the plane. Are you picking someone up? A husband? Or beau?"

My cheeks flame as I freeze with a start. I laugh uncomfortably. "No, sir. I mean, yes, I am here to pick someone up. Well, I'm here with my friends…" I gesture toward the active part of the airport. "They are up by security. Waiting for their brother to get off the plane." I swallow as I say, "But no, he's not my husband or beau… he's not my anything… just my friend."

His kind brown eyes crinkle at the corner as he nods. "Ah, I see. Your friend wouldn't happen to be a veteran, would he? Good looking fellow, with one leg?"

My throat goes dry. "Um, yes. Actually he is. I mean, he was injured while serving. That's why he's here…. home. But yes, that's probably him you're referring to."

He nods again. "Thought so. I served, too. I immediately recognized him as a brother." He stares at me. "It's good that he has his siblings… and you… he's going to need you all as he transitions." The conveyers wake up and start to move. We both look over before he looks back at me. I see him watching my face through my peripheral vision. My head turns to look at him. He says, "Be there for your friend, ma'am. It's not going to be easy for him and he's going to push all of you away and withdraw into himself. He's going to be angry with the world. That's normal. But don't let him wallow. Push back." He winks. "He'll come out on the other side."

His face lights up as he looks over my shoulder. Turning, I see why. A beautiful older woman is hurriedly walking towards him with her arms outstretched. He embraces her and kisses her softly on her pink lips. I hear her say, "I'm so happy you're home. Those five days felt like fifty."

He smiles and says, "Five days is the longest I can stay away from you, my love."

My heart pangs at their obvious affection and love for each other. He turns back to me and introduces me, "This beautiful woman is my lovely bride of almost sixty years. Honey, this young woman was kind enough to talk to me while we waited." His eyes crinkle again. "We didn't exchange names. I'm Howard and this is Marge."

Laughing, I introduce myself. "I'm Rea. It was lovely to meet you, Mr. Howard. And you, Mrs. Marge."

I hear an excited voice turn the corner and echo throughout the room. My head swivels and I see Leila walking beside, Laeten, as he pushes a wheelchair.

Luka.

I gasp and my eyes lock with the green eyes that captured my heart at about two years old.

My new friends are forgotten as I drink in the view in front of me... the Fitzgerald triplets together again, but mainly, just Luka.

His lower face is covered with a beard now, but it suits him. His shoulders and arms are still firm, though much broader and larger than I remember. His trim waist is still visible underneath the grey shirt he's wearing and his thighs are still impressive. His sitting position is doing nothing to hide that fact. He's wearing loose fitting athletic pants, and the toes of one tennis shoe are resting on the foot rest.

The other leg stops above where his knee used to be. The pants are tucked up and under his thigh on his right leg.

He looks so different, yet he doesn't...
He's still Luka.
And he's still gorgeous.
Oh shit...

* * *

Luka

I was pissed at Laeten after reading his text. He brought the girls to get me even though I asked that he come by himself.

Of course, I should have known that Leila wouldn't allow him to do that.

The airport worker helped me into the chair from the plane and then lightly chatted with me about the weather and he asked if I was an LSU fan as he pushed me from the gate to security.

As soon as I saw my siblings standing on the other side of the Plexiglas wall, emotion overcame me.

God, I've missed them.

Leila saw me at the same time and she covered her mouth as she screamed and then she and Laeten were racing to meet me.

The airport employee wheels me up to them. Laeten thanks him for bringing me out. Leila screams again and pushes Laeten out of the way to hug me before pulling back and cupping my cheeks so she can look into my eyes. Her eyes are glassy, but she smiles that Leila smile at me and whispers, "Hey, Luka. You're home." She hugs me again, hard, as her tears escape and roll down her cheeks before she stands and reaches for my hand to squeeze it. "I'm *so* glad to see you."

I nod and choke back the tears in my own throat. "I'm home, sis."

Laeten mutters sarcastically, "Ok, stop hogging this asshole. I've missed him, too," though his voice is husky, showing his own emotion.

Leaning down he cups the back of my neck and nods at me as his other hand reaches for the one Leila isn't clutching. "Hey, Luka. Welcome home, brother." His hand tightens on my neck. "I was awfully worried about you, but I should have known it would take more than that to take out your stubborn ass."

I swallow again and my chest tightens further. "Yeah... I'm home." I look down my body and my siblings follow my gaze. "Though, not all of me is home."

Leila squeezes my hand and kisses my hair. She says sharply, "Well, the most important parts of you are home and that's all that matters." Her eyes lock on mine. "*You* are home."

I nod again.

I am home. And I'm happy to be here. Around the people who matter to me and those who love me, no matter how broken I am.

Laeten steps behind me and pushes, "Ok, let's go. Rea is downstairs waiting for your bag and if I take any longer than absolutely necessary to get you home, Momma and Daddy will kill me! It took everything in me and all of my considerable charms to convince them that they did not need to come here with us to get you. I had to promise that I'd have you in the driveway immediately after landing. So, we need to go. I do not want Momma to grab that old wooden spoon and come at me for taking too long getting you to her."

Rea is here?

That surprises me.

Does it really, Luka? She's always been there. Of course she'd be here now, too.

The Fab Four are soon-to-be back together again, huh?

Well, not really.

Help Our Heroes

I didn't think she'd come with them to get me... Why would she?

I stopped responding to her letters and haven't heard from her in years.

But, you still know everything going on in her life because of Leila and Laeten.

Everything...

Of course she's here.

I nod. "Hell, I'd like to see Momma chase you around with that spoon."

Leila laughs. "Me, too!"

Laeten grumbles and is telling me that Rea and Mrs. Badeaux have cooked dinner for us tonight so our parents won't have to bother with it. Leila is joking and laughing at Laeten's attempt to tell her that Momma likes Rea better than her. I'm listening with half an ear as I try not to let the bumpy ride in the wheelchair bother me too much, but I'm already cramped and sore from traveling. I'm trying not to snap at my siblings though. It's not their fault that everything pisses me off and sours my mood these days.

I can go from fine to boiling point and wanting to break everything in my path in .001 seconds. The doctors have assured me that it's normal and all are part of my PTSD and that it'll get better with time.

I don't know why, but something tells me to look up.

My breath catches.

That's Rea?!

Of course that's Rea you idiot.

She looks exactly like she always has.

Does she though? Was she always that beautiful?

My eyes lock on hers and I see her freeze. I don't know if either one of us are breathing.

Her blue eyes are swirling and even with the space between us, our eyes stay locked for what seems like forever. Laeten and Leila are still talking, but I can't hear them or make out anything they're saying anymore. I don't care.

Her eyes leave mine and I see her breathing accelerate as she looks at my face, then my chest and arms. She swallows as she make her way down to my waist and then over my thighs. Her gaze goes to my shoe and then back to the absence of my leg. They widen and my heart pounds.

Yeah, it's gone.

She swallows slowly and meets my gaze again.

Laeten starts to wheel me over to her and I glance at the old couple beside her. The old man smiles as he looks at the side of her face and then at me. He nods in greeting. I nod back. I see him lean in to say something to Rea. Over the noise of the people from the plane, those there to pick them up, and the conveyer belt and sound of luggage being thrown onto it from the back, I barely hear him say, "Go on. Go greet your *friend*, Rea. It really was a pleasure to meet you."

Rea turns and nods at him. He cups her shoulder and then walks to the belt to reach for a bag.

Laeten stops me in front of her and says, "Stay here. I'll go grab your bag since they're coming out."

I laugh harshly, "Where would I go?"

Rea's brow crinkles at my hard tone, but she smiles at me and her beauty once again shocks me. She says, "Hello, Luka. The beard suits you." She leans down and hugs me. A soft scent wafts from her skin and hair and I inhale. Raising my arms, I hug her back.

She whispers in my ear, "Welcome home." My heart rate once again speeds up. It doesn't stop as she leans back and sends another burst of the smell of sunshine my way.

What the hell?

Home...

Chapter 8

Rea

I had Laeten drop me off at my house on the way to their parents. I don't need to be there for when their parents see Luka. Besides, I need to get home and get my insanely fluttering pulse and stomach in check.

I knew that it would be something to see Luka, but I wasn't prepared for the sheer amount of emotions that came roaring back to the surface like a damn freight train. The second I saw him, he was *all* I saw. It was literally as if the rest of the world faded away and he and I were the only people in it. He stared too as if he was taken aback.

Did he not know I was going to be there? Did he not want me there?

I mean, I didn't have any reason to really be there. But the look I saw for a moment… it was like he was seeing me for the first time.

That's crazy, Rea. He's known you his entire life.

Besides, you have a boyfriend and Luka Fitzgerald never has and never will see you as anything other than his friend.

So, stop it.

I'm stirring the white beans I put on this morning to go with the jambalaya I cooked. Momma is sitting at the bar with her phone laying in front of her, scrolling through Pinterest. Her famous dinner rolls and coconut cake are beside her.

I must have been muttering to myself because she calls out, "What, baby? What are you muttering about over there? Are you ok? How was Luka?"

I look up at her and smile. She asked me about Luka as well as Leila and Laeten when I first walked in, but I just said everyone was good.

I shrug. "Just overthinking some stuff."

She stares at me and then props her chin in her hand while she points to the coffee pot on the counter. "I made coffee. How about you top this one off for me and make yourself a cup? Come sit and talk to me."

I could drink a cup of coffee. Momma always has coffee on. Her house is guaranteed to have coffee in the pot, fresh coffee, no matter the time of day or night. It's a southern thing. I used to poke fun at her for it, but she'd always tell me, "Baby, coffee is for conversation. It can be verbal or silent. I always have coffee on and I always will because I want everyone to know that I'm always here for them. They know they are always welcome to stop by, have a cup of coffee, and it'll give them what they need. If they need to talk, we can talk over coffee. If they just need a friend to be there, we can do that, too. No conversation needed. If they're cold, coffee can warm them up. You'll learn one day."

And, I did. I tend to drink coffee all day now, too. Probably too much, but I also know that should I need it, the coffee is always there. Coffee is more than liquid love, it's knowing that someone cares. All the time. And if you need them, they'll be there. Sometimes, you don't even drink the coffee, but the coffee brings you together.

Setting the spoon down, I cross the kitchen and take her cup. I fill it and then my own, before setting both cups down and pulling out a bar stool. Momma looks at me and smiles as she sips her fresh cup. I do the same.

After she puts her cup down, she asks, "So, what's going on, baby?" Her eyes search my face. "What are you overthinking in that beautiful head of yours?"

I take another sip and then grimace. "Nothing really. Everything. I don't even know, Momma."

Her voice is soft as she says, "Luka Fitzgerald has you all twisted in knots again, huh?!"

My eyes widen and I gasp, "What.... No... I mean... I don't know... It's not... Why would you think it was about Luka?"

She chuckles and covers my hand with hers. "Because, I'm your momma. It's my job to know." She leans back and wraps her hands around her cup. "It's a mothers blessing *and* curse to know her child." She smiles at me. "It's always been about Luka Fitzgerald with you."

Well, son of a bitch.

I frown. "Momma, it can't be. I'm with Clive. I care about him... A lot. He's perfect. He cares for me so much and he is everything I've ever wanted. He's everything I deserve." I sigh. "Things are good with us." My eyes seek out hers for understanding. "He's amazing... so what does it say about me that the second Luka Fitzgerald comes home, after *years* of not even an email... I'm all messed up again?!"

She chuckles. "Oh, baby. You can't help who you care for. I know you care for Clive. And, you *are* dating Clive.

"I like Clive. I like him a lot. He's a good man and a great catch. You two have been together almost a year now, but none of that matters if you can't commit to him the same way he wants to commit to you." She smiles but it's not a happy smile. "I'm your mother. I want you to be happy. And as much as I'd like for Doctor Clive Evans to be the man for you... I just don't see it. And I know that *you* don't see it either." Her eyes show the wisdom of her words. "Your heart has belonged to Luka Fitzgerald forever. I know that. I've always known that. I also know that you two were only ever friends.

"That boy was a rascal. He was a good boy, but he was never going to settle down. His dreams were his love. People like that, focus on what they want to achieve and he accomplished his dreams.

"He made it to where he wanted to be and from the things you and his parents have told me over the years, he was good at what he did... damn good... until his accident. Now, that dream has been taken off the table. The one thing he always focused on, had that tunnel vision for, well, it's gone. He can't do it anymore.

"You work with veterans. You know what this is going to be like for him. His entire world is now in a tailspin and the only thing I ever knew he loved was ripped away from him. So, the things that he never focused on, well, he may see them differently now.

"I'm *not* telling you to do or not do anything, Rea." Her hand cups mine, over my tightly clenched fist. "You are an adult. You're my baby, but you are an adult, a smart one, too. I don't know exactly what's running through that head of yours, but I know that you'll do what's right for you.

"So, either you're going to have to make a real effort to *stop* letting Luka

Fitzgerald get in there or you're not. And whatever you decide to do, you have to think of the other people involved. You're choices affect other people, so while I want you to always think about you first and foremost, I also know that you won't want to hurt anyone else."

I sigh, "Well, ok then. You got all of that from me saying that I was slightly messed up at Luka being home?!"

She laughs. "I read between the lines." She points to her head. "It's that momma thing."

Laying my forehead in my hands, I groan.

Well, screw me six ways from Sunday.

* * *

Luka

Dinner was good. I picked at it, but my appetite isn't fully back yet and I'm just so tired. Rea arrived about an hour ago, with the boyfriend, I've heard so much about, in tow, and my family, she, and her boyfriend all ate the food she and her momma had prepared for me. For me being home...

Home... where everything is the same and everything is different. I'm different.

Luckily, Daddy was able to get a wheelchair from the hospital, he works at, for me to use until mine comes in. I'm really hoping that the wheelchair is a very temporary thing for me. My doctors at the base let me know my options and as soon as my leg is fully healed, probably another couple of weeks, I'll be fitted for a prosthesis. Of course, I'll need therapy to strengthen the muscles that have been only slightly worked over the past almost eight weeks. And then I'll need to learn how to walk with the prosthetic leg.

Is that all it's been? It seems so short... and so long...

It's so hard to believe that just under two months ago, I was overseas, doing what I was born to do. What I've always wanted to do. What I thought I'd do forever or at least until I was too old to be good at it anymore.

I was a Marine... no, dammit, I was a fucking Raider. I was one of the elite. I made choices and was assigned to the missions that really mattered. The super dangerous stuff. The things I did affected a lot of people. It kept my country and those I loved safe. While I risked my neck without a second thought, I did it willingly and eagerly because my doing that... my doing that protected others.

And now... now, I'm useless. I'm not a Marine. I'm not a Raider. That life I worked so hard for, that I sacrificed everything for, gladly, so it didn't seem like such a sacrifice, well, that's gone. Now, I'm just a fucking former Raider, injured in the field, disabled and unable to do what I love... and I have nothing to show for it. Sure, I can reminisce on the missions, the details, the patches and insignia on my uniform... but that's all it is...

Now... now, I'm nothing.

My parents have cleared out the dining room and created a bedroom for me downstairs. After all, it's not like I can get my damn wheelchair up the stairs. Laeten is talking about renting his apartment in New Orleans out and moving back home, into the small house he has near LSU, now. Some college kids are renting it for the semester, but he said they were late on their rent anyway. Leila offered me a room at her house, but I refuse to take her up on that offer and burden her with a disabled brother.

So, here I'll be... twenty-seven years old and back living with my parents, dependent on them and my siblings to get me to and from where I need to go. My appointments, physical therapies, and mandated therapy sessions start in six days. My life will be nothing but appointments. Doctors, therapists, nurses, and psychiatrists and counselors are all I have to look forward to.

Everyone is here and they are so happy that I'm home and I'm alive. I'm glad they're so damn happy, but I don't want to do this shit right now. I'm exhausted. My whole body hurts and I need to pee. Something else I'm probably too fucking tired to do on my own at this point.

I just want them to shut up and leave. I want to go in my room and take something to help me sleep, then I want to sleep for days!

But, that won't happen.
Because, I'm being celebrated like I'm some goddamn hero.
Shut up, just shut up! All of you!

It takes me a second to realize that the room is deathly quiet and everyone is staring at me slack jawed.

Why are they fucking staring at me?

Son of a bitch...

I snap, "I said that out loud?"

My mom's face is white as she stares at me. My dad is glaring, but he looks upset. Laeten is frowning at me and his eyes are asking me what's wrong. Leila's jaw is practically touching her chest. Rea looks shocked and her cheeks are pink... and then, there's the guy I don't know. Rea's boyfriend, the fucking perfect doctor, looking very uncomfortable.

Why the hell is he even here? Why would he be here at my apparent "Welcome Home" dinner?

I DON'T KNOW HIM!

Laeten is the one who speaks. "What the hell, Luka? Ok, you're obviously exhausted, but seriously?!"

I glare at him without looking around the table again. I don't want to see everyone else right now. I don't want to see the censure and disappointment on my family's faces. "I have to take a wizz. Can you please help me to the bathroom, Laeten?"

My Dad stands, "I'll help you, son. Look, I know things are different and we're all making adjustments here. But we're glad you're home. We love you and we're glad you're here and alive. The surliness we can deal with, but you remember the manners you were brought up with."

Great, now I'm being reprimanded at the dinner table by my father in front of my siblings and Rea... *and* her perfect ass boyfriend.

Why do I keep calling him that?

I don't even know him. He's obviously a good dude. Rea is with him.

Why the hell is that pissing me off so badly?

Nodding, I make eye contact with everyone at the table, one by one, as I reply, "You're right. And I'm sorry. I'm just tired. The traveling and all were just a bit much today. But, I shouldn't be rude to y'all. You're here because you love me and I'm grateful and appreciative of that." My eyes stay on Rea's as I say the last part. I refuse to look away.

Help Our Heroes

Her eyes widen and her mouth forms a small "o".

Finally, she clears her throat and says, "We all care about you, Luka." She hurriedly stands and her boyfriend, *what was his name,* stands to help move her chair. She smiles at him and the urge to grab my butter knife and fling it at his jugular overcomes me.

What is wrong with you?

Jesus!

I say nothing as she says, "We'd better be heading out anyway. It's getting late."

Everyone thanks her and tells her to also thank her mom for dinner. I nod. "Yes, thank you. It was delicious."

Her boyfriend says goodnight to everyone, who apparently do know him, before he looks at me. "It was good to finally meet you, Luka. I've heard many, many stories about you so it's nice to actually meet the man behind the fame. We'll be seeing you at the clinic next week I believe?"

I nod, "Yup." Before looking at my dad, "I need that bathroom, Dad." Backing myself away from the table, I turn away as Rea and her boyfriend leave.

My dad grabs the chair handles and takes over. We hear the front door close and I hear him sigh.

Chapter 9

Rea

Two days later

My phone rang a few minutes ago and Leila is pleading with me. "I hate to ask, Rea. But Mom and Dad are in New Orleans with Laeten, trying to get him all packed up and ready to move back to his place here. And I don't want to go around him since this damn illness sprung up on me so fast. If it's the flu, you know I'm the most contagious right now and with his still recovering and all…" She sighs. "If you can't, that's totally ok. He'll be there alone for a few hours, that's all. I just know he won't eat and his attitude is *atrocious*. So, he probably won't even leave his room. Yeah, he'll be fine…"

Dammit. Of course I'm not going to leave Luka at his parents' house alone. He'll be fine. He's an adult, not a child, but his burst of anger at dinner Friday night was just so out of character for him.

Leila says his mood has not improved since then.

He's dealing with everything the only way he knows how, with anger, and I know that it's eating him up that he's being such a bear because he can't really get around by himself yet.

I nod, though Leila can't see me through the phone. "Of course I'll go keep him company. He probably won't be very happy about it, but I'm going." I sigh. "I just need to call Clive and tell him that I can't make the brunch at his parent's house."

You know you're relieved about that anyway, Rea! This dinner is a big deal and he's going to be really disappointed.

He's been wanting me to meet his extended family for a few months now, but I have always been able to come up with a reason not to. Today is his grandmother's seventy-fifth birthday, so everyone will be there. I've met his parents and he's met mine. But this is like... everyone. Grandparents, aunts, uncles, nieces, nephews, cousins, etc...

Dammit! He likes me enough to want me to meet those the most important to him. But I know that we're not there... I don't know if we'll ever be there if I'm being honest... or, I know I won't.

Especially not now.

Leila cusses, "Shit! I'm sorry. I completely forgot that was today. No, you go. Luka will be ok."

"You need to go to the family thing with Clive. He's your man."

"I'm sorry I forgot..."

But, I interrupt her. "No, it's ok. He'll understand. He understands everything and he knows that Luka is having a rough go."

He does.

Friday night, we left after Luka's outburst. Clive didn't say a word about it, which is so like him, but as he drove back to my place from the Fitzgerald's, I brought it up. "I'm sorry about the way Luka acted... He was never like that."

He looked over at me and smiled before reaching for my hand as he focused back on the road. "It's ok." I shook my head and was about to apologize again, but he didn't let me. "It's really ok, Rea. He's home after something pretty traumatic. He has PTSD. Of course he's going to have bouts of rage. His treatments will help him learn to cope and eventually he WILL be back to the old Luka that y'all loved." He caught himself and grimaced. I saw because my eyes were watching his handsome profile. "Well, obviously he won't be exactly like the old Luka. Because he's not the old Luka. He's grown and matured. He's seen things and probably done things." He looked over at me again and his hand tightened on mine. "But the things that made you all love him before this happened... those are still there. They're just buried beneath the anger and frustration right now. He's probably blaming himself for what happened." His lips lift in a sad smile. "I know some of how he's feeling. When I was a field doctor, I blamed myself a lot for the ones I couldn't save. I even rationally knew that it wasn't my fault, but it didn't stop the self-reproach." He squeezed my hand again.

"He WILL be ok, Rea. He's tough. I saw it tonight. He's tough and that is going to be his blessing and curse as he learns to accept his new life. All you can do as someone who loves him is love him and be the great friend you always were. Between his family and you, he'll see the light."

I felt so guilty. That was my perfect opportunity to tell him that the love he thought I had for Luka wasn't right. I absolutely love Luka and I'll always be there for him, but my love for him is so much deeper than Clive knew.

I didn't say anything though. I just squeezed his hand back and when he asked if I wanted him to come in for the night, I said I was exhausted.

I WAS exhausted, but I also didn't want to invite my boyfriend into my home for the night when my thoughts were so focused on another man... a man he knew was in my life, but not the extent of it.

He kissed me softly and told me to get some rest and he'd see me the next day and then reminded me about the brunch today... the brunch I'm about to back out of.

Leila is trying to convince me that Luka will be ok and I should go with Clive. But, I stand firm. After hanging up with her a short time later, I call Clive. He's very understanding about why I'm not coming, but I can hear the disappointment in his voice.

Rea, you need to tell him the truth.

Not right now. I don't want to drop that bomb on him before he heads to a joyous family gathering. That would be selfish of me.

Would it now? Would it really?

Oh, shut up.

I once again lie to myself about why I'm not telling Clive.

It takes me about twenty minutes to get ready to head over to Luka's. I bet he doesn't know I'm coming, so I can only guess what his reaction will be.

The entire drive from my place to the Fitzgerald's is only about seven minutes. I bought a house in the neighborhood adjacent to the one we grew up in. Glancing at my phone, I debate on calling my momma to let her know that I'll be across the street from their house. If they're working out in the yard, readying the flower beds for spring, or even if they come or go while I'm there, they'll see my car.

I'll just text her when I get there.

I don't have to though. When I turn onto the street, I see both of my parents in the backyard. I decide to park in their driveway and just walk over to the Fitzgerald's so they can all pull in their own driveway when they come home. My daddy hears the car engine and pops his head over the iron gate to see who it is. I wave as I get out. He says, "Hey, sweet pea. What are you doing here? Momma didn't mention you were coming by."

I laugh and shake my head... "Because I'm not here to see y'all." His brows crease and I laugh as I walk over to give him a kiss. Leaning back, I point over my shoulder. "I'm actually heading to the Fitzgerald's. Luka is there alone since Mr. and Mrs. Fitzgerald are helping Laeten pack up his place in New Orleans and Leila thinks she may have the flu so she doesn't want to risk getting him sick. She called me and I said I'd come over to keep him company."

Momma appears beside Daddy and she watches me with a knowing look. "I see. Weren't you supposed to be with Clive today?"

My cheeks heat and I nod. "Yeah, but Luka is not adjusting well and I'm not sure he needs to be alone right now." I cough. "Clive understood."

Momma nods and Daddy says, "Yeah, Frank walked over this morning when he was getting the paper. I asked how Luka was doing and he said it wasn't exactly smooth sailing."

I immediately defend him. "He's been through a lot. And his life is nothing like he expected. He's doing the best he can right now. He'll get better…"

Daddy holds his hands up from my harsh tone. "I know that, sweet pea. Go on over there. But just call us if you need something. We're right here and Luka was here so often as a youngster, I feel like he's my kid. I want him to get better, too." I blush again. I cannot believe I snapped at my daddy. "He'll get back to being a hellion who breaks rules, bones, and hearts soon enough. Just going to take a little time to wrap that stubborn head of his around the changes. But, he will…He's too damn mule headed not to."

Leaning in, I kiss his cheek again. "I think so, too. Ok, I better get over there. Love y'all! I'll stop back by before I head home."

They call out, "Love you," and watch as I run across the street, like I did so many times as a child.

I wave as I reach the front door and knock. He doesn't answer, but I'm not surprised. I don't know how well he can navigate the house in his wheelchair. Leila said he's still refusing to use his crutches. I try the handle and find it stuck. Leaning down, I grab the Hide-A-Key, from the spot it's been in forever, and open the door. Turning, I again wave at my still watching parents. They wave back.

Shutting the door, I softly call out, "Luka? Luka, are you awake?"

There's no answer.

Setting the Hide-A-Key, my keys, and my purse on the foyer table, I call out again. "Luka? Where are you?" I don't want to spook him.

Since he still doesn't answer me, I check the living room, only to find it empty so I head down the hall to the dining room, now serving as his bedroom. I softly call out the entire way "Luka? Luka, I'm coming down here…"

I can hear music. It's coming from his room. It's a booming rock song and that's all I can make out. It sounds angry.

As I reach the door, I take a deep breath. I am not certain he's going to be happy to see me. Knocking as loud as I can, I call his name again, "Luka!"

He doesn't hear me over the music, or he's ignoring me. Slowly, I open the door and call his name again.

Still no response.

Well, shit!

Pushing it open the rest of the way, I peek into the room. The bed is unmade and looks like he's not sleeping well, judging from the way the comforter and sheets are tangled in knots and falling to the floor. His wheelchair is next to it, but he's not in it. A dresser is against the wall with the window that I know overlooks the backyard. Heavy black curtains are over it now. They're tightly closed but rays of light are still peeking through in places, accentuating dust bunnies flying in the air. The music is loud, really loud, but I can hear the clank of metal and my eyes follow the sound.

I gasp as my eyes fly over Luka's exposed skin. His beard has glimmers of sweat in it and they drip onto the brown skin and taunt muscle of his shoulders and chest. He has raised pink scars from burns on both arms and a section of his lower abdomen on the right side. There's also a white scar on the left side of his chest, centered between his ribs that I know to be from a chest tube. My eyes follow the washboard abs that the scars do nothing to diminish, and see his hips covered in low riding athletic shorts. They've raised up over his thighs, both of which are bumpy with burn scars. My eyes transfix on the most notable change... his leg, or rather his lack of a leg under his right thigh. I can see the scar from the amputation and it looks like a clean incision. Whomever did the surgery did a good job at minimizing the scarring. The stub is pink and white from the new skin and the healing.

I'm so focused on staring at him and realizing the extent of his injuries, and that it doesn't detract from his beauty, I don't realize he's noticed I'm standing there.

The music suddenly stops and I jump in the blinding quiet as I raise my eyes to see that I'm caught.

Luka's green eyes are blazing and his mouth is tight as his nostrils flare. His anger is extremely obvious.

His breath hisses from between his teeth before he growls, "What the fuck are you doing here, Rea? Come to see the extent of my injuries?" His hands harshly gesture down his body. "Well, here you go. Grotesque, isn't it?!"

* * *

Luka

The sound of a gasp broke through the fury of my workout and I dropped my weights as I turned to see who dared to brave my wrath.

Shock coursed through me as I saw Rea standing there, staring at me with her mouth open. Her eyes followed every line, sinew, and scar of my body. I felt her gaze as if she was touching me.

My body reacted.

Stop it! She's not looking at you like that because she wants you, you fucking idiot.

No woman will ever look at you like that again. Why would they?!

It's been so long since any woman has looked at my naked flesh without being a nurse, doctor, surgeon, or therapist of some kind... am I really getting aroused because Rea is looking at me?!

Besides, dumbass, Rea IS a nurse. She's probably just assessing my injuries with a professional eye.

Stop it! Stop looking at me, Rea. I don't want you to see me like this.

Stop it!

Reaching for the remote to the stereo, I push the button to mute the music. As they room is silenced, she gasps and her eyes fly to meet mine. Her tongue dips out to wet her lips and my body responds again.

Her eyes widen as she sees my face. Rage courses through me, both at myself for having a sexual reaction to Rea looking at me and at her for being here, in my space, seeing me in a way I don't want to be seen. My jaw clenches and I snap at her. "What the fuck are you doing here, Rea? Come to see the extent of my injuries?" I flail my hands and encompass my body. "Well, here you go. Grotesque, isn't it?!"

My breathing is harsh with my ire.

I don't want anyone I care about to see me like this. I can't handle the disgust... or pity that will show on their faces. It's bad enough that I see how sorry for me my dad is every night, as he helps me into and out of the shower.

Rea's eyes widen farther and her hand reaches for her throat. She stares at me in shock before her eyes harden to blue ice. She glares and I can see the anger in them. "Are you *kidding* me, Luka? I'm *here* because I didn't want you to be all alone. I'm here in case you need me. I'm here because I care about you, you freaking rude asshole!" My own eyes widen with shock as her voice rises.

She just called me an asshole...

Rea never cusses. She never has. My siblings have called me an asshole my whole life, but Rea never has. Not once. Not even when I deserved it.

Until now... and I know I deserve it.

I don't say anything and then I sigh. "I'm sorry. I'm sorry I snapped at you. I just didn't know anyone was here and well... I don't exactly want you to see me like this, Rea."

Her head cocks to the side and she stares at me some more. Finally she says, "You know I'm a nurse, Luka."

Help Our Heroes

Of course. I knew it. She's looking at me as a nurse... not as a man. Because you disgust her. Your scars disgust her...

She gestures to me, encompassing my body, but her eyes stay locked on mine. "Do you know how many of my patients are injured while serving? Or even after? There is nothing here that I haven't seen before."

Yet, you can't even look at me. Yeah, ok.

My anger flares again. "Well thanks so much, but I don't need a fucking babysitter. Go home... or better, yet, go to your *boyfriend*.

"I don't care who else you've seen, I don't want you seeing *me*. I don't want you bothering me. I don't *need* you here. So go on, go on. Go off with Doctor Perfect and leave me the fuck alone."

Every time I *mention* her boyfriend or I *think* about her and her boyfriend or I think about her *at all*, I get *angry*.

Why am I so damn angry?

I've always been around Rea. She's always been a good friend to me, so why don't I want her here now?

"Go away, Rea. Leave me the hell alone!"

Her eyes snap and she points at me. "You know what? I *should* leave! I should walk out of here and leave you to your misery. I *had* plans with Clive today! I had plans that I canceled because I decided to come here and spend some time with *you*." She's crossing the room in her tirade. "And you know what else? He *is* perfect. He treats me amazing. He makes time for me. He wants to include me in things that are important to him. I canceled going to a huge family function with him to come here. And for what?! To be yelled at by you." She yells at me. "He *is* perfect. He's absolutely the stuff that dreams are made of and I should be there with him!"

She's right in front of me. Her eyes are blue fire, her cheeks are flushed with anger, and she's absolutely beautiful.

God, she's so beautiful. She's so beautiful and you're screaming at her.

My hands reach out and catch her arms. Her eyes widen and she gasps. My voice is husky as I pull her closer to me. "So if he's so fucking perfect, Rea, why are you *here* right now? *With me?*"

Emotions I can't read are racing over her face and through her eyes. I know what I want them to be. I know what I want the reason to be as to why she's here and not there.

But, I have no right to want that.

Rea is a friend. She's one of my best friends. And she has a boyfriend.

I know that. I've seen it. I've heard about how amazing and perfect he is.

But he's not good enough for her... he's not.

She's always been important to me, but right this instant, I'm realizing just *how* important.

Chapter 10

Rea

Is it hot in here? Does Luka have the heat up?
Why the hell is it so hot?
What does he mean if Clive is so perfect, why am I here and not there?
Why AM I here and not there!?
Oh, you know why and it seems as if Luka knows, too.
But, so what? Nothing is any different now that it's ever been. Ever.
Well, a lot of things are different...
Oh, God.

Luka's hands are wrapped around my wrists and shock waves are shooting up my arms like lightning bolts. His rough thumbs are stroking the skin over my veins. I know he can feel my heartbeat. My entire body feels... electric. I need to answer him, to set him straight.

Set him straight on what exactly? The fact that his touch is making me crazy. Or that I've loved him my entire life and my brain has decided that now is the time it decides to short circuit. Better yet, how about I just don't tell him a damn thing and I straddle him and kiss him like I've longed to do for over twenty years.

You can't DO that, Rea!
He's right. You DO have a boyfriend.
Shit! I still have a boyfriend.
A boyfriend who is a wonderful man and deserves someone much better than me.

Oh my God.

Swallowing, I stare at Luka. My eyes are wide and I know that he can see the emotions racing through them. There's no telling what he's thinking. His voice is husky as he asks again, "Why are you *here*, Rea?"

I can't tell him. I can't.

Sighing, I gently pull on my wrists. Luka doesn't release them. "I'm here because I care about you. You already know that. I've always cared about you, Luka. I'm here because you're dealing with some major stuff and you need people around you who care." He stiffens and I see something happen in his eyes. It's as if I see a wall descend. "Luka…"

He flings my wrist and it's so unexpected, I stumble. His voice is harsh. "I'm fine. You can go."

My foot bumps into something behind me and I yell out as I trip. I'm falling. My hands reach behind me, but there's nothing there to break my fall. I bounce as my rear hits the floor and I howl as I look around to see what the hell I tripped over.

A crutch?!

My eyes fly to Luka's.

He's using his crutches. I should have known that. The wheelchair is by the bed… across the room. How would he have gotten here without using it?!

His face is full of alarm as he stares down at me. "Oh, shit! Rea! Are you ok? Shit! I'm so sorry." Moving quickly, he tries out of instinct, to stand. I see the moment he realizes he can't… not without the crutch.

I reach out with my hand and try to scramble to my knees to catch him. "Luka, dammit! Oh shit!"

He's going down and there's nothing I can do about it.

Neither of us is fast enough and he falls… Luckily, I'm able to roll enough so that he doesn't fall onto the floor.

He's able to keep most of his weight off me, but his body is still pressed against mine. His wrists absorb the impact that my body beneath him can't. His hands are planted on either side of my head and my arms are wrapped around his waist.

Well, I tried my best to catch him.

It worked, Rea…

Only now the adrenaline and panic are fading and raw awareness is taking over. Luka's skin is slightly sweaty and warm beneath the skin of my arms and under my palms. His chest and abdomen are pressed against mine and my body is so hot from the contact, I fear I'm going to spontaneously combust. I'm already breathless from exerting myself to catch him, then his body hit mine... Only now my lungs are incapable of inflating because I've forgotten the basics of breathing. I freeze.

My eyes are locked on his face. They travel over the perfect plains and angles. I can see the individual beads of sweat on his face. My eyes lift to his and I freeze further. His green eyes are blazing with awareness. I'm as certain as I've ever been that his are reading the exact same emotion in mine.

I exhale shakily and feel him shiver against me as my breath moves in his beard. His eyes bore into mine and though I can clearly decipher what's about to happen, I do nothing to prevent it.

I don't want to prevent it.

His head lowers and my own raises. He breathes and the warmth of his breath sends shiver down my spine and tingles across my lips. He groans, "Rea..."

Do it... don't think... Don't do anything... But this...

Do it...

My head raises and my hands flatten on the small of his back. He growls and swoops in to capture my lips. His beard is slightly scratchy against my face but his lips are soft, and warm. They nibble at my lower lip before he brushes his against mine slowly, concentrating on touching every section. I gasp and he pauses for just a second before his tongue slips between my parted lips. My own darts out and tentatively touches his.

Whatever force inside of us that was keeping us calm and controlled is vanquished at that first touch of tongue to tongue. My hands leave the small of his back to travel over every inch of skin I can touch and pull him tighter into me as my mouth opens and my head angles, allowing him to deepen the kiss. He growls into my mouth and I respond by sucking on his tongue and kneading his shoulders. He moans again and presses his hips into mine.

I can vividly feel the length of his erection as he moves against me in rhythm with the dance of our tongues. My thighs part, allowing him to settle more fully against my screaming core.

Oh, God... This is amazing. This is everything I've ever wanted and so much more.

Luka slowly pulls back. He sucks my lip into his mouth. The blood pulses there. Just when it's almost painful, he releases it and gently presses a soft kiss against them.

My fingers are digging into his back as I moan, "Oh, Luka..."

His mouth leaves mine. He presses wet, open mouthed kisses to my chin and then my neck. The straps of the thin tank top I'm wearing and my light cardigan are pushed to the side as his mouth trails over my shoulder and then back to my neck.

I feel him shaking above me and he lifts his head to look down at me. "You're so beautiful, Rea... so fucking beautiful."

My hand tightens on his back again before slowly traveling over his shoulder and cupping his bearded cheek. "I'm the same as I've always been, Luka."

He shakes his head. "I know that and I also know that I'm a fucking idiot for refusing to acknowledge it before now." Leaning down, he kisses me again. My lips cling to his and then crushing guilt crashes over me. I stiffen beneath him and my head falls back, breaking the kiss, and to the floor to look up at him.

I can't do this... not like this.

I'm not this woman.

I can't be here like this with Luka until I'm honest with Clive. He deserves that much.

"Luka, you have to get off me. We can't... we can't do this." He freezes above me. His eyes travel over my flushed face and heaving chest before settling back on my face. I feel the burn of desire and shame on my face so I know he can see it. The harshness returns to his face.

He quickly rolls off me. I watch him as he flops on the floor on his back with his chest heaving. Throwing his arm over his head, he says without looking at me, "You're right. We can't. You're disgusted and you feel sorry for me. I already knew that. So, thanks for the pity foreplay. I think you need to leave now."

What? Is he serious?

Help Our Heroes

Disgusting?
Pity Foreplay?
That is NOT true.

* * *

Luka

Rage and humiliation are burning through me as I stare at the ceiling, I can't bear to look at Rea again.

Rea tripped because of me. I was so afraid she'd hurt herself. At that moment, I completely forgot that I couldn't stand. I made a fool of myself and then I fell on top of her. I was so worried about her... I just had to make certain she was ok.

And then, she caught me.

I saw her roll to keep me from landing on the floor. Thank God, I was able to catch some of my weight. I could have really hurt her.

But that kiss... that passion.

That was real. I've known her for over twenty-five years and I know that she meant it.

That wasn't a pity kiss. Her hands were all over me and she was losing herself, just like I was.

She stopped though. And I lashed out.

That's all I do now. I lash out at those who mean the most to me.

Glancing over at her, I see she's sitting on her knees, looking at me with no color in her face. Her mouth is swollen. Her cheeks, chin, and neck have marks from my beard. But her eyes... I put that look there.

DAMMIT!

Her hand falls from her hair where she's twisting it and she looks at me. "Luka, I don't pity you. I don't find you disgusting..." She looks away from me and at the wall. Her hands knot in the material of her sweater and she takes deep breaths. Finally, she looks back at me. "You know I don't. I could never..." Her lip is sucked into her mouth and then she releases it and my eyes are glued to the spot. "But, I can't be with you... not like this..."

My heart pangs and my stomach knots.

"I can't be that woman that cheats on a wonderful man who adores her..."

Son of a bitch. Yeah, she's not a cheater... but she kissed me. Ok, so her boyfriend is wonderful, yet, she's here with me, right now. She was just kissing me.

I nod and roll to lean on one elbow as I face her. "Understood. And, I agree. That's not you. That's not your nature. But, here you are, Rea. And you kissed me."

She nods at me and one corner of her mouth turns up, but it's not a happy twist. "I did... but that doesn't change the fact that Clive doesn't deserve to be cheated on."

Dammit!

Of course he doesn't. But, now that I've kissed you, Rea, I don't plan on stopping.

Yet, that's not your right, Luka.

She's dating another man! She's happy. And here you are, a total asshole to be around, only half a man, and treating her like shit...

I don't deserve her.

I know the right thing to do and I hear her and myself. She's right and I don't deserve her.

That doesn't mean I don't want her. Or that I have to be happy about the fact that she's off limits.

I struggle on my elbow and use the muscles in my core that I've been working so hard on to try to pull myself to sit. She sees what I'm trying to do and reaches for me, but I slap her hand away and growl, "No. I don't need your help. Let me do it!"

Her lips thin and her eyes harden, but she leans back. She watches me the entire time. Finally, I'm able to sit. I'm sweaty and my body is spent, but I did it. I look at her and raise my brows like, "! See, I did it."

She smirks. "Proud of yourself?"

I grunt. "Yeah, actually, I am."

We stare at each other for a while and then both of us just smile. It's a great feeling. I did it. Alone. Sure, it's just sitting upright from the floor, but, I did it. And she saw me, offering her support. Like she always has.

Always...

The urge to lean over and kiss her again comes on so suddenly, I almost give in. But I don't. Instead, I look at the crutch that's responsible for both of us being on the floor. Rea follows my gaze. Her brow arches and I nod, "Yeah, I don't think I can do that by myself. At least not yet, but I will." He sighs, "Will you help me up, Rea?"

God, that was so hard to do.
To ask for help with something as simple as standing up...
But, it's Rea.
She's always there.
She always has been...

Her eyes crinkle at the corners as she smiles at me and nods. "Of course I will, Luka." Gracefully, she stands and walks over to me. She leans over to pick up the crutch as I hand it to her and leans it against the weight bench Laeten and my dad moved in here so I could work on my strength in private. Then, she smiles down at me and says, "Ok, champ, let's do this. I'll grab you under the arms and you use your leg to push up, ok? They'll probably start working on that with you in therapy." She leans down as she's talking and only stops when she's in front of my face. Her arms slip under my arms and she helps me position myself to push up with my arms and put weight on my leg.

She's in nurse mode right now and determination is written all over her face. She looks into my eyes once she sees me position my foot. "On three, I'm going to pull and you push, ok?"

I hear her, but I can't make out what she's saying as I stare into the blue of her eyes. They're swirling and this close to her, I can make out what appear to be golden specs in them. I feel like they're hypnotizing me.

She slightly shakes me and I snap back to reality. "Luka, are you ok?"

I nod and grit my teeth. "I am, Rea. I'm ready when you are."

Her eyes search my face, but I cover my feelings and try to leave it blank. She smiles at me and I grin back. Then, she counts. "Ok, on three... one... two... three."

Her slight but strong body lifts as I concentrate and focus on my leg. I hop once when I'm upright and she reaches for my crutch. She slips it to me and I exhale as I slide it under my arm. It's not comfortable at all. But, I'm standing.

Rea steps back so she can look at me. Happiness and pride are radiating from her eyes. She claps. "Look at you!" Her eyes narrow on me. "So, if you can do this... why is Leila telling me you're refusing to use your crutches?!" Her arms cross over her chest and my eyes drift to the cleavage it pushes up.

Stop it, Luka. Stop objectifying the gorgeous woman in the room that you cannot touch!

She chuckles and I look up. She's looking at me sarcastically. "Really?! So now that we've kissed one time, you're going to look at my chest like you've never noticed I've had one before?"

Uh, that's not true...

I noticed. I always noticed, I just never "NOTICED" noticed.

Luka, you are such a damn idiot.

I feel my face flush and it annoys me that I'm embarrassed about being caught ogling one of my best friends. I shrug. "Well, I noticed you had tits. I've just never wanted to suck on them before."

Why did I say that?!

Probably because it's true!

Her eyes widen and her mouth falls open. *"Luka!"*

Ah, I see she remembers how to yell.

She's outraged, but is that also a hint of desire I see on her face? Her chest is heaving again and her cheeks are pink.

You need to leave Rea or I'm going to forget all about respecting that boyfriend of yours. The boyfriend I want to pulverize...

I shrug again and stare at her, "You're beautiful. You already know that I want you. You felt the evidence of that against you when we were devouring each other's mouths. Yet, you have a boyfriend. A seemingly wonderful, perfect boyfriend who needs to be on the cover of Hot Doctor's Weekly or some shit. You don't want to cheat on him and realistically, I don't want you to either, though my body and head are warring over that.

"So, you have three choices here, Rea. One, you leave. Two, you stay and the sexual tension in this room will remedy itself. Or three, you leave and get rid of that boyfriend and then come back…"

Well, there.

I just laid it out.

Point blank. I want you, Rea. If you want me, then dump the doctor.

Or she could just realize that he has much more to offer her and decide my hot and cold PTSD, half of a man isn't enough for her…

If her mouth was open any further, it would be resting on those boobs that are fascinating me so much.

Her eyes lock with mine and she sighs. Her mouth closes and she opens it to speak. No words come out. She closes it and swallows before she tries again.

"I'm not leaving you here alone, Luka. I promised Leila I'd stay with you until your… er, family… got home." Her eyes implore me to let what I just said go. I don't listen.

"Ok, so you stay. But, if you stay, we're going to talk…"

Her breath is shaky as she whispers, "Talk about what?"

I stare at her. "Everything."

Everything, Rea… We're going to talk about everything.

Me. You. What happened with me. What's happening with us. And something IS happening.

Chapter 11

Rea

Talk? About everything?
What's everything?

I nod and exhale shakily. My eyes are locked on Luka's face, but I see the slight tremor in his body. My eyes focus on his hands and see the hand on the crutch is white-knuckling it.

Standing like this is exhausting him.

"Ok, I'll stay and we'll talk. About whatever you want. But you need to sit down before you fall again."

I'm expecting an argument just because he's stubborn and won't like being told what to do. But, he just jerks his chin and slowly turns to hobble back over to his bed. I watch him as both a woman who cares about him, probably far too much, and a nurse looking out for his physical and mental well-being. His gait is slow, but he's pretty good with the crutch. He must be practicing in the privacy of his room. He sets the crutch next to the wheelchair and rests both palms on his mattress before turning his body and bending to sit gingerly. He's out of breath when he looks up and catches me watching him. He smirks. "Were you checking out my ass, Rea?" do it

My eyes roll and I chuckle at him. "No. I most certainly was not."

He laughs out loud and I glare at him as he mutters, "Liar."

Shaking my head, I cross the room and glance at the bed uncertainly before looking at the wheelchair.

Nope. Not sitting on the bed with him. Because my will is seriously being tested right now and I'm not doing that... at least not today... I certainly hope we do it some other time... soon even.

Not until you talk to Clive!

I cough to stem my unruly thoughts and slide into the wheelchair. Luka's brow raises. "You don't have to sit in that thing."

Shaking my head, I mutter, "Oh, yeah, I do."

A huge grin covers his face and my stomach does somersaults.

Gah, that smile... Luka was stationed overseas.

How the hell did that smile not bring peace to the Middle East?!

That smile and that face... Hell, I'm about to surrender all of my morals...

Nope! No, you are not.

That's the smile I remember... the smile I wasn't sure I'd see again. But, there it is...

Oh shit.

I roll my eyes again before frowning at him, but it's only to cover a smile. He isn't fooled. It takes him a minute, but he settles on the bed by propping his back against the headboard. He asks, "You sure you don't want to sit up here with me? It's a hell of a lot more comfortable than that piece of crap?" He grimaces at the chair before looking at me again. "I'll behave. I promise, Rea."

My heart pitter patters at his sincerity.

I don't doubt he'll behave. He's an honorable man. My fear isn't him... it's me.

I put off talking to Clive and put it off and now I'm so wishing I hadn't done that... but, I did. And, I'm not going to betray him.

Hell, it's bad enough I kissed Luka.

My heart and body are both just screaming at me that it's been my dream for forever, so what the hell am I waiting for?! But, my head knows that I can't.

Not yet.

I settle back in the chair and lace my fingers on my lap. "I'm fine over here. It's not uncomfortable."

Luka's eyes are knowing, but he doesn't push. "Ok, if you say so. I've spent enough time in that damn contraption to know you're lying, but whatever."

I chuckle at his sarcasm. "I'm good, Luka. So, you wanted to talk... let's talk. You start."

His eyes widen and then he nods. He takes a minute and then he says, "Can

I tell you what happened?" He gestures at himself and grimaces. My breathing catches.

He wants to voluntarily talk about his injuries? I'm not a psychologist, but I know enough about PTSD from working at the VA that I know just volunteering the info isn't all that common.

I'm breathy as I say, "Luka, you don't have to… I know that has to be incredibly hard for you…" His expression is wry as I continue. "I mean, if you *want* to, you can, but are you sure you don't want to talk to your family… Laeten, Leila… you parents?!"

His eyes never leave mine. "Rea, there is no one I want to tell… but you."

Oh, shit…

Well, ok then…

I nod. "Ok… then, of course, you can."

He sighs and looks at the stub of his leg. I follow his gaze and try to see it as he must be seeing it. Where once was a strong and muscular thigh and then a scarred knee from his many falls as a kid, led down to an equally muscled calf, strong ankles, and a foot. And now, it's just a thigh with a scar that must vividly remind him of what used to be.

He says slowly, "You know I can still feel it sometimes?!"

My forehead creases as I reach out to cover his hand with mine. His scarred, calloused, tanned skin is a stark contrast to my paler white one. Mine aren't smooth since I work at the clinic and I wash my hands so much, but they're softer than his are.

My palm closes over the top of his fisted one on the sheet top. It's a simple gesture to say, "I'm here. Whatever you need from me. I'm here."

He looks at me and I angle my head and smile at him. "Feel what, Luka? Your leg?"

He nods again and his hand turns underneath mine to lace our fingers together as our eyes lock. "Yeah. Not all the time and I know it's not there… but sometimes… sometimes it *feels* like it is. It's crazy. I feel my leg and then I look… and it's not there."

"Yeah, that's common. It's called phantom feeling. They should have explained it to you in the hospital. Did they?"

He looks away and stares at the empty space beneath his thigh. "They did. It's just weird."

Ok, this is nice. This is like when we were kids. We could talk about anything. Well, not anything. I never wanted to hear anything about his dates or girlfriends and I never talked about my handful of dates except with Leila... and occasionally Laeten.

Never Luka. That topic was off limits.

A hard limit.

* * *

Luka

Luka, why are you stalling?

You wanted to talk to Rea about that day, yet now... I can't. I don't know how to start.

Rea is holding my hand and it's giving me strength. There's nothing romantic in it, it's just simple human comfort and companionship.

This is the way it's always been between us.

She's always been there and I've always just expected her to be. Take now for example. I haven't seen or spoken to her in far too long. I broke off contact so I could focus on my military career, my dreams... I never forgot about her, but I honestly never stopped to actively think about her either.

Sure, I'd ask my parents or siblings how she was when I'd talk to them, but I could have just as easily reached out to her... I could have spoken to her and checked in.

I didn't want to... And now I'm realizing it was because maybe I knew she was always more than just a friend. And that would have been a distraction...

Yet, here she is. I came home, broken and angry, and she's here... she has a boyfriend that I'm pretty certain is in love with her, yet she's here with me.

I'm such a selfish asshole.

Just like when we were younger... I counted on her but I was never there FOR her.

Instead of being there for her and allowing her to be with a man much better for her than me, here I am, asking her to stay... to listen to me... to take on my burdens... to choose me...

I'm not doing that.

For the first time ever, I'm going to do what's right for her.

Watching the wall, I unlink our fingers and jerk my hand away. I can tell it startles her. She gasps, "Luka? What's wrong?"

My eyes turn and meet hers. It's taking everything in me to make them as cold as I need them to be. She jerks back. "What's wrong? What happened? Are you ok?"

My voice is gravelly as I snap at her. "Everything is fine, Rea. I don't need you to fix me. You did that enough as a kid. You were always there... bandaging me up, coddling me, following me around."

I have to push her away. And I know that the only way to do that is to hurt her.

"Is that why you're here now, Rea? Did you *love* me back then? Do, you want to *save* me now?"

Of course she loved me. We're friends. We've always been friends.

I laugh harshly, "I didn't need you then and I don't need you now..." She gasps.

"I don't know why you're here... I've been in the desert and the hospital for a long time. For a long time, I was medicated and immobile and now I'm not." I look at the chair she's sitting in and the crutch beside it. "Well, not entirely. But parts of me that have been ignored for a long time are now waking up." I point at my groin. "You're the first pretty girl that I've had contact with in any way other than a medical capacity. Of course my dick woke up. And he's more than happy to show you that he works just fine... but then again, pretty much anything, including a waft of air could raise my flag right now."

I'm being so mean. So hateful. I'm lying to her face.

And she's believing every word.

Her face is pale. Her cheeks are literally devoid of all color and her eyes are stark and shocked as she stares at me. Her mouth is open in a wide "O".

She doesn't say anything. She doesn't move.

Help Our Heroes

We both jump when her cell phone rings. She jerks to the side and pulls it out of her back pocket.

I didn't know she stuffed it in there.

Still staring at me, she answers it. "Hel—lo." Her voice wavers. "Hello, this is Rea." It was clear that time. "Oh, hey. Yeah, I'm here with him now, but I'm leaving… Yeah, how was the party… that's good… yes, I'm going home… about half an hour. I have to get my car from my parents. Yes… no. Can you meet me at me place? No, they've just been outside all day and I need to see you. Great… ok. Half an hour. Drive safe."

How was the party? She needs to see him?
That's Clive. She's leaving here to go see Clive.
That's what you wanted, Luka. That's what she deserves.
That's why you just hurt her like that… just pushed her away.

She hangs up and looks away from me before swallowing. She says nothing as she stands and smoothes her jeans down her thighs. Finally she turns to me. "Your family should be home soon. Just stay here and don't try to do anything that could hurt you. If you do need someone, my parents are home and can be here in less than a minute. I'll write their number down for you."

I snap, "I know their number. It's the same fucking number it's been for twenty years."

She jerks at my tone and walks toward the door. I watch her go.

When she reaches it, she stops. "I'm glad you're getting around, Luka. I know it seems overwhelming right now, but you'll get it. The harder you work, the stronger you'll get and eventually, you'll be able to get around all by yourself. You won't need anyone.

"That should make you very happy…" She opens the door and walks out. It closes softly behind her, so I know that she closed it.

I stare at the door as rage builds within me. I'm so angry at Rea for making me realize what I really feel, at the military for giving me my dream, but taking my leg, at Clive for being the man I'm not, and at my family for being so goddamned considerate and loving even when I don't deserve it. But the person I'm angriest at is myself. Because I just hurt the one person who has always gone out of her way to make certain that I'm ok.

I just hurt the woman I love… and the fact that I know I love her and I just pushed her to walk out pisses me off most of all.

Grabbing the lamp off the nightstand, I hurl it across the room. The glass hits the door and shatters. It's so satisfying that I grab the next thing I can reach, my alarm clock, and fling it, too. It bounces off the door, but not before leaving a huge dent.

My eyes take in the shards and chunks of shattered glass and the busted lampshade before once again looking at the damage I caused to the door.

Resignation and shame course through me.

Dammit!

I need to clean that up. My parents don't deserve to come home to this shit all because I'm a grown ass man throwing a tantrum like a toddler.

I look at my leg and the crutch before muttering out loud. "Son of a bitch, you asshole. God job. Now how the hell am I supposed to get over there, on to the floor, clean that up without shredding my skin, and then get back up?!"

Leaning my head back, I yell at the ceiling, *"FUCK!"*

* * *

Laeten sweeps the last of the shards into the dustpan and then stands. "Yeah, how about you not break shit next time you're home alone and pissy?!"

I glare at him from my bed, where he helped me to sit when he and my parents got home half an hour ago. I was on the floor trying to balance on my knee while holding the dustpan with one hand and sweeping with the other.

It wasn't going well.

He walks into the bathroom across the hall and dumps the dustpan before calling down the hall, "Momma, where's the vacuum?"

She yells back and he points at me. "You don't move. I'm going get that heavy ass thing and then once I vacuum the carpet, you're telling me why you threw the lamp in the first place."

I roll my eyes and yell after him, "Yeah, where the hell am I going to go!?"

Now, do I tell him the truth or do I just blame my anger issues from my PTSD?

Of course I'm going to tell him the damn truth…

Chapter 12

Rea

A week and a half later

I'm in my office, entering information into the computer from the week's charts.

Stopping to pinch the bridge of my nose, I sigh. Things have been awkward between Clive and I. We're both professionals and we work very well together, but since I ended things, he's keeping his distance. Not that I can blame him.

He arrived at my house about ten minutes after I did last Sunday. Thankfully, I was able to get home in time to splash some water on my face and try to organize my thoughts. I knew that I had to break up with him. I had to be honest with him. He deserved that.

I was in the living room, perched on the edge of the couch, a bundle of nervous energy, when he knocked on the door. I'd heard his car pull into the drive, so I knew he was there. I opened the door for him and he was there, smiling like always. He was holding a bouquet of daisies. He leaned down to press his lips to mine and I let him, though I didn't return his kiss.

He pulled back and searched my face. Then, he sighed and said, "Ah, I can't say that I'm surprised."

I immediately felt like shit, but I held my hand out for him to come in. He handed me the flowers and said, "These are for you, so if you want them, you probably need to put them in some water."

I sighed and led him to the couch with me. I sat facing him and he just stared at me as I tried to think of how to start the conversation. It ended up that I didn't have to. He said, "It's Luka, isn't it? You're in love with him?"

I swallowed and nodded. "I am. I'm so sorry." I leaned forward. "Clive, I've loved him my whole life. But, it was just me... We never... I mean, he and I...

we never...

"He left and I was ready to move on. I like you. I care about you... so much."

He smiled sadly. "But, not as much as him."

I didn't know what to say. I sighed. "I don't know if I can ever love anyone as much as I love that stubborn man." I smiled sadly. "But, we aren't together... he and I... I mean..."

He saved me from further humiliation by covering my hand with his. "Rea, it's ok. I always knew you weren't as invested as I was in the relationship." My mouth fell open to contradict him, but he kept going. "I went all in... you always held back and I was ok with it... I am ok with it. We tried.

"I know you cared about me. That you care about me. And I care about you... that's why I'm willing to let you go. I want you to be happy, Rea.

"That's what caring about someone is."

I started crying and he wiped my tears with his thumb. "We're ok, Rea. You are more than my girlfriend. You're my friend. That's not going to change. And we work together." He smiled at me. "You're my best nurse and the patients love you... I'm not going to lose you over the fact that we didn't work as a couple."

Everything he said... his maturity and understanding... and he meant it... he really did.

It's just one more reason that I cannot believe that out of him and Luka Fitzgerald, my stupid heart decided on Luka Fitzgerald.

Pressing the heels of my hands into my eyes, I groan. "Ugh! Stupid ass!"

A slight chuckle at my office door has my turning my head. Leila points to my desk and then circles my face with her finger. "Something tells me that the 'stupid ass' is not directed at anyone in those charts."

Groaning again, I bury my head in my hands. I feel her perch on the edge of my desk, near my elbow. I peek at her through my fingers. She's looking at her fingernails. She smiles at me. "So, who's a stupid ass?"

I ignore her and she chuckles. "It wouldn't be a certain brother of mine, that is right this very second, sitting in the waiting room, awaiting being called back to see the dreamy doctor, that you are no longer dating, now would it?"

Help Our Heroes

My hands fall and I slap my desk. "Luka is not here. He's not supposed to be here until Friday."

Leila grins at me. "Oh, but he is. There was a cancellation for this afternoon and I just so happened to slide him into the spot." She crosses her arms and looks down at me. "You know he's started his therapy and he was fitted for his prosthesis yesterday…"

Of course I know that… I see the charts and you keep telling me everything about him.

Hell, I probably know how many times he peed today!

Ok, not really, but Leila has been keeping me plenty informed.

So has Laeten for that matter.

I haven't been back to the Fitzgerald house since the day we kissed… the day he told me quite clearly that he was aware of my lifelong adoration and that he was not interested.

I don't fully believe him, but my feelings were hurt enough that I didn't want to chance it.

I might have ended things with Clive, but I'm not looking to have my heart broken.

So… I've just avoided all things Luka Fitzgerald. Or tried to… it's a little difficult when my two best friends are his siblings.

Flipping the page in the chart I was working on, I start reading down the document, or trying to. I can't see the words and codes.

My ruse isn't fooling Leila. "Really? You better not actually enter anything on the damn screen right now, Rea. You're just going to have to redo it. I bet you don't even know what you just read."

I mutter, "I do, too. Go away. I'm busy."

She snatches the chart from me and I growl at her as she looks briefly before closing it and asking sarcastically, "What's this patient's name?" I glare and sit back in my chair before crossing my arms morosely. She arches her brow. "Well?"

I snap, "I don't know, ok!"

She smirks. "Uh huh. I knew that." She taps the folder to her mouth while her eyes flit over my face. "Ok, so when are you going to tell me what happened between you and Luka?"

I gasp, "Who said anything happened between us? He said something?"

She laughs. "No. You just did." She leans down and her hair cocoons us. "So, something did happen?" Her eyes search mine. "Rea, I'm your best friend. I've been your best friend since we were freaking embryos. You've been in love with my beloved, idiot brother for about that long, too. Only, well, he was stupid so he never noticed. And you were too scared to tell him.

"You broke up with Clive and that happened right *after* you spent the day with my mule-headed, though women find that attractive, brother… You try to change the subject when either Laeten or I mention Luka or his recovery, though I see you filing every little detail away in that pretty head of yours.

"And… Luka is an *angry* elf!" I look at her and smirk. She laughs and shakes her head, "No, he is horrid, Rea. Like even worse than his previous peachy self. If I didn't love him so much, I'd stab him in the eye with a fork or kick him in the balls. But, he's had enough trauma, so, I figure I wouldn't do that."

I can't help it. I laugh. "Please don't kick him in the balls. Or stab him in the eye. His eyes are so pretty."

She grins at me. "You think everything about him is pretty." She sobers. "No, really, Rea. Something happened… I don't know what, because neither of you have told me. You both suck by the way. But, I'm not stupid."

She sighs. "So, I'm going to assume that you two got naked…"

I gasp and quickly look at the door. It's closed. "Leila! We did not! Oh, my God! I was with Clive. I didn't… we didn't… *NO!*" She grins at me. "But something happened."

Rolling my eyes, I snap. "Yes, we kissed, ok?!"

She claps, but I wave off her glee. "No, don't. It was nothing. In fact, he told me he wasn't interested and that the only reason he kissed was because I was there and he was hard up."

That still hurts.

Her mouth drops open. "I'm *going* to kick him in the balls."

She turns to the door and I call out, "Oh my, God. Leila stop. No. You're at work, you fool. Besides, it's ok."

Help Our Heroes

She glares at me. "No, it's not and I know that you know he didn't mean that. I don't know why he said that to you, but you know damn well he didn't mean it."

I do know that...

Doesn't make it any less scary. In fact, it makes it scarier.

* * *

Luka

Laeten is at my appointment with me. Leila called this morning and said they had a cancelation and she was putting me in it. She didn't ask, she just told; but, I'm used to that.

She wouldn't be Leila if she wasn't bossy.

He was at the house with me anyway since they still refuse to leave me alone for more than a few hours at a time. It's like they're all worried I'll hurt myself or break more shit. Which I haven't... not since the lamp... and the clock.

He glances at his watch and I fidget as I look around the room. The waiting room is pretty packed.

They see all these people every day here? Holy shit!

Everything is in the same building, so I was actually here yesterday when I was measured for my prosthesis. My leg is finally healed enough, or it should be, to start my physical therapy with the prosthetic once it's ready. I'm seeing Doctor Evans today...

Of course it would be Clive. And since it's Clive, will Rea be there, too?

I haven't seen or heard from her since I said those hateful things to her and made her leave. Neither Laeten nor Leila have mentioned her either. Which now that I'm really thinking about it is not good.

Does she hate me?

Is that why they won't answer me or why she hasn't checked in.

Well, neither have you, Luka.

The door opens a heavy nurse in blue scrubs calls out five names. Mine is one of them.

Laeten looks over at me and hands me my crutch. Since Rea left the other day, I haven't been in the wheelchair. I've been working hard every day to re-strengthen my arms and my good leg. My abs are solid steel again and I'm proud of that.

Every day I'm stronger. I've also started my physical therapy and once my prosthesis comes in, it'll focus on teaching me to walk again. Eventually, I plan to run.

Group therapy is different. It's a whole bunch of veterans in a room with a counselor who is also a veteran. I haven't participated in it yet other than to tell the group my name and rank. Maybe next week…

Reaching out, I take the crutch from him and use my other hand to steady myself as I stand. I'm getting good at this. Every time, it's a little easier, a little more natural. A little less strenuous.

Laeten lets go and says, "You good, bro? Still want me to tag along?"

He knows that I'm stubborn. Besides, if I see Rea in a minute, I want to be doing this all on my own.

I nod. "Yup. I'm golden. But, I would really appreciate it if you would come with me." He nods. "Thanks, bro."

We follow everyone else through the doors to the back. The nurse is pointing at doors and calling out numbers. "Willis… four… Fitzgerald… you're in five, but let's go get your weight, ok?"

I follow her to the scale and try to inconspicuously look around. I don't see Rea.

So, is she not going to be my nurse?

I ask the nurse before I can think better of it. "Is Rea here today?"

The nurse looks up from her chart and her eyes widen as she really looks at me. She grins. "Ah, yes indeed. She is. Rea is here every day. That girl never takes a break. She's everyone's favorite around here."

Including the damn doctor. That she's dating.

But, she's here…

She gestures to the room. "Go on and get undressed. Put the paper gown on and hop up on the table. Be in shortly." Before I can ask anything else, she disappears into a room after sharply rapping on the door.

* * *

Help Our Heroes

Laeten is joking about the drab walls and see through paper gown I have on when there's a knock at the door. I call out, expecting to see the heavy nurse from earlier, but instead, my eyes widen as I look into the wide blue eyes I last saw ten day ago.

Rea looks at me and calmly says, "Luka." She looks over at Laeten and smiles at him. "Hey, Laeten."

She didn't smile at me.

She wheels in a blood pressure machine. "I need to check your pressure and temperature and then Dr. Evans will be in shortly to check your leg… it should be mostly healed, but he needs to check it thoroughly before he can sign off on your therapy with your prosthetic. If any area is not fully healed, the therapy can cause friction and that can cause an infection."

Really? We're playing this game?
She's going to act like she doesn't even know me?

Glancing over, I see Laeten hiding a smirk behind his hand.

Oh, so he's picked up on this, too.

"Lift your arm, please. I just need to get this cuff around." She wraps it and tightens the Velcro. "Is that too tight?"

I stare at her, but she doesn't look up. "It's great." She pushes the button and the cuff tightens around my bicep while she readies the thermometer. She holds it up and says without looking at me again. "I'm just going to slip this under your tongue." She's looking at my chin.

I don't open my mouth. She sighs and says, "Can you open your mouth, Luka?!"

I still don't do it. Finally, she looks at me and the fire in her eyes makes my heart pound. "Why are you treating me like you don't know me?" I look at the door pointedly and then back at her. "Is Doctor Perfect going to get mad?"

Laeten snickers and I look at him in annoyance. Rea looks at him sharply and then back at me. She rolls her eyes, "Why would my boss, Doctor Evans, get mad that I'm talking to a patient?"

I snort, "Because I don't think you kiss all of your patients like you kissed me..." I arch my brow at her and dare her, "or do you?!"

She scowls. "I think not. Can you just open your mouth so I can take your temperature, Luka? I have other patients…"

Laeten is outright enjoying this. He's grinning behind a magazine, but it's so obvious that he's laughing. I snap at him, "Why are you laughing?"

He shrugs. "No reason."

I ignore him and lean in to try to talk to Rea without him hearing. A feat in this cramped ass room. "I'm sorry. I'm sorry for what I said, Rea. I didn't mean it. I was pissed and I said things to deliberately drive you away."

Her eyes raise to meet mine and I can see the anger there. "That's neither here nor there. I'm at work, Luka. You are a patient. Either let me take your damn temperature or I can grab one of the other girls and she can come do it." She's pissed.

I frown, "You don't care that I'm sorry?"

She mutters, "Not really, no." But her body is giving her away. Her chest is heaving beneath her blue scrubs in tune with her heightened breathing.

Reaching out, I gently touch her arm. "Rea, I don't believe you. You care. And again, I'm sorry. I just wanted to tell you that." I look at the door again and says, "Can you acknowledge that before your boyfriend walks in?"

She looks at me and says calmly, "I don't have a boyfriend… now, can you open your freaking mouth?"

What? She doesn't have a boyfriend?
Since when?

My hand tightens on her hand. She looks at it sharply and I hurriedly say, "You don't? You and Clive…"

Rea's shoulders slump and she sighs again as she looks at me. "No. There is no me and Clive. I work with Doctor Evans… that's all. Now open your mouth or I'm leaving."

Before I can overthink it, I blurt out, "Have dinner with me? Like a date? You and me?"

Pure shock covers her face, but she shakes her head. "If I say yes, will you let me do my job?"

I nod and mutter "Yup."

She rolls her eyes. "Great, open up." This time I gladly open my mouth for

Help Our Heroes

her to stick the thermometer in.

Chapter 13

Rea

Three weeks later

I groan as I rummage through my closet for the umpteenth time in twenty minutes. It's been three weeks since I agreed to go out with Luka. I had conditions. He agreed to them.

His face was not happy as I listed them out and he argued with me over some of them, but in the end, he reluctantly agreed to them all.

Condition One: Go to group therapy and actually participate. After all you can't heal if you don't share.

Condition Two: Stop goading me about Clive. We've broken up. But I want to give it two weeks before we actually go on the date. I just broke up with Clive and I respect him too much to rub a new relationship or even a date in his face.

Condition Three: Since we aren't going on a date, no kissing or anything else. Just talking and getting to know each other again. He of course argued that we've known each other our entire lives, and that was stupid. I said we talked about things for three weeks or there would be no date.

Condition Four: Our date had to take place somewhere that would slightly challenge him.

Condition Five: He would respect the other conditions.

I laugh as I remember his face when I said that we couldn't kiss or anything else. He was so shocked. He tried to argue with me but in the end, I won.

And now... it's date day and I'm freaking out.

Why am I so nervous?

This is Luka.

EXACTLY!

This is Luka! The one male I've loved forever and now I'm going on a date with him.

My cell phone buzzes and I glance at it, expecting to see some GIF from Leila teasing me, or insinuating that Luka and I will be having sex tonight.

It's neither. It's Luka.

"Luka

Be ready at 5PM on the dot. Laeten will drop me off at your place. You're driving. I'm supplying the rest. Wear something comfortable yet pretty and shoes you can remove."

What?

I text him back.

"Rea

What? Where are we going?"

The dots appear that show he's typing and then a winking emoji pops up.

"Luka

Now why would I tell you that and spoil the surprise?"

Ugh.

Comfortable yet pretty?!

Suddenly, I know exactly what I'm going to wear. Reaching into the closet, I pull out the dress. Looking down, I see brown booties that will give it just enough edge to keep it from looking too little girly.

Yes, that's perfect.

Now, I just need to get ready.

* * *

Looking in the gold beveled mirror in my small foyer, I apply my light pink lip gloss and press my lips together. I hear a car in the driveway and then a door. My heart is racing as I stand and wait in breathless anticipation for the knock I've waited my entire life for.

I hear Luka call something out and another voice answer him, Laeten and then *rap rap rap*. Luka knocks three times.

Taking one last look in the mirror, I smooth my hair. I've left it down and the dirty blonde waves are caressing from my shoulders to the middle of my back.

Yes, you look nice, Rea.

Reaching out, I open the door. My breath leaves my chest as I stare at the gorgeous man on my doorstep. His light brown hair is perfectly styled to look tousled and his beard is neatly trimmed. He's wearing a crisp white button up shirt with the cuffs rolled and light worn, denim jeans. He's using his crutch for support, but he's standing on two legs. One real and one prosthetic. He's had it about two weeks now and he's doing fantastic with it.

I'm so busy losing myself in his appearance that I don't realize he's doing the same thing to me… until Laeten calls out from beside my car. "Good lord, you two! Stop eye fucking each other on the doorstep. At least take it inside."

Why is he by my car?!

He sets a picnic basket and a large blanket on the hood and laughs. "Y'all better use this." He points at the basket. "Have fun." He waggles his brows and waves as he gets back into his car. Luka and I watch as Laeten backs out. He waves again before driving off.

I look at Luka and then the basket on my car.

It's just us now…

We're really doing this then.

Luka clears his throat. "You look beautiful, Rea. I'd forgotten how long your hair was."

My hands immediately raise to smooth it. "That's because it's always up." I laugh nervously until Luka catches my hand. His thumb rubs over my tattoo. I have two and both are visible in this dress, but normally only the arrow on the side of my left palm can be seen, and only if people happen to be looking for it. He asks, "Why an arrow?"

I shrug. "Arrows are used for defense and archers were generally at the front of the line in battle. Archers were brave. They had courage. The arrow is a reminder that no matter what, if I proceed with courage, I can get through it."

He nods and his finger continues to trace it. Shivers race up my arm. "Is this your only one?"

My breathing hitches as I shake my head. Using my other hand, I pull my hair to the side and drape it over my right shoulder. "No, I also have this one." He lets my hand go and I turn my back to show him. His fingers reach out and he traces the feathers on my shoulder. Leaning down, he presses a kiss to the feathers. I gasp. And my nipples bead against the fabric of my dress. Thank God for the beading, since I've forgone a bra.

His breath caresses my back and neck as he leans over me. "Rea, I think we should get in the car and go now... if not, I'm going to push you into the house and against the door."

My breathing accelerates and I lock eyes with him, over my shoulder, "Would that be so bad, Luka?"

He growls and says, "No, it wouldn't. But you asked for a date that challenges me and though I have a feeling we'll be explosive together, I don't think it'll be challenging. So, let's go."

Part of me wants to say "Screw what I said," but the other part of me really wants to see what Luka has come up with.

Either way... I have no plans of ending this night *without* Luka between my thighs.

* * *

Luka

Dear lord. Never have I wanted a woman as much as I want Rea.

How can someone who has literally been there my entire life suddenly make up my entire world?

Rea is following the directions I plugged into her GPS. She didn't recognize the address and I didn't want to give it away by just telling her where it was.

It's a place we know well though.

She makes the turn onto the River Road and says, "Are we going someplace on the river?"

I shrug and tell her to follow the GPS. She laughs and does. As the GPS says we've reached our destination, she turns to me with a frown after looking around. "Where are we? This is nowhere, Luka? It says we're here... where is here?"

Smiling at her, I nod. "We're at the right place." She frowns again and I point out of the windshield. "See that trail… Take that."

Her eyes are wide as she looks at me in uncertainty. "I don't know about this, Luka. This looks like the setting of every horror movie ever."

No, no horror movie, Rea.

Trust me.

I look at her and lean over the console. "I forgot to tell you… you look beautiful."

She smiles at me and mutters, "Thank you. You look pretty good yourself." My heart speeds up.

"Rea?"

Her nose wrinkles, "Yeah, Luka?"

I lean in closer and whisper, "You've made me wait three weeks… I don't think I want to wait another second to taste those lips again."

I see her cheeks flush and her chest rises as her breathing accelerates. She leans in and angles her head. Her lips are level with mine. She breathes and her breath tickles my lips. She whispers, "Neither can I."

My mouth closes over hers. I intended for it to be soft and sweet but the second her plump lips touched mine, all of my good intentions flew out of the window. I growl against her mouth and she responds to my call by parting her lips. Her tongue meets mine and together, we war to see who can discover the deepest recesses of the others mouth fastest. Her hands grip both sides of my head and her fingers bury themselves in my hair. Our moans are bouncing around the small space of her car.

Reaching over, I try to touch her, but the console is in the way. Rea must share my urgency. She pulls her mouth from mine and gasps as she wriggles enough to climb over the console. I laugh, "Rea, this is crazy."

She looks down at me as she straddles me. "I can stop…" Her breasts are trying to burst out of the sparkles at the top of her short off white dress. They're heaving and her blue eyes are almost navy.

Her hands are resting on my shoulders as she waits for my response.

My hands slide up her bare thighs and under the flowy skirt. I feel the delicate cotton of her panties as I trail my hands up. She shivers and stares at me from between her lashes as she sucks on her bottom lip.

Pulling her against me, I let her feel what she's doing to me. Her head falls back slightly and she moans, "Ohhh, Luka…"

I groan as I rub against her again. "Rea, God… you're killing me, Smalls."

She stops and grins down at me. "Really, a Sandlot reference? Right now?"

Pulling her hips again, my eyes almost cross as the pressure builds against my fly. I gasp. "No, seriously. You have to get off me… I'm going to come in my pants."

She freezes and my eyes crack open. A smile I've never seen from her is on her face. She looks like a temptress with her hair fanning out over us and the sun at her back. Her skirt is around her waist and my hands are under the elastic of her panties, squeezing her ass.

I'm seriously about to embarrass myself.

Don't you dare, Luka.

She's too beautiful. Too tempting. Too… everything…

I'm expecting her to slide off me, so I jerk in shock as she straightens her thighs and kneels on the seat. She reaches between us and pops my fly. It doesn't need much help. The force of my erection parts the zipper and my engorged cock springs free. It slaps against her thigh and I feel my cheeks heat. "Um, yeah… I think you should put that up."

Her hand wraps around the base and she strokes me from root to tip. My head falls back and my jaw opens. "Ohhhhh, Rea… Damn you…"

She chuckles and strokes me again. My hips lift out of instinct. Leaning down, she brushes her mouth against mine as she continues to stroke me. My hands grasp her head to hold her in place as my tongue slips past her lips. It thrusts into her mouth and duels with her tongue in tandem with her strokes.

I break the kiss and groan, "I'm going to cum all over your hand, Rea. I'm so serious."

She stops stroking me and we both look down. Her pale hand is wrapped around my heated shaft and the sight alone is almost enough to send me over the edge.

Her eyes raise and she looks into my eyes. "Luka, I want you. I've wanted you my entire life." Her hand squeezes me and I try to concentrate on what she's saying. "It certainly appears as if you want me, too." Her hand stills and I see the vulnerability on her gorgeous face as she says, "If I'm just the first woman who has been available, since you know…" She looks at my thighs. "I need to know that. I can't… I can't settle for just being someone who was handy…"

Luka, you're such an idiot…

Of course she thinks that… You SAID that… To her.

My hand cups her cheek and I pour everything I'm feeling into my touch and my words. "I know I said that, Rea. But, I lied. I'm sorry. I lied to you." I sigh. "I realized what I was feeling for you and that I've probably always felt that way, but I've been too stupid and selfish to realize it." I smile wryly. "I didn't know that you loved me… back then. I mean, I did. I loved you, too. But, I didn't know that you *loved* me. If I had, I'd probably have gotten my head out of my ass and admitted that I loved you, too." Her eyes are glued to mine. My voice lowers, "Are you the first woman who's been available since my *accident*… yes. But, even if you weren't and there'd been ten or twenty or one hundred… it would still be you."

I'm going all in.

"Do you understand what I'm saying, Rea?" My voice is husky with my emotion. She nods, but I want to make certain she *knows*. My hand tremors where it's cupping her cheek. "The Raiders motto is 'Always Faithful, Always Forward'." I smile. "You are always faithful. You've been my faithful companion and friend my whole life, Rea. You've been there for me and cleaned up my messes even when you should have told me to screw off. And I want to go forward… *with you.*

"The Raiders was always my dream. It was all I thought I needed in my life. But, I was so wrong. Losing my leg is teaching me that. That wasn't a dream… that was a goal. A goal I accomplished. Losing the goal helped me understand the dream.

"You… *you're* the dream. I love you, Rea. I love you and I want you by my side as I go forward with this life." Her eyes are glassy as she holds back tears. Her smile wobbles but she doesn't say anything.

Uh, is she going to say anything?

Help Our Heroes

She's still holding my dick...
Does she know that?
Shit, I didn't!
I must really love her to forget about the fact that my dick is in her hand.

I have to know. "Rea... Do you have anything you want to say about what I just told you?"

She smiles and tears flow down her cheeks. She looks down and her smile widens. She looks back at me and grins. "You aren't just telling me you love me because your penis is in my hand, are you?"

Shaking my head, I laugh. "I am not. In fact, I love you so much that I gave you some big, romantic, awesome speech about why I love you *while* my penis was in your hand. A speech you have not commented on..."

Her hand tightens around my cock and it wakes back up. She strokes it once and stares into my eyes. "I heard every word. I filed it away. And I'm so glad, because I love you, too. I've always loved you, Luka."

I groan. "That's awesome, but can you hop back into the seat and take that trail? Right now? That's our spot... from when we were kids. Where we used to swim and play and I did a thousand asinine things that I shouldn't have and you doctored me up after every single one. So, I'd like to do something right now that's way past due and make love to you back there."

Her eyes leave my face to look over her shoulder and then back at me. "Our spot?"

I nod. "Our spot. It's the spot I should have kissed you for the first time, but I'll settle for it being the spot where I make you mine for the first time. That is, if you want to let go of my dick for the two minutes it takes to get there. You can have it right back though... I promise."

She leans down and kisses me breathless before releasing my dick. Grabbing her head, I pull her back down for another kiss. She fans her cheeks when I'm done. "I love you, Rea Badeaux." Her eyes show her love for me as she says, "God, I never thought I'd hear that from you. I love you, Luka," and she climbs over the console to drive down the trail and into the sand where so much happened when we were kids... and so much more will happen now that we're adults.

A Military Anthology

Epilogue

Rea

For as hot as we both were for each other, Luka made me park and he insisted he was unpacking the car and setting up our "date" himself. I've been watching him from the hood of my car, where I'm perched.

He's getting along very well on his prosthesis. I can tell he's been working hard.

He bends and sets the basket of food on one corner of the blanket he's spread on the river sand. I can't help but admire his firm backside in the light jeans he's wearing.

Holy, mother… no ass should look that good in a simple pair of jeans.

Luka turns and catches me admiring him. He smirks. "Are you admiring my *ass…ets*?!"

I feel a blush cover my cheeks, but I merely nod once and shrug as I grin back at him. "Why, yes. Yes, I am. I'm totally objectifying you, Luka. You have a mighty fine ass. In fact, why don't you bend over again so I can make sure to soak it all in."

Oh, my God. I never flirt this outrageously.

It's because it's Luka…

His green gaze locks on mine and my breath catches at the sudden fire in his eyes. All hint of joking is gone and white hot, desire has taken its place. His nostrils flare as he straightens to his full height and my heart feels like it's going to leave my chest.

My nipples bead against the front of my dress and a slight breeze lifts my hair and caresses my skin. I shiver in molten awareness.

Luka's eyes darken and he starts toward me. His gait is determined though still slightly unsteady. It's the sexiest thing I've ever seen.

I'm watching him stalk me as if it's in slow motion. Every step is pronounced and my heart is thumping in tandem with his feet in the sand. He stops about a foot in front of me and his eyes follow my body from my head to my chest. My chest heaves under his scrutiny and he smiles. His eyes leave my breasts and trail over my waist and then my hips. He slowly looks down the expanse of my bare legs, showcased by the short hem of the white fabric and to the tips of my pink painted toenails before he slowly and deliberately looks back up my body. He's a foot away, but it feels as if he's touching me.

His eyes once again lock on mine and he steps closer as he growls, "Rea, I feel like I've waited a lifetime for this moment."

His hands reach for my hair and his fingers weave into the long, loose strands, slowly tugging so my head angles back. I gasp at him as my scalp tingles and electricity invades my entire body. My hands reach for him, fisting in the fabric of his shirt. Breathlessly, I whisper, "I *have* waited a lifetime for you, Luka."

His eyes flare and his head swoops down. His mouth crashes to mine, but I'm ready for him. My head angles as my lips part, welcoming the thrust of his tongue. He traces my teeth with his velvet tongue and slides it alongside mine. Every touch of it sends a pang of desire to my core and I moan. He swallows it and an answering moan leaves him and ricochets in my mouth.

My hands leave the fabric of his shirt to slip underneath. As they flatten against his abdomen, I can feel the raised skin from his healed injuries where they cover the firm muscle. He shudders and ends the kiss. His voice is ragged as he leans his forehead against mine. "Rea... don't... I don't want you to touch that... to see that... it's ugly..."

Pulling my head back, I look at him. His eyes are squeezed tightly shut and I can see the grimace on his beautiful face. I softly say his name, "Luka... look at me." My fingertips gently trace the scars beneath his shirt. He doesn't open his eyes.

My hands still on his body and then I remove them from his skin. He exhales harshly, but his breath hitches as I start to unbutton the material. When I'm done with the last button, I look up and see him staring down at me intently. My

Help Our Heroes

eyes stay locked on his as I push his shirt from his shoulders and down his arms. He allows me to push the fabric over his clenched hands. It falls to the ground. My hands immediately return to his abdomen and I once again find the evidence of his bravery, that he doesn't want me to see.

His breath hisses out from between his teeth, "Rea…"

With our eyes still locked, I lean in and find one of his scars with my lips. His body jerks as I slowly slide my lips over it before finding the next one. His body is tight and I feel his hands shaking where he's clutching my shoulders. Raising my lips, I whisper against his skin, "Nothing about you is ugly, Luka. Never think that." My fingers trace the ridge of imperfect skin. "These are beautiful. You are beautiful. I love every inch of you. The perfect and the imperfect… because I love *you*."

He stares at me and I can see the war within his beautiful eyes. Finally, he nods and reaches for me again. He leans down and kisses me. His mouth is soft as it clings to mine. As fast as he leans down, he leans back and smiles at me. "I love you, Rea Badeaux. I have no idea what I did to have you love me, but this is one thing in my life, I'm not going to fuck up."

I smirk at him as my hands trail down his back and settle on the soft denim covering that ass I love to ogle. As I cup him, he groans and one brow raises. Leaning in, I press a kiss to his chest, over his heart and then look up at him. My eyes are alight with love and I suck my lip into my mouth as my fingers trail up his back and then back down to the curve of his delectable ass. "Good to know. Now… I've waited my whole life for this moment, Luka Fitzgerald. I think it's time you deliver."

His brows raise and then he smirks at me. "Yes, Ma'am." He lifts me and my legs wrap around his trim waist. My bare thighs are clutching at his warm skin and my breathing is erratic.

Luka turns with me in his arms and he stumbles, but the car allows him to right himself. He growls. "See what you do to me… I keep forgetting I'm not the man I used to be."

My hands cup his face and I look into his eyes. "No, you're not. But, go ahead and take your time. I trust you, Luka. I love the man that you *are*."

His steps are more deliberate as he makes his way to the blanket he's laid out for us, but I'm not worried. I trust him. I feel safe. I feel loved.

He stops at the edge and his cheeks flush as he mutters, "I'm not sure I can bend down with you in my arms and not drop you, Rea. I think that might be out of my skill set... for now..."

Reaching up, I press my lips to his. "Raincheck..."

He smiles at me as he gingerly shifts me to allow me to slide down his body and stand in front of him. We're both breathless as my feet touch the softness of the blanket. He winks at me. "You bet..."

His hands are on my waist and mine are on his forearms as we stand. Finally he glances at the blanket. I can see he's nervous. He chuckles. "Shall we sit?!"

A smirk escapes me and I step back from him. Watching him, I reach for the hem of my dress and slowly raise it. I hear his breathing stop as I raise the white material over my waist and then my head. My hair fans over my shoulders as I drop the dress and look at him.

Here I am, Luka. I'm exposed... in the open.

Oh my God...

Luka's eyes drink me in. My scant white panties are the only thing covering me from his gaze. My hands fist at my sides as I fight the urge to cover my chest.

Finally, he groans. "Ok, so we're not sitting..."

I can't help it, I laugh. "I don't want to *sit*." His eyes crinkle at the corners as I take a step toward him and reach for the clasp on his jeans. They widen as I pop it and my hands slide inside. His skin is like a furnace. He moans my name, "Rea... Oh, God, baby," and elation fills me. I push the material down and it catches. Looking down, I see what it's caught on.

Dropping to my knees, I help the jeans over the prosthesis and slowly remove his shoes so I can get the jeans off.

His eyes are vulnerable and unsure as he watches me. Finally, he takes a shaky breath and says, "Rea... I haven't... I mean... this is the first time since... everything... what if I can't?!"

My eyes lock on his throbbing length. I smirk and lean out to stroke him.

His breath hisses from between his teeth. "Luka, I really don't think you'll have that problem. Stop overthinking it and just be here... with me... finally. I love you."

He still looks uncertain, but want is overriding it. Slowly, he bends down. He takes his time and I just watch him... want building in me as I watch the man I love, who's trying so hard, who was injured doing what he always wanted to do, and serving his country... join me on the blanket. Stretching out beside me, he pulls me to him and for the first time, my practically nude body is pressed against his. We rub against each other and I groan as I feel him at the apex of my thighs. I can't prevent myself from acting wanton. He grins and reaches between us to trace the elastic at the top of my panties. "Sweetheart, why on earth do you still have these on?"

I grin back at him though it's hard to concentrate with him so close to where I most want him. "Well, I can't do *all* of the work, Luka."

Throwing his head back, he laughs. Leaning down his eyes lock on mine and he mutters, "Fair enough." His hands slide my panties down, though I help him. I want him too badly not to. When they reach my ankles, I kick them off but before I can do anything, Luka pushes me back and traces my folds with his finger. I gasp as he dips one inside of me. His strokes are slow and shallow as he plays my body. The sounds he's creating within me, as he fingers me and readies me for him, are not common.

I sound so breathless... so free.

Finally, he leans over me. I part my thighs. He freezes as his forehead leans on mine. He looks at me, asking me if this is what I want. In answer, my back arches and my feet lock around his waist. Our eyes stay connected as he enters me.

I gasp as he stops. "Ohhhhhh."

His breathing is just as ragged and then, still watching me, he moves. I move in perfect synchronicity and we find our rhythm.

Our gasps, groans, and the sound of sex and love fill the night air.

I'm so close.,.

He reaches between us and finds my clit. It sends me over the edge and I scream out his name, *"Luka,"* as stars that rival the night sky explode behind my eyelids. My release seems to be the sign he was waiting for. His pace quickens and he yells against the skin of my neck, "Rea... oh, baby. Rea..." His body spasms above me and then he stills.

He rolls us both so we're side by side on the blanket, a tangle of arms and legs... his prosthesis is resting against my calf and it's the most natural feeling in the world for me.

Finally, he sighs. I can feel him looking at me, so with a contented smile I turn and face him. He smiles back and then he grins.

I can't help but grin back, "What?"

He laughs and presses a kiss to my shoulder before pulling me closer to him. "You were right, baby." My brow wrinkles and I look at him in confusion. He winks at me. "I didn't have a problem. It's like riding a bike..."

Slapping his shoulder, I laugh with him. "Oh, my God, Luka!"

He rolls slightly so he's up on his elbow, looking down at me. The dusk light is accentuating his face and my breathing hitches at his beauty. His eyes light up as he watches me and I can read the emotion in them. He confirms it. "I love you, Rea."

Help Our Heroes

No Beginning

Sam Destiny

First Lieutenant Micah McCain lost his best friend and wasn't around to tell him goodbye. When finally visiting Timber's grave, Micah meets timber's little sister. It's as pleasant as it's unexpected, and Micah cannot help but follow her home and meet the people who raised his best friend.

Lost without a course, this could be his chance at a better life, but will he take it?

Sarah Timber lost everything when she lost her big brother. He'd been her support, her best friend, her protector. Drifting in a sea of sadness and despair, all she has left is to fulfill her brother's last wish.

But will Micah stay and let her heal him, or is the solider too afraid of deep-felt connections and runs the other way?

Help Our Heroes

Chapter 1

First Lieutenant Micah McCain walked up the tree-lined road toward the Ashburn Military cemetery. He'd just returned from his latest deployment, and his first stop was to the grave of a soldier he'd known for almost his entire service time.

Staff Sergeant Elton Timber and him had been in basic training together, and Micah remembered the first few weeks, wading through mud, carrying the heaviest backpacks through rain and rivers, and yet Timber had been almost like a brother. They'd done their first tour together at twenty-three, had seen their first death, had done their first killing shots, all side by side.

When they'd been twenty-six Timber had demanded to move bases because he'd met someone online.

Micah had been jealous and happy, all wrapped in one. While they'd gained an edge, Timber had kept his sunny personality, brightening up every party, every gathering he went to.

He'd also ended up happily married at twenty-eight, and no matter how much Micah had wished he could've been there, another tour had kept him away.

There hadn't been much for him at home in the states, and whenever he was on leave, he spent his time with his brother and his family. Their parents had died when he'd been just out of basic training, and although the time had been hard, it had caused him to dedicate everything he had to his life in the army.

The gates to the Ashburn cemetery came into view and his steps faltered.

At thirty-two Elton Timber should've been high on life, holding his children and his wife, not being buried in the cold, unyielding ground.

They'd lost touch for eighteen months, and yet it had been that way before, with them not having spoken for a length of time. Still, meeting again then had been as if they'd never been apart. It was what made true friendship.

Micah closed his eyes before pushing the gate open. It gave way to his touch easily and silently, the hinges well oiled, and he almost wished it would've kept him out.

God, regrets flooded him as he made his way to Timber's slot.

They should've talked more.

He should've made time for him last time he'd been home.

Maybe they should've exchanged letters.

Micah should've asked more about the wife and the kids.

It was then he realized he had known Elton for so long, but he couldn't recall his wife's name, or how many children they had, and if any, how old they were.

They'd talked about tours, lost comrades, regrets, and the fact that Micah tended to not get serious with women.

Then again, why would he, knowing he was still going to do tours as often as the Army allowed him to? He hadn't met anyone he considered captivating enough to keep him in the US forever.

"God, El, you would've loved it. They had this raw rock sound, the edge you always enjoyed when listening to music. I was going to play some songs for you, but they aren't on YouTube yet, and all the recordings I did on my phone were so horrible you'd turn in your grave."

Micah froze as he spotted a dark-haired girl sitting next to his friend's headstone. She had two blankets she sat on, wrapped in an army-green jacket that definitely was way too big for her because he saw the sleeves reach down to the middle of her hands, which she had wrapped around her shoulders.

"I'm considering getting a new phone, but really, where's the fun in that? I can no longer complain then." She laughed softly, and then seemed to listen to something.

Micah knew he probably should've made himself known, but he feared she'd interrupt herself the moment she knew he was there, and he wanted to give her the chance to talk to Timber.

"I miss you. I miss you so much, you have no idea. I'm still driving your truck, but don't worry, I haven't forgotten I promised you to give it up."

He remembered the truck. Or rather he remembered the one Timber bought when they were out of basic training. It was a rusty red and sounded like it was constantly broken, but he'd loved it. They'd spent many nights on the back of it, drinking beer and reminiscing about how their lives would turn out.

Micah knew Elton had family back here in Ashburn, but during those first years he'd been home rather seldom, wanting to live the life, hang out with comrades and go to clubs. He knew they'd talked often, and he'd seen pictures of them, but most had been old. As in, he couldn't have been more than twelve on them, his siblings even smaller, and all had the same haircut. To this day Micah had no idea if he had three brothers, or brothers and sisters instead.

Maybe he should've asked, but since his own family had been so disastrously broken, he never had bothered listening to his comrades talking about Christmases and Thanksgiving.

In fact, when it came to their non-army life he'd pretty much shut them out. For those first years he'd hardly spoken to his own family left, so why should he have cared about other people's families?

Deciding to give the girl her space, he stepped back, his eyes on her profile, and as if she'd seen the movement from the corner of her eye, she jumped up, taking on a defensive stance that more looked like a weird dancing position than anything keeping her safe.

Her blue eyes narrowed before widening and she relaxed. Micah took less than ten seconds to take her in.

The jacket had Timber's name still on it and reached down to the middle of her thighs. She wore skinny jeans and black, high-heeled boots, making him think without them she would maybe come up to his shoulder, if at all.

"Lieutenant McCain... Micah..." She shook her head as if recognizing him, and Micah blinked.

Shaking her head, she came forward, holding out her hand. "I'm sorry and so impolite. I'm Sarah Timber. I didn't think you'd be... you'd..." She thought for a second, a blush creeping along her cheeks. "I just didn't think you'd look like you do. I mean, of course, but... I'm babbling."

He smirked, not being able to help himself. "First Lieutenant Micah McCain, at your service." He touched his hat the way he'd learned it and then still smiled at her while her eyes roamed his body in a curious and not at all insulting way.

She shook her head. "I didn't think you'd be that tall. Naturally I know everything about you, but also know you know nothing about us, so…" Shrugging, she drowned her hands in the pockets of the jacket and then turned to the grave. "He's so different than you always made us believe," she hissed toward the headstone and he lowered his eyes.

Where he hadn't listened to him talk about home, home seemed to have listened to Timber talking about him, and damn if that didn't release a fresh wave of guilt.

* * *

Sarah stared at her brother's friend and couldn't reconcile him with the guy Elton had always spoken about.

The way it had sounded he'd been as outgoing and fun as Elton always was, but the man in front of her looked serious, life-worn and weathered. She knew the two hadn't seen each other in two years or so, but still…

Then again, a lot could happen in two years. She knew that better than anyone.

"I'm sorry, but Timber… I mean Elton never—"

She smiled softly. "Timber is fine. He'd been called by his last name since he was what? Ten?" She winked at him and then cleared her throat. "I'm going to gather my stuff and let you have your moment, okay?"

She bent to retrieve her blankets, folding them and holding them close to her body as she eyed Micah McCain again. He was tall, about a head and a half taller than she, shoulders wide, his back straight. He had blond hair that was a little longer at the top and shorter at the sides, and his eyes were green, shimmering like freshly mowed grass until he shifted and the sun no longer hit his face. Then they seemed to be almost forest green.

"He was an amazing person," he announced and she nodded briefly, then smiled at the headstone.

She'd picked up talking to him because with him being the oldest and she being the youngest sibling, they'd always had a special bond.

Sarah had no intention letting that lessen because he no longer walked this Earth.

Making her way through the headstones, she was surprised to find her truck still to be the only one in the parking lot. It made her curious as to how Lieutenant McCain had gotten there.

It took less than ten minutes for him to leave the cemetery, his head lowered, his steps hurried, as if he couldn't get away fast enough.

She had waited for him because there were some things she needed to talk to him about, but now she hurried after him.

"Lieutenant McCain, please, wait." He stopped and glanced up, his eyes bright as if he was biting back tears.

"It's two miles back into town. How did you get here?"

His eyes swept the length of the road as if he saw it for the first time. "I walked. It was nice moving my feet. I've been on planes for the better part of two days," he explained and she realized he'd just come home from war and his first stop had been to her brother's grave.

"Let me drive you. I'm sure you remember the beast?" She pointed over her shoulder at the truck and his eyes went over her head, the smallest of smiles playing over his lips.

"Good memories," he muttered and she nodded at the truck again.

"We have some things to talk about anyway," she then added and it was what seemed to be the deciding argument for him.

Together they made their way back, and she held out the keys. "Wanna drive it, Lieutenant McCain?"

"It's Micah," he said absentmindedly and then took the keys from her, his hand warm and calloused.

"Micah." She smiled and he paused for a second, his eyes lingering on her face until she all but blushed, and his gaze dropped.

"I'm sorry for the loss of your husband," he whispered and she instantly shook her head.

"Elton was my brother. His wife's name is Cathy, and she moved away with the kids three months ago. Said she couldn't handle the memories, the pain, our family without him. It wasn't pretty and my parents were devastated, but if things work out, we'll still be seeing my nephews, I hope."

She tried to hide the pain in her voice, but when he reached out and squeezed her shoulder, she realized she'd probably done a bad job.

Getting into the car, she gave him a moment, and then arched a brow when he still didn't start the truck.

"I'm sorry for your loss, Micah," she eventually offered and he met her eyes, his full of pain and emotions she couldn't place.

They'd been friends, close friends, probably closer than Micah had realized so far, and still seeing him the way he sat next to her that moment, she shifted until she was on the seat and could wrap her arms around him. She felt Micah reach around her shoulder, as if he was trying to wipe away tears while squeezing her tightly, and wished she could do something.

For her, Elton's death had been harsh reality for half a year now.

It seemed Micah hadn't realized the truth of it until that moment. He didn't let go, and neither did she, thinking she could give him all the comfort he needed.

And that seemed to be a lot.

* * *

Micah couldn't let go of Timber's little sister because he worried he'd fully fall apart then. He didn't even know what had caused the onslaught of emotion the moment he'd sat behind the wheel because he was trained in compartmentalizing and usually did well, but that day it seemed impossible.

She smelled of roses and vanilla and faintly of cookies and coffee, and it was a scent he found comforting and confusing all at the same time.

"I'm sorry, soldier," she whispered, her lips brushing the outer shell of his ear as she spoke and it was what made him realize how damn close he was holding her.

Easing his grip on her, she pulled back the moment he had let go. Her face was full of compassion as he bit his lip. She reached out and brushed a tear from his cheek, making him feel as if he was five years old.

He cleared his throat, moving his hat on his head, then finally started the truck. "Okay, where to?"

She watched him from the side, her eyes kind, and he forced himself to look away because this was Timber's little sister and he needed to stay away from thoughts like how sweet she was and how well she'd fit into his arms—despite being so small.

"Back roads maybe? This truck has seen a lot of wild rides. Are you up for it, soldier?" She buckled up and he grinned, liking the idea.

"Our first year at base Timber would always take me out to the forests. He loved the mud and the dirt," he recalled and she nodded.

"Dad used to get so pissed when El borrowed his truck after he turned sixteen and went through the backwoods with me. Okay, go straight and then the first turn into the forest is the one you can take."

He arched a brow at her. "Sure we won't get lost?"

There was a sparkle in her eye. "My brother taught me well, you'll see."

He didn't have the slightest doubt and yet knew he wouldn't go as wild as Elton was known to, because his friend would never forgive him if his little sister was hurt in anyway, and Micah could all but see Timber haunting him from his grave.

That thought almost made him smile.

Chapter 2

Sarah turned on the porch, wondering if maybe she should've given Micah the time to get over seeing his friend's grave first, but she worried he wouldn't come back then.

He rubbed his hands along his pants before standing straighter, the army green reminding her of her brother so much, she felt the need to scream and cry. Micah surprised her by opening his arms for her.

"Hey, come on. Had I known I'd be seeing anyone, I'd have changed into normal clothes," he whispered as she went into the arms he held open for her.

God, she was really small compared to him she realized as her head didn't even reach his chin. Instead she heard his heart race under her ear.

They'd spent two hours in the forest and the truck until she'd had the feeling he was more relaxed, and then she'd asked him to come and meet her parents because everyone had heard so much about him, it was as if they knew him.

Micah had admitted to having planned on offering her parents his condolences anyway, so convincing him had been somewhat easy.

Stepping back, she took his hand, drawing him up to the porch, but she felt as if she was tugging on a mountain.

"It'll be okay," she promised when the door opened and her mother came out. Sarah dropped his hand as he saluted.

"First Lieutenant Micah McCain. Ma'am, I came to offer you my condolences. I am sorry I am late, but I just now returned from Iraq."

"He came straight to Ashburn," Sarah explained, her eyes on her mother.

"We know who you are, soldier. Come on in, we are about to have dinner and everyone will be delighted to have you here," she announced and then turned in the door.

Micah looked honestly frightened.

Sarah stepped up to him, tilting her head back until he met her eyes. "You are going to war zones all over the world regularly, and yet you're afraid to step into a house with people who'll welcome you like a friend?" she asked and he sighed.

"It's different. I suddenly feel ignorant because I never wanted to hear his family stories. I don't know anything about you. I couldn't even have said if he had brothers or sisters or both," he admitted and she turned on the second step leading up to the porch.

She knew his story, knew more about him than he was probably aware, and her heart went out to him.

"We've heard about your loss, soldier." It was one of the reasons why her brother had put in his will what he had, but Sarah wasn't sure Micah was ready for that yet.

"Sarah…" It was the first time he'd said her name and something inside of her clicked, as if she'd waited a lifetime to hear that one word spoken the way he had.

Lowering her eyes, she wondered if maybe she should drive him back into town after all.

The Timber-Farm was a little outside of Ashburn, contrary direction of the cemetery, and she knew he had a room at a small B&B in town for the night.

She didn't know what he'd planned for the day after, but when they'd talked earlier—or rather with what little he'd offered—she guessed he didn't know where he wanted to go and what he wanted to do.

At thirty-two the soldier before her was lost, drifting in a sea of loneliness, and it had taken her less than two hours to see it.

Shaking her head, she turned away from him, feeling his hand on her arm, his warmth burning through her jacket.

"Sarah," he repeated, this time imploring. She turned to him, both of them the same height now, and held his eyes.

"What is it, Micah? Are you scared you could actually enjoy being here? Or worried it could suck donkey balls?"

It used to be Elton's favorite expression and she saw Micah smirk.

"I don't belong here."

She placed her hand on his chest. "You belonged here after basic training. You weren't just a brother-in-arms to Elton, Micah. You were his brother. He loved you like one. He talked about you like he would about a brother. All we're missing are your half naked baby pictures. Come inside. Give us a chance to welcome you into the family the way Elton wished he could've done." She bit her tongue to not say more and Micah gritted his teeth, his jaw moving, until finally nodding.

"Stay by my side. I hold you personally responsible if this turns into a disaster." His expression was serious, but his tone held a hint of amusement.

"Then don't mess up." And with that she vanished inside the house, knowing he'd follow, and hoping he'd feel comfortable with them all at some point.

* * *

"It was you with the bikini, wasn't it?" Micah couldn't help the laugh bursting from his lips, staring at Timber's oldest sister. Tara was taller than Sarah, her eyes blue, her hair dark wavy in contrary to her sister's. Timber's had always been so short, Micah didn't know it if was curly or straight.

"I cannot believe he told you about that," he exclaimed, but really, it was obvious Timber had told his family *everything*.

Sarah sat to his right, quieter than he'd anticipated while her family watched him.

Joe and Margie Timber, Timber's parents, were the kind you always saw on TV: friendly, welcoming, warm, and full of love for their children. Timber's middle sister, Jenny, was missing from the family dinner, but he'd been assured it was for good reasons.

It sounded as if this family hardly ever ate separated.

"Why would you run around base in a bikini?" Tara asked and he shifted in his chair.

"I lost a bet, and I'm a man of my word."

Sarah cleared her throat next to me. "Timber would've let you get away without doing it," she stated and met his eyes. There was something in her gaze he couldn't place, then she stood and excused herself.

Silence fell over the room as she exited it and Micah followed her with his eyes until she had vanished from his view.

"She was the youngest, and Elton the oldest. He adored her, protected her, hung out with her. Losing him has been harder on her than on anyone else, and we don't even need to pretend otherwise," Margie explained and Micah shrugged.

"I can see why he would feel that way about her." If she'd be his sister, he'd go all protective over her, too. She was sunshine in a small package, but the way she'd looked just before leaving made him wish he could do something to ease the pain.

However, they had talked about Timber the whole time in the car. He didn't understand why this was any different.

"I should get going," he eventually muttered. He'd still have to walk a few miles unless he found someone ready to drive him.

"We didn't have dessert yet," Tara protested and Micah laughed. He shouldn't be surprised, and yet he couldn't have another bite. There'd been a roast he'd had three helpings of, along with mashed potatoes and veggies, and it was probably the best meal he'd ever had.

"Thank you, but I feel like a turkey on Thanksgiving." He got to his feet and so did the rest of the family. "I'm going to head out."

And he planned on finding Sarah first. "I'll just go and say goodbye." The three other Timbers nodded while he went in search of the youngest family member, surprised no one had offered him directions, yet when he'd made his ways up the stairs he found a long hallway and one door half open, Timber's favorite band playing, and he knew where to go.

He knocked, finding Sarah by a window. She turned to him while he ignored the room that clearly had been Timber's for all his life. With a passing glance he'd seen discarded shoes and teenager's posters, faded and out-dated.

"I'm… I should go."

Sarah seemed small and breakable as she smiled at him through a curtain of tears, wiping at her cheeks. Something squeezed inside of him and he almost pressed his hand onto his chest to check if he was still complete.

"Yeah. Listen… come to dinner tomorrow. We're having barbecue and you aren't in a hurry."

He hadn't said it like that, but feared she'd deducted that—correctly—from his confession about not knowing where best to go.

The thing was, he wasn't sure he wanted to stay.

"Sarah," he whispered and she closed her eyes, then forced another smile, nodding toward the door.

"I'm gonna bring you downstairs, okay?"

He hesitated for a moment, wondering if there was something he should say, but then just nodded and stepped aside, this time letting her lead the way.

"It was good having you here, son," Joe said in earnest, meeting them at the door, and hugged him. Micah couldn't remember the last time he'd gotten a hearty hug like that.

"I told him to come for the barbecue tomorrow," Sarah explained from the stairs and Joe instantly nodded.

"We'd love to have you," he agreed, then it was Margie's turn to hug him before Tara threw her arms around him.

"It was so good meeting you!"

He gave the sentiment back, then opened the door, hoping Sarah would follow and therefore drive him because he really didn't feel like walking, although it was easy enough to find his way. To the end of the driveway, left, and then always straight until reaching the Ashburn city limits.

To his luck she followed him, being on the porch steps as he turned. Behind her the doorway was empty, yet he felt as if they were being watched.

This was worse than returning Lena Mittens after their first dance in High school, and he hadn't even been on a date with Sarah.

She reached into her pocket, hesitating for a moment, then she handed over the truck keys. "Here, take the beast back," she ordered and he reached out for the keys although he knew it meant he had to return here at least once, if he wanted to or not.

"Don't get lost," she winked and he grinned, wondering why her hug was the only one he didn't seem to get—and yet suddenly craved.

"I'm sure I can find the way." He forced his hands into his pockets,

Help Our Heroes

reluctant to go, no matter how ridiculous that was.

"Thank you for having been here," she eventually said into the silence and Micah nodded.

"It was fun and... well, cozy. I cannot remember the last time I'd had such a pleasant dinner." Because whenever he was at his sister's, things were quiet, rather sterile. They used to be like the Timbers, loud and boisterous, before his parents had died.

It was only when standing there, looking at the Timbers' farm, that he considered that maybe they should've been like that after their parents' death, too, to honor their memories.

"My family's something else," she agreed and he realized she couldn't meet his eyes any longer. Stepping closer again, he grabbed her chin, forcing her eyes to meet his. It was like she was a totally changed person, had been from the moment they'd entered together.

"Sarah, what is going on?"

She lowered her eyes, but he just squeezed a little more, not enough to hurt her, but enough to catch her attention again.

"I'm lost... Have been since he died. I don't know who I am any longer, and being with my family without him is... I feel like I'm fourteen all over again, having to manage my life without him there."

She looked young then, so much younger than she had before, grief-stricken and lost, and Micah felt a wave of tenderness rush through him.

"Come here," he whispered and drew her in. "He wouldn't want that, you know that, right?"

He felt the way her fingers curled into his jacket at his back, holding onto him tighter, but staying silent.

"I'll see you tomorrow, okay?" he asked as she didn't say anything.

"Okay."

Stepping back from her was harder than it ever had been to step back from his own sister.

He got into the truck, wondering why in the world he hadn't refused to take it, but instead had even promised to come back, and surely not just to drop off the truck.

Chapter 3

Sarah made her way to the inside of the house the next day. She loved working on the farm, loved being close to home and in contrary to most people, she didn't mind living at home again at twenty-four.

"Sarah, darling, can you please come here for a second?" her mother called and Sarah gritted her teeth. This was the reason she tried to avoid being inside the house as much as possible.

"Coming." Maybe she shouldn't have given up her small apartment in Ashburn. Then again, her parents wouldn't have left her alone there, either.

She entered the kitchen, smiling as she saw the chicken wings marinating while her mother worked over the patties for the burgers.

"Would you mind helping me with the potato salad?" she asked innocently enough and Sarah nodded, washing up before getting out a knife.

They worked in silence for a while, Sarah's task the same it had been since she'd turned twelve, and yet it took only twenty minutes until her mother cleaned her hands and sat down in a chair.

"I thought you didn't go to the cemetery every day anymore," she started and Sarah made sure she kept her features neutral.

"I don't. Luckily I'd been there yesterday or we wouldn't have known Micah was in town," she replied.

"He said he'd wanted to come by anyway," her mother pointed out.

Sarah wasn't sure about that. She'd seen the hesitation in him, and wasn't the least bit surprised.

When Elton had mentioned Micah hardly ever listened to back-home stories, she'd thought it was an understatement, but that man was more scared of family and connections than anyone she'd ever met.

"Maybe," Sarah conceded, hoping that was the end of the talk, but she should've known better.

"He reminds me of you, you know?"

Sarah's head snapped up. "*Micah* reminds you of *me*?" The notion was ridiculous. He stood with both feet on the ground, his life sorted and orderly, had reached something in the army and definitely wasn't as bubbly as Sarah normally was.

"Yes. You're both adrift in a sea of loneliness, no light to guide you, no place to hold onto. You don't have anywhere you two belong, and it couldn't be more obvious."

Sarah laughed, the sound incredulous, and she knew it. "I have a place I belong. Right here."

"You should be in an office, doing paralegal work the way you learned it instead of working on a farm. You should meet people you're not related to. You should be dating and breaking hearts. You should spread sunshine, and you haven't since it happened."

"Since Elton died. You can say it. I'm not gonna break down. I'm okay. I love being on the farm, and I don't need to see people."

No, she didn't want to hang out with her friends because they didn't understand her, hadn't been touched by pain the way she had.

"You're not okay, and it's worrying your father and me."

Sarah placed the knife down louder than was necessary. "If you want me to move out, just say so. I'll find a place. No worries." She didn't say that she was being paid by her father only and that it would make it impossible to pay rent and feed herself. She also didn't say that she was terrified of moving away from home again and forgetting Elton altogether.

Neither did she point out that she was drowning, and people didn't realize it most of the time because she smiled and beamed and sang anyway.

Only with Micah there it had been impossible, because the way he'd talked, the way everyone had acted around him was exactly how it would've been with Elton.

It had caused her to miss Elton more than all the other days, even if she was acutely aware of the fact that Micah wasn't Elton.

They didn't look anything alike, but for a few minutes last night during dinner Sarah had been able to catch a glimpse at the easy-going guy her brother had considered his best friend even when life had pulled them apart.

Her mother sighed in exasperation. "We don't want you to move out. We want you to wear an honest smile. We want you happy. We want you to remember El would've wanted you to live, and not wither away. I—"

"I'm fine, Mom. Excuse me." She left the kitchen, went straight to the front door and back out. She hesitated a moment, wondering where to go, and went for the barn. It had been her hiding place during her teenage years, and the only person who'd ever sought her there had been El when he'd been home. Those first years after he'd joined the Army had been the worst. After that he'd been home much more, doing shorter tours and spending the time then with his family.

They'd gotten even closer—until he'd been shot while being out of the country.

War sucked, and Sarah sighed as she climbed the steps in the barn.

She'd always hated knowing her brother was away and in danger, but in the end it all hadn't mattered because it had been what he'd loved above all… and even his wife hadn't been able to ground him fully.

She assumed that was what happened if you fell in love with a soldier. It would always be the Army first, and everything else after.

* * *

Micah hadn't been able to find any sleep. The bed in the Bed and Breakfast he'd stayed in had been comfortable enough, but his mind had been on Timber's little sister.

And she, too, was the first thing he saw when returning to the farm, but she seemed to be preoccupied, almost in distress. Micah considered giving her privacy as he watched her vanish inside the barn, but something within him urged him to follow her, to make sure she was ok.

Almost as if Timber was by his side, telling him it was what he'd do.

There were a few horses inside the barn, as well as an old tractor, and yet Micah didn't spot Sarah downstairs, leading him to believe she'd made her way up to the hayloft. It was almost fully filled, and it took him a moment until he heard shuffling to his left, following the noise.

He found her by a window, overlooking pastures and paddocks, her dark hair blowing in the breeze coming in through the wide window.

"Sarah," he muttered as he stood almost directly next to her, and she winced, taking a step back. Micah reached out instantly as her heel caught on a bent floorboard, causing her to stumble. Drawing her against his chest, he kept her from falling out of the window, and his heart did a panicked jolt at the thought of her hurt.

Her face darkened and she pushed herself off him. "Micah! Are you trying to kill me?"

He almost smirked as her eyes went over him, and he liked the appreciation he saw in hem—before they darkened with anger again.

"I didn't expect anyone to be up here. You could've called my name before or so," she snapped and he reached for her arm as she wanted to pass him.

"You didn't hear the truck coming, and that makes me think something's wrong. I..." He trailed off, unsure of what to say because he usually left people alone. If someone wanted to talk to him, they would.

Only with Sarah he didn't see himself ever letting her run off, upset.

And that almost sounded as if he planned on sticking around.

"What's going on?" he asked gently and she sighed, combing her fingers through her hair.

"I had a fight with mom. Supposedly dad and she are worried and... You know, it doesn't matter."

It mattered to him. "Because you're hiding?"

She blinked up at him, those blue eyes suspicious, and he almost smiled.

"I'm not hiding."

"You're what? Twenty-five? You shouldn't be living at home. You shouldn't be looking like a seventeen-year-old. You cannot get back your teenage years, even if you throw temper tantrums like one."

She gaped at him. "I don't."

He cocked his head. "Running out into the barn because you didn't like what your mother said? Temper tantrum like a teen," he pointed out. He wanted to antagonize her to maybe get her to scream and cry, because it would make her feel better, and then she could talk to him and maybe tell him what was going on, but it was working only half way.

"You don't know me, Micah. And no matter what, you're not my big brother. I can do what I want and you—"

"Care," he finished for her because he did. He had no idea why or how or when, but he did.

She watched him in silence for a moment and then shook her head, wanting to leave him standing, but he wouldn't have that.

"Why am I here, Sarah?" She froze with her back to him, needing a second, then she turned.

"Because you had the truck?" she offered and he closed the distance between them.

"No, why did you take me back to the house? Why did you give me the keys to the truck in the first place? Why invite me to dinner again?"

She lowered her head and he touched her arm, wanting her to look at him.

"Elton knew you'd come. Elton prepared for you to come. I don't know if he changed his will regularly, or if he had planned on leaving it the way it was forever and ever, but I know he wrote letters every year. They were with his will. I got one, and so did the family," she admitted.

He wasn't surprised she'd gotten a special one.

"And so did I, didn't I?" he asked.

A small smile played over her lips. "Snooping in a car that's not yours?" she questioned and he shrugged.

"I didn't snoop. There was a lamp lighting up and I figured there had to be a handbook somewhere. The truck is so old, I didn't even know what it meant."

She grinned now, making him grin in return. "And, did you fill it up with gas?"

"Sure did. However, it's not exactly the polite way, is it? Letting the stranger go in an empty truck."

Sarah sobered. "I'll pay you back. I didn't realize it was so low after our trip through the forest."

"That thing burns gas like crazy," he accused and she nodded, then she sighed.

"I didn't read your letter. Just put it in the truck because…" She shrugged and he realized there was something else she didn't say, but he didn't press.

"Wanna know what it said?" he asked and then waited as she considered the offer.

Eventually she pointed over to the wall, nodding him to follow her. "Let me hear."

He took the paper out of his pocket while she slid down on the wall, looking at him, waiting.

"Ready?"

She nodded, albeit hesitant. Micah cleared his throat, then he started reading.

"Mic,

You've been my brother for the better part of my life. Not the better part as in years, but as in quality time and... you know, it doesn't matter. You reading this means I'm dead. I hope it was with Cathy by my side while we did the deed. You know, it would be an epic death.

Then again, it most likely wasn't.

Thank you for having seen my family. Is Sarah okay? Tell me she's okay. Hell, she most likely isn't.

I couldn't move away because of her. She's the baby of the family, the most emotional one, the one with the biggest heart... the one easily broken. I need you to look out for her, okay? Beat up the guys that want to date her. Find the idiots who hurt her.

Talk to her.

Someone has to because I can't any longer.

But... don't hug her. I want her to remember my hugs. And remember, she's my sister.

My family needs you, okay? Watch out for them occasionally.

Take care, Lieutenant.

Timber."

"How could you forget that I'm his sister?" she asked, confused, as he lowered the letter, and Micah grinned to himself.

"No idea." He had a very good idea what Timber had meant, but didn't think Sarah needed to know. Especially because he wasn't looking for a quick adventure.

No, he was there to indeed make sure she'd be okay, and somehow, seeing her that afternoon, he knew she definitely wasn't.

* * *

Being with the family, spending time with them, had become the center point of Sarah's life. She was terrified of losing more relatives, no matter how distant. She knew it wasn't normal, the anxiety she felt at that thought, or the need to stay where she was, but it didn't matter.

She'd be okay in a few weeks, that much she was sure of.

"S?"

She turned on the porch, wiping her tears away. She hadn't even realized they were falling.

"Tara. Is the food ready yet?" No matter how early they started, her father had a tendency to wait too long and draw out dinner until half of the family was starving.

"Surprisingly yes. Micah took over, and it seems he knew what he was doing. The steaks are perfect. You'll love them. Come on. Don't stand around alone here in the front while everyone else is in the back."

Tara took her hand, drawing her along, but as much as Sarah had looked forward to the food, she suddenly didn't see herself eating any of it.

She found her family at the table, Micah standing by the grill, and she took his side.

He wore his pain and solitude like armor, and it made her feel as if she could be lonely with him because he'd understand.

"Eat, Sarah," he muttered while turning some patties on the grill.

"I'm not hungry really," she replied and he took a plate to put a patty on, handing it to her.

"Do me the favor and eat, okay?" he pleaded and she sighed.

The things to prepare the burger were on a table nearby and she watched him as she prepared her food the way she liked it most: no onions, but more than enough cheese, some bacon and lettuce on top of the sauces.

Her mouth watered and still she didn't sit down with her family.

"I swear they have manners," she announced before biting into her burger. Micah looked up at her.

"Who?"

Sarah nodded her head over to her family. "Them," she said around a mouthful and swallowed before continuing. "Normally you don't let the guest do the hard work."

He laughed, his eyes sparkling with amusement, then he shrugged. "I honestly don't mind. I fear Timber told too many embarrassing stories about me, so I rather stay away from the dinner table where everyone's going to try and remind me of them."

Sarah grinned, chewing before she cleared her throat. "He didn't only tell us the fun stuff. He also told us about the hard parts. Losing comrades and how you made it all better by keeping your head focused and not letting everyone fall apart. It makes me wonder though…"

She watched him as he turned the last patties, deciding they were done. He placed them on a cooking grate a little higher and then closed the smoker to keep them warm and finish the chicken wings off.

She followed him over to the porch steps and sat down while he took a sip of his beer.

"Makes you wonder what?" he asked.

"When did you allow yourself to fall apart and feel the loss?"

She rested her head on her arms, watching him from the side, but he was no longer focused on her, and the smile had left his face.

"Who said you have to fall apart?"

She shrugged. "Yeah, who says a soldier has to have feelings and live them?"

He snorted, almost sounding disbelieving. "I have feelings," he insisted.

She leveled him with a hard stare. "You do? Can't remember Elton ever telling us that you showed weakness, or emotions and—"

"When I heard Elton had fallen, I beat up a private for being an ass."

She arched a brow. "What did he do?"

"Crowded a female soldier and was trying to grope her."

She snorted. "He deserved it."

Micah shook his head, guilt written all over his face. "I shouldn't have lost it with him. I should be better than that. However, lucky for me there won't be repercussions. It could've cost me everything."

"You can lose it here, Micah. You can kick trees and the barn, and the truck even. Elton used to do that. You can scream and cry. You can miss all those people and—"

"I'm fine."

She didn't believe that and wondered how far to push him.

"Are you? Is that why you don't date, why you don't have a girlfriend? Or a boyfriend? Is that why you aren't spending that much time with your family? Is that—"

He stood so suddenly, she winced. His eyes were hard as they met her gaze. "What did you say earlier? You don't know me? Yeah, same. Just because your brother told you tons about me, or so you think, doesn't mean you know anything about me," he forced out and then hesitated before placing the bottle of beer down and walking around the house. She glanced at her family, but they acted oblivious, making it clear they expected her to get him back.

But… did she even want that? Having him there confused her because she had no idea what Elton had thought she could do for Micah.

Besides, she didn't have the feeling Micah even knew how much he absolutely *wasn't* okay.

* * *

Micah fumed as he walked away from the Timber's farm. Who exactly was Sarah to think she'd pecked him fully? Knew what he was or wasn't feeling?

He couldn't believe Timber had told his family so much about him, especially because it had been years since they'd last met.

"Micah, wait."

No, he didn't want to wait, especially not for Sarah. He saw the sunshine within her, saw the cracks in the broken exterior, and could imagine vividly how she'd been before Timber had died.

He could all but see her laughing out loud, dancing around and enjoying the rain falling on her face. She'd probably been ever-smiling, and would joke and wink all the time.

Sometimes he saw it on her face, a playful wink there, and it twisted a knife in his heart because he could understand why Timber had been as protective of her as he'd been.

Someone like her needed a good guy, and no guy could ever reach up to the standard required. He was sure about that because in his mind no one would be able to match up. Suddenly a small hand wrapped around his wrist and she pulled him to a stop.

"I'm sorry," Sarah said, her cheeks flushed while he almost smirked. He'd forgotten how much distance he could cover when he was angry. "Come back."

At this he shook his head because he'd been there too long anyway. He'd wanted to do nothing more than give Timber's parents his condolences.

Two days there had been two days too long.

"I'm not coming back. Tell your family thank you for everything, will you?"

Her brows furrowed and he wanted to reach out to smooth her forehead.

"That's it? You're running? Was that why you didn't talk to Timber anymore? Because he said things you didn't like and didn't want to hear? Is that why you don't face your family?"

He coughed in disbelief, wondering what he could say to her, but then decided her accusations weren't even worth a reply. Instead he stepped around her.

"You need us, Micah, just like we need you," she called after him.

"I'm not Timber, and I'm certainly not here to fill the shoes you expect me to fill." He didn't bother turning for that, just hoped the wind would carry it back.

"You couldn't be Timber because he let people close, and you're a block of ice."

Finally he threw up his hands, turning to her. "What do you want me to say, Sarah? You have me all figured out. You know what I feel and think. You know how I am. After just a little over twenty-four hours around me, you figured me out." He walked back to her, surprised to see angry tears in her eyes, but then he assumed it was the sarcasm dripping from his voice.

"Where are you gonna go, huh? What are you gonna do?" she asked harshly.

He didn't know, but considered just driving a car across the country roads, pausing only occasionally to check out the landscape, and then he'd count down the days until his next deployment.

Or could he stay there? Because that was ultimately what she was asking for, wasn't it?

For a moment he entertained the idea. Being on the farm, helping out. Visiting Timber's grave regularly, talking to him.

Having a place and a reason to be in the US besides counting down the days.

Then again, this wasn't his place to be. Timber should be standing where he was standing.

"See my family." And that literally meant to drop by, say hi and show he was alive, then he'd be off.

She arched a brow. "And then?"

"You piss me off. I can't remember when I last met someone who managed so easily to rile me up. I don't owe you explanations." But he suddenly wanted to give them to her, and that was what sealed the deal for him.

No more wondering, no more what ifs.

"I piss you off because you know I'm right, and because—"

"No," he interrupted. "You piss me off because you think you have a right to talk about me being closed off and all, but you're hiding here. Go and work. Date. Live. Don't stay here, and maybe when you do, so will I."

He wouldn't. He belonged in the army and that was what he'd live for until they didn't want him any longer.

Tears were streaming down her face and it caused him to lick his lips, acknowledging the fact that he wanted to make her feel better.

"The letter was in the truck because he wanted you to have it. Take it. No matter where, take it. You were like his brother, and he gave something to his family, to each of us. You got the truck," she whispered.

Micah gaped at her, knowing how her heart was stuck to that truck, and he couldn't believe Timber would've put that in his will, wanted Micah to own that truck. He stepped even closer to her, framing her face.

Help Our Heroes

"No, you keep it. I couldn't bring it anywhere with me and—"

"Stay and drive it here. Work the farm with my dad. Help us out. We need it. Do something normal, something that has nothing to do with weapons or desert heat. Please, Micah. Please."

He should've let go of her face, should've stopped brushing the tears from her cheeks, but he didn't.

He should've also wondered why she was so insistent, but he didn't do that, either.

"I cannot stay, Sarah. I'm not ready to…" He trailed off, not sure what he wanted to say.

"Be whole?" she offered and he rested his forehead against hers.

The gesture felt so right and yet so foreign, making him realize that he'd never before felt the need to be close to a woman that way.

"Keep the truck safe for me until I'm back, okay?" He knew he was lying about coming back, but it seemed to placate her.

Someone like Sarah deserved more than another soldier in her life, because she'd been through enough with losing her brother, and if Micah stayed around, the whole family was at risk of losing someone else they'd included.

"You have some weeks before you have to leave. I know they ground you before letting you go again. Stay," she begged again.

"No." The word wasn't more than a breath because he was tempted. Having her so close he wanted to stick around just to tickle Timber's Sarah out of the broken girl, but that bore a whole new danger.

"Yes."

"Sarah."

New tears started to fall then, hitting his fingers where they still lay against her cheeks, framing her face.

"I'll light a candle for you and put it my window so you'll you find your way back no matter how far you're lost in darkness. You were Elton's best friend. You have a place with this family, Micah, whenever you need it. Promise me you won't forget that," she begged and he did something he probably shouldn't have done.

He kissed her, kissed her until he was breathless.

He didn't believe she'd put on a candle every night, but he also knew he'd never find out because…

Sarah was a woman to fall in love with and Micah had no mind to risk something like that.

"Goodbye, Sarah," he whispered against her lips and then pulled back.

She didn't let go, and he grabbed her wrists, wanting to make her let go without hurting her.

"Just don't fucking die because we'd never find out," she called after him and he hung his head, wondering if he should be putting her name in where they asked about who should be informed in case of him being killed in action.

Then again, he hoped to forget about her soon. Women were a distraction he couldn't deal with when trying to free kidnapped people; to fight in a war that wasn't his own and yet could be decided by a single man.

Micah wasn't made for relationships and perfect images.

Micah was made to help young soldiers out in situations that were all about killing dreams.

His life was about making sure others survived long enough to see their dreams come true.

* * *

She'd failed. That was all Sarah could think as she watched Micah's retreating back. She knew when a fight was lost, and Micah didn't want anyone in his world.

He'd not be back, either, but she hadn't thought telling him she knew would've changed anything.

However, she knew it wouldn't keep her from lighting a candle because holy hell, she was lost in darkness, but at least she saw stars occasionally.

Micah on the other hand? He had nothing to guide him home safely, and that was what truly broke her heart.

Epilogue

Sarah,

When he's there. Don't let him go. Micah is on a one-way-street to self-destruct, and keeping people at arm's length is his specialty.

Yours is touching hearts, so do your magic, touch his.

He gave up on his family when his parents died, gave up on the notion of happiness when he was too young to give it up.

His sister gave up on him, too, I think. She no longer tries, but I know our family. We have so much room for lost people, so I know you can get him to feel something, to not risk it all.

Sarah, I owe him everything. Many people do. He's my best friend, was from the moment we started basic training together.

Don't let him get killed, without him ever knowing what it meant to love, to hope, because he forgot.

He forgot what it was like to truly smile, too.

I found my smile in Cathy.

He can find his in our family.

Dad needs the help on the farm.

Mom needs someone to take care of.

You are the only one who can convince him to stay.

Do it.

He needs a family, and I need to know you'll heal each other.

I'm sorry I left before you ever got married. I love you, Sarah. I love you so much, and I'll haunt all the idiots trying to date you because no one is good enough.

Find someone who almost is.

Love, El

Man Down

Alice La Roux

Corporal James Rees is trapped in a world of pain. Injured in an attack upon his convoy in Afghanistan, he refuses to believe that he will ever heal. As his life crumbles around him, his parents struggling, his fiancée in denial, in walks his new physio, Beatrice. She's a sassy, smart-mouthed optimist who takes crap from no one, including him. When these two butt heads over his recovery, sparks fly. But will the man who is afraid of being burned accept that his prison is partly of his own making. Self-pity will get him nowhere where Beatrice Taylor is concerned.

* * *

Note from the Author

What you're about to read is the beginning of Man Down. What started as a short story has now grown and the full length book will be released later this year but this means that there's a bit of a cliff-hanger. If you want raw and gritty with just a hint of alpha male, then please give Man Down a chance and enjoy this little taster of what's to come!

Help Our Heroes

Chapter 1

Beatrice

"Come on big boy, stop being a wimp," I call out across the room, standing with my hands on my hips.

"I am not a wimp—I have fought in wars!"

"And yet you're chickening out of a little leg action?" I raise my eyebrow at the soldier sat in his chair before me. I was goading him, of course I was. If these army boys responded to anything it was a challenge, daring them to do something. Proving me wrong over the next few weeks would be the only thing that kept him going some days, that's why it was important to build a good relationship with my clients. I wasn't just their physio—I was the person who kept on at them. It was easy to push away a family member, to shut yourself in a cocoon of hurt—not so easy with a stranger who is holding you accountable. That would mean defeat and these soldiers, they weren't quitters, and they'd merely had a stumble is all.

Scowling, Lieutenant William Keen, put one foot on the floor, followed by the other and very slowly stood. I could hear his breathing speed up as the knee pain kicked in but I was here to see progress so I couldn't let him sit his arse back down.

"See was that so hard? Now take a step towards me, gently—and use the bars if you need to," I say indicating to the bars either side of him.

"If I need to. Pffft!" He scoffs, taking that step.

We had been working on building up strength in his leg after the accident so far with swimming and using a peddling exerciser, but this was the first time he had his whole weight behind him and I was impressed. I nodded to my colleague and quickly jotted down some notes on my clipboard about how the knee was looking. It was going to take weeks of little movements, a step or two and then resting, swimming and exercising the muscle before he would see a huge improvement but these men don't need huge—they just need that first step. I can see the determination on his face and that's when I know he's realised that the treatment plan works. The sweat beading on his forehead is an indicator that he's getting tired; his body isn't ready to be pushed hard just yet.

"Take a seat Lieutenant, we're done on the bars for a moment. Let's do some stretches on the floor shall we?"

I help him lower himself onto the mats and plonk myself down beside him. Now was the hard part, reining him in from his victory so that he didn't cause further damage to himself by trying to do too much in one go. Reading body language and facial expressions is a large part of this job, the body tells you what the patient won't. So the giant shit eating grin on his face told me that I was in for a long afternoon.

* * *

"Bea is that you?" A voice calls out into the darkness.

"Who else is it going to be Poppy?" I sigh, wondering why the hell the flat was having a blackout.

"Did you forget to pay the electric again?" She asks, stumbling out into the hallway.

"I pay the water and the gas, you pay the electric!"

"I do?" I can practically hear her head tilt and the puppy dog eyes burning into me, even in the pitch black.

"Ohhhh Bea...I'm sorry! I'm so sorry. I'll sort something."

Groaning I dump my bag into the hallway, today had been a very, very long day. My current patient was making a promising recovery but he was also starting to push hard and was at risk of tearing a ligament. I just needed the man to walk but he was determined to fly. I had seen the pain he was in after our session, his wife had told me the agony he'd endured the next day as if it was my fault, but I'm only there to guide him. What does she want me to do, chain him down?

I hear gentle footsteps moving towards me, my flatmate shuffling around the kitchen trying to find a torch. I hear a triumphant "yay!", followed by "shit" as she realises we never replaced the batteries after the last time. I love Poppy, she

Help Our Heroes

was the happiest, brightest soul but she was also absent minded and very, *very* scatty. It had only gotten worse since she'd lost her job at the dentist surgery last month. I could cover her half of the rent, barely, but we'd manage and then she'd forget to actually pay the bills. Taking a deep breath I reach out and try to find her in the blackness, my hand clasps around something soft and I'm touching her hair, she's crouched on the floor by our sink.

Wrapping my arms around her I whisper "It's going to be okay, I'll fix this."

I feel her tremble beneath me as she gives a silent sob, this month has been hard on both of us but I was always the stronger one, it was my job to make sure she was okay. I stumble back out by the door, dig my phone out of the bottom of my bag and use it to light the way, Poppy following close behind.

"Why didn't I think of that?" she says with a small chuckle as she wipes away a tear, pulling her phone out of her cardigan pocket, "Oh. It's dead."

"Because you never remember to charge it," I say laughing.

When we're in my room I dig out a lighter from the drawer, load Poppy up with all the candles I have and send her around the flat to make sure we have some sort of light for the night while I call the electric company who promise to have everything up and running by the morning. With that done and dusted I jump in the shower, thanking god that we had a boiler to power it and not an electric one like Poppy's dad wanted installed.

* * *

Getting into work early, I'm desperate to charge my phone and use a kettle. A cup of tea always helps everything. My phone finally plugged in, it buzzes to life and within seconds it begins ringing. I frown when I see who it is but reluctantly I answer.

"Edith, why are you calling?" I ask with a sigh. I'd worked for Edith when I was training on placement. She was a tough nut, but ultimately one of the best in our field. She always called me foolish for taking a job in the public sector; the NHS didn't deserve me apparently.

"I have a job for you," she states, bold as brass.

"I don't work for you anymore, remember?"

"Don't be awkward Bea, I'm calling because I have a case that isn't improving and I think I need some of your magic tough-love and charm act."

"I can't, I'm swamped helping patients at St Jude's."

"Private sector pays more sweetie, you know that. And *I know* you need the money."

"Edith...I can't just drop everything."

"Look, use your holidays. I know you need to take them by April and I bet you haven't even used one. Come and work with Corporal Rees."

I hesitate, the money would be nice - especially with Poppy losing her job at the dental clinic.

Edith keeps pushing, "The pay is phenomenal."

"Yeah, for a reason. So spit it out."

"He's a refuser."

"Is that all?" I'd worked with stubborn soldiers refusing to take physio seriously but before the day was out I had them exercising and moving those damaged limbs. There had to be more to it than that because Edith was one hell of a stubborn woman, refusers crumbled beneath her critical gaze and big baby blue eyes.

"He's a refuser with extensive injuries to his right side. IED went off underneath his transport."

"Mental health?"

"He's very assertive..."

"You mean he's hostile don't you?"

"Not as such. Just very...determined."

Chapter 2

James

Fuck them. The whole lot of them. Bloody-bastarding-cunts. Why can't they just leave me alone? I've done my duty, I served my Queen and now all I want is to soak in my pain like the miserable twat I am. Why does everyone want to poke and prod the cripple?

Four physiotherapists have been by today, thanks to my doctor, my mother and my ex-fiancée who still won't believe me when I say we're over. Tiffany means well, I get that. But I am not the same person I was, when will she understand that? The parade of specialists isn't helping. I know my body, I know that it will never be the same and I don't need some dick in soft, non-slip shoes and a gentle voice to tell me how to fucking stretch. I need rest and to be alone in the dark, hidden. I don't need their pity when they see my scarring. I don't need the false optimism. I need them to face the harsh reality that my body is broken beyond repair.

"Corporal Rees? Your mother sent me through…"

"Get out. I don't need to see anyone else today. I'm not a fucking sideshow."

"Damn Edith," she hisses under her breath, is she talking to herself? Have they run out of sane physiotherapists that we're now on to the nut jobs? Scraping the bottom of the barrel aren't we there mother.

"Corporal Rees...James. I've just come to talk," she says gently as she pushes open the door and creeps into my darkened room.

"You want to see my injuries. You only want to look at the freak in his natural habitat."

I wait for her to placate me, like the others did. Try to reassure me that I'm not a freak but instead she gives a short laugh.

"Well, that is quite enough of that. Pity party for one, anyone?"

I growl, fuck where did that come from? I'm turning into more of a monster every day.

I flick a switch and the lights come on, revealing my broken limbs, scarred and disfigured. I expect her to gasp—the last one did. Instead she squats down beside my wheelchair and examines my leg and arm up close. After a moment she runs her hand carefully down my leg and I can almost imagine the weight of her fingertips as they move over the thick ridges of skin, but I feel nothing. I watch her carefully, she's younger than the last one—pretty even, with her strawberry blonde hair scraped back into a ponytail and big green almond shaped eyes squinting as she takes in the damage.

"Are you done now? Realised I'm a hopeless case yet?" I say, manoeuvring my chair away from her and into the shadows.

She sighs, before putting her hands on her hips, "Corporal Rees, the only thing I'm able to diagnose from this is that you're a grumpy arse who's hindering his own recovery."

I blink, shocked at her attitude. She's mouthy, normally I like that but I don't need a physio. I don't fucking want one.

"Get out." I say my voice low and steady. I am not a mental case; I'm not an injured man unsure of what he's doing. This isn't PTSD. I want solitude. I want to be left alone. I look over at her and see the corners of her mouth quirk and for the briefest moment I feel something almost twinge in my groin. But I can't want her. I don't.

"What?" I hiss. Is she taking the piss out of me? Laughing at me in my wheelchair?

"I didn't think you'd give up so easily. For a stubborn guy, a guy who served in the army, you sure are a coward."

"I am not afraid. Do not mistake what this is for cowardice."

"Then explain it to me, what is it? Why are you stopping yourself from healing?"

"You think I'll ever heal from this?" I wave a scarred hand feebly over an even more scarred leg, "Fucking crazy—I knew it." I turn away from her now. I am tired, this conversation has worn me out and I'm done. I think she can sense my defeat as she moves away quietly.

"Chicken," I hear her mutter under her breath as she leaves, the door closing softly.

* * *

The heat is unbearable, unlike anything I've ever felt. It's like I've been eating the sand I'm surrounded by, my tongue thick and dry in my mouth. Sweat forms on my forehead and it isn't long before fat beads of moisture are rolling down my face. Fuck, the desert is a ballache. The dirt roads don't help as we're thrown about in the shitty tin can they call a Land Rover Wolf. Every bounce, every pothole, every pissing rock is being felt through my whole body as we drive back to camp.

Camp. The hellhole I've called home for the last five months is just a speck in the distance. A mirage in this oven called Afghan. But I'm good at my job, a good little soldier and that's why I'm here again. It's my third deployment and I doubt it'll be my last. A young soldier named Jones gives a groan as the next bump causes his helmet to bounce against the roof of the Wolf.

A voice crackles over the radio, it's the convoy vehicle in front. Our pace slows as we enter a village. Everyone is on alert, us, the driver, the men, the women, the children playing in the streets. Even the man with the goats up on the hill is staring. Tension so thick you could scoop it up and apply it like a fucking mud mask. This is what I hate, it's like everyone is waiting until they can breathe again, the air heavy as we all try to hold our oxygen selfishly. The silence that surrounds us like a shroud is a testament to our stubbornness. No sudden moves. The car in front rolls forward a bit faster now, picking up speed as it scouts out our path. We follow slower, cautiously. Something is wrong, I can taste it.

"Contact. Wait out." is the last thing I hear.

* * *

"James, love, it's time to get up." My mother's soft voice fills the room and it feels like I'm a child all over again as she pulls up the blinds and sunlight warms my face. I don't want to open my eyes, because I know what will confront me when I do. I try to roll over, the stiffness sending pain through my limbs. A reminder that I am not a child. I dreamed of Camp Bastion last night, I always do.

Always bits of my memory from the camp, my attack wrapped up with nightmares of being on fire. Oh wait, I was on fire. That's why I know what it feels like, but at least in my dreams I can still feel. Is it sick that some nights I relish that? Am I fucked up that I want to go back to a moment, any moment, where my body is still my own, even if it's the one seconds before I lost it forever?

"Tiffany will be here at 10 and then the new physio Beatrice will be here at 11. We have quite a busy day ahead," she chatters on oblivious to the fact that her crippled son is not even looking at her, let alone responding.

Beatrice? She didn't look like a Beatrice. That was an old woman's name and she couldn't have been more than 28. Didn't I tell her to go away? Was she coming back to taunt me some more because if she was I had a few choice words that would make her sweat like a nun in a whorehouse. Making people uncomfortable was an art I'd been perfecting since my attack. You could get away with almost anything when people pitied you, hell I've said things that would've earned me a slap before but now people just turn red and look away as if they're the asshole. Confined to my chair I have to entertain myself somehow and being a dick seems to come naturally these days. They say it's the pain, I say that's bullshit.

"Your father will be along in a moment to help you shower. Is there anything else I can do?" She says gently as she sits on the edge of my bed and pushes strands of overgrown hair out of my eyes. My hair hasn't been a priority in months. I want to scream at her to get the fuck away from me but I can't bring myself to do it. I look at her dark eyes, bags making her look like she hasn't slept since God knows when, and I want to cry. My mother is a strong woman but I'm the reason she's struggling to hold it all together. I'm the cause of the lines around her eyes, the way her hands tremble when she touches me, the reason she sits outside my door and sobs on the nights when it's really bad. I'm not just destroying myself but all those around me, this is why Tiffany needs to leave. Why they all do.

Chapter 3

Beatrice

I'm greeted by sombre faces when I get to Corporal Rees' home the next morning. His mother's eyes are red ringed, she's obviously been crying and as for his fiancée she looks pissed off rather than sad but I'm not surprised. When you join the army it's all about the glory, the camaraderie and they don't tell you about the aftermath. His family are struggling to adjust, he is clearly struggling—refuser my arse—he's shut down completely, but it's to be expected when something like this flips your world upside down. There is *no* normal now, no right way to handle this because every case is different. If I'm going to make any headway I need to do a full assessment and I need some sort of cooperation from him, something I have a feeling I'm going to have to fight for.

Looking around I give a small smile, James Rees is a lucky man. He's alive, his family clearly want to support him because they've transformed the garage into living quarters for him and his wife-to-be has stuck by him even though he's quite clearly being a dick right now. There's only so much shit a family can put up with and I can tell by the look of exhaustion on their faces, James is toeing a thin line. He can't keep pushing and expect them not to break. Well I guess that's why I'm here, to make him see that he can heal with a little—okay—a lot of work. When I left yesterday his mother seemed amazed that I hadn't been made to cry or that I hadn't declared him a lost cause and invited me back straight away. Tiffany, the fiancée was a little more hesitant but she agreed that something needed to change and so here I was. I had four weeks to make some headway before I returned to St Jude's and the niggling suspicion in back of my head was that it wasn't going to be enough.

"Can I get you a cup of tea?" his mother, Grace, kindly asks.

I shake my head and smile, "No, thank you. How long has he been like this?"

Tiffany snorts, "What disabled? Or an asshole?"

"His mental state seems very erratic but that's to be expected." I say watching her carefully. She doesn't comfort his mother at all and seems to be distancing herself as she deliberately looks away when Grace begins to sniffle. She sits in silence, her face black for a moment before she eventually stands.

"I need to go to work, I'll call by after Grace. Nice meeting you Beatrice, good luck with him." she scoops up her handbag and is gone before either Grace or myself can reply.

"She doesn't really think he's an asshole, she's just finding it hard at the moment. They were meant to be getting married next month."

I nod, this is part of my job. I'm here to listen, to help ease the burden so that my patients can work on building themselves back up and sometimes that means caring for their family too.

"I think after the incident she thought he would get better...I think..."

"She thought the wedding would still happen?"

Grace just nods, tears falling freely down her cheeks now.

"She wouldn't let me cancel anything, it's all still booked....I think it's finally dawning on her...he could be like this forever...."

I sit and rub her back gently, "This is why I'm here. First we need to assess him and then we can get a management plan in place."

Wiping away her tears she tries to be positive, taking a deep breath and putting on a fake smile as a small part of my heart breaks.

"We have to start somewhere." she says firmly as her husband comes from James' room to let me know he's ready to start. I'm already in too deep with this family, my heart strings clutched tightly in their desperate hands like a bouquet of helium balloons but I'm about to walk into a hurricane and I don't even know it.

* * *

"If you want me to bend down and pander to you then you chose the wrong physio," I say almost forcefully as I stretch out James' right leg. I'm sat in front of his chair assessing how much movement he has. His paperwork said I was dealing with peripheral neuropathy, damage to his nerves, but I still needed to see to what extent he could feel and move his own limbs. At the moment the impairment looked severe, but he was making zero effort so getting a good read was almost impossible.

"I didn't choose you and I didn't ask you to pander. I asked you to fuck off and leave me alone," he growls, "Oww that hurts!"

"Well it would hurt less if you actually tried," I sigh, frustrated at the grown man moaning in front of me as his leg is lowered gently back down.

"I am," he hisses.

"Stop lying." I sit back with my hands on my hips and glare at him for a moment. His hair has obviously seen better days, but the rugged look is working for him. Dark strands fall down in front of his face, partially hiding his sharp nose, strong jaw line and sharp eyes. Those dark eyes have been watching me like a hawk ever since I entered the room, and even though it looks like he isn't watching now, I know he is. James Rees is too much the soldier to relax around me and right now I need to play on that, I need him to be a fighter, to prove me wrong. It'd been six months since his attack, he spent almost a month in a coma and yet the man still manage to look like a bloody Davidoff advert. Well, until you noticed the scarring that covered the right side of his body. His arm and leg clearly bore the brunt of it, angry raised flesh bloomed there and up his neck but his face seemed have healed remarkably well. Blinking slowly I realise he's openly examining me now as I had been him. It's not unusual, new patients always try to get a read on me so they can see if I'm a pushover, but there's something in the intensity of his gaze that unnerves me. It's like he's trying to burn my flesh with just a look and it almost works, the hair on the back of my neck raising. His lips twist into a slow smile as if he knows the effect he's having on me.

"You ready to stop being lazy?" I ask breaking the tension and he snorts.

I carefully wrap my hands back around his ankle, his skin warm beneath my touch and stretch out his leg once again, only this time it's easier. It looks like someone has finally realised I'm not going anywhere. I quickly scribble some notes down. The damage is bad, but with a proper exercise plan in place his mobility could be greatly improved. The way his finger twitches involuntarily as I hold his wrist also has me hopeful that some of the nerves have begun to repair. Nerve problems are always the hardest because there are no hard or fast rules, the nerves might be rehabilitated but on the other hand they may be irrevocably damaged. It was just a waiting game and maximising the chances for recovery through therapy. I'm not a fool, I know that he won't be magically fixed under my care but I can definitely help him if only he'd let me.

"Why did you come back? Am I going to be the pride of your portfolio? Think you can cure the cripple?" He asks as he raises his arm with my help.

"Look at me," I crouch down in front of him so we're eye level, "You are not a cripple. I have worked with cripples. What you are, is a defeatist, but I'm going to change that Corporal Rees so you better get on board and quit whining."

"Bossy cunt," I hear him mumble under his breath and I grin because he didn't argue back, challenge me or tell me to 'fuck off'. I'd call that progress.

Chapter 4

James

Fuckkkkk everything burns. Everything. Up my thighs are the worst, I feel like she's been peeling my tendons apart with jagged claws before trying to rip off my ballbag. I'm not even joking. It goes all the way up my side and back down my arms. It's like I've been on one of those medieval racks and I'm seriously resisting the urge to bite off her nose as she moves in front of me and lifts my arms above my head. Truth be told, it's the only part of her I could reach with minimal movement right now. God, my thoughts are messed up. I groan in pain, I can't help it, it leaves my mouth before I even realise and she eases my arms back down and steps away.

"I'd say we're done for today," she sounds a little out of breath and that's when I understand it isn't just me being pulled like Stretch Armstrong, she's right there alongside me.

Nodding my eyes never leave her as she does a few stretches of her own. Her back must be killing her. I hope her boyfriend rubs it when she gets home, it must be shit working a job like this every day, helping others move but then finishing as stiff as a board. I used to rub Tiffany's feet after a long day at the office and I feel angry that I'll never be able to do that again. Anger is an emotion I've become very familiar with these days, it's my constant companion. It's like a rotten seed in my chest, pushing poisonous vines out from my centre through every limb and there's nothing I can do.

"I'll be back tomorrow, the same time. I recommend a bath this evening because you're going to be a little tender," she says as she pulls her jacket on and zips it up.

I scoff, "Tender my arse."

Grinning she picks up her bag and slings it over her shoulder, "Good, I take it that means you're already feeling it."

I say nothing but I scowl, I can't help it. Admittedly I am feeling something besides the pain, I notice that I'm a little less stiff. It's like when you get up early and have that first stretch, that one where it feels like all your joints are popping out of the sockets before slotting back in again. I want to feel hopeful, like she clearly does but I know that there is no fixing what I've become. I'm trapped in this fleshy prison and she doesn't have the key, despite what she may think.

* * *

"I was talking to the venue today; they said they'd be willing to push back the wedding until the end of the year."

I say nothing, just keep staring out the window of my ground floor prison. Yesterday's burning agony is now just a throbbing ache.

"They said because you're a veteran they won't even charge us for changing the date, we just need to sign the new contract this week," she says excitedly and I finally look at her.

Her platinum blonde hair is swept up into an elegant bun but her normally immaculate face looks tired. Sometimes I wonder if she wants this wedding more than me. Does she realise what being married to a cripple looks like? I'm not magically going to stand and walk back up the aisle with her, there will be no first dance, no carrying her over the threshold of our house. I haven't been back there since before my accident. They decided it wasn't suited to someone with my 'complex needs' while I worked on my recovery. I snort, recovery? Yeah, right.

"What?" Tiffany demands, her blue eyes watching my carefully, "Why did you make that noise?"

"Look, Tiff..." I place my good hand over hers.

"Don't. You're going to tell me that I'm being silly, but I *need* this." She exhales slowly, as if she is calming some inner turmoil and my heart breaks for the woman I had planned to spend the rest of my life with.

"You need to plan a wedding that will never happen?" I quirk an eyebrow at her, it's all she ever talks about when we're together. It's like there's nothing else between us now.

"Why can't you just try? You have that new physio coming again today and—"

A sudden flash of anger fills me, why do they all assume that I don't want to get better? Just because I'm being realistic, I'm the bad guy.

"You think I'm not? You think I want to be like this?"

Now it's her turn to sit in silence as a tear rolls down her cheek and plops on to her blouse. We're done here.

"I think it's best if you leave Tiffany."

My mother fusses around me after Tiffany storms from the house, door slamming behind her.

"She loves you James, she's just struggling—we all are," she says gently as she makes my bed.

"Mum, she loved me when I was her big strong soldier. I was away for six months at a time and when I was on leave I spoiled her. I took her dancing, out for fancy dinners and planned an extravagant wedding. I can't go back to that. She doesn't accept me as I am now— how is that love?" I turn my chair to the window and watch as she climbs into her Audi and speeds out of the drive.

She sighs, "It's complicated…"

"I know."

* * *

The tension in the house since Tiffany left is palpable; you could cut it with a spoon never mind a knife. My parents have been hiding in the kitchen waiting for Beatrice to show and even I find myself feeling some sort of weird anticipation. Yesterday was hard, brutal and all we'd done was stretch but I slept like the dead after, dreamless and in darkness. It was my own special kind of bliss.

"Sorry I'm late," she babbles as she bursts in through my door. She quickly dumps down her sports bag and moves my chair to face her.

"I have something for you," she says with a wicked smile. Slowly she unzips her jacket, was my physio about to flash me? Admittedly, she was cute but she was also a no-go.

Finally she shrugs off the bulky hoodie and I laugh. Actually laugh for the first time in months. She's wearing a tight white t-shirt that clings to every curve and dip of her body but emblazoned across her perky tits it reads 'Bossy Cunt' in bold red writing.

"See, I knew you weren't a grumpy arse all of the time," she grins.

Sitting on the bed before me, she pulls out her notes. I knew this was coming after yesterday's torture. It was my care plan.

"Okay, down to business. I think we have to be realistic with your goals here, after all I'm only here for a month."

Something tightens in my chest, only a month? That's not enough time.

"So today we're going to work on some muscle massage, I can show your mum how to help with that. But my aim by the end of the month is to have you standing, maybe even a step or two."

"Right. I always said you were fucking crazy."

Beatrice sighs, "Corporal Rees, you have the potential to walk again with a lot of work but that's not going to happen if you keep being a miserable bastard."

"But being miserable looks so good on me," I say with a grumble.

She shrugs, "Actually, I preferred you when you laughed. Hell, even when you were being stubborn yesterday you looked more attractive than you do now."

"You think I'm attractive? Don't you see my scars?" She was definitely crazy. I was a mangled mess of fleshy lumps and bumps.

"Of course I do. But you're an idiot if you think they define you."

The sass I could deal with, but the blunt honesty she shows time and time again knocks me for six. It's like she's deflated the angry, self-loathing air in my sails. I look at her through narrowed eyes, there's this positivity that seems to emanate from her no matter how hard I push. I mean, just look at that t-shirt. I insult her and she wears it like a badge of fucking honour. I think my respect for her has just grown by several notches.

"Okay, so now we're going to get you on the floor and work on an all over body massage to loosen you up from yesterday."

I'm lowered out of my chair on down onto the carpet with help from her and the bars around my room. With a cushion under my head I watch carefully as she stretches across my chest to reach my bad arm, breasts brushing against me, her arse in the air.

The thought of those hands all over my broken body, touching me in ways I haven't been touched in months spark something in my brain and dirty thoughts flood in about the innocent, cheery physio in the tight t-shirt. Fuck, I think I just almost died. Again.

Riding Out the Storm

Lucy Felthouse

Cecelia is on a week-long artist's retreat in the North Yorkshire Moors. She's eager to capture the beauty of the local landscape on paper and is looking forward to the inspiration the area will provide. But a howler of a storm is due to hit the area, so she's stuck indoors until it passes by. She's not too concerned, until an unexpected visitor arrives.

Clark, a sexy soldier, is helping to evacuate residents from at risk properties in the area. Only, when it comes to helping Cecelia, things aren't straightforward, and the pair end up stranded. They have no choice but to ride out the storm together.

Help Our Heroes

Riding Out the Storm

When Cecelia had first seen the weather outlook for her week-long retreat in the North Yorkshire Moors, she'd been devastated. The idea had been to get into the great outdoors with her painting materials and capture the beauty and majesty of the countryside. To commit to paper the play of light, of clouds, upon trees, grass, moors, sheep.

At first, she'd thrown a childish tantrum and ranted about cancelling. But since the trip was only days away, she'd have lost all the money she'd paid, so when her initial anger and disappointment had drained away, she'd decided to go anyway. With any luck, the storm would blow itself out quickly and she could spend the remainder of her week painting outside, as she'd planned. Who knew, the devastation the weather left behind might even provide some inspirational subject matter. Broken tree branches and fences, mud-slides, puddles… yes, she was definitely going to make the best of a crappy situation.

But she hadn't expected inspiration to strike *during* the storm.

The rain lashed ferociously and relentlessly against the windows, but Cecelia didn't care. Let it rain, she thought; let the wind howl around the building, causing alarming creaking sounds and forcing cold draughts in through the tiniest of crevices. She didn't care. She'd come here to paint, and that's precisely what she was doing.

Granted, the thick cloud cover meant that the natural light flowing into her studio was poor—abysmal, in fact—so she was working by electric light, but she didn't care about that, either. It seemed to lend an air of mystery, of obscurity, to her work—as though she could see it, but not truly *see* it until the horrendous weather front finally passed over and the sun was allowed to shine once more. But that wouldn't be for a while yet.

She'd arrived at her rental property before the nasty weather hit and unloaded her car, before going grocery shopping, then settling in to wait out the storm. She'd brought books, magazines, her Kindle, tablet, and some DVDs along for her downtime—she wouldn't be painting twenty-four seven, after all—so she wasn't worried about being bored. But when the storm had arrived, fairly mild at first, then rapidly growing in intensity, some invisible force had drawn her upstairs, to the lovely room that had made her choose the property as her retreat in the first place. As soon as she'd walked in and checked out the view from the window—grey and ominous looking as it was—she'd hurried back down to the hallway to retrieve her painting materials.

That had been several hours ago, and she'd barely moved from her stool since—only for the necessary food, drink, and bathroom breaks, when she couldn't ignore her body's pleas any longer.

Now, she was well and truly *in the zone,* so when she heard what she thought was a knock on the door, she paused for a second, then shook her head. *Don't be ridiculous.* Nobody was crazy enough to be out in this weather, and nobody around here knew her anyway, so she dismissed it. Maybe there was a loose fence panel rattling around in the garden or something.

She carried on painting, carefully capturing in watercolour the majesty of what she was seeing through the large window she'd positioned herself in front of. It faced out across the moors, and so far her image was about two-thirds done. She'd worked her way from the ground up, and was now putting down on paper the last of the treetops in her view. Next, she would move on to the sky which, considering the way the fierce wind was dragging clouds across it, making its appearance change constantly, was going to be quite the challenge. And then there was the rain—that was a whole other ball game.

The knocking sound came again; louder this time. Cecelia sighed and, after a moment, put down her paintbrush. Maybe she should go and investigate. If she could secure whatever it was that was making the noise, she probably ought to. It wasn't her property, but it *was* the decent thing to do. She wouldn't like it if the roles were reversed and somebody else ignored it, after all.

Getting reluctantly to her feet—there was no way she wanted to go out in this hideous weather—she made her way down the stairs. Just as she reached the bottom, the thumping came yet again.

But this time it was accompanied by something else, something she'd never have believed had she not been right on the other side of the door. A voice. A man's voice, if she wasn't mistaken. "Hello? *Hello?* Are you in there? If you're there, please answer the door! I'm here to help you!" Yes, it was definitely a man's voice. Deep, and growing increasingly frustrated.

Help me? Unless you're going to cook me some dinner and bring me cups of tea while I get on with my painting, how can you possibly help me?

She crossed to the door. It didn't have a peephole, so she couldn't surreptitiously check out her mysterious visitor. It *did* have a security chain, however, so she slipped it on before opening the door a crack. The wind gusted through the tiny gap, making Cecelia gasp at its ferocity and chill. Her instinct was to take the chain off and fling the door open to let the man in out of the cold and the wet, but the sensible part of her stood firm, reminding her that just because he *said* he was here to help, didn't mean he was telling the truth. He could be a psychotic serial killer for all she knew, stalking the moors, seeking out people in remote places and—

Her wild imaginings were cut off when the man said, "Thank God! I was beginning to think you'd actually gone out in this, and that we were going to have to send out mountain rescue to find you."

Her visitor was covered from head to foot in heavy duty waterproof gear. All she could make out was part of his face, which was barely visible inside the hood he had pulled tightly around it. He shifted from foot to foot, and she saw the flash of teeth as he smiled. "Can I come in, please? It'll be a lot easier to help you if I can explain without shouting over this wind and rain."

Cecelia frowned. "I'm sorry, I think you've got the wrong house. I don't need any help—I'm perfectly all right, thank you."

"No." He shook his head. "No, you're not. Or you won't be, anyway. The area is starting to flood, and the rain is showing no sign of abating any time soon. This house is a huge flood risk. You need to get your belongings upstairs, and… where's your car?"

"Flood? Car?" Now it was her turn to shake her head. What the hell was he talking about?

"*Please,* let me in. I realise I'm some random stranger at your door, but I'm not here to hurt you—I'm here to help. And time is of the essence. Look," he loosened the ties of his hood and shoved it down, "why don't you take my photograph on your phone and post it online somewhere? Or send it to a friend? There's no phone signal out here, but you're logged into the WiFi, right? Just for your peace of mind."

He seemed to be well informed about the area. But that didn't mean he was genuine. He could just be a serial killer who had done his research. Would a serial killer be encouraging her to take his photograph and post it online, though? Highly unlikely.

Just then, movement behind him drew her gaze. There was water, lots of water, flowing across the driveway of her rented house, heading right for the man's feet. He had on rubber boots, but still… surely even a psychotic serial killer wasn't crazy enough to be out in this?

She quickly closed the door, only to whip off the security chain, then open it again, wide enough to admit the man. "Come on in," she said, her heart pounding. Christ, she hoped her instincts were right—if he was lying, it'd be the end of the week, when she was due to vacate the premises, before anyone even knew she was missing.

He hurried in, then spun on his heel and quickly closed the door behind him. He then turned back to her, but remained standing on the doormat. Water dripped off his clothing and his hair, which had become soaked in the mere seconds he'd had his hood down before she'd let him in. "Thank you," he said, smiling again. "I'm sorry to drop in on you like this. I understand your reticence to let me in. In most cases, I'd agree that you shouldn't allow a stranger in to your property, but this is an emergency. We need to get your belongings upstairs, then get out of here—preferably in your car, so we can get it to higher ground."

"Are you sure? It's just a bit of a storm. It was forecast. I wasn't planning on going out in it."

The man, who'd remained relatively cheerful—considering he was wet and had to be cold—now sighed and rolled his eyes. "Yes, I'm sure. And yes, it was forecast. That's why I'm here. I'm from the army. This area, and this house, are incredibly prone to flooding—and I'm not just talking about roads being blocked off. I'm talking ground floors being submerged. We're being deployed to all the at risk places in the area to check on the residents, make their properties as flood-proof as possible, then escort them to safety."

"So why haven't the owners of the property been in touch with me?" she asked, folding her arms across her chest.

The man narrowed his eyes. "Because they're busy doing to their main residence what we should be doing here! That's why they sent me to help you. Please, I don't mean to be rude, but we need to get a move on here, otherwise it's going to be too late."

Well, it explained why he was so confident she had a car—he'd already spoken to the owners of the property, and they'd told him. "A-all right. I'm sorry, I didn't mean to be difficult, I just… I didn't realise. So, what do you want me to do? Do you need a hot drink? You must be freezing."

He shook his head again, sending droplets of rainwater flying around. "I'd love one, but we seriously don't have time for that. First of all, you need to go and get changed into the warmest, most outdoor appropriate clothing you've got with you. And waterproofs, if you've got them. Then you need to start moving what belongings you've got down here up to the first floor. As fast as you can. It won't be too much longer before the lane is flooded and we won't be able to get your car out. If that happens, we'll have to walk all the way to the main road and get picked up there."

"Okay. I definitely don't want to have to leave my car."

"Understood. Where is the key? I'm assuming it's in the garage."

She nodded. "The key is in my handbag."

"Get it. I'll drive it out of the garage."

"W-what? Why do you want to drive my car?"

"For fuck's sake!" he snapped, his dark eyes flashing. It seemed he'd finally lost his cool. "I don't *want* to drive your bloody car! I don't want to be here at all, but I am. People need help, we got called out, end of. We need to make a quick getaway, so the nearer the car is to the front door, the better. Plus, the sandbags are in the garage, so it'll be a damn sight quicker for me to get them out and start putting them in position if your car isn't in the way. This isn't some kind of elaborate car theft—it's a dangerous situation! And if you keep questioning me instead of getting your bloody arse in gear, we could end up stranded here until the flood waters recede."

His harsh words finally penetrated the brain fog she'd been experiencing, triggered by panic and disbelief. How the hell was this happening? Her heart raced. "Er, yes… right. Key. I'll get the key."

He gave a small smile now. "That would be great."

She scurried into the living room and retrieved her handbag, then jogged back into the hallway, digging around for the key as she did so. She made a sound of triumph as she felt cold metal against her fingers, and she quickly withdrew the bundle—which also included her house key and a bunch of key rings—and handed it over.

Taking the set with a murmur of thanks, the man opened the door and stepped out. Just before the door closed behind him, he called out, "If I'm not back by the time you're done, please come out and help me."

"All right!" She all but ran up the stairs, still clutching her handbag, and into her bedroom. Fortunately she was the organised sort, so she knew exactly where everything was, and within a couple of minutes she'd replaced the clothes she'd been wearing with lined waterproof trousers, a couple of warm layers on the top, and thick socks. She also had a hat, coat, scarf, gloves, and wellington boots at the ready, but figured they could wait until she was actually heading outside—they'd only slow her down in the meantime.

That done, she grabbed a large, strong bag and jogged down the stairs. Back in the living room, she made the mistake of glancing out of the window. The rain was now coming down so heavily she could barely see past it, but she *could* see enough to realise that her rescuer—shit, she had no idea what his name was—had been telling the truth. The water level had already gone way beyond the first waves that had spurred her on to let him in the house. *Bloody hell—this is serious.*

She jumped as a shape hurried past the window, until she realised it was him, carrying what she assumed was a sandbag. The reminder spurred her back in to action, and she began dumping her stuff into the bag she'd brought down. The more she could carry in one go, the better. As she worked, she thought about what else needed to go upstairs. There wasn't much, actually, since her clothes and painting stuff were there already.

Help Our Heroes

A few minutes and a couple of journeys up and down the stairs later and everything important was safely on the first floor. Her rescuer hadn't said anything about moving any furniture or anything that belonged to the house—so she hadn't. She figured it was probably more helpful to go outside and help him with the sandbags than do that—it was better to try to keep the water out altogether, surely? She wouldn't be able to move much of the furniture by herself, in any case.

She dragged on her outer layer and her wellington boots, then gritted her teeth and headed outside. Immediately, she was almost blown off her feet by the force of the wind, which also drove what felt like a hundred needles into the exposed skin of her face. Muttering and cursing to herself, she pulled the drawstrings of her hood tighter around her face. Now wasn't the time to give a shit what she looked like.

Her car, as promised, sat on the driveway, pointing towards the exit track. The water level was already worryingly high on its tyres. Gulping, she hunched over and hurried around the side of the house in search of the army guy, clocking the multiple sandbags he'd already placed next to its walls. He wasn't messing around.

She almost bumped into him at the corner, and stopped abruptly.

"Hey," he said, raising his voice to be heard over the weather. His hood was back up and secured around his face now. "You all right?" He held a sandbag in his arms as though it weighed nothing.

She nodded. "Yes. I'm done in there. What do you need me to do?"

"Can you help with these?" He pointed with his chin to the sandbag.

"Yes, of course."

"Great. They're in the back of the garage. You can see what I'm doing with them, how I'm laying them out, so just continue with that, all right? It'll be much quicker with the two of us. Once we're done with that, we'll jump in the car and head into the village and the community centre." He glanced around, then down at the brown water swirling around his boots. "I know it looks bad, but we'll be all right to get out at the moment. Just be careful, all right? They're pretty heavy."

She nodded again. "All right."

He continued on his way, and she splashed to the garage and immediately homed in on the pile of sandbags. She hurried over and braced herself for the weight—glad her rescuer wasn't there to see her struggle. Bizarrely, in the circumstances, she remembered what she knew about lifting, and she bent her knees, hooked her arms under the topmost bag, then straightened her legs. It was incredibly heavy, particularly given her lack of upper body strength, but she managed it, letting out a grunt as she turned and walked back around to the front of the building, trying not to panic at the sight of the water, the volume and ferocity of which appeared to be increasing by the second. God, what would happen if her car couldn't get through it? Would they get swept away? She'd seen it on the news before—people stuck in their cars in flash floods, being rescued by firemen, and others not so lucky.

With a shudder, she picked up her pace. The sooner they got out of here, the better. She had no idea where the community centre was, but it seemed it was being used as a base, so it was presumably safe and on higher ground.

She and the man shared a smile—which was actually more like a grimace of shared discomfort—as they passed each other, and Cecelia moved to where he'd left his last bag and plopped hers down next to it. Then she spun around and prepared to repeat the whole action all over again. And again—however many times it took to position all the bags, and hopefully keep her lovely holiday home safe from the increasing flood water, which was now lapping against the first layer of sandbags.

After about fifteen minutes, when she and the army bloke passed again, he stopped. "Do you need to get anything from inside? We're almost done now—there's only the front door to go."

She thought for a moment. "Yes, if there's time, I could probably do with grabbing some stuff, since I don't know how long I'll be away from the house."

He nodded. "Go for it. There's a little time, but not much." He glanced at the wheels of her car, which were nearly half covered with water. "Hurry."

"Okay." She moved as fast as she could through the water and headed back into the house, her mind racing. What did she need? *Really* need? Her rescuer would probably throttle her if she came out carrying her paintbrushes; though it would be a wrench to leave them behind, common sense told her that they'd be perfectly safe where they were—there was no way the flood water would reach the first floor.

She decided to rely on her instincts, and grabbed her small wheeled suitcase and threw in toiletries, clean clothes and underwear, her pyjamas, and the book she was reading—telling herself it was *right next* to the pyjamas, so took minimal extra time to retrieve. Then she zipped the case almost to the top and scurried back down the stairs to the kitchen, where she stuffed a bunch of food and snacks through the gap she'd left in the zip. She had no idea how the community centre was set up—she'd never been in this kind of situation before—so it seemed like a good idea. Bags of crisps, crackers, and chocolate could be just what she and the other refugees needed as they waited out the weather and the havoc it was causing.

Finally, she zipped up the case and hefted it, along with her handbag, which she'd also brought down, to the front door. She opened it to find the army guy had stacked a load of sandbags, ready to be piled in front of the door once she was out of the house. Just then he appeared with another in his arms.

She barely made out the querying raise of his eyebrows within his hood as he called over the still-howling wind, "All ready?"

She nodded and indicated her case. "Yes. Do you have my keys? I'll put this and my bag in the car and come back to help you."

He dumped the sandbag he was carrying on the top of the pile and shook his head. "No need. Put your stuff in the car, then get in and wait for me. Start the engine. I won't be a minute now." He dug his hand into his coat pocket and removed her keys.

"Um, okay." With a shrug, she took the keys for the holiday home from the hook next to the door. Then she stepped out with her stuff, hurriedly closed and locked the door, pocketed the keys, took *her* keys from the army guy with a nod, then splashed over to her car, trying hard not to pay attention to how high the water level was on her tyres *now*. It didn't entirely work, since a flicker of anxiety worked its way through her body unbidden, but she ignored it and pushed on.

Moments later her stuff was safely in the back of the car, and she was in the front. She pulled on her seatbelt, then put the key in the ignition and turned it, heaving a sigh of relief as the engine instantly fired into life. Then she looked in the rear-view mirror to see how her rescuer was getting on. The window wipers were working hard to clear the still-pouring torrents of rain from the glass, and she could just about make out him placing what appeared to be the last sandbag on the stack in front of the door. He gave a nod, then spun on his heel and strode towards her car.

A second or two later, he opened the door and folded his large frame into the passenger seat, then quickly pulled the door shut behind him. Cecelia hadn't realised quite how big he was until he did that. Hunched over in her car, he looked like a giant. A dripping wet, heavy-breathing giant.

"Okay, let's go," he said.

Tearing her gaze away from him, she put the car in gear, disengaged the handbrake and put her foot down. "You'll have to direct me once we get to the road. I have no idea where I'm going."

"No problem."

A couple of hundred yards down the lane, Cecelia stomped on the brake.

"Oh, shit," they said as one as they took in the sight before them, then turned to look at each other, wide eyed.

"Er…" Cecelia said, clutching tightly onto the steering wheel, as though that would help the situation any. "What the fuck do we do now?"

Army Guy blew out a breath and shook his head. "Fucking hell, there's not a lot we can do, really. There's only one way in or out of this property—in a vehicle, anyway—and that…" he pointed at the mess of bricks and mud which used to be a bridge over a stream, "was it."

"B-but, my car… and… flooding… and… what the hell are we going to do?"

"Cecelia," the man said calmly, placing his right hand over her left on the steering wheel. "Try and stay calm for me, sweetheart. I know this is a scary situation, but I promise you everything is going to be all right."

She frowned. "How do you know my name?" It was hardly important, but the panic whizzing around her body was clearly getting into her brain, too, and messing up her priorities.

He chuckled. "The owners of the house told me. I'm Clark, by the way," he said with a gentle squeeze of her hand.

Help Our Heroes

"Is that your first or last name?"

"Let's discuss that later. Right now I need you to reverse the car, okay? We'll get it back in the garage—which is a fair bit higher than the house, as luck would have it—use the remaining sandbags to block the door, then get ourselves holed up in the house. We'll have to wait it out. We're much safer in there," he jerked his thumb over his shoulder, "than trying to get out of here on foot."

"O-okay." She ignored the pounding of her heart and tried hard to focus as she put the car in reverse gear, then slowly manoeuvred it towards the house. It was a narrow track, and reversing along it would be a challenge at the best of times, but with the surface beneath them being more water than ground, the wind buffeting the vehicle, and the rain lashing it, it was a task she was sure she'd never have completed if it hadn't been for Clark and his constant stream of help and encouragement.

"You're all right, Cecelia. Just keep the steering wheel straight, and your right foot steady. You're doing amazingly. Not far to go now. Right hand down a little… little bit more. That's it. So close. We're almost onto the drive. Left hand down a touch. Give her a bit more welly… and we're there. Well done!"

She turned to stare at him through slightly fuzzy eyes. "Shit. I never want to do that again."

"You won't have to. Right, I'm just going to jump out here and run and open the garage door, all right? Don't pull in until I say so, because I need to get the last few sandbags out to put in front of that door, okay?"

She nodded, then waited until he was clear of the vehicle before she slowly reversed it towards the garage. Her heart raced again as she heard and felt the swish of the water around the tyres. God, how much worse was it going to get? So much for heading out and doing some paintings of the aftermath of the storm—at this rate it'd be more like a dystopian world than one with the odd fence or tree blown down.

After a few minutes of gritting her teeth and forcing herself to keep going, Cecelia was safely inside the house. She stripped off her outer layers and left them in a pile on the hallway floor next to her bag and case, then hurried into the kitchen to make the two of them a hot drink while Clark shored up the front door once again. She wasn't sure, but she thought the rain seemed to be letting up a little. Not that it mattered at the moment, anyway—even if it stopped suddenly and the sun came out, their exit route wouldn't be magically repaired. No, they were stuck for the foreseeable. Thank God she'd already done the grocery shopping—at least they weren't in imminent danger of starvation.

She heard a clunk, then some shuffling. Clark joined her in the kitchen. He, too, had removed his soaked outer layer, giving her the opportunity to look at him—*really* look at him—for the first time. And, she realised with a jolt, he was *definitely* worth looking at. Despite the dark hair plastered to his head, he was obviously a handsome man, with deep blue eyes and a smile that could melt a woman's heart. His camouflage gear highlighted his athletic build, and she found herself wondering just what he looked like underneath all that green and brown.

The click of the kettle snapped her back to the task at hand, and she set about making two cups of tea. "Milk and sugar?"

Clark nodded. "Yes, please. Two sugars."

"Please, sit down." She nodded towards the kitchen table. "Or should we go upstairs?"

He quirked an eyebrow, and heat rushed to Cecelia's face as the implications of what she'd just said sunk in. "I-I meant, with the flooding. Do we need to get onto the first floor in case the water starts coming in to the house?"

With a chuckle, Clark shook his head and took a seat at the kitchen table. "I knew what you meant, and we'll be fine here for now. With any luck, it won't come in at all, but even if it does it won't suddenly burst in in gallons—we'll have some warning."

"Okay." She finished making the drinks, then joined him at the table, placing his mug in front of him then cupping her hands around her own. The heat seeped into her chilled, soggy skin and she closed her eyes for a moment, letting a shiver run through her body, both at the cold and the thought of their narrow escape.

"Hey," Clark said, drawing her attention. She opened her eyes again. "Are you shivering?"

Cecelia shrugged. "Yeah, a bit. I think it's mostly shock. My waterproofs did the job pretty well, I'm just a bit damp around the edges."

"We need to get you out of those wet clothes," he said, his blue eyes serious.

Now it was her turn for some eyebrow-raising. "Yeah?" she quipped, her mouth and tongue seeming to jump into action with very little input from her brain. "And what about you? You were out in the storm for much longer than me." *Cecelia, you outrageous flirt. Is now really the time for this?*

Clark pursed his lips and took on a thoughtful expression. "I really ought to contact the others and give them a status update. Let them know we're okay, but that we're stuck here until tomorrow at least."

"And then what?" She took a sip of her tea, hoping like hell he was on the same wavelength as her.

"Then," his lips curved slowly into a grin, "we should *both* get out of our wet clothes. Get dry, then warm."

"And how do you propose we do that?" *Seriously, Cecelia, what are you saying? Barely an hour ago, you were having palpitations about letting him into the house because you were worried he might be a serial killer. And now you're talking in sexual innuendos!*

"Oh," he said, his grin turning positively wicked, "I'm sure between us we can come up with something…"

She gulped down more of her drink, giving herself a moment to compose her thoughts. But it proved impossible—the dirty smile he was aiming in her direction had turned her insides to mush and her brain into an organ that could focus on only one thing—getting him upstairs and naked, and the sexy fun that would follow.

Everything else receded—the rain, the wind, the threat of flooding, their being cut off from the outside world. Abandoning her tea, she got to her feet and headed for the stairs, throwing over her shoulder, "You coming, then?"

"I was serious about the call, but I'll be right behind you."

"You'd better be."

He was.

The End.

A Military Anthology

Hunter

S.M Phillips

Hunter by name, Hunter by nature.
He used to be fierce, strong, loyal. Now he's damaged, broken and alone.

Sixteen years have passed.
Sixteen years spent blocking out bad memories and never-ending pain.
Hunter Dawson focused his time on building a new life; a life where he could become a better person, and for the most part he was succeeding—until now.

One letter.
One letter is all it took to unravel everything he tried so hard to forget.
Why now? Why, after all the years is he being asked to go back to a place which stole his soul and shattered the remaining pieces of his broken heart?

* * *

Reader Warning

I hope you enjoy the beginning of Hunter's story…
Please note, this is just the beginning of his story and I have released the prologue and first two chapters solely for this Anthology.

The remainder of Hunter's story will be released later this year, and once the Anthology is no longer on sale. If you enjoyed it, please add it to your TBR, and please don't shout at me when you get to the end ☐

Prologue

HUNTER

My eyes watch the flame flickering from side to side in the middle of the kitchen table, stealing my attention from what's happening around me.

"Hunter, eat your dinner before it gets cold." Mummy says calmly as she pulls out a chair and takes the seat next to me.

"I'm not hungry." I reply as I move my fork around my plate. I refuse to meet her gaze, as I don't want her to see the look of fear in my eyes—not when she looks so happy. I love it when mummy's happy, but I know it won't last for long. It never does, not when *he* comes around.

"But you've hardly touched it. Is everything okay? Has something happened at school?"

"No, school's fine." I reply truthfully. I love school. School is the only place I feel safe and I have my best friend Claire who always makes me happy when I get sad. I wish I could take mummy to school and keep her safe. I slowly raise my eyes to look at her and I smile. My mummy is very pretty, and she has long red hair and the brightest green eyes. Mummy smiles back at me and she has a lovely, kind smile especially for me.

"Are you sure, baby?" She places her hand on my head and then messes with my hair and I laugh, and I quickly lean over and hold onto her tightly, frightened that if I let go she'll be taken away from me forever, and I'll never see her again.

"I love you, mummy." I muffle into her shoulder and inhale deeply, breathing in her floral scent.

"I love you most." She whispers. "Now, let's get you cleaned up and ready for bed. Mummy's got her friend coming over, and he'll be here soon."

My whole body stiffens. I knew it. Mummy only ever wears make-up when her friend comes over. But he's not very nice, or very friendly and I don't know why mummy likes him so much.

I don't like him.

He shouts too much and says bad words.

I don't say anything to him because I'm too scared.

When he's here I'm sent to my room, but I don't want to go. I don't like leaving my mummy alone with him.

"Does he have to come over?" I say after a short while, and my voice cracks as I try not to cry. "He makes you sad mummy and upsets you all the time."

"Oh, Hunter," mummy cups my chin in her hand and slowly tilts my head back, so she can look into my eyes—eyes that match hers and says, "sometimes grown -ups are silly and say things they don't really mean, that's all. You're young sweetheart and you don't need to worry about any of that."

'But I do, mummy.' I think to myself. *'I worry about you all the time.'*

One day, when I'm old enough, I'll get a good job and take her out of this place. We'll live in a happy house and I'll look after her the way she deserves.

Chapter 1

The rain hammers down against the windows as the ferocious wind whistles loudly and rattles the damaged roof above me, and it's strong enough to rip the whole thing apart.

The beautiful and unique sound of mother nature doing her thing used to be a welcome distraction, a comfort even when I was younger. It used to calm me and help me escape my surroundings.

Surroundings I couldn't control, but for a short while I could zone off and pretend none of it was happening, and that life didn't truly exist. Man, I used to pretend I didn't exist at all—life was so much easier that way.

But that was then, and this is now, and I sit here in this small box of a room, all it does is awaken all kinds of memories...

Memories I tried so hard to shut out and forget.

Memories which won't let up and leave me the hell alone.

Why now?

Why, after all these years does he insist on seeing me now?

My hand twitches involuntarily and the letter, now scrunched up in my hand, falls to the ground and echoes all around me. A perfect demonstration of the emptiness of my damaged and broken soul.

A sudden rage consumes me, and I jump up and throw my arm out before I can stop myself, and my fist connects with the old, shabby mirror which hangs on the wall in front of me.

Pain shoots from my hand and begins to radiate up my arm, but I don't really feel it. Pain is something I'm used to, and now it feels more like and unsated itch I can't seem to get rid of.

Fuck!

I thought I was better than this.

I slowly raise my eyes back up towards the mirror after assessing my bloody hand, and see it's more than just cracked—it's shattered into a million pieces.

One letter.

One fucking letter after years and years of silence, and this is what the mother fucker does to me.

I don't recognize the man looking back at me. Sure, he looks familiar—but there's no denying he's changed. He's no longer the guy he used to be; the frightened little boy who was too scared to breathe out loud whenever *he* was home. Too scared his mom would suffer because this small boy was nothing but an unwanted inconvenience. Hell, I'd heard enough over the years to know exactly what the old man truly thought of me.

No, the person staring back at me isn't that boy any more. He's aged some, and he sure as hell looks like he's lived longer than his thirty-three years.

His eyes are tired and crinkled a little at the edges—a mapped story of his troubled past, but he wears them with pride; a reminder of what he's overcome. His eyes are a brilliant bright green, but they no longer hold the sparkle of innocence like they once did. Instead, they're hard and cold, completely void of any emotion—the perfect eyes of a monster.

These are the eyes of a man who has certainly made his fair share of mistakes, and then some. Many through no fault of his own, but when all's said and done, does any of that even matter?

Like fuck it does.

I turn on the tap and allow the cold water to trickle and graze my knuckles as it slowly washes away the blood, and I look down again at the crumpled piece of paper on the floor, and I know the only time I'll see that twisted son of a bitch again is in hell.

I used to be fierce... strong... and loyal

Now, I'm savage... broken... and alone.

Chapter 2

"I'm not leaving." My voice is strong, and I mean every goddamn word, but he's not having any of it. Well, tough shit, bud. It's my fucking decision, and it's been made.

"Hunter…"

I inhale slowly, trying to keep my resolve and look over to my buddy, Phoenix, and all I can do is shake my head at him. "I already told you. I'm not doing it, man. What's the fucking point?"

"Hey, I get that, really I do, but he obviously wants to see you for a reason."

No fucking shit. "Hell yeah, I bet he does. Probably so he can fuck my life up some more. You know, because my childhood wasn't enough."

I spent years and years putting up with his bullshit because I didn't have a choice back then. I was a kid. An innocent child, and one he made damn sure was to be seen and not heard.

I can sense Phoenix watching me. Clearly concerned about my well-being and I don't blame him because right now I'm so unpredictable—I'm like a mother fucking time bomb. But now isn't the time to get into all that bullshit. We've got work to do.

I think it's safe to say my life hasn't been a bed of roses, but shit happens and I'm sure there's a hell of a lot of people who'd say the same.

One thing I won't do is sit back and pull my small violin out. I don't need anyone's pity and I sure as hell don't dance along to anyone's tune but my own.

The bottom line is, life is hard, and I guess you've just got to handle the cards you've been dealt. Most of all, you need to be grateful you were dealt any to begin with.

"Maybe he wants to put it all right?" Phoenix says after a few moments of awkward silence between us. He says it so quietly I almost didn't catch it, and when I suddenly look up at him he refuses to meet my gaze. "All I'm saying is that people can change."

"Are you shitting me, right now?" I exclaim, my voice sharp and to the point as I struggle to reign in my emotions. I know there's no point getting mad at him. It's not his fault and I know he's only trying to help, and even though he's the closest thing to family that I've got, he still doesn't know half of what that son of a bitch put me through. Hell, it's probably for the best he doesn't know because that kind of shit, once it's out, it can't be unsaid.

"Hey man," Phoenix holds his hands out in surrender, and his brown eyes and boyish face is full of concern, and I fucking hate myself for snapping at him. "I just don't want you to do something you'll regret, is all."

Regret...

The only thing I regret is not killing the mother fucker back when I had the chance.

Usually, I'd listen to Phoenix. He's a smart kid and he always means well, but there's no way I'll ever live to regret this. How could I?

We're talking about a man who went out of his way to ruin my life at every possible turn, and even then, that wasn't enough for him. He utterly destroyed me, and any chance f happiness I ever had.

So why the hell would I want to make him happy now?

I look down at the SA80 which is laid out before me and I try to focus, but my minds on overdrive and it agitates the hell out of me. Usually, I'd be able to switch my unwanted thoughts off in an instant—totally shut them out. After years of practice I've mastered the art like the professional I am. But today, not so much.

I've spent the past sixteen years doing everything within my power to erase the hidden demons of my past, to try to make something of myself. To prove I deserve this life, and more importantly to prove I deserve a life worth living.

Of course, I've had my bad days. I'm still human after all, but only just. No matter what, I've always managed to pull through. This time though? I'm not so sure.

A whole barricade of emotions have been unleashed, let loose to cause damage on the life I've worked so hard to build for myself so far.

'I know I'm the last person you'd expect to hear from after all these years,

but please hear me out. Allow me a chance to explain. Hunter, I really need to see you...'

His words flutter in my minds eye and my hands grips the rifle, clenching so hard my veins in the back of my hand protrude profusely and begin to throb. I swear if I'd had this within my reach all those years ago, I wouldn't have thought twice about using it.

I've always had a good aim, possibly one of the best. One shot—that's all it would have taken, and the mother fucker would be gone—finished.

But then I guess that would have been too easy, and Lord knows I'm not lucky enough to get the easy ride.

A feral laugh escapes me as I think about how my life would have panned out so differently if he'd never been apart of it. I know nothing is certain or set in stone, but I'm pretty sure we would have been better off in every way possible.

I know I'd be happy, there's no doubt about it. I'd still have my mum. I know we would have had that beautiful bond a mother and son are supposed to have, and I know I would have made her proud. Jesus, there's not a day goes by where I don't stop and wonder if she's proud of what I've achieved so far.

When I ran, I put my heart and soul, everything I had left into my new role. I was a quick learner and discipline was my middle fucking name, and when I teamed that with my love of guns and machinery—hell, it was a no brainer.

I quickly found my feet within my new regiment, and that's when I first met Phoenix. I'll never forget looking at him and wanting nothing more than to knock the fucker out. He was all legs and arms, not a single ounce of muscle on him, and he was a cocky, arrogant son of a bitch.

After the first five minutes if being in his presence I had no choice but to take him under my wing and show him the ropes. He would have been beaten alive, hounded until he couldn't take anymore, until he was nothing but an empty shell—until I stepped in. He's been by my side ever since and I wouldn't have it any other way. He's had his fair share of being a complete prick over the years, but haven't we all? I trust him indefinitely, something I haven't really done before—well, with one exception…

Claire...

My breathing hitches and my chest tightens when I think about her.

Something I haven't allowed myself to do all that often since I turned my back on her and walked away.

I was a selfish son of a bitch, there's no denying it, but it was for the best. I did what I had to do—I did it for *her*. Claire really deserved the best of everything—a life I just couldn't give her.

I know I broke her trust and her heart that day. Jesus, my own heart shattered all around me and pierced my already damaged soul. As much as it pained me to do it, I had no choice but to turn away from the one person who kept my heart beating—my reason for living, before I destroyed her beautiful soul too.

She'll always be with me, even if she doesn't know it. I sure as hell made sure a part of her, no matter how small stayed with me forever. It was the least I could do.

My hand falls and presses against my chest, to the left, just where the last words she spoke to me are etched permanently onto my skin:

'If you allowed love to save you, you'd live forever...'

It's a little reminder of what we had, a unique connection which we shared, and for her to really live I needed to let her go. It's a painful reminder that I was too selfish and stupid not to give her love a chance to save me.

I didn't realise back then, but that's exactly what I needed—and now it's too late to go back and change it.

I stop and think about what could happen if I travelled back up to Manchester. To the place where I grew up and holds nothing but mainly bad memories for me. Would Claire still be there? I don't think so. It's been sixteen years and hopefully she's happy and settled with someone who can give her the world—exactly what I promised to give her a lifetime ago.

I know I failed her, just like I failed my mum—and myself.

"Shit!"

I throw the rifle back down with much more force than I intended as the anger consumes me once again, only this time I'm not alone. What the hell is happening to me? My guards down, one that I've protected only too well and now my uncontrollable emotions are taking over.

"Sergeant, is everything alright in here?"

Help Our Heroes

I look up instantly at the sound of his deep, cold voice and my eyes lock onto my squadron sergeant standing before me and he looks majorly pissed.

Fuck, fuck, fuck. Way to go Hunter...

A Military Anthology

Chopper
Broken Deeds MC #4.5
Esther E. Schmidt

Some scars run deeper than healed wounds on the body. Memories can be a tricky thing; they can be special or traumatic, especially when you have no control over the trigger. When they hit, they can hit hard.

When Chopper ends up in the ER, the memories start and the only thing that soothes his pain is a woman from his past that holds special meaning. Ivy fights for her patients, but when her teenage crush lands in her ER she is forced to handle her scalpel in a whole different way.

Life is a constant struggle and it can be difficult to realize that one tiny moment in time can be just the change you need. Nothing is more difficult than fighting an inner battle, one that has branded scars into pieces of your soul. Will Chopper allow Ivy into his fight? Or will he continue to face his battles alone?

Chapter 1

Chopper

"Stop fucking touching me," I bellow at the top of my lungs but it's no use.

I need to get out of here, and yet I damn well know I can't because they have to stitch me back up. *I fucking hate hospitals.* Hence the reason Lochlan is holding me down. I am determined to throw everything to the wind and crawl out of here if needed. Screw stitches. I always take them out myself anyway, so I can put them in just as easy.

"Can you nurses maybe find a doc who can knock him out? Would make your job easier because he's not going to cooperate," Lochlan grunts.

The nurse that was poking me scurries out of the room and I turn my fury on my brother. "You need to get me the fuck out of here."

"Chopper, you know I can't, man. Your leg has all kinds of lacerations. As soon as a doc has seen you and tells me there isn't any permanent damage, then I'll carry you out myself if I have to…you know I'd do it again." He adds that fucking last part to remind me he always has my back.

I don't need the fucking reminder. Lying here brings it all back. I'm sweating like a pig, out of breath, and nauseous as fuck. None of that has to do with the injuries I have except for the scars called memories that flare up in my head. *I hate it.* Hate feeling weak, like a lesser person with a truckload of damage that I'll never shake.

"I'm not the guy I was back then, asshole. These injuries I have now don't even compare. This shit is minor, my legs were fucking shattered when you had to carry me to get me the help I needed. We were so far off the…fuck." I close my eyes and try to contain the string of curses that wants to burst out of my mouth. "Why in the hell am I talking about this? Get me the fuck out of here."

"Ah, I hear we have a grumpy customer. Let's see if we can patch him up and push him out. Nora, can you give me a hand in a bit?" Great. Another damn nurse. And if you ask me, they dragged this one straight off a horse she was riding in the middle of Texas. Or so the thick accent tells me. And I damn well know because I grew up there. I can't see what she looks like because Lochlan is still holding me down.

"Ivy? When the hell did you start working here?" Lochlan quips and finally lets go of me.

"Jesus, Lochlan, is that you? You got big." The woman chuckles but I couldn't care less, because I'm outta here and this is my fucking chance.

"Not so fast, asshole," Lochlan grunts when he pushes me back on the bed.

"Mind telling me what's wrong with the runner I have on my hands? Is he a buddy of yours?" the woman Lochlan called Ivy says.

And then I fucking see dark green hair, like a fucking emerald. Thick, dark, shiny, pulled back in a tight braid. Damn stunning, and with that it makes her the biggest fucking gem I've ever seen in my life. Her eyes are on my leg. They've cut open my jeans to see the injury from when I crashed my bike. I already had the rundown with the nurses and X-rays and shit. Nothing broken, just lacerations. Or so they've told me but it seems like another doctor needs to double-check.

When she connects her gaze with mine, I notice her bright gray eyes. Fuck. They're like the sky when it's threatening to rain. A dark rim around her iris emphasizes the gray. Those eyes. I know them…they look familiar but for the life of me, I can't remember shit.

"Who the fuck are you?" I growl because she's hot and it pisses me off. I want out of here, in my own damn bed, and I want to know who the hell she is.

"Can it, idiot. This is Arthur's twin sister, Ivy. Don't you remember?" Lochlan growls at me.

Arthur's twin? Fuck. *Ivy.* That's why I recognized her eyes. "You were bald the last time I saw you…about ten years ago."

Yeah, that's the first thing I tell her because that's how I remember the last time I saw her. Maybe it was because she didn't have hair, or the fact that I thought it might be the last time I saw her, that I indefinitely branded her exquisite eyes into my memory. She's the one woman who made quite an impression on me, even if she was Arthur's sister and therefore off-limits, she still ruled every wet dream I had since then.

Who am I kidding…even when I was seventeen and Arthur and Ivy were sixteen, I couldn't keep my eyes off her. She was a stunner even then, and she was considered one of the guys because Arthur kept everyone at arm's length when it came to his twin sister. We all signed up for our first tour and I didn't see her for years. Not until I ran into her at the funeral where she was bald. Holy hell. Ten fucking years and what a world of difference.

"Yeah, the good ol'days. Less fuss in the morning, that's for sure." Ivy blows a puff of air up so a strand of that amazing dark green hair that escaped her braid falls away from her face. "Now keep still because I'm gonna take a look."

It's not that I listen to her, I'm simply frozen to the bed because my mind flashes back to her brother, Arthur, the reason why I saw her ten years ago…at his funeral. He's one of three we lost. "What the fuck, woman? Why don't you stick your head in there for a better view instead of just your fingers, huh?"

"I'm glad your mouth still works perfectly." Ivy chuckles. "Doesn't look too bad. I'll fix you up and have you on your way soon…what's your name, again? Because the information I had was all,"

"None of your damn business," I snap, although I feel shitty about doing so.

"Dammit, Chopper. Can you at least try to talk normal instead of ripping her head off? Ivy is only doing her job." Lochlan hits me with a disapproving look.

Why the fuck is he taking her side? I already felt shitty for snapping because I don't easily trust people and fucking hate hospitals. I was kinda opening up to letting her stitch me back up because I know her, might still have the hots for her, but fuck…I'm the one in pain and want to get the hell out of here while she's poking the shit out of me instead of fixing my leg so I can leave. And not to mention I'm fucking annoyed by the fact that she doesn't remember my fucking name or who I am.

I reach out and grab Lochlan's cut before I growl, "Why don't you go fuck her in the corner so I can sneak out of here. Show her some kindness and appreciation for the both of us."

Lochlan looks like I just punched him one in the face before he tells me in utter exasperation. "She's got no pussy, or tits, man."

Ivy chuckles.

What the hell? Why is he throwing the 'she's got no pussy, or tits' statement out there? What are we? Teenagers? We're grownups for fuck's sake, and we haven't seen each other in years, drifted a-fucking-part. "The way that white coat is stretching her front tells me there's some sinful pillow action hiding behind it," I growl at Lochlan before I lunge up and wrap my fingers around her throat. "Stop. Fucking. Touching. Me."

Her hand is gripping my wrist and she's leaning into my face, giving me some of her weight. Those bright gray, stormy eyes are locked on mine. "I'm going to touch you whether you like it or not. Now if you just suck in your personality for a few more minutes, then I'll be able to get my work done so you can let Lochlan get you the hell out of here. Deal?"

The sweet smell of jasmine wrapped with…pineapple? "Did you shove some pineapple down your throat before you,"

"Came to take care of your sorry ass? Yes. I had a slice of pineapple a moment ago. I kinda earned a little sweetness after my ten-hour shift. Like I said, calm down and let me take care of you so we can both get the hell out of here, because I need to get some sleep." Those gray orbs are mesmerizing, the dark ring around them seems to flare up when she's agitated. As if she's reaching out and smacking me on the back of my head to prove what an asshole I'm being in this moment.

"Fine," I snap and regretfully let go of her delicate neck because I could feel her pulse pick up underneath my touch from our banter.

Chapter 2

Ivy

I should have left over an hour ago. Dammit, why is Tuck always late or a no-show when he has to take over my shift? He should have been here already so he would have been the one to deal with this idiot. And I hate the fact that I'm reminded by Arthur's military buddies. It brings up so many hurtful memories. Arthur…my twin brother. My other half, the one I lost, still makes pain slice through my chest, even after all these years.

My patient wasn't lying when he said I was bald the last time he saw me. When Arthur signed up for his second tour, I shaved my head as a show of support. Or maybe I was just insane and it was easier going through med school not having to deal with my thick hair, with the long shifts and keeping it wrapped up to do my job.

Shit. I'm having a hard time focusing as it is because I remember this guy *very* vividly. He was the first one who made me aware of my own body when I was a teenager. Not that we ever did anything, because Arthur made it very clear to his friends that I was off-limits and just 'one of the guys.' But when I saw Chopper again at the funeral? Weeks after he was still on my mind. So much that I went out and bought my first vibrator. Okay, those thoughts need to leave my brain because like I said…*focus* on the job at hand.

"Nora, can you grab me a new set of gloves and then check why Tuck isn't here yet?" I stand up and throw my gloves in the trash. The idiot made me grab his wrist when he wrapped his fingers around my neck.

Though fear wasn't flowing through my veins. It was the thought of how huge his hand was and how strong his grip felt perfectly wrapped around my neck. Ugh. See? I need to get home and enjoy a long hot shower with my waterproof vibrator, have some food, and relax on my balcony while I sip on a nice cold beer.

Right when I've got a new pair of gloves on, the door swings open and a guy in a suit is standing in the doorway. Nora tries to pass but the guy holds his hand up, showing his badge. He talks softly and hands Nora some papers. Ignoring this, I get busy with sticking a needle with a sedative in Mr. Annoying so I can sew his leg back together.

It's nothing major, he was very lucky. Yet I saw his old scars and the X-rays of his legs and recognized the damage he has. Well, it's fixed but the bones show an old injury that's similar to an impact from a great height where bones shatter…jumpers.

Arthur was a SEAL. All of them go through a series of jump progressions, and seeing these guys worked together for years…a team…yeah. Needless to say, something went bad for this one. I mean, I can read it in his eyes. The bright bluish-green that flares when he speaks. He doesn't like hospitals and one look at his x-rays explains why.

Focus. Work, then get the hell out of here and suck in a week of relaxation. That's right, I've got seven days of nonstop doing nothing other than enjoying some peace and quiet. That is unless the hospital calls because that jerk Tuck is failing and the other ER doctors are packed.

I'm halfway with closing a wound when an idiot comes to stand next to me. "Ma'am, I need you to sign this first."

Is this guy for real? "And I need you to get the hell out of my space. Anything gets handled through administration or can be handled when I'm not standing over an open wound. Move you idiot, can't you see I'm busy trying to help this patient?"

The guy whose leg I'm talking about chuckles.

"You misheard me, ma'am. I need for you to sign this first. This patient of yours is a top security matter that demands a special kind of disclosure. If you don't sign right this second, I will have to take other actions," the suit says with a firm voice.

Since everything seemed to get screwed up the second I stepped foot inside this room, I snap off my gloves and smack the guy in the chest with a flat hand. Either he's caught off guard, or I've put every inch of strength into that one single push, making him stumble back.

"Go. Away. This patient is my first, and only, priority and you're endangering his health," I snap and step around him to grab my third pair of gloves.

"Drop the gloves, ma'am. I need for you to come with me. There are legal matters to settle first," the suit says.

I'm getting so annoyed in this moment that I might have reached my point of insanity. I've finally got my gloves on and snatch up the scalpel and point it in his direction. "You misheard me, asshole. I'm not leaving my patient, as I've said…this man here is my first, *and only*, priority. Legal matters or not, it can wait till I've closed every wound. See the scalpel in my hand? Not only did I make a vow, but I know how to handle this flawlessly."

The suit drops his papers and is now pointing a gun at me. Clearly the asswipe thinks I've lost my mind.

"Cool it, Stanley. She's an ol'lady." I risk a glance at the guy who said that. The one who's lying on the bed with his leg open and his eyes closed.

When I lock my gaze with Lochlan, I see his reaction matches mine. Surprise. Shock. There's only one woman in this room and she's most definitely not an ol'lady. She's the one holding a scalpel…*me*. I've never dated, never had a boyfriend, never had sex, so most definitely never been, am, or will be, an ol'lady.

"Stand down, Stanley. You heard Chopper. Put that gun away and let this ol'lady do her job," a guy with a leather cut and inked up forearms tells Stanley from the doorway.

Stanley only gives a tight nod before he tucks away his gun and takes his papers with him while he scurries out of the room.

The guy with the inked-up forearms closes the door and steps toward the bed. His leather cut says President. Awesome. This just keeps getting better. I know Lochlan is with an MC. He told me so at my brother's funeral, explaining how they would always be there for me if I needed anything. I never called though. I'm not one to reach out. I can take care of myself, always have, always will.

"Mind telling me whose ol'lady this is, Chopper? Yours or Lochlan's?" inked forearm dude says while I place my scalpel back down and sit to keep my hands busy with stitches. I'm actually thankful for the long-lasting period of silence that follows. And yes, I just carry on like nothing happened because the sooner his leg is taken care of, the faster I can leave for seven days of well-earned vacation time.

"He's delirious," I mutter when I put in the final few stitches. "He's been flipping out ever since they brought him in. No worries, though. I'm almost done, then you two can get him home."

"I just vouched for your ass, bitch." The President leans into my space. "I don't fucking know you."

I release an internal, very deep sigh while keeping an eye on what I'm doing. "They sure ripped open a can of assholes today," I mutter to myself.

Chopper chuckles. "Relax, Prez. She's not an ol'lady, she doesn't have any tits or pussy. Lochlan said so."

"No tits, or…what the fuck you idiot?" the President growls.

Okay, that's it. "I do have a pussy and stellar breasts that don't even need a damn push up bra to glance over the edge of my shirt, thank you very much. Now if you idiots would just mention that I'm off-limits because you were buddies with my brother instead of the ridiculous thing Arthur thought up when we were kids; buddies don't have dicks, sisters of buddies don't have tits or pussy. Arthur is dead, this idiot's leg is fixed. I'm going home and for the love of all that is holy or living in hell…stay out of my ER next time."

I tear off my gloves and walk out of the room.

Chapter 3

Chopper

"Dibs," Lochlan shouts as he watches the doctor leave the room.

What the fuck. Dibs? "You can't call dibs, she's Arthur's sister."

"Why not, you heard her, right?" Lochlan crosses his arms in front of his chest. "Arthur is dead, she's hot, and clearly wants it out there that the tits, pussy, and dick for that matter, are back in place."

Again, all my mind thinks is, "What the actual fuck?"

"Okay, let me spell it out for you then, because clearly the hot chick forgot to check that head of yours." Lochlan points into the direction of the door Ivy just left through. "I've called it. First dibs so I get to nail her first."

I stumble off the bed and grab the fucker by his cut. "Didn't you hear me say she's an ol'lady?"

"I heard that, loud and clear," Deeds quips, way too fucking cheerful if you ask me.

"You telling me that's yours?" Lochlan's eyes are as wide as when I voiced the words the first time.

"Yeah. If that gets you to back the fuck off, then yes, she's my ol'lady." I can easily claim her so Ivy is safe from any other brothers that want to fuck or go near her, because I have no intention of opening myself up, or committing myself, to a woman. *Ever.* I'm just not cut out for that shit because once you've seen what humans are capable of...let's just say I lack the ability to unsee shit.

Yet this one...this woman...she was branded in my head when I first saw her, sixteen fucking years old, and she even crawled deeper underneath my skin the last time we met...even if she was fucking bald. Then again today...how she handles herself and her actions just now? She fucking threatened a guy with a scalpel, defending me while the fucker pulled a gun on her and yet, she still didn't back down.

I've never met any other woman like her and that's the only reason I claimed her on the spot. I'm a fucking moron who had a brain fart because with my background and mindset, I'm clearly not cut out for that shit. I'm not able to let a woman, or any human being for that matter, get close to me. A chick for a quick fuck, sure, but when the cum has left my body, said body will leave the room.

I just simply can't, not with the nightmares that haunt me, my fucking legs, and the damn scars inside and out. And surely because I flat-out can't communicate, or connect for that matter. Women want all the right words and the actions that relate to the foundation of what they deserve and need. I tend to block and steer clear. Less disappointment, less chance to breach trust. I'm a cold-hearted asshole for a reason, so let's keep it that way.

But all of this sentimental, complicated life shit apart...deep down I have an unexpected urge to protect this little gem, to tie her to me. Or maybe deep down it's some form of guilt that flares up. I wasn't there for her brother, so I damn well am going to be there for her.

"You do realize that a claim made in front of two brothers stands, right? Not to mention the fact that the ol'lady in question needs to get fucking inked." Lochlan chuckles.

Shit. That might have slipped my mind. But I caught a glimpse of some ink peeking out from underneath the white sleeves of her coat so I know she's not a Virgin Mary when it comes to ink. Maybe she wouldn't mind getting another one, because that will give her protection for life. Kinda like a political immunity status that'll come in handy at some point in life. Holy fuck, I'm screwed. No woman in her right mind would do that. I mentioned my lack of communication skills, right?

"Ooooh, we have a new ol'lady, and I get to ink her? I need a name and I have time tomorrow. Is she a badass? She's gotta be a badass. Although Roan was a little timid, but she's fitting in so anything would work. Does she have a piercing? If not...I can,"

"What the fuck, Prez? Why the hell did you call Lips and put her on fucking speaker?" Dammit, my Prez's ol'lady is nosy as fuck. "Why don't you run a nationwide commercial while you're at it? Dammit man, the woman herself has no clue."

"Meh, we just went through some bad shit, this whole MC needs something to keep our minds occupied." Deeds shrugs and says goodbye to his ol'lady before he hangs up and tucks his phone away.

"At my, and mainly at this innocent woman's, expense? Just get me the fuck out of here," I growl and grab his cut for support.

Deeds shakes his head. "Want me to get a wheelchair for you?"

"One of the fucking perks we have of slipping in and out of shit is not to stick by the fucking rules. Fuck the wheelchair. I'm sure Stanley cleared the path for us, so shut up and get me home." I wince at the pain that shoots through my leg when I put some weight on it. I'm gonna be sore as fuck come morning, that's for sure.

"Come on, fucker. We've got you." Deeds throws his arm around me so I'm hanging in between my brothers as they gracefully drag me out of the hospital.

My fucking leg is throbbing and is tainting my sanity when I finally have my ass on the bed. I'm lying here with my leg up and my laptop on my lap. Before I know what I'm doing, I've got all the information in different windows open on my screen. *Ivy Demoroll*. Every single digital piece of information about her just entered my brain. Oh, yeah…I've got the world at my fingertips with just a few hits on the keyboard.

I didn't start off a computer nerd. Sit behind a damn screen? Fuck no. I was the epitome of adventure and action. A SEAL, fly a fucking chopper, or fuck…jumping out of one. I could handle any type of situation I was thrown into or got myself into. That all changed eleven years ago during a standard jump.

It wasn't even a combat jump in a warzone. Nope, during training. Getting your air stolen, that's what it's called. It's something that deep down you know and fear. Something that could happen. It did, and I should have pulled and slipped away. You're trained for these things, know you have to glide apart by somewhat steering. It didn't help one fucking bit because, yeah…I live to tell about it, but my legs were shattered and it took me months and months to be able to walk again. At first, they thought I wouldn't be able to.

The shit I saw and went through in Afghanistan…and then something like that happens during a fucking training and that's it. Lying in a bed for months with no future, only the now you're wrapped in and the vivid memories that haunt you day and night. It's like your brain is set on a loop of all the bad stuff you went through and saw in life.

And here I am a-fucking-gain...on a bed with my leg up and a damn computer on my lap. I know very well I can get up and go to the bathroom myself or do a fucking happy dance, but fuck...it triggers memories I thought I'd buried deep enough to walk the road they called living. Not balance on the edge just waiting to tip over.

My fingers run mindlessly over the keyboard until I'm staring at a black and white blurry video. Guess just looking up all the digital information I could find about Ivy wasn't enough. It's not like I know her through and through from when we were teenagers. But because she was the sister of one of my friends, I saw her a lot during that time.

Although it was just some teenage crush back then that I had to keep to myself because she was off-limits, that doesn't mean I never thought about her only as one of the guys. Hell no. I vigorously jerked off to her enough that I can't even give you a rough number of how many times I did so.

Seems like I'm right back down to where I was back then...because I found the location of her apartment. Across from her is a parking lot with cameras that have an angle that gives me the perfect view of her balcony. Stalker level, that's what it's come to. Again...hands off and just admire from a distance without anyone knowing.

Zooming in, I see she's sitting in a large chair that looks comfy with a book in one hand, a beer in the other. There are a lot of flowers and plants and shit crowding that small balcony. It looks like a tiny living room with a table and a candle, all romantic and girly. From the things I've found out about the past decade, it screams she's career driven and has been very successful.

She doesn't have any loans and her apartment is fully paid for. Her parents come from old money and probably paid for her education. Although it's none of my concern, I do think it's amazing how she's managed to climb up to being a highly respected ER doctor. From what I've discovered there is no history with a boyfriend. Like I said…career driven, hence the lack of information or anything about her private life.

I watch how she stands up and places her book on the chair she was sitting in and walks inside her house. Damn. From what I can tell, she's got the longest, finest legs I've seen in all my life. And that says a lot coming from a fucking black and white, blurry video stream. Seems like she's only wearing a large t-shirt. After a moment, she strolls out again holding a beer.

Movement at the bottom of my screen catches my gaze. There's a guy in a truck. That's not so special, except this one is leaning out the window holding a cup and his head is clearly staring in Ivy's direction. Can't blame the guy…if he's on a coffee break and a stunning woman is standing on her balcony…dudes appreciate the view, simple as that.

She grabs her book and sits her ass down before she places her feet up on the railing. Allowing me, and the fucker in the truck who's staring at her, a straight damn open view of her goddamned pussy. Fuck. I grab my cell and tap in her phone number. I watch as she leans to her right and places the book and beer on the table before she grabs, and answers, her phone.

Chapter 4

Ivy

"Ivy," I answer the phone and wait for the person to say something because it was an unknown number.

"Put your fucking feet on the ground," a voice barks.

I'm actually shocked by the tone of anger in his voice and don't even process the words until I'm standing with the phone still plastered to my ear.

"Better," the voice now tells me with a fragment less anger.

"Who is this?" I demand while glancing around me.

"Chopper," the voice snaps.

I'm still stunned, processing the whole phone call thing when it suddenly clicks. "Ah. Still the same grumpy one, huh? Thought you'd add a rude phone call and stalker issues to the pile now too? Where are you?"

"I'm rude?" And he's back to barking out his words. "You're all legs up, cunt on goddamned show for all to see."

Legs up? For all to…see? Wait, back the hell up…*he can see me?* I hang up, grab my book and beer and speed walk into my house. Closing the door to the balcony, I make fast work to close all the curtains before AC-DC's 'Thunderstruck' fills the room, indicating someone is calling me. I'm sooooo not going to answer that. Besides freaking out over the fact that he's observing me, called to tell me…

I glance down and check what I'm wearing. I'm not naked, but maybe it seems like it. When I got home I just took a long shower and put on a big t-shirt along with pink boy shorts. *I'm not naked.* Well, I'm not wearing a bra and maybe from his point of view…

What the hell am I thinking? I'm in my own freaking house, not naked, and he needs to leave me the hell alone. My phone stops ringing and shortly after dings, indicating I have an incoming message. I'm actually growling in anger at my phone at this point when I open the message.

Unknown: Answer the damn phone.

I stalk over to my window and shove my hand behind the curtains and flip him off. If he's watching, then that's all he's getting. Not only is Chopper grumpy and rude, he's also lacking some major social skills. Totally not the boy I used to know.

Taking a breath to calm myself, I think of a way to annoy him, or better yet…treat him as a child that needs to learn some manners. The corner of my mouth twitches as I add his number to my phone along with his name so I know it's him if he calls next time, and I reply to his message.

Me: You didn't say please; so, no.
Chopper: Rude.

What the? Is he dicking me? Remembering what he said earlier on the phone about me having my cunt on show…I click the camera app and hold the hem of my t-shirt between my teeth as I turn to the side and snap a picture of myself.

Me: Between me and you, I'm the nice one and you're the sociopath. And for the record, my cunt wasn't on show. See?!

I add the picture and when I hit sent and see the image again, my face flushes because I clearly didn't think this through. It does however make the texting stop, so that's a win, right? Nervously, I grab my beer and chug it down in one go. I'm about to grab a new one when my phone starts to ring.

Checking the caller, I see it's Chopper so this time I do pick up, trying to keep my voice steady because this guy is seriously making me nervous among a few other things. "Yes?"

"Please tell me you don't send pictures like that to guys on a regular basis, Ivy." I think this guy isn't capable of speaking normally because every word comes out like a stray dog who's barking at everything he sees and doesn't know.

"I most definitely do not," I gasp.

"Thank fuck." He sighs and with that, his voice changes into what I'm guessing is his normal one. "Just so we're clear, you can send them to me, any time day or night."

I roll my eyes and realize he can't see me so I add, "You wish."

"Actually, that isn't far from the truth." He chuckles.

And dammit, that sound is so sexy I have to swallow and plant my ass on the couch. Pulling my knees up, I try to change the subject. "So...did you work out that ol'lady thing with the others?"

"Nothing to work out," he gruffly says.

"Okay," I reply, unsure what to say next.

That is until he surprises me when he tells me, "Because you're still considered to be my ol'lady."

I'm standing back on my feet with my next breath. Pushing the end call button, I throw my phone on the couch and stalk to the windows to shove my hands in between the curtains and flip him off again, both hands this time, before I go the fridge to grab and chug down another beer. I hope he was still watching, well...not so much, and even if he wasn't, it soothes my anger in this moment.

This is so not happening. The one who was annoyingly dominating like this was my brother, and my father too, for that matter. Come to think of it...Arthur's friends were all like that when we used to hang out as teenagers. Even Chopper, although back then I used to know him as Rigby. Ugh. All of them were protective and fierce, placing my needs above theirs but acting like Neanderthals in the process. Basically, they were the reason why I was never asked out on a date or even thought about making a move toward a guy. It's been awhile since anyone acted like that on my behalf and I'm not sure what I think about all of this.

My phone starts to ring again but all I do is watch the thing vibrate while AC-DC's 'Thunderstruck' yet again fills the room. Taking a deep breath, I decide to focus on my vacation days. Meaning beer, a good book, and total relaxation. That certainly doesn't include annoying issues with guys who think they can claim to be in some sort of a relationship with me before even asking or going on a date first.

Help Our Heroes

   Grabbing my iPad, I order a pizza online before I snatch another beer from the fridge. With my phone on silent, book in hand, I plant my ass on the couch. Vacation mode: on.

Chapter 5

Chopper

My leg is throbbing like crazy and the painkillers I took do shit to mute the pain that is flaring up. I know...I should be in bed, leg up. Instead I'm knocking on this door with a bag slung over my shoulder. The door opens and the dark green haired beauty is standing in front of me. Her head is down while she fumbles with something and holds out her arm.

"Here you, go. No anchovies on there, right? Because..." Her head rears back when her gaze hits mine. "You're not the pizza guy."

"No," I snap. "I'm not." Stepping forward, she has no other choice but to step back so I can get inside.

Closing the door, she walks over to the table and clears away two beer bottles. "What are you doing here, Rigby? I don't remember inviting you."

I need to take a few breaths before I can get over the weird reaction of hearing my name falling from her lips. It's been a long fucking time since I've heard my given name. I decide to ignore her words and hold out a shot I printed from the video surveillance. "Any idea who this guy is?"

She glances at the shot for a microsecond and narrows her eyes at me. "Also, not the pizza guy."

What the hell? "Look closer, Doc," I snap.

Ivy glares at me. I don't fucking care, I'm still holding the paper up. She leans forward and snatches it away from me.

Her head tilts to the left. "Huh. That might look like Tuck. Except he should be at work right now."

She holds on to the paper and grabs up her phone, tapping it before she puts it close to her ear and stares at the paper again. "Yeah, hey, Ivy here...is Nora

Help Our Heroes

around? Good, can you put her on for me?"

It takes a moment because Ivy strolls over to the window and peeks through the curtains.

"The fucker isn't out there anymore. I just came from there." I sigh and drape myself over her couch, putting my leg up. It feels like someone is pounding on the thing with a hammer.

Ivy keeps staring out the window until she starts to talk. "Hey, it's me. Yes, I know it's vacation time, just listen, okay? Tuck...he was supposed to be at work but he wasn't there when I left. Did he show up?"

Now her eyes meet mine and she just shakes her head when she notices I'm lying comfortable on her couch.

"He's not sick, Nora...the idiot was in front of my house...no, I'm not kidding. I'm staring at a picture that puts him right there...yes, he's moved up to stalker classification...where did I get the picture? Well, to be honest, my other stalker gave it to me." She bursts out laughing. "Nah, I'm just kidding. He's a guy who's going to handle it for me. I've known him since I was sixteen, he was one of Arthur's friends...yes, I will...bye."

"Tuck was supposed to be at work, but he clearly wasn't...dodging shifts as usual." Ivy stalks over to the couch and looks down at me.

"What?" I question.

"Are you comfy? Because...dammit, your leg. If you ripped the stitches I'm going to be really pissed, mister," she says in a low, harsh voice before she bends over me and starts to pull on my sweatpants.

I can't help the laughter in my voice when I tell her, "Didn't expect you'd be stripping off my pants that fast."

Fuck. The way she's looking at me right now might be close to a death threat, and here comes my cock rising to get her attention as if he's willingly surrendering to his last seconds on this fucking earth.

I give her a cocky grin. "Looks like he wants a formal introduction."

Ivy rolls her eyes. "As an ER doctor, how many penises do you think I see in a normal week's work? I'll tell you...more than you think. But the bigger," she fucking winks before she continues, "question here is...how many were still functional? Because one time there was this girl holding her boyfriend's penis...and with this I don't mean palming it. Nope. Holding the guy's pride and joy in her hand because she accidentally bit it off while she was mid orgasm while giving him a blow job."

Yeah, my boner just left the fucking building with that little too much oversharing work shit. Her eyes slide down and she fucking chuckles.

"Hey, don't blame him. You're the one with the horror story. Any cock would fucking sympathize. Damn." I shudder at the thought. "I'm fine. Lemme up already, no need for you to check my damn leg."

She grips my cut and I'm surprised by her strength when she pulls me halfway up with one arm. "Shut up and let me look at it. I swear to God, if you made your leg worse I'll tie you to the bed and treat you Stephen King's Misery novel style. Get me?"

"You're gonna break my ankles if I leave. Gotcha. But for the record, Doc...I brought a bag, see," I point in the direction of the door where I left it, "I wasn't going to leave any time soon anyway."

"Shut up," she thunders before she checks out my leg and I swear she's doing it to inflict pain. No. That's a lie but she's not going all gentle on me, that's for damn sure. Ivy pins me with a fierce look. "Don't freaking move from this couch."

She grabs a few pillows to shove underneath my leg and covers me with a quilt that looks more like a spider web. She stalks off to the kitchen and returns with a bottle of beer in her hands.

"Are you gonna offer me one of those?" I question.

"Hell no," Ivy says with determination. "You need to take some pain meds and mixing them with alcohol won't be happening underneath my roof." She glares at me before she adds, "Now start talking about why you're here and why you have a picture of Tuck in front of my house."

I lean up on one elbow. "I was checking a camera feed that had a straight view of your house. There was this car parked with a dude in it leaning out of the window. He had a cup of coffee in his hand, so I thought he was just on a break from work or something. Then you flashed your cunt and,"

"I did not," she seethes before she adds, "And who's the creepy stalker in the first place? That's right...the one that's draped over my couch."

"Hey," I snap. "I resent that. I was just checking up on you. It's not like I was jerking off or something. It's what I do...I'm the intel guy of Broken Deeds MC. The computer guy who can get his hands on almost any type of information, no matter how deep it's hidden. That's why I hacked into the camera feed; because I was curious, that's all." I wait to see her reaction to my confession.

Ivy takes a few sips of her beer before she signals with her hand and adds, "Go on."

"Remember when you flipped me off the first time?" I watch as Ivy's mouth twitches.

Yeah, she remembers alright. "Well, that's when he threw down his coffee and almost got out of his truck. It spiked my attention that he wasn't just taking a break and enjoying the view while sipping his fucking coffee. Then you flipped me off again and he got out of his car and walked right up to the porch...but he stopped himself and the look he had on his face...yeah...I've seen that on lots of people. Built up anger that's been there for a while and threatening to blow any damn second. Even though the fucker got in his car and left...I couldn't ignore the situation. That's the reason I had Lochlan drop me off here. I'm not leaving until I've researched this fucker and know you're safe."

She's just staring at me; no fucking emotion on her face. I swallow that visual for a few minutes before I snap, "Well? Say something, dammit."

One eyebrow shoots for the ceiling before she raises her empty bottle. "I need another beer."

Chapter 6

Ivy

"You fucking what?" Chopper barks, clearly annoyed and I can tell he's about to get up from the couch.

Yes, I've decided to stick with the name he uses now because I saw a weird expression come over him when I used Rigby earlier. Kinda suits him though, Chopper. Because clearly Rigby, the teenager I knew, is far too different, in size and attitude, from the guy that's now lying on my couch.

I point at him while walking backwards into the kitchen. "Stay there. I said I needed another beer. I've got a few days of vacation time. I work shifts where I can't even count how many hours, or at what hour it is, for that matter. I'm allowed to drink beer right now…because I've looked forward to these days off ever since I asked for them months ago. Besides…all of what you just mentioned? *Weird.* Weird and most definitely insane enough that I need a little more liquid courage to talk more about this insanity."

Turning, I open the fridge and stroll back into the living room with a bottle of water for Chopper and a beer for me. "Tuck has the annoying habit of dodging shifts when he's supposed to work when I'm not. At first, I thought it was a coincidence. I mean the guy just started working at the hospital three months ago, but the last few weeks it's been getting more than annoying and now this."

I plunk down in an easy chair and put my feet on the table just as the doorbell rings, making me dash up. Except in the next instant Chopper is blocking my way to the door.

I see him palming a gun signaling at me without a sound. *I need to back up and let him handle this.*

I roll my eyes and whisper, "It's the pizza guy, doofus."

Help Our Heroes

He narrows his eyes and clearly waits for me to step back. I take a deep breath and finally do so as he checks the peephole before tucking away his piece because I'm right; it is the pizza dude. When he opens the door, I lean in, plastering myself against Chopper's back to hand the guy some money after Chopper takes the pizza.

Closing the door, he turns toward me and eyes the two boxes. "Two pizzas for a tiny woman like you…or did you have something planned?" I see him grit his teeth before he adds. "Some other dick I'm not aware of?"

I release a very unfeminine snort before taking the pizza boxes and mindlessly add, "The only dicks I've had, and own, are the jelly kind that come in all different colors, sizes, and speeds."

Oops. I manage to stalk away into the bedroom. Eating in bed while watching a movie sounds like a perfect way to start my night.

Chopper walks around the bed and plants his ass on the mattress and the second he does, I watch…horrified and gasp, "What are you doing?"

"We're having pizza in bed, apparently." Chopper shrugs. *Shrugs!*

"You're half right. *I* am having pizza in bed. *You* on the other hand can crash on the couch. I would say 'leave' but that nut, Tuck, was just brought to my attention and I can't do anything about it right now, so I'm going to get through this night and take action tomorrow." I open one pizza box and take out a slice.

Chopper eyes my pizza and asks, "What's in the other box?"

"Only cheese on that one." I make sure to put some steel in my voice before I add, "I'm not sharing the one with pineapple, but you can have a slice of the other one *if* you leave my bedroom."

"Hey, the pineapple shit is all yours. No way would I ever even try that combination." The man fake gags while he takes a slice of the other pizza.

"Why aren't you moving?" I mumble with a mouth filled with heavenly food.

Dammit. The smile he's now sporting almost makes me choke. It's absolutely stunning. His normally hard features, short hair, scruff, and strong jaw are now radiant, a warm welcome.

"Fine. Stay," I mutter and grab another slice.

Within minutes we've devoured the food, leaving me to stroll to the kitchen to grab us something else to drink. Soda for the both of us. I hand him one while I take a huge gulp from mine.

"Mind showing me your dick collection now?" Chopper asks me without one hint of humor, making me slap a hand over my mouth to keep the contents inside.

Swallowing to regain the function of drawing air into my lungs, I manage to free up my mouth and cough. "Excuse me?"

"Why? You didn't do anything wrong. Now show me." He crosses his thick arms in front of his chest...waiting.

I'm not easily embarrassed...but dammit...when I was sixteen he made me uncomfortable with the way my body reacted and he's this rough, huge, sexy biker that's just barged back into my life and demands that I just show him my stuff? The things I've collected over the years because I have no time to... "No."

He raises one eyebrow that he manages to evolve into a very hot action and repeats, "No?"

"That's right," I snap. "Be glad I'm not grabbing you by,"

"My dick?" He cuts me off mid-sentence, laughter and disbelief in his voice. "Because you only have rubber ones?"

I'm on my feet with my next breath and grab my lime colored vintage train case from underneath the bed where I keep my 'stash.' Screw shame, I don't owe this man anything, but I do want to show him how a girl has many more options than needing a man because only he can give her pleasure. Slipping my finger over the numbers, I take care of the lock and hold it upside down over the bed, making dick after colorful dick tumble out in a pile.

Did I not mention I have a huge collection? Some girls have lots of makeup. I'm the not so much virgin who likes to try stuff I order online...vibrators, dildos, plugs, beads, you name it, I've tried it...well, except for the real-life thing.

"Holy shit," Chopper mutters. "That's even more goddamned sexy than hearing a chick voice she watches porn every now and then." His eyes find mine. "Did you try every single one of them? Maybe two at a time?"

"Yes, but..." I lean over to the bedside table and grab my tiny clit vibrator and hold it up. "This one works best though. I think it's the fourth one I've bought. But that's only because I accidentally washed it along with the sheets. It's not water-resistant."

'Not..." He swallows before he croaks, "water-resistant." He rubs a hand over his face. "Dammit woman, do you have some kind of sex addiction or something?"

"No," I gasp. But I swallow my next words and think for a moment because this does look bad. I mean my bed is littered with all kinds of colorful sex toys. "That's all I have," I add in confession.

"Geez, that's comforting." Chopper chuckles. "So, no other cases filled with more dicks then?"

"I mean, I haven't shoved a real live one into my vagina, you idiot," I snap.

His eyes darken and it's then he realizes what I'm saying. "You mean, except for the fake stuff…you're telling me you're *a virgin*?"

Chapter 7

Chopper

"Put the fucking dicks away." My voice is filled with anger. Why? Maybe because I claimed a woman who no one has had before me. Un-fucking-touched and I've tied her to me.

To a broken person who can never be fully functional. I mean it's not due to my legs that were shattered and took months to heal, and still have a limp every now and then when I'm having a bad day. Some scars can fade but they will remain and I'm not talking about just the ones carved in my skin. There's more than that. The stuff I've seen and the guilt I have to live with, it's every-fucking-thing.

What the hell did I do, claiming her? I rip the case from her hand and start throwing those things she shoved in her cunt in there. Dammit. Now I've got that visual on a loop in my head.

"Get out." Ivy rips the bag out of my hands and shoves my shoulder. I'm caught by surprise and my leg fucking hurts. All of this makes me twist and turn, making me fall on my ass.

Every fucking ol'lady I know would have dropped down beside me to help. This lady doc here? She's glaring right at me while locking up her precious dicks and shoving them back underneath the bed. "Get up, and get out, Chopper." Her voice is as hard as stone.

Wincing at the pain, I manage to pull myself up by leaning on the bed. "By all means," I sneer, "don't raise a finger to help."

"Help? Help who? You?" She snorts and steps closer into my personal space. "You're beyond help because for one…you need to allow yourself to be of any value. That's something you couldn't do at the hospital when I tried to help you, so why would I give you a hand now? I've done enough already."

Somehow, that's a punch to my gut and I must have a look on my face because she shakes her head.

"Shit. Me and my big mouth," she mutters before she clears her throat and adds, "You're too damn annoying, you idiot." Ivy pokes her finger against my chest but this time I'm prepared for her hands-on tactics.

My fingers wrap around her wrist and in one smooth move I've got her turned and her back is plastered against my front. I've got a tight grip on her neck and my other arm around her waist preventing her from moving.

"Don't fucking judge me. You know nothing," I snarl.

Ivy struggles in my grip but it's useless. She just barely manages to draw in oxygen with my fingers wrapped tight around her neck. "I wonder how many times people threw a punch in your face," she mutters.

Stunned, I let her go and step back, planting my ass on the bed to remove the weight off my damn legs.

"Well? Go on, tell me. I shared my dick collection, so it's only fair you share something in return." She's toying with her necklace. There's a maple seed hanging from it.

Shit. I reach out and hold it. "Helicopter seed," I croak. What are the chances? "Why do you have this?"

"Quid pro quo," she tells me softly.

Share something. She's asking me to open up? I don't fucking know how to do that. So instead I just grunt the first thing that comes to mind…the last time I got punched. "I screwed up a while ago. Got slumped into a state where I was zoning out into the comfort of my brothers having my back. Didn't do my job, didn't protect an ol'lady and…let's just say I got my ass handed to me. That was a serious wakeup call."

"We all need a kick in the ass sometimes, keeps things real." Ivy gives me a tiny smile. "When I was little, me and my brother used to love throwing them in the air and watch how they…"

"Chopper down." I mirror her smile and release a deep sigh. "Can we just lie down and watch a movie?"

Ivy gives me a tiny nod before she whispers, "I'm sorry."

I shrug my shoulders.

"No, I mean it. I shouldn't have snapped at you, but you're very annoying, and when you indicated that I didn't jump to your rescue...let's just say you seem to be a guy who doesn't appreciate being pampered. I saw your X-rays. I know you were with Arthur when...I just...I can imagine, okay? My comment about you being beyond help was poorly stated. What I meant to say was you don't accept it in a kind matter. If I would have run to your side, you would have pushed me away. And dammit it's coming out all wrong and I can see by the way your jaw is ticking that I'm screwing it up even more. So yes, let's shut up and watch a movie." She sighs and slides underneath the covers.

Funny. I thought I was the communication nut. I supply information, it's part of my task in Broken Deeds MC, and yet keep my mouth shut most of the time, to anyone for that matter. Opening up isn't an option. You internalize the pain and you learn to embrace the flames that lash out at every angle. With everything I've been through, the shit I've seen...the human part of me has forgotten to live. Just a robot functioning on autopilot to get through the days.

I still have ghosts shattered in pieces running through my head and I need to set her straight. "I wasn't with Arthur when he died. I didn't sign up for a second tour. Medical discharge." Guilt swamps me because I should, and would have fucking been there, if it wasn't for that fucked up training incident.

"Right. Bone shattering matter, well duh." She rubs her eyes. "Clearly I forgot about that detail. Although you could have died too you know, from the accident you had or if you did sign up and...right. No need to tell you more details. I'm sure many options are branded in your brain as it is."

See? This woman doesn't tiptoe around me. She's a spark that could reboot my whole being...if I let her. Except after all these years, there might not be anything to reboot at all. I know damn well that denying a possibility is similar to standing in front of a door, being told it's locked. Do you try to find out for yourself? Or walk away without making sure? Right. That's why my ass, only covered with boxers, is sliding underneath the covers beside her.

Ivy grabs the remote and puts on a movie without asking for my opinion. Honestly, I couldn't care less because my mind is still processing the whole day.

Help Our Heroes

From giving chase on my bike, trying to save Ramrod from being gun downed by one of our own, to getting shot at that made my bike crash. Hence the reason I ended up in Ivy's hands.

And what are the chances? I mean they could have taken me to another hospital, could have been another doctor, but no…it had to be her. Arthur was one of the casualties that were killed during subsequent fighting on the ground. Lochlan was part of the team, he saw Arthur die. I should have been there too. *Would have been there*…if only…shit. I rub at the ache in my chest while vivid memories and guilt wash over me.

To my surprise, Ivy snuggles close, as if she can feel the turmoil running through me. Hell, maybe she can because I'm stiff as a board and yet soft lingering touches from her fingers sliding over my inked pecs makes the tension fade.

"So…" Ivy whispers before she clears her throat and adds in a firmer voice, "Do you slide into the beds of women often after coming to their rescue to chase off stalkers…while being a stalker yourself?"

Fuck. She's too damn much. Stunning, smart, witty, single, and lying in bed next to me. "Nah, Doc. That honor only belongs to you."

"Hmm," she hums. "So no secret girlfriends then?"

Placing two fingers underneath her chin, I lock our gaze so she can see the truth in my eyes. "I've never claimed an ol'lady, or had a girlfriend for that matter. You're the first and even that wasn't supposed to happen. Stanley harassing you, Lochlan calling dibs and wanting your pussy. Dammit, I'm not cut out for that shit but I couldn't just let those fuckers have you."

Ivy narrows her eyes. "Not cut out for that shit? What's that supposed to mean? And I didn't agree to be your…ol'lady thing because *I'm* not cut out for that boyfriend, man thing."

Chapter 8

Ivy

"No shit? I wonder what gave that away…lemme think…your bag of fake dicks?" He starts to laugh but I curl my fingers around his jaw and tighten my grip.

"We will never mention that ever again. I might have had a few too many beers but the pizza sobered me up some. I might lack in bedroom stuff but there's no reason at all to make fun of me, or make me uncomfortable, got it?" I let go and push myself away from him.

Or at least try because his arm is around my waist and pulling me back against him. "One question, if you give me an honest answer…I'll drop the fake dicks…fuck that sounds weird."

"What's the question?" I ask and glare at the annoying man.

"When and why did you buy the first one?" There's no smile or humor on his face.

Is he freaking serious? "What's it to you? And should I mention that's two questions instead of just one?"

I need to shut this conversation down. There's no way I'm going to answer why I bought the first one. With him being the reason I started craving a release that involved filling me up and…dammit. "I'm sleepy, the beer and food are,"

"Oh, no you don't. I need a name of the guy that got you addicted to dick shopping." Now he freaking chuckles.

"What would you like to hear? Right after I saw you the last time? Hmmm, that would stroke your…ego, right?" Ha, honesty and denial, perfect answer.

His breathing seems to stop when he takes his time watching me. I'm getting way uncomfortable with his staring.

"Fuck." Chopper rubs a hand over his head. "Why the hell did you say that? For fuck's sake woman, I know you're not lying, I can tell."

Shit, shit, and double shit. "What do you mean 'I can tell'? That's impossible."

"Don't gimme that," he growls. "Your eyes give me a step by step walk through. They light up, dim, bounce around, and fucking pierce straight through me. I might be lacking communication skills but I've been known to read people better than their own thought process. And you, Ivy…you might shield a lot from others, and it might be the beers you drank, but you're allowing me to read you thoroughly."

When did I lie down on my back and when did he cover his body with mine? Towering over me…shit, mental note…no more beers when I'm around this guy.

"What am I thinking now?" I breathe and watch his eyes dilate as if he's opening up to swallow me.

The corner of his mouth twitches. "That you're considering trading your fake stuff for the real thing."

"Geez, you make it sound so tempting." I roll my eyes and gasp when he grinds his hips against me.

"Nothing's more tempting than you," he mutters before he slams his mouth over mine.

My eyes close involuntarily and a moan escapes me, allowing him to swirl his tongue inside my mouth. There's so much raw intensity flowing around us that it's somehow overriding my brain and there's only animalistic instincts left. Hands roam, bodies grind, tongues dance, and it's not enough…we both need more.

Chopper pulls back, disconnecting our lips while his eyes stays locked on my mouth. "I need to bury myself inside you so bad right now. Tell me you want it too or else I'll,"

My hands slide up to cup his head. "Oh, yes," I mumble while I pull him down and move my leg in an effort to give him more room. Chopper hisses and it's then I realize I kicked his leg.

He leans his forehead against my shoulder. "Fuck. Gimme a second here."

I tighten my grip and pull his head up. "Roll over."

"Roll over?" Chopper snorts. "I think you've had a bit too much control,

I'm not one of your..."

"We weren't going to mention them again." I glare but suddenly I realize what he said earlier about my eyes and how he can read me...because I can clearly read him.

His mouth is tight and his eyes carry a hint of pain and yet they are overflowing with desire. My chest aches to soothe this beast who's shielding way too much.

"I'm not trying to take control." Swallowing my nerves, I add, "I've never done this, remember...can I just set the pace here?"

Okay, that might not have come out quite right but it's way better than 'you're hurt so lay down and let me do the work.' Right? Hell if I know how to seduce a guy in bed, but I do know the basics. *In theory*. Shit. My breath whooshes out when he rolls us over, making me straddle him in the process.

"How about we keep it to; *it's the first time for us*? But I advise you to embrace this moment because when my leg heals I won't give up much control again." There's a vow in his tone that makes me shiver.

The thought of letting him take full control over my body is an empowering thought. Although I have no clue where this is going, I'm embracing this moment as he said. Even if it's just to make a dusty lust filled dream from my past become reality. To have sex with the guy who made me crave sexual interaction.

I might have fantasized it was him every time I played with one of my toys...yet the one I'm seeing now as I pull down his boxer shorts is nothing compared to the rubber ones. I wasn't kidding when I told Chopper the number of dicks I've seen in my lifetime. Seen, handled, *as a doctor*...but now that I'm seeing his, it's through a whole different set of eyes.

Curious, I lean down and let my tongue trail over the tip. His curses flow through the air at the same time his fingers dive into my hair to keep my head locked in position. Opening, I take his dick into my mouth and move down until he hits the back of my throat. I'm barely halfway down because my hand is curled around his thick, hard length. Working in sync, I move up and down with my hand and mouth in slow strokes.

Chopper pulls my hair back and I watch how he replaces my hand with his, gripping his own dick and guiding it over my lips. "Fuck. Look at that…you have no idea how much strength it takes for me to hold back. I want to pin you in place while I jerk off and shoot my load all over your face. See how I boil over with that thought, sweetheart? It's already leaking out. Show me your tongue so I can give you a little taste…but beware, Ivy…you're not allowed to rip more cum from my body. Not until I've buried myself deep inside your sweet and tight cunt that you've saved especially, and only, for me. Understood?"

Breathe. I have to remember to breathe. How can anyone focus during sex? This man is taking away all my bodily functions and replacing them with blind lust.

"Understood, Ivy?" he grinds out through his teeth.

"Yes," I breathe and lick my lips before I stick my tongue out like he just asked me to.

Chapter 9

Chopper

My pre-cum painting her tongue is enough to tighten the grip I have on my cock. I'm basically trying to block the sucker from blowing my load. Damn. I want her. Badly enough to find the strength to make her crawl up my body. She's hovering that tight cunt above me. And it will be tight because the fake dicks won't be something to compare my cock with, but she'll find that out soon enough.

My fingertip brushes over her clit. "You're not going to sink down and swallow my cock with your slick cunt, Ivy. *Not yet*. Now take off your shirt and hold one of your tits up for me because my hands are busy and I want your nipple between my teeth while I finger-fuck you."

Her indrawn breaths are as raw as my voice. Feelings. How open and consuming they are…such a massive contrast. I'm unable to talk about shit but the language and voicing my thoughts, my feelings in this moment are endless. All because there's a need.

I knew she wasn't wearing a fucking bra but knowing and seeing are two very different things. Shamelessly she does as she's told, cupping that fine set of tits as she leans forward so I can let my tongue slide over a very hard peak.

"Damn," I hiss with my mouth filled with boob. "You're so wet for me but even then, it's hard for me to push a finger inside, sweetheart. No matter how slow we'll go, or how much I prepare this cunt, *that now belongs to me*, even with those rubber things you used…doesn't matter, taking my cock is going to burn. But I swear I'll make it good."

With one hand on her hip, the other palming my cock, I slowly guide her down. Just a few inches in and she starts to whimper. With a firm grip on her hip, I cup her face and drag her down for a kiss, one where I let her feel what she does to me. The longing to take care of her and cherish the essence of what life has to offer the both of us. Fuck. How can she do this to me? I'm thankful that these thoughts flow freely inside my head and yet there's no way I'll ever be able to voice them.

I feel her weight pressing down on me and her kiss turns hungry, greedy, as if she's craving something more. How I hate that my leg is stitched up and throbbing and yet I manage to shift the pain and let lust fill my veins. In this moment I feel invincible with my body fully charged to stake my claim. Brand her with my seed and show her cunt to whose cock she belongs to. She feels so damn good, it's never felt so good.

Fuck.

Condom. I'm bare inside of her and even if it's just a few inches it feels fucking magical. But how could I skip that fucking part and she's a doctor for Christ's sake. Guiding herself up on her knees, she sinks back down and I lose it. I don't fucking care about wrapping up to prevent pregnancy. I'm clean and this being her first time…

I roll us over and ignore the throbbing in my leg because my cock is overriding the pulsation. Catching both her wrists, I pin them above her head and keep them there. Her eyes are shut and her whole face is lighting up in ecstasy. I tweak her left nipple and start to thrust deep inside, pushing my body slightly up so I can watch how my cock is slamming back and forth into her tight heat.

Ivy struggles to get her arms free. Not a chance in hell, sweetheart. "Take it, Ivory. Take me." *As I am.* I mentally add.

Her eyes flash open and I know the very reason she's shocked. I voiced her full name, one I found buried in documents because even as a sixteen-year-old she was using Ivy already.

"Mine," I snarl and hover above her face.

Before she can spill words from her fuckable mouth, I slam my lips down over hers and find her clit with my fingers in the limited space between our bodies. All it takes is a mere touch before I'm allowed to swallow her screams as she strangles my cock in a vice grip.

My eyes roll back inside my skull when my balls draw up tight and cum fires off to brand the cunt that's got me hooked. How can I blow my load and with every pulse my cock gives it intensifies the need to do this again? As in right now, every pose, for an unforeseeable amount of time.

But my body has other thoughts. It's as if the orgasm drained all the energy straight out of me. I crash down but manage to twist and fall on the mattress beside Ivy. My hand lingers between her legs, my fingers sliding through her folds, and I swear my cock twitches from the feel of our mixed juices.

"I want to fuck you again so bad, but I can't." My voice sounds like a whine and I damn well know I'm acting like a kid who wants his next favorite toy.

Ivy chuckles and lifts herself up on her elbows. Her eyes slide down and remain on my cock before something else catches her attention, making her jump off the bed and curse.

"What?" I snap, annoyed by the way she jumped off the bed. Fuck, doesn't she realize? "I know we didn't use protection. Don't freak the fuck out on me. We'll handle what life throws in our path."

Her eyes widen and I get the impression that...

"Dammit, how stupid am I?" she mutters and shakes her head. "I didn't even think...but that's not why I freaked out, look." Ivy points at my leg and suddenly the throbbing makes sense when I see my leg is bleeding.

Without saying much more, she stalks into the bathroom and comes out with a first aid kit. "Just so you know, I'm on the pill. Have been for years. Oh, and clean. You?"

"I'd never would have fucked you bare if I wasn't clean." I manage to keep some of my anger back.

"Right," she mutters.

Ivy's eyes are down and I'm not liking it one fucking bit. "I mean it, Ivory. I've never dipped my cock into another body without a fucking condom." And again, I'm snapping at her. Christ, how fucked up am I?

Her gaze locks on mine. "No one calls me Ivory."

"I do," I state and don't add anything else.

She releases a deep breath and grabs my leg causing me to grunt and look at what the fuck she's doing.

"Dammit," we both snap.

My leg is obviously bleeding and I guess...

"You ripped a few stitches. Lay back down, let me close them with some strips. And don't you dare move that leg from now on." She's back to ordering me around and I'm feeling drained as it is, so I just close my eyes, lie back, and let her take care of me.

Chapter 10

Ivy

This time when I open my eyes, I see sunlight bursting through my bedroom. There were a few times during the night when Chopper was restless. Nightmares. His jerky movements and mumbling caused me to wake up. He only settled back to sleep when I would curl myself around him, stroking his chest with my cheek to snuggle as close as I could. Then he would wrap his arm around my waist and hold me tight. I'm not an idiot. I know very well the accident he had with his bike and hurting his leg brought back memories he must have buried deep.

Reaching out, I come up empty. Glancing to my left, I see Chopper left the bed at some point during the night because the left side of the bed is cold. The thought is unsettling and yet I hear noise coming from my kitchen. It would be worse if he left me here alone, right? At least he's still in the house.

Getting out of bed brings a smile to my face. My body aches in places I never knew was possible. Amazing sex. Most definitely on my to do list today. But first, coffee. And see what the morning brings because everything is new to me. Sex. A guy in my house…hell, a guy in my life because I asked him again about it and he won't budge…I'm his ol'lady. Would that make him my boyfriend? Okay, one day at a time. Grabbing some underwear, sweatpants, and a shirt, I make fast work to freshen up in the bathroom.

When I stroll into the kitchen I come to an abrupt stop. The guy standing in the kitchen isn't Chopper. "What are *you* doing here?" I gasp in shock.

"Making coffee," he says and adds, "we need to talk."

"No, we don't. I have no freaking clue what you think you're doing here, but you need to leave." I swing my arm in the direction of the door. "Right now, please." I can tell he's ready to argue so I continue, "Listen, Lochlan...I get it, your friend is an idiot. He was supposed to be here if he wanted a shot at me being his ol'lady. Clearly, he changed his mind because you're here instead. I'm not into the whole 'let's share' thing so I don't even care what you have to say, I just want you to leave."

"Tough shit," Lochlan tells me before he turns and pours himself a cup of coffee.

"Tough...*tough shit?* What the hell? Get out. Now, dammit," I snap and smack him on the back of his head.

Yeah, I grew up with a twin brother who was about the same size as Lochlan. And I've known this guy from my teenage years. No way I'm scared. And even more? I know how to handle myself in a fight. Well...I can put up a good fight, let's stick to that.

"No, Ivy. I said we need to talk. I'm here because Chopper gave me the task of keeping an eye on you. The way he gave me a warning that was about twenty minutes long, clearly stated you're the one for him. You know why?" Lochlan steps closer and his face hardens. "Ever since his medical discharge he's been moving along on autopilot. Broken Deeds MC is somewhat of a safe zone where we watch out for each other, and yet, he's never spoken about something so fierce as he did this morning. Or at the hospital for that matter. *You matter.* That little fact alone is a huge change. A long time ago he had some interest in a girl but that wasn't real. None of it. He just gave a little chase to piss someone off and I could see right through it. But you on the other hand...he mentioned that he would castrate me three times and one way was shoving my balls through my ass and out of my mouth. And that was just about getting in your personal space. He made more threats and some visual aspects of what would happen if I touched you."

The man chuckles while none of this is funny. "Okay, this might be all funny and special for you, but he left. Just jumped out of my bed and hauled his buddy over here to save face, so he didn't have to talk or be here with me. Yeah...like I said...*get out.*"

His gaze is still locked on mine when he pulls his phone out of his pocket, taps it and pushes it against his ear. "What would happen if she would put her hands on me?"

Holy crap, I can hear Chopper curse his friend off the face of the Earth from way over here.

"I mean, what would happen if she pushes me out her fucking house, man...because you fucked up, like I explained to you two times. You left, man...shouldn't have done that." Lochlan holds up his phone and offers it to me.

I glance around. Chopper's bag is gone, just like the man himself. *Good riddance.* My lip curls up in disgust as I shake my head.

The corner of Lochlan's mouth twitches as he puts the phone back to his ear. "Nope, like I said...screwed up...right. No worries, I will." He puts the phone back into his pocket and gives me a genuine smile. "Mind if I finish my coffee before I leave?"

I shrug. "Whatever, just move so I can get a cup myself."

"Since when did you start drinking coffee? I remember a time when you would never even taste the stuff," Lochlan says.

I have to bite my lip because the memory of me telling him I didn't drink coffee is still very vivid. He practically made it look as if I just confessed to the greatest crime ever.

"A few years ago. A friend of mine, Nora, screwed up our drinks and instead of giving me an iced tea, I got her caramel macchiato iced coffee and it was amazing. I gently grew accustomed to drinking it until I turned into the addict I currently am. Happy?" I quip.

"Very." He beams.

I can't help but smack his pecs. "Shut it. Oh, this tastes amazing. You can come over and make coffee anytime." I give him a wink and take another sip of my coffee.

Geez, I didn't realize how much I missed casual conversation in my home. I don't have any guy friends and this makes me miss my brother even more.

Lochlan steps closer. "Just for coffee, or maybe something more?"

Is he hitting on me? "Clearly, no more coffee for you. Feel free to leave now." I shake my head and step away. "Weirdo," I mutter. "Here for his buddy...talks in his defense and tries to get into my panties like it's freaking normal."

Help Our Heroes

I grip the doorknob and swing it open. "Out you go, asshole. Be sure to never return and keep that idiot, so called friend of yours, away from me too."

"What the fuck did you do?" Chopper's harsh words hit me by surprise, making me slam the door shut.

Except he's standing in the door opening so it bounces off his shoe, making it slam right into my face where my nose takes the brunt of it. Excruciating pain explodes and makes me grip my face with both hands.

"Get the fuck out, the both of you!" I seethe while I peek through my fingers and head for the bathroom.

I feel wetness trickling down my face and just know I'm bleeding. Fuckers. Yes, both of them. I'm supposed to have luxury time to myself. Relaxing vacation time with my feet up, watching Netflix, eating ice cream, and not having to deal with drama. Let alone guy drama I've never even faced in all my life.

"Dammit!" I snap while I look at myself in the mirror. Blood rushing out, tears in my eyes, while I gently...well, not so freaking gently because I need to know it's not broken, assess the damage.

When I'm sure nothing is broken, I firmly pinch the soft part of my nose shut and stalk into the kitchen where I grab an icepack before I head back into the living room. I need to know for sure that these assholes have left. And no, they haven't. They're standing toe to toe right next to the couch. There's some kind of silent discussion going on but I'm so freaking furious that I don't care one bit that they are massive males with some serious muscle.

"I said, out!" And dammit, is that my annoying, weird as hell voice coming from my mouth?

They're not moving. Not one single inch. Nope, they're staring right at me. The both of them. Tears sting my eyes and before I make an even bigger fool out of myself, I turn to head for the bedroom. Locking myself up in there sounds pretty damn good to me.

Chapter 11

Chopper

"Hang on a minute." I try to soften my tone but it comes out raw anyway. I throw an arm around her waist and drag her against me.

She tried to retreat into her bedroom when she saw Lochlan and me still standing in her living room where she caught us in the middle of a stare down. Lochlan said a few words when Ivy rushed off toward the bathroom to take care of her nose and those words hit me just as hard as the door that slammed into Ivy's face.

I knew I fucked up the moment I got up and out of the comfort of her bed and arms. I just couldn't handle it. Her. Me. This whole opening up thing. How can this wonderful, bright spirited woman take me into her home, her life, her fucking body? Comforting me when those haunting nightmares flare up again? The everlasting guilt and question of why Arthur and not me with the train of events that followed and impacted our lives and those around us.

I mean…I'm doing okay until life kicks my feet out from under me again and brings it all back. I feel like an oil leak that's spreading and covering her up so in the end it will suffocate the life right out of her.

If I didn't realize it a moment ago, I do now…I blew my shot with her because she doesn't even fight me, but just sags and basically gives up. Fuck. My chest feels so tight I feel the need to claw it right open and let her in…but I can't. I don't know how. So instead I swoop her up in my arms and carry her to the bed.

The way she slides into a fetal position when she hits the mattress makes me forget that I don't date and don't need a relationship, a damn ol'lady and sharing personal shit. Hell, she's the most positive influence my life has stumbled across since it all went to shit. Yet here I am looking down to the sunshine that

Help Our Heroes

I've ripped the purity right out of. *That's on me.*

I feel the need to reach out but Ivy catches my wrist. "Don't Chopper. Just leave, okay?"

My eyes trail over the bracelet she's wearing. The inscription states 'Trust me, I'm the doctor' and it makes me snort. Ivy takes the sound in a completely different interpretation and flashes up, her whole demeanor radiates anger.

"Now just wait," I tell her with my palms up. "I saw your bracelet, it just struck a nerve, that's it."

Ivy glances down as if she needs to check what bracelet she's wearing. She turns her attention back to me and it's clear she's going to stand by her words.

"I fucked up, I damn well know I did, but you didn't give me a choice." I rub my palm against my forehead. *Fuck.* That came out so wrong. "It's not you, okay?"

Ivy snorts. "It's not you, it's me. Oh, that's a classic. Can we just not do this? I mean, we had sex, a first for me. I had no clue what to expect but I did assume you'd be here when I woke up and not sneak off like that. Clearly, I was wrong. Oh, and let's not forget you planted a replacement in my kitchen who thought it was normal to see if he could get into my pants for some of your sloppy seconds. So yeah, *it is you.* Now leave."

Get into my pants...

Lochlan. That motherfucker.

I damn well know my brothers are allowed, and will, test an ol'lady that's been claimed but doesn't have her patch ink yet. But come the fuck on…I trusted him, if there's one person on this earth that knows what I've been through and what I struggle with, it's that guy.

Pure and utter rage fills me and I spin on my heels. I hear Ivy curse behind me but it fades when I reach the living room where Lochlan is standing. He sees me coming and yet there's only a fraction of time where he fails to react when my fist hits his jaw.

He stumbles back and I get ready to kick his ass when there's a touch as soft as a feather brushing my arm. A tiny dot starts to clear in my red haze when I glance back and lock with Ivy's eyes that are filled with concern. *For me.* She tightens her delicate hands that are now gripping my biceps. "Don't. It doesn't matter, Chopper. I was throwing him out but you were in the way when I opened the door." She takes a deep breath and steps back.

Somehow, with the loss of her touch on my skin, coldness washes over me. As if I know I've fucked up again in this moment.

"Listen. I'm tired and I don't have much free time. I really would like for the both of you to leave." Her voice is soft and there's a hint of defeat and sadness in her words that hits me harder than the punch I threw in Lochlan's face.

She's already holding the door open. Lochlan gives me a sympathetic pat on the shoulder and mutters low, "Come on, man. *Regroup*. Let's give her some space to breathe, huh?"

I don't want to do that. I want to throw Lochlan out and crawl back into bed with Ivy. Not to seek the comfort of her sweet cunt but to revel in the calm she pours into my body with a mere touch. Why the hell did I leave her bed this morning? Dammit. Why can't I just say the right things at the right time or make her see how things are?

Fuck this world where there's a constant need to communicate. And how the fuck can I, when everything is screwed up in my head or there's a filter in place that alters the shit that enters and goes out of my brain? The process, the trust, the reality that there's nothing out there so fucking screwed up as the human race.

I mean, when you try to protect people, work with them to keep them safe…then they turn around and throw a grenade. Killing best friends. Hell, it could have very well been me standing there if it wasn't for my medical discharge. Or hell, maybe I could have made a difference if I was there. Why him and not me?

That's what got me out of bed…because the incident that shattered my legs? Getting your air stolen? That was between me and Arthur. What if he would have been the one with his legs shattered? What if that would have given him the medical discharge…a fucked up 'trade places' my mind has been given me on a loop. The fucking reason I had to get out of bed and get some miles with the wind hitting my face.

Yeah, *that's reality*.

Help Our Heroes

Add that to the other long fucking list of haunting shit my mind allows me to process time and time again…how the fuck can a person open up ever again to another human being? The fact that I'm standing in front of her while her brother is in the ground. Does she know how in my mind me and her brother could have traded places? Would she want it to be the other way around?

I'm struggling with these things and it's eating me up. How can I pass that burden on to her, because in the end it doesn't make one lick of difference. Because I'm here and he's fucking not. How? Just…how? Tell me that and I might be able to take my next step forward in life and won't doubt things will literally blow up in my face.

Lochlan's almost out the door when I spin on my heels and head for the bedroom. It's a spur of the moment thing, I need to make some kind of statement; I'm taking the fake dicks and her vibrator. Her eyes are wide when I stroll past her with a smirk on my face.

"Gimme that," she snaps in a whisper. Probably to hide this incident from Lochlan who's standing nearby.

I shake my head. "No more dicks for you."

Fuck. My heartbeat picks up when I see her clenching her jaw. What a magnificent woman she is when she's angry and provoked. Even with dried up blood on her face. Yet she stays in full control.

"Keep 'em." She tries to shrug but the anger makes her body too tight, making it seem forced before she adds, "Shove them up that tight ass of yours. I'll just use my fingers to get myself off."

I have to refrain myself from the fury that's this time caused by jealousy. Of her own damn fingers might I add.

"Alright you two, cooling off period starts now." Lochlan grabs my cut and drags me out of her house but stops and addresses Ivy. "Just so you know, there will be a prospect standing guard. We need to check into this Tuck guy. Yeah?"

I watch how she gives Lochlan a tight nod before her eyes find mine again. Damn if there's longing and sadness swirling in her green eyes. Fuck. I'm such a damn asshole. Automatically I step forward, wanting to take her into my arms instead of the stash of fake dicks I'm holding but she slowly closes the door, making my whole being seem even emptier than I was before she walked back into my life.

Chapter 12

Ivy

It's been over two weeks since Chopper was in this bed with me. That's what's going through my mind when my body crashes down. I'm so damn tired from my long shift that I can't even find it in me to strip and shower. No. I just want to close my eyes and get at least six hours of nonstop sleep.

But apparently my mind has other ideas. Like reminding me of the man I had in my bed. Every damn second of the day I'm somehow reminded of him. The way he made me feel…and the way he bruised those feelings the morning after. Yeah. Hello shower, I'm ready for you now. Crap. And I was in a bad mood already.

Ever since that day that Chopper pointed out that Tuck was sitting right in front of my building, he's been MIA. So we're one doctor short. I'm also worried why he's missing and if Chopper had anything to do with it.

I could ask the guy across the street, because it seems I still have a stalker. Or is it considered a guard or something else when he's sitting there for my protection? Dammit. See? I don't need these worries after a long shift.

My clothes hit the floor and I pick them up and throw them in the hamper. It doesn't take long for the water to heat up and my whole body starts to relax while I'm surrounded by the warmth and comfort of the shower. For a person who didn't even have the energy to take a shower, I take a long freaking time before I stroll back into my bedroom. A towel is wrapped around my torso while I have another one in my hands to dry my hair.

I scream, like the girl I am, at the top of my lungs when I see Lochlan standing in my bedroom. "What the hell are you doing here?" The towel I was using to rub my head is now in front of me. Not that I needed it because I had all my good parts covered, but still. Wait… "How the hell did you get into my house?"

He freaking shrugs and says, "I picked the lock, no biggie."

No biggie? "Get out! And why the hell are those the only two words I have on repeat when it comes to guys in my own home?"

"Yeah, I have no answer to that one, Doc." Lochlan gives me a sheepish smile. "And no need to double layer the towel. You've got no pussy or tits. You're Chopper's ol'lady."

"Oh, cut it out with the tits and pussy statement. You already made a pass at me, remember?" I snap and stalk over to my closet to grab some sweatpants and a large sweater. I manage to put both on without flashing Lochlan and throw both towels in the bathroom.

"I know, but that was just a test." His face grows serious. "But that's not why I'm here."

"No." I step forward and poke him in the chest. "Hang on…what kind of test?"

Lochlan glances down at my finger before he meets my eyes. "One where we get to test a claimed ol'lady for her loyalty toward her ol'man and the club. He's laid a claim, you're his ol'lady and that means you have to get inked with the patch within two weeks. If you don't, then it shows you're not fully committed, so we get to run tests to see where your loyalty lies. If you don't get your ink within that time, you lose the right to pick the spot and we will make it happen."

My mind is reeling from the sound of the last word that falls out of his screwed-up head. "There's no way that's ever going to happen. You guys need to get the hell out of my life as easy as you stumbled into it."

"No can do. Well, maybe…let me ask you one question." Lochlan pierces me with his gaze.

"Lemme guess, another test?" I take a deep breath and shake my head. "Fine, get it over with. I'm tired and need sleep."

"If your answer is no, I'll leave this room and take the fuckers who are waiting outside along with me." The man tells me and makes me wonder who the hell is standing outside. The prospect who's keeping an eye out for me?

"Like I said, fine. Ask and I'll give you an honest answer." I rub my eyes in an effort to take away some of the burning from the lack of sleep.

"Chopper. He hasn't been on your mind in a longing matter?" Lochlan quirks an eyebrow. "I don't mean 'I need to find him and give the fucker a piece of my mind.' I'm talking about 'I miss and wish how things went different, give him a shot' kinda longing."

There's a lump as big as Mount Everest in my throat that prevents me from answering his question.

I must have a panicked expression on my face because his face softens and he steps forward. "Just be honest, Ivy. I'm not going to haul you over my shoulder and lock you up in his room."

"No," I squeak. And with that, it's Lochlan's face who shows slight panic.

"No, no…I was referring to the lock me up thing. I did think about him. Every damn day, it's so frustrating. I've had a crush on him ever since we were teenagers and then it came back again when I saw him at Arthur's funeral. Then we end up in bed together and it's amazing and the idiot leaves and you…you idiot, standing in my kitchen and it's all complicated and weird because I miss him so much and I don't need it with my line of work and the long hours and I can't sleep and it's making me itch and he took away all my dicks and," I'm stopped from mouth diarrhea when Lochlan slams his hand over my mouth.

"For the love of all that is holy and dipped in hell, please woman…shut the fuck up. You're just as off balance as Chopper." Lochlan sighs and steps back. "He's been off balance ever since that shit happened with your brother. That shook us all up, don't get me wrong, but I'm betting the fucker is loaded with guilt. The two involved in the jump incident where Chopper got his legs shattered were your brother and him. It doesn't take Einstein to figure out it could have easily been your brother who could have been medically discharged and him being killed. Add you in the fucking mix of things…and the shit he's seen during his time as a SEAL…yeah, the PTSD hit hard for him over the years. But you have to be in it, Ivy…I'm giving you an out because he's not all roses and sunshine, but you get the load of luggage he's carrying too."

"Post-traumatic stress disorder is real. Don't you think I know that?" Anger fills my veins. Who does he think he is throwing that at? Like I'm an idiot who doesn't know a thing about Chopper. Okay, I might not know him through and through, but from what I have seen about him, lusted after him…hell, he's been the reason I bought my first fake dick. And to throw up a discussion about his PTSD like I'm a kid who needs instructions. Freaking idiot. "It's a serious medical condition. But he needs to reach out, he needs to develop new skills to handle it, to overcome and move on…to cope. I'm not walking away because he has PTSD. Hell, no."

"So, you're walking away?" His voice rumbles in my face as if he's trying to scare me off some more.

Tough luck, I've had a hell of a shift and this feels like an awesome way to blow off some steam. "No, you overblown, insensitive asshole of a man. I'm not afraid to walk away, but I'm not going to run after him either. Any relationship needs to be built. Either from scratch with a solid foundation, or eased into. As for PTSD…it's a gradual, ongoing process. I know damn well it doesn't magically disappear overnight, and will flare up like they did with triggers. Hell, the memories will never disappear completely."

"Dandy," he cuts me off. "Seeing as we're on the same side…let's get you inked and then you need to come to the clubhouse because he's locked himself in his room. He won't go out and he needs,"

"That idiot," I seethe. "Let me guess…he's still got the stitches in, right? Or did he remove them himself?"

"I have no clue. That's why I'm here. Because he might open up when you knock on his door. Yeah, I could break down his door but that might not go so well because he's got a temper. Let's just say that the last time I tried to get him to go outside ended with him throwing stuff at my head." Lochlan cringes.

"Fine. I sigh. Let's do this. I'm already past my need for sleep so let's get that tattoo over with and then I can get to slap Chopper around. Right?" I've already got my arms tattooed with different flower vines. What's another tiny one added to the mix? Besides…all my ink has meaning and I've known Chopper for a long period of time. I have no problem with adding something personal that resembles him. I can just squeeze it in somewhere.

Lochlan steps to the door and lets a woman inside that's got a case with her and is followed by two other guys. One of them is the guy, Deeds, with the inked

Help Our Heroes

arms I met at the hospital two weeks ago.

"Hi, I'm Lips. Come on, let's chat." The woman with the dirty blonde hair gives me a warm smile, making me feel like I just gained a new friend.

I meet a lot of people in my line of work, and most times at the worst moment in their lives. So, you might say I have some angle in knowing people. This feels right. I know it's fast and some may judge me, but I've known Chopper and Lochlan for many years in the past and I've heard a lot of stories from Arthur about those two. I can honestly say I think they are good people. So yes…let's do this.

Chapter 13

Chopper

Finally. For the last two weeks I've been tracking down that Tuck fucker. He's been MIA ever since he drove off when he was watching Ivy's apartment. Not that I have him right now, but I have a solid lead. All I could do was lay down and let my leg heal. Well, that and retreat into my safety zone, shutting out all outer influences and keeping to myself. I took that time to retrace his steps, view every angle of video there was until it led me to a nameless town where he just disappeared.

So that's where I'm heading, to that town to check it out. Or maybe I need to hack into the system and check on some police or hospital reports first so I can...Fuck. Who the hell is knocking on my door? I've told Lochlan to keep everyone away, I don't need anything. What I do need is to solve this Tuck, stalker thing for Ivy so I can, or maybe, nah...I screwed that up.

"Stop fucking knocking. I'm not going to open anyway," I grumble.

"Chopper." My damn heart skips a beat from the sound of Ivy's voice saying my name. *She's here?* "Don't be a dick and open this door right now. Did you rip those stitches out yourself? Because then I'll really kick your ass, you thick headed, annoying, ignorant man."

My hands curl around the handle automatically and open the door. "If you're only here to take out those stitches, then feel free to leave."

"Oh?" She's got surprise and mischief bouncing off her gorgeous face.

And for fuck's sake, why did I say something like that? I mean, did I expect her to come here and throw herself at me to ask me to marry her or something? I could hit myself in the damn face. I want her and yet I'm absolutely selfish because she deserves a person who's whole and not...

Help Our Heroes

"Hey, we were talking, so focus on me and don't drift off in your head." Ivy pokes an accusing finger in my chest and strolls past me.

I close the door behind her and glance around my room, cringing at the lousy state.

"If we're going to have this thing where you call me your ol'lady…we clearly need to have a heart to heart about a few things." Ivy grabs the pizza boxes off the bed and places them on the table.

Yeah, I've been in bed since I've left her house and did nothing but kill time tracking Tuck and tearing his life to pieces, letting my leg heal in the process.

"I'm not normally like that," I grumble in my own defense.

"Well that's good to know. Now get your ass on the bed and let me look at your leg. Then we're going to have a long talk." She puts her tiny fists on her hips as if she's going to drag my massive ass on there if I deny her wishes.

The corner of my mouth twitches. I hate hospitals, hate doctors, all because the reminders and what I've been through and yet this woman is a doctor. She broke through my fucked-up brain when I was in the hospital last time and somehow, she's the only one I'm willing to have a look at my leg. Because she wasn't wrong when she asked if I already took out the stitches myself.

I was planning to do so today. I'm not a total idiot and know these things need to come out or else they're gonna get infected. But no way in hell was I gonna go to the clinic, or hospital, for that matter.

"Fine," I grumble and shove my pants down before I sit on the mattress.

Ivy grabs a chair and drags it closer to the bed. She takes her medical kit and lays shit down before she stalks off to the bathroom. When she returns I feel the need to say something and yet I have no clue where to start. So instead I close my eyes and try to relax.

The antiseptic enters my nose and the sound of gloves, all of it a recollection of getting ready to do medical stuff. My breathing picks up and my stomach rolls. Sweat starts to build like the nausea that overtakes me. I need to leave. I can't, it's…

"Hey," Ivy snaps and her breath strokes my face. Her scent reminds me of a flowery embrace, and yet not overwhelmingly thick. My eyes fly open the moment it hits me. It's just her, nothing or nobody else. I'm in my own fucking room. I have the use of my legs and no fucking pain. Well...not in my legs anyway.

"I'm right here, Chopper. Are you?" She gives me a stunning smile that has an amazingly relaxing effect more than any medicine I know of. "Can you let me near your body with some surgical scissors and some tweezers?"

"That depends," I croak. "Are you sure that's what you need?"

She snorts adorably and rolls her eyes. "Trust me, I'm the doctor," Ivy states and realization washes over her. I can tell by the look on her face and the way she's biting her lip that she regrets telling me those words.

Because I don't...trust anyone for that matter. Some on a high level, like Lochlan and my other brothers, others? Her?

My fingers wrap around her wrist where her bracelet is with that same line 'Trust me, I'm the doctor.' "I do," I tell her, shocking myself and yet deep down I know it's the truth. "Or at least my body does. Back at the hospital I let you, and I wouldn't have stepped up like that. Or hell...fucked up like that." Dammit I'm not making any sense.

I was sweating, heartbeat haywire and out of breath a moment ago where nausea ruled my body and yet there's anger rolling through my body because I have no fucking clue what to do and it's all so fucking frustrating.

"Have you been through therapy, or had help in any way when you were medically discharged, or in the years after?" Ivy gently takes my leg in her glove covered hand. "Oh, and lie still, I'm going to get those stitches out but we're going to talk while I'm doing it, okay?"

Her voice is soothing and I surprise myself yet again when I say, "I did. As all of us had at some point. It's just that..." I sigh and shut down the door that's called; opening up to people.

"Right. That's good. And I'm assuming Lochlan and those other guys who wear those leather vests are your support team. You're all there for each other, right?" Ivy doesn't look at me but is purely focused on doing her job.

It's not like she's prying or demanding I rip out my heart or brain and dissect it for her. "Yeah. Pumping iron is also something I use to blow off steam, it's..."

"Now that's something that shows." Her magnificent eyes hit mine and she fucking wiggles her eyebrows, making my mouth dry and I have to cough to mask a chuckle.

This reminds me yet again that I want her. I've been holding off with getting inked because I'm a selfish bastard and she deserves so much more. Something inside me wanted to let her off the hook and yet even the mere thought makes all the air rush out of my lungs. I need her. Her personality, her background, her connection. It's fucking everything, and if I let her go, there's no chance in hell I could ever find someone that will come even close to a person who can make me whole or make me feel worthy.

"You're fucking gorgeous." Wait, was that my voice? I'm a damn idiot. I can't even get my brain to function when I decide to take a step forward and seduce her, grovel, make her see I'm an asshole and then ask her to give me a shot…*give us a shot.*

She falls into a fit of full blown laughter.

Great. Can I fuck up even more?

Ivy catches her breath and rolls up her sleeve. Glancing toward her arm I see her new ink. As if I'm being hit full-frontal, something inside me shatters. An utter feeling of relief and a truckload of other feelings wash over me.

Her hands are cupping my face the next instant. "Hey." Her voice is filled with concern. "Shit. Don't cry."

Don't cry? What the fuck is she talking about? My eyes are burning but there's no way…I never cry. But I've also never…fuck…she's got…I glance down again. Ivy's hands fall from my face and I rub my own eyes because my sight is blurry. Wetness. I am fucking crying. It's her. She's managed to pierce through everything and hit me straight in the heart, allowing my feelings for her the room to flow and reach out. *She's mine.*

"When did you get it? How? This…it's…" Fucking words, when can they ever get in line when they need to?

"I've had a talk with Lochlan a few hours ago and he brought Lips over too. And if I had to get inked, it had to merge it with my other ink but also…" Now she's the one filling up with tears. Fuck we're a pair.

"Your brother…" I murmur and gently stroke her arm. "*In Flanders Fields*…the war poem he had on a piece of paper…always carrying it with him…fuck."

She's got the Broken Deeds patch with my name inked. But the round, red, distorted patch is the shape of *a poppy*. There are green vines around so it merges with her other ink and yet it stands out.

"Magnificent," I say in awe. And it is.

Chapter 14

Ivy

Unbeliveable. That's what it is. When I finished my shift this morning I would have never believed I would end up in Chopper's bed hours later. Yet I am. I've dozed off twice already.

After I removed his stitches and he saw my new tattoo, we crawled into bed and just cuddled without saying anything. When I saw the Broken Deeds patch I asked Lips if she could ink it in the shape of a poppy. Chopper was right, my brother loved that poem and I wanted the double reminder. Chopper and Arthur were friends since an early age, so if it wasn't for Arthur, I never would have known Chopper.

In the last few weeks, both Chopper and Arthur have been on my mind. Memories and moments of both of them flow through my head, but it was one thing Arthur mentioned to me years back that hit me the hardest. Because I didn't know back then who it was about…Arthur told me an accident happened during a training jump and that he blamed himself. Guilt ate at him, but he never gave me anything more than 'it should have been me, he could have died and yet it damaged his legs and he might never walk again.'

He never said it was Chopper but I put it together and it suddenly made sense. I bet Chopper feels the same guilt. Hell, it made me understand even more why he needed the space and left that morning. Even if he left Lochlan behind. Although all of that is in the past now. I mentioned it to Chopper and that lead to heavy conversation that ripped open both of our hearts and bared our feelings.

I could tell how hard it was for him to discuss it and hear Arthur's side…well, from the things my brother shared with me. After that Chopper pulled me down on the bed, putting us in a comfortable position, snuggled close to each other. Just the intense comfort of two people giving, without any expectations, dilemmas, or obligations in return.

We have a strong connection that was founded years ago where we each walked a path that crossed at the right time in our lives. I have no clue where it all will go but when it feels like you're bound in some way and life keeps throwing you at each other…it's enough to take the hint. *This feels right.*

We're far from perfect and maybe we never will be, but that's okay. Nobody is perfect and we all have flaws and scars. It's just what you're willing to accept and work with. The love you build together can have cracks and yet be strong enough to mend and heal to grow stronger over time.

"Are you hungry?" Chopper asks.

"Why? Do you have some leftover pizza from a few days ago you're gonna offer me if I say yes?" I mutter.

His laughter rumbles inside his chest and makes my insides go weak. My head is resting on his pecs where the sound and vibrations make it much more intense.

"I wouldn't dare." He places his finger underneath my chin and angles my head so our gazes lock. "I would order new ones."

"You know as a doctor I would advise to have more variety of food," I tell him with a stern voice.

"Let's just agree that when I have you in my bed, I'm the one who's always right. You might be the doctor," he taps on my bracelet I bought for myself as a mental boost a few months ago, "but I'm the one you can trust." His face turns serious before he adds, "I've screwed up, I know. It's hard for me to open up and trust people."

I can tell he's struggling with words and opening up, yet we have oceans of time ahead of us. And he opened up a hell of a lot a moment ago. That right there shoots straight to my heart. "I'm thankful you're giving me a shot. Well, I didn't actually have a choice to start with." I roll my eyes in an effort to lighten the mood.

He pushes me on my back and looms over me. His face still has the seriousness engraved in it and yet his eyes twinkle in a way I haven't noticed before. "My body and my brain didn't give me a choice when you walked back into my life. You caught me off guard and wormed yourself in without the both of us knowing. So, Doc…is my leg cleared? Full use and all? Do I have the ability to fuck my woman against the wall and support both our weights, or would that be too much to start with?"

My heart bounces around in my chest and tingles spread through my body at the mere thought of him…

"See? That right there, Doc. That's why I'm the one in charge in the bedroom." He has the nerve to chuckle but he's right.

I grab the bracelet I bought myself as a reminder when I lost a patient. A woman with a history of heart surgery that had a DNR in place. I didn't know about her history when they brought her in…she was in a bad car accident and I was trying to save her life when her heart gave up. I was right in the middle of CPR when a nurse rushed in with her medical history. I had to stop. DNR…I bought the bracelet as a reminder that even though I'm the doctor, the one they have to trust with their life…in the end, it's still their life.

I feel Chopper's lips nipping my neck, bringing me back to what I was going to do. Placing the bracelet on his wrist, I trace it with my finger for a moment before I add, "There. Now we have a reminder of our agreement in place."

Chopper looks at it before his eyes slide to mine, desire and something else swirling in his eyes. "You really are something," he mutters before his lips crash down over mine.

Our kiss is hungry as if we both need more. It's not just the emotional side to devouring each other. We had the soft cuddle, relax and enjoy the other person's company. This moment shifted into the longing of connecting our bodies. To possess and to claim.

His hand slides underneath my shirt where he pulls down my bra. A frustrated groan flows against my lips before he adds, "The clothes need to go."

Chopper grabs the hem of his own shirt and throws it down to the floor before he climbs off the bed. He unbuckles his jeans and raises his eyebrow at me expectantly. I shoot off the bed and remove my clothing before jumping back on.

"Someone is anxious," he mutters with satisfaction written all over his face. "Have you been missing me, or your substitutes that I took with me?"

"I don't need them anymore now that I got myself the real thing," I tell him while I've got my eyes set on that magnificent piece.

Thick, long, and so very hard. My fingers wrap around his dick that feels like velvet wrapped around steel and just the thought of him in my hand makes my body tremble in anticipation. I tug gently and watch how his head falls back. A groan of appreciation what I'm doing to him rumbles from his lips.

I lean forward and take him into my mouth. Sliding back, I try to take him deeper the second time, except I'm prevented from doing so when he wraps his fist in my hair and pulls me back.

"Not a chance, sweetheart." His voice thickens. "We have time later to put that mouth to good use. I need to bury my cock deep inside of your cunt, that's where my cum belongs. Because if you suck me off I won't last and it'll all be over in a blink of an eye and…fuck. I need to…"

"Shut up and jump into action?" I offer.

Chopper shakes his head but pushes me back on the bed as he looms over me. He hooks my leg over his shoulder, opening me up even more while he palms his dick and slides through my folds.

"I've dreamed about this cunt that's only seen and felt my cock. Being inside you feels so damn good." He gently slides in with short thrusts, letting me accommodate to his size.

My nails scrape down his back, urging him on.

"So impatient." Chopper chuckles and picks up his pace, surging deeper inside me.

Both our breathing picks up, the air between us thin and our bodies burning while sweat is building in an effort to soothe overheating. But it's a lost cause, it's undeniable, we literally burn for one another. The way our bodies move in sync, the building need in his gaze. Chopper bites down on my collarbone while he's tightening his grip on my hip to pin me in place.

I'm holding him close with both hands but he rips lose when he leans back and glances around him. *Why did he stop? What's he doing?*

"I need…" He leans to the left and grabs something off the bedside table. "Ah, that'll do."

Help Our Heroes

Before I can voice my questions, I feel how he grabs my wrists and pins me to the headboard while fabric wraps around my wrists and he locks my arms above my head. There's a hint of panic filling my veins before it flows into desire when his gaze meets mine.

"Absolutely gorgeous." His finger trails from my arm down to my breast where he rolls my nipple between his fingers. "I have to take my time with you. When I have your nails in my back urging me on, I lose control and will fuck you so hard that I'll blow my load way too fast. So, this," he taps my bound wrists, "is keeping the both of us in line. Just relax and enjoy, Ivory. I'm going to eat your cunt and when I've had my fill, and only then, I will slowly make both of us orgasm because I can't wait to have your cunt clench around my cock while I fill you up."

He trails a path of kisses down my body until he's hovering above my pussy. Chopper nips the skin of my inner thigh, making my ass shoot off the mattress. With one hand he pushes on my belly while I feel fingers sliding through my pussy.

There's a groan of contentment that vibrates against my folds when I feel his tongue slide through. Fingers pump slowly as he focuses his mouth on my clit. All of it is overwhelming. I want to slide my fingers in his hair, to pull him off, to bring him closer…anything to release the pressure of my orgasm that's being brought to the surface.

"Please," I beg and struggle against the restraints.

"All in good time, sweetheart. *Trust me*," he tells me in a husky voice with so many emotions that my body starts to tremble to surrender completely, for whatever he has in mind.

Chapter 15

Chopper

The way she clamps down on my fingers, her body shaking in anticipation, and her taste that's sweetening…all of this tells me she's close.

I pin my eyes on her face because I intend to watch her closely. "Ivory," I whisper against her sweet cunt before I have to add a little more volume and snap to my voice. "Ivy, eyes here." She responds beautifully.

Well, maybe with a hint of frustration because her eyes practically scream 'how dare you rip me out of my moment of surrendering to pleasure.'

"You're going to burn into the direction I'll guide you in. It's time, sweetheart." Gaze locked with mine, I show her body what I demand. I curl my finger slightly, find the right spot and rub on the inside while I hold her clit ransom in a way where she has to instantly surrender.

Her cum flows into my mouth as I watch how pure, intense pleasure washes over her face. Her eyes roll back and her struggling arms fall slack. I don't give her time to get her breathing under control when I crawl up her body. I'm balancing myself on my hands that are beside her breasts. Waiting. Yes, now I take my time to study how she comes down from the rush I gave her.

Ivy's bright gray eyes now flare with a darker ring around them. I fucking love I'm the one responsible for that change. She gives me a sheepish, post orgasm smile that I intend to see many times more before morning comes.

"You come beautifully," I tell her and with that, I bury myself to the hilt inside her.

She gasps and tugs on her arms. Suddenly I feel the need to have her nails dig into my skin. Leaning forward, I fumble for a moment to untie her before her arms go down. I curl one of my hands underneath her to grip her shoulder and pin her in place. This way I can pound into her with force, and I intend to because with her...I lose all sense of holding back.

Her cunt is slick, puffy, and so very welcoming. Every now and then my ears pick up a moan when she clenches in sync around me. So fucking enchanting. I manage to swallow the next one and yet I can't focus enough to continue the kiss when my balls start to draw up.

"Yes," Ivy breathes hot against my ear. "I need to feel you." Another sexy fucking moan before she adds between pants, "When you come inside me, I feel every pulse. Sooooo good." She moans again before she bites down on my shoulder as she starts to come.

Her words, her teeth and nails in my skin, the way her cunt strangles my cock in a way that rips the cum straight out of it...my whole body locks down to extract one task; claim my ol'lady with my cum.

That's taken every last bit of energy straight out of me. I manage to drop myself next to Ivy when I ease out of my orgasm fog. She turns, snuggles close and presses a kiss on my pecs. I feel how her breathing slows down and an instant later I notice she's out cold. A huge smile spreads my face. The knowledge that I fucked her into oblivion is fucking awesome.

Okay, I damn well know it's because she had a rough and long shift because I've been keeping tabs on her. Totally didn't wander from my stalker status. Well, not anymore because she's officially mine. She's wearing my fucking patch.

That reminds me. I need to handle two things to ease my mind. One is getting that ink on my body too; the other is finding Tuck. I also need to explain that one to Ivy but it's best that I find the fucker first.

Glancing at my ol'lady, I take a while to suck up this moment, enjoy the feel of her body against me before I slide out of bed. I know how exhausted she is and that she will be asleep for hours. That gives me enough time to wrap things up and slide right back against her body without her knowing I'm gone.

Chapter 16

Ivy

Slowly I stretch and wake up realizing I'm not in my own bed. The memory of Chopper doing crazy things with my body rushes back and makes me feel special. That is until I reach to my left, then right, and come up empty.

"That asshole, motherfucker," I mutter and push myself upright.

There's a chuckle before I hear his voice. "Would that be me?"

I have to swallow when I catch a glimpse of him. Chopper is standing in the doorway of the bathroom, rubbing a towel over his head, his hard body on display that's still got water drops sliding downwards…oh, God. Shit…he asked a question, right.

"Yes, you…for taking a shower without me." That wasn't why I was cursing, obviously I thought he left…again.

"You have every right to be angry. Because I did leave for a few hours. But I was sure you'd stay sleep and I hurried the hell back." His face shows concern and he's waiting for me to flip out, I can tell.

Instead I just let myself fall back on the bed. "Okay," I mutter.

It doesn't take long for him to loom over me. "Okay? Not one fucking extra curse or question why?"

"Nope," I tell him and manage to pop the P to add to the effect.

"I don't fuck and leave." He growls at me. "And I had Lips keep an eye on my room in case you came out. So she could have told you where I went and what I was doing. Well most of it because,"

"You got your ink," I squeak and jump upright again. He's got my name inked in the patch on his forearm.

"Yeah," he croaks, "that too."

His words make me think what else he was doing. "And…" I ask.

"And I was following up on Tuck. That's what kept my mind distracted from stalking you these two weeks," Chopper confesses.

There's pain written all over his face and yet there's no need because, "Hey, we're past that. So…" I try to hold in my laughter when I tease, "You didn't stalk me for those two weeks? Just Tuck?"

The guilt that washes over his face and makes his cheeks pink reminds me of a schoolboy who's been caught.

"I take that as a yes." I give him a smug smile before I realize he's serious about Tuck. "Wait…Tuck hasn't been to work in the last two weeks. Do you know where he is or why he's not at work?"

"Yeah." Chopper rubs a hand over his mouth and sits down on the bed. "I recently tracked him down to Arlington before he disappeared completely. I needed to check it out and I would have done so myself, but I hacked into the police records and then the hospital records…there was an accident. His car crashed, he died instantly. But Ivy…"

"He died?" I squeak. *Tuck is dead?*

Chopper walks over to a desk where he grabs a file and holds it out to me. I take it but keep my gaze locked on him, waiting for something…answers…instead he points at the file in my hands.

When I open it and glance at the first page, turn it and see pictures, another form with…oh, God. My signature. This is…no…it can't be…how's that even possible for me, or the hospital, not to know about this? "A few months ago…that woman I tried to save…she was his girlfriend? I…that…"

"Yeah, that right there explains a lot, huh? Well, not so much…except it explains why he was focused on you." Chopper takes the file out of my hands and places it on the bedside table before he crawls back in bed with me and pulls me into his arms.

"I tried so hard to save her." I can't help the tears that fall. "She was in a car accident and had internal bleeding. She had cardiac arrest when I was trying to…she…I couldn't." I sob against Chopper's chest while he just strokes my hair and murmurs soft words in comfort.

When I've finally got my breathing under control, I sit up and explain the rest. "When she was brought in we didn't have her medical records, so I tried like hell to save her life. I was right in the middle of CPR when a nurse rushed in with her medical history. *I had to stop.* I didn't have a choice…she had a DNR. *I had to respect her wishes.*"

"I know," Chopper tells me with a stern voice. "It wasn't your fault. Nothing makes sense because he was a doctor himself and would damn well know you did everything you could. Yet in some twisted way Tuck felt the need to…I don't know, stalk you for some reason. Hell, we will never find out the exact reason why he applied to the hospital and focused on you because he crashed his car."

"Why didn't he tell me? We could have gone over her file together, or talked things through…anything…I wish I would have known." I sigh.

"Yeah." He brushes his knuckles over my cheek. "But isn't that always the way of life? To know everything up front might make you do things differently, but in the end, it can still lead to fucked-up matters."

He's right. Yet it feels sometimes that life screws with every one of us no matter what the consequences. Everyone struggles with their own mess of things. Just how everyone in the end makes their own choices, like Tuck's girlfriend did with her DNR. The hard reality in all of this also shows that life can be over in a blink of an eye.

I launch myself at Chopper who gets knocked back into the mattress. I snuggle close and vow to myself and to him, "Let's agree to enjoy every minute life gives us for the very reason to be there for each other in a way that suits our needs."

"Hmmm," Chopper hums. "That sounds like a life motto." The man adds a groan. "And I do have…needs."

Crap. How can he make a joke of something so serious? Wait. He's right. "Good. Because I vow to tend to your needs, but Chopper…"

"Yeah, sweetheart," he croaks, his eyes filled with desire that's fully focused on me.

"You have obligations toward me too now," I carefully tell him.

I'm about to lighten the load because I meant it as a warning that it's not

Help Our Heroes

like he has to open up fully or rip open his head and chest and lay it all on me...but he does need to realize he doesn't have to do anything alone. That I'm right here for whatever he needs, and that I hope he will come to me when he needs...me. When he needs help.

"I know." The desire in his eyes shifts into determination when he adds, "I'm bound to fuck up but that shit falls under our needs. For you to tell me when I do, for me to make amends when needed. It's a road filled with uncertainties and it's bound to get some obstructions, but we're riding toward the sunset, right?"

Oh, wow.

"Right," I croak and kiss him fiercely.

Epilogue

Two years later

Chopper

I'm staring at my wife who is leaning in the doorway of the hospital room. Okay, I'm lying…it's the donation center but my mind always puts it in the same box. It's the smell, the needles, the poking and people in white coats. I'm donating blood. Ivy set this up for me two years ago and we've been doing it ever since.

It took a while before I started to feel at ease with the poking routine and the smell. I mean, when your wife works in a hospital…I needed to not freak out every time I picked her up or…fuck, when she gave birth to our babies…twins. So, this has been a tiny part in overcoming my hate for hospitals. Helping others while helping myself. And I've kept it going ever since.

"All done?" Ivy asks me as I stand up.

"Yeah," I croak and swoop her into my arms.

My fingers automatically slide to her ass. She's wearing jean shorts and they've been driving me crazy. I can practically slide my fingers between her legs, push them aside and…

Ivy giggles and smacks my hand away. "Okay, you can let me go now."

I've got my face buried into the crook of her neck and I don't want to let go. She's so fucking amazing. These two years we've been together have been a damn roller-coaster. I'm not going to say it's all roses and sunshine, fuck no. Life is filled with some kind of wicked balance in between the hard times and the times where you kiss the ground you're able to walk on.

I remember Ivy's face when I asked her to marry her. I surprised her when I showed up at her work with a sandwich in hand, sweating like a pig, and white as a fucking sheet but I did it because I love her. Overcoming fears and working on who we are and where we want to go, together.

I will never forget the moment we saw the lines appear on the pregnancy test confirming our assumptions. I remember when we heard the heartbeats and found out we were having twins. Every doctor's appointment since then, their birth…creating new memories together that makes life worth the effort we put in it. It might still be a fucked-up place but the good memories quiet your mind.

There will always be a part of me that's left behind and yet it's that very part that Ivy picks up and carries with her. For that reason alone, I could stare at her forever. She's magnificent in every way.

"What do you want?" she mumbles.

"You," I reply honestly.

Another giggle flows around us as she replies, "Silly man. Let's go home."

"Are the kids still good for another hour with Lips and Deeds?" I question.

We dropped them off before we got on my bike and came here. They're six months old. Although Leontine is one minute older that Asher.

Ivy steps back and laces her fingers with mine before she drags me along into the hallway. "Yes, why? Do you have something in mind?" She glances up at me with heated eyes.

"I don't care where, or what, as long as it involves you and me naked," I tell her and squeeze her hand.

She picks up speed and every step has a bounce to it. See what I mean? Enjoying life and each other. Moving forward and taking every possibility and turning it into something valuable for the both of us.

The cool breeze of a summer's day hits us as I straddle my bike and feel how Ivy slides on behind me. Every time she gets on the back of my bike the same heated flare of righteousness flows through my veins. She belongs there as my ol'lady, but there's more to it than that. She has my back. Literally.

It's in the little things where she understands or gives me space when I need it.

I know where I'm taking her and it doesn't take long to get there. It's a backroad where it's quiet but it holds the beauty of the raw nature that surrounds it. Parking my bike, I take her hand and stroll to a large tree. It's not like I planned every move but I did have one thing in mind…make out like fucking teenagers against a tree.

And I do just that, caging her against the tree while my mouth covers hers. My tongue slides between her lips to gather access and when she opens, allowing me to swirl inside, we both groan while I start to dry hump. See? We're parents who just dodged adulting and skipped straight into teenager mode. Fucking perfect if you asked me.

I slip my hand between our bodies and manage to push her shorts and thong to the side, allowing me access to that magnificent cunt. It's all and everything my cock wants and craves.

"Feel that, Ivory? You're practically drooling for me to give it to you, ain't ya, sweetheart?" The way my finger slides back and forth makes my cock thicken even more with the thought of being breaths away from doing the exact same. "I fucking love you," I add on a whisper.

Ivy grabs my cut in her fists and drags me even closer to her. "I damn well love you too, now give it to me, Chopper." She breathes as her cunt clenches around my fingers.

That's it. That's all it takes for me to unzip, unleash, and bring myself one step closer to unload.

With short thrusts we both revel in the sensation that gets us to a point we're it's hard to breathe as sweat is starting to build. Her legs curl around my waist and I gladly palm that tight ass of hers so I can fuck her harder. I should keep in mind that the bark of the tree I'm pinning her against could be imprinted on her back but somehow we both couldn't care less.

It's a damn teenager thing to come the next instant when I feel her cunt ripple as she starts to orgasm. Her head falls forward against my neck where she digs her teeth into my skin, muffling the sound of my name tumbling from her lips. My balls draw up and the cum flows with such force it seems like an endless supply that only Ivy can unleash from my body.

I'm shaking on my feet when I finally get some blood back into my brain. "Fuck. How does it keep getting better?"

"Because it's us," Ivy simply breathes out.

"Fuck yeah, it's us." And it is that simple… *it's us*. That's the bottom-line

Help Our Heroes

in the struggle that's called living. And I'm fucking thankful I risked a shot, opened up and let her in. Rooted in my past, present, and future.

* * *

Although fiction is a twist of reality, life does give us options.

Never hold back.

Take that step forward how tiny it might be because there will be someone who will reach out and be there for you.

The Do-Gooder and the Dropout

Bella Settarra

Chris Roberts is a dropout, living on the streets of London, begging for money to keep himself and his dog, Muttbags, alive. But it wasn't always like that. Hailed a hero of the British Army he saved the lives of a platoon of men by warning them of an oncoming ambush. The nightmares of seeing the men he *couldn't* save haunt him, though, and the black mist still blinds him when he gets riled or upset.

Kathy Johnson is a veterinary nurse who works for Street Vets, a charity that helps heal strays and pets of the homeless. She arrives at a bad time to help Muttbags, though, and is subjected to Chris' wrath. He sees her as a do-gooding nuisance and tells her to go.

When the mist clears, Chris realises that he's been a fool and ruined Muttbags' chances of having an expert examine the paw that's been hurting him for days. He's also foiled his chance of seeing Kathy again, the girl who's been on his mind ever since he yelled at her.

Chris lost his pride a long time ago, but not his compassion. Muttbags needs help. They go to find the charity workers the following night, only to hear that Kathy had been hurt by a homeless man.

When Chris and Muttbags are later set-upon by her attacker and his gang the black mist falls again. Chris desperately fights to save his dog and avenge Kathy's assault, but when Kathy witnesses the event will she see him as her hero or just another dropout?

Help Our Heroes

Chapter 1

It's cold tonight. Really cold. The kind of cold that seeps into your bones and goes right through your body, freezing up your organs so you can hardly breathe. I hate it. Like I hate begging for food. I hate life. *My* life. I thought about ending it but that wouldn't be fair on the others.

Muttbags whines, cuddling closer to me. He's feeling it tonight, too. I can tell by the way he's curling up, tucking his legs under him – and trying to swipe my fucking blanket.

"All right, boy; we'll share it."

My back's against a wall which feels like it's made of ice, but it was either that or let the wind whistle through the gap and freeze me even more. Muttbags' coat is soft against the top of my cheek, the only part of me still exposed. The ground we're lying on feels harder than ever, and I wouldn't be surprised if there's not a patch of ice there by morning, it's certainly cold enough.

Muttbags nuzzles into me and I squeeze him a little tighter. I often wonder if I'm doing him any favours keeping him with me. He's a stray mongrel who saved my bacon when the subway gang decided to choose me as their next victim. I've been bullied by worse people, but I feel so vulnerable out here. Muttbags appeared out of nowhere when they tried to steal my stuff. I'd gone for a pee, and nearly missed the whole thing. If it wasn't for the dog I'd have nothing by now, not that there's much here anyway. But what there is — a blanket, my cardboard and a plastic carrier bag with some half-eaten chocolate and stale crisps – is like gold dust. Muttbags barked at them, alerting passers-by, who stopped to watch. He bared his teeth and snarled, snapping at them when they tried to touch my stash. In the end they decided it wasn't worth it and left, but not without giving me the 'slit throat' sign on their way past.

Good old Muttbags. I'd only seen him a few times before then, just to say hello and give him a stroke. I wasn't sure if he was a stray or not, but by the way he latched on to me after that I realised he must be. He'd mine now. And I'm his.

We look out for each other. It's surprising how many people stop and give me food for him. They take more notice of me when he's by my side — not that I get anything out of it, mind, it's all about the dog.

He's a born wriggler, though.

"Shh, get some sleep, mate."

I wish *I* could. I have to admit I've had more zeds since he's been with me; it feels a bit safer, somehow, but I never get much. Not anymore. I snuggle into his fur and remember the days when I was a teenager and couldn't get out of bed on a Sunday morning. I'd be under that duvet until I smelled the roast dinner come out of the oven. That's the only time I'd make a move. That all changed once I joined the British Army, though. What a shock to the system that was!

"What's up mate?"

Muttbags is whimpering. I hate it when he does that. I furtle under the blanket and feel for his paw. He got something stuck in it — a thorn, I think — and it's been playing him up all day. I wrapped a piece of rag around it, tied with an elastic band I found, but I don't know if it's done any good. I thought it'd keep the germs out, but it might have introduced a few more as the fabric wasn't exactly clean. God, I feel so guilty. The mutt helped me when I needed it and I'm not sure I can ever repay the favour. I find his paw and notice my rendition of a bandage has gone. So much for that idea!

* * *

If it weren't for guilt and remorse I'd have no feelings at all. I'd rather that. Numb. Yeah, I could handle that, no worries. I close my eyes and breathe in his dog-breath. It's horrid, but not as horrid as the smell of death. Suddenly I'm back there in the desert banks of Helmand. We all knew it was the calm before the storm, and we savoured every second. Trouble was, it wasn't the sort of storm we hoped for — it was aimed at *us* and there was no escaping — for *them*, anyhow.

I can hear the pandemonium now, the yelling and shots firing all around us. We thought we were safe — well, as safe as you can be in the middle of a war. It was *us* who were supposed to surprise *them*. The order had come to wait for the signal from the other bunker — if you could call it that; mound of sand would be more accurate — and go in, all guns blazing.

Help Our Heroes

The screams of my comrades — my friends — haunt me even now. I'd gone for a pee so was a little way away from them. I heard everything and saw the bastard Taliban surround us. They weren't taking any prisoners. They just aimed to kill. Fuckers! Tommo, Kinky, Jonesy and the rest just yelled and fell to the ground for the last time. They didn't know I was there, though. I saw them home in on the others and realised I'd slipped under their radar. So I ran. I fucking well ran!

What sort of coward does that? I should've been chucked out of the Army with a dishonourable discharge. Instead they gave me a fucking medal! A medal! They said I'd done the right thing, alerting the other platoon so they could get the fuck out of there. They said I'd saved the lives of eight men that day. But I'd done fuck all for the seven in my platoon. I didn't even shoot any of the fuckers who did it — it all happened so fast, and I knew by the time I'd lined up a shot they'd have either seen me or gone.

That black mist's clouding up my eyes again. It's blacker than the night itself. I feel like I'm looking down into Hell, the place I should be. It's trying to suck me in but I don't want to go. I'm clinging to the edge of the abyss but I don't know why. Part of me's telling me to drop, let go, end it. But the other part tells me that if I do those guys died for nothing. It's all a mess. There's manic screaming in my ears and I can't see or feel anything. It's like...

"It's okay, it's all right. Just open your eyes."

I don't know that voice. It's sweet. A girl. But I don't know any girls. And this is no place for one — what's she doing here?

"It's all right. Please, wake up."

I open my eyes like a shot. My heart's practically pounding out of my chest and I can feel my whole body's covered in sweat, despite the cold night air.

"I'm sorry. Are you okay?"

It *is* a girl. She's got a torch that she's shining on Muttbags, but it's me she's talking to. Muttbags is licking her hand. But I've still got screaming in my ears and this mist's only just starting to clear from my eyes. I sit up straight, panting hard.

"What the fuck?" I can't believe the bitch woke me up!

"It's all right. You were having a bad dream, that's all." Her big eyes are staring at me in that pitying way the nurses at the hospital used to when I was at the Queen Elizabeth Birmingham Hospital.

"Bad dream?" I snap at her. "You've got no idea!"

"I'm sorry. I only wanted to help." She looks like she's about to cry. Fuck!

"Help? Well you can help by fucking off and leaving us alone. We're trying to get some sleep down here in case you hadn't noticed!" I can't believe her audacity. Sleep's hard enough to come by without the likes of Florence Nightingale here stealing it away from me.

"Is everything okay, Kathy?" A man comes over and frowns at me.

"Yes, it's fine, Joe. I just had to wake him up, that's all." She's nodding to the guy, but he doesn't look convinced. In fact, he looks ready to thump me.

"Who the fuck are you?" I stand up; ready to batter him as soon as he makes a move. My hands clench and my arms feel tight and eager for action. I puff my chest out. I might be a useless dropout but I can hold my own against the likes of him — or anyone else for that matter.

"I'm sorry, I should have said," the girl replies with a self-deprecating smile. "I'm Kathy Johnson. This is my friend, Joe Feckly. We're from Street Vets." She beams at me and I get the impression I'm supposed to know what the hell she's talking about.

"What?" I huff.

"Street Vets, she says. We help..."

"Don't tell me! You're one of those do-gooders who think they can help homeless war veterans by talking to them all bloody night." My blood boils. I've had this sort of shit countless times. They're a fucking nuisance.

She giggles. I have to admit it's a pretty sound — mind you, from what I can see of her she's a really nice-looking girl.

"No, nothing like that," she assures me. "We help with animals. Vets as in veterinarians. We go around and check on homeless people's pets, to see if there's anything we can do to help them. It's all free. We can get rid of fleas, protect them against lungworm, administer pain relief or even arrange surgery if necessary. Whatever they need."

"Yeah, well what we need right now is for you to fuck off so we can get some bloody sleep!" I sneer at her, wondering for a moment if I'm still dreaming. No-one does all that stuff for free — and I'm not waiting around to find out what the catch is!

"What about your dog, mate? Doesn't he deserve a bit of help? Looks like he's hurt his paw." Joe's face is tight as he speaks to me, as if daring me to deny my dog the help he needs. Well he can fuck off.

"My dog's just fine, so mind your own goddam business," I yell at him, the dark mist beginning to return to my eyes. "I look after him. He's mine — not yours. Just leave us alone!" My whole body is tense now, ready to fight this bastard if he doesn't fuck off soon. I know exactly what he's trying to do; he'll say I can't take care of my own mutt and insist the RSPCA come and take him away. But they're dealing with the wrong man this time. No-one's getting their hands on my dog — much less a do-gooding tosser like him!

"I can just take a look for you, if you like?" Kathy's giving me those puppy-dog eyes again but I won't be taken in by a pretty face.

"There's no need," I tell her bluntly. "Just go."

She bites her lip and I wonder if she's planning to say something else, but she doesn't. I can't help noticing how sad she looks as she turns away.

Joe scowls at me and goes with her. It's about fucking time.

"Come on, boy, let's get some kip." I get back down on my bed once they're far enough away.

Muttbags whines but joins me with a big huff. I can't help feeling sorry for him. I know that paw's hurting him but whatever it is they're offering I just can't afford it. And *nothing* comes for free!

Chapter 2

I feel like shit when I wake up next morning. Actually, I've woken up several times this morning already. It's just that it's getting light now so I can justify getting out of bed (if you can call it that). I'm not sure if I *couldn't* get back to sleep after our rude interruption last night, or if I just didn't *want* to. In either case that girl's to blame — Kathy whatever-her-name-is.

She said she woke me up because I was having a nightmare. I can well believe it. It's rare I get a whole night without reliving the hell of Afghanistan. Helmand Province was well-named. *Sheer hell!* Sometimes I shout out in my sleep — I wonder if that's what she meant? Maybe I was yelling? Muttbags usually alerts me by shoving me, or barking if I get really loud. I wouldn't have noticed if he'd been nudging me last night though, as he'd been doing it enough already with the pain of that damn paw of his.

After she'd left I couldn't stop thinking about her. Maybe because I wondered if she really *could* have helped the poor mutt without charging me the earth. I know that's what she claimed, but that's just too good to be true in anyone's book. There was something else about her, though. The way she looked at me. Apart from being a beautiful girl, she had an understanding expression, as though she didn't judge me for being here, or being... well, *rude,* I suppose. She couldn't hide the hurt in her eyes though when I shouted and swore at her and I feel really bad for doing that. I wouldn't normally speak to a girl that way; I was just so wound up from being woken up. Or maybe I was wound up *before* I'd woken up. I always feel in a crap mood when I think about what happened which is why I try not to remember it. You don't get a choice when you're asleep, though.

Muttbags licks me and I hope my morning-breath isn't as bad as his. I give him a cuddle and can't help wondering if he *has* got fleas that those do-gooders could get rid of. Poor boy must be really uncomfortable if he has, especially on top of that paw.

"Come on, boy. Let's go see if they've opened up the bogs yet."

He limps by my side as we wander down the next couple of streets to where the public toilet block is. I know they've got some of those automatic loos just over the way, but I somehow feel the need of a bit more luxury this morning. The block has proper sinks, not those weird metal machines, and it's a lot warmer with proper tiles instead of stainless steel sheeting everywhere. The only drawback is the cost. For the privilege of a decent loo and wash facilities I have to pay a whole fifty pence, as opposed to twenty for the other type. I'll bet the generous people who throw their coppers my way never imagine their hard-earned cash is paying me to use the bog. The thought makes me snigger. Of course, if I just need a pee I save my money and go against a wall or something – making sure there's no cops around first, of course.

It's the fat bloke on duty today, I'm pleased to see. He doesn't mind me coming in, but the other one tries to hurry me up and tells me I'm a bad advert for the place. It's a *bog*, for God's sake!

"Morning." He smiles at me.

"Hi, mate."

Some days he's the only person I get to talk to. Muttbags gets more attention than me when passers-by bother to stop. I leave him outside, guarding my stuff and lapping up water from a gutter, and go inside. I'm on my own, just how I like it. Not only do I make full use of the toilet facilities — including grabbing some bog roll for later — I strip off my layers and give myself a good wash. The soap in this place is actually quite nice and I use as much of it as I can to try to get rid of the stench of sweat. I don't know why, but I really feel in need of a good clean today. I know it won't do any good once I put my smelly clothes back on, though, and wish I could afford to go to one of those charity shops and get myself a new shirt or something.

I always keep my toothbrush and paste in a zip-up pocket in my jacket, and I pull them out and scrub my teeth over and over. Looking in the mirror I can see I desperately need a good shave and a haircut. It's odd, but I hadn't thought much about it before now.

A Military Anthology

The idea of a proper bed and a shower cross my mind and I close my eyes to savour the notion. One day I'll get there, I keep promising myself. A sound makes me quickly open my eyes again, as a bloke comes in to use the toilet. He gives me an odd look but says nothing. I glance back in the mirror and see what he sees. A dropout. A dirty scumbag.

The black mist begins to cloud my vision again as I pull on my clothes. I've got an old comb which still has half its teeth, and I put it under the tap before yanking it through my mop of dark hair. I remember when I was proud of my barnet; the girls used to love running their hands through it when I was out on the pull. Those were the days, I recall, grimly. It seems like a lifetime ago.

The mist in front of my eyes seems to get darker as I think how much that damn British Army stole from me. Not just my mates; my future, my pride, *me*. My hand grips the comb even tighter and I'm raking the teeth through my knots and into my scalp. The plastic tears at my skin as I yank it through relentlessly. The pain feels good. It starts to clear the mist. When I look back in the mirror I look different. My whole body seems more relaxed, my eyes not quite so sunken. My whole head stings and when I wash the comb the water turns pink with blood.

More men filter in and I can hear Muttbags whining outside. I suppose it's time I left the relative warmth of this place and got back to him. If we go now, we might be able to catch some of the commuters down by the subway — they're always good for a quid or two.

I take one last look in the mirror. I have to say I don't look as bad as a lot of them out there. My hair's slicked back now, but the waves are still curling around my ears. It's a far cry from the short-back-and sides I used to have, though I'm glad the British Army doesn't insist on buzz-cuts like the Americans. It'd be even colder out here with practically no hair. I'm even glad my moustache and beard have grown now, too, as it's amazing how much warmth they offer, though I never would have entertained any facial hair in my youth. I have to admit it rather suits me, too, although I'll admit it could all do with a good trim.

I pass a couple more men on my way out the door, and realise I must have been in there longer than I thought. I feel better for it, though, and even manage a smile for the attendant on my way past.

Help Our Heroes

"Come on, boy, let's go."

Muttbags is pleased to see me, and licks my hand as I grab the cardboard 'bed'. I give him a stroke before we make out way down the street. He's still limping and my thoughts immediately go back to that Kathy girl. She said they'd be in the area again for the next few nights, and I'm sorely tempted to find her and see if she really can help the poor mutt. I have to admit it's not the first time I've thought about it — maybe that's part of the reason I felt like getting properly cleaned up today — but I can't stand the thought of that guy that was with her, Joe, giving me an 'I told you so' look. I've had enough of that expression to last a lifetime!

I can see Muttbags is relieved when we reach the subway and he wastes no time in lying down by the wall. We receive some filthy looks from a gang over by the other end of the passageway and I stay standing until I'm satisfied they're not about to start any shit. The homeless get very territorial, but at this time in the morning even those fuckers can see they're better off wheedling loose change from passers-by than scrapping with the likes of me.

I sit down on the cardboard and stroke the dog. He's going to sleep now. Good. Neither of us had a good night, and at least while he's dreaming he's not feeling the pain in that damn paw. I glance down at his leg, not wanting to disturb him. My heart lurches. His skin's red and swollen. No wonder he was limping. If we can get a bit nearer to the Tube station there's a good chance I can find some water bottles that the commuters discard before they catch their connection. They never want to carry them around, so they usually chuck them in the bin half-full. I can use some clean water to wipe up the wound. Trouble is, it means making the poor guy walk a bit further and right now that's the last thing he needs.

We get a few quid more than I expected this morning, and I suppose it's because of his paw. No-one actually asks about it, but I can see them frown when they look at him. I know they're probably thinking I'm being cruel keeping him out here with me when he could be in a good home with people who can afford to pay vet's bills, but I can't say anything.

Muttbags and I met out here on the streets, so I can only assume he didn't have a home. He's expert at sniffing out the paper bags with good food in, so he must have been out here for a while before I came across him. That's why I gave him that name.

I wonder just how long he's been homeless. For me it's been a couple of years now. Two sodding Christmases I've spent out here. Occasionally I can get a bed in one of the shelters, but most don't allow pets so I stay on the street.

"For the dog." An old lady hands me a five pound note and I smile up at her, gratefully.

"Thanks. I'm going to try and get that paw looked at later," I promise her, tucking the money into my pocket.

"Good." She waddles off and as I watch her I notice the three thugs further down muttering and looking my way.

Damn. They must have seen her give me the money. I stand up, getting ready for the backlash. Muttbags must've felt me move, as he suddenly opens his eyes and gets to his feet, staring at the trouble-makers.

"Oi, you!" One of the guys shouts over to me and I clench my fists in readiness. "You're on our patch."

I sneer at him. "Says who?"

"Says us." The other two are right behind him now and they're striding menacingly towards me.

Shit! I recognise one of them as part of the gang that tried to steal my stuff before, when Muttbags scared them off. He's not going to do much scaring off today with that paw — and don't they know it?

I know I could probably make a good job of one of them, maybe two, but three's pushing it a bit — and Muttbags could get caught in the crossfire. I hate to back down, but the mutt has to come first. I put my hands up in the hope of placating them.

"All right, I'm off." I grab my carrier bag as swiftly as I can and turn to go.

"Not until you've paid us that money you stole from us, you're not!" The first guy's almost within spitting distance now and I feel my stomach churn. Every instinct tells me to stand and fight but I can't. Not today.

I twitch and the dog gets my instruction straight away. Run. We hurtle down the road with the bastards hot on our heels. It's raining, as usual, just to add to our misery. Muttbags barks but they take no notice. I know I can't outrun them, not without leaving him behind — and I'm not about to do that — so there's only one thing for it; I've got to outsmart them.

I dive down an alleyway with Muttbags and hear them following.

"You won't get away tosser!" Their voices tell me they're gaining on us.

We turn a corner and head down another passage that runs round the back of some terraces. One of the gates is slightly ajar and I push the dog through before pulling the bolt across. I know these houses. They have a gate out the back as well as one around the front, for taking the bins out. We don't hang around, we race up the garden and out the front gate and then down the main street, weaving in and out as shoppers swear and tut at us. There are a couple of blocks of flats just two streets away and we head for them like our lives depend on it — *they just might!*

I'm not sure how far away the fuckers are, as I don't waste time looking back. We head for the flats and get there just as a woman with a push-chair is coming out of one of them. I grab the main door.

"Here you go." I smile at her and she nods, gratefully as she struggles with the baby and a large bag.

"Thanks," she murmurs.

I should be thanking her, but I just help her out and then get Muttbags and myself inside as quickly as we can, careful to close the door behind us. We slip under the stairwell, the smell of urine and God-knows-what surrounding us. We're safe and dry, though. For now.

Chapter 3

We spend most of the day curled up under the stairs. Now and then someone from the flats goes in or out the main door, but they mainly ignore us, save the odd tut or rude remark. I don't listen to their shit. I know what they think, but it is what it is.

It's starting to get dark when my stomach finally insists it's time we made a move. We've eaten up the last of our stash and I've tucked the plastic bag in my pocket for later. If we're quick I might be able to get to the pound shop before they close; you can often pick up some good bargains there in the food aisle.

Luckily, no-one's around when we climb out from the stairwell, and we sneak out like the couple of thieves everyone assumes we are. Muttbags is limping really badly again, and my stomach churns at the thought of him being in so much pain.

It's been on my mind all day, whirring around like a cyclone. Do I go and find those do-gooders and ask for help? It totally goes against the grain, but I don't seem to have much choice. I know I'll get some filthy looks because of what I said last night, but this isn't about me — it's about the dog, and right now he's my priority. Besides, I lost my pride a long time ago.

I get some biscuits, chocolate and dog treats from the shop just before they close up for the night. Muttbags is happy to eat anything, and I know how he feels. It's rush hour and I know the Tube station will be packed with commuters, but Muttbags isn't up to the walk down there, so we sit in the doorway of one of the High Street shops and hope to get a few quid before the cops move us on.

I wonder what time those do-gooders will be around. They probably told me, but I wasn't taking much notice. I know they said they'd be around the Frimstone Road area though, which isn't far from here. It's raining again and I hope it doesn't put them off coming.

Help Our Heroes

I'm surprised how much I've been thinking about that girl, Kathy today. She was really quite pretty, from what I could see in the dark. Brown hair and big, chocolatey eyes. Nothing like Fiona.

"Thanks, mate."

I nod to a guy who just threw a two-pound coin onto the creased-up carrier bag I'd laid out in front of Muttbags. People would rather give money to a dog than the likes of me. The thought takes me back to the last row I had with Fiona, the one that landed me out here on the streets.

She didn't like the way I spoke to people — especially her. I'd only been back from my course a couple of weeks. It was part of the Army's rehabilitation programme to send us off to learn a different trade once we'd been discharged from service. I'd opted for plumbing. I don't know why, it just appealed more than electrics or decorating. Besides, I'd heard somewhere that there was a shortage of skilled plumbers and consequently they got paid a good whack.

I'd advertised my services in the local paper and got a couple of cash-in-hand jobs, mainly unblocking toilets, but the pay was good. When I declared my earnings I'd lost all my benefits, so I was left with the pressure of having to find more work to pay my way.

Fiona was very proud of the fact that the flat was hers. I'd only met her a few weeks after I'd been discharged, so had practically gone straight from the barracks to her place. I was grateful for the roof over my head and tried really hard to make some decent money. Problem was, most of the jobs I got meant travelling and I had to rely on public transport — not much use when someone rings saying it's an emergency. (Even the mobile phone I used was borrowed from Fiona). I was late getting to a flat where a burst pipe had wrecked the whole place, and the guy had the nerve to blame *me* for it. He wanted to claim against me for half the damage caused, saying if I'd got there on time I could've stopped it. I saw red. We had a massive row. Then I went home to Fiona and had another one. She said I shouldn't have lost my rag with the shithead; I should have just apologised and offered to do what I could to prevent any more damage. *Fuck that!* I told her I wasn't going to be treated like a dog by anyone — much less the fucker I'd just crossed half of London to help. She said I was useless and threw me out.

A horrid feeling in my stomach reminds me that that was exactly how I treated Kathy last night when she tried to help me. I was horrid to her. No wonder she looked so upset. I'll make it up to her tonight. I've still got a bar of chocolate in my pocket. I'll give it to her as a peace offering. Girls like chocolate.

We get up and I carefully put the change we've accumulated into my pocket, then put the rest of the biscuits and Muttbags' treats into the carrier bag before we make our way towards Frimstone Road. A clock in the distance chimes seven times and I hope we're not too early. The more I think about it, the more desperate I am to get that paw looked at. Poor Muttbags has been whining on and off all afternoon.

"I didn't expect to see you again."

I turn around to see the guy from last night.

"Joe, isn't it?" I ask, trying to sound casual.

"Yup. How's the dog?" He's looking disparagingly at Muttbags and I know exactly what he's thinking.

"Do you definitely do this stuff for free?" I stare at his sweatshirt which has Street Vets emblazoned across the front.

He nods. "Yeah. Like we said last night, we're all volunteers. We come out here four nights every week to see if we can help any of the pets of homeless people, or even strays. We don't charge a thing."

I'm mulling over his words. There has to be a catch.

"Why?" I frown at him while Muttbags start to whine at my feet.

Joe huffs. "We're not all heartless, you know. Some of us are actual animal-lovers who hate to think of the poor creatures being out here on the streets unable to get the help they need. We realise not everyone can afford to take their pets to the surgery when they're sick or injured." He looks pointedly at Muttbags' leg. "We just want to help them."

"Okay. Will you take a look at that paw, then?"

"Of course. We'd best get him to lie down over there." He points to a shop doorway with a streetlamp just outside. He crouches down and examines the paw before delving into his bag.

"He's been limping all day," I admit, as Joe takes a wipe to clean the wound. I crouch down, too, stroking the dog's back.

Help Our Heroes

"Looks like it's gone septic," Joe says. "I can give him some painkillers and a course of antibiotics but you'll need to come and find me for the next couple of nights."

I frown, wondering why I can't give them to the dog myself. Then he takes out a small syringe, answering my unasked question.

"Okay." I look around as he injects the mutt. Not that I'm squeamish or anything, it's just that given the choice I'd rather not watch. "You on your own tonight?"

It seems pretty quiet in the street, as the drizzle continues to soak us.

"Well, there's another team up the way," Joe says, nodding over the road. "We're not allowed to be out here on our own for safety reasons." He bites his lip and I sense something's wrong.

"So why isn't Kathy with you tonight?" For a minute I think about making a snarky comment about her maybe not wanting to get her hair wet, but I know that wouldn't be fair so I bite my tongue for once. Good job, too, when I see his angry expression.

"She's got the night off. Someone punched her last night when she went to help their dog." He scowls and I feel my stomach lurch.

"What? How the hell did that happen?" I stare at him, my body almost reaching boiling point.

"She said the guy agreed she could check the dog over, and when she did he went for her. Drunken good-for-nothing." Jo seethes, but manages to stroke Muttbags gently.

"Was she on her own?" I narrow my eyes. Joe was supposed to be with her last night.

He huffs, bandaging up the dog's paw. "She wasn't meant to be," he says, looking over at me. "I got a call from my wife. She's pregnant and was getting contractions. She thought the baby was coming so I said I had to go home. I told Kathy she should go home, too. She said she would." He shrugged. "I'd have given her a lift only..."

"Right." I'm staring at him.

He sighs. "Turns out she was on her way back to the Tube when she saw a guy with a dog down by the subway. The dog was whimpering so she asked if she could take a quick look. The rest, as they say, is history."

"Fuck!" I can't help it. It just slips out.

He nods. "I know. I shouldn't have left her. It wasn't that late, not long after we'd seen you, in fact. Luckily someone was passing that way and intervened. Kathy was okay, just a bit shaken up, and she's got a bruise on her forehead, but nothing drastic, thank God."

"She shouldn't have been on her own." I spit the words out.

"I know, man. You don't need to tell me. I feel as guilty as sin over it, trust me."

I watch his face cloud over and I know he's telling the truth. I'm an expert on guilt. We're silent for a few minutes.

"What did she have?" I speak first.

"What?"

"Your wife. Boy or girl?"

He rolls his eyes. "Braxton Hicks."

I suck a breath through my teeth. "Ouch!"

He nods. "In more ways than one. I have to admit they were quite convincing, even though we've still got another week. Poor thing was in agony. Nothing happening, though. She cried when they sent her back home from the hospital, but it wasn't her fault."

I shake my head, imagining the scene. I'd love to be a dad one day. Looks doubtful now, though.

"I didn't know about Kathy until I got to work this morning. You could've knocked me down with a feather when I saw her."

"You work together, then? Not just..." I gesture to his sweatshirt.

"Oh, yeah. She's a junior at my surgery. St. Patrick's down by the river."

"Oh." I'm still none the wiser.

"It's the really old building with the scaffolding at the side," he explains.

"I know the one." I frown. "I didn't know it was a vet's, though. I thought it was a ruin."

He sniggers. "It looks that way from the outside, but it's not really," he says. "My brother and I are into doing up old buildings. The vet's is a project as well as my business. We've done the inside and it's not half bad. You should take a look some time."

"Maybe I will."

"Kathy helped pick out the colour scheme for the reception area," he says with a smile. "She did a good job."

"And talking of her job, will she be back at work tomorrow night?" I ask, hopefully.

He smiles. "Yeah. I had a hard enough job keeping her away tonight."

"She seems very dedicated." I'm thinking aloud as I idly stroke Muttbags.

"She is." He sighs. "I feel so awful about last night." He clenches his fist. "I should never have..."

"I know how you feel, mate," I tell him. "But beating yourself up won't change a damn thing." I wish I could practice what I preach sometimes, but he looks grateful for the support.

"Sounds like you know a bit about the subject," he says with a weak grin.

"Oh yeah. Lost some buddies in Afghan." Saying it brings that lump back to my stomach.

Joe's eyes widen. "You're a soldier?"

"I was. They let me go saying I had PTSD. I'm not half as bad as some of them, mind, but they chucked me out anyway." I shake my head as memories come flooding back.

"God, I'm sorry." Joe actually looks shocked. I wonder what sort of no-mark he thought I was. "I had no idea."

"Why would you?" I give a self-deprecating grin. "Maybe I should get a sweatshirt made." I point at his logo and he laughs.

"Joe, we're about to go. You finished there yet?" Another guy comes up to us, closely followed by a younger one.

"Just about." He gives Muttbags another stroke on the nose and the dog licks his hand. "Will you come back this way tomorrow for another jab?" He looks expectantly and I notice his whole demeanour towards me has changed.

I nod. "Yeah, of course. We've got to get this fella back on his feet, haven't we?"

"You need to keep that wound as clean as you can," Joe says, putting his stuff back in his bag. "I know that's easier said than done, especially as he'll prefer walking on the soft mud instead of the street, but do what you can."

"I will." Last night I'd have come out with a smart-ass remark, but not now. This guy's a professional who's as human as I am, not some patronizing do-gooding prick like I first thought.

"I'll be down here around seven." Joe promises, giving Muttbags one last stroke on the head before standing up.

I stand up and shake his hand. "Thanks. And it's Chris, by the way."

As I watch the three guys make their way down the street I can't help feeling sorry for Joe. He clearly felt dreadful about leaving Kathy to make her own way home last night, but I really couldn't blame him. He must have been in a blind panic, thinking the baby was on its way.

I haven't the heart to make the poor mutt walk on that leg tonight, so I sit back down beside him on the pavement, pulling part of my coat under my arse. It's not just Brass Monkeys that suffer in this weather!

Chapter 4

I wake up the next morning in time to catch a few commuters who seem to take even more pity on Muttbags with that dressing on. We — or at least, *he* — makes enough to buy us a warm drink and a bacon roll from the street-vendor just down the road. It's great to get something hot inside me for a change, though I'm not sure if Muttbags appreciates the temperature of the food as he wolfs down half the roll and slurps the last of the tea.

I decide not to splash out on the public toilets this morning, as I've managed to find quite a few half-empty water bottles in the bins. The water's much colder than that in the taps yesterday, but at least it's clean and I feel much fresher once I've cleaned my teeth and drenched my face. I even use some to wash my hands after taking a pee in a back alley.

Whether it was the warm breakfast, or just a change in the weather, I'm not sure but it certainly doesn't feel quite as cold as we potter around the streets after that. Muttbags is putting that paw quite gingerly on the ground, and I know it must hurt him, but he still needs the exercise, and it's never a good idea to stay in one place for too long when you're on the streets.

It's a long and boring day, and I can't stop thinking about Kathy. She must have been terrified to get hit like that by a perfect stranger. I wonder if there's any way of finding out who the bastard was. Drunk or not, there's no excuse to hit a woman.

We take a stroll towards the subway near the Tube station. It's quite busy and we get jostled by passers-by who act like they don't even see us. Luckily, Muttbags has the sense to stay close to my side so he doesn't get too knocked about. He's a sensible mutt, that one.

I notice the gang that chased us yesterday are at the far opening, and stop short. There are more of them today and one of them's got a dog. I wouldn't put it past any of them to hit a woman. I'm not hanging around with Muttbags in this state, though, so turn him around and head back the way we came.

There's some of his treats still in the bag from last night, so I give him one to enjoy while I nip behind a shop and grab a large cardboard box from a pile of folded-up ones left in a stack by the rubbish. I'm thrilled to find it's quite thick, so hopefully we'll have a warmer night tonight.

We pick a spot at the side of a shopping street and try out luck, sitting on the folded box. I was right about it being warm, and I notice a nearby alleyway where I'll be stashing the box ready for our return tonight.

It's a good day for us; that bandage seems to be helping a lot, judging by the sympathetic looks Muttbags receives as passers-by throw their cash our way.

It's great to have his fur to snuggle up to as the dog snores quietly and I have a little daydream about seeing Kathy tonight. It's all that's keeping me going today, I realise.

By the time the clock chimes seven we've made quite a bit of cash and I spend the journey to Frimstone Road thinking about what to spend it on. The trick is not to put all your eggs in one basket, so to speak — you never know when you'll make your next quid.

We pass a chippy on the way and the smell beckons me in. Poor Muttbags has to wait outside the door but he doesn't seem to mind as he scavenges in a nearby bin. I treat us to a large portion of chips and we eat them as we walk. They've got salt and vinegar on, too, and they taste like heaven. I'm not sure the dog's all that keen on vinegar, though, by the look on his face, but he gobbles them down anyway.

I'm disappointed not to see anything of Kathy, Joe or the others despite walking the whole length of Frimstone Road. I know it's after seven but I've no idea how late it is and begin to wonder if we've missed them. Maybe we shouldn't have stopped for the chips on the way? Did Joe mean for us to get here bang on seven o'clock, like an appointment? *Damn!*

We try the next street and the one after that, but there's no sign. *Typical! Fucking liar!* I take deep breaths, trying to quell my anger. Although I know it's possible — and looking likelier by the minute — that Joe was bullshitting me about helping with a whole course of antibiotics, somehow I'm finding it hard to believe. Maybe I'm getting soft in my old age, but he certainly seemed sincere.

And besides, for him to have been lying meant that Kathy would have been, too and I just can't see that somehow.

"Come on, boy. If the mountain won't come to Muhammad..." I lead the mutt towards the river.

Luckily the area around this part of the Thames is quite well lit up and I can see the dilapidated building Joe was talking about. In fact, on closer inspection it doesn't look quite as bad as I thought. The building's in darkness and it occurs to me that maybe the surgery just ran over. I berate myself for getting so het up. I really need to stop getting angry so damn quickly. I had counselling when I left the Army, and they talked a lot about anger management. Trouble was, I stormed out in a huff one day and never went back!

Someone opens the front door as we approach, and torchlight floods out onto the steps leading up to it. A heavy-looking mat is flung over the banister-rail before we're even noticed, and I jump back to avoid being hit by it.

"Oh God, I'm so sorry!" Dim light from inside bounces off the shiny, brunette hair of a pretty girl, who I recognised as soon as she opened her mouth. "I didn't see you there."

"That's okay." I'm surprised and a little flattered that she seems so mortified at ignoring us — not that anyone could blame her.

Her eyes light up as I take a step closer and I feel a lurch in my stomach. Something that should know way better stirs in my jeans and I silently admonish myself.

"Hey, it's you!" At first I thought it was the dog she'd recognised, but she's actually looking right at *me*. No-one's looked that happy to see me in years.

"Chris." I nod. "Hi, Kathy. How are you?" I smile at her, then frown at the bruise on her forehead, half-hidden by her fringe. "Joe told me what happened."

She rolls her eyes. "Yeah, it wasn't as bad as it sounds," she assures me. "The guy was drunk and just lashed out. It was all over in seconds."

I shake my head. "It should never have happened, though."

"I know. Anyway, come on in." She opens the door wider, inviting us inside. "I didn't expect to see you here." She actually looks delighted to see us, and bends down to give Muttbags a stroke as he passes her in the hallway. "How's this fella?"

"Damn! His anti-biotics!" Joe struts towards us, torch in-hand and a sheepish look on his face. "I meant to bring them down tonight. I'm really sorry. We've had this flood, as you can probably see." He points the torch up at the ceiling. "It's even worse through here."

I look up as he focuses the light on a large, damp patch on the newly-painted ceiling. While Kathy fusses Muttbags I follow Joe through to a large room, feeling the carpet squelch under my feet. Part of the ceiling has broken through, and bits of plaster scatter the otherwise-stylish waiting room. Water is trickling down the walls and dripping through the gaping hole.

"Jeesh!"

"I know. Luckily it didn't happen while we were open. We were just getting ready to go out when there was a huge crash and the damn roof caved in!" Joe shakes his head.

There's giggling from the doorway, where Kathy's standing with Muttbags. "Maybe a *slight* exaggeration there, boss," she says. "It was a good job we didn't have any customers in, though."

"What's up there?" I point upwards.

"Just an old flat. We were going to do it up once we had chance, maybe let it out eventually. The pipe must have frozen then cracked when the place warmed up a bit. We've had to keep down here heated up more than usual these past couple of days as we've got a few animals staying over in the recovery cages."

"Have you switched off the water up there?" I assume he has, or it'd be pouring down here now.

He nods. "Yeah. We'll need to call a plumber out in the morning. We've already gone over-budget getting this place up and running, I don't know how we're going to afford the repairs on top — and we all know plumbers don't come cheap." He heaves a heavy sigh.

"I could take a look if you like?"

Joe stares at me. "Really?"

I nod. "I learned plumbing as soon as I left the Army. I'm not exactly an expert, but I know the basics." It feels good to see his impressed expression and I look over, hoping to see a similar look on Kathy's face. I'm not disappointed.

Help Our Heroes

She's beaming.

"Come this way." Joe eagerly leads me up the stairs.

The door to the flat's wide open and the bare floorboards are soaked. I'm surprised how big the place is, and peer into the kitchen. It's got plenty storage units and seems in quite good condition.

"It's the bathroom that's done it," Joe explains, pointing down the tiny hall.

I go over and see that the floor is completely drenched. Tiles have lifted from underfoot and there's a wet patch on the wall behind the pipe work. I quickly locate the shutoff valve and ensure that Joe has cut off the supply fully. Then I switch on the taps to drain the system. Meanwhile, I check the pipe for the damage.

"I could probably fix this with some epoxy and a rubber seal," I tell him. "Where's the nearest hardware shop?"

"B&Q's open late tonight, it's not far," he says, hopefully.

He leads me back downstairs where Kathy's giving Muttbags a good meal in the surgery's kitchen. She looks up and smiles when we arrive.

"We're just popping out to get some supplies," Joe tells her with a grin. "Can you give him a shot of antibiotics for me?"

She nods. "Of course."

I give the dog a quick stroke. "Be good for the lady, Muttbags," I tell him, "and mind your manners." I wink at her and am thrilled to see her blush before I head off after Joe.

It's not far to the DIY centre and I feel like a kid in a toyshop looking at all the tools and equipment stacked from floor to ceiling. Joe's quite happy for me to just select anything I think I'll need and I look forward to the day I can buy this sort of stuff for myself.

Most of the shoppers are men, dressed in overalls or scruffy jeans, some splattered in paint or filler. For once I feel quite at home here, and like no-one's judging me for the way I look.

Joe gets us all a Chinese take-away on the way back, and I'm surprised how much I look forward to seeing Kathy again. She's a beautiful girl, as well as being the kindest person I've met in my life.

Muttbags is pleased to see me, too, as always — not that we spend much time apart from each other these days. I take a torch and some rag and run upstairs to turn off the taps before we eat. I rub down the pipe as well as the wall behind it, leaving it to air-dry while we enjoy our meal. I feel more content than I've felt in years as we all enjoy our supper, chatting about anything that comes into our heads. There are some gas heaters burning in the back of the surgery to keep the recovering animals warm, so it's quite toasty and I relax more than I have in a long time.

"His paw's clearing up well," Kathy tells me with a smile. "And I've put another clean dressing on. I reckon one more shot of antibiotics and he'll be well on the mend."

"I still can't get over how you guys do this stuff for free," I tell her.

"Street Vets is quite a new thing," Joe informs me. "London's one of the few cities that has them, but we're hoping more and more surgeries will join in. There's certainly a high demand out there, and we're well aware how much homeless people depend on their dogs. You've all got enough to worry about without the added trauma of seeing your best friend suffering."

"Tell me about it." I get up. "Well, I'd best get this pipe fixed so you two can get off home." I didn't mean to put an edge in my voice, but I really didn't need to be reminded that, unlike them, I didn't have a home to go back to.

I take the new torch we just bought and head upstairs. As I'm checking the pipe, I'm surprised to hear light footsteps.

"Are you okay?" Kathy slowly comes into the tiny bathroom, carrying a small torch.

"Yeah. I'll be done in a minute," I tell her with a sigh. I know they're probably desperate to get out of here, but I have to admit it's the best night I've had in years. It's also a lot warmer here than out on the streets, even without the power on.

"There's no rush," she says with a shrug.

I use some epoxy, smearing it on with a flat putty knife.

"Haven't you got someone waiting for you at home?" I ask, as she crouches next to me on the hard floor.

She shakes her head. "No, it's just me. I'm not even allowed a pet as I'm renting, so no-one's missing me."

"Would you like a pet?"

She nods. "Yeah. We get so many cases in here I'd love to take home, but my landlady would have a fit."

"What about this place?" I ask, looking around the shadowy room. "Surely your boss could rent this out to you once it's done up?"

"*When* is a big word." Joe suddenly appears in the doorway. "I'd be only too happy to have Kathy living above the shop but it'll cost a small fortune to get this place habitable — especially now. My brother's an architect so buying up old places is just a hobby for us. I'm not qualified or anything, I just pitch in with a bit of painting and decorating when I get time — which isn't that often with everything going on downstairs."

"Business is good, then?" I ask, wrapping some rubber around the pipe.

"Yeah, much better than we expected, in fact. Only trouble is, we've got this one and couple of other properties that we're trying to do up and right now I haven't got much time. I suppose we should've thought about it before and got them sorted before the weather got so bad, but we hadn't even considered burst pipes and stuff until this happened." He tuts at himself.

"Well, I've got plenty of time on my hands if you need any help?" I offer. I feel quite excited at the idea.

"Yeah, that would be great." Joe sounds excited, too. "There's plenty of work needs doing, and if you're up for it, we could use a handyman for our other properties that we're renting already?"

I feel hope burn inside me for the first time in the two years since I've been on the streets. "I'd love to."

"In that case the job's yours." He grins, reaching out a hand to shake mine.

"Thanks, boss," I say with a snigger.

"Do you think that'll hold now?" he asks, nodding at the pipe as I attach a couple of clamps.

"You can always sack me if it doesn't," I tell him, cheekily. "It needs to settle like that for about an hour before I can put a waterproof seal over it – unless you want me to come back tomorrow? Then I'll need to check it for leaks before we can trust having the water switched back on."

"Well, I'll be here anyway as we've got animals staying overnight, so you're welcome to join me if you want a roof over your head for a change?" Joe offers. "Normally I'd have the TV on and a warm drink but you can see how we're fixed." He grimaces.

"It's okay. Why don't you get on home? I can stay here tonight. It'll save me having to walk back to the Tube on my own anyway," Kathy offers quickly.

My heart lurches.

"Well..." Joe doesn't look too sure.

"When did you say that baby's due?" I check.

He gets the message loud and clear. "You've got a point there, mate. Well, if you two are sure?"

"Yeah, we'll be fine. You get going, I'm sure Caroline'll be relieved to have you home tonight," Kathy says, clearly not taking no for an answer.

I smile, pleased to see she can be quite assertive when she's got her heart set on something – and I'm hoping that heart of hers is set on me.

Chapter 5

"As Joe said, usually have the little TV on when we stay over," Kathy explains."I hope it won't be too boring for you without it."

"I haven't watched any telly for a couple of years," I tell her. "I don't miss it."

She smiles. We've got the large torch on the coffee table in front of us, acting like a lamp. "It must be horrid being out in all weathers," she says, "does it make you feel vulnerable?"

I shrug, stoking Muttbags, who's curled up at my feet as I sit next to her on a padded sofa in the reception area. "Sometimes, I suppose, when we get rowdy drunks wandering the streets, but we can look after ourselves."

She nods. "It's a good job. I'd hate to be out there all night."

"You took a risk, approaching that man with the dog," I tell her.

Even in the limited light I can see her blush.

"I was just concerned about his dog. He looked like he was starving and he was whining," she tells me. "And the man was okay about it until I felt the poor mutt's ribs, then he yelled at me and swiped me across the face." She rubs her forehead, as though remembering the pain.

"What did he look like?"

She bites her lip. "He had a black beard and moustache. Much thicker and bushier than yours. And he was wearing a dark green coat. The dog looked really skinny — you'd have thought it was a whippet or a greyhound or something, but it wasn't. I think it was part lab, judging by its face. Poor thing."

I nod, anger roiling in my stomach. Definitely the guy I saw this morning by the subway. I'd thought — or rather, *hoped* — that the dog was one of those lean racing-types because of the way it looked, but it seems my suspicions were right. It was just malnourished. What makes the situation worse is knowing that when passers-by leave money it's usually for the dog, not us humans, so that bastard was clearly keeping it for himself. *Shithead!* Looks like he just uses the mutt to earn himself a good meal.

"Are you from around here?" I ask, trying to cheer her up a little. She's so sensitive; I can see that just thinking about that poor animal has brought her down.

"No, I came to London for my veterinary studies," she says. "Then I got the chance of this job so I took it. My family are down in Kent. How about you?"

"Yeah, I was brought up in Hammersmith," I tell her. "My parents moved up north, though, so I don't see anything of them. When I left the Army I thought I'd have a better chance of work down here so I came back."

She doesn't ask, but I go on to explain how I ended up on the streets anyway. That girl certainly wears her heart on her sleeve, as she looks like she's going to cry when I tell her how Fiona threw me out.

"I'd better go and see how that pipe's doing," I say after a while. I'm enjoying chatting with her — she's so easy to talk to, but I have to remember the reason why I'm here.

"I'll hold the torch," she offers, following me up.

The pipe's still dry and the rubber's set securely, so I bind some water resistant tape around it.

"And now for the moment of truth." I slowly turn the water valve back on and wait with bated breath. It's the first time I've actually done this job for real and I feel a flutter of excitement as I run my hand over the pipe and note that it's still bone dry.

"You did it!" Kathy flings herself into my arms, and I automatically hold her, stunned but not disappointed at her reaction. "You're a genius!"

I chuckle. "Well, I wouldn't go that far," I assure her, flattered. I don't think I've ever been called that in my life, and I'm thrilled that such a compliment is coming from someone as lovely as her.

She feels soft in my arms and I'm surrounded by the scent of her floral perfume. I hope I smell okay, and remember it's been a while since I had a shower. I slowly let go of her in the pretence of gathering up the equipment.

"Joe'll be really pleased," Kathy goes on, excitedly. "He was horrified when the ceiling came down. He was talking about having to close for a few days while we got it all sorted, and we just can't afford to do that with all the bookings we've got. It'd be a shame to lose all the customers when we've only just got them."

"I'll check the electrics in the morning," I tell her, following her downstairs. "As long as the sockets and fittings aren't flooded we should be okay to get the power back on. If we clean up the mess in the waiting room, do you think he'd mind cordoning off the part below the hole in the ceiling, just while I fix it? That way it'll be business as usual."

She turns around to beam at me. "He'll be so relieved. He was worried he might have to tell the kennel maid not to come in tomorrow — she's only part-time and needs the money. If we had to close down, even for a few days it would be awful for her."

I smile at her. She obviously cares a lot about this place and the people she works with. We go through to the back of the surgery where I leave the equipment on top of one of the work-surfaces.

"I'll just check on our patients," she says. "The other torch is on there if you want to go and get comfy again."

She shines the large torch on a smaller one which is lying on top of Joe's toolbox and I pick it up along with a screwdriver and go back through to the reception area. Muttbags has made himself at home on a dry patch of carpet and is splayed out, snoring his head off. While Kathy sees to the animals I quickly stand on a chair and unscrew the rosette in the centre ceiling light. It's bone-dry. The wall-sockets are dry, too, when I open them up. It's good to know the electricity should be safe to go back on, but I think I'll keep quiet about that for now. We don't need the TV on and it's much more romantic doing everything by torchlight.

Joe was right about Kathy doing a good job in furnishing this area. It's pale shades of mint and peach with warm wood on the table and ends of the large sofas. Everything has clean lines and looks comforting yet smart. The middle of the floor is taken up with a large, square deep brown carpet with a thick pile, but all around it the parquet floor has been polished up — I can just see the light of my torch bouncing off it. Practical, yet warm. A bit like the girl herself!

"They're all fine," she announces, coming into the room with a packet of chocolate biscuits and a huge quilt. She places the large torch on the coffee table again and sits back on the sofa next to me.

"Are you cold?" she asks, holding up the quilt.

Normally I might have quipped back with something snarky like 'you don't know what cold is!' but with her I don't want to be like that. She deserves better. And she'll get it, I've decided.

I'm not really chilly, but I can't deny that the thought of cuddling up with her under that quilt is making my insides melt.

"Yeah, want a hand?" I reach out and help her arrange it over us both. We kick off our shoes and get comfy, my arm around the back of the sofa, ready to drop onto her shoulder at any given moment.

Her body's warm and soft against mine and I'm smothered in that pretty perfume once again. We chat about our families and I'm surprised at how easy it is to open up to her.

"I was afraid I'd disappointed my folks when I had to leave the Army," I tell her, ruefully. "A lot of us left after our tour of Afghanistan with PTSD — some worse than others. It didn't really affect me, but they diagnosed me anyway."

"They must have had reason to think you had it," she says, clearly puzzled.

I shrug. "I suppose I was bit quick-tempered, and I had nightmares like you wouldn't believe, but that's about it." I grimace. "I'm not loopy or anything."

She giggles. "I know that."

I'm surprised how relieved I feel. "I went to counselling, too." I'm keen to assure her that she's got nothing to fear from me. I'm not some crazed lunatic or anything. In fact, I'm surprised that she's happy to stay with me tonight, being as she doesn't exactly know me — and especially after getting hit by that fuckwad the other night!

"Did it help?"

"I dunno." I shrug again. "I suppose I understood better why I felt the way I do. It doesn't stop me being guilty thought, does it?" The thought gives me that sinking feeling in my gut again. It always does that.

"I don't think you're guilty," she says matter-of-factly. "There was nothing you could've done to help those men, but you were able to help the ones in the other platoon. You saved their lives. I think that's wonderful."

She doesn't sound like she's trying to flatter me; she's just telling it how she sees it. The thought makes me snigger. Usually people tell me what they think I want to hear, or ask me probing questions to make me try to look at things differently, but not her. She just comes out with it, blunt as you like. It's all black and white with her and I can't help loving her attitude. I'm reminded how she reacted to me when I was suspicious of her the other night when she stopped by to help Muttbags. She shrugged it off when I misunderstood what she was there for, despite how rude I was. She only looked hurt when I got a bit personal. I hate myself for doing that.

Warmth floods my stomach. She's called me a genius and wonderful all in the space of a couple of hours. I never thought I'd be able to impress a girl this much in a million years. And I'm really glad it's *her* that thinks so highly of me.

Her head leans onto my shoulder and I hear her soft breathing right next to my ear. I allow my arm to sink down onto her as I drift into the most peaceful sleep of my life.

* * *

I'm not sure how long I slept before I feel a nudge. My befuddled brain is confused that it's not a wet nose that's stroking my face, but the soft hand of a beautiful woman. At first I think I must still be dreaming, but her soft voice permeates my mind and I quickly open my eyes.

"Chris, wake up." Kathy's smiling at me in the dim light of the torch. We must have left it on last night as it looks like the battery's running down. "I need some help."

I spring into action, suddenly getting my bearings. I don't remember ever waking up so warm — I'd been wearing my coat under the quilt and now I'm quite sticky. "What's up?"

"It's Lady. She's having her pups," Kathy says quickly. "I think she's okay, but I could use a hand."

"Of course."

I follow her into the back of the surgery where the large cages house the animals staying overnight.

"Can you grab some of that newspaper?" Kathy points to a large stack of the stuff behind the door and I grab what I can.

We spread it out around the pen, where a large bitch is quietly getting on with the job of giving birth. She's lying on a soft blanket and the pups seem to be slipping out quite easily. The newspaper is for the area around the blanket, just to catch the mess.

"I'll change the blanket when she's finished," Kathy explains, "this is just to make the clearing up a bit easier. The mess tends to spread a little."

Fascinated, I watch as the tiny, bald creatures emerge from their mother, blindly following the scent of her milk and latching on to feed as soon as they can.

"We won't touch them for a while, let them bond with her first," Kathy says softly. "But can you just pass over that bottle of water? Mum looks like she could do with a good drink."

I do as she asks, mesmerised by the sight before us. I've never witnessed anything so incredible. The gas heater's giving off a little light, shrouding the room in a pale, orange glow, and I remove my coat before settling back down on the floor beside Kathy. We keep our distance, just staying close enough to intervene if necessary, although Lady seems to be doing just fine without us.

Muttbags wanders through to take a look at what we're up to, but then meanders back to the reception area. I can't blame him. I've often wondered what use males are at a time like this.

Eight puppies later, we can't stop smiling as we watch them all fighting for space on their mother's stomach. She nuzzles them all lazily, and then sighs as she closes her eyes.

Kathy strokes Lady's nose, whispering words of encouragement, before turning back to me.

"Let's just replace the newspaper and then leave them for a while to get acquainted," she whispers.

I grab a bin-bag and stuff the soggy paper into it while Kathy lays out the dry sheets and then we quietly go into the kitchen.

"Sorry I can't offer you a cup of tea," she says, after washing her hands thoroughly.

"Actually, you might." I remember the situation with the electrics and check the sockets again, which are still perfectly dry.

I look around for the master switch and reinstate the power. Immediately

Help Our Heroes

the lights flicker on and the red dot on the microwave flashes into action.

"Great!" Kathy beams and grabs the kettle.

I remove my jumper, conscious of the stench of sweat, which embarrasses the hell out of me. Kathy doesn't seem to notice, though, and soon hands me a large mug of hot tea before grabbing more biscuits from the cupboard.

It's been two years since I did anything as 'normal' as sit in a kitchen drinking tea as the sun rose through the open blind. I sigh with contentment, wishing it could be like this every day. Kathy's very sweet and chatters quietly about how they found Lady on the street and brought her in, worried that she was malnourished and about to give birth. She talks enthusiastically about the other animals in the surgery's kennels and I'm touched at how much love she has for the helpless critters. I wonder if any of that devotion could ever be lavished my way.

Chapter 6

A while later we return to clean the pen where Lady and her pups are nudging and licking at each other. They seem a little more awake now, and more conscious of each other, which is lovely to see.

"I might need a hand moving Lady onto a clean blanket," Kathy explains as we remove the newspaper again.

I strip off my shirt and tee-shirt, hoping I don't smell too bad, and take the dog's weight as Kathy slides the dirty blanket from beneath her and replaces it with a clean one. Lady hardly seems to notice, still fussing over her pups, and we leave them in peace once we're happy they've got everything they need.

"There's a small bathroom through there," Kathy says, pointing down the corridor. "It's got a shower and everything. You can use anything you need. Not that..." She suddenly looks embarrassed, as though she's afraid of offending me.

I put a hand up to reassure her. "That's great to hear. You wouldn't believe how much I'd love a proper wash."

I grab my clothes and head in the direction she indicated. I'm glad I take my toothbrush everywhere, and can't believe my luck when I see how well-stocked the tiny bathroom is, with soap, towels, and even shaving foam and disposable razors. It seems Joe must spend a lot of time back here in between dealing with the animals.

"There are some spare clothes here if you need them," Kathy shouts through the door, just as I'm about to climb into the shower.

"Thanks." I call back, grateful at the thought of not having to put my dirty gear back on afterwards.

The hot water feels heavenly and I probably use a bit more shower gel and shampoo than I should have, but it's such a relief to actually feel clean for a change. The fresh scent of the gel surrounds me and I don't want to wash it off.

Help Our Heroes

My hair feels really greasy until I give it a good soak in the two-in-one shampoo and conditioner. I badly need a haircut and wonder when I'll ever be able to afford such a luxury.

Eventually, I emerge from the steamy shower and wrap a towel around me before scrubbing my teeth and having a shave. I haven't felt so human in a long time.

Kathy's left a pile of clean clothes outside the door for me — even underwear. I assume it's some stuff that Joe's left in case he ever needs it, and it's a bit tight on me but I'm not about to complain — it's sheer luxury.

"Wow — look at you!" Kathy's eyes are wide as she stares at me and I'm sure I detect a note of approval in her voice.

I feel great, like I could conquer the world right now. I'm fresh and clean and I've actually been useful for a change. I couldn't ask for more. I even had a good night's sleep and I don't think I dreamt about anything other than the pretty girl who spent the entire time in my arms.

I smile at her. "Thanks. You don't think Joe'll mind lending me his things, do you?"

She shakes her head. "He's got loads of stuff in his locker. He just keeps it there for emergencies — you never know when you're going to get peed on or whatever in this job." She giggles. "You suit green." She's nodding at the jumper I'm wearing.

I roll my eyes. "It's just as well. I wore enough of it in the Army."

"I'm sorry. I didn't mean to..." She looks mortified that she's upset me.

"It's fine," I assure her. "I was lucky. Some of the guys looked hideous in their uniform but I always thought it brought out the colour of my eyes." I grin.

She stares up into my eyes, which are dark green. "They're lovely," she whispers.

Warmth floods my whole stomach and I reach out for her, relieved that she walks straight into my arms. I gaze into her big, brown eyes before taking her lips in a lingering kiss. She kisses me back gently and meaningfully. My whole body feels like it's floating as I hold her and carefully lap at her lips before probing my tongue into her mouth, exploring tentatively.

We both gasp for air when we finally open our eyes again and take a step back, reluctantly pulling away from each other. I still have my arms around her soft frame, though. I don't ever want to let go. Her smile tells me she feels the same and I sigh with relief.

With a sudden shock she quickly puts her hand in front of her mouth. "Oh no. I haven't cleaned my teeth!" She dives into the bathroom, while I chuckle at her cute embarrassment. It looks like she feels the same as me about dental hygiene.

As I hear the water running I go back into the kitchen and make some more tea, sneaking a couple more chocolate Hobnobs while I'm there. I gaze out the window as the sun beams down on the frosty pavement. This time tomorrow I'll be back out there, curled up in a doorway somewhere, feeling every bite of cold air surround me and permeate my bones. For now, though, I want to savour every second of feeling like a normal human being.

* * *

Penny, the kennel maid arrives just after eight o' clock and is delighted to hear that Lady had her pups earlier.

"Trust me to miss all the fun!" She rushes into the back of the surgery to see the new arrivals and she and Kathy coo and swoon over the little creatures, who, to them, are the most beautiful things on God's earth right now. I can't help thinking they look naked and ugly, but, as I'm outnumbered, decide to keep quiet about my opinions.

Joe arrives not long after that, and is also thrilled about the pups. He's even more pleased to note that the electricity is back on and that the upstairs pipe's all fixed.

"You're a handy bloke to have around," he tells me, pulling out his wallet. "I told my brother about you and he's got quite a bit lined up for you, if you still fancy some work? And if you don't mind roughing it you can stay up in the flat while we get it renovated. Then I'm sure we'll sort something out. What d'you think?"

He grins, handing me a wad of notes. I can almost feel my jaw hit the floor as I take the money and stuff it into my back pocket without even counting it.

"That's a great idea!" Kathy jumps up, throws her arms around me and gives me a big peppermint-scented kiss on the cheek. "You've now got a job *and* somewhere to live!"

I nod. It's about all I can manage.

"Great. Why don't you guys go and get some breakfast and we'll talk about it all later?"

Joe doesn't seem at all surprised at Kathy's reaction and just smiles at us as we pull on our coats.

Kathy grabs my hand as we stroll down past the river to a small cafe. Muttbags seems much more comfortable walking on that paw now, and I think the comfy night in the warmth must have helped with his healing, too. The smell of bacon welcomes us inside and we order the full English with extra toast. I don't know why, but I'm starving this morning. It could be connected to my feeling so relaxed and happy, I suppose.

I save some of my breakfast for the mutt, who's waiting outside, drinking out of a water-bowl provided by the owners. It feels good to be able to pay for the meal, and I realise that Joe's given me a hundred quid for the job.

"Well, I'd best get back to work," Kathy says, turning to go back the way we just came.

"I'll catch you up," I tell her. "Muttbags needs a walk and I could use a barber." I feel the need to smarten myself right up and now I've got some cash I'm determined to do just that.

She reaches up and gives me a quick kiss on the cheek. "Okay. There's a place on Rosamund Street that Joe uses, if it's any help?"

"Thanks."

I watch her head back towards the surgery before going in the opposite direction. Rosamund Street is just the other side of the subway but I decide to go the long way around today. Not only because I don't want any trouble from the fuckwad with the emaciated mongrel, but also to give me and Muttbags some exercise. It's become our routine to have a good stroll first thing in the morning — at least, when he's not suffering from an injured paw — and I'm keen to keep it up.

As I walk down the street I feel like a totally different person. I'm clean. It makes such a difference. There's a second-hand shop on the High Street and I pop in and buy myself a new coat. It's not in bad condition and although it's priced at a tenner I manage to haggle the price down to eight pounds. I'm well aware of how much every penny is worth and I'm not going to waste any of it. After transferring my toothbrush and paste into the inside pocket, I discard the old one in a bin outside. Catching sight of my reflection in a shop window, I grin.

The barber's shop isn't too busy, and I leave Muttbags sniffing around the doorway while I head inside and take a seat. The guy acknowledges me and I pick up a magazine from the coffee table. A couple of guys next to me are talking about a football match, and some music's warbling in the background where the radio's been left on.

When it's my turn the guy frowns at my hair. I'm glad I washed it this morning, but there's no escaping the choppy way it's been hacked at with razor blades while I've been on the streets.

"It needs a good cut," I tell the guy before he can comment.

He nods and stares at me as though I've just made the understatement of the year. At least my face doesn't look too bad, I note, staring at my reflection in the large mirror. I shaved it close to my skin but left a thin layer of stubble – after all, I didn't want to overdo it.

The old man squirts some fancy-smelling water on my hair and sets to with the scissors and a fine-toothed comb. By the time he's finished there's more hair on the floor than on my head, but it looks good. He seems surprised when he sees the wad of notes I pull out of my pocket to pay him with, and asks if I want to buy some weird-looking gel he's got on the counter. Oddly enough, I decline the offer.

Muttbags has no difficulty recognising me when I leave the shop, so I figure the change can't have been all that drastic, and we head back for the surgery. My mind's reeling about everything that's happened over the past twenty-four hours and before I know it we're heading down the subway.

I realise all-too-late that the gang are down there, waiting at the far end, and they see me before I've got time to turn back.

"What the fuck?" The one with the dog sneers at me and the others laugh.

My blood starts to boil as they all square up to me and I wish I'd gone the other way. Muttbags barks at them and their mongrel yelps back. Shoppers hurry past, giving us all a wide berth, which makes me feel even more annoyed that I'm being tarred with the same brush as these delinquent shits.

"Did you want something?" I sneer at the ring-leader as they all make an arc blocking our way.

"Yeah. The money you stole from us." His breath's rancid and I hope mine was never that bad.

Damn. There are four of them and although it doesn't bother me so much, I don't want Muttbags getting caught in the cross-fire. I'm tempted to pull a fiver from my pocket and just give it to them to shut them up, but even *I* know that won't be the end of it. It's just an excuse. Besides, why the fuck should I? I don't owe them a bean.

"I didn't steal anything." The argument's just to buy me some time while I try to figure a way out of this mess.

Out of the corner of my eye I see one of the gang pick up a plank of wood. That's all I need. I suddenly regret buying my new coat – it's about to get ruined.

"You know exactly what you did, fucker and don't you deny it!" The head honcho narrows his eyes at me, menacingly. I can well imagine he was the one that hit Kathy, and my jaw tenses at the thought.

I nod towards his dog. "Your hound needs some help." I was hoping to divert his attention but he's having none of it.

"So will yours when we've finished with it." That wasn't the response I wanted and the threat hits me like a brick.

My fist rises with my anger and suddenly they're all onto me, thumping and kicking like wild animals. I hear Muttbags bark in the midst of it all and I shout at him to get away. At first I thought he'd made a run for it, but as a foot comes flying into my face I notice one of the fuckers grab hold of him.

"Leave him!" The black mist closes in on me and my fists flail, hitting whatever they can reach. I feel something wet run down my fingers and I hope it's not my own blood.

"Get the dog!" I recognise the voice of the ringleader and I want to kill him on the spot. Trust him to target a defenceless animal. He's obviously realised he's my Achilles heel, damn him!

I hear a yelp, which fires me up even more and my feet and fists thrash out indiscriminately, maiming whoever and wherever I can. Pain sears my body but I can't ascertain the exact location. Blood is flying through the air — I'm not sure whose — and the sounds of shouts and cursing echo in the murky walls of the underpass. A dog's whining spurs me on and I dread to think what they're doing to my poor pooch. I continue to smash whatever flesh I can lay my fists on, and I'm sure I hear the crack of a nose before an almighty yell.

    A woman's voice screams, reverberating around the subway, and I see a familiar face at the mouth of the entrance, as blood runs over my eyes. I'm about to shout at her to get away from here, when there's a sudden agonising burn across the back of my head and everything goes black and silent.

Chapter 7

I wake up in a hospital bed with the mother of all headaches. Even in my days of getting wasted on a Friday night I never felt anything this bad — and that's saying something!

"You're back with us, then?" A nurse with a strong Welsh accent peers at me before shining a torch in my eyes. *Fuck!* "You had us worried for a while, there," she goes on. "That was some hit you took."

I roll my eyes before realising how much that hurts.

"The police want a word with you." The woman never shuts up. "I'll tell them they can come in now." *Oh deep joy!*

A couple of burly constables saunter in. They look bored stiff and I wonder how long I've been in here.

"Good evening. Chris, isn't it?" *Well, that answers my question.*

I nod and immediately regret it when the pain ricochets through my head. "Yes. Chris Roberts."

"I'm PC Cage and this is PC Skinner," the eldest one says. "Can you remember what happened to you?"

I close my eyes momentarily. As if I'd ever forget! "The bastards tried to kill me," I mutter. My thoughts suddenly turn to Muttbags and all that whimpering. "How's my dog?" My heart thumps hard against my ribs as I fear the worst and I stare at them for what seems an eternity before the older one speaks again.

"He's been taken to St. Patricks, the vet by the river."

"Is he okay?"

"We're not sure. He was badly hurt."

"How badly?"

He takes a deep breath. "They're sorting him out. Good job one of them came by when they did."

"Kathy?" I groan, recalling her blood-curdling scream.

PC Cage checks his notebook. "Yes. She came looking for you, apparently. Saw you in the middle of a brawl and called us. She was in a right state."

Oh God!

"It wasn't a brawl. They wanted to rob me." I can just imagine how it must have looked to her.

"You knew these guys, then?" Skinner's found his voice.

"Not by choice."

I go on to explain about my past two years living on the streets and the ongoing battle with the gang who seem to think they own half the subways in London. It transpires that the cops are well aware of the thugs, and were currently holding them all in the local cells. Kathy had identified the instigator as the bastard that hit her the other night; something the cops take a very dim view of. Their poor dog's been taken to St. Patrick's too, and I'm glad it couldn't be in more caring hands.

"Someone from the vet's will drop by later to update you," PC Cage promises when they eventually leave.

I'm worried sick about Muttbags, and it's doing nothing to help the pain in my head. I'm grateful when the nurse returns a short while later with a couple of painkillers and a glass of water. The doctor follows her in.

"You're a very lucky man." The doctor, a grey-haired man who looks in need of a good night's sleep, nods at me after looking at my notes. "We scanned your brain but there's no swelling or anything. You had a fortunate escape."

"I've had a few of them," I mutter. I can't stop my snarky side escaping.

He frowns. "You were in the Army, weren't you?"

I stare at him in surprise. Kathy must have been talking about me. I hope that means she doesn't hate me. "Yes."

"Helmand Province?"

I nod. I really should stop doing that – it kills my head.

"You might know Father Donnelly. He's been out there a couple of times."

I gawp at him. "Yes." I remember the little fat padre well. For a man of God he had a wicked sense of humour and spoke a lot of sense. I've never been the religious type but he never held that against me. He was just a really good laugh and great company. I don't remember him ever spouting the Bible, though I suppose he must have done at some time.

"I'll get him to drop in on you if you like? He'll be doing the rounds later."

My heart lightens at the prospect of seeing him again. I didn't realise how constricted my chest had felt since I woke up, and I suspect it had more to do with Kathy than the fuckers who hit me. Hearing her scream like that, and knowing she must have thought I was nothing but a violent thug hurt me more than I'd care to admit.

The doctor goes on to say that they're keeping me in overnight for observation, since my head took such a battering, but he's not overly worried. I can eat and drink — which is good as I'm starving, I realise — and he's prescribed some stronger painkillers for tonight. I've never been one to pop pills, but I'll make an exception if it helps ease this almighty throb in my head.

Mercifully, the nurse isn't half as chatty when the doctor's around, and she scurries off to find me a sandwich as soon as he's made his assessment.

After my meal I must have fallen asleep for a short while, as I'm woken by light tapping on my door and a familiar face pokes his head around it.

"Well, I thought you'd dropped off the edge of the earth," Father Donnelly announces, that twinkle still in his eye.

I sit up slowly. "Father? What the hell are you doing here?"

He rolls his eyes in that familiar way he always did when we used to cuss in front of him, and saunters into the room.

"I could ask you the same thing." His broad Irish accent takes me back to happier times with my mates, and I feel a pang deep inside me.

"How are you, mucker?" I ask, as he comes over and gives me a big hug. Even my dad never put as much meaning into a hug as this guy and I love him for it.

"I'm fine, it's just these others." That was his stock reply all those years ago and it still made me giggle today.

He points at my head which has a huge bandage wrapped around it. "It's not the first time I've seen you looking like that," he remarks. "Though I'd hoped you'd be taking more care of yourself in civvy street."

For some inexplicable reason tears gush down my face and the squidgy old guy holds me tight as I bawl my eyes out. Everything comes rushing to my mind at once and I'm overcome with emotion. The past, the present, — my whole future just flows through my befuddled brain as he sits on the bed, gently rocking me like a baby.

It's ages before I can make any coherent sound, and then I find I can't stop talking. Everything pours out; how hard it was to cope when I left the Army, how I ended up on the streets — even the latest episode with those thugs and my fears about Kathy getting the wrong impression of me.

"You're very lucky," he says when he can finally get a word in edgeways. "It looks like you've got a bright future ahead of you, what with the new job and somewhere to live."

I nod. I know he's right. It meant the world to me this morning, but somehow it lost its shine when I heard Kathy scream. I want her to like me; to think I'm worth knowing. She was lovely last night and she really made me feel useful for once.

"What if the vet thinks I'm just a thug? Joe won't want to hire me then, will he? And Kathy won't want to know me. I'll be right back to where I started." Fresh tears stream down my cheeks and I brush them away irritably.

"Don't you think you're being a little unfair to judge them so harshly? After all, they haven't done or said anything to make you think that's the case, have they? Don't you owe it to them to hear what they think before you jump to conclusions?" Father Donnelly has a soft lilt which gives his voice a gentle edge. He never sounds judgemental and talks such sense it makes you wonder why you didn't think of that in the first place.

"You're right," I concede.

"Don't sound so surprised." He feigns indignance and we both chuckle.

I sniff. "I'll talk to them. Explain what happened." The thought makes me feel better already. The padre always had this affect on me — on all of us. There wasn't a man who knew him that didn't love the bones of the old priest.

The door opens and the Welsh nurse pops her head around it. I quickly wipe my face with my hands.

"Sorry to interrupt. There's a couple of people here from the vet's to see you." She's smiling. I hope that's an indication they brought good news. I couldn't bear anything to happen to Muttbags.

"I'll leave you to it," Father Donnelly says, standing slowly. "I'll look in on you in the morning if that's all right?"

I nod eagerly. "Yes, please, Father."

He smiles kindly at me. "Try to get a good night's sleep. You can face anything with a good rest behind you."

As soon as he leaves Kathy and Joe appear in the doorway. She looks pale but beautiful. I don't know why I didn't notice how gorgeous she was the first time I laid eyes on her.

"How are you feeling?" She looks nervous as she slowly walks into the room.

"I'm fine," I assure her, tapping the bed in the hope she'll take the padre's place beside me. "How's Muttbags?" I hold my breath.

"He's going to be fine," Joe says calmly, as he takes the chair by the side of the bed. "He was in quite a bit of pain as they'd given him a good kicking, but there's no permanent damage done and he's back on his feet and eating properly, so we're happy he's okay."

Kathy sits on the bed and smiles shyly at me. "We treated him for fleas, too, and gave him a bath."

I gawp at her. "How did he like that?" He's never had a bath in all the time I've known him and I hadn't actually noticed any fleas.

"He was trying to drink all the water while I was washing him, but he was really good," she says with a giggle. She looks a little more relaxed now.

I roll my eyes, then wince with the pain. Kathy's face falls.

"Is your head hurting? Should we go?"

"No." I grab her arm before she can hop off the bed. I like feeling her so close to me. "It's nothing serious, just a headache. Doc says I'll have it for a while. I'm being dosed up so I'll be fine soon."

She bites her lip. "I saw you look over at me just before that man hit you with a wooden plank." She looks strained. "I'm so sorry. I shouldn't have distracted you." Tears well in her beautiful dark eyes and I put a finger to her cheek to catch them as they fall.

"It wasn't your fault." It hadn't occurred to me that she'd think she was to blame for any of it. "He was just a fucker who took the first chance he got. I knew he was waiting for his moment. He'd have done it whether you were there or not."

"The doctor said you were lucky. It was a hefty whack," Joe pipes up.

"It wasn't that bad." I scowl at him. Kathy feels bad enough already; she doesn't need him making it sound any worse.

"You had concussion," Kathy says with a sniff.

"Where there's no sense there's no feeling," I tell her with a self-deprecating chuckle. "I'm fine, honestly. I was more worried that you'd got caught up in it."

She shakes her head. "I called the cops as soon as I saw what was happening," she said. "Lots of other people started crowding around when I screamed . Those men looked shocked when you fell to the ground — I think they thought you were dead."

Her voice trails off and I can see that she must have thought it, too.

"Only the good die young," I tell her, stroking her cheek.

"They tried to run for it when they heard the sirens," Joe says with a smirk.

Kathy looks a little brighter as she adds, "they couldn't get out of the subway. Everyone was gathered around both entrances, blocking their way. They were cursing and swearing but no-one took any notice. The cops came and arrested all of them."

"I heard you recognised one of them." I keep my voice soft.

She nods. "Yeah. The one with the dog was the one that hit me. The cop said he'd face charges for that on top of everything else."

"Good." I can't help thinking it's worked out well, despite my crashing headache.

"We'll keep Muttbags in for observation tonight," Joe says, standing up. "You don't have to worry about him."

"Thanks, mate. I appreciate it," I tell him, shaking his hand.

"No problem. You just get better. That flat's waiting for you when you're up to coming home and my brother and I have already starting compiling a list of jobs for you when you're back on your feet."

My heart sings. I was dreading him telling me he'd changed his mind, but the man's an absolute diamond.

"Just let me get out of this bed and I'm all yours," I promise him.

"I was rather hoping you'd be all mine," Kathy pipes up coyly.

I suddenly feel ten feet tall as I smile at her. "That's a given," I assure her, leaning over and kissing her on the nose.

"Only when you're ready. There's nothing urgent," Joe says with a chuckle. "The important thing is for you to get better."

I nod. *I really must stop doing that!*

"I'll drop by tomorrow with some clean clothes," Kathy promises, jumping down from the bed. She leans over to kiss me and I'm shrouded in her pretty, floral perfume. Her lips are soft and I don't want to ever stop feeling them on mine. Something stirs under the bedcovers, reminding me that it's time to let her go, and the giggle that emanates from her sweet mouth makes me wonder if she guessed my predicament.

"Sleep well," she whispers.

I watch them go. Somehow I think those nightmares might be kept at bay for another night yet.

Chapter 8

I'm straightening up my bed, ready to leave the hospital when there's a knock on the door.

"Morning Father. I thought you'd forgotten me." I grin at him.

"Never," he assures me. "But I'd like a quick word if you've got a minute?"

I nod, thankful that it doesn't hurt as much today. He takes the chair while I lean against the bed.

"You stopped the counselling," he says, matter-of-factly.

I feel a thud in my gut.

"Why don't you go back?"

I shake my head with a self-deprecating smirk. "I don't think they'd want me." The vision of me losing my rag and yelling at the guy springs to mind and I wince at the thought.

"Because you shouted at Paul Hudson?"

"Yep."

"Do you think you're the first?"

I consider it for a moment and suddenly feel really sorry for the poor guy. He's a very good listener and offers some sound advice, but I was having a really off-day and let rip at him. He must have thought I was about to hit him, but I thumped the desk instead. I shrug.

Father Donnelly sighs. "Chris, it's part of his job. And it's part of your recovery to let off steam occasionally. That's why you're there; to get it out in a safe, non-judgemental environment. You can't bottle it all up forever. He's well aware of that — it's what he's there for."

"He didn't deserve that."

"So, tell him if it bothers you."

I stare at him. "You think he'd listen?"

"It's what he does best."

"You're right." I think for a moment. It would be good to have someone to talk to, and Paul was a great counsellor. "It's worth a thought," I concede.

"I'm glad you said that. You've got an appointment with him on Thursday at ten o'clock."

I gape at the priest as though he's just sprouted another head or something. "What?"

He runs a hand through his hair. "You're still having nightmares, aren't you?"

"Who told you?"

"You don't have to go through this alone. There are plenty of other guys out there who know exactly what you've gone through, and could do with a chat now and then, too. Paul wants to see you on a one-to-one again, but he also thinks you'll benefit from some group discussions. It's a good way to meet new friends — and re-acquaint with some old ones."

I don't like the way the old man's looking at me and dread to think what's coming next.

"You remember Reidy and Tom Phillips?"

I gape at him. They're two of the guys from the other platoon; the ones I warned about the ambush.

"They've been seeing Paul for a while now, too. They'd love to meet up with you again. Maybe chat over old stuff." Father Donnelly looks at me sideways, as though judging my reaction.

"My God!"

"You're learning," he says, that twinkle dancing in his eyes again.

I roll my eyes at him, glad that that's another thing that doesn't hurt as much today. "They're back in London?"

"Yep. Both with honorary discharges, like yourself. They're desperate to meet up with their hero again — if you're up for it, of course?"

I balk. I'd never considered myself a hero and I'm surprised the guys saw me that way. I was just doing my job — badly, I thought.

Father Donnelly hands me an appointment card with details of the counselling arrangements on. He also hands me a Help For Heroes leaflet with all sorts of useful information on it.

"Thanks." I feel a lump in my throat.

"Oh, and don't forget this one." He hands me another card. It's got his name and number on. "In case you ever want to catch up." He stands up.

I put the papers on the bed and throw my arms around him. Not for the first time, this guy's offered me a lifeline and this time I don't intend to let go of it.

"Thank you," I whisper.

He smiles. "You need to thank that girl of yours, too," he tells me. "We had a good long talk last night after she'd left you. I hadn't realised you were still haunted by those damn nightmares. She's worried about you."

I sigh. "I was afraid she'd think I was a thug when she saw me fighting with those bastards in the subway."

"She was surprised how hard you fought, but at the same time she said she felt proud. You were vastly outnumbered and hindered by worrying about your dog. *Their* dog was an unknown quantity too —it could have been vicious for all you knew. It was brave of you to take them all on like that."

"I didn't have much choice."

"Isn't that so often the way? You have to act on instinct even if afterwards you think you did the wrong thing. You did what you had to." He smiles kindly at me and I get his message loud and clear.

"Thanks, mate." I pat him on the shoulder.

"Right, go and find that girl. Oh, and find me after you've seen Paul next week. I'd like to hear how it went."

"I will," I promise on both counts.

* * *

A week later my headache's actually gone. I'm living at the flat over the vet's and Kathy's helped me to get some second-hand furniture. I've now got a sofa to sit on, an old telly with a Freeview box to watch, and a fridge. I didn't bother with a cooker, but I've got an old microwave that Joe gave me, though I've got a feeling it's just a good excuse for the practice to get a new one. Either way, I'm happy.

Help Our Heroes

I'm pacing the floor waiting on the delivery of my new bed. Well, new to me. The good folks from the charity shop are supposed to bring it this morning and I can't wait. I've been sleeping on the sofa, which is absolute luxury after park benches and sheets of cardboard on the pavement, but I still can't wait for my own bed.

"Is it here yet?" Kathy runs up the stairs and bursts into the flat, as eager as a puppy. Her excitement rouses Muttbags who suddenly jumps and barks.

"No," I say with a frown. "They definitely said it would be this morning."

"It's only twelve, they're not really late," Kathy says, putting an arm around me. "We just have to be patient, that's all."

I had a good discussion about patience the other day with Paul Hudson, the counsellor. He was thrilled to see me again and welcomed me like a long-lost friend. Father Donnelly said he was really proud of me when we met for a drink a couple of days later, and we're going to meet up on a regular basis, too. That's something I'm really looking forward to.

"Is that them?"

I follow Kathy into the living room where she's peering through the window at a large white van which has just pulled up in the vet's car park.

"Yes!" I fist-pump the air before running down the stairs to give them a hand.

The damn thing proves to be a bastard to get up the narrow staircase, and at one stage we actually considered trying to get it in through the window instead. Still, with sheer determination, not to mention brute force, we manage to get it into the bedroom, which looked much bigger before we added the bed. It's a good job we went for a regular double instead of the king size I was considering. It would have meant waiting another week for delivery anyway and I just couldn't hold out that long.

Kathy offers the two guys a cup of tea, which, luckily, they decline and I slam the front door as soon as they're gone.

She's already picked out and bought some brand new bedding in a mint green shade, which I've realised is her favourite colour. We got a new duvet from the supermarket and I put the cover on it yesterday in readiness. The new pillows also have matching covers, so all that's left is to put the sheet on the mattress. It's fitted, so doesn't take a minute and then we throw on the cover and pillows.

"It looks great." Kathy beams at our handiwork.

I stare at her, wondering how long she's planning to just stand there admiring it. She looks up at me, her eyes wide and shining with anticipation.

"I've still got half an hour before I'm back on duty," she informs me, twirling her hair around her fingers.

"Great. We can do it twice, then," I say, almost jumping on her.

She giggles as we bounce on the soft springs, tugging at each others' clothes. Her skin feels soft beneath my fingers as I swiftly unbutton her blouse and she pulls her arms through the holes. Her breasts are caged in a pretty pink bra with white flowers on, her nipples protruding through the lace enticingly. I want to run my thumb over them but she's too quick and pulls my tee-shirt over my head instead. She yanks at my zip and tugs my jeans down my legs. I return the favour with hers and we lie on the bed in just our underwear.

"At last," she gasps.

We'd decided to wait until we had a proper bed to make love in, but the anticipation was almost too much to bear. Every night we'd kissed and cuddled, but there wasn't room for both of us to sleep on the sofa, and it made sense for her to go home to get a proper night's sleep being as she was working every day.

Her day off is tomorrow, and we're planning to spend it together, but no way can we wait until tonight with all this tension burning within us.

"I want you," I whisper between kisses.

"I want you, too." Her voice is muffled as she's kissing my neck and I arch my back, offering my whole body up to her.

Having her rub her soft skin next to mine is the best feeling ever — well, so far, anyway — and I can't get enough of it. My cock's been aching for this for days, and is letting its presence be known by nudging at her with its wet knob. Her giggle is melodical, and I know she's got the message loud and clear.

Gently, I rub her back before unfastening her bra, and feel her pert little breasts break free onto my chest. I let out a gasp at their sheer beauty and take one in my mouth, nipping at her nipple and sucking it hard.

"Ooh." She yelps, lying on top of me and rubbing her whole body up and

Help Our Heroes

down mine. My briefs are soaking wet and sticking to my cock like glue. I'm desperate to take them off, but don't want to overstep the mark, so I content myself with licking and sucking at her gorgeous breasts, and kissing her throat, making her moan uncontrollably.

She delights me by pulling off her panties, and I guess hers are as uncomfortable as my own. I follow suit, relieved to get the sodden material away from my tingling skin. My massive cock springs free, soaking my stomach with its sticky juice. Kathy grabs it and rubs it up and down, letting the liquid run over her fingers.

Her soft hand keeps up a steady rhythm while the other one roams up and down my torso, flicking at my nipples and stroking the hairs of my chest. I'm getting harder by the second and I know I won't be able to hold off much longer.

I'm relieved when she reaches for my jeans and pulls out the box of condoms we bought in preparation. I've already unwrapped the outer plastic — I'm not an idiot — and she easily opens the box and pulls out a tiny foil packet. With swift fingers she rolls the sheath over my throbbing dick and continues to rub it up and down as before.

I reach down for her pussy but there's no time for me to play, as she's astride me in a second and teetering on the head of my waiting cock. No longer coy and shy, she raises a questioning eyebrow, teasing the life out of me as she licks her lips and waits.

I nod. "Yes."

With a salacious wink she places the end of my knob inside her and slides down the shaft, enveloping me in her warm wetness. She rides me like I've never felt before, all the time maintaining eye contact and moaning loudly.

I can't believe the fervour she ignites in me and I hammer home as hard as I can, careful not to hurt her, but unable to hide my ardour as we both crash into an almighty climax that sends my whole brain into a spiral. My hot juice forces its way out of my body and into the rubber sack while her tongue penetrates my mouth, owning it with the power of a passionate woman.

"I love you," I gasp, realising the meaning of those words for the first time in my life. "My sweetheart!"

"I love you, too," she whispers, draping her languid body over mine. "My hero."

THE END

Help Our Heroes

A Military Anthology

Outranked In Love

JF Holland

All it took was one incident, and Adam Jones lost not only his mobility, but also his army career.

Adam is attracted to Hannah Summers, but as she's his best friend, Phil's sister, she's out of bounds. Unfortunately, Adam's feelings for her are no longer clear cut as lines he shouldn't cross begin to blur.

As Hannah tries to help Adam come to terms with his life changing injury, confusing dreams taunt him with all that is now out of his reach. Despondent over his losses, Adam sends her away.

Taunted by images Adam can't decide if fact or fiction, he begins to suspect he's either forgotten something important or else he's losing his mind

Can he unravel the mystery to what he's missing, or will he lose something even more important to him than his career?

Prologue

Hannah sat in her car outside of the base, unsure why she'd driven the four-hours to get here.

Who was she kidding.

She'd driven here as she'd needed to see Adam before he took off on tour. He'd not come home like he'd promised and she'd missed him. He'd also been a little distant, the tone of his correspondence had changed and she didn't know why.

As it would be at least another six-months before he came back off tour... Yeah, here she sat like a loser, unsure of her reception, but unable to stay away.

She'd tried for years to keep her distance, scared of becoming involved with a soldier.

However, it had happened anyway.

But, for some reason, he was now treating her as if it had never happened.

Just as she was about to turn the key in the ignition and drive away, a familiar figure appeared on the other side of the barrier. She'd recognise him anywhere, Tall, broad, and sporting a swagger born of confidence in his own abilities. He didn't seem hurt, nothing about him had changed, although, his caramel hair was shorter than she remembered. His head turned, putting his face in profile.

Damn.

Hannah's heart skipped a beat as he grinned, that familiar dimple appearing in his right cheek as he joked with one of his team. Before he could disappear – and she lost her nerve – Hannah jumped out of her car - keys in hand.

"Adam…" she yelled, running towards the barrier.

Adam was heading towards the truck, shooting the breeze with Nomad, kit slung over his shoulder when he heard someone yelling his name. Turning, he stared in disbelief as the one person he'd been trying to avoid since he came home, came running towards the barrier.

Hannah.

God give him strength.

He'd stayed away, his own desperation to see her had spooked him. She may no longer be an awkward, shy teenager, but she was still out of bounds being his brother-in-arms' little sister.

Not that it stopped him wanting her.

She went with him wherever he went, her image burned into his subconscious, from her short, chin length bobbed black hair, to her large, expressive green eyes.

Thoughts of her had kept him company on many a tour, even though she shouldn't. She was his weakness, but in those dark hours, she had also become not only his salvation but also his sanity.

Unfortunately, he couldn't have her, but taking her in, standing there in ripped fitted jeans and a t-shirt, his chest ached with longing. He saw how she watched him so warily. As he headed her way, it morphed, her mouth tilting up in a smile, and felt a tug on his memory.

Laughter, soft skin, whispers in the dark and closeness.

Frowning, he tried to tug at the strands to unravel the mystery.

Memory or dream?

Surely a dream, it had to be.

Help Our Heroes

She was out of bounds.

Although, that didn't stop him wanting her with a desperation stronger than his need for breath.

As he tugged, trying to unravel the fragments in his mind, his head began to ache. When the throb in his temple began to intensify, with a sigh he let it go.

He'd been having headaches since just before his last tour. However, he'd not sought treatment for them, putting it down to stress. Being a Sergeant came with a cost, decisions he made could affect the lives of many.

He needed to make sure his team was physically fit, well trained, and ready for anything.

Always stressful, especially on tour.

If he fucked up, the price paid could be lives lost.

Not something he wanted on his conscience.

He'd already done and seen enough for more than one life-time.

As he watched her, her smile faltered, and she turned, as if to leave.

His conviction to keep his distance weakened, especially when he caught the flash of disappointment enter her eyes. She looked at him as if he'd let her down and his restraint snapped.

"I won't be a minute," he told Nomad and jogged over to her.

"Hi."

"Hi yourself," she replied, her smile returning, although, it appeared forced, and her expression was a little guarded.

"Hannah, what are you doing here?"

"You didn't come home… and… I couldn't let you go off again without wishing you luck," she told him. Then standing on tiptoes, she reached over the barrier and wrapping her arms around him.

He felt the warmth of her arms on the back of his neck, her breath feathering over his throat and he froze, that buzz starting in his head. Tugging, he found shadows moving, but then she spoke and it vanished. "Promise me you'll be careful," she whispered in his ear, squeezing him before pulling back.

"Always princess," he told her, his pale blue eyes holding hers captive as he ran a finger over her cheek.

He instantly missed her closeness, but one touch was all he allowed himself.

A taste of the forbidden to keep him going.

As his finger lightly stroked the smooth skin of her cheek, the shadow moved again, laughter, moans, something....

"Hey, are you okay?" Hannah looked up at him with concern, teeth nibbling at her bottom lip as that wariness crept back into her eyes.

There is was again, that shadow, moving.

He was missing something, something important, but...

Shit.

His head hurt like a son of a bitch. The ache intensifying, his temples throbbing so badly now, his head felt like it had its own heart-beat.

"Yo, Serge, they're loading up," came Nomad's voice over his shoulder.

"I've got to go," Adam told Hannah, letting the shadow go.

His eyes roamed over her face, taking in her features one last time. Then, unable to resist, he dropped his kit and jumped the barrier.

Pulling her into his arms, he embraced her, absorbing the feel and weight of her body against his own. He squirreled away every nuance of the sensation to store away to take with him. Something he could pull it out and think of it when his job got to him. He absorbed everything about her, from how she felt to how she smelt and even the rasp of her breathing.

It was over in a second.

Gone, far too quickly, but he had to let go before he was tempted to do more… although.

Tug.

He pulled again on the thread, trying to shift the shadow and reveal what it was hiding in his subconscious, but again, he came up blank. All he got was that familiar ache behind his eyes.

Reluctantly, he released Hannah, holding himself rigid, fighting his need to keep touching her and with what he couldn't remember as he stepped back away from her.

"Don't forget to write," she told him, as he ducked back beneath the barrier. "And Adam, remember, you promised me you'd be careful."

When had he promised?

Again, he looked at her, but she wouldn't hold his gaze, her eyes staring over his shoulder. "Come home safe, do you hear!"

Her throat moved as she told him this, her smile once again in place but wavering.

Adam nodded, mouth grim, and with that, picked up his kit and walked away.

Hannah swallowed again, the lump in her throat so big, it threatened to choke her as she watched his retreating back.

Chapter 1

Four-Weeks Later: -

Adam lay listlessly in his hospital bed, eyes staring morosely at the ceiling. He didn't want to be here.

He was no longer whole.

Neither in body nor spirit.

The surgery had gone well – or so his surgeon and shrink kept telling him. Yes, he was still alive, but he wasn't sure he wanted to be at this point. He had nothing to look forward to but lying here listening to the incessant beeping of the machine at his side. The sound pounded in his skull like a drum, a loud proclamation that his heart was still beating, a relentless reminder.

It depressed the shit out of him as it continued to beep.

Oh, and there went the blood pressure cuff, the puff as it inflated, squeezing his bicep to check he was all 'A' okay.

Oh, joy.

God, what a mess.

He was half a man.

Well, that's how he felt.

It should have just been a routine patrol.

No big deal.

It should have been simple.

Help Our Heroes

A clean in and out as the baddies had already cleared out - or so their intel had informed them.

Unfortunately, they hadn't gotten the memo.

They'd been shooting the breeze and generally yanking each other's chains on the trip over to this supposedly deserted village on the outskirts of their base. It was something they did often to relieve tension as they moved out on these kinds of missions. Adam had gotten out of the truck first as he was in the lead, but when he was about ten-yards out, Norman Fielding, aka, Nomad - due to his wandering eyes and ever ready hard-on - had said something. It was just a smart-arse crack about Adam's refusal to fuck some random woman who'd propositioned him in a bar on their last night of R&R before they'd flew out. It was all done in jest, and chuckling, Adam turned back to tell him to fuck himself when the quiet made itself known. Sobering, his hand had rose in warning to the others as he looked around, listening to the silence, trying to get a bead on what was coming.

No indication though.

Just complete silence.

The type which had the hair on the back of your neck standing up to attention. The absence of noise was so complete it left your ears ringing - which was normally a warning in itself – but had a whole other connotation when its absence was interrupted by a familiar whistling in the air. As he hunkered down, making himself a smaller target, Adam warily eyed the derelict buildings surrounding them. However, as he edged upwards to make a run for cover, the whistling sound ended in a thud. On impact, Adam stumbled forward onto his knees, pain exploding in his right calf, buckling his leg and dropping him.

All hell broke loose then as his team scrambled to cover him as he tried getting to his feet. However, with his lower leg being smashed, he hit the deck again and his rifle fell to the floor as fresh agony bloomed up his leg. Teeth gritted, he rolled sideways and pulled his Glock from its holster on his left thigh. He rested on his elbows, lifting the gun, tracking the surrounding buildings as he tried to locate a target. From his prone position, he rubbed his eye with his shoulder to clear his wavering vision, and tried again, but it was no use, he couldn't see shit.

Nomad crab walked over to Adam, grabbed the webbing on his kit, and dragged him backwards towards the safety of the truck. Voices could be heard shouting, but it came out muffled, Adam's hearing off as the buzzing in his head got louder. Covering shots were fired towards the buildings, followed by a scream of pain as Nomad continued dragging him towards the open door of the truck. Adam dug his left boot into the dirt, trying to help Nomad shift his dead weight as his right leg lay sprawled out, mashed and useless. When the second shot hit, he knew he was in trouble, the ricochet of the round being fired filled him with dread - and that was before the pain had torn through his already damaged leg. His body jerked violently at the multiple rounds of buck shot more or less exploded his already damaged limb and sprayed up his thighs. The impact had been close range, a shadowy figure stood in a doorway not forty-feet away. Adam heard a shot fired from over his shoulder followed by a thud, just as a white-hot lance of inscrutable agony took his breath.

Nomad overbalanced and lost his hold as Adam's body went into spasm at the shattering impact. Unable to help himself as he writhed in pain, Nomad quickly righted himself, took a firmer grip on the webbing, and continued dragging Adam towards the safety of the vehicle. Groaning due to the rough ride, Adam ground his jaw to hold in his screams of agony, but after what felt like an eternity, he was finally pulled into the vehicle as other hands helped. Once inside, he was relieved of the Glock he'd never gotten to fire.

The last thing Adam saw as the vehicle took off was a boot lay in the crimson dirt still attached to camo material which was ragged, and flapping in the breeze. The bright red stain surrounding it trailed up towards the tyre tracks, and as Adam lay slumped against the seat - vision wavering - he was hit with the realisation as the door shut that it was his own foot which had been left behind with his rifle.

Help Our Heroes

Shouts went out for a medic, and Adam knew he'd not be keeping his promise to Hannah. He also knew that if Nomad hadn't been dragging him at the time, the shot would have been higher, possibly killing him outright. However, as pressure was applied to his fucked-up leg it he wasn't sure he'd have rather it had ended him. Mercifully, by that point it was lights out as the burning agony sucked him down into a black-void.

Chapter 2

Hannah rushed through the hospital, getting lost in the honeycomb maze of corridors. Finally, after what felt like a lifetime, she stepped onto the ICU ward. Sanitizing her hands at the entrance - as directed - she rubbed the astringent into her skin while heading for the nurse's station. No one was behind, but there was a dozen opened curtained cubicles along the back wall. When her eyes landed on the bed she searched for, her heart nearly stopped.

So many tubes, monitors and wires surrounded him.

Adam.

Her eyes flicked to the monitor showing his heart beating, and nearly collapsed in relief.

When she'd gotten the phone call, she'd been with a client. She'd apologized profusely and offered her a refund and a free treatment. She'd left happily enough, but then she'd had to cancel the rest of her afternoon book-ins before grabbing her coat and bag and rushing out.

Four hours was a long drive when you didn't know what you were heading into and your mind revelled in throwing up all kinds of scenario's.

As they'd given her no information over the phone, the top of her list was if he was still alive.

He was breathing.

Thank you, God.

So long as he kept breathing, everything else he could get over.

He was young enough and strong enough.

Her eyes traced down the covers trying to figure out exactly what had put him here, but found no clues. His face was pale, a little bruised and scraped, but apart from that, his lower half was covered with a sheet.

Although...

"Hi, are you Hannah?"

Help Our Heroes

"I am."

"Thank you for coming," the nurse told her stepping from the cubicle to the left of Adam's. She threw her plastic apron in the yellow bin, pulled off her gloves, which joined it, then sanitized her hands from the small hand pump hanging from her pocket before coming over.

"He's been asking for you."

Hannah hid her shock at the nurse's words.

He'd asked for her.

At least now she knew why she'd been called as normally only family members were notified or allowed onto the ICU ward due to how sick most of the patients were. Phil hadn't even been informed he was here, not in the ICU anyway. He knew he'd been sent home, but not the where or why as he was no longer in service, he wasn't privy to what went on. He'd only been informed as he was listed as Adam's contact in his paperwork as he had no family.

She'd tried contacting him since he'd gone on tour, but had not received anything back. Then again, mail from the Middle-East didn't exactly arrive by next day post, and internet could be sketchy. Add in differences in time zones and patrols and it was hit and miss with keeping in touch via that way too. Plus, with the reluctance she'd felt from Adam when she'd drove out to see him off, she'd not expected him to keep in touch so the call had come as a shock.

Her eyes went back to him.

What had happened?

"He's only here so we can keep a close watch on him after his temperature spiked. Apart from that, he's doing okay."

At the nurse's words, Hannah shook herself from her thoughts.

"I'm sorry, where are my manners. Are you Nurse Stevens?"

"I am, but just call me Mel. We're more informal in here," she told her as she held out a hand.

"Thanks for calling, Mel, what happened?"

"Have you not been told?"

"No. All I knew was that he'd been sent home early."

"I shouldn't discuss this with you, but as he asked for you personally..." Sighing, she broke off, then tiredly, looked to Hannah, taking in her wan features and worried gaze. "I take it you two are together?"

Hannah didn't know what they were, she'd thought they were heading in that direction but now... she didn't have a clue.

"Phil, my brother... or maybe you have him down as Corporal Summers. Anyway, Phil is classed as Adam's next of kin. Adam's has been part of our family since I was 12-years-old..." She broke off then, knowing she was rambling as she didn't know how to describe their relationship.

"You and Sergeant Jones aren't siblings though, are you?" she interrupted, a brow rising as she waited for Hannah to reply.

"No, not siblings," Hannah confirmed, unable to hold eye contact as her cheeks heated.

What she felt for Adam was most definitely not what you felt for a sibling.

"I don't see any point in keeping this from you because, to be honest, as soon as you get close enough, you're going to see what's happened to him anyway. He's lost part of his right leg.... Wow, are you okay?" She quickly stepped forward, her hands lifting and grabbing onto Hannah's arm as she swayed. Her stricken eyes jumped to Adam who lay so quietly beneath those covers and wires.

"Is he okay?" Hannah whispered, then coughed to clear her throat, swallowing the ball of emotion lodged there.

"He's healing, but as I said, his temperature has spiked, and I think he's a little depressed. That's why I called when he asked for you. I think if he can see someone familiar, it may help."

"Okay, good, he can survive that."

Hannah's eyes again went to the bed, her chest aching for what he must have been through, but he was alive and that was all that counted as far as she was concerned.

"Hannah... Hell, go see him. At this point I'm willing to go against protocol for the good of his recovery."

Help Our Heroes

"Thank you, Mel," and with that, Hannah made her way over to Adam's bedside.

She stood at the foot of the bed, her eyes going over his familiar features. His brow was puckered, frowning as his eyes flickered behind his closed lids. He had a sheen of sweat on his face and his mouth moved as if he was mumbling in his sleep. Without conscious thought, her eyes then dropped down his body, taking note of how the sheet was flattened on one side just below his knee.

"Here," Mel told her, placing a plastic seat by Adam's right side.

"Can I move it around to the other side, please? Only he's got a drip in his right arm and I'd rather not hold that hand and risk dislodging it. Plus, he's left handed."

With a smile, Mel moved the chair to the left-hand side of the bed and once Hannah was seated, she quickly checked his vitals before leaving her to it. Two other nurses had appeared from somewhere as Mel donned another apron and moved onto the next cubicle.

Hannah put her bag on the floor and pushed a hand through the safety rail so she could touch the back of Adam's hand. His head turned in her direction but his eyes didn't open.

"Hey, you came back, thank you," she whispered.

"Not sure I should have," Adam sighed, frowning. "Hannah?"

"Yeah, I'm here."

"Shouldn't have come," he sighed again.

"How could I not."

With that, he turned his hand over, twined his fingers with hers and drifted back into a fitful sleep.

Chapter 3

2 days later: -

Adam slowly opened his eyes as the cuff on his right bicep began to inflate. *Where was he?*

Frowning in incomprehension, he looked around.

ICU?

Oh, yes, he'd spiked a fever, and his heart had gone a little haywire after his blood pressure had dropped so he'd been moved him to ICU for monitoring and intravenous antibiotics. He didn't have a clue how long he'd been here, though.

Shivering, he dropped his hand, trying to tug the sheet up.

Something was missing?

A shadow moving around in his subconscious, a head resting against his chest, soft lips trailing butterfly kisses down his stomach. He groaned, eyes squeezing tightly closed as the ache began to pound behind his eyes. Dropping his mental search for answers, he rubbed the sheet between his thumb and fingers of his left hand. An echo of a memory appeared, but it was so insubstantial it left him unable grasp any real information, but a lingering feeling of loss echoed through him, as if he'd lost something important.

Releasing the sheet, he fingered the material.

Not as soft, he thought in confusion as his head turned towards the left-hand side of the bed.

Not as soft as what?

He again tried reaching for what he was missing but nothing came to him, just another echo of soft sultry laughter, and then it was again gone.

Frustrated, and his head now aching, he blinked, then saw a chair beside his bed.

Help Our Heroes

Maybe he was remembering Hannah sitting by him, then nearly snorted at the absurdity of where his head went. Then swallowed at the stab of regret that hit him.

They'd never be able to be more… well, maybe at one time it would have been possible if he could have spoken to Phil first, but not now.

Now it was impossible, he had nothing to offer, not even whole in body.

"Hey, welcome back. I've sent your girlfriend for a break. Poor thing has been sat by your side for the last 48-hours," his nurse told him as she checked his monitors and stuck a thermometer in his ear. "She was nearly dead on her feet, but she wouldn't leave your side until your temperature broke and your breathing eased."

Adam looked at her blankly, not sure whether he'd broadcasted what he wanted, rather than what was.

"Girlfriend?" he croaked, throat dry.

"Pretty, jet-black hair and big green eyes. You've got yourself a real looker there, Sergeant Jones."

"Hannah?"

"Yes, that's her name," she smiled, continuing with her checks.

"Just a friend, Phil Summer's sister," he told her, then frowned, some wisp of memory coming back and hovering at the periphery of his subconscious, but as his head began to throb once more, he let it go.

"Hey, are you okay?"

"Just a headache."

"Probably an after effect of the fever. Would you like some water?"

At his nod, she filled a glass with water out of the jug and put a straw in it, helping him to take a few sips. "Better?" at his nod, she put the glass back on the wheeled-tray that had been pushed to one side. "Talking of Phil Summers, he stopped by yesterday" she told him conversationally as she checked his urine output and lifted the sheet to check the bandaging on his leg… or what was left of it anyway. Dropping the sheet again and tucking him back in she continued. "He stayed with you for a couple of hours, but said to tell you he'd get back to see you again as soon as he could."

Adam tried to tune back into what the nurse was telling him, but he was a little fuzzy.

What had she been saying?

Oh, yes, Phil… now why did he get a stab of guilt when he thought about Phil?

He let it go, fatigue dragging at him, eyelids heavy as the nurse offered him another drink of water.

Hannah stopped behind the curtain allowing Adam some privacy as the nurse did his checks, her cheeks heating as she referred to her as Adam's girlfriend, but her heart broke a little as he refuted it.

She'd thought after…

Well, what was the point in thinking about it. It had happened, but now it seemed that Adam wanted to forget about it.

Obviously, she was back to just being Phil's little sister.

After hiding her feelings for him for all these years, it shouldn't hurt. However, she was shocked to realise just how much it did when it was verbalized.

Oh, well, time to pull up her big girl panties, and move on.

But not until he was back on his fe… healing, she amended, giving the nurse a tight smile as she passed her on her way out of his cubicle.

Taking a deep breath and straightening her shoulders, Hannah stepped back around the curtains.

"Hey, your back with us," Hannah smiled, moving towards the chair and sitting down again.

"Not sure how pleased I am about it," Adam murmured sleepily, his eyes trying to take in her features, but his vision was a little blurry. "Sorry, tired."

"It's okay, you sleep, like mum always says you heal while you sleep."

"Not enough sleep in the world to fix me this time," were the last words Adam murmured before his breathing evened out.

Chapter 4

2 week later: -

Adam had been transferred to a veteran's rehabilitation hospital closer to home. This meant Hannah could get back to work, but could still spend time at the hospital with Adam in the evenings.

Not that he was very responsive.

He was refusing to speak to the onsite psychiatrist about his injury, and was becoming more introverted and moody as time went on. His situation wasn't helped as he was bedbound due to refusing the use of the wheelchair he'd been provided with to get about. Although his injury was healing well - as he wasn't exercising and had been bed bound for a couple of weeks - he also didn't have the upper body strength to ambulate himself around with crutches either.

They were at an impasse.

"Hey, how are you doing?" Hannah asked as she came into the room. Adam just looked at her, his eyes returning to the television monitor. "Well, I've had a good day," she told him, ignoring his sullen attitude as she removed her coat and sat down. She folded her coat and placed it on the floor beside her chair with her bag.

"I have two new clients so my books are filling up."

"Ah-uh," was the only answer she got from him.

"Oh, I forgot, Phil said he'll be popping by on Friday as he's back after doing his training. He starts at his new security job in the next week or two."

"Ah-uh."

Instead of snapping at him, Hannah opened her bag and pulled out a large packet of jelly babies, his weakness.

"Here, I know you like them," she said putting them on his lap as he lay there. "So, what have you been up to today?"

Adam just turned his head and looked at her.

I mean, what did she think he'd been doing?

"I went for a jog around the block before I did a bit of tap-dancing down the ward. Then after lunch, I ran the stairs before doing cartwheels," he replied dryly.

"That's nice," she replied with a tight smile, biting her tongue instead of snapping at him.

Adam didn't know why he was taking it out on Hannah, it wasn't her fault. But then again, seeing her, whole and healthy was a slap in the face, it was like showing him a steak then telling him he couldn't eat red meat. He wanted her, and it was getting harder to see her without touching, without dragging her off that chair and into the bed. It was harder still as he wasn't even capable of having her, not unless she fancied getting up on the bed and taking the lead.

He ground his teeth at the thought.

Who the fuck was he kidding, he wasn't even sure he functioned anymore.

He'd certainly not been woken up with morning wood, so maybe that was fucked too.

Or not, as the case may be.

Wouldn't that be a kicker, not only was he a leg down, but he was also dickless.

"Oh, I forgot, I stopped at the shop on my lunch and picked you up a couple of books. I know you like thrillers, I'm not sure if you've read these or not," she told him, again reaching down and digging around in her large bag. She placed the paperbacks on the cabinet beside his bed, along with magazines she's brought him yesterday.

What she thought he wanted muscle car magazines for he didn't have a clue?

A bit hard to drive without an accelerator foot.

"So, what would you like to do?" she asked, sitting back in the chair, swiping invisible lint off her blouse. The action drew attention to her breasts and he ground his jaw.

"How about dancing?"

"Maybe we can go out dancing once you get out," Hannah replied.

"Yeah, I hear the hop is still really popular."

Hannah ignored him, but it was getting harder to bite her tongue.

"Mum says hi, and she's looking forward to you visiting once you get out."

Adam ground his jaw again at the thought of Kay, she was a nice woman, an older version of Hannah and an absolute sweetheart. He'd missed her, she made the best Sunday roast and hugged everyone. He'd been shocked the first-time Phil had taken him home on leave, Kay had made a fuss of him, she'd hugged him and made him sit at the table as she fed him home cooked food. He'd never had that, being brought up in care didn't often offer that kind of friendly atmosphere and openness, especially not for a kid that was constantly in trouble. Even the foster homes hadn't wanted him. He'd been kicked out as soon as he was of age, and his first stop had been to enlist, which was where he'd been ever since.

What the hell was he going to do, he wasn't trained to do anything but be a soldier, and now that was over. He was thirty-one and didn't have any skills to offer an employer.

He wasn't even whole now.

God, he was a real catch.

No job, no prospects of a job and probably incapable of even fucking.

He was living the dream.

"How are you sleeping?" she asked and he again ignored her, eyes on the television screen again. "I was thinking, once you are out, I could give you regular massages, it will keep your muscles supple.

Yeah, he would certainly enjoy her hands on him, but he wasn't planning on getting that close. She was a constant reminder of what he'd never have.

He turned his back, and closed his eyes.

The nurse passed his bed, her mouth thinning as she looked in Adam's direction before she smiled sadly at Hannah.

Hannah sat there for another ten-minutes checking her e-mails and social media. When gentle snores came from Adam, she gave up. Standing, she leaned over and went to run her hand over his hair, but pulled it back at the last minute.

Never a good idea to touch a sleeping man who'd come back from tour.

Sighing, she picked up her bag and coat and left the ward.

"Hi," she interrupted the orderly who sat behind the nurse's station checking through files. "Could you tell Sergeant Jones, I'll be back tomorrow and that if he needs anything bringing to ring me?"

The orderly nodded, and she walked off out of the ward.

Help Our Heroes

Fast food was required on her way home, maybe some chocolate too as she needed cheering up, he wasn't improving and she was at a loss of how to help him.

Google would be her evening companion as she searched for some answers.

Chapter 5

Adam lay back, lip between his teeth and eyes squeezed tightly closed as a groan of pleasure was pulled from his throat. Her hand delicately trailed over his chest, a nail scraping across a beaded nipple as her lips butterfly kissed a path down to his stomach. Her mouth moved lower, and his hand now tangled in her hair, controlling the pace as his hips lifted. Her tongue stroked over the head of his cock before her lips slid over him, tongue flattening so that as he slid in and out of the tight wet heat of her mouth it caressed the underside.

Heaven.

Fuck, the suction and warmth was killing him, his control snapping as his balls tightened, drawing up close to his body.

Teeth gritted, he reluctantly used the hand in her hair to pull her off him as he felt the familiar tingle start in the base of his spine. Pale blue eyes now dark with lust, stared into her slumberous, green gaze, and couldn't help grinning at the pretty pout she wore.

"My turn," he growled, dragging her up his body, and startling a surprised squeak out of her, which morphed into a gasp as he took her mouth. Tasting himself on her lips, he groaned, rolled, and put her under him as his hand moved to a breast. Slowly, he circled a long finger around the strawberry birthmark beside her left nipple, satisfaction strumming through his veins as he watched her arch into him. Pulling back, he rested on his elbows, staring hungrily down the length of the body now spread out and lay beneath him. A hiss of pleasure leaving him as his length brushed against her core, his eyes travelled up from the apex of her spread thighs, over her lush hips, tucked in waist, and finally landed on the tight tips of her breasts. "God, Hannah, you have no idea what you do to me," he rumbled huskily as her arms lifted, reaching for him.

Help Our Heroes

Adam moaned in his sleep, going willingly into her arms, but she was no longer there. Confused, he looked around and found that he wasn't just alone, he was also no longer naked. He was dressed in combats as he stood in the middle of a dirt packed, dusty street. Derelict buildings surrounded him, and as he turned, he heard the familiar whistle in the air.

He sprang upright in bed, panting, hand dropping to his fucked-up leg as the pain hit, tearing through him like the bullet and buckshot that had done the damage.

Dropping back, he lay there panting, sweat pouring off him, making the sheets stick to his now soaking skin. Eyes now squeezing tightly closed while heaving breaths sawed in and out of his lungs as he tried to push the memory away. Then frowning, he thought about what he'd been dreaming of before it had morphed into a nightmare.

Hannah.

God, it had felt so real.

Did she even have a birthmark?

And if she did, how did he know?

He was missing something - he knew he was.

Maybe he needed to talk to the shrink after all. Especially as the headache hit again when he tugged at the shadows in his mind. His head felt like it was being split in two.

Cautiously, he turned his head, the seat beside his bed empty, and the ward lights dimmed.

"Hey, you okay?" the nurse asked, tiptoeing over to him.

"Nightmare," he told her.

"Flashback?"

"Yeah," he admitted, trying to get comfortable, sucking in a breath as his head throbbed.

"Do you have a headache again?"

"Yes," he winced, a hand rubbing his temple.

"You didn't hurt your head in the ambush did you, there's nothing in the notes?"

"Manoeuvres a few months back."

"What happened?" she asked, moving around the bed and taking a seat.

"Exercises. I can't remember what I did exactly but I woke up beneath the wall. I must have fell somehow and knocked myself out... Well, I think I knocked myself. I must have as I woke up with a cut on the top of my head and a headache which had its own heartbeat... therefore, I assumed I must have landed on my head.

"Where you concussed?"

"Mildly, I guess, I was nauseous but not sick."

"Any memory loss?"

"I don't think so."

"Why isn't it in your notes?"

"Because I didn't feel it was important. I wasn't out for long and I don't seem to have had any other problems. I mean, I was well enough to carry on so I didn't see the point in going to the doc," he told her.

"I think it's worth mentioning."

"I had a thorough check up when I came in with missing pieces," he told her dryly.

"Yes, but they didn't have all the facts."

"It was months ago."

"But stil…"

"Honestly, I'll be fine," he told her, again rubbing at his temples.

"How about I get you something for the headache, and a hot chocolate, it may help you settle?"

"That would be great, thanks."

Adam lay there staring at the ceiling as he thought back to that stupid accident.

Surely…

No, if anything had happened with him and Hannah, he'd have remembered. Plus, he'd never have touched her… she was Phil's sister, Kay's daughter, if he had it would be tantamount to breaking an unspoken oath. You didn't mess with your brother-in-arms family, you just didn't.

Plus, she'd have said something.

Wouldn't she?

Chapter 6

Hannah came onto the ward the following night. She'd meant to do some research when she'd gotten home, but after a Chinese, a bottle of wine – and a few tears – she'd passed out.

As she got to the entrance of the six-bedded room where Adam was staying, Tim, the physio passed her, features grim.

"See if you can talk some sense into him will you. I still can't get him out of that bed."

"Isn't it too early?"

"No, not if he wants out of here, he needs to start rebuilding his strength."

"What do you need from me?"

"If you care for him, you have to stop pussyfooting around him."

"But he's injured."

"Yes, but he's still alive, it could have been so much worse."

Hannah's eyes moved to the young soldier who'd lost an arm and a leg, as well as having a serious case of road rash on his face after stepping on an IED. He was manoeuvring his wheelchair single handed down the corridor, grinning in triumph as she passed her.

Hannah's mouth firmed as she nodded at Tim, and headed into the room.

Help Our Heroes

"You're a stubborn sod, listen to your physio. Get in the damn chair," Hannah hissed at Adam as she sat down beside him and put her bag on the floor.

"Hello to you too."

"Why are you still not moving?"

"What is the point?" Adam told her, turning his head and staring at the television monitor again.

"You need to get out of that bed."

"I can't walk."

"You will once you've healed enough for a prosthetic."

"I don't want to be here."

"Well, tough shit, you are. Now stop sulking like a baby and get your stubborn arse out of that bed, and into that god, damn, chair."

"I think you need to work on your bedside manner."

"You lost your leg, not your life, now get up."

"Such sympathy," he drawled.

"I'm not your mother, I'm your friend, now get up and get moving. You cannot just lie in this bed."

"No, you're not my mother. She dumped me in the foster system and walked away when I was 2-years-old."

Hannah winced, but then her jaw firmed.

"Boohoo, now get up and get moving before you get sores on your arse. You need to rebuild the strength you've lost in your upper body and the only way to do that is to get up and in the gym."

"I don't want to be in a god damn wheelchair."

"So get off your arse and fight, then you can get back on your feet."

"Foot, singular, I only have one now."

"Yes, but you're still breathing."

"Mores the pity."

"Oh, for god sake, how many of your brothers have you buried. How many of them do you think would swap places with you in a heartbeat?"

It was his turn to wince at that one, and his head turned, glaring at her.

"I don't like you very much at the moment. Where's the shy kid gone who never talked."

"She grew the hell up. Now, I suggest you do the same, and GET UP out of that bed."

"I don't want to be like this," he told her, jaw rigid.

"I know, and I'm sorry, but I'm not sorry you're still here," she told him, sadly, placing her hand over his where it twisted in the bed sheet.

"Hannah, I can't be who I was. I'm sick of pretending, I think you need to leave."

He couldn't do this anymore, couldn't pretend that everything was going to be okay. He couldn't keep spending time with her, enjoying her company and weaving fantasies of a life with her. He wasn't capable of being what she needed.

He wasn't whole.

He was also uneasy over that dream last night… uncomfortable with how far his fantasies over her had weaved. He needed to get her to go and not come back, needed to let her go, sever the relationship with her like his leg.

A clean cut.

"What?"

"You need to leave, I'm grateful for all you've done, but I think you need to go home. Go back to your life and forget about me."

"Adam, we're frien…"

"I can't be anything for anyone right now," he interrupted. "I…" he sighed, a tick working at the side of his jaw. "Look it's better that you leave."

With that, he pulled his hand from beneath hers and turned over, giving her his back.

A nurse entered the room, coming towards him to do his checks and Adam spoke. "Nurse, can you escort my friend from the ward please, I no longer want to receive visitors." The nurse looked towards Hannah and back towards Adam, then sighing, mouth grim, nodded.

"Of course."

Hannah slowly sat back, blinking and swallowing the golf sized ball of emotion in her throat as she rose from the chair.

"Adam…" He just shook his head, and with a sigh, she bent and retrieved her bag from the floor. Then standing, she slowly walked around his bed, giving the nurse a shaky smile.

As she left the room and headed down the ward, she refused to look back. She did not want him to see that he'd broken her. He would not see the tears that slowly trickled over her bottom lashes and ran down her cheek as she left that room.

She walked past the nurses' station and, Tim, the physio turned to her, mouth grim as he moved around the counter.

"Hey, come on," he told her as he put his arm around her shoulders and lead her towards the family room. "It's not him, this is not him…"

"The sad thing is, I think it is, Tim. Adam, the man I knew is no longer here. He may have come back, but he didn't come home whole. He's left a part of himself over there and I don't mean his leg."

"It will just take time."

"He doesn't want me to give him the time."

Then, smiling sadly, Hannah lifted on her tiptoes and brushed her mouth across the cheek of the jovial big guy who gave his time to all those who needed it. "Thank you for your kindness. Take care of him, okay." With that, she moved left off the ward, and entered the maze of corridors that lead to the car park. She would not be back, not only had he specifically asked not to have visitors, she would not go back unless he called her himself.

It was time to go back to her life. She'd wasted too much time due to the stupid fantasy she'd had of Adam suddenly realising he had feelings for her.

It was over now.

She'd got the message loud and clear.

It had always been one sided on her part, a stupid, childish fantasy.

She was done waiting on him.

Yes, there was a huge part of her that would always wander 'what if,' but that wasn't all of her.

There was also a part of her that wanted to live, to love, to be whole too, and this wanting and waiting, this hoping had to end.

She wanted a family of her own, she wanted to be loved, and with the way she'd held back that had been impossible. Now, today, he'd set her free.

He would always hold a special part in her life, he was just never going to be the whole of it anymore.

She may have slipped once, but as he didn't even find it important enough to remember, why should she.

She was putting him back where he should have always stayed.

Help Our Heroes

He was now and forever, Sergeant Jones, friend and brother-in-arms to her beloved, nosey, and bossy big brother, Phil.

He was no longer her future he was her past.

Chapter 7

A week later: -

Adam shot up in bed, sweat dripping down his face, sheets tangled around and sticking to him.

"Hey, are you okay?"

He lay shaking, left arm over his eyes, trying to block the memory. He was back on patrol, the sound of the bullet like a crack of thunder as it took his leg out from under him. He felt the searing agony and ground his jaw, trembling with pain

"Adam?" the nurse spoke again.

"Flashback," he ground out, slamming his head into the pillow.

"You could do with talking to the…"

"I don't want to talk to the shrink," he gritted out. "I know what it is, it'll fade," he told her, pushing himself up in the bed.

"Do you enjoy the flashbacks?"

"What?" he asked her incredulously, the arm he'd flung over his eyes dropping as he stared at her.

"The flashbacks, the self-containment… is it working for you?"

"I'm not in the mood for this," Adam hissed, putting his arm back over his eyes, blocking her out.

"You are 31-years-old, you have a long life ahead of you. Are you intending to just lie there or are you going to work and get yourself out of here?"

Help Our Heroes

"I have nothing to go back to."

"You have a future. Don't waste it. Now, do you need anything?"

He just shook his head and with that, she walked away.

He lay there staring at the ceiling, shivering as the sweat began to dry on his body.

"Hey?"

Adam dropped his arm and pushed up, looking over as the young soldier who'd been put in with them the day before spoke to him. His bed was opposite, and as he watched, the lad, pushed himself up and managed to sit on the edge of his bed, grab his chair and after putting the brake on, manoeuvred himself into it. He then, painstakingly wheeled himself over to Adam's bed.

Adam sat up and shoved himself backwards, digging his left heel into the bed as leverage.

"What's wrong?"

"Daniel, my names Daniel, Private, Daniel Wiest," he told Adam as he arrived at the side of his bed. "Can I ask you something?"

"Sure, Adam said as he straightened his blankets.

"Why won't you use the chair?"

"I don't… shit, I don't know. I don't want to be like this."

"Me neither, but shit happens. I was like you at first you know. I didn't want to face what had happened."

"What changed for you?"

"I'm going to be a dad," he grinned.

"A dad?"

"Yeah, my girl, Nicola found out she was pregnant just before I was due to ship out for my second tour. She didn't want me worrying while I was away, so had planned to tell me when I returned. Obviously, I didn't come back the same way I'd left. I decided in my wisdom that I was no good for her, that she deserved someone whole. I sent her a text message saying that she wasn't' to come to the hospital and that we were over."

Adam winced and Daniel chuckled.

"Yeah, not my finest hour."

"So what changed?"

"She sent me a text back, no words, just a scan picture with 'your son' written on it."

"Wow."

"Yeah, I was stunned, I'd not had a clue." Daniel shook his head at that as if he still couldn't believe it. "She's clever my Nicola, she didn't message me again. However, a few days later, she came to the hospital to tell me that she still loved me, and that my injuries were just a part of me, not the whole. She also asked me to marry her."

"Congratulations."

"Thank you," Daniel grinned.

"So, the thought of becoming a dad is what made you…"

"Not just that. I love Nicola, I'm alive. I also want to walk down the aisle at my wedding under my own steam. I want to be able to hold my son, and then, when he's old enough play football with him."

"You're braver than me," Adam told him, feeling very small and cowardly in the face of Daniels strength and courage.

Help Our Heroes

"No I'm not, I'm scared shitless," Daniel admitted. "However, I'm more scared of losing Nicola, of not having a life with her and Davey."

"Davey?"

"That's what we're going to call him."

Adam nodded, and Daniel spoke again.

"Come to the gym with me, give it a try. What have you got to lose?" and with that, he wheeled himself towards the door.

Adam watched Daniel go, watched how he struggled to move his chair one handed. Jaw rigid with tension, he glared at the wheelchair sitting beside his bed, then slowly, shuffled around in his bed. He lowered the railing, and swung his legs around until he was balanced on the edge of the mattress. Left leg now on the floor, the bandage on his right leg became a beacon… a white galling reminder that he'd lost a portion of his leg. He ran his hand over it, feeling the rounded stump where the calf was cut off. Sighing, he sucked in a breath and leaned over, reaching for the wheelchair which had been sat there goading him for over a week. Putting his weight on his left leg he tried to pull the chair closer, but the brake was on and he couldn't move it. He tried pushing himself up off the bed and was shocked when it shook, weakened by the length of time he'd been in bed. Although, Tim, the physio had come around each day and tried to get him to do stretching exercises in bed, he'd refused even that.

Growling, he dropped back on the bed, shame swamping him as he realised he'd done this to himself.

"Adam?" he turned at the familiar voice as Phil came in the room.

"Hey."

"You okay?" Phil asked, warily watching him.

"I've been an ass," Adam agreed.

"Hell, you won't get an argument from me," Phil told him. "You ready to join the living?"

"Yeah, I think I am... although I'm not guaranteeing anything."

"It's a start," Phil told him. "Hang on a minute," and with that, he dropped a carrier bag on the bed and walked out again.

A minute later, Phil came back with a nurse in tow.

"I've been given permission to accompany you to the gym," Phil told him with a grin. "A Physio is already down there so they're going to let them know you're coming."

"Here you go Adam, take your time," the nurse told him as she released the brake on the chair and pushed it to him, turning it sideways. She then put the brake back on and removed the arm. "It's easier this way, until you gain some strength back. Then, you'll either be able to swing yourself into it or use crutches," she told him with a smile. "Now, lean on me, and we'll get you sorted," she told him.

Phil stood back and waited until the nurse had got Adam seated and had replaced the arm.

"Okay, all yours, Corporal Summers," she told him.

"Ex-Corporal," Phil told her.

"Snap," Adam added.

"You're out?" Phil asked as he began pushing him towards the door.

"I'll put this bag behind the nurse's station," the nurse told him as she picked it up off the bed.

"There's two containers of cookies in there," Phil told her. "One's for the nurses to have with a cuppa, courtesy of my mother."

"Your mum sent me cookies?" Adam asked as Phil wheeled him past the nurses station and out of the ward.

"She did, she also sent you a pasty and told me to tell you that she'd like to come visit."

"Why didn't she come with you?"

"Because some arsehole had informed the nursing staff that he didn't want visitors."

"So how come you're here?" Adam asked, looking over his shoulder.

"I was never very good at taking orders," Phil told him with a grin and Adam chuckled.

"I'm glad you came," he told him, sobering and turning as they came to the entrance.

"Me too, now let's get you back on your feet," Phil said, pushing Adam's chair into the gym.

Chapter 8

A month later: -

Adam gritted his teeth as he reached for the barres either side of him, then dropped his hands again, wiping his sweating palms on his t-shirt. Neil, his new physio, stood between the barres in front of Adam who still sat in his wheelchair.

"Okay, on three," he told Adam.

Nodding, Adam blew out a breath and again reached for the barres. Flexing his fingers, he took a firm grip as he used his left leg to push himself up and out of his chair. Standing upright after spending so much time either lay down or in a wheelchair was strange. He felt tall, like a kid who had stood on stilts for the first time, and then, when they looked down, the floor seemed to be miles away. Trying to ignore the peculiar sensation, Adam settled his weight wholly on his intact leg, slowly adjusting his stance, allowing the temporary prosthetic he'd been fitted with to take some of his weight. The stump was still a little tender, but that was more due to the unfamiliar feeling of the prosthetic than the injury itself. He'd been fitted with a special kind of cushioned sock that he had to roll over the stump to protect the scarred tissue from pressure.

"You've got this," Neil told him, taking a step back. "Now, lead with your left leg, take your weight and then bring the right leg forward. It's going to feel strange at first, kind of like your foot and ankle has gone to sleep, but you'll adjust. The fitting of the prosthetic is good, but again, it's going to feel strange, but you've got this. Just take your time. Walking is something we normally do without thinking, but, amputees must learn to think, to work out placement and balance before each move. In your case, you still have your knee so that should help. I'm not going to lie, it's never going to be as it was, but with practice and time, it will become easier and your new normal. Okay?"

Help Our Heroes

Adam nodded, then slowly shuffled the prosthetic forward, finding it strange not being able to feel his foot beneath him. He could work out where it was, though by the way his knee and thigh muscles bunched and the pressure on his stump.

"It feels weird."

"I know, but you'll get used to it. Once you have your balance and the scarring and swelling settles properly, you can be fitted for your proper prosthetic."

"That one will have an ankle joint, right?'

"Yes, there are many variations and limbs, each tailored to the specific needs of the wearer. Now, come on, let's get you to the end, then turn and back."

Adam moved along the barres feeling like a toddler, his gait off and his thighs shaking.

It had been a long and gruelling month. They'd worked him hard in the gym to improve not only the muscle tone in his arms and shoulders but also his core strength. Once he'd finally gotten over his aversion to the chair, Adam had spent a couple of hours a day in the gym. He'd pushed himself to gain back the mass and strength he'd lost while lying in that bed for weeks. He and Daniel had become closer; he was an inspiration, and his grit and determination had helped Adam to push himself further when he was ready to quit. With Daniel's help, he'd now not only gained back the muscle and strength he'd lost in his upper body, he'd also gained more.

He'd not seen Hannah since he'd sent her away. However, as the dreams persisted, he was becoming more convinced that he may well have forgotten or lost something important. The only problem was, he still wasn't up to talking to the shrink. He could only handle one thing at a time - and trying to get out of a wheelchair was taking all his energy.

He, lost his grip on the barre, and wobbled so Neil put his hands on his waist to steady him.

"You need to concentrate," Neil told him, and teeth gritted, sweat beading on his forehead Adam nodded. "You okay?"

"Yes, sorry, I was miles away."

"You can't afford to have your head anywhere else but the here and now, not If you want to stay upright. You fall now you could put yourself back weeks by doing further damage. Now concentrate."

Nodding, Adam tried to blank his mind, to only think about the way the muscles and tendons in his thighs bunched and stretched as he moved his left leg. He then tried to get his right leg to mimic the actions by mentally transferring the information. He may still have the leg to below his knee, but he didn't have full feeling. It was as if he had a short circuit somewhere in his neural pathway which made it kind of hit and miss on what he could or couldn't feel. This also happened with pain. Although he no longer had the lower part of his leg, ankle or foot, it didn't stop the limb from causing him excruciating pain. The surgeon had explained about nerve damage or trauma, saying it was where his brain wasn't registering that certain nerve endings were no longer there. It also hadn't helped when further trauma had been cause due to them having to dig around in his thighs to remove the buckshot that had peppered them.

Who turned a shotgun on someone?

Adam dropped the thoughts knowing it was pointless trying to search for answers that he'd never get.

As he got to the end of the Barres, he went to turn, but tried it too quickly, and as pain lanced through his left leg, he hissed in a shocked breath. Looking down, he realised that although he'd turned, his right leg hadn't. He wobbled, and nearly fell as his prosthetic stayed put, still pointing the way he'd come. The unnatural position wrenched on his stump, making his knee cap creak and his thigh muscles quiver and scream under the strain.

Once again, Neil's hands went to Adam's waist to steady him while he slowly edged his right leg around to point in the correct direction.

"Okay, take a breather. You can't just turn, not yet anyway. You need to do it slowly, work out how first, okay?"

"Yes," Adam huffed, his t-shirt now stuck to his soaked body with the amount of effort it had taken for him to get this far.

"Do you want to call it a day?" Neil asked.

Help Our Heroes

"No," Adam gritted out. "No pain, no gain, right?" and as Neil grinned, Adam carefully stepped off with his left foot, hands gripping the barre like a lifeline; which they were. He mapped out his movements in his mind before he executed them. It was slow progress, but he was on his feet, and just then, that was all that mattered to him.

He was physically exhausted, his limbs shaking with fatigue, but he was also elated as he finally reached his starting point.

"Well done," Neil told him, helping Adam to lower himself back into his chair.

"I'm beat," Adam admitted, lifting his hands out before him and showing Neil how much they shook.

"That just shows your working hard. You should be proud of yourself. If we keep at this daily, then in a week or so, you may be able to lose the safety of the barres and move over to crutches."

"I can't wait," Adam told him, grinning as he took the brake off and pushed the wheels backwards, before turning and then heading towards the door.

****

Hannah cleared up her work room as her last client left for the day. She loved what she did, had put in the work for her qualification and it was now paying off with regular bookings and returning clients. She was now a qualified masseuse, and although there was still some stigma attached to her profession, she ignored it. She'd seen for herself the benefits she could bring to a client in pain due to tense, stiff muscles or stress. She'd helped new mothers sleep better and even had a client that had recently started to come to her who'd gone through chemotherapy, the after effects of her treatment was aching bones. She'd had to learn what carrier oils she could use for different ailments, and how to mix them correctly. She'd also done a course on meditation and did a class once a month for pregnant mothers. The one person she'd love to help had still not contacted her and she missed him. She knew she was supposed to be moving on, but she seemed to be stuck. Phil had kept them updated on his progress and she was pleased to know that he was now using his chair and working out, but he still hadn't come to terms with the loss mentally. Until he did and sought help to deal with that, he was going to still have problems.

Sighing, she blew out the candles after brushing and mopping the floor and took the towels through to the little utility room.

She needed a night out.

Maybe blowing off some steam would help her to gain some perspective where Adam was concerned. With that thought, she pulled her phone out of her overcoat pocket, and rang a couple of her girlfriends'.

Help Our Heroes

Chapter 9

A fortnight later: -

Hannah pushed through the front door, pulled off her coat and hung it up.

"Call off the search party. I'm finally here, and starving as I got held up with a client. I'm also off out with the girls tonight," she called as she made her way into the family kitchen. She stopped dead in her tracks at the entrance.

"Hi baby, come on, sit down, we've been waiting on you. Isn't it nice to have Adam home," her mother beamed, wiping her hands on a tea-towel as she moved towards the cooker.

"Hannah," Adam looked at her, his eye tracing over her features, trying to reconcile what he kept seeing in his dreams with the woman before him.

"Adam," she replied, taking a seat at the table - the opposite end and side to him. Although it was only a couple of feet, it was the furthest she could get from him.

Why hadn't she kept her mouth shut when she'd come in. If she'd not said anything, she could have made an excuse about eating with the girls and left. Yes, her mother would have been disappointed, but she'd get over it. She liked them to get together once a month or more for an evening meal, plus a Sunday if they could. However, this was just going to be plain uncomfortable, and her appetite fled as she watched Adam from the corner of her eye. For a man in a wheelchair, he was intimidating, he had that edge of rawness that was often found with soldiers. Add to that that he'd widened out since the last time she'd seen him, and he had a harder edge. His upper body had widened, biceps now straining the lightweight sweater he wore. His caramel and golden hair had also grown out, now looking messy and rumpled. It looked as if he'd just gotten out of bed and ran his hands through it. That brought memories to the surface of her subconscious, gasps and moans, sweaty entwined limbs and running her own fingers through his hair. That was the clincher, her appetite vanished completely.

She couldn't do this.

She couldn't sit at this table with her family and pretend that everything was okay. About to get up again, Phil came in behind her.

"Hey squirt, where've you been?" he asked, grabbing a crusty roll off the table and moving his hand out of the way before his mother could hit the back of his knuckles with her wooden spoon.

"Phillip, Radlington, Summer, you just wait for your food."

"RADLINTON," Adam mouthed with a snicker and Phil gave him the finger.

"It's a good job you're already in a chair or I'd put you in one," he growled at Adam.

"Phillip," his mother hissed, shocked at her son's words.

"It's okay, Kay, he's only being brave now because he knows if I still had both legs I could kick his arse, twice," Adam winked at her. Head shaking, Kay went back to stirring the pot on the stove.

"You wish," Phil snorted, biting into his cob and chewing.

"I could take you with one hand tied behind my back," Adam told him, grinning.

The front door opened and a shout of "Nana, catch," was followed by a whistling sound as Phil's 2-year-old son, Alan threw his whizzing ball into the room ahead of him as he came running into the kitchen.

Adam's grin vanished as he froze, hands clawing the edge of the table as sweat broke out on his forehead. His eyes went huge, lids peeling wide just before he threw himself sideways, rolling out of his chair and coming up on his knees - hands up.

"Alan, freeze," Phil told his son. "April, take him in the front room," he told his wife who had stepped into the room behind their son.

Nodding, eyes dropping, April picked up Alan and took him into the other room out of the way.

"Mum, back away," Phil told her, "Slowly, no sudden moves, okay?" Kay began edging away from the stove, hands before her as she slowly moved around the table.

"Phil?"

"Not now squirt," Phil told Hannah as he began to get up from his seat.

"Oh, for god's sake," Hannah grumbled. "Adam, snap out of it, it's not a bullet, you're in mum's kitchen, there is no threat." She clicked her fingers, and pushed up from her place. Phil held his hand up to her and she turned, glaring at him. "Adam, come on I'm starving here, listen, you can hear the radio playing, feel the floor beneath you, it's tiles not sand.

Hannah couldn't stand sitting there and doing nothing. She may be trying to move on, but Adam was caught in some kind of flashback, a memory that had surfaced and was now more real to him than the here and now. She hated the look of pain and torment that covered his features, and how his body shook as sweat broke out across his forehead.

Adam had been joking with Phil one minute, trying not to stare at Hannah as she came through the door. Suddenly, that noise had registered, and bam, he was back on that dirt road. He went sideways as he felt the impact of the first bullet and came up on his knees, ears straining as he pulled his Glock up and waited for the cock of that shotgun. He wasn't tracking properly. He could see the room he was in now, but it was as if it was a mirage, wavering as another image superimposed itself over the top, trying to solidify. He could hear shuffling and mumbling around him, but couldn't make anything out... which left him disorientated.

Getting up, Hannah ignored Phil and approached Adam, her hand gently touching his shoulder where he knelt. However, he grabbed her arm, shoved, and knocked her off her feet and onto her back on the tiled floor. Hannah's breath left her in a whoosh as she landed, then Adam's weight came down on top of her, his forearm pressing down on her windpipe.

Shit.

The wrong move here and he'd crush her larynx.

A hand lightly touched his shoulder and Adam went on instinct. Grabbing the hand, he flipped his enemy over onto his back, then rolled over onto him, arm across his windpipe to subdue...

More noise, another hand on his shoulder trying to shake him, when he picked up a scent, a soft touch on his face before it covered his restraining forearm.

Adam froze, something familiar about the touch, and breathing deep he removed the pressure on the windpipe. The hand over his forearm dropped away and he lowered his head, face coming closer to the captive he held pinned beneath him.

Hannah tried to say Adam's name, but with the pressure on her throat she couldn't get the words out. Relaxing, she lay completely still, closed her eyes and tried to calm her breathing. Then, slowly - so as not to startle him - she lifted her right hand and touched his cheek. He didn't move as her fingers stroked over the rasp of his stubble, up the side of his face and over and behind his ear. Hannah, hoped to god this worked, and that somewhere deep in his subconscious he recognised her touch. Her fingers shook as she moved from his ear, down his throat and on down his chest until her own hand rested on top of Adam's forearm where it lay across her throat.

As Adam got closer, he felt the cushion beneath his chest...

Phil was off his chair and trying to physically manhandle Adam from her, but he wouldn't budge, it was like trying to move a statue. Hannah glared at him over Adam's shoulder, and mouth grim, he stepped back, fingers twined behind his head as he ground his jaw and looked on helplessly. Adam was his brother-in-arms, one of his closest friends. He trusted him with his life, but this wasn't him, this was his sister. He felt helpless to do anything because he knew first-hand how hard it was to shake off a flashback and come back to reality, especially when it held you so tightly within its grasp.

Hannah watched Adam frown as his nostrils flared. He began to blink rapidly... as if trying to clear his vision, then, in the next instance, the pressure was gone as he leaned towards her, nose running up her neck.

"Hannah," he whispered against her throat, his shoulders shaking as he squeezed his eyes closed. His arms dropped around her, holding her to him as his shoulders shook. Hannah swallowed, her sheened gaze meeting her brother's over Adam as her arms came up and held him back.

Adam's first response to coming back was shame. He couldn't believe he'd treated Hannah so roughly. Obviously, it wasn't enough that he'd upset her mentally, he'd had to compound it by hurting her physically also. Wiping the moisture from his face with his shoulder, he pushed back onto his knees and began to check her over, his features grim as he saw the reddening skin across her throat.

"I'm sorry," he told her, grabbing onto the table as Phil righted his wheelchair. With a heave, Adam managed to drop back into this chair and put the brake on before holding a hand out to Hannah to help her up.

However, Phil beat him to it. He plucked his sister up off the tiled floor, hands running over the back of her head, checking for injury.

"Shit, Han, you know better. You grew up around dad and me, coming back is never easy, you know that. You've also been warned not to approach us if unaware due to either being asleep or going through the after effects. Especially not until we've acclimatised. So, why in the hell would you think Adam would be any different. Are you hurt?" he asked, a finger beneath her chin, tilting her head back so he could get a good look at her throat.

"I'm fine. I think my ego took more of a beating," Hannah admitted with a shrug. "I'm sorry, Adam, I should have thought."

"I'm sorry, Phil, but do you think you could take me back to the rehab centre now, please?" Adam asked. He couldn't look at Hannah. Anger at himself was running like lava beneath the surface, bubbling and seething. He also felt chilled, and shaky due to the overload of adrenaline.

"Adam, I'm fine, honestly, I shouldn't have touched you. I know better."

"You shouldn't have had to know better, Hannah. This is all on me."

"Oh, please, get over yourself. You've been traumatised, and the only thing you damaged was my ego, so get over yours. You are human, therefore, not infallible. Plus, my arse is big enough to take the impact," she hissed, plonking herself back at the table.

"Mum, it's safe to come back. Adam's finished," Hannah shouted and Adam just stared at her, mouth open.

Phil grinned at the look of shock on Adam's face as he sat back down in his own seat. "Welcome home. It's the place where your family doesn't bat an eye at your crazy," he winked at Adam. "Hey, baby, how was your day?" Phil asked April, taking hold of her hand as she came back into the kitchen.

"It was good. The hotel is coming along," she told him as she leaned over and kissed his lips before taking the seat beside him. "Hi, Adam, now, Alan, come sit down," she told their son.

Help Our Heroes

"I, sorry," Alan told Adam, clambering onto the chair beside his aunt Hannah and sticking his thumb into his mouth.

"Right, can we eat now?" Kay asked walking back to the stove, stroking her hand over Adam's shoulder on her way passed.

"Yup, I'm starved," Hannah told her mother. "Workouts always give me an appetite," she grinned, winking at Adam as her mother began to dish up the big pan of stew. She then gave her attention to her nephew, pretending to take his nose. Alan's thumb popped out of his mouth as he giggled and Hannah smiled before blowing a raspberry on his cheek.

Adam looked around the table, not sure how to process what had just happened.

He'd had a complete freak out, a meltdown he'd not been prepared for, nearly choking Hannah in the process. However, this family just took it in their stride. He'd been prepared to leave, to crawl back to rehab and asked to be locked up for his own and others safety. Yet, here he sat, watching Hannah not only not blame him, but just accept it and move on as if it was no big deal.

"If it's any consolation, it took April and some other things happening to me until I got on an even keel. When you're ready to talk, we'll discuss what's available to help you deal. Okay?" Phil asked Adam.

Adam again looked around the table, his eyes once again on Hannah who was laughing as she played with Alan.

"I'll think about it," Adam told Phil, who nodded and thanked his mother as she passed him an overflowing bowl of stew.

"Dig in," Kay told them as she took her own seat beside Alan, her place as head of the table.

Chapter 10

Hannah sat in her yellow Bug, waiting as Phil stowed Adam's chair in the boot as he sat silently beside her. The boot dropped with a click and Phil tapped on it, his hand raised to them through the windscreen.

"Okay, you ready?" she asked Adam as she put her car in gear and set off.

"Do you not have an oh shit bar in here?" Adam asked, fingers digging into the dashboard.

"If you don't like the way I drive you could always push yourself the ten-miles or so back to the hospital," she sniffed. Then edging sideways turned up the volume on the radio.

"I'm sorry."

"That's okay," she told him not looking at him.

"I meant about earlier, not about your appalling driving."

"You're asking for an arse kicking," Hannah ground out, crunching the gears as she changed up.

"I doubt it, I've already managed to knock you on your arse, I think I've already won that one."

"Only because you got me unawares. Next time I'd be ready so I wouldn't make it so easy for you."

"What the hell was that thing Alan was playing with anyway?" Adam asked, deciding to let it go. Not wanting to remember how she'd felt beneath him, how the heat and scent of her skin had intoxicated him. Then nearly groaned as his cock came screaming back to life, swelling behind his fly, pushing against the material. He shuffled in his seat looking to get comfortable, trying to rearrange himself without making it obvious.

"Stop messing with your dick. Sheesh, could you at least wait until you're back in your room. What is it with men and their junk?" Hannah growled.

Yeah, he wasn't touching that one.

Then again, although it hurt like a son of a bitch, at least he knew he was back in working order. Now if only he could take it for a test-drive.

He turned in his seat and looked towards Hannah, her face in profile as she drove, then let it go.

Still not going there, he was already messed up where she was concerned. Add that to the way he was fucked in the head and learning how to walk on a prosthetic, he wasn't up to it.

"So, what was it?"

"What?" she asked, confused, her eyes dropping to his groin.

"No, I already know that's a hard-on. What was that thing Alan was playing with?"

"Not a clue what it's actual name is, he calls it his zoomy. It's kind of a rugby ball but it has a tail and makes a whistling sound as it's thrown.

"Yeah, I heard the whistle," Adam ground out.

"Is that what did it, the sound?"

"I think so. The sound it made was very like the sound a bullet makes when it's been fired from a gun. Especially if it's quiet."

"Okay, that makes sense."

"What, that's it, no questions?"

"I've been around army men all my life. Dad was in the army, we went from base to base as military brats, then Phil joined up…" Hannah shrugged.

"So you saw your dad like that with your mum?"

"Hell, no. Dad didn't need to have come back from tour to be like that, he was a real piece of work," she snorted.

"Phil never mentions him."

"Not exactly someone to be proud of. For a while, we thought Phil was going to head down the same path."

"Phil would never hit April."

"Oh, not the hitting, he'd never do that to a woman. Not after all the times he saw mum take a beating keeping dad from us. The drinking and fighting… that was all dad."

"Shit, I never knew."

"Again, not something we talk about. He's gone, and I can't say I'm sorry."

"How did he die, in service?"

"No. He staggered into the road one night pissed up and was hit head-on by a speeding car."

"Damn, I'm sorry."

"Nothing to be sorry for. The guy had a short fuse and a nasty temper… Hell, life was a lot better after he was gone, and I won't apologise for my feelings. If we didn't call him, Sir, we got a beating, same as mum… not exactly father of the year material."

"Why didn't she leave, get you all away from him?"

"Fear, plain and simple. He told her if she ever left, he'd track her down and kill us all."

Help Our Heroes

"I'm sorry," Adam told her, his hand moving and resting over hers on the gear stick. Hannah shrugged before slipping her hand from beneath his, flicking the indicator as she turned a corner.

Adam curled over, a grimace on his face as his hand went to his prosthetic.

"You okay?"

"Just stiff I think. I've been exercising and practicing walking on it. To be honest, I think I'm just generally stiff."

"Okay, change of plan," Hannah told him, checking her rear-view mirror, then indicating and doing a U-turn.

"Where are you going?"

"My place… or should I say, the studio below it anyway."

"Your place?"

"My studio, it's where I do massage."

"Massage…"

"Keep up, Adam. You may be a pain in the arse, but I'm not leaving you in pain when I can do something about it."

She may live to regret this, but she couldn't sit by and do nothing when she had the capabilities of being able to bring him some relief.

Chapter 11

Hannah dug her hands into his tense shoulders.

Bliss.

"I have something else that could use your attention. If I rolled over..." Adam cut off his words, mumbling as her fingers dug in a little harder. "Ouch, a little rough there."

"Stop being a pig," Hannah retorted as she worked on him.

"Aww, come on Hannah, don't be cruel. I've not gotten laid in months."

"Well, you aren't getting laid today either. Now be quiet while I sort out these knots, you're hard as steel."

"Tell me about it," Adam huffed, shuffling around and looking for a comfortable position. "Ouch, I'm sure you're not meant to abuse your patients," he laughed as Hannah smacked him around the back of the head before going back to digging into his tense muscles.

"You're not a patient. You're my bothers smart mouthed mate; and a pain in the arse," she retorted.

"Now you're just being mean as you won't let me... ouch. What was that for?"

"To save your life. If my brother ever hears you talking about doing me, he's going to remove that appendage you're now so fond of," she hissed leaning over him and once again digging her hands into his shoulders.

"You're the one who said I was a pain in your arse. All I was doing was offering to do it, literally."

"Shut up. Use your hand like a normal bloke." She blew out a breath, then leaned forward rubbing her forehead on her forearm to move her hair out of her face. Her bangs were getting long as she was overdue a cut, her bob the longest she'd ever had it.

"So, are you dating?" Adam asked, his question coming out muffled from where his face was wedged into the hole in the table.

He needed to know... it had been playing on his mind, especially after all the dreams.

"Be serious," she laughed.

"I am."

"Me too, none of your business. You'd tell Phil, then he'd hunt down whoever it was and scare the life out of him and I'd never see him again."

"He wouldn't do that."

"Please, he tied the last one to a chair in the dining room and held a knife to his nuts while he interrogated him. You lot are lunatics. You're not in the army now, you can't go around interrogating people for shits and giggles."

"And did he?" Adam asked, trying to lift his head up so he could look at her.

"Stay still," Hannah huffed, pushing his head back down.

"Well?"

"Well what?" she asked, digging into a particularly hard bit of muscle, using an elbow and rotating it to get it to release and making him grunt.

"Did he shit or giggle?" Adam asked after groaning in relief when the stiffness in his neck eased.

"Mum was furious, the guy pissed on her rug," Hannah fumed.

"He wasn't for you then," Adam told her with a shrug.

"Seriously, have you seen my brother. Mean son-of-a-bitch, built like a brick shit house."

"Yeah, I have, but I've seen bigger."

"Who? Oh, Jeff, yeah. Haneran is bigger, but Phil is meaner."

"Not really," Adam told her and she snorted. Adam sighed, conceding defeat. "Okay, he can be, but only where his baby sister is concerned."

"He needs to stay out of my love life. I swear, I'll be a born again virgin if he doesn't cut that shit out."

Adam groaned, thinking about Hannah and virgin in the same sentence. Shadows moved in his mind, laughter, but it cut off as she leaned over again and he felt her breasts rub against his back.

Tease.

He knew he shouldn't mess with her, but he couldn't help it, the dreams were making him crazy. He'd first laid eyes on her after he'd joined the army, way too many years back to think of. She'd been a pretty teenager, jet black hair, gangly legs and huge big green eyes. The next time he'd seen her had been two-years later and she'd most definitely filled out. By the time she was 18-years old she'd had the curves of a 50's pin-up, and nothing had changed about her looks in the last 7-years. Well, apart from now she was even more stunning because she'd gotten over her shyness. She'd come into her own, and wore her confidence like a designer gown.

Man, it looked good on her.

He felt his right leg go into cramp and hissed in a breath.

"Adam, you okay?"

"Cramp," he snarled, beginning to move around on the table. She stepped back, hands by her sides as she watched him in concern.

"Do you want to stretch your legs?"

"Don't you mean leg," he snarled.

"Oh pipe down, one leg is better than dead. Get over it," she sniped back.

"Always so sympathetic," he grunted, pushing himself upright and managing to sit, the jeans he wore riding low on his hips.

"Crutch or chair?" Hannah asked.

"Neither, I can't walk it off," he ground out.

"Why?"

"Because it's the fucking leg I no longer have."

"Phantom pain. Okay, what can I do?"

Her eyes slit, then a brow rose as she glared at him. "Jesus, Adam, get your mind out of your pants. What can I do to help you that doesn't include sex?" he grinned at her tone. "Or blow jobs either, sheesh, give it up."

"I will if you will," he told her, waggling his brows. She burst out laughing.

"You'd shit yourself if I ever took you up on your offer."

Help Our Heroes

"Probably," he grinned. "But the only way to find out is if you offered," he told her hopefully.

"Not happening." There was no way she was going down that rabbit hole again.

Seen the movie.

Got the t-shirt.

One go on that merry-go-round was enough.

She was just getting back on an even keel, learning to be friends with him again. Massaging him was hard enough, she had to keep him in his box.

Friends.

That was the only way she'd save herself from receiving a drudge down broken-hearted lane again as he walked away and never looked back.

"Now what can I do to help?" she asked.

"Not a damn thing," he ground out again. All signs of joking vanishing as he grimaced in pain. She saw his eyes close, squeezing tightly shut, pinched mouth whitened, showing her just how much pain he was in.

"Hang on, I've got an idea."

With that, Hannah rushed out of her treatment room, opened the connecting door, and could be heard running upstairs.

Adam began sweating, eyes squeezed tightly closed as his nostrils flared with his ragged breathing. He was in so much pain it was becoming unbearable. He'd had it before as he'd been working hard to get out of the chair, but, this was the worse it had been.

Bollocks.

He'd rather have been shot again than deal with this.

Jaw rigid, he heard Hannah come stumbling back into the room, panting.

"Right, this should do," Hannah said, standing up again, hands on hips as she blew her hair of out of eyes.

"A mirror! What the fuck is a mirror going to do?" Adam groused.

"Look in the mirror."

"Yeah, I try not to do that these days, not so pretty anymore."

"Oh shut up. Open your god, damn, eyes and look," Hannah ground back, mouth pinched as she glared at him.

"Hannah..."

"Adam, just trust me, okay. What harm can it do?"

Blowing out a breath, nostrils flaring, Adam stared at her, but the only emotion he saw in her eyes was empathy. That was one of the other things he liked about her, she didn't pity him nor was she repulsed by his injuries. If anything, she treated him no differently now than when he'd been whole... and not just in body.

"Okay, what do I do?"

"Look at yourself in the mirror."

His eyebrow rose at this, then he groaned, teeth grinding again as the pain intensified, sweat beading on his brow and upper lip.

"Adam, come on, trust me."

Eyes opening, he looked directly into her concerned green gaze.

"Come on," she took his left hand and gave it a squeeze before moving to the side and jumping on the massage table beside him. "Okay, now, look at your reflection in the mirror and tell me what you see."

His pain filled pale blue gaze met hers in the floor standing mirror she'd placed near the window at the side of the massage table.

"Eyes off my tits you pervert," Hannah laughed as his eyes dropped to her chest and flared. She had to clamp down on the prickle of awareness that bloomed. Clearing her throat and crossing her arms over her chest to hid her physical reaction to his perusal, she tried again. "Focus on my face, now your own, move down your body, your chest..."

"I hate my chest and thighs almost as much as my bloody missing leg," he bit out. He'd received mild second-degree burns after helping a family escape from their burning home. When you added that to the lost limb, the bump on his nose where he'd broken it as a kid and the pitting in his thighs...

Yeah, he was most definitely no longer pretty.

"Just scars Adam, they shouldn't bother you."

"Really..." he scoffed.

"Yes, really. They are another medal, a testament to your bravery and survival. Now, stop with the pity-party for one minute, and just look in the god, damn, mirror."

His eyes met hers again in the glass, just as the pain hit in another twisting wave of excruciating pain, strain in his missing limb as his calf and foot went into spasm. He desperately needed to move, to get up and make it stop, but couldn't.

"Adam, focus on your chest, then slowly lower your eyes to your left leg, focus on your knee, then your calf, and finally your toes."

"I can't see anything with my jeans on," he gritted out. His pant leg empty on one side as he'd slipped his prosthesis off and leaned it against the wall so he could lie flat on his front. The ankle had no movement on his temporary one, so it wasn't comfortable to lie down on his front while wearing it.

"Bollocks," Hannah mumbled, jumping down off the table and standing before him. "Okay, lift up," she told him, hands on the waistband of his loose jeans as she went for the button and zipper.

"You're trying to get me naked, now?" Adam ground out incredulously.

"Oh, get over yourself," Hannah ground out, hands shaking as she tried to ignore the feel of his skin on the backs of her fingers. "Now lift up your arse. I need to remove them so you can see your leg."

Jaw grinding, Adam lifted, leaning back, using his arms to brace himself. However, he had to close his eyes and suck in breath when Hannah's knuckles grazed over his stiff cock which was presently straining against his boxers as she pulled down his zipper.

Fuck.

Sex should be the last thing on his mind, but it seemed not. Especially as Hannah now knelt before him as she pulled the material down his legs – or at least one of them.

Adam squeezed his eyes tightly shut and thought about anything but the sight of her knelt before him, her face in line with his cock. Not that he had to think for long because just knowing she could now see the pitting in his thighs and his missing limb cooled his ardour as nothing else could have.

"Okay?" Hannah asked, clearing her throat and trying to ignore all the toned skin on show. She averted her gaze from his groin and stood, jeans in hand before jumping back up beside him on the massage table. She placed his jeans behind her giving herself a minute to recover her composure - allowing her blush to fade before she once again returned her attention to the mirror. "Okay, now look at your right leg, the leg that is hurting."

"It's not there, that's the problem. If I still had it, I'd be able to walk this off..."

"Shut up," she cut him off. "Now look in the mirror. Your knee, can you see your knee?"

Again, he nodded.

"Good, now move your eyes downwards, where's your calf, ankle and foot? Where are they, Adam?"

"Fucking missing, obviously," he spat resentfully.

"No shit. Now look, look at where your leg is missing and concentrate. You said the leg is hurting, but how can it hurt you when it's no longer there?"

Frowning, Adam stared at his reflections in the mirror. Staring at his knee on his right leg, his eyes moved downwards, chest tightening for a minute at the evidence of his lost limb. His eyes then moved to his left leg, taking in the calf, ankle and foot, and frowned. Then, looking again, his eyes moved from one leg to the other, and after a minute or two of this, the weirdest thing happened...

The pain began to subside.

He looked again.

Really looked, paying attention to each part, absorbing the visual evidence before him that his leg was no longer there.

Then, to his utter disbelief, the pain began easing.

"What the fuck..." he sputtered, blinking as he slowly turned his head to Hannah, awe in his pale-blue gaze.

"How did you... What..." he couldn't form a sentence, stunned at what he was feeling.

"Has it gone?" Hannah asked, uncertainly, biting her lip.

Help Our Heroes

"Yeah... well, no. Not exactly, but it's most definitely easing. How?"

"I've been doing a bit of research. New findings state that if you can get the person dealing with phantom limb pain to see that the limb in question is no longer there, it helps to reboot the brain – so to speak. The pain you feel isn't real, but your mind doesn't know that. By showing you that you no longer have the limb or area causing the issue, it slowly begins to accept it. Then, hopefully, the phantom pain vanishes. It's not a quick fix, but they state that if you do the exercise regularly, it will eventually no longer bother you."

Chapter 12

Hannah shrugged, uncomfortable with the way Adam continued to stare at her.

After a minute or two of uncomfortable silence, she spoke again.

"It's not exactly how it's done, but it was the only way I could think of doing it to help you. I'll give you all the information I have on mirror therapy so you can do the exercises at home. You know, as you're refusing the help being offered to you in rehab," she glared.

Adam held Hannah's gaze, then leaning sideways, gently brushed his lips over hers.

He'd only meant to give her a quick, chaste kiss. Just a token of thanks, but feeling her breath wash over his own lips from her soft exhale changed it all. Hannah gasped, her lashes lowering as her soft lips clung to his own, and groaning, Adam deepened the kiss. His mouth moving over hers, ravenous, but unable to get close enough from their present position. Shifting around, he raised a hand, cupping her jaw and angling her head where he needed it. Thrusting his tongue between her lips, he deepened the kiss, his thumb stroking the skin beside her mouth, losing himself in her taste and texture.

He was lost.

As Hannah moved restlessly against him, and her taste began to suffuse his system, the shadows that had been prowling around his confused mind began to dissipate. Once gone, the memories they'd covered began bombarding his mind, and breaking the kiss, Adam rested his forehead against Hannah's as he sucked in a breath.

Anguish tore through him at all he'd forgotten.

Hannah lay with him, head pillowed on his chest as her index finger traced over the scarring on the left side of his chest.

Laughter, whispers of love and forever followed by moans as they made love for hours in the hotel room she'd rented when she'd come to visit.

"We've been here before," he whispered against her lips.

Nodding, Hannah pulled back and Adam's hand dropped from her jaw. She jumped off the massage table and as he watched, she began to wander around the room, anxiety and fear eating her up.

"Why didn't you tell me?"

"I thought you'd just decided that it didn't matter… that I didn't matter. I thought you'd changed your mind."

"Jesus, Hannah, I told you that I loved you…" Adam exploded.

"I thought it was just a line," she shrugged unable to meet his hurt gaze.

"No. Fuck, not with anyone, but never with you. Not you, Hannah. I thought you knew me better than that."

"I thought I did too, but you didn't come back to my hotel room like you said you would. I didn't want to ring and sound needy, so I went home, angry. I kept in touch with you while you were on tour, but in your responses, you didn't mention anything. Then, when you didn't come to me when you finally returned from tour…" she went quiet, swallowing the lump of emotion in her throat. "I had to try to figure out what was happening, which is why I came to the base before you flew out. Even though I thought you didn't want me, I couldn't let you go without…" she broke off, swallowing again, her eyes sheened with unshed tears.

"I didn't remember," he groaned in true anguish.

"What do you mean?"

"I hit my head."

"How, when?"

"After I left you. I was distracted, wondering how to approach Phil…" he shrugged, staring at the ceiling thinking back to that morning now he could.

"I was leading exercises and ahead of the others. I scrambled up the wall, but somehow, when I reached the top, I overbalanced. I think my kit slipped, and it ended up dragging me straight over the top head first. I knocked myself out."

"What did the doctor say?"

"I never went to the doctor," he admitted with a wince. "I felt stupid about falling, and although I felt a little nauseous, I managed to carry on. I didn't realise I was missing anything major," he shook his head. "God, Hannah, I'm so sorry," he groaned.

"It doesn't matter, it is what it is," she shrugged, a tight smile on her face.

"Of course it matters, it's drove me batty. I began to think I was losing my goddamn mind. I'd get flashes and images that I couldn't figure out," he began to chuckle.

"What's funny?" she stiffened, frowning at him.

"I should have known…" he shook his head.

"Should have known what, Adam, you're not making sense?"

"When I was hit, Nomad was giving me shit about not taking some random woman up on her offer to f…" He broke off and winced at what he'd nearly said, running a hand around the back of his neck in discomfort.

"I can guess," Hannah told him dryly. "Hang on, you didn't?"

"No, I didn't. Somewhere, somehow I must have known," he admitted.

"It's okay Adam," she told him her arms wrapping around herself. "I know you're Phil's friend and that it makes this awkward for you."

"What are you talking about?"

"Us, I know it couldn't work."

"Why?"

"Phil."

"What about Phil?"

"You said you were distracted during exercise. You fell as you tried to figure out how to talk to Phil."

"Yes, but not with worry over us. I was trying to figure out the proper way to approach him, to ask if I could marry you. Jesus, Hannah, I told you that I loved you and I meant it. Have you any idea how frustrating it was getting little wisps of memory, but not knowing if it was real or not. I thought I was losing my mind. I stayed away when I came home last time as I was so god damn desperate to see you that it made me nervous. I felt like some kind of skeevy bastard after the things I had dreamed of doing to you. Jesus, I was worried that if I did see you, I wouldn't be able to stop myself from turning my dreams into reality. That's why I stayed away," he laughed mockingly. "I didn't realise that we'd already been together and more, and that there was a real reason for why I was so desperate to see you. That… Fuck, this is a mess."

"It's okay…"

"No, it's not, it will never be okay. I lost so much more than my fucking leg, I lost you too," he spat bitterly.

"What do you mean?"

"You said you were seeing someone and that you weren't going to tell me as I'd tell Phil."

"Of course I was seeing someone…"

"Fuck," he groaned again, head dropping forward as he sat there, shoulders collapsing in on himself as he rubbed his hands over his face.

Hannah stood across the room from where Adam sat so dejectedly on her massage table. He seemed devastated and hurt, but she couldn't figure out why… then realisation dawned.

Slowly, she took a hesitant step towards him, then another. Once within reach, she tentatively touched his left arm until he dropped his hands and looked at her.

"Adam, it's you who I was seeing. That's why I couldn't tell you, I didn't think you cared and I didn't want to look foolish. It's always been you. You're the only man I've ever loved," she admitted. His pale blue orbs practically glowed now as he gazed at her.

"Say it again?"

"What, that it's always been you?"

"I like that bit, but no, I want to hear you say you love me."

"I love you, I've always loved you."

Adam's hands shot out and grabbed her, pulling her into the cradle between his spread thighs as he wrapped his arms around her. Holding her securely against him, he squeezed her and closed his eyes, breathing her in and feeling his chest ease.

"I'm not letting go this time, Hannah. I may not have remembered what happened between us, but you were always with me. You are what kept me going, thoughts of you were with me wherever I went. You were also the last thing I thought of before I lost consciousness when I was hit. I hated that I wasn't going to be able to keep my promise to you to come back."

"You kept it, just a little late," she mumbled against his shoulder.

Adam held Hannah, his arms running up and down her back as he just soaked in the feel of her against him.

"Marry me?" he took hold of her arms and held her out so he could see her eyes. She swallowed, green eyes shiny as she nodded. "You're sure? It won't be a walk in the park. I still have some way to go with rehab and I think I may need some help in other areas, the flashbacks and such. Damn, I'm also unemployed, so I guess I'm not much of a cat…"

Hannah silenced his words with her lips, kissing him until neither of them could breathe.

"I'll take you any way I can get you," she told him breathlessly once they broke apart.

"You will," he beamed. "I think we need to celebrate, I need to feel you close to me. How about we give this table a test drive?"

"My sofa next door pulls out into a bed, more room and less time than climbing the stairs to my bedroom," she told him with a smile.

"Pass me my leg and clothes, and lead the way," Adam groaned.

Chapter 13

Hannah placed Adam's jeans and jumper on the floor beside the sofa as she unfolded the bed from the frame. She could feel his nearly naked body at her back, the heat pouring off him. She bit her lip, uncertainty and nerves getting the better of her as she straightened but didn't move.

"What's wrong, changed your mind?" Adam asked as she straightened up, her back still to him. He placed his hands on her shoulder, brushing her hair to the side as he placed butterfly kisses over the side of her neck. Groaning, Hannah's head fell backwards resting on his chest as his arms slid around her waist.

"No, it's just that…"

"I didn't come back the last time we were together," he finished for her and she sighed, nodding. "I promise, I will never forget again. I'll have your name tattooed on my chest so that it's on my skin as a permanent reminder."

"I know I'm being silly."

"Hey, no, it's fine. How about I just hold you for a while," he told her, resting his chin on the top of her head, his fingers entwining at her front as he rocked her.

At his words, Hannah placed her hands over his.

"Thank you."

"For?"

"Being understanding, but Adam?"

"Yes."

"I need this too."

"Thank god," he growled, tightening his arms on her stomach as his mouth once again began kissing the length of her neck.

Hannah chuckled at the relief she heard in his voice, but it turned into a groan as he sucked the sensitive skin above her collarbone while rubbing himself against her backside.

Stepping back, Adam took hold of the bottom of Hannah's jumper, and pulled it up her torso and over her head, dropping it on the floor. His fingers left a trail of fire as they stroked over her exposed skin, his mouth again on her shoulder as he unclipped her bra and slid the straps down her arms. He then turned her around to face him, his eyes dropping and finding she'd crossed her arms over her breasts. Eyebrow cocked, he waited until she dropped them.

"Now this, this I remembered," he told her, a finger lifting and tracing over the strawberry birthmark by the side of her left nipple. Lowering his head, he ran his tongue around it before flicking her tight nipple with his tongue then sucking the sensitive tip into his mouth. Hannah moaned, her hands lifting, running through his caramel hair, now long enough to fist. "I also remembered the sounds you make," he whispered against her breast, stroking over her with his tongue. Transferring his attention to her right breasts, he again suckled this side while his hand was busy kneading the plump flesh surrounding his mouth.

"I'd love to be able to lift you up and carry you. However, unfortunately, I don't think this leg's up to that," he admitted, after releasing her nipple with a pop, his hands still moulding and stroking the fleshy globes.

"So lie down," Hannah replied as her green eyes, now darkened with heat, rose to meet his.

Grinning, Adam's hands trailed from her waist to the waistband of her jeans, unclipping and unfastening them.

"You're overdressed," he told her, pushing them over her hips and waiting while she stepped out of them. He then stood there, eyes roaming over her body, reacquainting himself with every dip and curve. "I didn't forget a damn thing about how you look," he told her, hands going to her hips and holding her to him. "In my dreams I remembered every sigh, dip and hollow of your body," he groaned, fingers now kneading the soft skin of her arse, moulding and squeezing the cheeks in his palms.

Hannah dropped onto the bed behind her and Adam followed her down, then growled in frustration.

"What?"

"The ankle has no movement."

"So, take it off," she told him as her hand stroked the rough skin of his chest making him suck in a breath.

"I remembered that too," he told her, eyes closing in pleasure. Heavy lids lifting, he held her pinned in the dark depths of his gaze, the usually pale blue of his irises now nearly black. "You slept with your head on my chest, your fingers moving over the scars."

"I did, I found it comforting."

"How?"

"The scarring is a reminder to me that you are still here," she told him. A groan leaving her throat as he took her lips, leaning on his elbows, his prosthetic foot hanging off the end of the sofa bed. "I'd like to take this slow, but I don't think I can," he admitted.

"I don't need slow."

With that, she shoved at his shoulder until he landed on his back with an 'oomph.'

"How does this come off?" she asked, shuffling down the mattress and kneeling up at his side, her hand on his prosthetic.

"Just tug," he told her and she did, placing it on the floor with their clothing. She then leaned over him, her tongue stroking over the scars on his thighs. "Okay, playtime is over," Adam ground out, grabbing her under her arms and dragging her up his body. He then rolled, putting her beneath him as he settled between her thighs. Again, he kissed her, his weight held off by leaning on his elbows.

"I can't wait," Adam gritted out, his body raging at him.

"Then don't," Hannah whispered against his lips, her hand running between them and freeing him from his boxers.

Groaning, Adam pushed into her questing, stroking hand, then leaning sideways, ran his knuckles over her panties. Finding them damp, he tugged on the material, pushing them to one side.

Rolling back over, he took himself in hand and positioned himself at her entrance, then pushed forward, sliding into her body with a shudder.

He thanked god that he still had his knee as he pushed upwards onto them, from there he had the leverage to go deeper as he moved in and out of her body.

"Shit, no condom," he gritted out, desperate to keep moving but forcing himself to hold still. Mentally berating himself for not thinking. Then again, he'd not slept with anyone since Hannah, so hadn't needed to buy any.

"Still on the pill," Hannah told him as her legs hooked over his thighs. From there she could use his body to move her own, arching herself up and onto him.

"Thank fuck," Adam replied, as he again began to move, his hands holding the tops of her thighs as he pounded into her body.

Within what felt like minutes, he was gritting his teeth as he felt Hannah tighten around him, movement nearly impossible as her release hit. Her breath whooshed out as she stiffened beneath him, his name leaving her on a breathy moan as she shook.

Adam let go.

With each pump of his hips, his body emptying into Hannah's until he was done, nothing left but little aftershocks. He collapsed over her, boneless as he lay there, breath sawing in and out of his oxygen starved lungs.

"Shit, I'm sorry, I must be crushing you."

"No, I like it," she sighed, her hands stroking up and down his sweat soaked back as her shaky legs fell either side of his hips.

"Give me a minute and we'll…" Adam's words broke off, head turning towards the doorway as he heard footsteps.

Chapter 14

"Oh, my god, I need eye bleach. My sister, Adam, really. Fucking hell," Phil growled from the living room doorway, frozen, face like thunder.

"Can you give us a minute?"

"Adam, seriously, I'm about to rip you a new one."

"Oh, do shut up, I'm not scared of you. Plus, you're going to be my brother-in-law, and family shouldn't fight."

"What?"

"You heard me, I'd like to marry your sister."

"Finally, yes," Phil breathed, his scowl morphing into a grin.

"Excuse me?" Hannah asked, peeking from beneath Adam at her brother.

"It took you both long enough. I've been throwing you together for years. I'd begun to give up hope."

"But you hated everyone I dated. You…"

"They weren't for you, Han, I've seen the way you look at Adam and it hasn't changed since the first time I brought him home. Why would I allow you to settle? My job as your big brother is to protect you, to make sure you get what you want, and you wanted him." He bobbed his chin in Adam's direction. "Luckily, I also saw the way he watched you too, so it's all good. Well, this, not so much," he shuddered, angry eyes raking over Adam's nakedness and his sister lay beneath him.

"Turn your god, damn, back," Adam growled.

"So are you ready to come back to the land of the living?" Phil asked conversationally as he leaned against the door frame, back to them. "I won't lie, it's not easy, but I have a great therapist I can give you the details of. Haneran is seeing her too, she specialises in EMDR."

"What's EMDR?" Adam asked as he gently pulled out of Hannah and tucked himself away. Then, leaning sideways, he grabbed their clothes, passing

Hannah hers before tugging his lightweight jumper over his head. He then sat up, his body shielding hers as he dressed.

"Eye Movement Desensitisation and Reprocessing, it helps with flashbacks and other trauma or stress related issues. I use it. Well, that and kick boxing. Hey, maybe once you have a decent prosthetic, you can come along and join in. I'm also pretty sure I can find work for you too."

"Really, you can help me with employment?" Adam asked, sliding his prosthetic over his stump and checking it was secure before stepping into his jeans.

"Yes, they need more security staff at the hotel April manages."

"That would be great, or maybe we could look into starting our own security firm," Adam mumbled as he zipped up and waited for Hannah to finish dressing. A tap on his shoulder, and he looked around, grinning to find Hannah kneeling up on the bed, sadly, fully clothed. Sighing, he leaned down and kissed her lips one last time before returning his attention to Phil as he stood up. "Okay, you can look now."

"Good," Phil replied, pushing off from the doorframe, then turning, he came into the room. He strolled right up to Adam, pulled back his fist and punched him in the jaw, the force of the hit snapping his head back.

"Son of a bitch," Adam growled, shaking his head as his hand came up and rubbed over his jaw, waggling it from side to side, checking it wasn't dislocated.

"Phil," Hannah growled, clambering off the sofa bed and trying to push past Adam to get to her brother. Adam grabbed onto her arm to hold her back.

"It's okay, I deserved that."

"For what?"

"Come on baby, he found me with you. Think about it, he's your brother."

Help Our Heroes

"It doesn't make it right for him to hit you."

"He's protecting you."

"I don't care," Hannah told him, scowling at Phil, before turning her attention back to Adam. Standing on tiptoe, she stroked her fingers over his jaw, and Adam stood still under her inspection until she was finally happy he wasn't permanently damaged. Brushing a kiss over the red mark, she stepped back her eyes on his as she crossed her arms.

"See, I'm okay, honestly. Plus, he hits like a girl," Adam told her with a wink, giving her a smacking kiss on her pouting lips. "As for you," Adam looked at Phil as he spoke. "That's the only free shot you get. Next time, I hit back," he glowered at him.

"Fair enough," Phil grinned. "Now come on, I need to get you back to rehab.

"Why?" Hannah asked.

"They rang me to find out where he was. I only came here as I knew you were meant to be driving him. Obviously, with him not turning up, and you not answering your phone, I got worried.

"Yeah, I was...."

"Busy," Phil supplied dryly. "Yes, I know, I walked in on you," he scowled again then shuddered.

"I left my phone in my treatment room," Hannah scowled back. "Why does he have to go back to rehab?"

"Because I must finish my rehabilitation, but I'll be out soon, I promise," Adam assured her before hugging her and giving her a last lingering kiss.

"I'll take your car squirt, his chairs already in the back I take it?" At her nod, Phil gave her a quick hug, brushed a kiss across her cheek and left with Adam.

Hannah closed the door on them with a sigh before locking up and tiredly heading to bed. Phil would post her keys before taking his own car home.

Epilogue

A months later: -

"So how does it feel?"

Adam stood, stretching up and bouncing on the balls of his feet, feeling the give in the prosthetic's ankle joint as he balanced his weight. He then lifted his own leg, putting all his weight on the prosthetic and felt it adjust and absorb the impact and extra weight. Shaking his head in wonder, he picked up his jeans.

"It feels great," he chuckled at the technician, turning a shit eating grin on Hannah as she sat smiling at him from her seat beside the desk.

"Just take it easy until you get used to it, Sergeant Jones," the technician told Adam.

"I'm no longer in service, so I'd say my fiancé outranks me now," Adam grinned.

"You better believe it," Hannah chuckled, flashing her solitaire ring.

"I get to walk down the aisle," Adam told the technician.

"That's wonderful news, congratulations."

"Thank you, and this, this is wonderful," he turned his leg this way and that staring at his shiny new leg. "Hey baby, maybe I can take you dancing now."

"I look forward to it," she told him with a smile.

"Are we done?"

"Yes, Sir, you're free to leave, just ring if you have any problems."

"I will, thank you," Adam told him as he pulled on his jeans and fastened them before slipping his feet back into his trainers.

"Are you ready to go home?" Hannah asked

"I am. I'm ready for anything now. Let's go look for a venue for our wedding," Adam told her, shrugging back into his jacket. Then, holding out a hand, Hannah rose from the chair and took his offering, twining her fingers with his as they left the office.

"Are you sure you're ready for marriage?"

"Honey, I've been waiting for you all my life. You are my next adventure, my last one."

"Good answer," Hannah told Adam, her other hand holding onto his arm as she hugged him.

"So, do I get laid for being a good patient?"

"Oh, I think you do," she laughed as he held the door open for her as they left the building.

The End.

Or should I say, Their beginning.

Help Our Heroes

A Military Anthology

Thank you

Thank you to all the authors that have been involved in this military anthology, without your hard work this wouldn't have been possible. Thank you just doesn't seem enough you have all been amazing.

I'd also like to say a big thank you to JC Clarke for designing the covers.

And most importantly thank you to you the READERS for buying this book and supporting these two worthy charities. I hope you have enjoyed reading it and found some new must-read authors along the way.

We will be back with a different themed charity anthology early in 2019.

Keep reading for a bonus real life true story.
WARNING
It is a true story and some might find it upsetting.

Help Our Heroes

An Army Brats Hero

As I look back on being an army brat, as people call us, I remember all the fun, heartache, nerves and excitement. I have been an army brat since birth! Yes, my dad was a TA solider but hey, who cares? It's still the army.

* * *

13 years old Flash back

"Daddy please don't go." I hear myself say to him and he is dressed in his combats. It's hard knowing that this will be two weeks without my dad, and who know what will happen.

"Sweetie it is only the two-week camp. I will be back before you know it and you will be too busy at school"

As I hear his words, I roll my eyes and pull a face. His laugh brings me back to the here and now. "Dad I don't like it though, please."

"You will be good for your mum, and help with your brothers?" I look at him and nod. He sees my hazel brown eyes shining up at him as my head moves up and down.

Being the eldest stinks sometimes. Yes, my brothers and I fight like all siblings do, and whoever says they don't are lying—it's natural.

I run into the room to play with my things, and when my dad shrugs his combat jacket on I run in with my little monkey teddy to keep him safe. "Thank you. I will look after him and think of you all. I will miss each of you, but I have to go as I am needed, and granddad Eddy is waiting for me."

My eyes light up knowing Granddad Eddy is there, because that means plenty of ration sweets.

"Yummy!" The thought of Boiled sweets and chocolate bars had my brothers and I jumping up and down for joy, and just then my mum comes in.

Help Our Heroes

"Kids, go play" She says.

With it being a sunny day my Brother Andrew shouts, "Let's play football. Come on!" I laugh as I run after him with my youngest brother Paul following close behind. I hear my mum saying good bye to him as he leaves the house.

My dad would be away sometimes, just for the weekends, or the main two weeks annual camp, and I hated these with a passion. My dad would be picked up and that would be the last image of him for two weeks. Being an army brat can be hard, but some rewards come with it too.

* * *

I would arrive home from school and before I was even let out to play, I had to change out of my uniform.

The first thing mum would say was, "Change and then homework. Then you can play" Damn, we would know if we didn't do as we were told. We would have our things taken off us, and we'd be sent to our rooms with no toys.

* * *

Snapping myself back to the here and now, I look around the dull drab classroom and carry on with my English work. As I finish the last piece of work I was completing, the school bell rings for lunch. I grab my school bag and pack my text books away before going to meet Claire—my best friend.

I greet her with my trade mark smile. Okay, I was always smiling. Well, apart from when I was being bullied. "Hi, girl." I call out, as I look at this beautiful, slim and stunning girl who always looked amazing in our school uniform of black pants, white shirt teamed with a snotty green jumper. Yes, I said snotty. Well, it was disgusting.

Claire smiles back at me. We became best friends the first day of upper school. She was trying to find the swipe machine to put money on her card for lunch when she walked up to me, and a shy voice came out "Excuse me? But do you know where the swipe machines are?"

I nodded back and looked at her before replying, "Sure, I can show you if you would like?"

She gave me a small nod, "Thank you. I am Claire. We are in Mr Smith's class."

I couldn't help but smile at her shyness "I am Ann. It's nice to meet you." I shake her hand, and I give her another smile as we make our way to the machine, talking and laughing as if we had been friends since first school, and not just that day.

She turned and asked me, "Ann, do you fancy going to get fish and chips from the chip shop at the bottom of the road tomorrow?" I turn to look at her, my face a little glum. I had already put my dinner money on my card, which left me with no spare cash. Claire knew my parents didn't have a lot of money, what with them being on benefits.

Yes, they were looking for work, but it was hard. Not that I cared—I had two parents who loved me and my two brothers, and we had a roof over our heads, with food in our bellies.

Yes, I had pass me down clothes. I didn't have any top of the range gadgets, or the latest brands. I remember giving her a sad smile. "Sorry Claire, I had put all my money on my lunch card"

At my words, she smiled over to me as If she didn't care. Not one little bit. "Hey don't worry. It is on me." My eyes snap to hers. I didn't feel comfortable about this, but all I saw was a dear friend looking back at me expectantly. "You don't need to, Claire."

When the bell rings, we make our way to our next class after our lunch.

* * *

The weekend went fast, as always. From playing out, visiting my nana and granddad, and my cousins would always play on the streets with us.

I run in to check the time, and I run towards my mum. "Mum, when will daddy be home?" I ask her, then she turns to smile at me as she finished up cooking our tea of sausage, mash and beans,

"I am not sure, Ann." she plates up our food.

"Okay, mum. Shall I call the boys in?" She nods at me and I run out shouting as I always did for my brothers "AMANDA" I laugh as I shout his nick name. He runs in with Paul and they start to fight. It doesn't take long before my mum tells them both off, and as she does Dad walks through the door. We turn as we hear the door and shout "DADDY" in unison. He smiles tiredly and says hello to my mum, with a kiss and then comes to kiss us all on the heads.

Help Our Heroes

* * *

My memories flashes to the Remembrance Sunday.

Hearing my mum shout upstairs, "Will you three hurry up?" I hurry up and apply my make-up, tie my hair back and leave my bedroom, before making my way downstairs and help Paul get ready.

I grab my black high heels and put them on, just as our taxi pulls up outside our house. I always felt excited to go to the Barracks. I always had fun.

I look at my mum as we get into the taxi and give our location. "Mum, when we get there can I go see dad? "

She nods and tells me, "If he is in the kitchen, then yes." Smiling, I know he will be there. I remember all the hiding places my friends and I used to use. As the driver pulls up to the gate of the Barracks, I have a big grin upon my face.

My mum pays the driver as Andrew, Paul and myself go to the gate to tell them we are here and to let us through. I run through the gate as it opens and run to the doors and run up the stairs to my dad's kitchen. When I get there, I wash my hands. It's our number one rule, and then I see my dad smiling as I do.

"Hi dad. Can I help at all?" He turns from cutting onions, and smiles. "I am fine, thank you. Why don't you go to the Ors mess and I will be there very soon? I am just finishing up, okay?"

I nod and smile as I turn to walk out calling behind me "Okay, daddy" I turn around the corner and make my way along the cream balcony and push the double doors open, which makes my way to the ORS mess, where all the army personal are drinking cans of beer or larger and having a laugh. I see all the other army brats playing together. I go and greet everyone I know and love with a hug.

The day passes as it always does. The lads always teasing me and my mum or finding myself being squadron child care service with a group of 20 kids at a time.

I can't help but grin as I remember all these flash backs from my youth, and now, as a thirty-year-old woman I look back on the love and solid grounds I was brought up on and the family values I still hold to this day.

* * *

A Military Anthology

August 2014 my worst nightmare began

As I enjoy my day off from work, I feel my phone vibrate and I reach into my pocket before pressing the accept button. When I look down at my phone, I can see it's my mum and she's saying my dad had gone to hospital.

I grabbed my coat and walked out of the house, locking up and made my way to the hospital. The 614 and 619 buses seemed to take twice as long to get me to the hospital, and my mind was already on overdrive.

I arrive at the hospital 45 minutes after receiving the call. I make my way to the ward my dad was on, and when I locate it, I find his bed and see him laying on top of the covers. He gives me a small smile, I walk straight to his side and kiss his cool cheek and then I sit down in the chair beside his bed.

"Ann." His voice is deep as he starts to talk. "the doctors have discovered I have two tubes connected to my right Kidney."

I can't help but chuckle and face him. "You greedy sod, dad." His chuckle was low but also sounded off, I look up at him instantly.

"Ann, they have also found a mass in my bowel and they want me to have tests when they remove the extra tube" My world stands still as I hear the word *mass*. I shake it off and think it will be nothing.

"It will be nothing dad" My voice is unsure, but I need to be thinking positive when he turns to face me.

"Ann it could be Cancer. The doctors want to remove my extra tube as soon as they treat me for Sepsis."

I look at him as he says the word sepsis. *Oh my god, not blood poisoning too!* "You don't do it by halves do you dad?" I joke but deep down my heart is breaking and I want to curl up in his arms like when I was a kid and cry, but I knew I had to stay strong in front of him. After chatting for an hour or so about everything, I say good bye to him with a kiss to the cheek. I leave his room and ward where I ring my area manager to inform her of what my dad has told me and that I will be back to work as normal, but I will be having my phone on me in case I was needed.

Working in a different town to where you lived was hard, but now felt the

Help Our Heroes

worst. My days would consist of working 9 till 5.30 and the travelling to visit my dad at the hospital.

* * *

A week later my phone rings whilst I am in the stock room sorting our point of sale out for the shop floor, when I see it's my brother Pauls name, and I quickly answer it.

"Hi Paul, what's up?" As he talks it sounds hoarse from crying.

When he says, "Ann, dad has Cancer." I break down and cry with my brother for a few minutes. When I dry my eyes, I say, "Paul, I am going to hang up and call Lis and I will be on my way."

I hang up the call as my Assistant manager walks in and sees me sat on the floor as I cry some more, and she rushes over to me as hugs me. "Ann, what has happened?" As I explain, she hugs me more. "Ann, go home. Be with your family and dad"

I look at her "Sab, I need to call Lis." She leaves me to call Lis, as I dial her number I get her voicemail. "Lis it's Ann. I need you to call me ASAP." My voice breaking as I speak with unshed tears, I hang up and I try her again. I still get her voicemail.

As I do, I hear Sab call in to the stock room. "Ann, go home." I get up and dry my eyes and walk towards the door.

"No, honey, I need to speak to Lis," I go to grab my things ready for when I can go to my dad's side, and just then the store phone starts to ring.

I answer in my normal greeting, only this time with a fake happiness, to hear it is Lis. My heart breaks again as I start to speak and I rush back into the stockroom. "Lis, it is my dad. The Doctors have confirmed" I start to sob again as I talk. "that he has cancer."

I hear Lis gasp as I tell her. "Ann, go be with your family and he will be ok. I am praying for your family honey, and I am here if you need me." I dry my eyes, but my voice is laced with hurt and emotion.

"Thank you, Lis" I hang up and grab my things and put my coat on as I rush out of the store to the bus station—desperate to make my way back to my home town, so I can get to the hospital.

The whole hour and half journey, I kept praying that he will beat this, and he will be okay. I make my way into the ward two hours after leaving my store, placing a fake smile on my face once again, and as I look at my dad I know he sees right through me. But he knows I am doing it for my mum's sake as I kiss her head and kiss my dad's cheek.

My brother Andrew is happily married and has a little girl, Elise who lights us all up when we see her, especially my dad.

* * *

Andrew brings my niece into the room and my dad automatically sits up with a big smile on his face. Even though Andrew is three years younger than me, he helps me keep my mum busy whilst dad is in hospital.

* * *

October 2015

I start to see my dad get worse.

He had lost at least two stone in two weeks, and his pain was getting worse—more than he let on, but I can see right through him.

Andrew brings my niece Ella and goes right to her sick granddad and she starts to play with him, to cheer him up even though she is only one and half, she knows her granddad is sick.

The sight of them melts my heart, knowing full well that if and when I have kids they will never meet this amazing man.

I get up from the couch and smile. "Mum, Dad, Andy, Paul, would you guys like a drink?" My mum nods and my dad, far too busy playing, he just shakes his head, and Paul says, "No thanks." Andrew shakes his head.

I walk in to the kitchen and take the kettle, making sure there is enough water in before bringing it back and put it on to boil. I grab the sugar and tea bags and then start to pour the boiling water to make myself a drink.

* * *

All I seem to do is work all the time. Visiting my Dad and mum, and sleep, I have no time to sleep.

I was so drained and tired. My friends would always ask me if I wanted to

Help Our Heroes

go out and get drunk, so as the month passed by into November I decided to take my mum out of the house and do some Christmas shopping. That way we could have some mother, daughter time, and to help her de-stress.

We all laugh and cry and as December rolls around, work starts to get busy as it is our busiest time of the year.

Because we have worked so hard, and my team have been so amazing and supportive with me, on the twentieth of December I took them all out for a Christmas meal.

The next day after finishing work I go to see my hero—my dad.

When entering the room, it hits me every time I see my hero, he's all skin and bones. I try to keep strong, but it's hard.

I see the nurse making my Dad more comfortable and administer the Morphine as he is unable to eat and barely drinking anything now.

My brother Andrew is at work, Paul is speaking with the nurses and my sister-in-law Shari is calling for updates, so Paul keeps relaying the information.

I get told to go home at eleven-thirty, to my empty place and curl up.

I wake up to the sound of my phone as it starts to ring and vibrate. I answer, half asleep and as I glance at the clock, I can see it's twenty past four in the morning.

I would be getting up within the next hour. Deep down, I know what this call is.

On the December 22nd at 4.20, my dad was taking his last few breaths.

"Andy?" His voice is full of hurt and tears "Ann, we think dad is ready to go. You need to get here fast."

I put the phone down after saying okay and call a taxi and I rush to get ready. As I get to my parent's place, I walk in and see the doctor attending to my dad and calling his time of death at 4:25 am.

I had missed his last breath, but I know he had gone while I was asleep as I was sure I had felt a gentle kiss on my cheek and thought I heard the words *"I love you Ann"*

I burst into tears as I rushed to his cold, lifeless body on the couch and kissed his head and I kept asking why they had to take my hero. I finally left his side to call my boss, to tell her and notify my team to run the store for me.

Christmas was so hard without him there, but we had to put on a brave face for my niece. She knew her granddad was not there, and she was pointing to my dad's photos. She was running around pulling me into the kitchen to play with my mum's fridge magnets.

* * *

January came and my friends finally persuaded me to go out to take my mind off things, when I accidently bumped into a tall handsome bloke. I almost stutter but calm down before I speak to him.

"I am so sorry about that." He smiles at me and tells me "Are you okay ?" He looks at me as he speaks, "I'm Michael."

I smile shyly back at him "Hi Michael I'm Ann,"

He offers to buy me a drink. "I am with my friends, but they say no-go have one." and push me away grinning, and so I do, and we start to talk and laugh, I look over a few times.

* * *

EPILOGUE

Wow I cannot believe Michael and I are living together and are very happy. He has been so supportive and held my hand at my dad's funeral as I said goodbye to my dad. My hero who was given a guard of honour. Michael was my rock, my light at in my darkest time of my life. It turned out that we knew of each other at school.

"What a small world" He kneels down on one knee, and I look down at him in shock as he starts to speak.

"Ann, will you marry me?" He holds out a beautiful retro style cluster engagement ring, and my hand flies straight to my gasping mouth as I nod my head.

"Yes, I will Marry you, Michael" I cry out as I jump into his arms.

* * *

1 year later

Help Our Heroes

As I am ready to make my way down the aisle to the man I love, I have a moment of unhappiness as my dad should be here to do this honour and walk me to my husband to be and give me away. Andy looks at me knowing what I am thinking "Ann, Sis you look so beautiful and dad would be so happy and proud of you today. Shall we get you down that aisle to Michael?" I nod and look at him. "yes, I am and I know dad is here with us right now smiling at us both" I Link my arm with his we start to walk down the aisle as mine and Michael's friends and as my man stands in Cream whilst our ushers are in charcoal grey. "Yes, you all heard me In Cream!!!!" But DARM he looks hot my bridesmaids had entered before me down to the song Christina Perri's A Thousand years, In My beautiful princess wedding dress. He looks at me totally stunned at how I looked as he leans closer to me and whispers "You look stunning baby" We say our vows and place our wedding rings on and then enjoys our wedding reception.

Made in the USA
Lexington, KY
25 March 2018